Bedford Cultural Editions

W9-BZA-805

NATHANIEL HAWTHORNE
The Blithedale Romance

EDITED BY

William E. Cain

Wellesley College

BEDFORD BOOKS *of* ST. MARTIN'S PRESS ✿ BOSTON

For Bedford Books

President and Publisher: Charles H. Christensen
General Manager and Associate Publisher: Joan E. Feinberg
Managing Editor: Elizabeth M. Schaaf
Developmental Editor: Katherine A. Retan
Editorial Assistant: Alanya Harter
Copyeditor: Barbara Sutton
Cover Design: Susan Pace and Donna Lee Dennison
Cover Photograph: Art: Brook Farm by M. G. Cutter, 1910, after a contemporary drawing. Reproduced by permission of the Concord Free Public Library.

Library of Congress Catalog Card Number: 95–80790

Manufactured in the United States of America.

0   9   8   7
f   e   d   c   b

For information, write: St. Martin's Press, Inc.
175 Fifth Avenue, New York, NY 10010

Editorial Offices: Bedford Books *of* St. Martin's Press
75 Arlington Street, Boston, MA 02116

ISBN: 0–312–11803–1

Published and distributed outside North America by:

MACMILLAN PRESS LTD.
Houndmills, Basingstoke, Hampshire RG21 2XS and London
Companies and representatives throughout the world.

ISBN: 0–333–65705–5

About the Series

The need to "historicize" literary texts — and even more to analyze the historical and cultural issues all texts embody — is now embraced by almost all teachers, scholars, critics, and theoreticians. But the question of how to teach such issues in the undergraduate classroom is still a difficult one. Teachers do not always have the historical information they need for a given text, and contextual documents and sources are not always readily available in the library — even if the teacher has the expertise (and students have the energy) to ferret them out. The Bedford Cultural Editions represent an effort to make available for the classroom the kinds of facts and documents that will enable teachers to use the latest historical approaches to textual analysis and cultural criticism. The best scholarly and theoretical work has for many years gone well beyond the "new critical" practices of formalist analysis and close reading, and we offer here a practical classroom model of the ways that many different kinds of issues can be engaged when texts are not thought of as islands unto themselves.

The impetus for the recent cultural and historical emphasis has come from many directions: the so-called new historicism of the late 1980s, the dominant historical versions of both feminism and Marxism, the cultural studies movement, and a sharply changed focus in older movements such as reader response, structuralism, deconstruction, and psychoanalytic theory. Emphases differ, of course, among schools and individuals, but what these movements and approaches have in common is a commitment to explore — and to have students in the classroom study interactively — texts in their full historical and cultural dimensions. The aim is to discover how older texts (and those from other traditions) differ from our own assumptions and expectations, and thus the focus in teaching falls on cultural and historical difference rather than on similarity or continuity.

The most striking feature of the Bedford Cultural Editions — and the one most likely to promote creative classroom discussion — is the inclusion of a generous selection of historical documents that contextualize the main text in a variety of ways. Each volume contains works (or passages from works) that are contemporary with the main text: legal and social documents, journalistic and autobiographical accounts, histories, sections from conduct books, travel books, poems, novels, and other historical sources. These materials have several uses. Often they provide information beyond what the main text offers. They provide, too, different perspectives on a particular theme, issue, or event central to the text, suggesting the range of opinions contemporary readers would have brought to their reading and allowing students to experience for themselves the details of cultural disagreement and debate. The documents are organized in thematic units — each with an introduction by the volume editor that historicizes a particular issue and suggests the ways in which individual selections work to contextualize the main text.

Each volume also contains a general introduction that provides students with information concerning the political, social, and intellectual contexts for the work as well as information concerning the material aspects of the text's creation, production, and distribution. There are also relevant illustrations, a chronology of important events, and, when helpful, an account of the reception history of the text. Finally, both the main work and its accompanying documents are carefully annotated in order to enable students to grasp the significance of historical references, literary allusions, and unfamiliar terms. Everywhere we have tried to keep the special needs of the modern student — especially the culturally conscious student of the turn of the millenium — in mind.

For each title, the volume editor has chosen the best teaching text of the main work and explained his or her choice. Old spellings and capitalizations have been preserved (except that the long "s" has been regularized to the modern "s") — the overwhelming preference of the two hundred teacher-scholars we surveyed in preparing the series.

Original habits of punctuation have also been kept, except for occasional places where the unusual usage would obscure the syntax for modern readers. Whenever possible, the supplementary texts and documents are reprinted from the first edition or the one most relevant to the issue at hand. We have thus meant to preserve — rather than counter — for modern students the sense of "strangeness" in older texts, expecting that the oddness will help students to see where older texts are *not* like modern ones, and expecting too that today's historically informed teachers will find their own creative ways to make something of such historical and cultural differences.

In developing this series, our goal has been to foreground the kinds of issues that typically engage teachers and students of literature and history now. We have not tried to move readers toward a particular ideological, political, or social position or to be exhaustive in our choice of contextual materials. Rather, our aim has been to be provocative — to enable teachers and students of literature to raise the most pressing political, economic, social, religious, intellectual, and artistic issues on a larger field than any single text can offer.

J. Paul Hunter, University of Chicago
William E. Cain, Wellesley College
Series Editors

About This Volume

The Blithedale Romance is complex in form and content, and a key reason for its complexity is the absorbing but elusive relationship between Hawthorne and Miles Coverdale, the narrator who describes his membership in the utopian community of Blithedale. This is the only novel that Hawthorne wrote with a first-person narrator, and because he spent seven months at Brook Farm, a cooperative community begun in 1841 in West Roxbury, Massachusetts, he seems to be prompting readers to identify Coverdale with himself. But one of the challenges of *The Blithedale Romance* is that Coverdale's attitude toward reform is an ambivalent one in which hope and despair are merged, and Hawthorne's own views about both Brook Farm and the subject of reform are filtered through his narrator. Hawthorne and Coverdale are connected to, yet independent of, one another, and the novel needs to be read with its biographical context in mind but not made equivalent to it.

The documents included in this edition are designed to contextualize the novel in two senses. A number of them bear directly on Brook Farm and Hawthorne's experiences there. But many are aimed more generally to enable readers to situate *The Blithedale Romance* in the midst of nineteenth-century reform movements, utopian communities, and discussion of gender roles and feminist issues. The novel gains in power and richness when we know more about the broad social and cultural scene in the 1830s, 1840s, and 1850s, especially the personalities of reformers, the bold ideas and radical proposals that they advanced, and the communities in which they tried to exemplify a better form of life.

The Blithedale Romance is, then, a book that emerged in an era of debate about reforms and utopias and the motivations for them. But its concerns remain vital today. It probes the nature of meaningful work; the relationship between the sexes; the responsibility of intellectuals for social change; the desire that many persons feel for a life better than the one they have experienced; and the disenchantment that follows when reformers realize that they have not achieved their goals.

A NOTE ON THE TEXT

The text of this volume is that of *The Blithedale Romance* in the Centenary Edition of the Works of Nathaniel Hawthorne, volume III, published in 1964 by the Ohio State University Press for the Ohio State University Center for Textual Studies. The Center for Editions of American Authors of the Modern Language Association has given its approval of this text, and it is authoritative.

Students should be aware that this text preserves certain usages, archaic idioms and antiquated terms, and peculiarities in spelling that reflect the Centenary editors' effort to be faithful to Hawthorne's mid-nineteenth-century style. When the meaning of a word or phrase is unclear, I have explained it in my annotations. In addition, I have noted several places in the text where the Centenary editors restored material that was included in Hawthorne's manuscript but not in prior editions of the novel.

Wherever possible, the text of the documents in Part Two is that of the original edition or of the most authoritative scholarly edition. Unless otherwise indicated in the headnote for a document, the text used is that of the original edition.

ACKNOWLEDGMENTS

My preparation of this book benefited from the excellent biographical work on Hawthorne that Edwin Haviland Miller, James R. Mellow, Randall Stewart, and Arlin Turner have done. I am also indebted to the many fine scholars and editors involved with the Centenary Edition of the Works of Nathaniel Hawthorne, published by the Ohio State University Center for Textual Studies. They have carefully established the texts for Hawthorne's novels and stories, notebooks, and letters (from which I have quoted in my Introduction) and provided much helpful annotation.

For cogent readings of the manuscript, I am grateful to Gillian Brown, Evan Carton, Joel Myerson, Robert Levine, Dana Nelson, and Ross Posnock. I have also learned from others who have edited *The Blithedale Romance*, including Maurice Aaron Crane, Seymour Gross and Rosalie Murphy, Annette Kolodny, and Tony Tanner and John Dugdale. Less directly but still importantly, my approach to this edition has profited from conversations and correspondence with Sylvan Barnet, Gerald Graff, and Eric Sundquist.

My research was also aided on many occasions by the staff of Clapp Library at Wellesley College, particularly in the Interlibrary Loan Office, Reference, and Special Collections. My thanks to Joan Stockard, Karen H. Jensen, Ruth R. Rogers, and Jill Triplett. I am glad to mention, too, my stellar student assistants, Amy Burns and Maureen Paulsen, who helped me locate materials and often gave me good advice.

I would also like to express my thanks to the staff at Bedford Books for their support and encouragement. In particular, I am very grateful to Chuck Christensen and Joan Feinberg for inviting me to edit Hawthorne's novel and make it part of the Bedford Cultural Editions series. Elizabeth Schaaf guided the book through the production process with great care and attention to detail; Kim Chabot handled permissions; and Adrian Harris and Alanya Harter ably assisted on many matters along the way. Above all, my editor, Kathy Retan, merits special acknowledgment for her expertise and dedication to this project from beginning to end. Kathy was a source of countless good ideas and suggestions; I feel fortunate indeed to have worked with such a rigorous, thoughtful, patient, and perceptive editor.

Most important of all, I am grateful to my wife, Barbara, and my daughters, Julia and Isabel. They are part of every book that I write.

William E. Cain
Wellesley College

Contents

Illustrations

Part One

The Blithedale Romance
The Complete Text

Introduction:
Cultural and
Historical Background

"Do you despise woman?" the "brilliant" Zenobia asks the reformer Hollingsworth in a crucial scene in Chapter 14 of *The Blithedale Romance*. "Despise her? No!" he replies. "She is the most admirable handiwork of God, in her true place and character. Her place is at man's side. Her office, that of the Sympathizer; the unreserved, unquestioning Believer." Hollingsworth's language then becomes fierce as he condemns as "monsters" women who seek separation from men. If necessary, he declares, men must use "physical force, that unmistakable evidence of sovereignty, to scourge them back within their proper bounds."

Miles Coverdale, Hawthorne's narrator, assumes that Zenobia will "resent" such "intensity of masculine egotism." Yet to his "surprise" and "indignation," she does not challenge Hollingsworth but responds, he notes, all too mildly, with tears of "grief": "Let man be but manly and godlike, and woman is only too ready to become to him what you say!"

Coverdale, however, neither perceives Zenobia's tone nor catches the drift of her statement and hence he misunderstands her response. In fact, Zenobia *is* grieving over and resenting Hollingsworth's "masculine egotism." She is not saying that Hollingsworth's view is acceptable but, rather, is agreeing that when men invoke their authority and rule with "force," women succumb to the part that patriarchy assigns them. Zenobia acknowledges the accuracy, if not the justice, of Hollingsworth's words because she feels herself attracted to him and to the domineering drive of his masculine rhetoric. She resents it for the sake of all women, and she resents it in herself because she feels its power. Men command the culture and, Zenobia knows, can enlist their size and strength to execute their will over women. Violence ("scourge them back," like unruly slaves) is the underside of the cult of domesticity.

This scene suggests the complexity of Hawthorne's exploration of gender and sexuality and the keenness of his inquiry into the nature of reform and social change. *The Blithedale Romance* draws upon Hawthorne's own experiences in 1841 as a resident of the cooperative utopian community of Brook Farm, in West Roxbury, Massachusetts, projecting them through the recollections of the fictional bachelor-poet Coverdale "twelve long years" later. But Brook Farm serves for Hawthorne as a dramatic occasion, an artistic opportunity, for studying reform and reformers, utopian communities, and the mixed motives that impel (and break down and ruin) programs for social improvement; personal, political, and economic renewal; and reorientation of gender roles.

Spurred on by the religious revivalism of the Second Great Awakening, reform caught fire in the 1820s and 1830s and extended across many fronts, including abolitionism, women's rights, temperance, education, labor and rights for workers, and improvement in prisons. Hawthorne witnessed this passion for reform and took part in it at Brook Farm. He knew the appeal of the call to embrace a new self, and also the tempting prospect of living in a community of like-minded persons inspired with the hopeful dream of a better world. It was because Hawthorne had felt the soul-stirring of reform himself, and scrutinized it in the nation and among many people with whom he was acquainted, that he was led to criticize it as dangerous and portray its tragic consequences in his novel. Scholars have wondered why the reclusive, skeptical Hawthorne was led to join Brook Farm, but the important question is not why he went but what he discovered there about the price to persons that radical change could exact.

TRANSCENDENTALISM

As *The Blithedale Romance* testifies, the 1830s and 1840s were filled with reforms and utopian experiments, and one noteworthy point of departure for them was the Transcendental Club, which met in Boston and Concord, Massachusetts. Begun in 1836 as Hedge's Club — the name derived from F. H. Hedge, a Unitarian minister from Maine who organized meetings of scholars and ministers — it included Ralph Waldo Emerson, the scholar and reformer Theodore Parker, the writer Margaret Fuller, the teacher-philosopher Amos Bronson Alcott, the poet Jones Very, and the Boston minister George Ripley, Emerson's cousin and later the founder of Brook Farm.

It is both inevitable and misleading to speak of transcendentalism as a literary, religious, and philosophical *movement*. The persons usually grouped within it differed on many points, criticized and sometimes even renounced the term, and shaded their transcendentalist views a lot or a little depending on their relationship to evangelical revivalism, romanticism, and specific social reforms. This much can be said: transcendentalism represented an effort to break free from the heritage of Calvinism, which emphasized mankind's innate sinfulness, and, furthermore, from philosophical rationalism, which maintained that knowledge was independent of sense experience. Evolving from such important German thinkers as Immanuel Kant and Johann Wolfgang von Goethe, transcendentalism stressed the correspondences between each person and nature and the sheer indwelling presence of the divine in all men and women. It exalted individual conscience, honored the imagination, and insisted on personal autonomy. Transcendentalism entailed an openness to and faith in truths that men and women could intuit, and a rapt gaze outward to a nature illuminated everywhere by a higher, "transcendent" reality.

Elizabeth Palmer Peabody and her sister, Sophia (whom Hawthorne would marry in 1842), were among those interested in transcendentalism, and they took part in the Transcendental Club. Elizabeth Peabody kept house and managed a bookstore at 13 West Street in Boston, close to the Common, where she sold periodicals and books from abroad and where, beginning in November 1839 and extending into 1841, Margaret Fuller held a series of "Conversations" on Greek mythology and the fine arts, meeting weekly with about twenty-five women for two hours or more.

Despite his closeness to the Peabodys, Hawthorne's relation to the club and to transcendentalist thought was marginal. He was aware of the attention being paid to German literature and philosophy, including such key thinkers as Johann Gottfried von Herder, Friedrich Schleiermacher, Jean Paul Richter, and especially Goethe, whom Emerson, Ripley, and Fuller read avidly. He took a few lessons in the

German language in a course at the Peabody house, and thumbed through a German dictionary that the poet Henry Wadsworth Longfellow loaned him. But it was more than Hawthorne had patience or energy for; according to Sophia, "he said he wished he could read German, but could not take the trouble" (qtd. in Stewart 58).

Central documents in transcendentalism include Emerson's *Nature* (1836), "The American Scholar" (August 1837), and the Divinity School address (July 1838), and there are many testimonies by transcendentalists, reformers, and Brook Farmers to Emerson's impact on their lives. This resulted not only from his lectures and writings but also from the controversies he sparked and the actions he took, particularly his resignation from the ministry in 1832 and his disputes with eminent conservative Unitarians in the 1830s.

Ripley's contribution should not be underestimated, however. His ten articles for *The Christian Examiner* in the 1830s and six essays collected in *Discourses on the Philosophy of Religion* (1836) laid much of the foundation for transcendentalism. He supplemented these writings with an important public address, "Jesus Christ, the Same, Yesterday, Today, and Forever," which he delivered more than a half dozen times between 1834 and 1839.

Ripley disseminated texts by German and other European writers, overseeing a fourteen-volume collection, *Specimens of Foreign Standard Literature*, begun in 1838 and completed in 1842. In his Introduction to *Philosophical Miscellanies*, the first two volumes in this series, Ripley states, "The office of the true scholar in our republic is to connect himself in the most intimate and congenial relations with the energetic and busy population of which he is too often merely an insignificant unit. He is never to stand aloof from the concerns of the people. . . . He is never to set himself above them as their condescending instructor" (1:35–36). This desire for contact with "the concerns of the people" points not only to the motivation for Ripley's work as an editor and translator but also to the quest for community that led him to Brook Farm.

CONTEXTS FOR REFORM

By the late 1830s, the United States was in economic crisis. Even as Emerson in 1837 summoned up the duties of "the American scholar," the nation as a whole was suffering a financial panic triggered by rampant, risky speculation in western lands, canals, and railroad operations, and by huge state debts and overextended lines of credit by banks. The consequences included many bank failures (618 in 1837 alone) and slow-downs in public works. The price of cotton fell by one-half in New Orleans; in New York City, there were demonstrations protesting the high cost of food, housing, and fuel, and mobs ransacked food and supply warehouses. Unemployment was widespread, and between 1836 and 1842, for those fortunate enough to find work, wages plummeted by one-third.

The panic of 1837 forced reformers, cultural critics, and intellectuals to scrutinize the American social and economic order and consider how it might be modified, both to relieve mass distress and to enable men and women to create conditions within which they could realize their higher selves. In *Democracy in America*, the French aristocrat Alexis de Tocqueville fastened on a fact that troubled many Americans — the transformation of persons, and separation of classes, that the ever-increasing division of labor had caused (2:169). When Karl Marx and Friedrich Engels described and analyzed the effects of capitalism in England and Europe, they made intensified versions of this same point. It was not only the miserable, inhumane physical conditions of the workers' lives that Marx and Engels deplored, but also the alienation from work — from life itself. (See Part Two, Chapter 1, in this book.)

Sometimes the indictments by Americans of the flawed social order were extreme, even apocalyptic. Orestes A. Brownson, for example, stressed in a two-part essay on "the laboring classes" that America was characterized by poverty for the many, exploitative forms of labor, and failure in practice to live up to the tenets of Christianity that the nation claimed to embrace. He concluded that evils had become embedded in the structure of society and that government must therefore repeal laws that oppress laborers, pass new ones that bring these classes to equality with the fortunate and privileged, and destroy monopolies and banks and inherited property. Brownson conceded that "the rich, the business community," would never consent to such reform without desperately battling against it, and "it will come, if it ever come at all, only at the conclusion of war, the like of which the world as yet has never witnessed, and from which, however inevitable it may seem to the eye of philosophy, the heart of Humanity recoils with horror" (see Part Two, p. 246 in this book).

Brownson's article was met with angry rebuttals — he was said to be instigating class war — and his fellow Democrats disavowed it.

But class war, or at least class strife and struggle, was already under way, as the newspaper writings of the workers'-rights and land-reform advocate George Henry Evans demonstrate (see Part Two, Chapter 1). Reformers argued as to whether it was possible to change the socioeconomic order from within and provide alternatives to it before violence became the only recourse. They asked what would be the shape of change, what reform would necessitate, and what would mark its limits.

These questions are especially pointed when one recalls that the 1830s and 1840s were the decades in which abolitionism began its steady, difficult rise. William Lloyd Garrison started his abolitionist newspaper, *The Liberator,* in January 1831 (see Part Two, Chapter 1); the New England Anti-Slavery Society was formed in Boston in January 1832; and a national organization, the American Anti-Slavery Society, was established in Philadelphia in December 1833. As mob attacks on abolitionists in the 1830s showed (Garrison was nearly killed in Boston in October 1835), this reform struck many as dangerous and subversive. It would mean incalculable changes for both the Southern states, where millions of blacks were held in bondage, and the Northern states, which depended on the cotton crop that slave labor produced.

Many reformers were hesitant about abolitionism. Garrison was often labeled a fanatic and was criticized for focusing more on the sufferings of African Americans in the South than on the oppressed lives of whites nearby in the North. Brownson in "The Laboring Classes," George Henry Evans, and the utopian theorist Albert Brisbane in *Social Destiny of Man* (see Part Two, Chapters 1 and 2) contended that black slaves were actually better off than white workingmen: slaves lacked legal freedom but could count on a measure of security. They argued that "wage slavery," which made poor workers and their families dependent on hard jobs at low pay, was worse than "black slavery" and should be remedied first.[1]

Southerners saw no reason to attack black slavery at all. But pro-slavery theorists were quick to register that capitalism was rife with the exploitation and abuse of workers and their families. In ways that might surprise us, the pro-slavery argument thus overlapped with the

---

[1]Needless to say, African Americans did not share the notion that bondage meant tolerable work, a decent life, and security. In his *Narrative* (1853), Solomon Northrup, who had been held in slavery in Louisiana, presents a cogent rebuttal (see Part Two, Chapter 1).

proscriptions against white wage slavery and the evils of industrialism made by Brownson and other reformers and friends of workingmen.

The temperance movement was another powerful force for social change. To reformers, excessive drinking was a serious social problem that led to joblessness, poor performance at work, lost wages, and mistreatment of wives and children, and they banded together in thousands of state and local temperance groups and organizations. By 1835, the American Temperance Society, begun by evangelicals in Boston a decade earlier, claimed 1.5 million members — more than 10 percent of the free population of the country. The Washingtonian Temperance Society, which got under way in the late 1830s and concentrated on reforming drunkards and persuading them to take an abstinence pledge, was also extremely popular. Abraham Lincoln delivered one of his most important early speeches before the Washingtonian Temperance Society of Springfield, Illinois, in February 1842 (see Part Two, Chapter 1). Hawthorne's writing and publication of *The Blithedale Romance* coincided with the midcentury climax of the temperance cause — the passage in 1851 of the "Maine law" that prohibited the manufacture and sale of intoxicating liquors in that state.

The women's movement took early root in temperance activism. By seeking to moderate or eliminate the use of hard liquor, women could be advocates for reform and agents of change without seeming to step outside their socially prescribed roles of defender of the home and protector of their children. In the 1820s and 1830s, women formed roughly half the membership of American Temperance Society auxiliaries and state societies. They ran societies of their own as well as joining others with a mixed membership.

The "woman question" emerged most dramatically, however, as a by-product of abolitionism. As Lydia Maria Child, Margaret Fuller, and Elizabeth Cady Stanton pointed out, it was the struggle for freedom for African Americans that clarified for white, middle-class women the nature of their own oppression and lack of full equality — that they had, for example, no control of their property once they married and were excluded from most occupations and from advanced schooling (see Part Two, Chapter 4).

The Blithedale Romance studies divisions and tensions within individual gender roles and conflicts within male and female friendships, as these began to loom with the rise of women's rights campaigns. As his depiction of Zenobia shows, Hawthorne was drawn to the idea of powerful, passionate women but, at the same time, was highly ambivalent about the challenge to traditional gender roles that such women represented. He was both attracted to and threatened, and even repelled, by women reformers and activists.

Another urgent issue of the era, and again one that figures in *The Blithedale Romance*, was prison reform. American prisons, it was generally agreed, were a disgrace, and two new systems — organized and orderly but extremely rigid — competed for acceptance. The first (the "Pennsylvania" or "separate" system) stressed the total isolation of prisoners, who lived in windowless cells, could not speak with other prisoners (they were prevented even from knowing the identities of other inmates), and were denied outside visitors. A model institution of this type was Eastern Penitentiary in Philadelphia, which opened in 1829. The second (the "Auburn" or "congregate" system), begun at Auburn and Ossining (Sing Sing) prisons in New York in the early 1820s, enforced isolation at night and forbade conversation but allowed prisoners to work together, under strict supervision, during the day.

Samuel Gridley Howe and Theodore Parker were among the reformers who made specific recommendations for improving prisons and transforming criminals into good citizens (see Part Two, Chapter 1), and in *The Blithedale Romance*, Hollingsworth shares their broad concerns. Hawthorne, however, is not specific about the kind of prison reform that his character Hollingsworth espouses. Exactly what Hollingsworth wants matters less to Hawthorne than the fact that this reformer desires it so adamantly and cannot tolerate any opposition or disagreement.

The reformers of Hawthorne's era made American society better than it was — at least that is how we would view the progressive results of anti-slavery and women's rights, and, to an extent, the moral betterment and humane policies that temperance and prison reform instilled. But for Hawthorne, reform too often led to narrowness of vision, intolerance, and fanaticism, as Hollingsworth's conduct reveals. It brought with it, he believed, bad consequences for persons that the reformers, wedded to the changes they demanded, failed to anticipate and cared little about. Hawthorne was skeptical about proposals for social change and skeptical, too, about new communities and movements based on these proposals. Detached, ironic, critical, Hawthorne was nonetheless a skeptic with an insider's experience, having lived as a reformer himself in the utopian community of Brook Farm.

BROOK FARM AND
UTOPIAN COMMUNITIES

The scholar-minister George Ripley was deeply affected by the scenes of unemployment, poverty, and human degradation he glimpsed in cities and towns in the 1830s. He visited religious communities in the Midwest and admired their sense of common purpose and absence of class distinctions even as he regretted that they placed so little emphasis on the individual. Many reformers — the diverse men and women among the transcendentalists in particular — were vexed by the question of how to reshape the social order without obliging persons to compromise their freedom and curtail their own development. Ripley wanted to design and develop a community that would fulfill both personal and social goals, not sacrifice one for the other.

In the summer of 1840, Ripley attended a convention of "The Friends of Universal Reform" in Groton, Massachusetts, and soon thereafter another reform convention that met on Chardon Street in Boston. During this same summer, he and his wife vacationed at Ellis Farm, the future site of Brook Farm, in West Roxbury, about eight miles southwest of Boston. Ripley perused books on agriculture, and he met with the Christian reformer Adin Ballou, who launched the community of Hopedale, in Milford, Massachusetts, in the 1840s. He held weekly meetings in his Boston home, in the winter of 1840–41, to discuss his interest in settling with a group of people at Ellis Farm. These conversations included Margaret Fuller, Theodore Parker, the Harvard graduate and former minister John Sullivan Dwight, and the Unitarian clergyman William Henry Channing, and soon they branched outward to Emerson's residence in Concord.

The main document in the background of Brook Farm is Ripley's "Letter to the Church in Purchase Street," addressed to his Boston congregation on October 1, 1840. In it Ripley said that it was imperative that the Gospel be put into practice "in the living present," and his words about the ideal church expressed the principles he would aim to implement at Brook Farm: "the true followers of Jesus are a band of brothers; they compose one family; they attach no importance whatever to the petty distinctions of birth, rank, wealth, and station." For Ripley, the "great fact" was "human equality before God," and it was this fact that American society ignored (Frothingham 73–74).

In his letter to his congregation, Ripley identified himself as a transcendentalist. Both Christiantity and transcendentalism, he declared,

uphold the belief that "there is a light . . . which enlighteneth every
man that cometh into the world." It is therefore not surprising that as
Ripley moved forward with his Brook Farm experiment, he turned to
Emerson. Writing to Emerson on November 9, 1840, Ripley outlined
the goals of Brook Farm — among them, securing "union between
intellectual and manual labour" (qtd. in Frothingham 307) — and he
noted that this venture, though small at first, would illuminate the
path for entire nations to follow.

Replying sometime in mid-December, Emerson wished Ripley well
but said he would not join the community himself. As Emerson made
clear in an address, "Man the Reformer," which he delivered in
Boston in January 1841 and later published in *The Dial,* he had always judged manual labor and agricultural work important — there
was an "education" in them (see Part Two, Chapter 3). But Brook
Farm, he told Ripley, was not right for him: "I must assume my own
vows" (qtd. in Frothingham 315). Emerson believed that his situation
in Concord was nearly ideal for his writing and studies, and he was
wary of the plan that Ripley favored.

This response no doubt disappointed Ripley, but he moved forward. On January 1, 1841, he resigned as minister of the Purchase
Street Church, where he had served since November 8, 1826, and
preached his final sermon on March 28. Yet Ripley was taking his
ministry to a new location rather than abandoning it altogether. For
him, "Brook Farm was simply the logical completion of the pulpit
ministration; a final proof of the speaker's sincerity" (Frothingham
108–9). In sermons at his church, Ripley had spoken about the ever-
widening gap between the rich and the poor; he had decried capitalist
domination of political, legal, and economic institutions; and he had
evoked for his congregation the bitter plight of the workingman. At
Brook Farm, he hoped to nourish brotherhood and sisterhood in an
atmosphere that would combine rewarding work, study, and leisure.
People would cooperate and share with one another, in line with the
verses in the Acts of the Apostles: "And all that believed were together, and had all things common. . . . And the multitude of them
that believed were of one heart and of one soul: neither said any of
them that aught of the things which he possessed was his own; but
they had all things common" (2:44; 4:32).

Brook Farm was only one of many utopias, religious or secular,
undertaken in the first half of the nineteenth century. These included
communities set up by Robert Owen and his son Robert Dale Owen
at New Harmony, Indiana; Frances Wright at Nashoba, Tennessee;

and John Humphrey Noyes in Putney, Vermont, and later in Oneida, New York. In addition, there were many "phalanxes" — communities based on the ideas of the French theorist Charles Fourier — some of which were fairly prosperous and others of which lasted only a short while before being riven by factionalism or undercut by debt. Perhaps the most extraordinary of the utopian communities began with the settlements in the Midwest founded by the Mormon prophet Joseph Smith. These culminated in the great migration westward, led by Brigham Young, to Salt Lake City, Utah, which became the Mormon headquarters and center for the Church of Jesus Christ of Latter-Day Saints. For scholars and students of American literature, however, Brook Farm has always seemed special, because of its connection to *The Blithedale Romance,* and because its residents and visitors included many gifted writers, artists, and intellectuals, such as Emerson, Ripley, Brownson, Peabody, and Fuller, who described it in memorable terms (see Part Two).

For Ripley, his wife and sister, and the fifteen or so original members, life at Brook Farm seems to have been delightful but difficult. Though well-intentioned, Ripley had made a poor choice of site. The landscape was indeed beautiful — wide pastures and an expanse of woods, with the Charles River nearby; an elm and sycamore providing shade by the main farmhouse (which residents named "the Hive"); and terraces that led to a brook. But the soil was rocky and poor for farming and needed to be cleared and cultivated. Most members were inexperienced at farming, and, as Hawthorne discovered, the labor placed demands on time and energy that never ended.

In addition to farming, Brook Farm revolved around a school, with primary, elementary, and preparatory levels. Ripley noted that "we are a company of teachers. . . . The branch of industry we pursue, as our primary object and chief means of support, is teaching" (qtd. in Cooke 54). The faculty was a good one: Ripley taught philosophy and mathematics; Dwight, music and Latin; and Charles A. Dana, German and Greek. Field work, the study of plant and animal life, and lab experiments were also woven into the curriculum.

Brook Farm members (eventually peaking at about one hundred) could either pay their board or work for it — the men as teachers in the school and laborers in the farms and small shops, and the women as teachers, houseworkers, and preparers of food for market. The older boys and girls who attended school performed one to two hours per day of manual labor, such as hoeing or dishwashing. Autobiographies, memoirs, letters, and journals describe pleasant conversations at the six tables in Brook Farm's main dining room, good music, walking trips to concerts in Boston, boating, skating, and dancing. John Sullivan Dwight did much in his lectures and writings to promote appreciation of Beethoven, Mozart, Handel, and Haydn; he said that "the great music came in because it was in full affinity with the best thoughts stirring in fresh, earnest souls" (qtd. in Cooke 68). There were readings of Dante in Italian; Ripley lectured on the philosophers Kant and Spinoza; and visitors such as Emerson, Alcott, and Fuller gave lectures and led discussions. Other favorite pastimes were dramatic readings, costume parties, and the staging of plays.

By 1842, Brook Farm included the main building, the "Hive"; the Eyrie House (where the Ripleys and six new members lived); the Cottage and Pilgrim houses; and two large sheds. Women took care of most of the domestic chores and arranged trips and joint activities, but men assisted them. Women also voted and held office in the community. (It took a two-thirds vote, after a two-month probationary period, for a new member to be accepted.) In her reminiscences of Brook Farm, Rebecca Codman Butterfield, who lived there from 1843 to 1847, said that its central idea was socialism — "by which I mean," she explained, "the enlargement and improvement of the Home." Women did most of the housework and men the outdoor work, she observed, yet labor was not always divided along traditional gender lines. Above all, what stood out was that "no one questioned the right or propriety of a woman's doing any act, following any vocation, taking part in any enterprise in which men were engaged, that she felt fitted for or was disposed to undertake" (see Part Two, p. 454).

HAWTHORNE AT BROOK FARM

In March 1837, Hawthorne published *Twice-Told Tales,* a collection of eighteen stories that had previously appeared in periodicals. He sent a copy to Elizabeth Peabody, and she reviewed the work of this "first rate genius" in March 1838 (Peabody, *Letters* 199). In November 1837, the thirty-three-year-old Hawthorne had made his first call on the Peabody family, and shortly thereafter he met Elizabeth's sister, Sophia, whom he courted and to whom he became secretly engaged. By July 1839, Hawthorne was referring to himself in letters to Sophia as "thy husband."[2]

---

[2]For detailed information on Hawthorne's life, see the Chronology in this volume.

Hawthorne's desire to marry Sophia intensified his already pressing need for a reliable income. In January 1839, through friends in the Democratic party, he was appointed the weigher and gauger at the Boston Custom House at $1,500 per year. Hawthorne performed his job well but found it tedious and irritating. He resigned from his post in November 1840 and decided in this same month to join Brook Farm. He arrived on April 12, 1841, traveling from Boston in the middle of a snowstorm, as does Coverdale, his narrator in *The Blithedale Romance*. He hoped to find a home he could share with Sophia, to whom he had been engaged for nearly two years, and a source of a modest but sufficient income that would allow him private time for his literary craft in a small, supportive community.

On his arrival at Brook Farm, Hawthorne faced a pile of 320 wagonloads of manure that needed to be spread, and soon he and the others were busy cutting and carrying wood, chopping hay, and plowing and planting the fields. In his first letter to Sophia, April 13, 1841, Hawthorne assured her, "Think that I am gone before, to prepare a home for my Dove, and will return for her, all in good time." He signed his first letter to his sisters Elizabeth and Louisa (who were unsympathetic to his Brook Farm foray) "Nath. Hawthorne, Ploughman." He said he enjoyed the countryside, the routine, and the fellowship, and he marveled at the tasks he performed, exclaiming in an April 16 letter to Sophia, "Thy husband has milked a cow!!!" (For Hawthorne's letters while at Brook Farm, see Part Two, Chapter 3.)

Hawthorne's dedication inspired everybody. Elizabeth Peabody remarked in an April 26, 1841, letter to John Sullivan Dwight that "Hawthorne has taken hold with the greatest spirit and proves a fine workman" (qtd. in Haraszti 17). In a May 6 letter to Dwight, Ripley's wife, Sophia, proclaimed, "Hawthorne is one to reverence, to admire with that deep admiration so refreshing to the soul. He is our prince — prince in everything — yet despising no labour and very athletic and able-bodied in the barnyard and field" (qtd. in Haraszti 18). George Ripley was very pleased that Hawthorne had chosen to join the community and said that he "worked like a dragon" (qtd. in Lathrop 186).

Yet Hawthorne's signs of discontent were evident as early as April 22, when he apologized to Sophia for his "abominable" handwriting — the result of having chopped wood and turned a grindstone for long hours. "It is an endless surprise to me," he admitted, "how much work there is to be done in the world." He declared himself fit, and said that he took delight in the landscape. "I am transformed into a complete farmer," he remarked in a May 3 letter to his sister Louisa, and in the midst of "one of the most beautiful places I ever saw in my life." The next day, writing to Sophia, he announced he was "engaged in a righteous and heaven-blessed way of life." But on June 1, he confessed that he had been "too busy to write thee a long letter. . . . I think this present life of mine gives me an antipathy to pen and ink, even more than my Custom House experience did," and he went on to bemoan the onerous work he was obliged to perform. On July 16, he had to tell G. S. Hillard, editor of *The Token,* that he could not submit a story he had promised: "Now, I have no quiet at all."

"Thou and I must form other plans for ourselves," Hawthorne observed to Sophia in an August 22 letter, "for I can see few or no signs that Providence purposes to give us a home here." In several letters to Sophia, he referred to his bondage and enslavement at Brook Farm, and in his letter of September 3, he went so far as to profess that "the real Me was never an associate of the community." At the same time — his ambivalence and uncertainty showing — Hawthorne intimated that he and Sophia might reside there after all, saying this in letters in September and again in mid-October.

By August, Hawthorne had become a boarder, paying his own way (four dollars per week), and thereby freeing himself from manual labor. He spent the first three weeks of September at home in Salem, but was back at Brook Farm by September 22. He still had not given up on the community. How otherwise to explain the curious fact that in a letter to Sophia of September 30 he reported that he had been elected a trustee of Brook Farm and chairman of the Committee of Finance? Hawthorne accepted these posts and, furthermore, purchased two shares in the Brook Farm Institute of Agriculture and Education for $1,000 — money he had saved while working at the Custom House in Boston.

In December 1842, six months after marrying Sophia, Hawthorne resigned his position as trustee and sought to recover his $1,000 investment (it appears he had also invested $500 toward the purchase of a home), but at this time Ripley and Charles A. Dana could give him only $475.95. In the fall of 1845, Hawthorne filed suit to recover his money, and on February 21, 1846, as the date of the trial approached, he wrote the following in a letter to his friend Horatio Bridge: "Brook Farm, I suspect, is soon to see worse times than it ever has yet — at least, so men of business appear to think. Let it sink, say I; — it has long since ceased to have any sympathy from me, though individually I wish well to all concerned."

The trial itself took place in Concord, on March 7 or 9, 1846 — a few days after the new main building at Brook Farm was destroyed by fire. The decision of the court went in Hawthorne's favor, but it is not certain whether the debt to him was actually paid. Probably it was not, despite the efforts that the court continued to make as late as August 1849.

FOURIERISM

By the time Hawthorne wrote *The Blithedale Romance* in 1851–52, he had seen how Brook Farm had evolved and ended. In the novel, Hawthorne blends his own experiences with allusions and references to the later history of Brook Farm, when its members aligned themselves with the utopian principles of the French socialist Charles Fourier.

The central figure in outlining and promoting Fourierism in the United States was Albert Brisbane, termed by Brook Farmers the "Great Apostle." Brisbane had studied under the philosopher G. W. F. Hegel in Berlin and under the liberal French philosopher Victor Cousin in Paris, and he had known Fourier personally. He presented Fourier's views in *Social Destiny of Man* (1840), *A Concise Exposition of the Doctrine of Association* (1843), and in a regular column for Horace Greeley's paper, the New York *Tribune,* from 1842 to 1844.

Fourier, as Brisbane showed, emphasized not the city, town, or single farm or farms but, rather, the "phalanx," a highly organized community of 1,600 persons, and the "phalanstery," the large building where life would be centered. Fourier favored a complex, multiple division of labor, with many tasks and occupations, and with each person belonging to as many as thirty to forty work groups. As no person would spend much time in any one group, no job would come to seem tedious. The systematic character of Fourierism, with its precise timetables and plans for the formation of work teams, provided blueprints for community life unlike any previous plans that had been followed at Brook Farm. (For selections by Fourier and Brisbane, see Part Two, Chapter 2.)

The Brook Farmers did not follow Fourier uncritically. They were not in agreement, for example, with his proposals for a more open and experimental marital and sexual life. But Fourierism was consistent with Brook Farm's theme of cooperation, and it included features, such as care for the sick and aged, that had been central to Brook Farm since its inception. Inevitably, too, the earlier phase of Brook Farm had devoted some attention to the scheduling and monitoring of work.

In January 1844, a Fourierist constitution was announced for the "Brook Farm Association," and the Fourierist journal, *The Phalanx,* reported on February 5, 1844, that Brook Farm was in "process of transformation and extension from its former condition of an educational establishment mainly, to a regularly organized association — embracing the various departments of industry, art, and science." This purpose was made clear in the "Introductory Statement" to the Constitution of the Brook Farm Association: "we yield an unqualified assent to that doctrine of universal unity which Fourier teaches." The Brook Farmers' new position, the statement added, was one that their observations and experiences had prepared for and validated: "The law of groups and series is . . . the law of human nature, and when men are in true social relations, their industrial organization will necessarily assume those forms" ("Introductory" 80–81).

Why did Brook Farm transform itself into a Fourierist phalanx? In part it did because some members and frequent visitors were discontented and judged a new direction was necessary. The English reformer Charles Lane, commenting on the state of affairs at Brook Farm in January 1844, concluded that "it is not a community: it is not truly an association: it is merely an aggregation of persons, and lacks that oneness of spirit, which is probably needful to make it of deep and lasting value to mankind" (354). But Brook Farm was also in financial trouble. There was no local market for its trade goods, and the cost of the interest payments on loans was a heavy burden. Something drastic had to be done, and, by early 1843, the community was already diversifying work to make it more productive and profitable, requiring sixty hours of labor per week by each adult, planning a central building, and making efforts at fund-raising.

The context for reform throughout the nation had altered, too, as the effects of the financial panic of 1837 wore off. Reform movements picked up speed — especially abolitionism, which was now making its way into national politics, and the temperance movement, which had many supporters. But alternative communities, though they did not disappear altogether, now seemed less urgent. "What put a stop to these co-operative experiments was not only their bad management," notes the scholar Zoltan Haraszti, "but also the fact that with the return of better times people lost interest in them" (11).

The final blow to Brook Farm came on the evening of March 3, 1846, when fire destroyed the phalanstery just as its construction — begun in the summer of 1844 — neared completion. The building — 175 feet long, three stories high, with a dining hall designed to seat three hundred to four hundred persons — was paid for by a $7,000 loan, at high interest. There was no insurance policy on it, and the financial loss was devastating. Ripley and his wife left on September 6, 1847, and the Brook Farm Association, deeply in debt, was dissolved in October 1847.

RELATIONSHIPS BETWEEN BROOK FARM AND *THE BLITHEDALE ROMANCE*

In his Preface, Hawthorne identifies *The Blithedale Romance* as a "romance" and explains that his "present concern with the Socialist Community is merely to establish a theatre, a little removed from the highway of ordinary travel," on which his characters can perform without "too close a comparison with the actual events of real lives." He says that Brook Farm was "certainly, the most romantic episode" of his life; it was "essentially a day-dream, and yet a fact" and thus offers "an available foothold between fiction and reality."

Using these words as a key, many scholars have explored the romance as a genre, with Hawthorne as its foremost theorist and practitioner.[3] But as Nina Baym has pointed out, the term is both inescapable and hard to define with precision. From 1820 to 1860, she explains, "romance" was used inconsistently and often as a synonym for "novel." When reviewers and essayists did make distinctions, as in commentaries on Hawthorne's fiction and prefaces, their usage varied from one piece to the next. Like others in these decades, Hawthorne was a writer of romances, but his understanding of the term was his own (see Baym, *Feminism* 57–70, and *Novels, Readers* 224–48).

In the Preface to *The House of the Seven Gables,* Hawthorne observes that the *novel* aims at "a very minute fidelity" to the possible

---

[3]Studies of the romance include the books by Bell; Carton; Levine, Pease (49–107); and Porte.

and probable, to the "ordinary course of man's experience," whereas in the *romance* the writer is free to be more fanciful and enjoys greater "latitude" as long as he respects "the truth of the human heart." In a November 3, 1850, letter to the publisher J. T. Fields, he stated, "In writing a romance, a man is always — or always ought to be — careering on the utmost verge of a precipitous absurdity, and the skill lies in coming as close as possible, without actually tumbling over."

Hawthorne creates such a doubleness about his subject in *The Blithedale Romance* — fictional yet real, distant yet close by — through combining two ranges of language. His narrator, Coverdale, uses words and phrases that are archaic, quaint, far from the America of the 1840s and 1850s. The archaic "shoon," for example, is used as the plural for "shoes"; "winged people" and "feathered citizens" are used for "birds"; "leafy tongues" is the phrase given for "foliage." Other phrases from earlier centuries include "as my conscience whispered me," "it rejoices me," "whom we wot of," "canst lift." But these and many similar instances are presented in the midst of Coverdale's references to Emerson, Fuller, transcendentalism, *The Dial*, Fourier, mesmerism, lyceum meetings, *The North American Review*, the California Gold Rush, the Mormon leader Joseph Smith, the literary critic Rufus Griswold, and the Hungarian revolutionary Lajos Kossuth, all of which cast the story into Hawthorne's own day.[4]

There is a doubleness, too, in Hawthorne's presentation of his central characters, by which the reader is prompted to seek sources for them only to remain unsure about the identities of the sources. The scholar Maurice Crane has noted with dismay that readers seem unable to resist the temptation "to find prototypes in the Brook Farm community for the characters in *The Blithedale Romance*" (lxxv). But this temptation is built into the novel itself from the Preface forward, as Hawthorne/Coverdale cites and alludes to an array of Brook Farmers and transcendentalists.

"Hollingsworth" was the title that Hawthorne nearly selected for his book. As he said in a May 2, 1852, letter to the literary critic E. P. Whipple, he hoped thereby to call attention to "the original figure about which the rest of the book clustered itself." This has induced scholars to be especially intent on finding the person on whom Hollingsworth was based, and they have proposed a dozen possibilities, including George Ripley, Orestes Brownson, Albert Brisbane, and Theodore Parker.

---

[4]For this point, I am indebted to the discussion in Crane (lxvii–lxxi).

Parker is a likely choice, both because of his intense personality and because of his interest in prison reform. As noted earlier, much attention was paid in the 1830s and 1840s to competing models for prison reform, and Hollingsworth's concern for the treatment of criminals is a skewed reflection of this. In their study of the penitentiary system in the United States (1833), the French travelers Gustave de Beaumont and Alexis de Tocqueville wrote that some reformers they encountered "occupy themselves continually with prisons; it is the subject to which all the labors of their life bear reference. Philanthropy has become for them a kind of profession, and they have caught the *monomanie* of the penitentiary system, which to them seems the remedy for all the evils of society" (80).

Parker — Ripley's good friend and a frequent visitor to Brook Farm — was among the persons gripped by the passion for improving prisons. In his sermon on "the dangerous classes in society," delivered at the Melodeon in Boston on January 31, 1847, he argued that whereas a few men were "born criminals," under the sway of a "bad nature," the vast majority of criminals were the product of vile social circumstances, particularly in cities. Parker maintained that criminals should receive neither cruel punishment nor hopeless incarceration but, instead, Christian teaching and training — not "force" but "love" that would instruct and cure them (see Part Two, pp. 298–99).

But perhaps the source for Hollingsworth was not a person whom Hawthorne knew at Brook Farm but someone whom many there admired — Charles Fourier. Hawthorne and his wife, Sophia, read Fourier's writings in the summer of 1844, and a year later, Sophia complained about one of Fourier's volumes that it was "abominable, immoral, irreligious, and void of all delicate sentiment." She added, "To make as much money and luxury and enjoyment out of man's lowest passions as possible, — this is the aim and end of his system. . . . My husband read the whole volume, and was entirely disgusted" (qtd. in J. Hawthorne 1:268–69). Despite his distaste, Hawthorne read several books by Fourier again in late summer and early fall of 1851.

In *The Blithedale Romance*, it is Hollingsworth who renders judgment on Fourier, in words that echo those used by Sophia in her letter. For him, the scandal lies not only in the perversity of desire and sexual motive that he claims to detect in Fourier's ideas but also in the distraction from authentic reform (i.e., *his* reform) that all other programs and utopian plans create.

It is interesting that Hawthorne makes Hollingsworth a reformer, not a political revolutionary, or public leader of men. No doubt he realized that his gifts as a novelist did not extend to depicting large-scale social upheaval and panoramic political action of the kind that Charles Dickens, for example, caught in *A Tale of Two Cities* (1859). The point is worth bringing up, however, because Hawthorne was writing not long after the explosion of revolutions throughout Europe in 1848 and the bloody suppressions that followed, which Margaret Fuller had reported on from Italy in newspaper columns for the New York *Tribune*. Near the end of *The Blithedale Romance*, Hawthorne refers briefly to the revolutionary Kossuth, who toured the United States in 1851–52 after the failure of the Hungarian republic, and whose Boston lecture Hawthorne attended. He thereby brings before the reader for a moment the specter of revolution and reaction, even as he allows Coverdale an ironic tone toward it, and dramatizes by contrast the narrower scope of his own novel.

Hawthorne believed that reformers like Hollingsworth, transfixed by an idea, crave to take possession of others and neutralize their individual agency. This perception of reform may help to account for the presence in *The Blithedale Romance* of mesmerism — a strange, complex theory and practice of possession, influence, and domination that both captivated and disturbed Hawthorne.

The Austrian physician Franz Mesmer (1734–1815) sketched his theory of "animal magnetism" in the late eighteenth century, and the term *mesmerism* was associated with other forms of spiritualism, hypnotic experiments and cures, and séances. Both Hawthorne's wife, Sophia, and her sister, Elizabeth, were interested in this pseudo-science, and such eminent writers as Harriet Martineau and Fuller recounted its beneficial effects for them (see Part Two, Chapter 1). Hawthorne alludes to and depicts mesmerism's powers in "The Artist of the Beautiful" (1844) and in greater detail in *The House of the Seven Gables* (1851).

Mesmerism and related spiritualist phenomena became widespread by the mid- to late 1840s. In 1845, Andrew Jackson Davis, a nineteen-year-old illiterate shoemaker from Poughkeepsie, New York, was revealed after tests and experiments to possess mesmeric powers; and the book he dictated, *The Principles of Nature, Her Divine Revelations, and a Voice to Mankind,* published in 1847, was a major sensation. Shortly thereafter, in the winter and spring of 1848, the Fox sisters, Maggie and Kate, in northern New York, after hearing rappings and knockings, began their communications with the world of spirits. The influential Horace Greeley vouched for their honesty in the New York *Tribune,* and they displayed their prowess in a series of public appearances and tours in 1849–50. They and many other mesmerists and mediums provided a very popular form of entertainment while also satisfying an authentic interest in spiritual mysteries and the afterlife.

For Hawthorne, mesmerism was yet another reform that had dangerous consequences. It meant the seizure of and control over one person by another, a form of control undertaken in the self-deluded expectation that transcendent good would be the result. Mesmerism functioned for Hawthorne as a context in which to assess the reformer's relationship to his or her audiences, and as a means, too, to probe the nature of the lover and the beloved. It also gave him additional terms for delving into the themes of privacy, secrecy, hypocrisy, and the evil influences that preyed on human gullibility and for exposing the hazards of scientific method.

Readers of *The Blithedale Romance* have also been curious about the source for Zenobia, the book's feminist reformer, and have often identified her with Margaret Fuller. Fuller took part in the early discussions about Brook Farm and visited it regularly. But "Utopia it is impossible to build up," she concluded, and she viewed Brook Farm not as a place with a real future but, rather, as a site for good talks about principles (qtd. in Emerson 2:29). Fuller conducted such talks at Brook Farm after the community was under way, leading one resident, Amelia Russell, to remark, "When listening to her wonderful conversations, which, by the way, were limited to one person — herself — and straining my mind to comprehend her meaning, I must own I have sometimes wished her English was rather plainer" (qtd. in Swift 212). A student at the school playfully observed that "there is no end to her talk" (qtd. in Codman 260). On the other hand, the Brook Farmer Georgiana Bruce Kirby paid tribute to Fuller's "wonderfully comprehensive judgment and tenderness" (173), and many shared this high esteem for her.

Like Fuller, Zenobia advocates women's rights, is full of passionate energy, and is self-dramatizing. In the final analysis, however, Zenobia should not be tied to a specific person but interpreted in the context of nineteenth-century feminism and the many voices who spoke in support of, or in resistance to, the women's movement. Fuller was in the company of Harriet Beecher Stowe, Angelina E. Grimké, Catharine Beecher, Harriet Farley, Lydia Maria Child, and Elizabeth Cady Stanton, all of whom articulated a conception of women's life and work that can be placed alongside Fuller's and profitably brought to bear when examining Hawthorne's portrayal of Zenobia. (See Part Two, Chapters 2 and 4.)

Still, the specific Zenobia/Fuller link is a difficult issue to resolve — present and absent at the same time. Some critics have even said that Hawthorne shows his dislike of Fuller by engineering a dreadful fate for Zenobia, and those who have made this argument have cited Hawthorne's hostile portrait in his notebook, where he depicts Fuller as "a great humbug" with many moral and intellectual defects (see Part Two, Chapter 4). But even this does not displace the fact that Zenobia is the most complicated character in *The Blithedale Romance*. She has a radiant personality and acute intelligence, and yet she lacks insight into the effects of her power and its meanings for herself. Hawthorne represents her as a woman for whom independence is crucial, even as she longs to defer to Hollingsworth and ally herself with his zealously prosecuted plan to improve the prisons. Here, as in his novel as a whole, Hawthorne explores reform and reformers in depth, studying their beliefs, feelings, values, and relationships, balancing his judgments and reaching complex conclusions.

WORKS CITED

Baym, Nina. *Feminism and American Literary History: Essays.* New Brunswick, N.J.: Rutgers UP, 1992.
———. *Novels, Readers, and Reviewers: Responses to Fiction in Antebellum America.* Ithaca: Cornell UP, 1984.
Beaumont, Gustave de, and Alexis de Tocqueville. *On the Penitentiary System in the United States and Its Application in France.* Trans., with an introduction, notes, and additions by Francis Lieber. Philadelphia: Carey, Lea, and Blanchard, 1833. Rpt. Carbondale: Southern Illinois UP, n.d.
Bell, Michael Davitt. *Hawthorne and the Historical Romance of New England.* Princeton: Princeton UP, 1971.
Brook Farm Papers. Massachusetts Historical Society.
Carton, Evan. *The Rhetoric of American Romance: Dialectic and Identity in Emerson, Dickinson, Poe, and Hawthorne.* Baltimore: Johns Hopkins UP, 1985.
Codman, John Thomas. *Brook Farm: Historic and Personal Memoirs.* Boston: Arena, 1894.
Cooke, George Willis. *John Sullivan Dwight: Brook-Farmer, Editor, and Critic of Music.* Boston: Small, Maynard, 1898.

Crane, Maurice Aaron. "A Textual and Critical Edition of Hawthorne's *Blithedale Romance*." Diss. U of Illinois, 1953.

Emerson, R. W., W. H. Channing, and J. F. Clarke, eds. *Memoirs of Margaret Fuller Ossoli*. 2 vols. Boston: Phillips, Sampson, 1852.

Frothingham, Octavius. *George Ripley*. Boston: Houghton Mifflin, 1883.

Haraszti, Zoltan. *Idyll of Brook Farm, as Revealed by Unpublished Letters in the Boston Public Library*. Boston: Trustees of the Public Library, 1937.

Hawthorne, Julian. *Nathaniel Hawthorne and His Wife: A Biography*. 2 vols. Boston: Osgood, 1884.

"Introductory Statement." "Constitution of the Brook Farm Association for Industry and Education." January 18, 1844. *The Phalanx* 1 (March 1, 1844): 80–82.

Kirby, Georgiana Bruce. *Years of Experience: An Autobiographical Narrative*. New York: Putnam, 1887.

Lane, Charles. "Brook Farm." *The Dial* 4 (January 1844): 351–57.

Lathrop, George Parsons. *A Study of Hawthorne*. 1876. New York: AMS, 1969.

Levine, Robert S. *Conspiracy and Romance: Studies in Brockden Brown, Cooper, Hawthorne, and Melville*. New York: Cambridge UP, 1989.

Peabody, Elizabeth. *Letters*. Ed. Bruce A. Ronda. Middletown, Conn.: Wesleyan UP, 1984.

Pease, Donald E. *Visionary Compacts: American Renaissance Writings in Cultural Context*. Madison: U of Wisconsin P, 1987.

Porte, Joel. *The Romance in America: Studies in Cooper, Poe, Hawthorne, Melville, and James*. Middletown, Conn.: Wesleyan UP, 1969.

Ripley, George, ed. *Philosophical Miscellanies*. 2 vols. Boston, Hilliard, Gray, 1838.

Stewart, Randall. *Nathaniel Hawthorne: A Biography*. New Haven: Yale UP, 1948.

Swift, Lindsay. *Brook Farm: Its Members, Scholars, and Visitors*. New York: Macmillan, 1900.

Tocqueville, Alexis de. *Democracy in America*. 1835, 1840. 2 vols. New York: Vintage, 1945.

Chronology of
Hawthorne's Life and Times

1804

July 4: Nathaniel Hawthorne born in Salem, Massachusetts, second of three children of Nathaniel (1775–1808) and Elizabeth Manning Hathorne (1780–1849). Two sisters: Elizabeth (1802–1883) and Maria Louisa (1808–1852). (Hawthorne added a "w" to the family name sometime in the late 1820s.) Colonial ancestors include William Hathorne (1606?–1681), who pronounced judgment on Quakers, and John Hathorne (1641–1717), a magistrate in the Salem witch trials.

1808

March: Father dies of yellow fever in Surinam (Dutch Guiana).

April: Report of father's death arrives, and Hawthorne's mother takes the children and moves in with her relatives, the Mannings, in the family home in Salem.

1813

November: Hawthorne injures foot, suffers lameness, and is confined to house, unable to attend school for fourteen months.

1818

October: Family moves to Raymond, Maine; Hawthorne attends school in Portland.

1819–21

Lives with Manning relatives and attends school in Salem.

1820

March: Missouri Compromise enacted whereby Missouri is admitted to the Union as a slave state, Maine as a free state; slavery is prohibited in Louisiana Territory north of 36°30' latitude.

1821–25

Hawthorne attends Bowdoin College. Friends include Franklin Pierce (1804–1869), later a U.S. president (1852–56), and Henry Wadsworth Longfellow (1807–1882), later an eminent poet and translator. Begins writing stories and a novel.

1825–37

Lives with mother and sisters in Salem.

1825–28

Robert Owen (1771–1858) founds New Harmony community in Indiana. Frances Wright (1795–1852) founds Nashoba community in western Tennessee.

1826

James Fenimore Cooper (1789–1851), *The Last of the Mohicans.*

1827

Freedom's Journal, first African American newspaper, begins publication in New York.

1828

Hawthorne publishes *Fanshawe* anonymously in Boston at his own expense. (He disliked this book, and it was not republished until 1876.)
William Ladd (1778–1841) founds the American Peace Society.

1830–32

Hawthorne begins publishing stories and sketches, anonymously, in the *Salem Gazette* and in *The Token* (including "The Gentle Boy," "My Kinsman, Major Molineux," and "Roger Malvin's Burial").

1831

January: William Lloyd Garrison (1805–1879) begins the abolitionist newspaper *The Liberator.*

1832

January: New England Anti-Slavery Society is formed in Boston.
July: Controversy over the future of the Bank of the United States

between President Andrew Jackson (1767–1845), who refuses to recharter it, and bank president Nicholas Biddle (1786–1844).

December: Nullification crisis: President Jackson issues proclamation in reply to South Carolina's declaring federal tariff null and void and its threat to secede from the Union.

1833

December: American Anti-Slavery Society is organized in Philadelphia.

Lydia Maria Child (1802–1880), *An Appeal in Favor of That Class of Americans Called Africans.*

1835–36

Hawthorne's publications include "The Minister's Black Veil" and "The May-Pole of Merry Mount" in *The Token* and "Young Goodman Brown," "The Ambitious Guest," and "Wakefield" in *New-England Magazine.*

1836

March-August: Hawthorne is editor of the *American Magazine of Useful and Entertaining Knowledge* in Boston; fails to receive salary when magazine goes bankrupt.

Ralph Waldo Emerson (1803–1882), *Nature.*

1837

Under his own name, Hawthorne publishes *Twice-Told Tales,* a collection of eighteen stories previously published in periodicals.

May: U.S. suffers financial panic, economic collapse, and beginnings of mass unemployment; effects linger for the next seven years.

October: Hawthorne begins contributing stories and sketches (twenty-four over the next seven years) to the *United States Magazine and Democratic Review.*

November: Meets Sophia Peabody (1809–1871), his future wife, in Salem.

Emerson, "The American Scholar."

1838

Trail of Tears: The U.S. government forces the Cherokee nation to march from its native home in Georgia to Indian Territory (Oklahoma); thousands die. John Humphrey Noyes (1811–1886), founds a utopian community in Putney, Vermont.

Edgar Allan Poe (1809–1849), *Narrative of A. Gordon Pym.* Alexis de Tocqueville (1805–1859), first American edition of *Democracy in America* (2 vols., 1835).

1839

January: Through friends in the Democratic Party, Hawthorne is appointed weigher and gauger (a measurer of salt and coal) at the Boston Custom House at $1,200 per year.

July: Proposes marriage to Sophia Peabody.

1840–41

Hawthorne publishes three children's books: *Grandfather's Chair, Famous Old People,* and *Liberty Tree.*

1840

June: World's Anti-Slavery Convention, meeting in London, refuses to admit women delegates from America.

July: First issue of the transcendentalist journal, *The Dial.*

Washington Temperance Society is formed; within three years, it claims to have reformed five hundred thousand intemperate drinkers and one hundred thousand alcoholics.

Richard Henry Dana, Jr. (1815–1882), *Two Years before the Mast.* Poe, *Tales of the Grotesque and Arabesque.*

1841

January 1: Hawthorne resigns from the Custom House (submitted November 1840).

April–October: Member of and investor in Brook Farm community in West Roxbury, Massachusetts.

April: The New York *Tribune,* edited by Horace Greeley (1811–1872), begins publication.

Dorothea Dix (1802–1887) begins campaign in Massachusetts to reform prisons and insane asylums.

Emerson, *Essays* (first series).

1842

January: English novelist Charles Dickens (1812–1870) begins five-month tour of United States.

July 9: Hawthorne marries Sophia and rents Old Manse, owned by Emerson family, in Concord, Massachusetts.

Adin Ballou (1803–1890) founds Hopedale community in Milford, Massachusetts. Massachusetts Supreme Court, in *Commonwealth* v. *Hunt,* establishes legality of labor unions. Massachusetts's child labor law limits workday of children under twelve to ten hours.

New edition of *Twice-Told Tales*. Longfellow, *Ballads and Other Poems*.

1842–45

Hawthorne meets members of Emerson's circle, including Amos Bronson Alcott (1799–1888), Margaret Fuller (1810–1850), and Henry David Thoreau (1817–1862). Publishes twenty sketches and stories, including "The Artist of the Beautiful," "The Birth-mark," "The Christmas Banquet," "Earth's Holocaust," and "Rappaccini's Daughter." Also edits *Journal of an African Cruiser*, by Horatio Bridge (1806–1893), a friend from Bowdoin.

1843

June: Amos Bronson Alcott and Charles Lane found Fruitlands community in Harvard, Massachusetts.

A utopian community, based on principles of French theorist Charles Fourier (1772–1837), is established at Red Bank, New Jersey. Many other Fourierist communities begun in the East and Midwest in 1840s and 1850s. Association for Improving the Condition of the Poor of New York City is founded.

William Hickling Prescott (1796–1859), *The History of the Conquest of Mexico*.

1844

January: John A. Collins (1810–1879), founds Skaneateles community in central New York.

March 3: Hawthorne's daughter Una born (d. 1877).

April: Texas Annexation Treaty provides for admission of Texas as a territory; is resisted in the U.S. Senate.

June: Mormon leader Joseph Smith (1805–1844) is murdered by a mob in Carthage, Illinois; Brigham Young (1801–1877) leads Mormons on westward migration (1846–47) to Utah territory.

December: Democrat James K. Polk (1795–1849) wins presidential election, defeating Whig candidate Henry Clay (1777–1852) and abolitionist Liberty Party candidate James Birney (1792–1857).

New York Prison Association is established. *The Dial* suspends publication.

Emerson, *Essays* (second series).

1845

June: Congress accepts annexation of Texas. Andrew Jackson — former president, Democratic party leader, and military hero — dies.

July: The *United States Magazine and Democratic Review* describes United States' "manifest destiny to overspread the continent."

October: Hawthorne moves family to Salem and lives with his mother and sisters.

December: Texas is admitted to the Union, the twenty-eighth state.

National Reform Association, advocating the rights of workingmen, established. Industrial Congress of the United States, a labor organization, established in New York City.

Frederick Douglass (1817–1895), *Narrative of the Life*. Fuller, *Woman in the Nineteenth Century*. Poe, *Tales*; *The Raven and Other Poems*.

1846

January: *De Bow's Review,* a pro-slavery periodical devoted to studies of southern social and economic life, begins publication.

April: Hawthorne is appointed surveyor in the Salem Custom House and sworn in on April 9. Publishes *Mosses from an Old Manse*.

May: United States declares war on Mexico.

June 22: Hawthorne's son, Julian, born (d. 1934).

August: Wilmot Proviso, proposed by Pennsylvania's Democratic congressman David Wilmot (1814–1868), states that slavery should be prohibited in any territory acquired during the war with Mexico.

Abraham Lincoln (1809–1865) elected to Congress from Illinois; serves 1847–49.

Herman Melville (1819–1891), *Typee*.

1847

May: American Medical Association is organized in Philadelphia.

Longfellow, *Evangeline*.

1848

January: Gold is discovered near a sawmill in California owned by John Sutter (1803–1880); start of the Gold Rush.

February: Treaty of Guadalupe Hidalgo ends the Mexican War; Mexico cedes five hundred thousand square miles of territory to the United States.

July: American women, led by Lucretia Mott (1793–1880) and Elizabeth Cady Stanton (1815–1902), meet at a convention in Seneca Falls, New York, to call for women's rights.

November: Boston Female Medical School, first medical school for women, opens.

John Humphrey Noyes establishes a utopian community in Oneida in central New York. Icarian utopian community is begun in Texas.

James Russell Lowell (1819–1891), *The Biglow Papers*; *A Fable for Critics*.

1849

June: Hawthorne loses surveyor's post following election of the Whig candidate for president, Zachary Taylor (1784–1850).

July 31: Mother dies.

September: Begins work on *The Scarlet Letter*.

Thoreau, *A Week on the Concord and Merrimack Rivers*; "Resistance to Civil Government" (republished in 1866 as "Civil Disobedience").

1850

March: *The Scarlet Letter* published.

May 1850–November 1851: Lives in Lenox, in western Massachusetts.

August: Hawthorne meets Herman Melville, who dedicates *Moby-Dick* (1851) to him.

September: Congress passes series of compromise measures designed to end the crisis over slavery; includes a more restrictive law for recapture of fugitive slaves.

Emerson, *Representative Men*. Susan Warner (1819–1895), *The Wide, Wide World*.

1851

Hawthorne publishes a new edition of *Twice-Told Tales* (March); *The House of the Seven Gables* (April); *A Wonder-Book for Girls and Boys* (November); and *The Snow-Image, and Other Twice-Told Tales* (December), which includes "Main Street" and "Ethan Brand."

May 20: Daughter, Rose, born (d. 1926).

November: Family moves to West Newton, Massachusetts.

New York *Daily Times* (name changed in 1857 to the *Times*) begins publication. Young Men's Christian Association (organized in England in 1844) opens chapters in Boston, Massachusetts, and Montreal, Canada. Asylum for Friendless Boys founded in New York City. "Maine Law" prohibits manufacture and sale of intoxicating liquors; by 1855, thirteen states have such laws. Josiah Warren (1798–1874), establishes the Modern Times community on Long Island, New York.

Melville, *Moby-Dick*.

1852

May: Hawthorne returns to Concord and lives in The Wayside, a house formerly owned by Amos Bronson Alcott.

July: *The Blithedale Romance* published.

July 27: Sister Louisa dies in a steamboat accident on the Hudson River.

September: Hawthorne publishes a campaign biography of Franklin Pierce.

November: Franklin Pierce, a Democrat, is elected U.S. president.

Massachusetts enacts school attendance law.

Oliver Wendell Holmes (1809–1894), *Poetical Works*. Melville, *Pierre*. Harriet Beecher Stowe (1811–1896), *Uncle Tom's Cabin*.

1853

March: Hawthorne is named American consul at Liverpool, England, by President Pierce. Leaves United States in July.

The American, or Know-Nothing, Party is formed; the party contends that only the native-born should hold public office and calls for repeal of naturalization laws. The Crystal Palace Exhibition of the Industry of All Nations held in New York City, to demonstrate U.S. industrial and technological progress.

Melville, "Bartleby the Scrivener."

1853–57

Hawthorne serves as Liverpool consul from August 1853 to October 1857. Keeps detailed notebooks.

1854

May: Kansas-Nebraska Act, sponsored by Senator Stephen A. Douglas (1813–1861) of Illinois, calls for "popular sovereignty" (that is, let the people decide) on the slavery question in the territories; the act heightens the slavery crisis.

July: Republican Party formed in Jackson, Michigan.

August: Hawthorne's *Tanglewood Tales,* a book for children, is published.

September: New edition of *Mosses from an Old Manse.*

Boston Public Library opens. Children's Aid Society is founded in New York City.

Thoreau, *Walden.*

1855

Hawthorne travels in England; in September, he makes his first visit to London.

May: Feminist and abolitionist Lucy Stone (1818–1893) becomes the first woman officially to keep maiden name in marriage.

New York *Daily News* established. *American Journal of Education* is begun by Henry Barnard (1811–1900). Violence erupts in Kansas territory over the slavery question.

John Bartlett (1820–1905), *Bartlett's Familiar Quotations*. Thomas Bullfinch (1796–1867), *The Age of Fable* (known as *Bullfinch's Mythology*). Douglass, *My Bondage and My Freedom*. Fanny Fern [Sara Payson Willis] (1811–1872), *Ruth Hall*. Longfellow, *Song of Hiawatha*. Walt Whitman (1819–1892), *Leaves of Grass*.

1856

Still traveling in England, Hawthorne meets British poets Robert Browning (1812–1889) and Elizabeth Barrett Browning (1806–1861) and other literary figures.

May: Congressman Preston Brooks (1819–1857) of South Carolina assaults Senator Charles Sumner (1811–1874) of Massachusetts for his anti-slavery "Crime against Kansas" speech.

Emerson, *English Traits*. Melville, *The Piazza Tales*. John Motley (1814–1877), *The Rise of the Dutch Republic*. Stowe, *Dred: A Tale of the Great Dismal Swamp*.

1857

February: Hawthorne resigns consulship.

March: In *Dred Scott* case, the Supreme Court declares that slaves are not citizens and that Congress cannot prohibit slavery in the territories.

May: Hawthorne is visited by Melville on May 4.

June/July: Hawthorne tours England and Scotland.

August: Widespread banking failures and financial panic.

Channing Home, a hospital for poverty-stricken women, opens in Boston.

The Atlantic Monthly, edited by James Russell Lowell, and *Harper's Weekly*, edited by George William Curtis (1824–1892), begin publication.

1858

Hawthorne travels to France and Italy. Lives in Rome (January–

May), Florence (June–October), and Rome (October–May 1859). Works on romance, *The Ancestral Footstep,* left unfinished. Compiles notebook entries. Begins *The Marble Faun.*

August–October: Stephen Douglas and Abraham Lincoln, candidates for U.S. Senate seat from Illinois, debate; Douglas wins reelection.

Cooper Union, an adult educational institution for the working class, opens in New York City. Religious revivalism sweeps across United States.

Holmes, *The Autocrat of the Breakfast Table.*

1859

April: Serious illness of daughter Una in Rome. Family returns in summer to England.

October: Anti-slavery forces led by John Brown (1800–1859) attempt to seize federal arsenal in Harpers Ferry, Virginia; Brown executed in December.

Harriet Wilson (1808?–1870), *Our Nig,* first novel by an African American to appear in the United States.

1860

February: Strikes and labor unrest erupt, beginning with a shoemakers' strike over wages and working conditions in Lynn, Massachusetts.

February/March: Hawthorne publishes *The Marble Faun* (titled *Transformation* in England).

June: Family returns to United States.

November: Lincoln elected U.S. president.

December: South Carolina secedes from the Union.

Emerson, *The Conduct of Life.* Thoreau, "A Plea for Captain John Brown."

1860–62

Hawthorne lives in Concord; works on two romances — *Dr. Grimshawe's Secret* and *Septimus Felton* — both left unfinished.

1861

April 1: Civil War begins with the Confederate attack on Fort Sumter, in Charleston Harbor, South Carolina.

Massachusetts Institute of Technology chartered in Boston, Massachusetts (and opened in 1865).

Rebecca Harding Davis (1831–1910), *Life in the Iron Mills.* Harriet

Jacobs (1813–1897), *Incidents in the Life of a Slave Girl.* Frederick Law Olmsted (1822–1903), *The Cotton Kingdom.*

1862

March: Hawthorne meets Abraham Lincoln in Washington, D.C.

July: "Chiefly about War-Matters," an essay on the Civil War, is published in *The Atlantic Monthly.*

October 1862–August 1863: Hawthorne contributes essays to *The Atlantic Monthly* on experiences while in England.

1863

January: Lincoln issues Emancipation Proclamation, freeing slaves in territory controlled by the Confederacy.

September: *Our Old Home,* a collection of articles on England, is published.

Louisa May Alcott (1832–1888), *Hospital Sketches.*

1864

May 19: Hawthorne dies in Plymouth, New Hampshire, while on trip with Franklin Pierce. Buried May 23 in Sleepy Hollow cemetery, Concord.

July: *The Atlantic Monthly* publishes parts of work-in-progress as "Scenes from 'The Dolliver Romance.'"

The Blithedale Romance

PREFACE

In the 'BLITHEDALE'[1] of this volume, many readers will probably suspect a faint and not very faithful shadowing of BROOK FARM, in Roxbury,[2] which (now a little more than ten years ago) was occupied and cultivated by a company of socialists.[3] The Author does not wish to deny, that he had this Community in his mind, and that (having had the good fortune, for a time, to be personally connected with it) he has occasionally availed himself of his actual reminiscences, in the hope of giving a more lifelike tint to the fancy-sketch in the following pages. He begs it to be understood, however, that he has considered

[1]'BLITHEDALE': the word combines *blithe,* meaning happy, joyous, contented, cheerful, and *dale,* meaning a portion of land or, more specifically, a river valley running between hills or through high land. Hawthorne coined the word; there is no entry for it in *The Oxford English Dictionary.* Compare *Rasselas* (1759), a philosophical romance by Samuel Johnson (1709–1784), whose protagonist dwells in the "happy valley" but finds it suffocating and escapes from it. Hawthorne refers to Johnson's book in *Fanshawe* (1828), ch. 1, and *The House of the Seven Gables* (1851), ch. 9.

[2]BROOK FARM, *in Roxbury:* Cooperative community (1841–1847), emerging from transcendentalist movement, located in West Roxbury, Massachusetts, about eight miles southwest of Boston. Hawthorne resided there from April to November 1841.

[3]*socialists:* In the broad sense used here, refers to theory and practice of collective, communal life, in opposition to the competitive, market-driven system of capitalism. Socialism also means joint or collective ownership of property — which Brook Farm did not advocate.

the Institution itself as not less fairly the subject of fictitious handling, than the imaginary personages whom he has introduced there. His whole treatment of the affair is altogether incidental to the main purpose of the Romance;[4] nor does he put forward the slightest pretensions to illustrate a theory, or elicit a conclusion, favorable or otherwise, in respect to Socialism.

In short, his present concern with the Socialist Community is merely to establish a theatre, a little removed from the highway of ordinary travel, where the creatures of his brain may play their phantasmagorical antics, without exposing them to too close a comparison with the actual events of real lives. In the old countries, with which Fiction has long been conversant, a certain conventional privilege seems to be awarded to the romancer; his work is not put exactly side by side with nature; and he is allowed a license with regard to every-day Probability, in view of the improved effects which he is bound to produce thereby. Among ourselves, on the contrary, there is as yet no such Faery Land, so like the real world, that, in a suitable remoteness, one cannot well tell the difference, but with an atmosphere of strange enchantment, beheld through which the inhabitants have a propriety of their own. This atmosphere is what the American romancer needs. In its absence, the beings of imagination are compelled to show themselves in the same category as actually living mortals; a necessity that generally renders the paint and pasteboard of their composition but too painfully discernible. With the idea of partially obviating this difficulty, (the sense of which has always pressed very heavily upon him,) the Author has ventured to make free with his old, and affectionately remembered home, at BROOK FARM, as being, certainly, the most romantic episode of his own life — essentially a day-dream, and yet a fact — and thus offering an available foothold between fiction and reality. Furthermore, the scene was in good keeping with the personages whom he desired to introduce.

These characters, he feels it right to say, are entirely fictitious. It would, indeed, (considering how few amiable qualities it distributes among his imaginary progeny,) be a most grievous wrong to his former excellent associates, were the Auther to allow it to be supposed that he has been sketching any of their likenesses. Had he attempted it, they would at least have recognized the touches of a friendly pen-

---

[4]*Romance:* Hawthorne's term for the kind of prose fiction he wrote. See also Hawthorne, "The Custom-House," Introductory to *The Scarlet Letter* (1850), and Preface to *The House of the Seven Gables*; and Henry James, Preface to the New York edition of *The American* (1877, 1907).

cil. But he has done nothing of the kind. The self-concentrated Philanthropist; the high-spirited Woman, bruising herself against the narrow limitations of her sex; the weakly Maiden, whose tremulous nerves endow her with Sibylline attributes;[5] the Minor Poet, beginning life with strenuous aspirations, which die out with his youthful fervor — all these might have been looked for, at BROOK FARM, but, by some accident, never made their appearance there.

The Author cannot close his reference to this subject, without expressing a most earnest wish that some one of the many cultivated and philosophic minds, which took an interest in that enterprise, might now give the world its history. Ripley, with whom rests the honorable paternity of the Institution, Dana, Dwight, Channing, Burton, Parker,[6] for instance — with others, whom he dares not name, because they veil themselves from the public eye — among these is the ability to convey both the outward narrative and the inner truth and spirit of the whole affair, together with the lessons which those years of thought and toil must have elaborated, for the behoof of future experimentalists. Even the brilliant Howadji[7] might find as rich a theme in his youthful reminiscences of BROOK FARM, and a more novel one — close at hand as it lies — than those which he has since made so distant a pilgrimage to seek, in Syria, and along the current of the Nile.

CONCORD (Mass.), May, 1852.

---

[5]*Sibylline attributes:* Sibyls are prophetic women in Greek and Roman mythology.

[6]*Ripley, Dana, Dwight, Channing, Burton, Parker:* George Ripley (1802–1880), Unitarian minister, reformer, and founder of Brook Farm; Charles A. Dana (1819–1897), Brook Farm member from 1841 to 1846, and later the editor of the New York *Sun*; John Sullivan Dwight (1813–1893), gifted music critic and Brook Farm member from 1841 to 1847; Warren Burton (1800–1866), Unitarian minister and Brook Farm member from 1841 to 1844. William Henry Channing (1810–1884) and Theodore Parker (1810–1860) were Unitarian ministers and reformers and visitors to Brook Farm, but neither was a resident of the community.

[7]*Howadji:* The word means "traveler" and refers to the travel writings of George William Curtis (1824–1892), who was a student at Brook Farm (1842–1843) and correspondent for the New York *Tribune*. His books under this pen name include *Nile Notes of a Howadji* (1851) and *Howadji in Syria* (1852).

I. OLD MOODIE

The evening before my departure for Blithedale, I was returning to
my bachelor-apartments, after attending the wonderful exhibition of
the Veiled Lady, when an elderly-man of rather shabby appearance
met me in an obscure part of the street.

"Mr. Coverdale,"[1] said he, softly, "can I speak with you a moment?"

As I have casually alluded to the Veiled Lady, it may not be amiss
to mention, for the benefit of such of my readers as are unacquainted
with her now forgotten celebrity, that she was a phenomenon in the
mesmeric line;[2] one of the earliest that had indicated the birth of a
new science, or the revival of an old humbug. Since those times, her
sisterhood have grown too numerous to attract much individual notice; nor, in fact, has any one of them ever come before the public
under such skilfully contrived circumstances of stage-effect, as those
which at once mystified and illuminated the remarkable performances
of the lady in question. Now-a-days, in the management of his 'subject,' 'clairvoyant,' or 'medium,' the exhibitor affects the simplicity
and openness of scientific experiment; and even if he profess to tread
a step or two across the boundaries of the spiritual world, yet carries
with him the laws of our actual life, and extends them over his preternatural conquests. Twelve or fifteen years ago, on the contrary, all
the arts of mysterious arrangement, of picturesque disposition, and
artistically contrasted light and shade, were made available in order
to set the apparent miracle in the strongest attitude of opposition to
ordinary facts. In the case of the Veiled Lady, moreover, the interest
of the spectator was further wrought up by the enigma of her identity, and an absurd rumor (probably set afloat by the exhibitor, and
at one time very prevalent) that a beautiful young lady, of family and
fortune, was enshrouded within the misty drapery of the veil. It was
white, with somewhat of a subdued silver sheen, like the sunny side

---

[1]*Coverdale:* The historical Miles (or Myles) Coverdale (1488–1568) was a Protestant priest, bishop, reformer, and scholar, whose works include the first complete English Bible (1535) and the English version of the Psalms in the Book of Common Prayer.

[2]*mesmeric line:* The Austrian physician Franz Mesmer (1734–1815) described his
theory of "animal magnetism" in the late eighteenth century. Mesmerism was one of
many forms of nineteenth-century spiritualism, a very popular broad trend that included hypnotic experiments and cures, spirit "rapping," and séances. Both
Hawthorne's wife, Sophia Peabody, and her sister, Elizabeth, were interested in this
pseudoscience, as was Margaret Fuller.

of a cloud; and falling over the wearer, from head to foot, was supposed to insulate her from the material world, from time and space, and to endow her with many of the privileges of a disembodied spirit.

Her pretensions, however, whether miraculous or otherwise, have little to do with the present narrative; except, indeed, that I had propounded, for the Veiled Lady's prophetic solution, a query as to the success of our Blithedale enterprise. The response, by-the-by, was of the true Sibylline stamp, nonsensical in its first aspect, yet, on closer study, unfolding a variety of interpretations, one of which has certainly accorded with the event. I was turning over this riddle in my mind, and trying to catch its slippery purport by the tail, when the old man, above-mentioned, interrupted me.

"Mr. Coverdale! — Mr. Coverdale!" said he, repeating my name twice, in order to make up for the hesitating and ineffectual way in which he uttered it — "I ask your pardon, sir — but I hear you are going to Blithedale tomorrow?"

I knew the pale, elderly face, with the red-tipt nose, and the patch over one eye, and likewise saw something characteristic in the old fellow's way of standing under the arch of a gate, only revealing enough of himself to make me recognize him as an acquaintance. He was a very shy personage, this Mr. Moodie; and the trait was the more singular, as his mode of getting his bread necessarily brought him into the stir and hubbub of the world, more than the generality of men.

"Yes, Mr. Moodie," I answered, wondering what interest he could take in the fact, "it is my intention to go to Blithedale tomorrow. Can I be of any service to you, before my departure?"

"If you pleased, Mr. Coverdale," said he, "you might do me a very great favor."

"A very great one!" repeated I, in a tone that must have expressed but little alacrity of beneficence, although I was ready to do the old man any amount of kindness involving no special trouble to myself. "A very great favor, do you say? My time is brief, Mr. Moodie, and I have a good many preparations to make. But be good enough to tell me what you wish."

"Ah, sir," replied old Moodie, "I don't quite like to do that; and, on further thoughts, Mr. Coverdale, perhaps I had better apply to some older gentleman, or to some lady, if you would have the kindness to make me known to one, who may happen to be going to Blithedale. You are a young man, sir!"

"Does that fact lessen my availability for your purpose?" asked I. "However, if an older man will suit you better, there is Mr.

Hollingsworth,[3] who has three or four years the advantage of me in age, and is a much more solid character, and a philanthropist to boot. I am only a poet, and, so the critics tell me, no great affair at that! But what can this business be, Mr. Moodie? It begins to interest me; especially since your hint that a lady's influence might be found desirable. Come; I am really anxious to be of service to you."

But the old fellow, in his civil and demure manner, was both freakish and obstinate; and he had now taken some notion or other into his head that made him hesitate in his former design.

"I wonder, sir," said he, "whether you know a lady whom they call Zenobia?"[4]

"Not personally," I answered, "although I expect that pleasure tomorrow, as she has got the start of the rest of us, and is already a resident at Blithedale. But have you a literary turn, Mr. Moodie? — or have you taken up the advocacy of women's rights? — or what else can have interested you in this lady? Zenobia, by-the-by, as I suppose you know, is merely her public name; a sort of mask in which she comes before the world, retaining all the privileges of privacy — a contrivance, in short, like the white drapery of the Veiled Lady, only a little more transparent. But it is late! Will you tell me what I can do for you?"

"Please to excuse me to-night, Mr. Coverdale," said Moodie. "You are very kind; but I am afraid I have troubled you, when, after all, there may be no need. Perhaps, with your good leave, I will come to your lodgings tomorrow-morning, before you set out for Blithedale. I wish you a good-night, sir, and beg pardon for stopping you."

And so he slipt away; and, as he did not show himself, the next morning, it was only through subsequent events that I ever arrived at a plausible conjecture as to what his business could have been. Arriving at my room, I threw a lump of cannel coal[5] upon the grate,

---

[3]*Hollingsworth:* The name may echo Thomas Holcroft (1745–1809), English author, translator, dramatist, and radical, who was indicted for high treason in 1794 and imprisoned for two months before being discharged.

[4]*Zenobia:* Third-century princess and later queen of Palmyra, who in 271–72 heroically resisted the forces of the Roman emperor Aurelian before being defeated by them. *Lemprière's Classical Dictionary* (1788) describes her as "the mistress of the east" and notes that she was greatly admired for her "literary talents" as well as for her "military abilities." See John C. Hirsh, "Zenobia as Queen: The Background Sources to Hawthorne's *The Blithedale Romance*," *Nathaniel Hawthorne Journal* (1971): 182–90, and Richard Stoneman, *Palmyra and Its Enemies: Zenobia's Revolt against Rome* (Ann Arbor: U of Michigan P, 1992).

[5]*cannel coal:* Bright burning, smoky fuel.

lighted a cigar, and spent an hour in musings of every hue, from the brightest to the most sombre; being, in truth, not so very confident as at some former periods, that this final step, which would mix me up irrevocably with the Blithedale affair, was the wisest that could possibly be taken. It was nothing short of midnight when I went to bed, after drinking a glass of particularly fine Sherry, on which I used to pride myself, in those days. It was the very last bottle; and I finished it, with a friend, the next forenoon, before setting out for Blithedale.

II. BLITHEDALE

There can hardly remain for me, (who am really getting to be a frosty bachelor, with another white hair, every week or so, in my moustache,) there can hardly flicker up again so cheery a blaze upon the hearth, as that which I remember, the next day, at Blithedale. It was a wood-fire, in the parlor of an old farm-house, on an April afternoon, but with the fitful gusts of a wintry snow-storm roaring in the chimney. Vividly does that fireside re-create itself, as I rake away the ashes from the embers in my memory, and blow them up with a sigh, for lack of more inspiring breath. Vividly, for an instant, but, anon, with the dimmest gleam, and with just as little fervency for my heart as for my finger-ends! The staunch oaken-logs were long ago burnt out. Their genial glow must be represented, if at all, by the merest phosphoric glimmer, like that which exudes, rather than shines, from damp fragments of decayed trees, deluding the benighted wanderer through a forest. Around such chill mockery of a fire, some few of us might sit on the withered leaves, spreading out each a palm towards the imaginary warmth, and talk over our exploded scheme for beginning the life of Paradise anew.

Paradise, indeed! Nobody else in the world, I am bold to affirm — nobody, at least, in our bleak little world of New England — had dreamed of Paradise, that day, except as the pole suggests the tropic. Nor, with such materials as were at hand, could the most skilful architect have constructed any better imitation of Eve's bower, than might be seen in the snow-hut of an Esquimaux.[1] But we made a summer of it, in spite of the wild drifts.

[1]*Esquimaux:* Eskimo.

It was an April day, as already hinted, and well towards the middle of the month. When morning dawned upon me, in town, its temperature was mild enough to be pronounced even balmy, by a lodger — like myself — in one of the midmost houses of a brick-block; each house partaking of the warmth of all the rest, besides the sultriness of its individual furnace-heat. But, towards noon, there had come snow, driven along the street by a north-easterly blast, and whitening the roofs and sidewalks with a business-like perseverance that would have done credit to our severest January tempest. It set about its task, apparently as much in earnest as if it had been guaranteed from a thaw, for months to come. The greater, surely, was my heroism, when, puffing out a final whiff of cigar-smoke, I quitted my cosey pair of bachelor-rooms — with a good fire burning in the grate, and a closet right at hand, where there was still a bottle or two in the champagne-basket, and a residuum of claret in a box, and somewhat of proof in the concavity of a big demijohn[2] — quitted, I say, these comfortable quarters, and plunged into the heart of the pitiless snow-storm, in quest of a better life.

The better life! Possibly, it would hardly look so, now; it is enough if it looked so, then. The greatest obstacle to being heroic, is the doubt whether one may not be going to prove one's self a fool; the truest heroism is, to resist the doubt — and the profoundest wisdom, to know when it ought to be resisted, and when to be obeyed.

Yet, after all, let us acknowledge it wiser, if not more sagacious, to follow out one's day-dream to its natural consummation, although, if the vision have been worth the having, it is certain never to be consummated otherwise than by a failure. And what of that! Its airiest fragments, impalpable as they may be, will possess a value that lurks not in the most ponderous realities of any practicable scheme. They are not the rubbish of the mind. Whatever else I may repent of, therefore, let it be reckoned neither among my sins nor follies, that I once had faith and force enough to form generous hopes of the world's destiny — yes! — and to do what in me lay for their accomplishment; even to the extent of quitting a warm fireside, flinging away a freshly lighted cigar, and travelling far beyond the strike of city-clocks, through a drifting snow-storm.

There were four of us who rode together through the storm; and

---

[2]*demijohn:* Narrow-necked bottle enclosed in wickerwork, commonly used for containing whiskey. The part of the sentence with this word in it was deleted in the original manuscript but restored in the Centenary edition.

Hollingsworth, who had agreed to be of the number, was accidentally delayed, and set forth at a later hour, alone. As we threaded the
streets, I remember how the buildings, on either side, seemed to press
too closely upon us, insomuch that our mighty hearts found barely
room enough to throb between them. The snow-fall, too, looked inexpressibly dreary, (I had almost called it dingy), coming down
through an atmosphere of city-smoke, and alighting on the sidewalk,
only to be moulded into the impress of somebody's patched boot or
over-shoe. Thus, the track of an old conventionalism was visible on
what was freshest from the sky. But — when we left the pavements,
and our muffled hoof-tramps beat upon a desolate extent of country-
road, and were effaced by the unfettered blast, as soon as stamped —
then, there was better air to breathe. Air, that had not been breathed,
once and again! Air, that had not been spoken into words of falsehood, formality, and error, like all the air of the dusky city!

"How pleasant it is!" remarked I, while the snow-flakes flew into
my mouth, the moment it was opened. "How very mild and balmy is
this country-air!"

"Ah, Coverdale, don't laugh at what little enthusiasm you have
left," said one of my companions. "I maintain that this nitrous atmosphere[3] is really exhilarating; and, at any rate, we can never call
ourselves regenerated men, till a February north-easter shall be as
grateful to us as the softest breeze of June."

So we all of us took courage, riding fleetly and merrily along, by
stone-fences that were half-buried in the wave-like drifts; and
through patches of woodland, where the tree-trunks opposed a snow-
encrusted side towards the north-east; and within ken of deserted vil-
las, with no foot-prints in their avenues; and past scattered dwellings,
whence puffed the smoke of country fires, strongly impregnated with
the pungent aroma of burning peat. Sometimes, encountering a traveller, we shouted a friendly greeting; and he, unmuffling his ears to
the bluster and the snow-spray, and listening eagerly, appeared to
think our courtesy worth less than the trouble which it cost him. The
churl! He understood the shrill whistle of the blast, but had no intelligence for our blithe tones of brotherhood. This lack of faith in our
cordial sympathy, on the traveller's part, was one among the innumerable tokens how difficult a task we had in hand, for the reformation of the world. We rode on, however, with still unflagging spirits,

---

[3]*nitrous atmosphere:* Nitre or niter is potassium nitrate, used in making gunpowder. Here *nitrous* implies exhilarating, invigorating.

and made such good companionship with the tempest, that, at our journey's end, we professed ourselves almost loth to bid the rude blusterer good bye. But, to own the truth, I was little better than an icicle, and began to be suspicious that I had caught a fearful cold.

And, now, we were seated by the brisk fireside of the old farm-house; the same fire that glimmers so faintly among my reminis-cences, at the beginning of this chapter. There we sat, with the snow melting out of our hair and beards, and our faces all a-blaze, what with the past inclemency and present warmth. It was, indeed, a right good fire that we found awaiting us, built up of great, rough logs, and knotty limbs, and splintered fragments of an oak-tree, such as farmers are wont to keep for their own hearths; since these crooked and unmanageable boughs could never be measured into mer-chantable cords for the market. A family of the old Pilgrims might have swung their kettle over precisely such a fire as this, only, no doubt, a bigger one; and, contrasting it with my coal-grate, I felt, so much the more, that we had transported ourselves a world-wide distance from the system of society that shackled us at breakfast-time.

Good, comfortable Mrs. Foster (the wife of stout Silas Foster, who was to manage the farm, at a fair stipend, and be our tutor in the arts of husbandry) bade us a hearty welcome. At her back — a back of generous breadth — appeared two young women, smiling most hos-pitably, but looking rather awkward withal, as not well knowing what to be their position in our new arrangement of the world. We shook hands affectionately, all round, and congratulated our-selves that the blessed state of brotherhood and sisterhood, at which we aimed, might fairly be dated from this moment. Our greetings were hardly concluded, when the door opened, and Zenobia — whom I had never before seen, important as was her place in our en-terprise — Zenobia entered the parlor.

This (as the reader, if at all acquainted with our literary biography, need scarcely be told) was not her real name. She had assumed it, in the first instance, as her magazine-signature; and as it accorded well with something imperial which her friends attributed to this lady's figure and deportment, they, half-laughingly, adopted it in their fa-miliar intercourse with her. She took the appellation in good part, and even encouraged its constant use, which, in fact, was thus far ap-propriate, that our Zenobia — however humble looked her new phi-losophy — had as much native pride as any queen would have known what to do with.

III. A KNOT OF DREAMERS

Zenobia bade us welcome, in a fine, frank, mellow voice, and gave each of us her hand, which was very soft and warm. She had something appropriate, I recollect, to say to every individual; and what she said to myself was this: —

"I have long wished to know you, Mr. Coverdale, and to thank you for your beautiful poetry, some of which I have learned by heart; — or, rather, it has stolen into my memory, without my exercising any choice or volition about the matter. Of course — permit me to say — you do not think of relinquishing an occupation in which you have done yourself so much credit. I would almost rather give you up, as an associate, than that the world should lose one of its true poets!"

"Ah, no; there will not be the slightest danger of that, especially after this inestimable praise from Zenobia!" said I, smiling and blushing, no doubt, with excess of pleasure. "I hope, on the contrary, now, to produce something that shall really deserve to be called poetry — true, strong, natural, and sweet, as is the life which we are going to lead — something that shall have the notes of wild-birds twittering through it, or a strain like the wind-anthems in the woods, as the case may be!"

"Is it irksome to you to hear your own verses sung?" asked Zenobia, with a gracious smile. "If so, I am very sorry; for you will certainly hear me singing them, sometimes, in the summer evenings."

"Of all things," answered I, "that is what will delight me most."

While this passed, and while she spoke to my companions, I was taking note of Zenobia's aspect; and it impressed itself on me so distinctly, that I can now summon her up like a ghost, a little wanner than the life, but otherwise identical with it. She was dressed as simply as possible, in an American print, (I think the dry-goods people call it so,) but with a silken kerchief, between which and her gown there was one glimpse of a white shoulder. It struck me as a great piece of good-fortune that there should be just that glimpse. Her hair — which was dark, glossy, and of singular abundance — was put up rather soberly and primly, without curls, or other ornament, except a single flower. It was an exotic, of rare beauty, and as fresh as if the hot-house gardener had just clipt it from the stem. That flower has struck deep root into my memory. I can both see it and smell it, at this moment. So brilliant, so rare, so costly as it must have been, and yet enduring only for a day, it was more indicative of the

pride and pomp, which had a luxuriant growth in Zenobia's character, than if a great diamond had sparkled among her hair.

Her hand, though very soft, was larger than most women would
like to have — or than they could afford to have — though not a
whit too large in proportion with the spacious plan of Zenobia's entire development. It did one good to see a fine intellect (as hers really
was, although its natural tendency lay in another direction than towards literature) so fitly cased. She was, indeed, an admirable figure
of a woman, just on the hither verge of her richest maturity, with a
combination of features which it is safe to call remarkably beautiful,
even if some fastidious persons might pronounce them a little defi-
cient in softness and delicacy. But we find enough of those attributes,
everywhere. Preferable — by way of variety, at least — was Zenobia's bloom, health, and vigor, which she possessed in such overflow
that a man might well have fallen in love with her for their sake only.
In her quiet moods, she seemed rather indolent; but when really in
earnest, particularly if there were a spice of bitter feeling, she grew all
alive, to her finger-tips.

"I am the first-comer," Zenobia went on to say, while her smile
beamed warmth upon us all; "so I take the part of hostess, for to-day,
and welcome you as if to my own fireside. You shall be my guests,
too, at supper. Tomorrow, if you please, we will be brethren and sisters, and begin our new life from day-break."

"Have we our various parts assigned?" asked some one.

"Oh, we of the softer sex," responded Zenobia, with her mellow,
almost broad laugh — most delectable to hear, but not in the least
like an ordinary woman's laugh — "we women (there are four of us
here, already) will take the domestic and indoor part of the business,
as a matter of course. To bake, to boil, to roast, to fry, to stew — to
wash, and iron, and scrub, and sweep, and, at our idler intervals, to
repose ourselves on knitting and sewing — these, I suppose, must be
feminine occupations for the present. By-and-by, perhaps, when our
individual adaptations begin to develop themselves, it may be that
some of us, who wear the petticoat, will go afield, and leave the
weaker brethren to take our places in the kitchen!"

"What a pity," I remarked, "that the kitchen, and the house-work
generally, cannot be left out of our system altogether! It is odd
enough, that the kind of labor which falls to the lot of women is just
that which chiefly distinguishes artificial life — the life of degenerated
mortals — from the life of Paradise. Eve had no dinner-pot, and no
clothes to mend, and no washing-day."

"I am afraid," said Zenobia, with mirth gleaming out of her eyes, "we shall find some difficulty in adopting the Paradisiacal system, for at least a month to come. Look at that snow-drift sweeping past the window! Are there any figs ripe, do you think? Have the pine-apples been gathered, to-day? Would you like a bread-fruit, or a cocoa-nut? Shall I run out and pluck you some roses? No, no, Mr. Coverdale, the only flower hereabouts is the one in my hair, which I got out of a green-house, this morning. As for the garb of Eden," added she, shivering playfully, "I shall not assume it till after May-day!"

Assuredly, Zenobia could not have intended it — the fault must have been entirely in my imagination — but these last words, together with something in her manner, irresistibly brought up a picture of that fine, perfectly developed figure, in Eve's earliest garment. I almost fancied myself actually beholding it.[1] Her free, careless, generous modes of expression often had this effect of creating images which, though pure, are hardly felt to be quite decorous, when born of a thought that passes between man and woman. I imputed it, at that time, to Zenobia's noble courage, conscious of no harm, and scorning the petty restraints which take the life and color out of other women's conversation. There was another peculiarity about her. We seldom meet with women, now-a-days, and in this country, who impress us as being women at all; their sex fades away and goes for nothing, in ordinary intercourse. Not so with Zenobia. One felt an influence breathing out of her, such as we might suppose to come from Eve, when she was just made, and her Creator brought her to Adam,[2] saying — 'Behold, here is a woman!' Not that I would convey the idea of especial gentleness, grace, modesty, and shyness, but of a certain warm and rich characteristic, which seems, for the most part, to have been refined away out of the feminine system.

"And now," continued Zenobia, "I must go and help get supper. Do you think you can be content — instead of figs, pine-apples, and all the other delicacies of Adam's supper-table — with tea and toast, and a certain modest supply of ham and tongue, which, with the instinct of a housewife, I brought hither in a basket? And there shall be bread-and-milk, too, if the innocence of your taste demands it."

The whole sisterhood now went about their domestic avocations,

---

[1] *I almost fancied myself actually beholding it:* This sentence was deleted from the original manuscript and restored in the Centenary edition.

[2] *Creator brought her to Adam:* See Genesis 2–3; and John Milton (1608–1674), *Paradise Lost* 8:452–520. See also Hawthorne's story, "The New Adam and Eve" (1843).

utterly declining our offers to assist, farther than by bringing wood, for the kitchen-fire, from a huge pile in the back-yard. After heaping up more than a sufficient quantity, we returned to the sitting-room, drew our chairs closer to the hearth, and began to talk over our prospects. Soon, with a tremendous stamping in the entry, appeared Silas Foster, lank, stalwart, uncouth, and grisly-bearded. He came from foddering the cattle, in the barn, and from the field, where he had been ploughing, until the depth of the snow rendered it impossible to draw a furrow. He greeted us in pretty much the same tone as if he were speaking to his oxen, took a quid[3] from his iron tobacco-box, pulled off his wet cow-hide boots, and sat down before the fire in his stocking-feet. The steam arose from his soaked garments, so that the stout yeoman looked vaporous and spectre-like.

"Well, folks," remarked Silas, "you'll be wishing yourselves back to town again, if this weather holds!"

And, true enough, there was a look of gloom, as the twilight fell silently and sadly out of the sky, its gray or sable flakes intermingling themselves with the fast descending snow. The storm, in its evening aspect, was decidedly dreary. It seemed to have arisen for our especial behoof; a symbol of the cold, desolate, distrustful phantoms that invariably haunt the mind, on the eve of adventurous enterprises, to warn us back within the boundaries of ordinary life.

But our courage did not quail. We would not allow ourselves to be depressed by the snow-drift, trailing past the window, any more than if it had been the sigh of a summer wind among rustling boughs. There have been few brighter seasons for us, than that. If ever men might lawfully dream awake, and give utterance to their wildest visions, without dread of laughter or scorn on the part of the audience — yes, and speak of earthly happiness, for themselves and mankind, as an object to be hopefully striven for, and probably attained — we, who made that little semi-circle round the blazing fire, were those very men. We had left the rusty iron frame-work of society behind us. We had broken through many hindrances that are powerful enough to keep most people on the weary tread-mill of the established system, even while they feel its irksomeness almost as intolerable as we did. We had stept down from the pulpit; we had flung aside the pen; we had shut up the ledger; we had thrown off that sweet, bewitching, enervating indolence, which is better, after all, than most of the enjoyments within mortal grasp. It was our

---

[3]*quid:* A cut or wad of chewing tobacco.

purpose — a generous one, certainly, and absurd, no doubt, in full proportion with its generosity — to give up whatever we had heretofore attained, for the sake of showing mankind the example of a life governed by other than the false and cruel principles, on which human society has all along been based.

And, first of all, we had divorced ourselves from Pride, and were striving to supply its place with familiar love. We meant to lessen the laboring man's great burthen of toil, by performing our due share of it at the cost of our own thews[4] and sinews. We sought our profit by mutual aid, instead of wresting it by the strong hand from an enemy, or filching it craftily from those less shrewd than ourselves, (if, indeed, there were any such, in New England,) or winning it by selfish competition with a neighbor; in one or another of which fashions, every son of woman both perpetrates and suffers his share of the common evil, whether he chooses it or no. And, as the basis of our institution, we purposed to offer up the earnest toil of our bodies, as a prayer, no less than an effort, for the advancement of our race.

Therefore, if we built splendid castles (phalansteries,[5] perhaps, they might be more fitly called,) and pictured beautiful scenes, among the fervid coals of the hearth around which we were clustering — and if all went to rack with the crumbling embers, and have never since arisen out of the ashes — let us take to ourselves no shame. In my own behalf, I rejoice that I could once think better of the world's improvability than it deserved. It is a mistake into which men seldom fall twice, in a lifetime; or, if so, the rarer and higher is the nature that can thus magnanimously persist in error.

Stout Silas Foster mingled little in our conversation; but when he did speak, it was very much to some practical purpose. For instance: —

"Which man among you," quoth he, "is the best judge of swine? Some of us must go to the next Brighton fair, and buy half-a-dozen pigs!"

Pigs! Good heavens, had we come out from among the swinish multitude, for this? And again, in reference to some discussion about raising early vegetables for the market: —

---

[4]*thews:* Muscles.

[5]*phalansteries:* The phalanstery — the word combines *phalanx* and *monastery* — was the large central building in the reform community described in the French utopian Charles Fourier's writings. It was designed to house the 1,600 persons in a phalanx, the name Fourier (1772–1837) gave to the basic social unit of his program.

"We shall never make any hand at market-gardening," said Silas Foster, "unless the women-folks will undertake to do all the weeding. We haven't team enough for that and the regular farm-work, reckoning three of you city-folks as worth one common field-hand. No, no, I tell you, we should have to get up a little too early in the morning, to compete with the market-gardeners round Boston!"

It struck me as rather odd, that one of the first questions raised, after our separation from the greedy, struggling, self-seeking world, should relate to the possibility of getting the advantage over the outside barbarians, in their own field of labor. But, to own the truth, I very soon became sensible, that, as regarded society at large, we stood in a position of new hostility, rather than new brotherhood. Nor could this fail to be the case, in some degree, until the bigger and better half of society should range itself on our side. Constituting so pitiful a minority as now, we were inevitably estranged from the rest of mankind, in pretty fair proportion with the strictness of our mutual bond among ourselves.

This dawning idea, however, was driven back into my inner consciousness by the entrance of Zenobia. She came with the welcome intelligence that supper was on the table. Looking at herself in the glass, and perceiving that her one magnificent flower had grown rather languid, (probably by being exposed to the fervency of the kitchen-fire), she flung it on the floor, as unconcernedly as a village-girl would throw away a faded violet. The action seemed proper to her character; although, methought, it would still more have befitted the bounteous nature of this beautiful woman to scatter fresh flowers from her hand, and to revive faded ones by her touch. Nevertheless — it was a singular, but irresistible effect — the presence of Zenobia caused our heroic enterprise to show like an illusion, a masquerade, a pastoral, a counterfeit Arcadia,[6] in which we grown-up men and women were making a play-day of the years that were given us to live in. I tried to analyze this impression, but not with much success.

"It really vexes me," observed Zenobia, as we left the room, "that Mr. Hollingsworth should be such a laggard. I should not have thought him at all the sort of person to be turned back by a puff of contrary wind, or a few snow-flakes drifting into his face."

[6]*Arcadia:* In classical and Renaissance poetry, Arcadia (originally a region of ancient Greece) is the place of pastoral peace and tranquility and rustic innocence. See Theocritus (310–250 B.C.), *Idylls;* Virgil (70–19 B.C.), *Eclogues.*

"Do you know Hollingsworth personally?" I inquired.

"No; only as an auditor — auditress, I mean — of some of his lectures," said she. "What a voice he has! And what a man he is! Yet not so much an intellectual man, I should say, as a great heart; at least, he moved me more deeply than I think myself capable of being moved, except by the stroke of a true, strong heart against my own. It is a sad pity that he should have devoted his glorious powers to such a grimy, unbeautiful, and positively hopeless object as this reformation of criminals, about which he makes himself and his wretchedly small audiences so very miserable. To tell you a secret, I never could tolerate a philanthropist before. Could you?"

"By no means," I answered; "neither can I now!"

"They are, indeed, an odiously disagreeable set of mortals," continued Zenobia. "I should like Mr. Hollingsworth a great deal better, if the philanthropy had been left out. At all events, as a mere matter of taste, I wish he would let the bad people alone, and try to benefit those who are not already past his help. Do you suppose he will be content to spend his life — or even a few months of it — among tolerably virtuous and comfortable individuals, like ourselves?"

"Upon my word, I doubt it," said I. "If we wish to keep him with us, we must systematically commit at least one crime apiece! Mere peccadillos will not satisfy him."

Zenobia turned, sidelong, a strange kind of a glance upon me; but, before I could make out what it meant, w— ad entered the kitchen, where, in accordance with the rust— v of our new life, the supper-table was spread.

SUPPER-TABLE

The pleasant firelight! I must still keep harping on it.

The kitchen-hearth had an old-fashioned breadth, depth, and spaciousness, far within which lay what seemed the butt of a good-sized oak-tree, with the moisture bubbling merrily out of both ends. It was now half-an-hour beyond dusk. The blaze from an armfull of substantial sticks, rendered more combustible by brush-wood and pine, flickered powerfully on the smoke-blackened walls, and so cheered our spirits that we cared not what inclemency might rage and roar, on the other side of our illuminated windows. A yet sultrier warmth was bestowed by a goodly quantity of peat, which was crumbling to white ashes among the burning brands, and incensed the kitchen with

its not ungrateful fragrance. The exuberance of this household fire
would alone have sufficed to bespeak us no true farmers; for the New
England yeoman, if he have the misfortune to dwell within practicable distance of a wood-market, is as niggardly of each stick as if it
were a bar of California gold.[1]

But it was fortunate for us, on that wintry eve of our untried life,
to enjoy the warm and radiant luxury of a somewhat too abundant
fire. If it served no other purpose, it made the men look so full of
youth, warm blood, and hope, and the women — such of them, at
least, as were anywise convertible by its magic — so very beautiful,
that I would cheerfully have spent my last dollar to prolong the blaze.
As for Zenobia, there was a glow in her cheeks that made me think of
Pandora,[2] fresh from Vulcan's workshop, and full of the celestial
warmth by dint of which he had tempered and moulded her.

"Take your places, my dear friends all," cried she; "seat yourselves
without ceremony — and you shall be made happy with such tea as
not many of the world's working-people, except yourselves, will find
in their cups to-night. After this one supper, you may drink butter-
milk, if you please. To-night, we will quaff this nectar, which, I assure you, could not be bought with gold."

We all sat down — grisly Silas Foster, his rotund helpmate, and
the two bouncing handmaidens, included — and looked at one another in a friendly, but rather awkward way. It was the first practical
trial of our theories of equal brotherhood and sisterhood; and we
people of superior cultivation and refinement (for as such, I presume,
we unhesitatingly reckoned ourselves) felt as if something were already accomplished towards the millennium of love. The truth is,
however, that the laboring oar was with our unpolished companions;
it being far easier to condescend, than to accept of condescension.
Neither did I refrain from questioning, in secret, whether some of
us — and Zenobia among the rest — would so quietly have taken our
places among these good people, save for the cherished consciousness
that it was not by necessity, but choice. Though we saw fit to drink

---

[1]*bar of California gold:* In August 1848, the New York *Herald* reported the discovery of gold at Sutter's Mill, and this report was confirmed by President James Polk
a month later. During the next several years, tens of thousands of gold seekers journeyed to California in a quest for riches.
[2]*Pandora:* Figure in Greek mythology created from clay by Vulcan, the god of fire,
in his workshop. Zeus gave Pandora a beautiful box on her wedding day. By breaking
his command not to open it, she let loose the torments that have afflicted mankind. See
Hesiod, *Theogony,* 570–612; and *Works and Days,* 47–105.

our tea out of earthen cups to-night, and in earthen company, it was at our own option to use pictured porcelain and handle silver forks again, tomorrow. This same salvo, as to the power of regaining our former position, contributed much, I fear, to the equanimity with which we subsequently bore many of the hardships and humiliations of a life of toil. If ever I have deserved — (which has not often been the case, and, I think, never) — but if ever I did deserve to be soundly cuffed by a fellow-mortal, for secretly putting weight upon some imaginary social advantage, it must have been while I was striving to prove myself ostentatiously his equal, and no more. It was while I sat beside him on his cobbler's bench, or clinked my hoe against his own, in the cornfield, or broke the same crust of bread, my earth-grimed hand to his, at our noontide lunch. The poor, proud man should look at both sides of sympathy like this.

The silence, which followed upon our sitting down to table, grew rather oppressive; indeed, it was hardly broken by a word, during the first round of Zenobia's fragrant tea.

"I hope," said I, at last, "that our blazing windows will be visible a great way off. There is nothing so pleasant and encouraging to a solitary traveller, on a stormy night, as a flood of firelight, seen amid the gloom. These ruddy window-panes cannot fail to cheer the hearts of all that look at them. Are they not warm and bright with the beacon-fire which we have kindled for humanity?"

"The blaze of that brush-wood will only last a minute or two longer," observed Silas Foster; but whether he meant to insinuate that our moral illumination would have as brief a term, I cannot say.

"Meantime," said Zenobia, "it may serve to guide some wayfarer to a shelter."

And, just as she said this, there came a knock at the house-door.

"There is one of the world's wayfarers!" said I.

"Aye, aye, just so!" quoth Silas Foster. "Our firelight will draw stragglers, just as a candle draws dor-bugs,[3] on a summer night."

Whether to enjoy a dramatic suspense, or that we were selfishly contrasting our own comfort with the chill and dreary situation of the unknown person at the threshold — or that some of us city-folk felt a little startled at the knock which came so unseasonably, through night and storm, to the door of the lonely farm-house — so it happened, that nobody, for an instant or two, arose to answer the summons. Pretty soon, there came another knock. The first had been

[3]*dor-bugs:* A common dung beetle.

moderately loud; the second was smitten so forcibly that the knuckles of the applicant must have left their mark in the door-panel.

"He knocks as if he had a right to come in," said Zenobia, laughing. "And what are we thinking of? It must be Mr. Hollingsworth!"

Hereupon, I went to the door, unbolted, and flung it wide open. There, sure enough, stood Hollingsworth, his shaggy great-coat all covered with snow; so that he looked quite as much like a polar bear as a modern philanthropist.

"Sluggish hospitality, this!" said he, in those deep tones of his, which seemed to come out of a chest as capacious as a barrel. "It would have served you right if I had lain down and spent the night on the door-step, just for the sake of putting you to shame. But here is a guest, who will need a warmer and softer bed."

And stepping back to the wagon, in which he had journeyed hither, Hollingsworth received into his arms, and deposited on the door-step, a figure enveloped in a cloak. It was evidently a woman; or rather — judging from the ease with which he lifted her, and the little space which she seemed to fill in his arms — a slim and unsubstantial girl. As she showed some hesitation about entering the door, Hollingsworth, with his usual directness and lack of ceremony, urged her forward, not merely within the entry, but into the warm and strongly lighted kitchen.

"Who is this?" whispered I, remaining behind with him, while he was taking off his great-coat.

"Who? Really, I don't know," answered Hollingsworth, looking at me with some surprise. "It is a young person who belongs here, however; and, no doubt, she has been expected. Zenobia, or some of the women-folks, can tell you all about it."

"I think not," said I, glancing towards the new-comer and the other occupants of the kitchen. "Nobody seems to welcome her. I should hardly judge that she was an expected guest."

"Well, well," said Hollingsworth, quietly. "We'll make it right."

The stranger, or whatever she were, remained standing precisely on that spot of the kitchen-floor, to which Hollingsworth's kindly hand had impelled her. The cloak falling partly off, she was seen to be a very young woman, dressed in a poor, but decent gown, made high in the neck, and without any regard to fashion or smartness. Her brown hair fell down from beneath a hood, not in curls, but with only a slight wave; her face was of a wan, almost sickly hue, betokening habitual seclusion from the sun and free atmosphere, like a flower-shrub that had done its best to blossom in too scanty light. To complete the pitiableness of her aspect, she shivered either with cold, or fear, or nervous excitement, so that you might have beheld her shadow vibrating on the fire-lighted wall. In short, there has seldom been seen so depressed and sad a figure as this young girl's; and it was hardly possible to help being angry with her, from mere despair of doing anything for her comfort. The fantasy occurred to me, that she was some desolate kind of a creature, doomed to wander about in snow-storms, and that, though the ruddiness of our window-panes had tempted her into a human dwelling, she would not remain long enough to melt the icicles out of her hair.

Another conjecture likewise came into my mind. Recollecting Hollingsworth's sphere of philanthropic action, I deemed it possible that he might have brought one of his guilty patients, to be wrought upon, and restored to spiritual health, by the pure influences which our mode of life would create.

As yet, the girl had not stirred. She stood near the door, fixing a pair of large, brown, melancholy eyes upon Zenobia — only upon Zenobia! — she evidently saw nothing else in the room save that bright, fair, rosy, beautiful woman. It was the strangest look I ever witnessed; long a mystery to me, and forever a memory. Once, she seemed about to move forward and greet her — I know not with what warmth, or with what words; — but, finally, instead of doing so, she drooped down upon her knees, clasped her hands, and gazed piteously into Zenobia's face. Meeting no kindly reception, her head fell on her bosom.

I never thoroughly forgave Zenobia for her conduct on this occasion. But women are always more cautious, in their casual hospitalities, than men.

"What does the girl mean?" cried she, in rather a sharp tone. "Is she crazy? Has she no tongue?"

And here Hollingsworth stept forward.

"No wonder if the poor child's tongue is frozen in her mouth," said he — and I think he positively frowned at Zenobia — "The very heart will be frozen in her bosom, unless you women can warm it, among you, with the warmth that ought to be in your own!"

Hollingsworth's appearance was very striking, at this moment. He was then about thirty years old, but looked several years older, with his great shaggy head, his heavy brow, his dark complexion, his abundant beard, and the rude strength with which his features seemed to have been hammered out of iron, rather than chiselled or moulded from any finer or softer material. His figure was not tall, but massive and brawny, and well befitting his original occupation, which — as the reader probably knows — was that of a blacksmith. As for external polish, or mere courtesy of manner, he never possessed more than a tolerably educated bear; although, in his gentler moods, there was a tenderness in his voice, eyes, mouth, in his gesture, and in every indescribable manifestation, which few men could resist, and no woman. But he now looked stern and reproachful; and it was with that inauspicious meaning in his glance, that Hollingsworth first met Zenobia's eyes, and began his influence upon her life.

To my surprise, Zenobia — of whose haughty spirit I had been told so many examples — absolutely changed color, and seemed mortified and confused.

"You do not quite do me justice, Mr. Hollingsworth," said she, almost humbly. "I am willing to be kind to the poor girl. Is she a protégée of yours? What can I do for her?"

"Have you anything to ask of this lady?" said Hollingsworth, kindly, to the girl. "I remember you mentioned her name, before we left town."

"Only that she will shelter me," replied the girl, tremulously. "Only that she will let me be always near her!"

"Well, indeed," exclaimed Zenobia, recovering herself, and laughing, "this is an adventure, and well worthy to be the first incident in our life of love and free-heartedness! But I accept it, for the present, without further question — only," added she, "it would be a convenience if we knew your name!"

"Priscilla," said the girl; and it appeared to me that she hesitated whether to add anything more, and decided in the negative. "Pray do not ask me my other name — at least, not yet — if you will be so kind to a forlorn creature."

Priscilla! Priscilla! I repeated the name to myself, three or four times; and, in that little space, this quaint and prim cognomen had so amalgamated itself with my idea of the girl, that it seemed as if no other name could have adhered to her for a moment. Heretofore, the poor thing had not shed any tears; but now that she found herself received, and at least temporarily established, the big drops began to ooze out from beneath her eyelids, as if she were full of them. Perhaps it showed the iron substance of my heart, that I could not help smiling at this odd scene of unknown and unaccountable calamity, into which our cheerful party had been entrapped, without the liberty of choosing whether to sympathize or no. Hollingsworth's behavior was certainly a great deal more creditable than mine.

"Let us not pry farther into her secrets," he said to Zenobia and the rest of us, apart — and his dark, shaggy face looked really beautiful with its expression of thoughtful benevolence — "Let us conclude that Providence has sent her to us, as the first fruits of the world, which we have undertaken to make happier than we find it. Let us warm her poor, shivering body with this good fire, and her poor, shivering heart with our best kindness. Let us feed her, and make her one of us. As we do by this friendless girl, so shall we prosper! And, in good time, whatever is desirable for us to know will be melted out of her, as inevitably as those tears which we see now."

"At least," remarked I, "you may tell us how and where you met with her."

"An old man brought her to my lodgings," answered Hollingsworth, "and begged me to convey her to Blithedale, where — so I understood him — she had friends. And this is positively all I know about the matter."

Grim Silas Foster, all this while, had been busy at the supper-table, pouring out his own tea, and gulping it down with no more sense of its exquisiteness than if it were a decoction of catnip; helping himself to pieces of dipt toast on the flat of his knife-blade, and dropping half of it on the table-cloth; using the same serviceable implement to cut slice after slice of ham; perpetrating terrible enormities with the butter-plate; and, in all other respects, behaving less like a civilized Christian than the worst kind of an ogre. Being, by this time, fully gorged, he crowned his amiable exploits with a draught from the water-pitcher, and then favored us with his opinion about the business in hand. And, certainly, though they proceeded out of an unwiped mouth, his expressions did him honor.

"Give the girl a hot cup of tea, and a thick slice of this first-rate bacon," said Silas, like a sensible man as he was. "That's what she wants. Let her stay with us as long as she likes, and help in the kitchen, and take the cow-breath at milking-time; and, in a week or two, she'll begin to look like a creature of this world!"

So we sat down again to supper, and Priscilla along with us.

V. UNTIL BEDTIME

Silas Foster, by the time we concluded our meal, had stript off his coat and planted himself on a low chair by the kitchen-fire, with a lap-stone, a hammer, a piece of sole-leather, and some waxed ends, in order to cobble an old pair of cow-hide boots; he being, in his own phrase, 'something of a dab'[1] (whatever degree of skill that may imply) at the shoemaking-business. We heard the tap of his hammer, at intervals, for the rest of the evening. The remainder of the party adjourned to the sitting-room. Good Mrs. Foster took her knitting-work, and soon fell fast asleep, still keeping her needles in brisk movement, and, to the best of my observation, absolutely footing a stocking out of the texture of a dream. And a very substantial stocking it seemed to be. One of the two handmaidens hemmed a towel, and the other appeared to be making a ruffle, for her Sunday's wear, out of a little bit of embroidered muslin, which Zenobia had probably given her.

It was curious to observe how trustingly, and yet how timidly, our poor Priscilla betook herself into the shadow of Zenobia's protection. She sat beside her on a stool, looking up, every now and then, with an expression of humble delight at her new friend's beauty. A brilliant woman is often an object of the devoted admiration — it might almost be termed worship, or idolatry — of some young girl, who perhaps beholds the cynosure only at an awful distance, and has as little hope of personal intercourse as of climbing among the stars of heaven. We men are too gross to comprehend it. Even a woman, of mature age, despises or laughs at such a passion. There occurred to me no mode of accounting for Priscilla's behavior, except by supposing that she had read some of Zenobia's stories (as such literature goes everywhere,) or her tracts in defence of the sex, and had come hither with the one purpose of being her slave. There is nothing parallel to this, I believe — nothing so foolishly disinterested, and hardly anything so beautiful — in the masculine nature, at whatever epoch of life; or, if there be, a fine and rare development of character might reasonably be looked for, from the youth who should prove himself capable of such self-forgetful affection.

Zenobia happening to change her seat, I took the opportunity, in an under tone, to suggest some such notion as the above.

"Since you see the young woman in so poetical a light," replied she, in the same tone, "you had better turn the affair into a ballad. It is a grand subject, and worthy of supernatural machinery. The storm, the startling knock at the door, the entrance of the sable knight Hollingsworth and this shadowy snow-maiden, who, precisely at the stroke of midnight, shall melt away at my feet, in a pool of ice-cold water, and give me my death with a pair of wet slippers! And when

---

[1]*dab:* A skilled hand.

the verses are written, and polished quite to your mind, I will favor you with my idea as to what the girl really is."

"Pray let me have it now," said I. "It shall be woven into the ballad."

"She is neither more nor less," answered Zenobia, "than a seamstress from the city, and she has probably no more transcendental purpose than to do my miscellaneous sewing; for I suppose she will hardly expect to make my dresses."

"How can you decide upon her so easily?" I inquired.

"Oh, we women judge one another by tokens that escape the obtuseness of masculine perceptions," said Zenobia. "There is no proof, which you would be likely to appreciate, except the needle marks on the tip of her forefinger. Then, my supposition perfectly accounts for her paleness, her nervousness, and her wretched fragility. Poor thing! She has been stifled with the heat of a salamander-stove,[2] in a small, close room, and has drunk coffee, and fed upon dough-nuts, raisins, candy, and all such trash, till she is scarcely half-alive; and so, as she has hardly any physique, a poet, like Mr. Miles Coverdale, may be allowed to think her spiritual!"

"Look at her now!" whispered I.

Priscilla was gazing towards us, with an inexpressible sorrow in her wan face, and great tears running down her cheeks. It was difficult to resist the impression, that, cautiously as we had lowered our voices, she must have overheard and been wounded by Zenobia's scornful estimate of her character and purposes.

"What ears the girl must have!" whispered Zenobia, with a look of vexation, partly comic and partly real. "I will confess to you that I cannot quite make her out. However, I am positively not an ill-natured person, unless when very grievously provoked; and as you, and especially Mr. Hollingsworth, take so much interest in this odd creature — and as she knocks, with a very slight tap, against my own heart, likewise — why, I mean to let her in! From this moment, I will be reasonably kind to her. There is no pleasure in tormenting a person of one's own sex, even if she do favor one with a little more love than one can conveniently dispose of; — and that, let me say, Mr. Coverdale, is the most troublesome offence you can offer to a woman."

"Thank you!" said I, smiling. "I don't mean to be guilty of it."

She went towards Priscilla, took her hand, and passed her own

[2]*salamander-stove:* Small, portable stove having no chimney.

rosy finger-tips, with a pretty, caressing movement, over the girl's hair. The touch had a magical effect. So vivid a look of joy flushed up beneath those fingers, that it seemed as if the sad and wan Priscilla had been snatched away, and another kind of creature substituted in her place. This one caress, bestowed voluntarily by Zenobia, was evidently received as a pledge of all that the stranger sought from her, whatever the unuttered boon might be. From that instant, too, she melted in quietly amongst us, and was no longer a foreign element. Though always an object of peculiar interest, a riddle, and a theme of frequent discussion, her tenure at Blithedale was thenceforth fixed; we no more thought of questioning it, than if Priscilla had been recognized as a domestic sprite, who had haunted the rustic fireside, of old, before we had ever been warmed by its blaze.

She now produced, out of a work-bag that she had with her, some little wooden instruments, (what they are called, I never knew,) and proceeded to knit, or net, an article which ultimately took the shape of a silk purse. As the work went on, I remembered to have seen just such purses, before. Indeed, I was the possessor of one. Their peculiar excellence, besides the great delicacy and beauty of the manufacture, lay in the almost impossibility that any uninitiated person should discover the aperture; although, to a practised touch, they would open as wide as charity or prodigality might wish. I wondered if it were not a symbol of Priscilla's own mystery.

Notwithstanding the new confidence with which Zenobia had inspired her, our guest showed herself disquieted by the storm. When the strong puffs of wind spattered the snow against the windows, and made the oaken frame of the farm-house creak, she looked at us apprehensively, as if to inquire whether these tempestuous outbreaks did not betoken some unusual mischief in the shrieking blast. She had been bred up, no doubt, in some close nook, some inauspiciously sheltered court of the city, where the uttermost rage of a tempest, though it might scatter down the slates of the roof into the bricked area, could not shake the casement of her little room. The sense of vast, undefined space, pressing from the outside against the black panes of our uncurtained windows, was fearful to the poor girl, heretofore accustomed to the narrowness of human limits, with the lamps of neighboring tenements glimmering across the street. The house probably seemed to her adrift on the great ocean of the night. A little parallelogram of sky was all that she had hitherto known of nature; so that she felt the awfulness that really exists in its limitless extent. Once, while the blast was bellowing, she caught hold of

Zenobia's robe, with precisely the air of one who hears her own name spoken, at a distance, but is unutterably reluctant to obey the call.

We spent rather an incommunicative evening. Hollingsworth hardly said a word, unless when repeatedly and pertinaciously addressed. Then, indeed, he would glare upon us from the thick shrubbery of his meditations, like a tiger out of a jungle, make the briefest reply possible, and betake himself back into the solitude of his heart and mind. The poor fellow had contracted this ungracious habit from the intensity with which he contemplated his own ideas, and the infrequent sympathy which they met with from his auditors; a circumstance that seemed only to strengthen the implicit confidence that he awarded to them. His heart, I imagine, was never really interested in our socialist scheme, but was forever busy with his strange, and, as most people thought it, impracticable plan for the reformation of criminals, through an appeal to their higher instincts. Much as I liked Hollingsworth, it cost me many a groan to tolerate him on this point. He ought to have commenced his investigation of the subject by perpetrating some huge sin, in his proper person, and examining the condition of his higher instincts, afterwards.

The rest of us formed ourselves into a committee for providing our infant Community with an appropriate name; a matter of greatly more difficulty than the uninitiated reader would suppose. Blithedale was neither good nor bad. We should have resumed the old Indian name of the premises, had it possessed the oil-and-honey flow which the aborigines were so often happy in communicating to their local appellations; but it chanced to be a harsh, ill-connected, and interminable word, which seemed to fill the mouth with a mixture of very stiff clay and very crumbly pebbles. Zenobia suggested 'Sunny Glimpse,' as expressive of a vista into a better system of society. This we turned over and over, for awhile, acknowledging its prettiness, but concluded it to be rather too fine and sentimental a name (a fault inevitable by literary ladies, in such attempts) for sun-burnt men to work under. I ventured to whisper 'Utopia,'[3] which, however, was unanimously scouted down,[4] and the proposer very harshly maltreated, as if he had intended a latent satire. Some were for calling

[3]*Utopia:* Literally means "no place" or "nowhere"; more generally, with a pun on "eutopia" ("good place"), imaginary land of ideal laws and social conditions. Derives from Thomas More (1478–1535), *Utopia* (1516), a speculative work on the best form of government.

[4]*scouted down:* Etymologically, a "scout" is someone who "listens." In this context, heard and then overruled, dismissed.

our institution 'The Oasis,' in view of its being the one green spot in the moral sand-waste of the world; but others insisted on a proviso for reconsidering the matter, at a twelvemonth's end; when a final decision might be had, whether to name it 'The Oasis,' or 'Saharah.' So, at last, finding it impracticable to hammer out anything better, we resolved that the spot should still be Blithedale, as being of good augury enough.

The evening wore on, and the outer solitude looked in upon us through the windows, gloomy, wild, and vague, like another state of existence, close beside the littler sphere of warmth and light in which we were the prattlers and bustlers of a moment. By-and-by, the door was opened by Silas Foster, with a cotton handkerchief about his head, and a tallow candle in his hand.

"Take my advice, brother-farmers," said he, with a great, broad, bottomless yawn, "and get to bed as soon as you can. I shall sound the horn at day-break; and we've got the cattle to fodder, and nine cows to milk, and a dozen other things to do, before breakfast."

Thus ended the first evening at Blithedale. I went shivering to my fireless chamber, with the miserable consciousness (which had been growing upon me for several hours past) that I had caught a tremendous cold, and should probably awaken, at the blast of the horn, a fit subject for a hospital. The night proved a feverish one. During the greater part of it, I was in that vilest of states when a fixed idea remains in the mind, like the nail in Sisera's brain,[5] while innumerable other ideas go and come, and flutter to-and-fro, combining constant transition with intolerable sameness. Had I made a record of that night's half-waking dreams, it is my belief that it would have anticipated several of the chief incidents of this narrative, including a dim shadow of its catastrophe. Starting up in bed, at length, I saw that the storm was past, and the moon was shining on the snowy landscape, which looked like a lifeless copy of the world in marble.

From the bank of the distant river, which was shimmering in the moonlight, came the black shadow of the only cloud in heaven, driven swiftly by the wind, and passing over meadow and hillock — vanishing amid tufts of leafless trees, but reappearing on the hither side — until it swept across our door-step.

How cold an Arcadia was this!

---

[5]*the nail in Sisera's brain:* In Judges 4, the heroic woman Jael drives a tent nail into the head of Sisera, the leader of the Canaanite enemies of the Israelites. See also Hawthorne's *The Marble Faun* (1860), ch. 5.

VI. COVERDALE'S SICK-CHAMBER

The horn sounded at day-break, as Silas Foster had forewarned us, harsh, uproarious, inexorably drawn out, and as sleep-dispelling as if this hard-hearted old yeoman had got hold of the trump of doom.

On all sides, I could hear the creaking of the bedsteads, as the brethren of Blithedale started from slumber, and thrust themselves into their habiliments, all awry, no doubt, in their haste to begin the reformation of the world. Zenobia put her head into the entry, and besought Silas Foster to cease his clamor, and to be kind enough to leave an armful of firewood and a pail of water at her chamber-door. Of the whole household — unless, indeed, it were Priscilla, for whose habits, in this particular, I cannot vouch — of all our apostolic society, whose mission was to bless mankind, Hollingsworth, I apprehend, was the only one who began the enterprise with prayer. My sleeping-room being but thinly partitioned from his, the solemn murmur of his voice made its way to my ears, compelling me to be an auditor of his awful privacy with the Creator. It affected me with a deep reverence for Hollingsworth, which no familiarity then existing, or that afterwards grew more intimate between us — no, nor my subsequent perception of his own great errors — ever quite effaced. It is so rare, in these times, to meet with a man of prayerful habits, (except, of course, in the pulpit,) that such an one is decidedly marked out by a light of transfiguration, shed upon him in the divine interview from which he passes into his daily life.

As for me, I lay abed, and, if I said my prayers, it was backward, cursing my day as bitterly as patient Job[1] himself. The truth was, the hot-house warmth of a town-residence, and the luxurious life in which I indulged myself, had taken much of the pith out of my physical system; and the wintry blast of the preceding day, together with the general chill of our airy old farm-house, had got fairly into my heart and the marrow of my bones. In this predicament, I seriously wished — selfish as it may appear — that the reformation of society had been postponed about half-a-century, or at all events, to such a date as should have put my intermeddling with it entirely out of the question.

What, in the name of common-sense, had I to do with any better society than I had always lived in! It had satisfied me well enough. My pleasant bachelor-parlor, sunny and shadowy, curtained and

---

[1]*patient Job:* The suffering Old Testament figure, whose faith is sorely tested.

carpeted, with the bed-chamber adjoining; my centre-table, strewn with books and periodicals; my writing-desk, with a half-finished poem in a stanza of my own contrivance; my morning lounge at the reading-room or picture-gallery; my noontide walk along the cheery pavement, with the suggestive succession of human faces, and the brisk throb of human life, in which I shared; my dinner at the Albion, where I had a hundred dishes at command, and could banquet as delicately as the wizard Michael Scott,[2] when the devil fed him from the King of France's kitchen; my evening at the billiard-club, the concert, the theatre, or at somebody's party, if I pleased: — what could be better than all this? Was it better to hoe, to mow, to toil and moil amidst the accumulations of a barn-yard, to be the chambermaid of two yoke of oxen and a dozen cows, to eat salt-beef and earn it with the sweat of my brow, and thereby take the tough morsel out of some wretch's mouth, into whose vocation I had thrust myself? Above all, was it better to have a fever, and die blaspheming, as I was like to do?

In this wretched plight, with a furnace in my heart, and another in my head, by the heat of which I was kept constantly at the boiling point — yet shivering at the bare idea of extruding so much as a finger into the icy atmosphere of the room — I kept my bed until breakfast-time, when Hollingsworth knocked at the door, and entered.

"Well, Coverdale," cried he, "you bid fair to make an admirable farmer! Don't you mean to get up to-day?"

"Neither to-day nor tomorrow," said I, hopelessly. "I doubt if I ever rise again!"

"What is the matter now?" he asked.

I told him my piteous case, and besought him to send me back to town, in a close carriage.

"No, no!" said Hollingsworth, with kindly seriousness. "If you are really sick, we must take care of you."

Accordingly, he built a fire in my chamber, and having little else to do while the snow lay on the ground, established himself as my nurse. A doctor was sent for, who, being homeopathic,[3] gave me as much medicine, in the course of a fortnight's attendance, as would have lain on the point of a needle. They fed me on water-gruel,[4] and I

---

[2]*Michael Scott:* Scholar, translator, astrologer, alchemist, and magician (1175–1230) who was said to command devils and possess the power to feed dinner guests with food from the courts of Europe.

[3]*homeopathic:* Homeopathy involves treatment with small doses of medicine similar or related to the illness itself.

[4]*water-gruel:* A thin cereal or porridge made chiefly with water.

speedily became a skeleton above ground. But, after all, I have many precious recollections connected with that fit of sickness.

Hollingsworth's more than brotherly attendance gave me inexpressible comfort. Most men — and, certainly, I could not always claim to be one of the exceptions — have a natural indifference, if not an absolutely hostile feeling, towards those whom disease, or weakness, or calamity of any kind, causes to faulter and faint amid the rude jostle of our selfish existence. The education of Christianity, it is true, the sympathy of a like experience, and the example of women, may soften, and possibly subvert, this ugly characteristic of our sex. But it is originally there, and has likewise its analogy in the practice of our brute brethren, who hunt the sick or disabled member of the herd from among them, as an enemy. It is for this reason that the stricken deer goes apart, and the sick lion grimly withdraws himself into his den. Except in love, or the attachments of kindred, or other very long and habitual affection, we really have no tenderness. But there was something of the woman moulded into the great, stalwart frame of Hollingsworth; nor was he ashamed of it, as men often are of what is best in them, nor seemed ever to know that there was such a soft place in his heart. I knew it well, however, at that time; although, afterwards, it came nigh to be forgotten. Methought there could not be two such men alive, as Hollingsworth. There never was any blaze of a fireside that warmed and cheered me, in the downsinkings and shiverings of my spirit, so effectually as did the light out of those eyes, which lay so deep and dark under his shaggy brows.

Happy the man that has such a friend beside him, when he comes to die! And unless a friend like Hollingsworth be at hand, as most probably there will not, he had better make up his mind to die alone. How many men, I wonder, does one meet with, in a lifetime, whom he would choose for his death-bed companions! At the crisis of my fever, I besought Hollingsworth to let nobody else enter the room, but continually to make me sensible of his own presence by a grasp of the hand, a word — a prayer, if he thought good to utter it — and that then he should be the witness how courageously I would encounter the worst. It still impresses me as almost a matter of regret, that I did not die, then, when I had tolerably made up my mind to it; for Hollingsworth would have gone with me to the hither verge of life, and have sent his friendly and hopeful accents far over on the other side, while I should be treading the unknown path. Now, were I to send for him, he would hardly come to my bedside; nor should I depart the easier, for his presence.

"You are not going to die, this time," said he, gravely smiling. "You know nothing about sickness, and think your case a great deal more desperate than it is."

"Death should take me while I am in the mood," replied I, with a little of my customary levity.

"Have you nothing to do in life," asked Hollingsworth, "that you fancy yourself so ready to leave it?"

"Nothing," answered I — "nothing, that I know of, unless to make pretty verses, and play a part, with Zenobia and the rest of the amateurs, in our pastoral. It seems but an unsubstantial sort of business, as viewed through a mist of fever. But, dear Hollingsworth, your own vocation is evidently to be a priest, and to spend your days and nights in helping your fellow-creatures to draw peaceful dying-breaths."

"And by which of my qualities," inquired he, "can you suppose me fitted for this awful ministry?"

"By your tenderness," I said. "It seems to me the reflection of God's own love."

"And you call me tender!" repeated Hollingsworth, thoughtfully. "I should rather say, that the most marked trait in my character is an inflexible severity of purpose. Mortal man has no right to be so inflexible, as it is my nature and necessity to be!"

"I do not believe it," I replied.

But, in due time, I remembered what he said.

Probably, as Hollingsworth suggested, my disorder was never so serious as, in my ignorance of such matters, I was inclined to consider it. After so much tragical preparation, it was positively rather mortifying to find myself on the mending hand.

All the other members of the Community showed me kindness, according to the full measure of their capacity. Zenobia brought me my gruel, every day, made by her own hands, (not very skilfully, if the truth must be told,) and, whenever I seemed inclined to converse, would sit by my bedside, and talk with so much vivacity as to add several gratuitous throbs to my pulse. Her poor little stories and tracts never half did justice to her intellect; it was only the lack of a fitter avenue that drove her to seek development in literature. She was made (among a thousand other things that she might have been) for a stump-oratress. I recognized no severe culture in Zenobia; her mind was full of weeds. It startled me, sometimes, in my state of moral, as well as bodily faint-heartedness, to observe the hardihood of her philosophy; she made no scruple of oversetting all human institutions, and scattering them as with a breeze from her fan. A female reformer, in her attacks upon society, has an instinctive sense of where the life lies, and is inclined to aim directly at that spot. Especially, the relation between the sexes is naturally among the earliest to attract her notice.

Zenobia was truly a magnificent woman. The homely simplicity of her dress could not conceal, nor scarcely diminish, the queenliness of her presence. The image of her form and face should have been multiplied all over the earth. It was wronging the rest of mankind, to retain her as the spectacle of only a few. The stage would have been her proper sphere. She should have made it a point of duty, moreover, to sit endlessly to painters and sculptors, and preferably to the latter; because the cold decorum of the marble would consist with the utmost scantiness of drapery, so that the eye might chastely be gladdened with her material perfection, in its entireness. I know not well how to express, that the native glow of coloring in her cheeks, and even the flesh-warmth over her round arms, and what was visible of her full bust — in a word, her womanliness incarnated — compelled me sometimes to close my eyes, as if it were not quite the privilege of modesty to gaze at her. Illness and exhaustion, no doubt, had made me morbidly sensitive.

I noticed — and wondered how Zenobia contrived it — that she had always a new flower in her hair. And still it was a hot-house flower — an outlandish flower — a flower of the tropics, such as appeared to have sprung passionately out of a soil, the very weeds of which would be fervid and spicy. Unlike as was the flower of each successive day to the preceding one, it yet so assimilated its richness to the rich beauty of the woman, that I thought it the only flower fit to be worn; so fit, indeed, that Nature had evidently created this floral gem, in a happy exuberance, for the one purpose of worthily adorning Zenobia's head. It might be, that my feverish fantasies clustered themselves about this peculiarity, and caused it to look more gorgeous and wonderful than if beheld with temperate eyes. In the height of my illness, as I well recollect, I went so far as to pronounce it preternatural.

"Zenobia is an enchantress!" whispered I once to Hollingsworth. "She is a sister of the Veiled Lady! That flower in her hair is a talisman. If you were to snatch it away, she would vanish, or be transformed into something else!"

"What does he say?" asked Zenobia.

"Nothing that has an atom of sense in it," answered Hollingsworth. "He is a little beside himself, I believe, and talks about your being a witch, and of some magical property in the flower that you wear in your hair."

"It is an idea worthy of a feverish poet," said she, laughing, rather compassionately, and taking out the flower. "I scorn to owe anything to magic. Here, Mr. Hollingsworth: — you may keep the spell, while it has any virtue in it; but I cannot promise you not to appear with a new one, tomorrow. It is the one relic of my more brilliant, my happier days!"

The most curious part of the matter was, that, long after my slight delirium had passed away — as long, indeed, as I continued to know this remarkable woman — her daily flower affected my imagination, though more slightly, yet in very much the same way. The reason must have been, that, whether intentionally on her part, or not, this favorite ornament was actually a subtile expression of Zenobia's character.

One subject, about which — very impertinently, moreover — I perplexed myself with a great many conjectures, was, whether Zenobia had ever been married. The idea, it must be understood, was unauthorized by any circumstance or suggestion that had made its way to my ears. So young as I beheld her, and the freshest and rosiest woman of a thousand, there was certainly no need of imputing to her a destiny already accomplished; the probability was far greater, that her coming years had all life's richest gifts to bring. If the great event of a woman's existence had been consummated, the world knew nothing of it, although the world seemed to know Zenobia well. It was a ridiculous piece of romance, undoubtedly, to imagine that this beautiful personage, wealthy as she was, and holding a position that might fairly enough be called distinguished, could have given herself away so privately, but that some whisper and suspicion, and, by degrees, a full understanding of the fact, would eventually be blown abroad. But, then, as I failed not to consider, her original home was at a distance of many hundred miles. Rumors might fill the social atmosphere, or might once have filled it, there, which would travel but slowly, against the wind, towards our north-eastern metropolis, and perhaps melt into thin air before reaching it.

There was not, and I distinctly repeat it, the slightest foundation in my knowledge for any surmise of the kind. But there is a species of intuition — either a spiritual lie, or the subtile recognition of a fact — which comes to us in a reduced state of the corporeal system. The soul gets the better of the body, after wasting illness, or when a vegetable diet[5] may have mingled too much ether in the blood. Vapors then rise up to the brain, and take shapes that often image falsehood, but sometimes truth. The spheres of our companions have, at such periods, a vastly greater influence upon our own, than when robust health gives us a repellent and self-defensive energy. Zenobia's sphere, I imagine, impressed itself powerfully on mine, and transformed me, during this period of my weakness, into something like a mesmerical clairvoyant.

Then, also, as anybody could observe, the freedom of her deportment (though, to some tastes, it might commend itself as the utmost perfection of manner, in a youthful widow, or a blooming matron) was not exactly maidenlike. What girl had ever laughed as Zenobia did! What girl had ever spoken in her mellow tones! Her unconstrained and inevitable manifestation, I said often to myself, was that of a woman to whom wedlock had thrown wide the gates of mystery. Yet, sometimes, I strove to be ashamed of these conjectures. I acknowledged it as a masculine grossness — a sin of wicked interpretation, of which man is often guilty towards the other sex — thus to mistake the sweet, liberal, but womanly frankness of a noble and generous disposition. Still, it was of no avail to reason with myself, nor to upbraid myself. Pertinaciously the thought — 'Zenobia is a wife! Zenobia has lived, and loved! There is no folded petal, no latent dew-drop, in this perfectly developed rose!' — irresistibly that thought drove out all other conclusions, as often as my mind reverted to the subject.

Zenobia was conscious of my observation, though not, I presume, of the point to which it led me.

"Mr. Coverdale," said she, one day, as she saw me watching her, while she arranged my gruel on the table, "I have been exposed to a great deal of eye-shot in the few years of my mixing in the world, but never, I think, to precisely such glances as you are in the habit of favoring me with. I seem to interest you very much; and yet — or else a woman's instinct is for once deceived — I cannot reckon you as an admirer. What are you seeking to discover in me?"

"The mystery of your life," answered I, surprised into the truth by the unexpectedness of her attack. "And you will never tell me."

She bent her head towards me, and let me look into her eyes, as if challenging me to drop a plummet-line down into the depths of her consciousness.

---

[5]*a vegetable diet:* In Hawthorne's day, a meatless diet was said to produce an "ether" in the body that made a person more spiritual, less earthly and carnal.

"I see nothing now," said I, closing my own eyes, "unless it be the face of a sprite, laughing at me from the bottom of a deep well."

A bachelor always feels himself defrauded, when he knows, or suspects, that any woman of his acquaintance has given herself away. Otherwise, the matter could have been no concern of mine. It was purely speculative; for I should not, under any circumstances, have fallen in love with Zenobia. The riddle made me so nervous, however, in my sensitive condition of mind and body, that I most ungratefully began to wish that she would let me alone. Then, too, her gruel was very wretched stuff, with almost invariably the smell of pine-smoke upon it, like the evil taste that is said to mix itself up with a witch's best concocted dainties. Why could not she have allowed one of the other women to take the gruel in charge? Whatever else might be her gifts, Nature certainly never intended Zenobia for a cook. Or, if so, she should have meddled only with the richest and spiciest dishes, and such as are to be tasted at banquets, between draughts of intoxicating wine.

VII. THE CONVALESCENT

As soon as my incommodities allowed me to think of past occurrences, I failed not to inquire what had become of the odd little guest, whom Hollingsworth had been the medium of introducing among us. It now appeared, that poor Priscilla had not so literally fallen out of the clouds, as we were at first inclined to suppose. A letter, which should have introduced her, had since been received from one of the city-missionaries, containing a certificate of character, and an allusion to circumstances which, in the writer's judgment, made it especially desirable that she should find shelter in our Community. There was a hint, not very intelligible, implying either that Priscilla had recently escaped from some particular peril, or irksomeness of position, or else that she was still liable to this danger or difficulty, whatever it might be. We should ill have deserved the reputation of a benevolent fraternity, had we hesitated to entertain a petitioner in such need, and so strongly recommended to our kindness; not to mention, moreover, that the strange maiden had set herself diligently to work, and was doing good service with her needle. But a slight mist of uncertainty still floated about Priscilla, and kept her, as yet, from taking a very decided place among creatures of flesh and blood.

The mysterious attraction, which, from her first entrance on our scene, she evinced for Zenobia, had lost nothing of its force. I often heard her footsteps, soft and low, accompanying the light, but decided tread of the latter, up the staircase, stealing along the passageway by her new friend's side, and pausing while Zenobia entered my chamber. Occasionally, Zenobia would be a little annoyed by Priscilla's too close attendance. In an authoritative and not very kindly tone, she would advise her to breathe the pleasant air in a walk, or to go with her work into the barn, holding out half a promise to come and sit on the hay with her, when at leisure. Evidently, Priscilla found but scanty requital for her love. Hollingsworth was likewise a great favorite with her. For several minutes together, sometimes, while my auditory nerves retained the susceptibility of delicate health, I used to hear a low, pleasant murmur, ascending from the room below, and at last ascertained it to be Priscilla's voice, babbling like a little brook to Hollingsworth. She talked more largely and freely with him than with Zenobia, towards whom, indeed, her feelings seemed not so much to be confidence, as involuntary affection. I should have thought all the better of my own qualities, had Priscilla marked me out for the third place in her regards. But, though she appeared to like me tolerably well, I could never flatter myself with being distinguished by her, as Hollingsworth and Zenobia were.

One forenoon, during my convalescence, there came a gentle tap at my chamber-door. I immediately said — "Come in, Priscilla!" — with an acute sense of the applicant's identity. Nor was I deceived. It was really Priscilla, a pale, large-eyed little woman, (for she had gone far enough into her teens to be, at least, on the outer limit of girlhood,) but much less wan than at my previous view of her, and far better conditioned both as to health and spirits. As I first saw her, she had reminded me of plants that one sometimes observes doing their best to vegetate among the bricks of an enclosed court, where there is scanty soil, and never any sunshine. At present, though with no approach to bloom, there were indications that the girl had human blood in her veins.

Priscilla came softly to my bedside, and held out an article of snow-white linen, very carefully and smoothly ironed. She did not seem bashful, nor anywise embarrassed. My weakly condition, I suppose, supplied a medium in which she could approach me.

"Do you not need this?" asked she. "I have made it for you."

It was a night-cap!

"My dear Priscilla," said I, smiling, "I never had on a night-cap in my life! But perhaps it will be better for me to wear one, now that I

am a miserable invalid. How admirably you have done it! No, no; I
never can think of wearing such an exquisitely wrought night-cap as
this, unless it be in the day-time, when I sit up to receive company!"

"It is for use, not beauty," answered Priscilla. "I could have embroidered it and made it much prettier, if I pleased."

While holding up the night-cap, and admiring the fine needle-
work, I perceived that Priscilla had a sealed letter, which she was
waiting for me to take. It had arrived from the village post-office,
that morning. As I did not immediately offer to receive the letter, she
drew it back, and held it against her bosom, with both hands clasped
over it, in a way that had probably grown habitual to her. Now, on
turning my eyes from the night-cap to Priscilla, it forcibly struck me
that her air, though not her figure, and the expression of her face, but
not its features, had a resemblance to what I had often seen in a
friend of mine, one of the most gifted women of the age. I cannot describe it. The points, easiest to convey to the reader, were, a certain
curve of the shoulders, and a partial closing of the eyes, which
seemed to look more penetratingly into my own eyes, through the
narrowed apertures, than if they had been open at full width. It was a
singular anomaly of likeness co-existing with perfect dissimilitude.

"Will you give me the letter, Priscilla?" said I.

She started, put the letter into my hand, and quite lost the look
that had drawn my notice.

"Priscilla," I inquired, "did you ever see Miss Margaret Fuller?"[1]

"No," she answered.

"Because," said I, "you reminded me of her, just now, and it happens, strangely enough, that this very letter is from her!"

Priscilla, for whatever reason, looked very much discomposed.

"I wish people would not fancy such odd things in me!" she said,
rather petulantly. "How could I possibly make myself resemble this
lady, merely by holding her letter in my hand?"

"Certainly, Priscilla, it would puzzle me to explain it," I replied.
"Nor do I suppose that the letter had anything to do with it. It was
just a coincidence — nothing more."

She hastened out of the room; and this was the last that I saw of
Priscilla, until I ceased to be an invalid.

Being much alone, during my recovery, I read interminably in Mr.

---

[1]*Miss Margaret Fuller:* Margaret Fuller (1810–1850) was an important transcendentalist essayist, translator, editor, literary critic, and journalist. She visited Brook
Farm often but was never a member of the community.

Emerson's Essays, the Dial, Carlyle's works, George Sand's romances,[2] (lent me by Zenobia,) and other books which one or another of the brethren or sisterhood had brought with them. Agreeing in little else, most of these utterances were like the cry of some solitary sentinel, whose station was on the outposts of the advance-guard of human progression; or, sometimes, the voice came sadly from among the shattered ruins of the past, but yet had a hopeful echo in the future. They were well adapted (better, at least, than any other intellectual products, the volatile essence of which had heretofore tinctured a printed page) to pilgrims like ourselves, whose present bivouâc was considerably farther into the waste of chaos than any mortal army of crusaders had ever marched before. Fourier's works,[3] also, in a series of horribly tedious volumes, attracted a good deal of my attention, from the analogy which I could not but recognize between his system and our own. There was far less resemblance, it is true, than the world chose to imagine; inasmuch as the two theories differed, as widely as the zenith from the nadir, in their main principles.

I talked about Fourier to Hollingsworth, and translated, for his benefit, some of the passages that chiefly impressed me.

"When, as a consequence of human improvement," said I, "the globe shall arrive at its final perfection, the great ocean is to be converted into a particular kind of lemonade, such as was fashionable at Paris in Fourier's time. He calls it *limonade à cèdre*.[4] It is positively a fact! Just imagine the city-docks filled, every day, with a flood-tide of this delectable beverage!"

"Why did not the Frenchman make punch of it, at once?" asked Hollingsworth. "The jack-tars[5] would be delighted to go down in ships, and do business in such an element."

[2]*Mr. Emerson's Essays, the Dial, Carlyle's works, George Sand's romances:* Ralph Waldo Emerson (1803–1882), transcendentalist writer and philosopher, whose works include two volumes of *Essays* (1841, 1844); *The Dial,* transcendentalist journal, edited by Margaret Fuller and Emerson and published from 1840 to 1844; Thomas Carlyle (1795–1881), Scottish literary and cultural critic and historian whose influential early book, *Sartor Resartus* (1836), Emerson helped to publish in the United States; George Sand (1803–1876), French spokeswoman for feminism and socialism whose novel *Consuelo* (1842–1843) was translated by Francis G. Shaw for *The Harbinger,* Brook Farm's journal.

[3]*Fourier's works:* Charles Fourier, French theorist, author of many utopian socialist works, advocate of reorganization of society into cooperative, self-sufficient units (phalanxes).

[4]*limonade à cèdre:* The correct French passage is *aigre de cèdre,* a tart French lemonade, to which, according to Fourier, the oceans would be converted in the era of social harmony.

[5]*jack-tars:* Sailors.

I further proceeded to explain, as well as I modestly could, several points of Fourier's system, illustrating them with here and there a page or two, and asking Hollingsworth's opinion as to the expediency of introducing these beautiful peculiarities into our own practice.

"Let me hear no more of it!" cried he, in utter disgust. "I never will forgive this fellow! He has committed the Unpardonable Sin! For what more monstrous iniquity could the Devil himself contrive, than to choose the selfish principle — the principle of all human wrong, the very blackness of man's heart, the portion of ourselves which we shudder at, and which it is the whole aim of spiritual discipline to eradicate — to choose it as the master-workman of his system? To seize upon and foster whatever vile, petty, sordid, filthy, bestial, and abominable corruptions have cankered into our nature, to be the efficient instruments of his infernal regeneration! And his consummated Paradise, as he pictures it, would be worthy of the agency which he counts upon for establishing it. The nauseous villain!"

"Nevertheless," remarked I, "in consideration of the promised delights of his system — so very proper, as they certainly are, to be appreciated by Fourier's countrymen — I cannot but wonder that universal France did not adopt his theory, at a moment's warning. But is there not something very characteristic of his nation in Fourier's manner of putting forth his views? He makes no claim to inspiration. He has not persuaded himself — as Swedenborg[6] did, and as any other than a Frenchman would, with a mission of like importance to communicate — that he speaks with authority from above. He promulgates his system, so far as I can perceive, entirely on his own responsibility. He has searched out and discovered the whole counsel of the Almighty, in respect to mankind, past, present, and for exactly seventy thousand years to come, by the mere force and cunning of his individual intellect!"

"Take the book out of my sight!" said Hollingsworth, with great virulence of expression, "or, I tell you fairly, I shall fling it in the fire! And as for Fourier, let him make a Paradise, if he can, of Gehenna,[7] where, as I conscientiously believe, he is floundering at this moment!"

"And bellowing, I suppose," said I — not that I felt any ill-will towards Fourier, but merely wanted to give the finishing touch to

[6]*Swedenborg:* Emmanuel Swedenborg (1688–1772), Swedish theologian, mystic, and scientist, argued that each natural object is permeated by a higher, spiritual reality. He was read and admired by Emerson and other transcendentalists.
[7]*Gehenna:* Hell, the place where souls suffer for their sins; more generally, the realm of death.

Hollingsworth's image — "bellowing for the least drop of his beloved *limonade à cèdre!*"

There is but little profit to be expected in attempting to argue with a man who allows himself to declaim in this manner; so I dropt the subject, and never took it up again.

But had the system, at which he was so enraged, combined almost any amount of human wisdom, spiritual insight, and imaginative beauty, I question whether Hollingsworth's mind was in a fit condition to receive it. I began to discern that he had come among us, actuated by no real sympathy with our feelings and our hopes, but chiefly because we were estranging ourselves from the world, with which his lonely and exclusive object in life had already put him at odds. Hollingsworth must have been originally endowed with a great spirit of benevolence, deep enough, and warm enough, to be the source of as much disinterested good, as Providence often allows a human being the privilege of conferring upon his fellows. This native instinct yet lived within him. I myself had profited by it, in my necessity. It was seen, too, in his treatment of Priscilla. Such casual circumstances, as were here involved, would quicken his divine power of sympathy, and make him seem, while their influence lasted, the tenderest man and the truest friend on earth. But, by-and-by, you missed the tenderness of yesterday, and grew drearily conscious that Hollingsworth had a closer friend than ever you could be. And this friend was the cold, spectral monster which he had himself conjured up, and on which he was wasting all the warmth of his heart, and of which, at last — as these men of a mighty purpose so invariably do — he had grown to be the bond-slave. It was his philanthropic theory!

This was a result exceedingly sad to contemplate, considering that it had been mainly brought about by the very ardor and exuberance of his philanthropy. Sad, indeed, but by no means unusual. He had taught his benevolence to pour its warm tide exclusively through one channel; so that there was nothing to spare for other great manifestations of love to man, nor scarcely for the nutriment of individual attachments, unless they could minister, in some way, to the terrible egotism which he mistook for an angel of God. Had Hollingsworth's education been more enlarged, he might not so inevitably have stumbled into this pit-fall. But this identical pursuit had educated him. He knew absolutely nothing, except in a single direction, where he had thought so energetically, and felt to such a depth, that, no doubt, the entire reason and justice of the universe appeared to be concentrated thitherward.

It is my private opinion, that, at this period of his life, Hollingsworth was fast going mad; and, as with other crazy people, (among whom I include humorists of every degree,) it required all the constancy of friendship to restrain his associates from pronouncing him an intolerable bore. Such prolonged fiddling upon one string; such multiform presentation of one idea! His specific object (of which he made the public more than sufficiently aware, through the medium of lectures and pamphlets) was to obtain funds for the construction of an edifice, with a sort of collegiate endowment. On this foundation, he purposed to devote himself and a few disciples to the reform and mental culture of our criminal brethren. His visionary edifice was Hollingsworth's one castle in the air; it was the material type, in which his philanthropic dream strove to embody itself; and he made the scheme more definite, and caught hold of it the more strongly, and kept his clutch the more pertinaciously, by rendering it visible to the bodily eye. I have seen him, a hundred times, with a pencil and sheet of paper, sketching the façade, the side-view, or the rear of the structure, or planning the internal arrangements, as lovingly as another man might plan those of the projected home, where he meant to be happy with his wife and children. I have known him to begin a model of the building with little stones, gathered at the brookside, whither we had gone to cool ourselves in the sultry noon of haying-time. Unlike all other ghosts, his spirit haunted an edifice which, instead of being time-worn, and full of storied love, and joy, and sorrow, had never yet come into existence.

"Dear friend," said I, once, to Hollingsworth, before leaving my sick-chamber, "I heartily wish that I could make your schemes my schemes, because it would be so great a happiness to find myself treading the same path with you. But I am afraid there is not stuff in me stern enough for a philanthropist — or not in this peculiar direction — or, at all events, not solely in this. Can you bear with me, if such should prove to be the case?"

"I will, at least, wait awhile," answered Hollingsworth, gazing at me sternly and gloomily. "But how can you be my life-long friend, except you strive with me towards the great object of my life?"

Heaven forgive me! A horrible suspicion crept into my heart, and stung the very core of it as with the fangs of an adder. I wondered whether it were possible that Hollingsworth could have watched by my bedside, with all that devoted care, only for the ulterior purpose of making me a proselyte to his views!

VIII. A MODERN ARCADIA

May-Day[1] — I forget whether by Zenobia's sole decree, or by the unanimous vote of our Community — had been declared a moveable festival. It was deferred until the sun should have had a reasonable time to clear away the snow-drifts, along the lee of the stone-walls, and bring out a few of the readiest wild-flowers. On the forenoon of the substituted day, after admitting some of the balmy air into my chamber, I decided that it was nonsense and effeminacy to keep myself a prisoner any longer. So I descended to the sitting-room, and finding nobody there, proceeded to the barn, whence I had already heard Zenobia's voice, and along with it a girlish laugh, which was not so certainly recognizable. Arriving at the spot, it a little surprised me to discover that these merry outbreaks came from Priscilla.

The two had been a-maying together. They had found anemones in abundance, houstonias[2] by the handfull, some columbines, a few long-stalked violets, and a quantity of white everlasting-flowers, and had filled up their basket with the delicate spray of shrubs and trees. None were prettier than the maple-twigs, the leaf of which looks like a scarlet-bud, in May, and like a plate of vegetable gold in October. Zenobia — who showed no conscience in such matters — had also rifled a cherry-tree of one of its blossomed boughs; and, with all this variety of sylvan ornament, had been decking out Priscilla. Being done with a good deal of taste, it made her look more charming than I should have thought possible, with my recollection of the wan, frost-nipt girl, as heretofore described. Nevertheless, among those fragrant blossoms, and conspicuously, too, had been stuck a weed of evil odor and ugly aspect, which, as soon as I detected it, destroyed the effect of all the rest. There was a gleam of latent mischief — not to call it deviltry — in Zenobia's eye, which seemed to indicate a slightly malicious purpose in the arrangement.

As for herself, she scorned the rural buds and leaflets, and wore nothing but her invariable flower of the tropics.

"What do you think of Priscilla now, Mr. Coverdale?" asked she, surveying her as a child does its doll. "Is not she worth a verse or two?"

---

[1]*May-Day:* The celebration or festival marking the beginning of spring, from the pagan festival for Maia, mother of Mercury. See Hawthorne's story "The May-Pole of Merry Mount" (1835).

[2]*houstonias:* North American herb with blue, lilac, or white flowers.

"There is only one thing amiss," answered I.

Zenobia laughed, and flung the malignant weed away.

"Yes; she deserves some verses now," said I, "and from a better poet than myself. She is the very picture of the New England spring, subdued in tint, and rather cool, but with a capacity of sunshine, and bringing us a few alpine blossoms, as earnest of something richer, though hardly more beautiful, hereafter. The best type of her is one of those anemones."

"What I find most singular in Priscilla, as her health improves," observed Zenobia, "is her wildness. Such a quiet little body as she seemed, one would not have expected that! Why, as we strolled the woods together, I could hardly keep her from scrambling up the trees like a squirrel! She has never before known what it is to live in the free air, and so it intoxicates her as if she were sipping wine. And she thinks it such a Paradise here, and all of us, particularly Mr. Hollingsworth and myself, such angels! It is quite ridiculous, and provokes one's malice, almost, to see a creature so happy — especially a feminine creature."

"They are always happier than male creatures," said I.

"You must correct that opinion, Mr. Coverdale," replied Zenobia, contemptuously, "or I shall think you lack the poetic insight. Did you ever see a happy woman in your life? Of course, I do not mean a girl — like Priscilla, and a thousand others, for they are all alike, while on the sunny side of experience — but a grown woman. How can she be happy, after discovering that fate has assigned her but one single event, which she must contrive to make the substance of her whole life? A man has his choice of innumerable events."

"A woman, I suppose," answered I, "by constant repetition of her one event, may compensate for the lack of variety."

"Indeed!" said Zenobia.

While we were talking, Priscilla caught sight of Hollingsworth, at a distance, in a blue frock[3] and with a hoe over his shoulder, returning from the field. She immediately set out to meet him, running and skipping, with spirits as light as the breeze of the May-morning, but with limbs too little exercised to be quite responsive; she clapt her hands, too, with great exuberance of gesture, as is the custom of young girls, when their electricity overcharges them. But, all at once, midway to Hollingsworth, she paused, looked round about her, towards the river, the road, the woods, and back towards us, appearing

---

[3]*blue frock:* A workman's long, loose shirt.

to listen, as if she heard some one calling her name, and knew not precisely in what direction.

"Have you bewitched her?" I exclaimed.

"It is no sorcery of mine," said Zenobia. "But I have seen the girl do that identical thing, once or twice before. Can you imagine what is the matter with her?"

"No; unless," said I, "she has the gift of hearing those 'airy tongues that syllable men's names' — which Milton tells about."[4]

From whatever cause, Priscilla's animation seemed entirely to have deserted her. She seated herself on a rock, and remained there until Hollingsworth came up; and when he took her hand and led her back to us, she rather resembled my original image of the wan and spiritless Priscilla, than the flowery May Queen of a few moments ago. These sudden transformations, only to be accounted for by an extreme nervous susceptibility, always continued to characterize the girl, though with diminished frequency, as her health progressively grew more robust.

I was now on my legs again. My fit of illness had been an avenue between two existences; the low-arched and darksome doorway, through which I crept out of a life of old conventionalisms, on my hands and knees, as it were, and gained admittance into the freer region that lay beyond. In this respect, it was like death. And, as with death, too, it was good to have gone through it. No otherwise could I have rid myself of a thousand follies, fripperies, prejudices, habits, and other such worldly dust as inevitably settles upon the crowd along the broad highway, giving them all one sordid aspect, before noontime, however freshly they may have begun their pilgrimage, in the dewy morning. The very substance upon my bones had not been fit to live with, in any better, truer, or more energetic mode than that to which I was accustomed. So it was taken off me and flung aside, like any other worn out or unseasonable garment; and, after shivering a little while in my skeleton, I began to be clothed anew, and much more satisfactorily than in my previous suit. In literal and physical truth, I was quite another man. I had a lively sense of the exultation with which the spirit will enter on the next stage of its eternal progress, after leaving the heavy burthen of its mortality in an earthly grave, with as little concern for what may become of it, as now affected me for the flesh which I had lost.

[4] *"airy tongues that syllable men's names"*: See John Milton's *Comus* (1634), line 208, the story of a maiden whose Christian virtue protects her from a wicked enchanter. Note the reference to "the crew of Comus" in Hawthorne's "The May-Pole of Merry Mount." See also *The House of the Seven Gables*, ch. 18.

Emerging into the genial sunshine, I half fancied that the labors of the brotherhood had already realized some of Fourier's predictions. Their enlightened culture of the soil, and the virtues with which they sanctified their life, had begun to produce an effect upon the material world and its climate. In my new enthusiasm, man looked strong and stately! — and woman, oh, how beautiful! — and the earth, a green garden, blossoming with many-colored delights! Thus Nature, whose laws I had broken in various artificial ways, comported herself towards me as a strict, but loving mother, who uses the rod upon her little boy for his naughtiness, and then gives him a smile, a kiss, and some pretty playthings, to console the urchin for her severity.

In the interval of my seclusion, there had been a number of recruits to our little army of saints and martyrs. They were mostly individuals who had gone through such an experience as to disgust them with ordinary pursuits, but who were not yet so old, nor had suffered so deeply, as to lose their faith in the better time to come. On comparing their minds, one with another, they often discovered that this idea of a Community had been growing up, in silent and unknown sympathy, for years. Thoughtful, strongly-lined faces were among them, sombre brows, but eyes that did not require spectacles, unless prematurely dimmed by the student's lamplight, and hair that seldom showed a thread of silver. Age, wedded to the past, incrusted over with a stony layer of habits, and retaining nothing fluid in its possibilities, would have been absurdly out of place in an enterprise like this. Youth, too, in its early dawn, was hardly more adapted to our purpose; for it would behold the morning radiance of its own spirit beaming over the very same spots of withered grass and barren sand, whence most of us had seen it vanish. We had very young people with us, it is true — downy lads, rosy girls in their first teens, and children of all heights above one's knee; — but these had chiefly been sent hither for education, which it was one of the objects and methods of our institution to supply. Then we had boarders, from town and elsewhere, who lived with us in a familiar way, sympathized more or less in our theories, and sometimes shared in our labors.

On the whole, it was a society such as has seldom met together; nor, perhaps, could it reasonably be expected to hold together long. Persons of marked individuality — crooked sticks, as some of us might be called — are not exactly the easiest to bind up into a faggot.[5] But, so long as our union should subsist, a man of intellect and feeling,

[5]*faggot:* Bundle of sticks or twigs, especially for fuel.

with a free nature in him, might have sought far and near, without finding so many points of attraction as would allure him hitherward. We were of all creeds and opinions, and generally tolerant of all, on every imaginable subject. Our bond, it seems to me, was not affirmative, but negative. We had individually found one thing or another to quarrel with, in our past life, and were pretty well agreed as to the inexpediency of lumbering along with the old system any farther. As to what should be substituted, there was much less unanimity. We did not greatly care — at least, I never did — for the written constitution under which our millennium had commenced. My hope was, that, between theory and practice, a true and available mode of life might be struck out, and that, even should we ultimately fail, the months or years spent in the trial would not have been wasted, either as regarded passing enjoyment, or the experience which makes men wise.

Arcadians though we were, our costume bore no resemblance to the be-ribboned doublets, silk breeches and stockings, and slippers fastened with artificial roses, that distinguish the pastoral people of poetry and the stage. In outward show, I humbly conceive, we looked rather like a gang of beggars or banditti, than either a company of honest laboring men or a conclave of philosophers. Whatever might be our points of difference, we all of us seemed to have come to Blithedale with the one thrifty and laudable idea of wearing out our old clothes. Such garments as had an airing, whenever we strode afield! Coats with high collars, and with no collars, broad-skirted or swallow-tailed, and with the waist at every point between the hip and armpit; pantaloons of a dozen successive epochs, and greatly defaced at the knees by the humiliations of the wearer before his lady-love; — in short, we were a living epitome of defunct fashions, and the very raggedest presentment of men who had seen better days. It was gentility in tatters. Often retaining a scholarlike or clerical air, you might have taken us for the denizens of Grub-street,[6] intent on getting a comfortable livelihood by agricultural labor; or Coleridge's projected Pantisocracy,[7] in full experiment; or Candide[8] and his motley asso-

---

[6]*Grub-street:* Street in London associated with poor, struggling hack writers.

[7]*Coleridge's projected Pantisocracy:* Derives from Greek word meaning "all to rule equally." The name for the utopian community that the English poets Samuel Taylor Coleridge (1772–1834) and Robert Southey (1774–1843) projected in the 1790s and hoped to establish along the Susquehanna River in Pennsylvania.

[8]*Candide: Candide, ou L'Optimisme* (1759), a satiric philosophical novel by Voltaire (1694–1778), in which the main characters, after a series of disasters, finally settle on a small farm where they cultivate their garden.

ciates, at work in their cabbage-garden; or anything else that was miserably out at elbows, and most clumsily patched in the rear. We might have been sworn comrades to Falstaff's ragged regiment.[9] Little skill as we boasted in other points of husbandry, every mother's son of us would have served admirably to stick up for a scarecrow. And the worst of the matter was, that the first energetic movement, essential to one downright stroke of real labor, was sure to put a finish to these poor habiliments. So we gradually flung them all aside, and took to honest homespun and linsey-woolsey,[10] as preferable, on the whole, to the plan recommended, I think, by Virgil — '*Ara nudus; sere nudus*'[11] — which, as Silas Foster remarked when I translated the maxim, would be apt to astonish the women-folks.

After a reasonable training, the yeoman-life throve well with us. Our faces took the sunburn kindly; our chests gained in compass, and our shoulders in breadth and squareness; our great brown fists looked as if they had never been capable of kid gloves. The plough, the hoe, the scythe, and the hay-fork, grew familiar in our grasp. The oxen responded to our voices. We could do almost as fair a day's work as Silas Foster himself, sleep dreamlessly after it, and awake at daybreak with only a little stiffness of the joints, which was usually quite gone by breakfast-time.

To be sure, our next neighbors pretended to be incredulous as to our real proficiency in the business which we had taken in hand. They told slanderous fables about our inability to yoke our own oxen, or to drive them afield, when yoked, or to release the poor brutes from their conjugal bond at nightfall. They had the face to say, too, that the cows laughed at our awkwardness at milking-time, and invariably kicked over the pails; partly in consequence of our putting the stool on the wrong side, and partly because, taking offence at the whisking of their tails, we were in the habit of holding these natural flyflappers with one hand, and milking with the other. They further averred, that we hoed up whole acres of Indian corn and other crops, and drew the earth carefully about the weeds; and that we raised five hundred tufts of burdock,[12] mistaking them for cabbages; and that,

---

[9]*Falstaff's ragged regiment:* See Falstaff's account of his 150 tattered, ragged soldiers in Shakespeare's *Henry IV, Part 1*, 4.2.

[10]*linsey-woolsey:* A coarse, sturdy fabric "spun at home" and mixing wool and linen; used for work clothes.

[11]*"Ara nudus; sere nudus":* "Strip to plough and strip to sow," from Virgil's *Georgics* (37–30), trans. L. P. Wilkinson (New York: Penguin, 1982), 1:299.

[12]*burdock:* A weed-like plant with purple flowers.

by dint of unskilful planting, few of our seeds ever came up at all, or if they did come up, it was stern foremost, and that we spent the better part of the month of June in reversing a field of beans, which had thrust themselves out of the ground in this unseemly way. They quoted it as nothing more than an ordinary occurrence for one or other of us to crop off two or three fingers, of a morning, by our clumsy use of the hay-cutter. Finally, and as an ultimate catastrophe, these mendacious rogues circulated a report that we Communitarians[13] were exterminated, to the last man, by severing ourselves asunder with the sweep of our own scythes! — and that the world had lost nothing by this little accident.

But this was pure envy and malice on the part of the neighboring farmers. The peril of our new way of life was not lest we should fail in becoming practical agriculturalists, but that we should probably cease to be anything else. While our enterprise lay all in theory, we had pleased ourselves with delectable visions of the spiritualization of labor. It was to be our form of prayer, and ceremonial of worship. Each stroke of the hoe was to uncover some aromatic root of wisdom, heretofore hidden from the sun. Pausing in the field, to let the wind exhale the moisture from our foreheads, we were to look upward, and catch glimpses into the far-off soul of truth. In this point of view, matters did not turn out quite so well as we anticipated. It is very true, that, sometimes, gazing casually around me, out of the midst of my toil, I used to discern a richer picturesqueness in the visible scene of earth and sky. There was, at such moments, a novelty, an unwonted aspect on the face of Nature, as if she had been taken by surprise and seen at unawares, with no opportunity to put off her real look, and assume the mask with which she mysteriously hides herself from mortals. But this was all. The clods of earth, which we so constantly belabored and turned over and over, were never etherealized into thought. Our thoughts, on the contrary, were fast becoming cloddish. Our labor symbolized nothing, and left us mentally sluggish in the dusk of the evening. Intellectual activity is incompatible with any large amount of bodily exercise. The yeoman and the scholar — the yeoman and the man of finest moral culture, though not the man of sturdiest sense and integrity — are two distinct individuals, and can never be melted or welded into one substance.

Zenobia soon saw this truth, and gibed me about it, one evening, as Hollingsworth and I lay on the grass, after a hard day's work.

---

[13]*Communitarians:* Members of a small cooperative community.

"I am afraid you did not make a song, to-day, while loading the hay-cart," said she, "as Burns did,[14] when he was reaping barley."

"Burns never made a song in haying-time," I answered, very positively. "He was no poet while a farmer, and no farmer while a poet."

"And, on the whole, which of the two characters do you like best?" asked Zenobia. "For I have an idea that you cannot combine them, any better than Burns did. Ah, I see, in my mind's eye, what sort of an individual you are to be, two or three years hence! Grim Silas Foster is your prototype, with his palm of sole-leather, and his joints of rusty iron, (which, all through summer, keep the stiffness of what he calls his winter's rheumatize,) and his brain of — I don't know what his brain is made of, unless it be a Savoy cabbage;[15] but yours may be cauliflower, as a rather more delicate variety. Your physical man will be transmuted into salt-beef and fried pork, at the rate, I should imagine, of a pound and a half a day; that being about the average which we find necessary in the kitchen. You will make your toilet for the day (still like this delightful Silas Foster) by rinsing your fingers and the front part of your face in a little tin-pan of water, at the door-step, and teasing your hair with a wooden pocket-comb, before a seven-by-nine-inch looking-glass. Your only pastime will be, to smoke some very vile tobacco in the black stump of a pipe!"

"Pray spare me!" cried I. "But the pipe is not Silas's only mode of solacing himself with the weed."

"Your literature," continued Zenobia, apparently delighted with her description, "will be the Farmer's Almanac;[16] for, I observe, our friend Foster never gets so far as the newspaper. When you happen to sit down, at odd moments, you will fall asleep, and make nasal proclamation of the fact, as he does; and invariably you must be jogged out of a nap, after supper, by the future Mrs. Coverdale, and persuaded to go regularly to bed. And on Sundays; when you put on a blue coat with brass buttons, you will think of nothing else to do,

---

[14]*as Burns did:* Robert Burns (1759–1796), Scottish poet who experienced difficult work as a farm laborer and ploughman.

[15]*Savoy cabbage:* A form of cabbage or spinach with wrinkled leaves, grown for use in winter.

[16]*Farmer's Almanac:* Massachusetts almanac, begun by Robert Bailey Thomas (1766–1846) in 1793. It included weather forecasts, poems, recipes, and other pieces of lore and information (e.g., about crops and livestock). It is still published today. See G. L. Kittredge, *The Old Farmer and His Almanack* (1904).

but to go and lounge over the stone-walls and rail-fences, and stare at the corn growing. And you will look with a knowing eye at oxen, and will have a tendency to clamber over into pig-sties, and feel of the hogs, and give a guess how much they will weigh, after you shall have stuck and dressed them. Already, I have noticed, you begin to speak through your nose, and with a drawl. Pray, if you really did make any poetry to-day, let us hear it in that kind of utterance!"

"Coverdale has given up making verses, now," said Hollingsworth, who never had the slightest appreciation of my poetry. "Just think of him penning a sonnet, with a fist like that! There is at least this good in a life of toil, that it takes the nonsense and fancy-work out of a man, and leaves nothing but what truly belongs to him. If a farmer can make poetry at the plough-tail, it must be because his nature insists on it; and if that be the case, let him make it, in Heaven's name!"

"And how is it with you?" asked Zenobia, in a different voice; for she never laughed at Hollingsworth, as she often did at me. — "You, I think, cannot have ceased to live a life of thought and feeling."

"I have always been in earnest," answered Hollingsworth. "I have hammered thought out of iron, after heating the iron in my heart! It matters little what my outward toil may be. Were I a slave at the bottom of a mine, I should keep the same purpose — the same faith in its ultimate accomplishment — that I do now. Miles Coverdale is not in earnest, either as a poet or a laborer."

"You give me hard measure, Hollingsworth," said I, a little hurt. "I have kept pace with you in the field; and my bones feel as if I had been in earnest, whatever may be the case with my brain!"

"I cannot conceive," observed Zenobia, with great emphasis — and, no doubt, she spoke fairly the feeling of the moment — "I cannot conceive of being, so continually as Mr. Coverdale is, within the sphere of a strong and noble nature, without being strengthened and ennobled by its influence!"

This amiable remark of the fair Zenobia confirmed me in what I had already begun to suspect — that Hollingsworth, like many other illustrious prophets, reformers, and philanthropists, was likely to make at least two proselytes, among the women, to one among the men. Zenobia and Priscilla! These, I believe, (unless my unworthy self might be reckoned for a third,) were the only disciples of his mission; and I spent a great deal of time, uselessly, in trying to conjecture what Hollingsworth meant to do with them — and they with him!

IX. HOLLINGSWORTH,
ZENOBIA, PRISCILLA

It is not, I apprehend, a healthy kind of mental occupation, to devote ourselves too exclusively to the study of individual men and women. If the person under examination be one's self, the result is pretty certain to be diseased action of the heart, almost before we can snatch a second glance. Or, if we take the freedom to put a friend under our microscope, we thereby insulate him from many of his true relations, magnify his peculiarities, inevitably tear him into parts, and, of course, patch him very clumsily together again. What wonder, then, should we be frightened by the aspect of a monster, which, after all — though we can point to every feature of his deformity in the real personage — may be said to have been created mainly by ourselves!

Thus, as my conscience has often whispered me, I did Hollingsworth a great wrong by prying into his character, and am perhaps doing him as great a one, at this moment, by putting faith in the discoveries which I seemed to make. But I could not help it. Had I loved him less, I might have used him better. He — and Zenobia and Priscilla, both for their own sakes and as connected with him — were separated from the rest of the Community, to my imagination, and stood forth as the indices of a problem which it was my business to solve. Other associates had a portion of my time; other matters amused me; passing occurrences carried me along with them, while they lasted. But here was the vortex of my meditations around which they revolved, and whitherward they too continually tended. In the midst of cheerful society, I had often a feeling of loneliness. For it was impossible not to be sensible, that, while these three characters figured so largely on my private theatre, I — though probably reckoned as a friend by all — was at best but a secondary or tertiary personage with either of them.

I loved Hollingsworth, as has already been enough expressed. But it impressed me, more and more, that there was a stern and dreadful peculiarity in this man, such as could not prove otherwise than pernicious to the happiness of those who should be drawn into too intimate a connection with him. He was not altogether human. There was something else in Hollingsworth, besides flesh and blood, and sympathies and affections, and celestial spirit.

This is always true of those men who have surrendered themselves to an over-ruling purpose. It does not so much impel them from without, nor even operate as a motive power within, but grows incorporate with all that they think and feel, and finally converts them into little else save that one principle. When such begins to be the predicament, it is not cowardice, but wisdom, to avoid these victims. They have no heart, no sympathy, no reason, no conscience. They will keep no friend, unless he make himself the mirror of their purpose; they will smite and slay you, and trample your dead corpse under foot, all the more readily, if you take the first step with them, and cannot take the second, and the third, and every other step of their terribly straight path. They have an idol, to which they consecrate themselves high-priest, and deem it holy work to offer sacrifices of whatever is most precious, and never once seem to suspect — so cunning has the Devil been with them — that this false deity, in whose iron features, immitigable to all the rest of mankind, they see only benignity and love, is but a spectrum of the very priest himself, projected upon the surrounding darkness. And the higher and purer the original object, and the more unselfishly it may have been taken up, the slighter is the probability that they can be led to recognize the process, by which godlike benevolence has been debased into all-devouring egotism.

Of course, I am perfectly aware that the above statement is exaggerated, in the attempt to make it adequate. Professed philanthropists have gone far; but no originally good man, I presume, ever went quite so far as this. Let the reader abate whatever he deems fit. The paragraph may remain, however, both for its truth and its exaggeration, as strongly expressive of the tendencies which were really operative in Hollingsworth, and as exemplifying the kind of error into which my mode of observation was calculated to lead me. The issue was, that, in solitude, I often shuddered at my friend. In my recollection of his dark and impressive countenance, the features grew more sternly prominent than the reality, duskier in their depth and shadow, and more lurid in their light; the frown, that had merely flitted across his brow, seemed to have contorted it with an adamantine wrinkle. On meeting him again, I was often filled with remorse, when his deep eyes beamed kindly upon me, as with the glow of a household fire that was burning in a cave. — "He is a man, after all!" thought I — "his Maker's own truest image, a philanthropic man! — not that steel engine of the Devil's contrivance, a philanthropist!" — But, in my wood-walks, and in my silent chamber, the dark face frowned at me again.

When a young girl comes within the sphere of such a man, she is as perilously situated as the maiden whom, in the old classical myths, the people used to expose to a dragon. If I had any duty whatever, in reference to Hollingsworth, it was, to endeavor to save Priscilla from that kind of personal worship which her sex is generally prone to lavish upon saints and heroes. It often requires but one smile, out of the hero's eyes into the girl's or woman's heart, to transform this devotion, from a sentiment of the highest approval and confidence, into passionate love. Now, Hollingsworth smiled much upon Priscilla; more than upon any other person. If she thought him beautiful, it was no wonder. I often thought him so, with the expression of tender, human care, and gentlest sympathy, which she alone seemed to have power to call out upon his features. Zenobia, I suspect, would have given her eyes, bright as they were, for such a look; it was the least that our poor Priscilla could do, to give her heart for a great many of them. There was the more danger of this, inasmuch as the footing, on which we all associated at Blithedale, was widely different from that of conventional society. While inclining us to the soft affections of the Golden Age,[1] it seemed to authorize any individual, of either sex, to fall in love with any other, regardless of what would elsewhere be judged suitable and prudent. Accordingly, the tender passion was very rife among us, in various degrees of mildness or virulence, but mostly passing away with the state of things that had given it origin. This was all well enough; but, for a girl like Priscilla, and a woman like Zenobia, to jostle one another in their love of a man like Hollingsworth, was likely to be no child's play.

Had I been as cold-hearted as I sometimes thought myself, nothing would have interested me more than to witness the play of passions that must thus have been evolved. But, in honest truth, I would really have gone far to save Priscilla, at least, from the catastrophe in which such a drama would be apt to terminate.

Priscilla had now grown to be a very pretty girl, and still kept budding and blossoming, and daily putting on some new charm, which you no sooner became sensible of, than you thought it worth all that she had previously possessed. So unformed, vague, and without substance, as she had come to us, it seemed as if we could see Nature

---

[1] *the Golden Age:* According to classical mythology, an idyllic state of nature that existed when men alone lived on earth; women had not yet been created. Also used to describe the ideal state of perfection that mankind would eventually achieve. See Hesiod, *Works and Days;* Virgil, *Eclogue* 4; Ovid, *Metamorphoses* 1:89–150. See also Harry Levin, *The Myth of the Golden Age in the Renaissance* (Bloomington: Indiana UP, 1969).

shaping out a woman before our very eyes, and yet had only a more reverential sense of the mystery of a woman's soul and frame. Yesterday, her cheek was pale; to-day, it had a bloom. Priscilla's smile, like a baby's first one, was a wondrous novelty. Her imperfections and short-comings affected me with a kind of playful pathos, which was as absolutely bewitching a sensation as ever I experienced. After she had been a month or two at Blithedale, her animal spirits waxed high, and kept her pretty constantly in a state of bubble and ferment, impelling her to far more bodily activity than she had yet strength to endure. She was very fond of playing with the other girls, out-of-doors. There is hardly another sight in the world so pretty, as that of a company of young girls, almost women grown, at play, and so giving themselves up to their airy impulse that their tiptoes barely touch the ground.

Girls are incomparably wilder and more effervescent than boys, more untameable, and regardless of rule and limit, with an ever-shifting variety, breaking continually into new modes of fun, yet with a harmonious propriety through all. Their steps, their voices, appear free as the wind, but keep consonance with a strain of music, inaudible to us. Young men and boys, on the other hand, play according to recognized law, old, traditional games, permitting no caprioles[2] of fancy, but with scope enough for the outbreak of savage instincts. For, young or old, in play or in earnest, man is prone to be a brute.

Especially is it delightful to see a vigorous young girl run a race, with her head thrown back, her limbs moving more friskily than they need, and an air between that of a bird and a young colt. But Priscilla's peculiar charm, in a foot-race, was the weakness and irregularity with which she ran. Growing up without exercise, except to her poor little fingers, she had never yet acquired the perfect use of her legs. Setting buoyantly forth, therefore, as if no rival less swift than Atalanta[3] could compete with her, she ran faulteringly, and often tumbled on the grass. Such an incident — though it seems too slight to think of — was a thing to laugh at, but which brought the water into one's eyes, and lingered in the memory after far greater joys and sorrows were swept out of it, as antiquated trash. Priscilla's life, as I beheld it, was full of trifles that affected me in just this way.

[2]*caprioles:* Literally, a vertical leap with a backward kick of the legs; leap or flight.

[3]*Atalanta:* In Greek legend, the beautiful maiden who defeats all of her suitors in races, until Melanion slows her by dropping three golden apples in her path and thus wins her as his wife. See Ovid, *Metamorphoses,* 10:560–704.

When she had come to be quite at home among us, I used to fancy that Priscilla played more pranks, and perpetrated more mischief, than any other girl in the Community. For example, I once heard Silas Foster, in a very gruff voice, threatening to rivet three horse-shoes round Priscilla's neck and chain her to a post, because she, with some other young people, had clambered upon a load of hay and caused it to slide off the cart. How she made her peace, I never knew; but very soon afterwards, I saw old Silas, with his brawny hands round Priscilla's waist, swinging her to-and-fro and finally depositing her on one of the oxen, to take her first lesson in riding. She met with terrible mishaps in her efforts to milk a cow; she let the poultry into the garden; she generally spoilt whatever part of the dinner she took in charge; she broke crockery; she dropt our biggest pitcher into the well; and — except with her needle, and those little wooden instruments for purse-making — was as unserviceable a member of society as any young lady in the land. There was no other sort of efficiency about her. Yet everybody was kind to Priscilla; everybody loved her, and laughed at her, to her face, and did not laugh, behind her back; everybody would have given her half of his last crust, or the bigger share of his plum-cake. These were pretty certain indications that we were all conscious of a pleasant weakness in the girl, and considered her not quite able to look after her own interests, or fight her battle with the world. And Hollingsworth — perhaps because he had been the means of introducing Priscilla to her new abode — appeared to recognize her as his own especial charge.

Her simple, careless, childish flow of spirits often made me sad. She seemed to me like a butterfly, at play in a flickering bit of sunshine, and mistaking it for a broad and eternal summer. We sometimes hold mirth to a stricter accountability than sorrow; it must show good cause, or the echo of its laughter comes back drearily. Priscilla's gaiety, moreover, was of a nature that showed me how delicate an instrument she was, and what fragile harp-strings were her nerves. As they made sweet music at the airiest touch, it would require but a stronger one to burst them all asunder. Absurd as it might be, I tried to reason with her, and persuade her not to be so joyous, thinking that, if she would draw less lavishly upon her fund of happiness, it would last the longer. I remember doing so, one summer evening, when we tired laborers sat looking on, like Goldsmith's old folks[4] under the village thorn-tree, while the young people were at their sports.

---

[4]*Goldsmith's old folks:* Refers to "The Deserted Village" (1770), by Oliver Goldsmith (1730–1774), a poem that examines the conditions of English rural life.

"What is the use or sense of being so very gay?" I said to Priscilla, while she was taking breath after a great frolic. "I love to see a sufficient cause for everything; and I can see none for this. Pray tell me, now, what kind of a world you imagine this to be, which you are so merry in?"

"I never think about it at all," answered Priscilla, laughing. "But this I am sure of — that it is a world where everybody is kind to me, and where I love everybody. My heart keeps dancing within me; and all the foolish things, which you see me do, are only the motions of my heart. How can I be dismal, if my heart will not let me?"

"Have you nothing dismal to remember?" I suggested. "If not, then, indeed, you are very fortunate!"

"Ah!" said Priscilla, slowly.

And then came that unintelligible gesture, when she seemed to be listening to a distant voice.

"For my part," I continued, beneficently seeking to over-shadow her with my own sombre humor, "my past life has been a tiresome one enough; yet I would rather look backward ten times than forward once. For, little as we know of our life to come, we may be very sure, for one thing, that the good we aim at will not be attained. People never do get just the good they seek. If it come at all, it is something else, which they never dreamed of, and did not particularly want. Then, again, we may rest certain that our friends of today will not be our friends of a few years hence; but, if we keep one of them, it will be at the expense of the others — and, most probably, we shall keep none. To be sure, there are more to be had! But who cares about making a new set of friends, even should they be better than those around us?"

"Not I!" said Priscilla. "I will live and die with these!"

"Well; but let the future go!" resumed I. "As for the present moment, if we could look into the hearts where we wish to be most valued, what should you expect to see? One's own likeness, in the innermost, holiest niche? Ah, I don't know! It may not be there at all. It may be a dusty image, thrust aside into a corner, and by-and-by to be flung out-of-doors, where any foot may trample upon it. If not today, then tomorrow! And so, Priscilla, I do not see much wisdom in being so very merry in this kind of a world!"

It had taken me nearly seven years of worldly life, to hive up the bitter honey which I here offered to Priscilla. And she rejected it!

"I don't believe one word of what you say!" she replied, laughing anew. "You made me sad, for a minute, by talking about the past.

But the past never comes back again. Do we dream the same dream twice? There is nothing else that I am afraid of."

So away she ran, and fell down on the green grass, as it was often her luck to do, but got up again without any harm.

"Priscilla, Priscilla!" cried Hollingsworth, who was sitting on the door-step. "You had better not run any more to-night. You will weary yourself too much. And do not sit down out of doors; for there is a heavy dew beginning to fall!"

At his first word, she went and sat down under the porch, at Hollingsworth's feet, entirely contented and happy. What charm was there, in his rude massiveness, that so attracted and soothed this shadowlike girl? It appeared to me — who have always been curious in such matters — that Priscilla's vague and seemingly causeless flow of felicitous feeling was that with which love blesses inexperienced hearts, before they begin to suspect what is going on within them. It transports them to the seventh heaven;[5] and if you ask what brought them thither, they neither can tell nor care to learn, but cherish an ecstatic faith that there they shall abide forever.

Zenobia was in the door-way, not far from Hollingsworth. She gazed at Priscilla, in a very singular way. Indeed, it was a sight worth gazing at, and a beautiful sight too, as the fair girl sat at the feet of that dark, powerful figure. Her air, while perfectly modest, delicate, and virginlike, denoted her as swayed by Hollingsworth, attracted to him, and unconsciously seeking to rest upon his strength. I could not turn away my own eyes, but hoped that nobody, save Zenobia and myself, were witnessing this picture. It is before me now, with the evening twilight a little deepened by the dusk of memory.

"Come hither, Priscilla!" said Zenobia. "I have something to say to you!"

She spoke in little more than a whisper. But it is strange how expressive of moods a whisper may often be. Priscilla felt at once that something had gone wrong.

"Are you angry with me?" she asked, rising slowly and standing before Zenobia in a drooping attitude. "What have I done? I hope you are not angry!"

"No, no, Priscilla!" said Hollingsworth, smiling. "I will answer for it, she is not. You are the one little person in the world, with whom nobody can be angry!"

---

[5]*seventh heaven:* The last and highest of the abodes of bliss of the Muslim and of the cabalist systems.

"Angry with you, child? What a silly idea!" exclaimed Zenobia, laughing. "No, indeed! But, my dear Priscilla, you are getting to be so very pretty that you absolutely need a duenna;[6] and as I am older than you, and have had my own little experience of life, and think myself exceedingly sage, I intend to fill the place of a maiden-aunt. Every day, I shall give you a lecture, a quarter-of-an-hour in length, on the morals, manners, and proprieties of social life. When our pastoral shall be quite played out, Priscilla, my worldly wisdom may stand you in good stead!"

"I am afraid you are angry with me," repeated Priscilla, sadly; for, while she seemed as impressible as wax, the girl often showed a persistency in her own ideas, as stubborn as it was gentle.

"Dear me, what can I say to the child!" cried Zenobia, in a tone of humorous vexation. "Well, well; since you insist on my being angry, come to my room, this moment, and let me beat you!"

Zenobia bade Hollingsworth good night very sweetly, and nodded to me with a smile. But, just as she turned aside with Priscilla into the dimness of the porch, I caught another glance at her countenance. It would have made the fortune of a tragic actress, could she have borrowed it for the moment when she fumbles in her bosom for the concealed dagger, or the exceedingly sharp bodkin,[7] or mingles the ratsbane[8] in her lover's bowl of wine, or her rival's cup of tea. Not that I in the least anticipated any such catastrophe; it being a remarkable truth, that custom has in no one point a greater sway than over our modes of wreaking our wild passions. And, besides, had we been in Italy, instead of New England, it was hardly yet a crisis for the dagger or the bowl.

It often amazed me, however, that Hollingsworth should show himself so recklessly tender towards Priscilla, and never once seem to think of the effect which it might have upon her heart. But the man, as I have endeavored to explain, was thrown completely off his moral balance, and quite bewildered as to his personal relations, by his great excrescence of a philanthropic scheme. I used to see, or fancy, indications that he was not altogether obtuse to Zenobia's influence as a woman. No doubt, however, he had a still more exquisite enjoyment of Priscilla's silent sympathy with his purposes, so unalloyed with criticism, and therefore more grateful than any intellectual

---

[6]*duenna:* Spanish term for elderly woman who serves as governess and companion to a younger one.

[7]*bodkin:* A slender, sharply pointed instrument for making small holes in cloth.

[8]*ratsbane:* Arsenic.

approbation, which always involves a possible reserve of latent cen-
sure. A man — poet, prophet, or whatever he may be — readily per-
suades himself of his right to all the worship that is voluntarily ten-
dered. In requital of so rich benefits as he was to confer upon
mankind, it would have been hard to deny Hollingsworth the simple
solace of a young girl's heart, which he held in his hand, and smelled
to, like a rosebud. But what if, while pressing out its fragrance, he
should crush the tender rosebud in his grasp!

As for Zenobia, I saw no occasion to give myself any trouble. With
her native strength, and her experience of the world, she could not be
supposed to need any help of mine. Nevertheless, I was really generous enough to feel some little interest likewise for Zenobia. With all
her faults, (which might have been a great many, besides the abundance that I knew of,) she possessed noble traits, and a heart which
must at least have been valuable while new. And she seemed ready to
fling it away, as uncalculatingly as Priscilla herself. I could not but
suspect, that, if merely at play with Hollingsworth, she was sporting
with a power which she did not fully estimate. Or, if in earnest, it
might chance, between Zenobia's passionate force and his dark, self-
delusive egotism, to turn out such earnest as would develop itself in
some sufficiently tragic catastrophe, though the dagger and the bowl
should go for nothing in it.

Meantime, the gossip of the Community set them down as a pair
of lovers. They took walks together, and were not seldom encountered in the wood-paths; Hollingsworth deeply discoursing, in tones
solemn and sternly pathetic. Zenobia, with a rich glow on her cheeks,
and her eyes softened from their ordinary brightness, looked so beautiful, that, had her companion been ten times a philanthropist, it
seemed impossible but that one glance should melt him back into a
man. Oftener than anywhere else, they went to a certain point on the
slope of a pasture, commanding nearly the whole of our own domain, besides a view of the river and an airy prospect of many distant
hills. The bond of our Community was such, that the members had
the privilege of building cottages for their own residence, within our
precincts, thus laying a hearthstone and fencing in a home, private
and peculiar, to all desirable extent; while yet the inhabitants should
continue to share the advantages of an associated life. It was inferred,
that Hollingsworth and Zenobia intended to rear their dwelling on
this favorite spot.

I mentioned these rumors to Hollingsworth in a playful way.

"Had you consulted me," I went on to observe, "I should have recommended a site further to the left, just a little withdrawn into the wood, with two or three peeps at the prospect, among the trees. You will be in the shady vale of years, long before you can raise any better kind of shade around your cottage, if you build it on this bare slope."

"But I offer my edifice as a spectacle to the world," said Hollingsworth, "that it may take example and build many another like it. Therefore I mean to set it on the open hill-side."

Twist these words how I might, they offered no very satisfactory import. It seemed hardly probable that Hollingsworth should care about educating the public taste in the department of cottage-architecture, desirable as such improvement certainly was.

X. A VISITOR FROM TOWN

Hollingsworth and I — we had been hoeing potatoes, that forenoon, while the rest of the fraternity were engaged in a distant quarter of the farm — sat under a clump of maples, eating our eleven o'clock lunch, when we saw a stranger approaching along the edge of the field. He had admitted himself from the road-side, through a turnstile, and seemed to have a purpose of speaking with us.

And, by-the-by, we were favored with many visits at Blithedale; especially from people who sympathized with our theories, and perhaps held themselves ready to unite in our actual experiment, as soon as there should appear a reliable promise of its success. It was rather ludicrous, indeed, (to me, at least, whose enthusiasm had insensibly been exhaled, together with the perspiration of many a hard day's toil,) it was absolutely funny, therefore, to observe what a glory was shed about our life and labors, in the imagination of these longing proselytes. In their view, we were as poetical as Arcadians, besides being as practical as the hardest-fisted husbandmen in Massachusetts. We did not, it is true, spend much time in piping to our sheep, or warbling our innocent loves to the sisterhood. But they gave us credit for imbuing the ordinary rustic occupations with a kind of religious poetry, insomuch that our very cow-yards and pig-sties were as delightfully fragrant as a flower-garden. Nothing used to please me more than to see one of these lay enthusiasts snatch up a hoe, as they were very prone to do, and set to work with a vigor that perhaps carried him through about a dozen ill-directed strokes. Men are wonderfully soon satisfied, in this day of shameful bodily enervation, when, from one end of life to the other, such multitudes never taste the sweet weariness that follows accustomed toil. I seldom saw the new enthusiasm that did not grow as flimsy and flaccid as the proselyte's moistened shirt-collar, with a quarter-of-an-hour's active labor, under a July sun.

But the person, now at hand, had not at all the air of one of these amiable visionaries. He was an elderly man, dressed rather shabbily, yet decently enough, in a gray frock-coat, faded towards a brown hue, and wore a broad-brimmed white hat, of the fashion of several years gone by. His hair was perfect silver, without a dark thread in the whole of it; his nose, though it had a scarlet tip, by no means indicated the jollity of which a red nose is the generally admitted symbol. He was a subdued, undemonstrative old man, who would doubtless drink a glass of liquor, now and then, and probably more than was good for him; not, however, with a purpose of undue exhilaration, but in the hope of bringing his spirits up to the ordinary level of the world's cheerfulness. Drawing nearer, there was a shy look about him, as if he were ashamed of his poverty, or, at any rate, for some reason or other, would rather have us glance at him sidelong than take a full-front view. He had a queer appearance of hiding himself behind the patch on his left eye.[1]

"I know this old gentleman," said I to Hollingsworth, as we sat observing him — "that is, I have met him a hundred times, in town, and have often amused my fancy with wondering what he was, before he came to be what he is. He haunts restaurants and such places, and has an odd way of lurking in corners or getting behind a door, whenever practicable, and holding out his hand, with some little article in it, which he wishes you to buy. The eye of the world seems to trouble him, although he necessarily lives so much in it. I never expected to see him in an open field."

"Have you learned anything of his history?" asked Hollingsworth.

"Not a circumstance," I answered. "But there must be something curious in it. I take him to be a harmless sort of a person, and a tolerably honest one; but his manners, being so furtive, remind me of those of a rat — a rat without the mischief, the fierce eye, the teeth to bite with, or the desire to bite. See, now! He means to skulk along that fringe of bushes, and approach us on the other side of our clump of maples."

---

[1]*the patch on his left eye:* On p. 169, the patch is over his right eye.

We soon heard the old man's velvet tread on the grass, indicating that he had arrived within a few feet of where we sat.

"Good morning, Mr. Moodie," said Hollingsworth, addressing the stranger as an acquaintance. "You must have had a hot and tiresome walk from the city. Sit down, and take a morsel of our bread and cheese!"

The visitor made a grateful little murmur of acquiescence, and sat down in a spot somewhat removed; so that, glancing round, I could see his gray pantaloons and dusty shoes, while his upper part was mostly hidden behind the shrubbery. Nor did he come forth from this retirement during the whole of the interview that followed. We handed him such food as we had, together with a brown jug of molasses-and-water, (would that it had been brandy, or something better, for the sake of his chill old heart!) like priests offering dainty sacrifice to an enshrined and invisible idol. I have no idea that he really lacked sustenance; but it was quite touching, nevertheless, to hear him nibbling away at our crusts.

"Mr. Moodie," said I, "do you remember selling me one of those very pretty little silk purses, of which you seem to have a monopoly in the market? I keep it, to this day, I can assure you."

"Ah, thank you!" said our guest. "Yes, Mr. Coverdale, I used to sell a good many of those little purses."

He spoke languidly, and only those few words, like a watch with an inelastic spring, that just ticks, a moment or two, and stops again. He seemed a very forlorn old man. In the wantonness of youth, strength, and comfortable condition — making my prey of people's individualities, as my custom was — I tried to identify my mind with the old fellow's, and take his view of the world, as if looking through a smoke-blackened glass at the sun. It robbed the landscape of all its life. Those pleasantly swelling slopes of our farm, descending towards the wide meadows, through which sluggishly circled the brimfull tide of the Charles, bathing the long sedges on its hither and farther shores; the broad, sunny gleam over the winding water; that peculiar picturesqueness of the scene, where capes and headlands put themselves boldly forth upon the perfect level of the meadow, as into a green lake, with inlets between the promontories; the shadowy woodland, with twinkling showers of light falling into its depths; the sultry heat-vapor, which rose everywhere like incense, and in which my soul delighted, as indicating so rich a fervor in the passionate day, and in the earth that was burning with its love: — I beheld all these things as through old Moodie's eyes. When my eyes are dimmer than they have yet come to be, I will go thither again, and see if I did not catch the tone of his mind aright, and if the cold and lifeless tint of his perceptions be not then repeated in my own.

Yet it was unaccountable to myself, the interest that I felt in him.

"Have you any objection," said I, "to telling me who made those little purses?"

"Gentlemen have often asked me that," said Moodie, slowly; "but I shake my head, and say little or nothing, and creep out of the way, as well as I can. I am a man of few words; and if gentlemen were to be told one thing, they would be very apt, I suppose, to ask me another. But it happens, just now, Mr. Coverdale, that you can tell me more about the maker of those little purses, than I can tell you."

"Why do you trouble him with needless questions, Coverdale?" interrupted Hollingsworth. "You must have known, long ago, that it was Priscilla. And so, my good friend, you have come to see her? Well, I am glad of it. You will find her altered very much for the better, since that wintry evening when you put her into my charge. Why, Priscilla has a bloom in her cheeks, now!"

"Has my pale little girl a bloom?" repeated Moodie, with a kind of slow wonder. "Priscilla with a bloom in her cheeks! Ah, I am afraid I shall not know my little girl. And is she happy?"

"Just as happy as a bird," answered Hollingsworth.

"Then, gentlemen," said our guest, apprehensively, "I don't think it well for me to go any further. I crept hitherward only to ask about Priscilla; and now that you have told me such good news, perhaps I can do no better than to creep back again. If she were to see this old face of mine, the child would remember some very sad times which we have spent together. Some very sad times indeed! She has forgotten them, I know — them and me — else she could not be so happy, nor have a bloom in her cheeks. Yes — yes — yes," continued he, still with the same torpid utterance; "with many thanks to you, Mr. Hollingsworth, I will creep back to town again."

"You shall do no such thing, Mr. Moodie!" said Hollingsworth, bluffly. "Priscilla often speaks of you; and if there lacks anything to make her cheeks bloom like two damask[2] roses, I'll venture to say, it is just the sight of your face. Come; we will go and find her."

---

[2]*damask:* Grayish red.

"Mr. Hollingsworth!" said the old man, in his hesitating way.

"Well!" answered Hollingsworth.

"Has there been any call for Priscilla?" asked Moodie; and though his face was hidden from us, his tone gave a sure indication of the mysterious nod and wink with which he put the question. "You know, I think, sir, what I mean."

"I have not the remotest suspicion what you mean, Mr. Moodie," replied Hollingsworth. "Nobody, to my knowledge, has called for Priscilla, except yourself. But, come; we are losing time, and I have several things to say to you, by the way."

"And, Mr. Hollingsworth!" repeated Moodie.

"Well, again!" cried my friend, rather impatiently. "What now?"

"There is a lady here," said the old man; and his voice lost some of its wearisome hesitation. "You will account it a very strange matter for me to talk about; but I chanced to know this lady, when she was but a little child. If I am rightly informed, she has grown to be a very fine woman, and makes a brilliant figure in the world, with her beauty, and her talents, and her noble way of spending her riches. I should recognize this lady, so people tell me, by a magnificent flower in her hair!"

"What a rich tinge it gives to his colorless ideas, when he speaks of Zenobia!" I whispered to Hollingsworth. "But how can there possibly be any interest or connecting link between him and her?"

"The old man, for years past," whispered Hollingsworth, "has been a little out of his right mind, as you probably see."

"What I would inquire," resumed Moodie, "is, whether this beautiful lady is kind to my poor Priscilla."

"Very kind," said Hollingsworth.

"Does she love her?" asked Moodie.

"It should seem so," answered my friend. "They are always together."

"Like a gentlewoman and her maid servant, I fancy?" suggested the old man.

There was something so singular in his way of saying this, that I could not resist the impulse to turn quite round, so as to catch a glimpse of his face; almost imagining that I should see another person than old Moodie. But there he sat, with the patched side of his face towards me.

"Like an elder and younger sister, rather," replied Hollingsworth.

"Ah," said Moodie, more complaisantly[3] — for his latter tones had harshness and acidity in them — "it would gladden my old heart to witness that. If one thing would make me happier than another, Mr. Hollingsworth, it would be, to see that beautiful lady holding my little girl by the hand."

"Come along," said Hollingsworth, "and perhaps you may."

After a little more delay on the part of our freakish visitor, they set forth together; old Moodie keeping a step or two behind Hollingsworth, so that the latter could not very conveniently look him in the face. I remained under the tuft of maples, doing my utmost to draw an inference from the scene that had just passed. In spite of Hollingsworth's off-hand explanation, it did not strike me that our strange guest was really beside himself, but only that his mind needed screwing up, like an instrument long out of tune, the strings of which have ceased to vibrate smartly and sharply. Methought it would be profitable for us, projectors of a happy life, to welcome this old gray shadow, and cherish him as one of us, and let him creep about our domain, in order that he might be a little merrier for our sakes, and we, sometimes, a little sadder for his. Human destinies look ominous, without some perceptible intermixture of the sable or the gray. And then, too, should any of our fraternity grow feverish with an over-exulting sense of prosperity, it would be a sort of cooling regimen to slink off into the woods, and spend an hour, or a day, or as many days as might be requisite to the cure, in uninterrupted communion with this deplorable old Moodie!

Going homeward to dinner, I had a glimpse of him behind the trunk of a tree, gazing earnestly towards a a particular window of the farm-house. And, by-and-by, Priscilla appeared at this window, play-fully drawing along Zenobia, who looked as bright as the very day that was blazing down upon us, only not, by many degrees, so well advanced towards her noon. I was convinced that this pretty sight must have been purposely arranged by Priscilla, for the old man to see. But either the girl held her too long, or her fondness was resented as too great a freedom; for Zenobia suddenly put Priscilla decidedly away, and gave her a haughty look, as from a mistress to a dependent. Old Moodie shook his head — and again, and again, I saw him shake it, as he withdrew along the road — and, at the last point whence the farm-house was visible, he turned, and shook his uplifted staff.

---

[3]*complaisantly:* The first edition has "complacently," but this was changed in the Centenary edition to "complaisantly."

XI. THE WOOD-PATH

Not long after the preceding incident, in order to get the ache of too constant labor out of my bones, and to relieve my spirit of the irksomeness of a settled routine, I took a holiday. It was my purpose to spend it, all alone, from breakfast-time till twilight, in the deepest wood-seclusion that lay anywhere around us. Though fond of society, I was so constituted as to need these occasional retirements, even in a life like that of Blithedale, which was itself characterized by a remoteness from the world. Unless renewed by a yet farther withdrawal towards the inner circle of self-communion, I lost the better part of my individuality. My thoughts became of little worth, and my sensibilities grew as arid as a tuft of moss, (a thing whose life is in the shade, the rain, or the noontide dew,) crumbling in the sunshine, after long expectance of a shower. So, with my heart full of a drowsy pleasure, and cautious not to dissipate my mood by previous intercourse with any one, I hurried away, and was soon pacing a wood-path, arched overhead with boughs, and dusky brown beneath my feet.

At first, I walked very swiftly, as if the heavy floodtide of social life were roaring at my heels, and would outstrip and overwhelm me, without all the better diligence in my escape. But, threading the more distant windings of the track, I abated my pace and looked about me for some side-aisle, that should admit me into the innermost sanctuary of this green cathedral; just as, in human acquaintanceship, a casual opening sometimes lets us, all of a sudden, into the long-sought intimacy of a mysterious heart. So much was I absorbed in my reflections — or rather, in my mood, the substance of which was as yet too shapeless to be called thought — that footsteps rustled on the leaves, and a figure passed me by, almost without impressing either the sound or sight upon my consciousness.

A moment afterwards, I heard a voice at a little distance behind me, speaking so sharply and impertinently that it made a complete discord with my spiritual state, and caused the latter to vanish, as abruptly as when you thrust a finger into a soap-bubble.

"Halloo, friend!" cried this most unseasonable voice. "Stop a moment, I say! I must have a word with you!"

I turned about, in a humor ludicrously irate. In the first place, the interruption, at any rate, was a grievous injury; then, the tone displeased me. And, finally, unless there be real affection in his heart, a man cannot — such is the bad state to which the world has brought itself — cannot more effectually show his contempt for a brother-mortal, nor more gallingly assume a position of superiority, than by addressing him as "friend." Especially does the misapplication of this phrase bring out that latent hostility, which is sure to animate peculiar sects, and those who, with however generous a purpose, have sequestered themselves from the crowd; a feeling, it is true, which may be hidden in some dog-kennel of the heart, grumbling there in the darkness, but is never quite extinct, until the dissenting party have gained power and scope enough to treat the world generously. For my part, I should have taken it as far less an insult to be styled "fellow," "clown," or "bumpkin." To either of these appellations, my rustic garb (it was a linen blouse, with checked shirt and striped pantaloons, a chip-hat[1] on my head, and a rough hickory-stick in my hand) very fairly entitled me. As the case stood, my temper darted at once to the opposite pole; not friend, but enemy!

"What do you want with me?" said I, facing about.

"Come a little nearer, friend!" said the stranger, beckoning.

"No," answered I. "If I can do anything for you, without too much trouble to myself, say so. But recollect, if you please, that you are not speaking to an acquaintance, much less a friend!"

"Upon my word, I believe not!" retorted he, looking at me with some curiosity; and lifting his hat, he made me a salute, which had enough of sarcasm to be offensive, and just enough of doubtful courtesy to render any resentment of it absurd. — "But I ask your pardon! I recognize a little mistake. If I may take the liberty to suppose it, you, sir, are probably one of the Æsthetic — or shall I rather say ecstatic? — laborers, who have planted themselves hereabouts. This is your forest of Arden; and you are either the banished Duke, in person, or one of the chief nobles in his train. The melancholy Jacques,[2] perhaps? Be it so! In that case, you can probably do me a favor."

I never, in my life, felt less inclined to confer a favor on any man.

"I am busy!" said I.

So unexpectedly had the stranger made me sensible of his presence, that he had almost the effect of an apparition, and certainly a less appropriate one (taking into view the dim woodland solitude about us)

---

[1]*chip-hat:* Brimmed hat made from palm leaves.
[2]*forest of Arden, melancholy Jacques:* Refers to Shakespeare's pastoral comedy *As You Like It* (1599), which describes the experiences of an exiled Duke, his followers, and the discontented courtier Jaques (not "Jacques") in the Forest of Arden.

than if the salvage man of antiquity,[3] hirsute and cinctured[4] with a leafy girdle, had started out of a thicket. He was still young, seemingly a little under thirty, of a tall and well-developed figure, and as handsome a man as ever I beheld. The style of his beauty, however, though a masculine style, did not at all commend itself to my taste. His countenance — I hardly know how to describe the peculiarity — had an indecorum in it, a kind of rudeness, a hard, coarse, forthputting freedom of expression, which no degree of external polish could have abated, one single jot. Not that it was vulgar. But he had no fineness of nature; there was in his eyes (although they might have artifice enough of another sort) the naked exposure of something that ought not to be left prominent. With these vague allusions to what I have seen in other faces, as well as his, I leave the quality to be comprehended best — because with an intuitive repugnance — by those who possess least of it.

His hair, as well as his beard and moustache, was coal-black; his eyes, too, were black and sparkling, and his teeth remarkably brilliant. He was rather carelessly, but well and fashionably dressed, in a summer-morning costume. There was a gold chain, exquisitely wrought, across his vest. I never saw a smoother or whiter gloss than that upon his shirt-bosom, which had a pin in it, set with a gem that glimmered, in the leafy shadow where he stood, like a living tip of fire. He carried a stick with a wooden head, carved in vivid imitation of that of a serpent. I hated him, partly, I do believe, from a comparison of my own homely garb with his well-ordered foppishness.

"Well, sir," said I, a little ashamed of my first irritation, but still with no waste of civility, "be pleased to speak at once, as I have my own business in hand."

"I regret that my mode of addressing you was a little unfortunate," said the stranger, smiling; for he seemed a very acute sort of person, and saw, in some degree, how I stood affected towards him. "I intended no offence, and shall certainly comport myself with due ceremony hereafter. I merely wish to make a few inquiries respecting a lady, formerly of my acquaintance, who is now resident in your Community, and, I believe, largely concerned in your social enterprise. You call her, I think, Zenobia."

---

[3]*the salvage man of antiquity:* The "savage" or wild, hairy ("hirsute") man of the woods was clothed only in garments of leaves. Caliban, the half-human slave of Prospero in Shakespeare's *The Tempest* (1611), is listed in the "names of the Actors" of the First Folio as "a salvage and deformed slave."

[4]*cinctured:* Wearing a belt.

"That is her name in literature," observed I — "a name, too, which possibly she may permit her private friends to know and address her by; — but not one which they feel at liberty to recognize, when used of her, personally, by a stranger or casual acquaintance."

"Indeed!" answered this disagreeable person; and he turned aside his face, for an instant, with a brief laugh, which struck me as a noteworthy expression of his character. "Perhaps I might put forward a claim, on your own grounds, to call the lady by a name so appropriate to her splendid qualities. But I am willing to know her by any cognomen that you may suggest."

Heartily wishing that he would be either a little more offensive, or a good deal less so, or break off our intercourse altogether, I mentioned Zenobia's real name.

"True," said he; "and, in general society, I have never heard her called otherwise. And, after all, our discussion of the point has been gratuitous. My object is only to inquire when, where, and how, this lady may most conveniently be seen?"

"At her present residence, of course," I replied. "You have but to go thither and ask for her. This very path will lead you within sight of the house; — so I wish you good morning."

"One moment, if you please," said the stranger. "The course you indicate would certainly be the proper one, in an ordinary morning-call. But my business is private, personal, and somewhat peculiar. Now, in a Community like this, I should judge that any little occurrence is likely to be discussed rather more minutely than would quite suit my views. I refer solely to myself, you understand, and without intimating that it would be other than a matter of entire indifference to the lady. In short, I especially desire to see her in private. If her habits are such as I have known them, she is probably often to be met with in the woods, or by the river-side; and I think you could do me the favor to point out some favorite walk, where, about this hour, I might be fortunate enough to gain an interview."

I reflected, that it would be quite a super-erogatory[5] piece of quixotism,[6] in me, to undertake the guardianship of Zenobia, who, for my pains, would only make me the butt of endless ridicule, should the fact ever come to her knowledge. I therefore described a spot which, as often as any other, was Zenobia's resort, at this period of

[5]*super-erogatory:* Superfluous, nonessential.
[6]*quixotism:* Lofty romantic or chivalric idea, doomed to fail; from the satirical romance *Don Quixote* (1605, 1615), by Miguel de Cervantes (1547–1616).

the day; nor was it so remote from the farm-house as to leave her in much peril, whatever might be the stranger's character.

"A single word more!" said he; and his black eyes sparkled at me, whether with fun or malice I knew not, but certainly as if the Devil were peeping out of them. "Among your fraternity, I understand, there is a certain holy and benevolent blacksmith; a man of iron, in more senses than one; a rough, cross-grained, well-meaning individual, rather boorish in his manners — as might be expected — and by no means of the highest intellectual cultivation. He is a philanthropical lecturer, with two or three disciples, and a scheme of his own, the preliminary step in which involves a large purchase of land, and the erection of a spacious edifice, at an expense considerably beyond his means; inasmuch as these are to be reckoned in copper or old iron, much more conveniently than in gold or silver. He hammers away upon his one topic, as lustily as ever he did upon a horse-shoe! Do you know such a person?"

I shook my head, and was turning away.

"Our friend," he continued, "is described to me as a brawny, shaggy, grim, and ill-favored personage, not particularly well-calculated, one would say, to insinuate himself with the softer sex. Yet, so far has this honest fellow succeeded with one lady, whom we wot of,[7] that he anticipates, from her abundant resources, the necessary funds for realizing his plan in brick and mortar!"

Here the stranger seemed to be so much amused with his sketch of Hollingsworth's character and purposes, that he burst into a fit of merriment, of the same nature as the brief, metallic laugh already alluded to, but immensely prolonged and enlarged. In the excess of his delight, he opened his mouth wide, and disclosed a gold band around the upper part of his teeth; thereby making it apparent that every one of his brilliant grinders and incisors was a sham. This discovery affected me very oddly. I felt as if the whole man were a moral and physical humbug; his wonderful beauty of face, for aught I knew, might be removeable like a mask; and, tall and comely as his figure looked, he was perhaps but a wizened little elf, gray and decrepit, with nothing genuine about him, save the wicked expression of his grin. The fantasy of his spectral character so wrought upon me, together with the contagion of his strange mirth on my sympathies, that I soon began to laugh as loudly as himself.

---

[7]*whom we wot of:* "Whom we know of."

By-and-by, he paused, all at once; so suddenly, indeed, that my own cachinnation[8] lasted a moment longer.

"Ah, excuse me!" said he. "Our interview seems to proceed more merrily than it began."

"It ends here," answered I. "And I take shame to myself, that my folly has lost me the right of resenting your ridicule of a friend."

"Pray allow me," said the stranger, approaching a step nearer, and laying his gloved hand on my sleeve. "One other favor I must ask of you. You have a young person, here at Blithedale, of whom I have heard — whom, perhaps, I have known — and in whom, at all events, I take a peculiar interest. She is one of those delicate, nervous young creatures, not uncommon in New England, and whom I suppose to have become what we find them by the gradual refining away of the physical system, among your women. Some philosophers choose to glorify this habit of body by terming it spiritual; but, in my opinion, it is rather the effect of unwholesome food, bad air, lack of out-door exercise, and neglect of bathing, on the part of these damsels and their female progenitors; all resulting in a kind of hereditary dyspepsia. Zenobia, even with her uncomfortable surplus of vitality, is far the better model of womanhood. But — to revert again to this young person — she goes among you by the name of Priscilla. Could you possibly afford me the means of speaking with her?"

"You have made so many inquiries of me," I observed, "that I may at least trouble you with one. What is your name?"

He offered me a card, with "Professor Westervelt" engraved on it. At the same time, as if to vindicate his claim to the professorial dignity, so often assumed on very questionable grounds, he put on a pair of spectacles, which so altered the character of his face that I hardly knew him again. But I liked the present aspect no better than the former one.

"I must decline any further connection with your affairs," said I, drawing back. "I have told you where to find Zenobia. As for Priscilla, she has closer friends than myself, through whom, if they see fit, you can gain access to her."

"In that case," returned the Professor, ceremoniously raising his hat, "good morning to you."

He took his departure, and was soon out of sight among the windings of the wood-path. But, after a little reflection, I could not help regretting that I had so peremptorily broken off the interview, while

---

[8]*cachinnation:* Loud, convulsive laughter.

the stranger seemed inclined to continue it. His evident knowledge of matters, affecting my three friends, might have led to disclosures, or inferences, that would perhaps have been serviceable. I was particularly struck with the fact, that, ever since the appearance of Priscilla, it had been the tendency of events to suggest and establish a connection between Zenobia and her. She had come, in the first instance, as if with the sole purpose of claiming Zenobia's protection. Old Moodie's visit, it appeared, was chiefly to ascertain whether this object had been accomplished. And here, to-day, was the questionable Professor, linking one with the other in his inquiries, and seeking communication with both.

Meanwhile, my inclination for a ramble having been baulked, I lingered in the vicinity of the farm, with perhaps a vague idea that some new event would grow out of Westervelt's proposed interview with Zenobia. My own part, in these transactions, was singularly subordinate. It resembled that of the Chorus[9] in a classic play, which seems to be set aloof from the possibility of personal concernment, and bestows the whole measure of its hope or fear, its exultation or sorrow, on the fortunes of others, between whom and itself this sympathy is the only bond. Destiny, it may be — the most skilful of stage-managers — seldom chooses to arrange its scenes, and carry forward its drama, without securing the presence of at least one calm observer. It is his office to give applause, when due, and sometimes an inevitable tear, to detect the final fitness of incident to character, and distil, in his long-brooding thought, the whole morality of the performance.

Not to be out of the way, in case there were need of me in my vocation, and, at the same time, to avoid thrusting myself where neither Destiny nor mortals might desire my presence, I remained pretty near the verge of the woodlands. My position was off the track of Zenobia's customary walk, yet not so remote but that a recognized occasion might speedily have brought me thither.

XII. COVERDALE'S HERMITAGE

Long since, in this part of our circumjacent wood, I had found out for myself a little hermitage. It was a kind of leafy cave, high upward into the air, among the midmost branches of a white-pine tree. A wild

---

[9]*Chorus:* In Greek tragedy (e.g., the plays of Aeschylus and Sophocles), the voices commenting on the action, expressing traditional social, political, and moral attitudes.

grape-vine, of unusual size and luxuriance, had twined and twisted itself up into the tree, and, after wreathing the entanglement of its tendrils around almost every bough, had caught hold of three or four
neighboring trees, and married the whole clump with a perfectly inextricable knot of polygamy. Once, while sheltering myself from a
summer shower, the fancy had taken me to clamber up into this
seemingly impervious mass of foliage. The branches yielded me a passage, and closed again, beneath, as if only a squirrel or a bird had
passed. Far aloft, around the stem of the central pine, behold, a perfect nest for Robinson Crusoe or King Charles![1] A hollow chamber,
of rare seclusion, had been formed by the decay of some of the pine-
branches, which the vine had lovingly strangled with its embrace,
burying them from the light of day in an aerial sepulchre of its own
leaves. It cost me but little ingenuity to enlarge the interior, and open
loop-holes through the verdant walls. Had it ever been my fortune to
spend a honey-moon, I should have thought seriously of inviting my
bride up thither, where our next neighbors would have been two ori-
oles in another part of the clump.

It was an admirable place to make verses, tuning the rhythm to
the breezy symphony that so often stirred among the vine-leaves; or
to meditate an essay for the Dial, in which the many tongues of Nature whispered mysteries, and seemed to ask only a little stronger
puff of wind, to speak out the solution of its riddle. Being so pervious
to air currents, it was just the nook, too, for the enjoyment of a cigar.
This hermitage was my one exclusive possession, while I counted myself a brother of the socialists. It symbolized my individuality, and
aided me in keeping it inviolate. None ever found me out in it, except, once, a squirrel. I brought thither no guest, because, after
Hollingsworth failed me, there was no longer the man alive with
whom I could think of sharing all. So there I used to sit, owl-like, yet
not without liberal and hospitable thoughts. I counted the innumerable clusters of my vine, and fore-reckoned the abundance of my vintage. It gladdened me to anticipate the surprise of the Community,
when, like an allegorical figure of rich October, I should make my
appearance, with shoulders bent beneath the burthen of ripe grapes,

---

[1]*Robinson Crusoe or King Charles:* In *Robinson Crusoe* (1719), by Daniel Defoe
(1660–1731), the title character is marooned on a desert island and gazes for ships
from a platform he builds in a tree; Charles II (1630–1685), king of England, sought
refuge in an oak tree after being defeated in the battle of Worcester by Oliver
Cromwell's Puritan army (September 1651).

and some of the crushed ones crimsoning my brow as with a blood-stain.[2]

Ascending into this natural turret, I peeped, in turn, out of several of its small windows. The pine-tree, being ancient, rose high above the rest of the wood, which was of comparatively recent growth. Even where I sat, about midway between the root and the topmost bough, my position was lofty enough to serve as an observatory, not for starry investigations, but for those sublunary matters in which lay a lore as infinite as that of the planets. Through one loop-hole, I saw the river lapsing calmly onward, while, in the meadow near its brink, a few of the brethren were digging peat for our winter's fuel. On the interior cart-road of our farm, I discerned Hollingsworth, with a yoke of oxen hitched to a drag of stones, that were to be piled into a fence, on which we employed ourselves at the odd intervals of other labor. The harsh tones of his voice, shouting to the sluggish steers, made me sensible, even at such a distance, that he was ill at ease, and that the baulked philanthropist had the battle-spirit in his heart.

"Haw Buck!" quoth he. "Come along there, ye lazy ones! What are ye about now? Gee!"

"Mankind, in Hollingsworth's opinion," thought I, "is but another yoke of oxen, as stubborn, stupid, and sluggish, as our old Brown and Bright. He vituperates us aloud, and curses us in his heart, and will begin to prick us with the goad stick, by-and-by. But, are we his oxen? And what right has he to be the driver? And why, when there is enough else to do, should we waste our strength in dragging home the ponderous load of his philanthropic absurdities? At my height above the earth, the whole matter looks ridiculous!"

Turning towards the farm-house, I saw Priscilla (for, though a great way off, the eye of faith assured me that it was she) sitting at Zenobia's window, and making little purses, I suppose, or perhaps mending the Community's old linen. A bird flew past my tree; and as it clove its way onward into the sunny atmosphere, I flung it a message for Priscilla.

"Tell her," said I, "that her fragile thread of life has inextricably knotted itself with other and tougher threads, and most likely it will be broken. Tell her that Zenobia will not be long her friend. Say that Hollingsworth's heart is on fire with his own purpose, but icy for all

[2]*ripe grapes . . . blood-stain:* See "The Mutability Cantos," fragment of book 7 of *The Faerie Queene* (1590, 1596), an allegorical epic by Edmund Spenser (1552–1599). The figure of October is presented as gleeful and carrying a plowshare (vii, 39).

human affection, and that, if she has given him her love, it is like casting a flower into a sepulchre. And say, that, if any mortal really cares for her, it is myself, and not even I, for her realities — poor little seamstress, as Zenobia rightly called her! — but for the fancy-work with which I have idly decked her out!"

The pleasant scent of the wood, evolved by the hot sun, stole up to my nostrils, as if I had been an idol in its niche. Many trees mingled their fragrance into a thousand-fold odor. Possibly, there was a sensual influence in the broad light of noon that lay beneath me. It may have been the cause, in part, that I suddenly found myself possessed by a mood of disbelief in moral beauty or heroism, and a conviction of the folly of attempting to benefit the world. Our especial scheme of reform, which, from my observatory, I could take in with the bodily eye, looked so ridiculous that it was impossible not to laugh aloud.

"But the joke is a little too heavy," thought I. "If I were wise, I should get out of the scrape, with all diligence, and then laugh at my companions for remaining in it!"

While thus musing, I heard, with perfect distinctness, somewhere in the wood beneath, the peculiar laugh, which I have described as one of the disagreeable characteristics of Professor Westervelt. It brought my thoughts back to our recent interview. I recognized, as chiefly due to this man's influence, the sceptical and sneering view which, just now, had filled my mental vision in regard to all life's better purposes. And it was through his eyes, more than my own, that I was looking at Hollingsworth, with his glorious, if impracticable dream, and at the noble earthliness of Zenobia's character, and even at Priscilla, whose impalpable grace lay so singularly between disease and beauty. The essential charm of each had vanished. There are some spheres, the contact with which inevitably degrades the high, debases the pure, deforms the beautiful. It must be a mind of uncommon strength, and little impressibility, that can permit itself the habit of such intercourse, and not be permanently deteriorated; and yet the Professor's tone represented that of worldly society at large, where a cold scepticism smothers what it can of our spiritual aspirations, and makes the rest ridiculous. I detested this kind of man, and all the more, because a part of my own nature showed itself responsive to him.

Voices were now approaching, through the region of the wood which lay in the vicinity of my tree. Soon, I caught glimpses of two figures — a woman and a man — Zenobia and the stranger — earnestly talking together as they advanced.

Zenobia had a rich, though varying color. It was, most of the while, a flame, and anon a sudden paleness. Here eyes glowed, so that their light sometimes flashed upward to me, as when the sun throws a dazzle from some bright object on the ground. Her gestures were free, and strikingly impressive. The whole woman was alive with a passionate intensity, which I now perceived to be the phase in which her beauty culminated. Any passion would have become her well, and passionate love, perhaps, the best of all. This was not love, but anger, largely intermixed with scorn. Yet the idea strangely forced itself upon me, that there was a sort of familiarity between these two companions, necessarily the result of an intimate love — on Zenobia's part, at least — in days gone by, but which had prolonged itself into as intimate a hatred, for all futurity. As they passed among the trees, reckless as her movement was, she took good heed that even the hem of her garment should not brush against the stranger's person. I wondered whether there had always been a chasm, guarded so religiously, betwixt these two.

As for Westervelt, he was not a whit more warmed by Zenobia's passion, than a salamander by the heat of its native furnace.[3] He would have been absolutely statuesque, save for a look of slight perplexity tinctured strongly with derision. It was a crisis in which his intellectual perceptions could not altogether help him out. He failed to comprehend, and cared but little for comprehending, why Zenobia should put herself into such a fume; but satisfied his mind that it was all folly, and only another shape of a woman's manifold absurdity, which men can never understand. How many a woman's evil fate has yoked her with a man like this! Nature thrusts some of us into the world miserably incomplete, on the emotional side, with hardly any sensibilities except what pertain to us as animals. No passion, save of the senses; no holy tenderness, nor the delicacy that results from this. Externally, they bear a close resemblance to other men, and have perhaps all save the finest grace; but when a woman wrecks herself on such a being, she ultimately finds that the real womanhood, within her, has no corresponding part in him. Her deepest voice lacks a response; the deeper her cry, the more dead his silence. The fault may be none of his; he cannot give her what never lived within his soul. But the wretchedness, on her side, and the moral deterioration attendant on a false and shallow life, without strength enough to keep itself sweet, are among the most pitiable wrongs that mortals suffer.

[3] *a salamander by the heat of its native furnace:* A common folk belief was that the salamander was so cold-blooded that it could survive exposure to fire.

Now, as I looked down from my upper region at this man and woman — outwardly so fair a sight, and wandering like two lovers in the wood — I imagined that Zenobia, at an earlier period of youth, might have fallen into the misfortune above indicated. And when her passionate womanhood, as was inevitable, had discovered its mistake, there had ensued the character of eccentricity and defiance, which distinguished the more public portion of her life.

Seeing how aptly matters had chanced, thus far, I began to think it the design of fate to let me into all Zenobia's secrets, and that therefore the couple would sit down beneath my tree, and carry on a conversation which would leave me nothing to inquire. No doubt, however, had it so happened, I should have deemed myself honorably bound to warn them of a listener's presence by flinging down a handful of unripe grapes; or by sending an unearthly groan out of my hiding-place, as if this were one of the trees of Dante's ghostly forest.[4] But real life never arranges itself exactly like a romance. In the first place, they did not sit down at all. Secondly, even while they passed beneath the tree, Zenobia's utterance was so hasty and broken, and Westervelt's so cool and low, that I hardly could make out an intelligible sentence, on either side. What I seem to remember, I yet suspect may have been patched together by my fancy, in brooding over the matter, afterwards.

"Why not fling the girl off," said Westervelt, "and let her go?"

"She clung to me from the first," replied Zenobia. "I neither know nor care what it is in me that so attaches her. But she loves me, and I will not fail her."

"She will plague you, then," said he, "in more ways than one."

"The poor child!" exclaimed Zenobia. "She can do me neither good nor harm. How should she?"

I know not what reply Westervelt whispered; nor did Zenobia's subsequent exclamation give me any clue, except that it evidently inspired her with horror and disgust.

"With what kind of a being am I linked!" cried she. "If my Creator cares aught for my soul, let him release me from this miserable bond!"

"I did not think it weighed so heavily," said her companion.

"Nevertheless," answered Zenobia, "it will strangle me at last!"

---

[4]*Dante's ghostly forest:* At the beginning of the *Inferno,* part of his epic poem the *Divine Comedy* (completed 1321), Dante (1265–1321) depicts himself wandering in a wood.

And then I heard her utter a helpless sort of moan; a sound which, struggling out of the heart of a person of her pride and strength, affected me more than if she had made the wood dolorously vocal with a thousand shrieks and wails.

Other mysterious words, besides what are above-written, they spoke together; but I understood no more, and even question whether I fairly understood so much as this. By long brooding over our recollections, we subtilize them into something akin to imaginary stuff, and hardly capable of being distinguished from it. In a few moments, they were completely beyond ear-shot. A breeze stirred after them, and awoke the leafy tongues of the surrounding trees, which forthwith began to babble, as if innumerable gossips had all at once got wind of Zenobia's secret. But, as the breeze grew stronger, its voice among the branches was as if it said — "Hush! Hush!" — and I resolved that to no mortal would I disclose what I had heard. And, though there might be room for casuistry,[5] such, I conceive, is the most equitable rule in all similar conjunctures.

XIII. ZENOBIA'S LEGEND

The illustrious Society of Blithedale, though it toiled in downright earnest for the good of mankind, yet not unfrequently illuminated its laborious life with an afternoon or evening of pastime. Pic-nics under the trees were considerably in vogue; and, within doors, fragmentary bits of theatrical performance, such as single acts of tragedy or comedy, or dramatic proverbs and charades. Zenobia, besides, was fond of giving us readings from Shakspeare, and often with a depth of tragic power, or breadth of comic effect, that made one feel it an intolerable wrong to the world, that she did not at once go upon the stage. *Tableaux vivants*[1] were another of our occasional modes of amusement, in which scarlet shawls, old silken robes, ruffs, velvets, furs, and all kinds of miscellaneous trumpery, converted our familiar companions into the people of a pictorial world. We had been thus engaged, on the evening after the incident narrated in the last chapter. Several splendid works of art — either arranged after engravings

---

[5]*casuistry:* Study of cases of conscience; also refers to specious or sophistical reasoning.
[1]*Tableaux vivants:* French, meaning "living pictures"; a static depiction on a stage of a literary, historical, or cultural event in which the participants appear in costume.

from the Old Masters,[2] or original illustrations of scenes in history or romance — had been presented, and we were earnestly entreating Zenobia for more.

She stood, with a meditative air, holding a large piece of gauze, or some such ethereal stuff, as if considering what picture should next occupy the frame; while at her feet lay a heap of many-colored garments, which her quick fancy and magic skill could so easily convert into gorgeous draperies for heroes and princesses.

"I am getting weary of this," said she, after a moment's thought. "Our own features, and our own figures and airs, show a little too intrusively through all the characters we assume. We have so much familiarity with one another's realities, that we cannot remove ourselves, at pleasure, into an imaginary sphere. Let us have no more pictures, to-night; but, to make you what poor amends I can, how would you like to have me trump up a wild, spectral legend, on the spur of the moment?"

Zenobia had the gift of telling a fanciful little story, off hand, in a way that made it greatly more effective, than it was usually found to be, when she afterwards elaborated the same production with her pen. Her proposal, therefore, was greeted with acclamation.

"Oh, a story, a story, by all means!" cried the young girls. "No matter how marvellous, we will believe it, every word! And let it be a ghost-story, if you please!"

"No; not exactly a ghost-story," answered Zenobia; "but something so nearly like it that you shall hardly tell the difference. And, Priscilla, stand you before me, where I may look at you, and get my inspiration out of your eyes. They are very deep and dreamy, to-night!"

I know not whether the following version of her story will retain any portion of its pristine character. But, as Zenobia told it, wildly and rapidly, hesitating at no extravagance, and dashing at absurdities which I am too timorous to repeat — giving it the varied emphasis of her inimitable voice, and the pictorial illustration of her mobile face, while, through it all, we caught the freshest aroma of the thoughts, as they came bubbling out of her mind — thus narrated, and thus heard, the legend seemed quite a remarkable affair. I scarcely knew, at the time, whether she intended us to laugh, or be more seriously impressed. From beginning to end it was undeniable nonsense, but not necessarily the worse for that.

---

[2]*Old Masters:* Refers to distinguished European painters of the sixteenth, seventeenth, and early eighteenth centuries.

The Silvery Veil

You have heard, my dear friends, of the Veiled Lady, who grew suddenly so very famous, a few months ago. And have you never thought how remarkable it was, that this marvellous creature should vanish, all at once, while her renown was on the increase, before the public had grown weary of her, and when the enigma of her character, instead of being solved, presented itself more mystically at every exhibition? Her last appearance, as you know, was before a crowded audience. The next evening — although the bills had announced her, at the corner of every street, in red letters of a gigantic size — there was no Veiled Lady to be seen! Now, listen to my simple little tale; and you shall hear the very latest incident in the known life — (if life it may be called, which seemed to have no more reality than the candlelight image of one's self, which peeps at us outside of a dark window-pane) — the life of this shadowy phenomenon.

A party of young gentlemen, you are to understand, were enjoying themselves, one afternoon, as young gentlemen are sometimes fond of doing, over a bottle or two of champagne; and — among other ladies less mysterious — the subject of the Veiled Lady, as was very natural, happened to come up before them for discussion. She rose, as it were, with the sparkling effervescence of their wine, and appeared in a more airy and fantastic light, on account of the medium through which they saw her. They repeated to one another, between jest and earnest, all the wild stories that were in vogue; nor, I presume, did they hesitate to add any small circumstance that the inventive whim of the moment might suggest, to heighten the marvellousness of their theme.

"But what an audacious report was that," observed one, "which pretended to assert the identity of this strange creature with a young lady" — and here he mentioned her name — "the daughter of one of our most distinguished families!"

"Ah, there is more in that story than can well be accounted for!" remarked another. "I have it on good authority, that the young lady in question is invariably out of sight, and not to be traced, even by her own family, at the hours when the Veiled Lady is before the public; nor can any satisfactory explanation be given of her disappearance. And just look at the thing! Her brother is a young fellow of spirit. He cannot but be aware of these rumors in reference to his sister. Why, then, does he not come forward to defend her character, unless he is conscious that an investigation would only make the matter worse?"

It is essential to the purposes of my legend to distinguish one of these young gentlemen from his companions; so, for the sake of a soft and pretty name, (such as we, of the literary sisterhood, invariably bestow upon our heroes,) I deem it fit to call him 'Theodore.'

"Pshaw!" exclaimed Theodore. "Her brother is no such fool! No-body, unless his brain be as full of bubbles as this wine, can seriously think of crediting that ridiculous rumor. Why, if my senses did not play me false, (which never was the case yet,) I affirm that I saw that very lady, last evening, at the exhibition, while this veiled phenome-non was playing off her juggling tricks! What can you say to that?"

"Oh, it was a spectral illusion that you saw!" replied his friends, with a general laugh. "The Veiled Lady is quite up to such a thing."

However, as the above-mentioned fable could not hold its ground against Theodore's downright refutation, they went on to speak of other stories, which the wild babble of the town had set afloat. Some upheld, that the veil covered the most beautiful countenance in the world; others — and certainly with more reason, considering the sex of the Veiled Lady — that the face was the most hideous and hor-rible, and that this was her sole motive for hiding it. It was the face of a corpse; it was the head of a skeleton; it was a monstrous visage, with snaky locks, like Medusa's,[3] and one great red eye in the centre of the forehead. Again, it was affirmed, that there was no single and unchangeable set of features, beneath the veil, but that whosoever should be bold enough to lift it, would behold the features of that person, in all the world, who was destined to be his fate; perhaps he would be greeted by the tender smile of the woman he loved; or, quite as probably, the deadly scowl of his bitterest enemy would throw a blight over his life. They quoted, moreover, this startling ex-planation of the whole affair: — that the Magician (who exhibited the Veiled Lady, and who, by-the-by, was the handsomest man in the whole world) had bartered his own soul for seven years' possession of a familiar fiend, and that the last year of the contract was wearing towards its close.

If it were worth our while, I could keep you till an hour beyond midnight, listening to a thousand such absurdities as these. But, fi-nally, our friend Theodore, who prided himself upon his common-sense, found the matter getting quite beyond his patience.

---

[3]*like Medusa's:* In Greek mythology, Medusa was a female monster, with snakes for hair, whose gaze turned men into stone. See Ovid, *Metamorphoses,* 4:614–20, 770–803.

"I offer any wager you like," cried he, setting down his glass so forcibly as to break the stem of it, "that, this very evening, I find out the mystery of the Veiled Lady!"

Young men, I am told, boggle at nothing, over their wine. So, after a little more talk, a wager of considerable amount was actually laid, the money staked, and Theodore left to choose his own method of settling the dispute.

How he managed it, I know not, nor is it of any great importance to this veracious legend; the most natural way, to be sure, was by bribing the door-keeper, or, possibly, he preferred clambering in at the window. But, at any rate, that very evening, while the exhibition was going forward in the hall, Theodore contrived to gain admittance into the private withdrawing-room, whither the Veiled Lady was accustomed to retire, at the close of her performances. There he waited, listening, I suppose, to the stifled hum of the great audience; and, no doubt, he could distinguish the deep tones of the Magician, causing the wonders that he wrought to appear more dark and intricate, by his mystic pretence of an explanation; perhaps, too, in the intervals of the wild, breezy music which accompanied the exhibition, he might hear the low voice of the Veiled Lady, conveying her Sibylline responses. Firm as Theodore's nerves might be, and much as he prided himself on his sturdy perception of realities, I should not be surprised if his heart throbbed at a little more than its ordinary rate!

Theodore concealed himself behind a screen. In due time, the performance was brought to a close; and whether the door was softly opened, or whether her bodiless presence came through the wall, is more than I can say; but, all at once, without the young man's knowing how it happened, a veiled figure stood in the centre of the room. It was one thing to be in the presence of this mystery, in the hall of exhibition, where the warm, dense life of hundreds of other mortals kept up the beholder's courage, and distributed her influence among so many; it was another thing to be quite alone with her, and that, too, with a hostile, or, at least, an unauthorized and unjustifiable purpose. I rather imagine that Theodore now began to be sensible of something more serious in his enterprise than he had been quite aware of, while he sat with his boon-companions over their sparkling wine.

Very strange, it must be confessed, was the movement with which the figure floated to-and-fro over the carpet, with the silvery veil covering her from head to foot; so impalpable, so ethereal, so without substance, as the texture seemed, yet hiding her every outline in an impenetrability like that of midnight. Surely, she did not walk! She floated, and flitted, and hovered about the room; — no sound of a footstep, no perceptible motion of a limb; — it was as if a wandering breeze wafted her before it, at its own wild and gentle pleasure. But, by-and-by, a purpose began to be discernible, throughout the seeming vagueness of her unrest. She was in quest of something! Could it be, that a subtile presentiment had informed her of the young man's presence? And, if so, did the Veiled Lady seek, or did she shun him? The doubt in Theodore's mind was speedily resolved; for, after a moment or two of these erratic flutterings, she advanced, more decidedly, and stood motionless before the screen.

"Thou art here!" said a soft, low voice. "Come forth, Theodore!"

Thus summoned by his name, Theodore, as a man of courage, had no choice. He emerged from his concealment, and presented himself before the Veiled Lady, with the wine-flush, it may be, quite gone out of his cheeks.

"What wouldst thou with me?" she inquired, with the same gentle composure that was in her former utterance.

"Mysterious creature," replied Theodore, "I would know who and what you are!"

"My lips are forbidden to betray the secret!" said the Veiled Lady.

"At whatever risk, I must discover it!" rejoined Theodore.

"Then," said the Mystery, "there is no way, save to lift my veil!"

And Theodore, partly recovering his audacity, stept forward, on the instant, to do as the Veiled Lady had suggested. But she floated backward to the opposite side of the room, as if the young man's breath had possessed power enough to waft her away.

"Pause, one little instant," said the soft, low voice, "and learn the conditions of what thou art so bold to undertake! Thou canst go hence, and think of me no more; or, at thy option, thou canst lift this mysterious veil, beneath which I am a sad and lonely prisoner, in a bondage which is worse to me than death. But, before raising it, I entreat thee, in all maiden modesty, to bend forward, and impress a kiss, where my breath stirs the veil; and my virgin lips shall come forward to meet thy lips; and from that instant, Theodore, thou shalt be mine, and I thine, with never more a veil between us! And all the felicity of earth and of the future world shall be thine and mine together. So much may a maiden say behind the veil. If thou shrinkest from this, there is yet another way."

"And what is that?" asked Theodore.

"Dost thou hesitate," said the Veiled Lady, "to pledge thyself to me, by meeting these lips of mine, while the veil yet hides my face? Has not thy heart recognized me? Dost thou come hither, not in holy faith, nor with a pure and generous purpose, but in scornful scepticism and idle curiosity? Still, thou mayst lift the veil! But from that instant, Theodore, I am doomed to be thy evil fate; nor wilt thou ever taste another breath of happiness!"

There was a shade of inexpressible sadness in the utterance of these last words. But Theodore, whose natural tendency was towards scepticism, felt himself almost injured and insulted by the Veiled Lady's proposal that he should pledge himself, for life and eternity, to so questionable a creature as herself; or even that she should suggest an inconsequential kiss, taking into view the probability that her face was none of the most bewitching. A delightful idea, truly, that he should salute the lips of a dead girl, or the jaws of a skeleton, or the grinning cavity of a monster's mouth! Even should she prove a comely maiden enough, in other respects, the odds were ten to one that her teeth were defective; a terrible drawback on the delectableness of a kiss!

"Excuse me, fair lady," said Theodore — and I think he nearly burst into a laugh — "if I prefer to lift the veil first; and for this affair of the kiss, we may decide upon it, afterwards!"

"Thou has made thy choice," said the sweet, sad voice, behind the veil; and there seemed a tender, but unresentful sense of wrong done to womanhood by the young man's contemptuous interpretation of her offer. "I must not counsel thee to pause; although thy fate is still in thine own hand!"

Grasping at the veil, he flung it upward, and caught a glimpse of a pale, lovely face, beneath; just one momentary glimpse; and then the apparition vanished, and the silvery veil fluttered slowly down, and lay upon the floor. Theodore was alone. Our legend leaves him there. His retribution was, to pine, forever and ever, for another sight of that dim, mournful face — which might have been his life-long, household, fireside joy — to desire, and waste life in a feverish quest, and never meet it more!

But what, in good sooth, had become of the Veiled Lady? Had all her existence been comprehended within that mysterious veil, and was she now annihilated? Or was she a spirit, with a heavenly essence, but which might have been tamed down to human bliss, had Theodore been brave and true enough to claim her? Hearken, my sweet friends — and hearken, dear Priscilla — and you shall learn the little more that Zenobia can tell you!

Just at the moment, so far as can be ascertained, when the Veiled

Lady vanished, a maiden, pale and shadowy, rose up amid a knot of visionary people, who were seeking for the better life. She was so gentle and so sad — a nameless melancholy gave her such hold upon their sympathies — that they never thought of questioning whence she came. She might have heretofore existed; or her thin substance might have been moulded out of air, at the very instant when they first beheld her. It was all one to them; they took her to their hearts. Among them was a lady, to whom, more than to all the rest, this pale, mysterious girl attached herself.

But, one morning, the lady was wandering in the woods, and there met her a figure in an Oriental robe, with a dark beard, and holding in his hand a silvery veil. He motioned her to stay. Being a woman of some nerve, she did not shriek, nor run away, nor faint, as many ladies would have been apt to do, but stood quietly, and bade him speak. The truth was, she had seen his face before, but had never feared it, although she knew him to be a terrible magician.

"Lady," said he, with a warning gesture, "you are in peril!"

"Peril!" she exclaimed. "And of what nature?"

"There is a certain maiden," replied the Magician, "who has come out of the realm of Mystery, and made herself your most intimate companion. Now, the fates have so ordained it, that, whether by her own will, or no, this stranger is your deadliest enemy. In love, in worldly fortune, in all your pursuit of happiness, she is doomed to fling a blight over your prospects. There is but one possibility of thwarting her disastrous influence."

"Then, tell me that one method," said the lady.

"Take this veil!" he answered, holding forth the silvery texture. "It is a spell; it is a powerful enchantment, which I wrought for her sake, and beneath which she was once my prisoner. Throw it, at unawares, over the head of this secret foe, stamp your foot, and cry — 'Arise, Magician, here is the Veiled Lady' — and immediately I will rise up through the earth, and seize her. And from that moment, you are safe!"

So the lady took the silvery veil, which was like woven air, or like some substance airier than nothing, and that would float upward and be lost among the clouds, were she once to let it go. Returning homeward, she found the shadowy girl, amid the knot of visionary transcendentalists,[4] who were still seeking for the better life. She was

---

[4]*visionary transcendentalists:* Transcendentalism was the name of the literary and cultural movement, centered in the Boston/Cambridge/Concord area and associated with Emerson, Ripley, Fuller, and others, that arose in the 1830s.

joyous, now, and had a rose-bloom in her cheeks, and was one of the prettiest creatures, and seemed one of the happiest, that the world could show. But the lady stole noiselessly behind her, and threw the veil over her head. As the slight, ethereal texture sank inevitably down over her figure, the poor girl strove to raise it, and met her dear friend's eyes with one glance of mortal terror, and deep, deep reproach. It could not change her purpose.

"Arise, Magician!" she exclaimed, stamping her foot upon the earth. "Here is the Veiled Lady!"

At the word, uprose the bearded man in the Oriental robes — the beautiful! — the dark Magician, who had bartered away his soul! He threw his arms around the Veiled Lady; and she was his bond-slave, forever more!

Zenobia, all this while, had been holding the piece of gauze, and so managed it as greatly to increase the dramatic effect of the legend, at those points where the magic veil was to be described. Arriving at the catastrophe, and uttering the fatal words, she flung the gauze over Priscilla's head; and, for an instant, her auditors held their breath, half expecting, I verily believe, that the Magician would start up through the floor, and carry off our poor little friend, before our eyes.

As for Priscilla, she stood, droopingly, in the midst of us, making no attempt to remove the veil.

"How do you find yourself, my love?" said Zenobia, lifting a corner of the gauze, and peeping beneath it, with a mischievous smile. "Ah, the dear little soul! Why, she is really going to faint! Mr. Coverdale, Mr. Coverdale, pray bring a glass of water!"

Her nerves being none of the strongest, Priscilla hardly recovered her equanimity during the rest of the evening. This, to be sure, was a great pity; but, nevertheless, we thought it a very bright idea of Zenobia's, to bring her legend to so effective a conclusion.

XIV. ELIOT'S PULPIT

Our Sundays, at Blithedale, were not ordinarily kept with such rigid observance as might have befitted the descendants of the Pilgrims, whose high enterprise, as we sometimes flattered ourselves, we had taken up, and were carrying it onward and aloft, to a point which they never dreamed of attaining.

On that hallowed day, it is true, we rested from our labors. Our oxen, relieved from their week-day yoke, roamed at large through the pasture; each yoke-fellow, however, keeping close beside his mate, and continuing to acknowledge, from the force of habit and sluggish sympathy, the union which the taskmaster had imposed for his own hard ends. As for us, human yoke-fellows, chosen companions of toil, whose hoes had clinked together throughout the week, we wandered off, in various directions, to enjoy our interval of repose. Some, I believe, went devoutly to the village-church. Others, it may be, ascended a city or a country-pulpit, wearing the clerical robe with so much dignity that you would scarcely have suspected the yeoman's frock to have been flung off, only since milking-time. Others took long rambles among the rustic lanes and by-paths, pausing to look at black, old farm-houses, with their sloping roofs; and at the modern cottage, so like a plaything that it seemed as if real joy or sorrow could have no scope within; and at the more pretending villa, with its range of wooden columns, supporting the needless insolence of a great portico. Some betook themselves into the wide, dusky barn, and lay there, for hours together, on the odorous hay; while the sun-streaks and the shadows strove together — these to make the barn solemn, those to make it cheerful — and both were conquerors; and the swallows twittered a cheery anthem, flashing into sight, or vanishing, as they darted to-and-fro among the golden rules of sunshine. And others went a little way into the woods, and threw themselves on Mother Earth, pillowing their heads on a heap of moss, the green decay of an old log; and dropping asleep, the humble-bees and mus-quitoes sung and buzzed about their ears, causing the slumberers to twitch and start, without awakening.

With Hollingsworth, Zenobia, Priscilla, and myself, it grew to be a custom to spend the Sabbath-afternoon at a certain rock. It was known to us under the name of Eliot's pulpit, from a tradition that the venerable Apostle Eliot[1] had preached there, two centuries gone by, to an Indian auditory. The old pine-forest, through which the Apostle's voice was wont to sound, had fallen, an immemorial time ago. But the soil, being of the rudest and most broken surface, had apparently never been brought under tillage; other growths, maple, and beech, and birch, had succeeded to the primeval trees; so that it

---

[1]*Apostle Eliot:* John Eliot (1604–1690), pastor and teacher in Roxbury, Massachusetts, was a missionary to the Indians and translated the Bible into their language. In *The Scarlet Letter,* Reverend Dimmesdale goes for a visit to "Apostle Eliot, among his Indian converts" (ch. 16).

was still as wild a tract of woodland as the great-great-great-great grandson of one of Eliot's Indians (had any such posterity been in existence) could have desired, for the site and shelter of his wigwam. These after-growths, indeed, lose the stately solemnity of the original forest. If left in due neglect, however, they run into an entanglement of softer wildness, among the rustling leaves of which the sun can scatter cheerfulness, as it never could among the dark-browed pines.

The rock itself rose some twenty or thirty feet, a shattered granite boulder, or heap of boulders, with an irregular outline and many fissures, out of which sprang shrubs, bushes, and even trees; as if the scanty soil, within those crevices, were sweeter to their roots than any other earth. At the base of the pulpit, the broken boulders inclined towards each other, so as to form a shallow cave, within which our little party had sometimes found protection from a summer shower. On the threshold, or just across it, grew a tuft of pale columbines, in their season, and violets, sad and shadowy recluses, such as Priscilla was, when we first knew her; children of the sun, who had never seen their father, but dwelt among damp mosses, though not akin to them. At the summit, the rock was overshadowed by the canopy of a birch-tree, which served as a sounding-board for the pulpit. Beneath this shade, (with my eyes of sense half shut, and those of the imagination widely opened,) I used to see the holy Apostle of the Indians, with the sunlight flickering down upon him through the leaves, and glorifying his figure as with the half-perceptible glow of a transfiguration.

I the more minutely describe the rock, and this little Sabbath solitude, because Hollingsworth, at our solicitation, often ascended Eliot's pulpit, and — not exactly preached — but talked to us, his few disciples, in a strain that rose and fell as naturally as the wind's breath among the leaves of the birch-tree. No other speech of man has ever moved me like some of those discourses. It seemed most pitiful — a positive calamity to the world — that a treasury of golden thoughts should thus be scattered, by the liberal handful, down among us three, when a thousand hearers might have been the richer for them; and Hollingsworth the richer, likewise, by the sympathy of multitudes. After speaking much or little, as might happen, he would descend from his gray pulpit, and generally fling himself at full length on the ground, face downward. Meanwhile, we talked around him, on such topics as were suggested by the discourse.

Since her interview with Westervelt, Zenobia's continual inequalities of temper had been rather difficult for her friends to bear. On the first Sunday after that incident, when Hollingsworth had clambered down from Eliot's pulpit, she declaimed with great earnestness and passion, nothing short of anger, on the injustice which the world did to women, and equally to itself, by not allowing them, in freedom and honor, and with the fullest welcome, their natural utterance in public.

"It shall not always be so!"cried she. "If I live another year, I will lift up my own voice, in behalf of woman's wider liberty."

She, perhaps, saw me smile.

"What matter of ridicule do you find in this, Miles Coverdale?" exclaimed Zenobia, with a flash of anger in her eyes. "That smile, permit me to say, makes me suspicious of a low tone of feeling, and shallow thought. It is my belief — yes, and my prophecy, should I die before it happens — that, when my sex shall achieve its rights, there will be ten eloquent women, where there is now one eloquent man. Thus far, no woman in the world has ever once spoken out her whole heart and her whole mind. The mistrust and disapproval of the vast bulk of society throttles us, as with two gigantic hands at our throats! We mumble a few weak words, and leave a thousand better ones unsaid. You let us write a little, it is true, on a limited range of subjects. But the pen is not for woman. Her power is too natural and immediate. It is with the living voice, alone, that she can compel the world to recognize the light of her intellect and the depth of her heart!"

Now — though I could not well say so to Zenobia — I had not smiled from any unworthy estimate of woman, or in denial of the claims which she is beginning to put forth. What amused and puzzled me, was the fact, that women, however intellectually superior, so seldom disquiet themselves about the rights or wrongs of their sex, unless their own individual affections chance to lie in idleness, or to be ill at ease. They are not natural reformers, but become such by the pressure of exceptional misfortune. I could measure Zenobia's inward trouble, by the animosity with which she now took up the general quarrel of woman against man.

"I will give you leave, Zenobia," replied I, "to fling your utmost scorn upon me, if you ever hear me utter a sentiment unfavorable to the widest liberty which woman has yet dreamed of. I would give her all she asks, and add a great deal more, which she will not be the party to demand, but which men, if they were generous and wise, would grant of their own free motion. For instance, I should love dearly — for the next thousand years, at least — to have all government devolve into the hands of women. I hate to be ruled by my own sex; it excites my jealousy and wounds my pride. It is the iron sway of bodily force, which abases us, in our compelled submission. But, how sweet the free, generous courtesy, with which I would kneel before a woman-ruler!"

"Yes; if she were young and beautiful," said Zenobia, laughing. "But how if she were sixty, and a fright?"

"Ah; it is you that rate womanhood low," said I. "But let me go on. I have never found it possible to suffer a bearded priest so near my heart and conscience, as to do me any spiritual good. I blush at the very thought! Oh, in the better order of things, Heaven grant that the ministry of souls may be left in charge of women! The gates of the Blessed City will be thronged with the multitude that enter in, when that day comes! The task belongs to woman. God meant it for her. He has endowed her with the religious sentiment in its utmost depth and purity, refined from that gross, intellectual alloy, with which every masculine theologian — save only One, who merely veiled Himself in mortal and masculine shape, but was, in truth, divine — has been prone to mingle it. I have always envied the Catholics their faith in that sweet, sacred Virgin Mother, who stands between them and the Deity, intercepting somewhat of His awful splendor, but permitting His love to stream upon the worshipper, more intelligibly to human comprehension, through the medium of a woman's tenderness. Have I not said enough, Zenobia?"

"I cannot think that this is true," observed Priscilla, who had been gazing at me with great, disapproving eyes. "And I am sure I do not wish it to be true!"

"Poor child!" exclaimed Zenobia, rather contemptuously. "She is the type of womanhood, such as man has spent centuries in making it. He is never content, unless he can degrade himself by stooping towards what he loves. In denying us our rights, he betrays even more blindness to his own interests, than profligate disregard of ours!"

"Is this true?" asked Priscilla, with simplicity, turning to Hollingsworth. "Is it all true that Mr. Coverdale and Zenobia have been saying?"

"No, Priscilla," answered Hollingsworth, with his customary bluntness. "They have neither of them spoken one true word yet."

"Do you despise woman?" said Zenobia. "Ah, Hollingsworth, that would be most ungrateful!"

"Despise her? — No!" cried Hollingsworth, lifting his great shaggy head and shaking it at us, while his eyes glowed almost fiercely. "She is the most admirable handiwork of God, in her true place and character. Her place is at man's side. Her office, that of the Sympathizer;

the unreserved, unquestioning Believer; the Recognition, withheld in every other manner, but given, in pity, through woman's heart, lest man should utterly lose faith in himself; the Echo of God's own voice, pronouncing — 'It is well done!' All the separate action of woman is, and ever has been, and always shall be, false, foolish, vain, destructive of her own best and holiest qualities, void of every good effect, and productive of intolerable mischiefs! Man is a wretch without woman; but woman is a monster — and, thank Heaven, an almost impossible and hitherto imaginary monster — without man, as her acknowledged principal! As true as I had once a mother, whom I loved, were there any possible prospect of woman's taking the social stand which some of them — poor, miserable, abortive creatures, who only dream of such things because they have missed woman's peculiar happiness, or because Nature made them really neither man nor woman! — if there were a chance of their attaining the end which these petticoated monstrosities have in view, I would call upon my own sex to use its physical force, that unmistakeable evidence of sovereignty, to scourge them back within their proper bounds! But it will not be needful. The heart of true womanhood knows where its own sphere is, and never seeks to stray beyond it!"

Never was mortal blessed — if blessing it were — with a glance of such entire acquiescence and unquestioning faith, happy in its completeness, as our little Priscilla unconsciously bestowed on Hollingsworth. She seemed to take the sentiment from his lips into her heart, and brood over it in perfect content. The very woman whom he pictured — the gentle parasite, the soft reflection of a more powerful existence — sat there at his feet.

I looked at Zenobia, however, fully expecting her to resent — as I felt, by the indignant ebullition of my own blood, that she ought — this outrageous affirmation of what struck me as the intensity of masculine egotism. It centred everything in itself, and deprived woman of her very soul, her inexpressible and unfathomable all, to make it a mere incident in the great sum of man. Hollingsworth had boldly uttered what he, and millions of despots like him, really felt. Without intending it, he had disclosed the well-spring of all these troubled waters. Now, if ever, it surely behoved Zenobia to be the champion of her sex.

But, to my surprise, and indignation too, she only looked humbled. Some tears sparkled in her eyes, but they were wholly of grief, not anger.

"Well; be it so," was all she said. "I, at least, have deep cause to think you right. Let man be but manly and godlike, and woman is only too ready to become to him what you say!"

I smiled — somewhat bitterly, it is true — in contemplation of my own ill-luck. How little did these two women care for me, who had freely conceded all their claims, and a great deal more, out of the fulness of my heart; while Hollingsworth, by some necromancy[2] of his horrible injustice, seemed to have brought them both to his feet!

"Women almost invariably behave thus!" thought I. "What does the fact mean? Is it their nature? Or is it, at last, the result of ages of compelled degradation? And, in either case, will it be possible ever to redeem them?"

An intuition now appeared to possess all the party, that, for this time, at least, there was no more to be said. With one accord, we arose from the ground, and made our way through the tangled undergrowth towards one of those pleasant wood-paths, that wound among the over-arching trees. Some of the branches hung so low as partly to conceal the figures that went before, from those who followed. Priscilla had leaped up more lightly than the rest of us, and ran along in advance, with as much airy activity of spirit as was typified in the motion of a bird, which chanced to be flitting from tree to tree, in the same direction as herself. Never did she seem so happy as that afternoon. She skipt, and could not help it, from very playfulness of heart.

Zenobia and Hollingsworth went next, in close contiguity, but not with arm in arm. Now, just when they had passed the impending bough of a birch-tree, I plainly saw Zenobia take the hand of Hollingsworth in both her own, press it to her bosom, and let it fall again!

The gesture was sudden and full of passion; the impulse had evidently taken her by surprise; it expressed all! Had Zenobia knelt before him, or flung herself upon his breast, and gasped out — "I love you, Hollingsworth!" — I could not have been more certain of what it meant. They then walked onward, as before. But, methought, as the declining sun threw Zenobia's magnified shadow along the path, I beheld it tremulous; and the delicate stem of the flower, which she wore in her hair, was likewise responsive to her agitation.

Priscilla — through the medium of her eyes, at least — could not possibly have been aware of the gesture above-described. Yet, at that instant, I saw her droop. The buoyancy, which just before had been so birdlike, was utterly departed; the life seemed to pass out of her,

---

[2]*necromancy:* Magic, witchcraft, sorcery.

and even the substance of her figure to grow thin and gray. I almost imagined her a shadow, fading gradually into the dimness of the wood. Her pace became so slow, that Hollingsworth and Zenobia passed by, and I, without hastening my steps, overtook her.

"Come, Priscilla," said I, looking her intently in the face, which was very pale and sorrowful, "we must make haste after our friends. Do you feel suddenly ill? A moment ago, you flitted along so lightly that I was comparing you to a bird. Now, on the contrary, it is as if you had a heavy heart, and very little strength to bear it with. Pray take my arm!"

"No," said Priscilla, "I do not think it would help me. It is my heart, as you say, that makes me heavy; and I know not why. Just now, I felt very happy."

No doubt, it was a kind of sacrilege in me to attempt to come within her maidenly mystery. But as she appeared to be tossed aside by her other friends, or carelessly let fall, like a flower which they had done with, I could not resist the impulse to take just one peep beneath her folded petals.

"Zenobia and yourself are dear friends, of late," I remarked. "At first — that first evening when you came to us — she did not receive you quite so warmly as might have been wished."

"I remember it," said Priscilla. "No wonder she hesitated to love me, who was then a stranger to her, and a girl of no grace or beauty; she being herself so beautiful!"

"But she loves you now, of course," suggested I. "And, at this very instant, you feel her to be your dearest friend?"

"Why do you ask me that question?" exclaimed Priscilla, as if frightened at the scrutiny into her feelings which I compelled her to make. "It somehow puts strange thoughts into my mind. But I do love Zenobia dearly! If she only loves me half as well, I shall be happy!"

"How is it possible to doubt that, Priscilla?" I rejoined. "But, observe how pleasantly and happily Zenobia and Hollingsworth are walking together! I call it a delightful spectacle. It truly rejoices me that Hollingsworth has found so fit and affectionate a friend! So many people in the world mistrust him — so many disbelieve and ridicule, while hardly any do him justice, or acknowledge him for the wonderful man he is — that it is really a blessed thing for him to have won the sympathy of such a woman as Zenobia. Any man might be proud of that. Any man, even if he be as great as Hollingsworth, might love so magnificent a woman. How very beautiful Zenobia is! And Hollingsworth knows it, too!"

There may have been some petty malice in what I said. Generosity is a very fine thing, at a proper time, and within due limits. But it is an insufferable bore, to see one man engrossing every thought of all the women, and leaving his friend to shiver in outer seclusion, without even the alternative of solacing himself with what the more fortunate individual has rejected. Yes; it was out of a foolish bitterness of heart that I had spoken.

"Go on before!" said Priscilla, abruptly, and with true feminine imperiousness, which heretofore I had never seen her exercise. "It pleases me best to loiter along by myself. I do not walk so fast as you."

With her hand, she made a little gesture of dismissal. It provoked me, yet, on the whole, was the most bewitching thing that Priscilla had ever done. I obeyed her, and strolled moodily homeward, wondering — as I had wondered a thousand times, already — how Hollingsworth meant to dispose of these two hearts, which (plainly to my perception, and, as I could not but now suppose, to his) he had engrossed into his own huge egotism.

There was likewise another subject, hardly less fruitful of speculation. In what attitude did Zenobia present herself to Hollingsworth? Was it in that of a free woman, with no mortgage on her affections nor claimant to her hand, but fully at liberty to surrender both, in exchange for the heart and hand which she apparently expected to receive? But, was it a vision that I had witnessed in the wood? Was Westervelt a goblin? Were those words of passion and agony, which Zenobia had uttered in my hearing, a mere stage-declamation? Were they formed of a material lighter than common air? Or, supposing them to bear sterling weight, was it not a perilous and dreadful wrong, which she was meditating towards herself and Hollingsworth?

Arriving nearly at the farm-house, I looked back over the long slope of pasture-land, and beheld them standing together, in the light of sunset, just on the spot where, according to the gossip of the Community, they meant to built their cottage. Priscilla, alone and forgotten, was lingering in the shadow of the wood.

XV. A CRISIS

Thus the summer was passing away; a summer of toil, of interest, of something that was not pleasure, but which went deep into my heart, and there became a rich experience. I found myself looking forward to years, if not to a lifetime, to be spent on the same system.

The Community were now beginning to form their permanent plans. One of our purposes was to erect a Phalanstery (as I think we called it, after Fourier; but the phraseology of those days is not very fresh in my remembrance) where the great and general family should have its abiding-place. Individual members, too, who made it a point of religion to preserve the sanctity of an exclusive home, were selecting sites for their cottages, by the wood-side, or on the breezy swells, or in the sheltered nook of some little valley, according as their taste might lean towards snugness or the picturesque. Altogether, by projecting our minds outward, we had imparted a show of novelty to existence, and contemplated it as hopefully as if the soil, beneath our feet, had not been fathom-deep with the dust of deluded generations, on every one of which, as on ourselves, the world had imposed itself as a hitherto unwedded bride.

Hollingsworth and myself had often discussed these prospects. It was easy to perceive, however, that he spoke with little or no fervor, but either as questioning the fulfilment of our anticipations, or, at any rate, with a quiet consciousness that it was no personal concern of his. Shortly after the scene at Eliot's pulpit, while he and I were repairing an old stone-fence, I amused myself with sallying forward into the future time.

"When we come to be old men," I said, "they will call us Uncles, or Fathers — Father Hollingsworth and Uncle Coverdale — and we will look back cheerfully to these early days, and make a romantic story for the young people (and if a little more romantic than truth may warrant, it will be no harm) out of our severe trials and hardships. In a century or two, we shall every one of us be mythical personages, or exceedingly picturesque and poetical ones, at all events. They will have a great public hall, in which your portrait, and mine, and twenty other faces that are living now, shall be hung up; and as for me, I will be painted in my shirt-sleeves, and with the sleeves rolled up, to show my muscular development. What stories will be rife among them about our mighty strength," continued I, lifting a big stone and putting it into its place; "though our posterity will really be far stronger than ourselves, after several generations of a simple, natural, and active life! What legends of Zenobia's beauty, and Priscilla's slender and shadowy grace, and those mysterious qualities which make her seem diaphanous with spiritual light! In due course of ages, we must all figure heroically in an Epic Poem; and we will ourselves — at least, I will — bend unseen over the future poet, and lend him inspiration, while he writes it."

"You seem," said Hollingsworth, "to be trying how much non-sense you can pour out in a breath."

"I wish you would see fit to comprehend," retorted I, "that the profoundest wisdom must be mingled with nine-tenths of nonsense; else it is not worth the breath that utters it. But I do long for the cottages to be built, that the creeping plants may begin to run over them, and the moss to gather on the walls, and the trees — which we will set out — to cover them with a breadth of shadow. This spick-and-span novelty does not quite suit my taste. It is time, too, for children to be born among us. The first-born child is still to come! And I shall never feel as if this were a real, practical, as well as poetical, system of human life, until somebody has sanctified it by death."

"A pretty occasion for martyrdom, truly!" said Hollingsworth.

"As good as any other!" I replied. "I wonder, Hollingsworth, who, of all these strong men, and fair women and maidens, is doomed the first to die. Would it not be well, even before we have absolute need of it, to fix upon a spot for a cemetery? Let us choose the rudest, roughest, most uncultivable spot, for Death's garden-ground; and Death shall teach us to beautify it, grave by grave. By our sweet, calm way of dying, and the airy elegance out of which we will shape our funeral rites, and the cheerful allegories which we will model into tombstones, the final scene shall lose its terrors; so that, hereafter, it may be happiness to live, and bliss to die. None of us must die young. Yet, should Providence ordain it so, the event shall not be sorrowful, but affect us with a tender, delicious, only half-melancholy, and almost smiling pathos!"

"That is to say," muttered Hollingsworth, "you will die like a Heathen, as you certainly live like one! But, listen to me, Coverdale. Your fantastic anticipations make me discern, all the more forcibly, what a wretched, unsubstantial scheme is this, on which we have wasted a precious summer of our lives. Do you seriously imagine that any such realities as you, and many others here, have dreamed of, will ever be brought to pass?"

"Certainly, I do," said I. "Of course, when the reality comes, it will wear the every-day, common-place, dusty, and rather homely garb, that reality always does put on. But, setting aside the ideal charm, I hold, that our highest anticipations have a solid footing on common-sense."

"You only half believe what you say," rejoined Hollingsworth; "and as for me, I neither have faith in your dream, nor would care the value of this pebble for its realization, were that possible. And what more do you want of it? It has given you a theme for poetry. Let that content you. But, now, I ask you to be, at last, a man of sobriety and earnestness, and aid me in an enterprise which is worth all our strength, and the strength of a thousand mightier than we!"

There can be no need of giving, in detail, the conversation that ensued. It is enough to say, that Hollingsworth once more brought forward his rigid and unconquerable idea; a scheme for the reformation of the wicked by methods moral, intellectual, and industrial, by the sympathy of pure, humble, and yet exalted minds, and by opening to his pupils the possibility of a worthier life than that which had become their fate. It appeared, unless he over-estimated his own means, that Hollingsworth held it at his choice (and he did so choose) to obtain possession of the very ground on which we had planted our Community, and which had not yet been made irrevocably ours, by purchase. It was just the foundation that he desired. Our beginnings might readily be adapted to his great end. The arrangements, already completed, would work quietly into his system. So plausible looked his theory, and, more than that, so practical; such an air of reasonableness had he, by patient thought, thrown over it; each segment of it was contrived to dove-tail into all the rest, with such a complicated applicability; and so ready was he with a response for every objection — that, really, so far as logic and argument went, he had the matter all his own way.

"But," said I, "whence can you, having no means of your own, derive the enormous capital which is essential to this experiment? State-street,[1] I imagine, would not draw its purse-strings very liberally, in aid of such a speculation."

"I have the funds — as much, at least, as is needed for a commencement — at command," he answered. "They can be produced within a month, if necessary."

My thoughts reverted to Zenobia. It could only be her wealth which Hollingsworth was appropriating so lavishly. And on what conditions was it to be had? Did she fling it into the scheme, with the uncalculating generosity that characterizes a woman, when it is her impulse to be generous at all? And did she fling herself along with it? But Hollingsworth did not volunteer an explanation.

"And have you no regrets," I inquired, "in overthrowing this fair system of our new life, which has been planned so deeply, and is now beginning to flourish so hopefully around us? How beautiful it is,

---

[1]*State-street:* The center of finance, banking, and commerce in Boston.

and, so far as we can yet see, how practicable! The Ages have waited for us, and here we are — the very first that have essayed to carry on our mortal existence, in love, and mutual help! Hollingsworth, I would be loth to take the ruin of this enterprise upon my conscience!"

"Then let it rest wholly upon mine!" he answered, knitting his black brows. "I see through the system. It is full of defects — irremediable and damning ones! — from first to last, there is nothing else! I grasp it in my hand, and find no substance whatever. There is not human nature in it!"

"Why are you so secret in your operations?" I asked. "God forbid that I should accuse you of intentional wrong; but the besetting sin of a philanthropist, it appears to me, is apt to be a moral obliquity. His sense of honor ceases to be the sense of other honorable men. At some point of his course — I know not exactly when nor where — he is tempted to palter with the right, and can scarcely forbear persuading himself that the importance of his public ends renders it allowable to throw aside his private conscience. Oh, my dear friend, beware this error! If you meditate the overthrow of this establishment, call together our companions, state your design, support it with all your eloquence, but allow them an opportunity of defending themselves!"

"It does not suit me," said Hollingsworth. "Nor is it my duty to do so."

"I think it is!" replied I.

Hollingsworth frowned; not in passion, but like Fate, inexorably.

"I will not argue the point," said he. "What I desire to know of you is — and you can tell me in one word — whether I am to look for your co-operation in this great scheme of good. Take it up with me! Be my brother in it! It offers you (what you have told me, over and over again, that you most need) a purpose in life, worthy of the extremest self-devotion — worthy of martyrdom, should God so order it! In this view, I present it to you. You can greatly benefit mankind. Your peculiar faculties, as I shall direct them, are capable of being so wrought into this enterprise, that not one of them need lie idle. Strike hands with me; and, from this moment, you shall never again feel the languor and vague wretchedness of an indolent or half-occupied man! There may be no more aimless beauty in your life; but, in its stead, there shall be strength, courage, immitigable will — everything that a manly and generous nature should desire! We shall succeed! We shall have done our best for this miserable world; and happiness (which never comes but incidentally) will come to us unawares!"

It seemed his intention to say no more. But, after he had quite broken off, his deep eyes filled with tears, and he held out both his hands to me.

"Coverdale," he murmured, "there is not the man in this wide world, whom I can love as I could you. Do not forsake me!"

As I look back upon this scene, through the coldness and dimness of so many years, there is still a sensation as if Hollingsworth had caught hold of my heart, and were pulling it towards him with an almost irresistible force. It is a mystery to me, how I withstood it. But, in truth, I saw in his scheme of philanthropy nothing but what was odious. A loathsomeness that was to be forever in my daily work! A great, black ugliness of sin, which he proposed to collect out of a thousand human hearts, and that we should spend our lives in an experiment of transmuting it into virtue! Had I but touched his extended hand, Hollingsworth's magnetism would perhaps have penetrated me with his own conception of all these matters. But I stood aloof. I fortified myself with doubts whether his strength of purpose had not been too gigantic for his integrity, impelling him to trample on considerations that should have been paramount to every other.

"Is Zenobia to take a part in your enterprise?" I asked.

"She is," said Hollingsworth.

"She! — the beautiful! — the gorgeous!" I exclaimed. "And how have you prevailed with such a woman to work in this squalid element?"

"Through no base methods, as you seem to suspect," he answered, "but by addressing whatever is best and noblest in her."

Hollingsworth was looking on the ground. But, as he often did so — generally, indeed, in his habitual moods of thought — I could not judge whether it was from any special unwillingness now to meet my eyes. What it was that dictated my next question, I cannot precisely say. Nevertheless, it rose so inevitably into my mouth, and, as it were, asked itself, so involuntarily, that there must needs have been an aptness in it.

"What is to become of Priscilla?"

Hollingsworth looked at me fiercely, and with glowing eyes. He could not have shown any other kind of expression than that, had he meant to strike me with a sword.

"Why do you bring in the names of these women?" said he, after a moment of pregnant silence. "What have they to do with the proposal which I make you? I must have your answer! Will you devote yourself, and sacrifice all to this great end, and be my friend of friends, forever?"

"In Heaven's name, Hollingsworth," cried I, getting angry, and glad to be angry, because so only was it possible to oppose his tremendous concentrativeness and indomitable will, "cannot you conceive that a man may wish well to the world, and struggle for its good, on some other plan than precisely that which you have laid down? And will you cast off a friend, for no unworthiness, but merely because he stands upon his right, as an individual being, and looks at matters through his own optics, instead of yours?"

"Be with me," said Hollingsworth, "or be against me! There is no third choice for you."

"Take this, then, as my decision," I answered. "I doubt the wisdom of your scheme. Furthermore, I greatly fear that the methods, by which you allow yourself to pursue it, are such as cannot stand the scrutiny of an unbiassed conscience."

"And you will not join me?"

"No!"

I never said the word — and certainly can never have it to say, hereafter — that cost me a thousandth part so hard an effort as did that one syllable. The heart-pang was not merely figurative, but an absolute torture of the breast. I was gazing steadfastly at Hollingsworth. It seemed to me that it struck him, too, like a bullet. A ghastly paleness — always so terrific on a swarthy face — overspread his features. There was a convulsive movement of his throat, as if he were forcing down some words that struggled and fought for utterance. Whether words of anger, or words of grief, I cannot tell; although, many and many a time, I have vainly tormented myself with conjecturing which of the two they were. One other appeal to my friendship — such as once, already, Hollingsworth had made — taking me in the revulsion that followed a strenuous exercise of opposing will, would completely have subdued me. But he left the matter there.

"Well!" said he.

And that was all! I should have been thankful for one word more, even had it shot me through the heart, as mine did him. But he did not speak it; and, after a few moments, with one accord, we set to work again, repairing the stone-fence. Hollingsworth, I observed, wrought like a Titan,[2] and, for my own part, I lifted stones which, at

---

[2]*Titan:* In ancient Greek mythology, the family or race of giants whom Zeus and the Olympian gods deposed. See Hesiod's *Theogony.*

this day — or, in a calmer mood, at that one — I should no more have thought it possible to stir, than to carry off the gates of Gaza[3] on my back.

XVI. LEAVE-TAKINGS

A few days after the tragic passage-at-arms between Hollingsworth and me, I appeared at the dinner-table, actually dressed in a coat, instead of my customary blouse; with a satin cravat, too, a white vest, and several other things that made me seem strange and outlandish to myself. As for my companions, this unwonted spectacle caused a great stir upon the wooden benches, that bordered either side of our homely board.

"What's in the wind now, Miles?" asked one of them. "Are you deserting us?"

"Yes, for a week or two," said I. "It strikes me that my health demands a little relaxation of labor, and a short visit to the seaside, during the dog-days."[1]

"You look like it!" grumbled Silas Foster, not greatly pleased with the idea of losing an efficient laborer, before the stress of the season was well over. "Now, here's a pretty fellow! His shoulders have broadened, a matter of six inches, since he came among us; he can do his day's work, if he likes, with any man or ox on the farm; — and yet he talks about going to the seashore for his health! Well, well, old woman," added he to his wife, "let me have a platefull of that pork and cabbage! I begin to feel in a very weakly way. When the others have had their turn, you and I will take a jaunt to Newport or Saratoga!"[2]

"Well, but, Mr. Foster," said I, "you must allow me to take a little breath."

"Breath!" retorted the old yeoman. "Your lungs have the play of a pair of blacksmith's bellows, already. What on earth do you want more? But go along! I understand the business. We shall never see your face here again. Here ends the reformation of the world, so far as Miles Coverdale has a hand in it!"

---

[3]*the gates of Gaza:* See Judges 16:1–3. The inhabitants of Gaza tried to trap the mighty hero Samson by locking the city gates, but he lifted off the gates and carried them away on his shoulders.

[1]*dog-days:* The period of hot, sultry days from July to September.

[2]*Newport or Saratoga:* Popular summer resorts were located in Newport, Rhode Island, and Saratoga, New York.

"By no means," I replied. "I am resolute to die in the last ditch, for the good of the cause."

"Die in a ditch!" muttered gruff Silas, with genuine Yankee intolerance of any intermission of toil, except on Sunday, the Fourth of July, the autumnal Cattle-show, Thanksgiving, or the annual Fast.[3] "Die in a ditch! I believe in my conscience you would, if there were no steadier means than your own labor to keep you out of it!"

The truth was, that an intolerable discontent and irksomeness had come over me. Blithedale was no longer what it had been. Everything was suddenly faded. The sun-burnt and arid aspect of our woods and pastures, beneath the August sky, did but imperfectly symbolize the lack of dew and moisture that, since yesterday, as it were, had blighted my fields of thought, and penetrated to the innermost and shadiest of my contemplative recesses. The change will be recognized by many, who, after a period of happiness, have endeavored to go on with the same kind of life, in the same scene, in spite of the alteration or withdrawal of some principal circumstance. They discover (what heretofore, perhaps, they had not known) that it was this which gave the bright color and vivid reality to the whole affair.

I stood on other terms than before, not only with Hollingsworth, but with Zenobia and Priscilla. As regarded the two latter, it was that dreamlike and miserable sort of change that denies you the privilege to complain, because you can assert no positive injury, nor lay your finger on anything tangible. It is a matter which you do not see, but feel, and which, when you try to analyze it, seems to lose its very existence, and resolve itself into a sickly humor of your own. Your understanding, possibly, may put faith in this denial. But your heart will not so easily rest satisfied. It incessantly remonstrates, though, most of the time, in a bass-note, which you do not separately distinguish; but, now-and-then, with a sharp cry, importunate to be heard, and resolute to claim belief. 'Things are not as they were!' — it keeps saying — 'You shall not impose on me! I will never be quiet! I will throb painfully! I will be heavy, and desolate, and shiver with cold! For I, your deep heart, know when to be miserable, as once I knew when to be happy! All is changed for us! You are beloved no more!' And, were my life to be spent over again, I

---

[3]*the annual Fast:* The custom of an annual "fast day" for prayer and repentance began among the Puritans in the seventeenth century.

would invariably lend my ear to this Cassandra[4] of the inward depths, however clamorous the music and the merriment of a more superficial region.

My outbreak with Hollingsworth, though never definitely known to our associates, had really an effect upon the moral atmosphere of the Community. It was incidental to the closeness of relationship, into which we had brought ourselves, that an unfriendly state of feeling could not occur between any two members, without the whole society being more or less commoted[5] and made uncomfortable thereby. This species of nervous sympathy (though a pretty characteristic enough, sentimentally considered, and apparently betokening an actual bond of love among us) was yet found rather inconvenient in its practical operation; mortal tempers being so infirm and variable as they are. If one of us happened to give his neighbor a box on the ear, the tingle was immediately felt, on the same side of everybody's head. Thus, even on the supposition that we were far less quarrelsome than the rest of the world, a great deal of time was necessarily wasted in rubbing our ears.

Musing on all these matters, I felt an inexpressible longing for at least a temporary novelty. I thought of going across the Rocky Mountains, or to Europe, or up the Nile — of offering myself a volunteer on the Exploring Expedition[6] — of taking a ramble of years, no matter in what direction, and coming back on the other side of the world. Then, should the colonists of Blithedale have established their enterprise on a permanent basis, I might fling aside my pilgrim-staff and dusty shoon,[7] and rest as peacefully here as elsewhere. Or, in case Hollingsworth should occupy the ground with his School of Reform, as he now purposed, I might plead earthly guilt enough, by that time, to give me what I was inclined to think the only trustworthy hold on his affections. Meanwhile, before deciding on any ultimate plan, I determined to remove myself to a little distance, and take an exterior view of what we had all been about.

In truth, it was dizzy work, amid such fermentation of opinions as was going on in the general brain of the Community. It was a kind of

---

[4]*Cassandra:* Daughter of King Priam of Troy, whose prophecies and warnings were not believed. See Homer, *Iliad*, 6:252, 13:361–82, 24:699.

[5]*commoted:* Agitated, upset, confused.

[6]*the Exploring Expedition:* In the spring of 1837, Hawthorne's friends, including Horatio Bridge and Franklin Pierce, tried unsuccessfully to secure for him the post of official historian on an exploring expedition to the South Seas and Antarctica.

[7]*shoon:* Shoes.

Bedlam,[8] for the time being; although, out of the very thoughts that were wildest and most destructive, might grow a wisdom, holy, calm, and pure, and that should incarnate itself with the substance of a noble and happy life. But, as matters now were, I felt myself (and having a decided tendency toward the actual, I never liked to feel it) getting quite out of my reckoning, with regard to the existing state of the world. I was beginning to lose the sense of what kind of a world it was, among innumerable schemes of what it might or ought to be. It was impossible, situated as we were, not to imbibe the idea that everything in nature and human existence was fluid, or fast becoming so; that the crust of the Earth, in many places, was broken, and its whole surface portentously upheaving; that it was a day of crisis, and that we ourselves were in the critical vortex. Our great globe floated in the atmosphere of infinite space like an unsubstantial bubble. No sagacious man will long retain his sagacity, if he live exclusively among reformers and progressive people, without periodically returning into the settled system of things, to correct himself by a new observation from that old stand-point.

It was now time for me, therefore, to go and hold a little talk with the conservatives, the writers of the North American Review,[9] the merchants, the politicians, the Cambridge men,[10] and all those respectable old blockheads, who still, in this intangibility and mistiness of affairs, kept a death-grip on one or two ideas which had not come into vogue since yesterday-morning.

The brethren took leave of me with cordial kindness; and as for the sisterhood, I had serious thoughts of kissing them all round, but forbore to do so, because, in all such general salutations, the penance is fully equal to the pleasure. So I kissed none of them, and nobody, to say the truth, seemed to expect it.

"Do you wish me," I said to Zenobia, "to announce, in town, and at the watering-places,[11] your purpose to deliver a course of lectures on the rights of women?"

"Women possess no rights," said Zenobia, with a half-melancholy

---

[8]*Bedlam:* Popular name for the Hospital of St. Mary of Bethlehem in London, an insane asylum.

[9]*North American Review:* Quarterly, published in Boston (founded 1815), devoted to literature, criticism, history, and social/political commentary; generally conservative in its views.

[10]*Cambridge men:* Men affiliated with or connected in some way to Harvard University, in Cambridge, Massachusetts.

[11]*watering-places:* Health or recreational resorts.

smile; "or, at all events, only little girls and grandmothers would have the force to exercise them."

She gave me her hand, freely and kindly, and looked at me, I thought, with a pitying expression in her eyes; nor was there any settled light of joy in them, on her own behalf, but a troubled and passionate flame, flickering and fitful.

"I regret, on the whole, that you are leaving us," she said; "and all the more, since I feel that this phase of our life is finished, and can never be lived over again. Do you know, Mr. Coverdale, that I have been several times on the point of making you my confidant, for lack of a better and wiser one? But you are too young to be my Father Confessor; and you would not thank me for treating you like one of those good little handmaidens, who share the bosom-secrets of a tragedy-queen!"

"I would at least be loyal and faithful," answered I, "and would counsel you with an honest purpose, if not wisely."

"Yes," said Zenobia, "you would be only too wise — too honest. Honesty and wisdom are such a delightful pastime, at another person's expense!"

"Ah, Zenobia," I exclaimed, "if you would but let me speak!"

"By no means," she replied; "especially when you have just resumed the whole series of social conventionalisms, together with that straight-bodied coat. I would as lief open my heart to a lawyer or a clergyman! No, no, Mr. Coverdale; if I choose a counsellor, in the present aspect of my affairs, it must be either an angel or a madman; and I rather apprehend that the latter would be likeliest of the two to speak the fitting word. It needs a wild steersman when we voyage through Chaos![12] The anchor is up! Farewell!"

Priscilla, as soon as dinner was over, had betaken herself into a corner, and set to work on a little purse. As I approached her, she let her eyes rest on me, with a calm, serious look; for, with all her delicacy of nerves, there was a singular self-possession in Priscilla, and her sensibilities seemed to lie sheltered from ordinary commotion, like the water in a deep well.

"Will you give me that purse, Priscilla," said I, "as a parting keepsake?"

"Yes," she answered; "if you will wait till it is finished."

---

[12]*Chaos:* In Greek mythology, the confused, unorganized state of primordial matter before creation.

"I must not wait, even for that," I replied. "Shall I find you here, on my return?"

"I never wish to go away," said she.

"I have sometimes thought," observed I, smiling, "that you, Priscilla, are a little prophetess; or, at least, that you have spiritual intimations respecting matters which are dark to us grosser people. If that be the case, I should like to ask you what is about to happen. For I am tormented with a strong foreboding, that, were I to return even so soon as tomorrow morning, I should find everything changed. Have you any impressions of this nature?"

"Ah, no!" said Priscilla, looking at me apprehensively. "If any such misfortune is coming, the shadow has not reached me yet. Heaven forbid! I should be glad if there might never be any change, but one summer follow another, and all just like this!"

"No summer ever came back, and no two summers ever were alike," said I, with a degree of Orphic wisdom[13] that astonished myself. "Times change, and people change; and if our hearts do not change as readily, so much the worse for us! Good bye, Priscilla!"

I gave her hand a pressure, which, I think, she neither resisted nor returned. Priscilla's heart was deep, but of small compass; it had room but for a very few dearest ones, among whom she never reckoned me.

On the door-step, I met Hollingsworth. I had a momentary impulse to hold out my hand, or, at least, to give a parting nod, but resisted both. When a real and strong affection has come to an end, it is not well to mock the sacred past with any show of those commonplace civilities that belong to ordinary intercourse. Being dead henceforth to him, and he to me, there could be no propriety in our chilling one another with the touch of two corpse-like hands, or playing at looks of courtesy with eyes that were impenetrable beneath the glaze and the film. We passed, therefore, as if mutually invisible.

I can nowise explain what sort of whim, prank, or perversity it was, that, after all these leave-takings, induced me to go to the pig-stye and take leave of the swine! There they lay, buried as deeply among the straw as they could burrow, four huge black grunters, the very symbols of slothful ease and sensual comfort. They were asleep, drawing short and heavy breaths, which heaved their big sides up and

---

[13]*Orphic wisdom:* Mystic, esoteric, oracular wisdom; from Orphism, ancient Greek religion, deriving from Orpheus, its founder, the poet-musician of Greek mythology. See Ovid, *Metamorphoses*, 10:1–105, 11:1–84.

down. Unclosing their eyes, however, at my approach, they looked dimly forth at the outer world, and simultaneously uttered a gentle grunt; not putting themselves to the trouble of an additional breath for that particular purpose, but grunting with their ordinary inhalation. They were involved, and almost stifled, and buried alive, in their own corporeal substance. The very unreadiness and oppression, wherewith these greasy citizens gained breath enough to keep their life-machinery in sluggish movement, appeared to make them only the more sensible of the ponderous and fat satisfaction of their existence. Peeping at me, an instant, out of their small, red, hardly perceptible eyes, they dropt asleep again; yet not so far asleep but that their unctuous bliss was still present to them, betwixt dream and reality.

"You must come back in season to eat part of a spare-rib," said Silas Foster, giving my hand a mighty squeeze. "I shall have these fat fellows hanging up by the heels, heads downward, pretty soon, I tell you!"

"Oh, cruel Silas, what a horrible idea!" cried I. "All the rest of us, men, women, and live-stock, save only these four porkers, are bedevilled with one grief or another; they alone are happy — and you mean to cut their throats, and eat them! It would be more for the general comfort to let them eat us; and bitter and sour morsels we should be!"

XVII. THE HOTEL

Arriving in town, (where my bachelor-rooms, long before this time, had received some other occupant,) I established myself, for a day or two, in a certain respectable hotel. It was situated somewhat aloof from my former track in life; my present mood inclining me to avoid most of my old companions, from whom I was now sundered by other interests, and who would have been likely enough to amuse themselves at the expense of the amateur working-man. The hotel-keeper put me into a back-room of the third story of his spacious establishment. The day was lowering, with occasional gusts of rain, and an ugly-tempered east-wind, which seemed to come right off the chill and melancholy sea, hardly mitigated by sweeping over the roofs, and amalgamating itself with the dusky element of city-smoke. All the effeminacy of past days had returned upon me at once. Summer as it still was, I ordered a coal-fire in the rusty grate, and was glad to find myself growing a little too warm with an artificial temperature.

My sensations were those of a traveller, long sojourning in remote regions, and at length sitting down again amid customs once familiar. There was a newness and an oldness, oddly combining themselves into one impression. It made me acutely sensible how strange a piece of mosaic-work had lately been wrought into my life. True; if you look at it in one way, it had been only a summer in the country. But, considered in a profounder relation, it was part of another age, a different state of society, a segment of an existence peculiar in its aims and methods, a leaf of some mysterious volume, interpolated into the current history which Time was writing off. At one moment, the very circumstances now surrounding me — my coal-fire, and the dingy room in the bustling hotel — appeared far off and intangible. The next instant, Blithedale looked vague, as if it were at a distance both in time and space, and so shadowy, that a question might be raised whether the whole affair had been anything more than the thoughts of a speculative man. I had never before experienced a mood that so robbed the actual world of its solidity. It nevertheless involved a charm, on which — a devoted epicure of my own emotions — I resolved to pause, and enjoy the moral sillabub[1] until quite dissolved away.

Whatever had been my taste for solitude and natural scenery, yet the thick, foggy, stifled element of cities, the entangled life of many men together, sordid as it was, and empty of the beautiful, took quite as strenuous a hold upon my mind. I felt as if there could never be enough of it. Each characteristic sound was too suggestive to be passed over, unnoticed. Beneath and around me, I heard the stir of the hotel; the loud voices of guests, landlord, or barkeeper; steps echoing on the staircase; the ringing of a bell, announcing arrivals or departures; the porter lumbering past my door with baggage, which he thumped down upon the floors of neighboring chambers; the lighter feet of chamber-maids scudding along the passages; — it is ridiculous to think what an interest they had for me. From the street, came the tumult of the pavements, pervading the whole house with a continual uproar, so broad and deep that only an unaccustomed ear would dwell upon it. A company of city-soldiery, with a full military band, marched in front of the hotel, invisible to me, but stirringly audible both by its foot-tramp and the clangor of its instruments. Once

[1]*sillabub:* Sweet dessert made with cream and wine or liquor.

or twice, all the city-bells jangled together, announcing a fire, which brought out the engine-men and their machines, like an army with its artillery rushing to battle. Hour by hour, the clocks in many steeples responded one to another. In some public hall, not a great way off, there seemed to be an exhibition of a mechanical diorama;[2] for, three times during the day, occurred a repetition of obstreperous music, winding up with the rattle of imitative cannon and musketry, and a huge final explosion. Then ensued the applause of the spectators, with clap of hands, and thump of sticks, and the energetic pounding of their heels. All this was just as valuable, in its way, as the sighing of the breeze among the birch-trees, that overshadowed Eliot's pulpit.

Yet I felt a hesitation about plunging into this muddy tide of human activity and pastime. It suited me better, for the present, to linger on the brink, or hover in the air above it. So I spent the first day, and the greater part of the second, in the laziest manner possible, in a rocking-chair, inhaling the fragrance of a series of cigars, with my legs and slippered feet horizontally disposed, and in my hand a novel, purchased of a railroad bibliopolist.[3] The gradual waste of my cigar accomplished itself with an easy and gentle expenditure of breath. My book was of the dullest, yet had a sort of sluggish flow, like that of a stream in which your boat is as often aground as afloat. Had there been a more impetuous rush, a more absorbing passion of the narrative, I should the sooner have struggled out of its uneasy current, and have given myself up to the swell and subsidence of my thoughts. But, as it was, the torpid life of the book served as an unobtrusive accompaniment to the life within me and about me. At intervals, however, when its effect grew a little too soporific — not for my patience, but for the possibility of keeping my eyes open — I bestirred myself, started from the rocking-chair, and looked out of the window.

A gray sky; the weathercock of a steeple, that rose beyond the opposite range of buildings, pointing from the eastward; a sprinkle of small, spiteful-looking raindrops on the windowpane! In that ebb-tide of my energies, had I thought of venturing abroad, these tokens would have checked the abortive purpose.

After several such visits to the window, I found myself getting pretty well acquainted with that little portion of the backside of the universe which it presented to my view. Over against the hotel and its

[2]*diorama:* Miniature three-dimensional scenic representation.
[3]*bibliopolist:* Bookseller, especially a dealer in rare, strange, or curious books.

adjacent houses, at the distance of forty or fifty yards, was the rear of a range of buildings, which appeared to be spacious, modern, and calculated for fashionable residences. The interval between was apportioned into grass-plots, and here and there an apology for a garden, pertaining severally to these dwellings. There were apple-trees, and pear and peach-trees, too, the fruit on which looked singularly large, luxuriant, and abundant; as well it might, in a situation so warm and sheltered, and where the soil had doubtless been enriched to a more than natural fertility. In two or three places, grape-vines clambered upon trellises, and bore clusters already purple, and promising the richness of Malta or Madeira[4] in their ripened juice. The blighting winds of our rigid climate could not molest these trees and vines; the sunshine, though descending late into this area, and too early intercepted by the height of the surrounding houses, yet lay tropically there, even when less than temperate in every other region. Dreary as was the day, the scene was illuminated by not a few sparrows and other birds, which spread their wings, and flitted and fluttered, and alighted now here, now there, and busily scratched their food out of the wormy earth. Most of these winged people seemed to have their domicile in a robust and healthy buttonwood-tree.[5] It aspired upward, high above the roof of the houses, and spread a dense head of foliage half across the area.

There was a cat — as there invariably is, in such places — who evidently thought herself entitled to all the privileges of forest-life, in this close heart of city-conventionalisms. I watched her creeping along the low, flat roofs of the offices, descending a flight of wooden steps, gliding among the grass, and besieging the buttonwood-tree, with murderous purpose against its feathered citizens. But, after all, they were birds of city-breeding, and doubtless knew how to guard themselves against the peculiar perils of their position.

Bewitching to my fancy are all those nooks and crannies, where Nature, like a stray partridge, hides her head among the long-established haunts of men! It is likewise to be remarked, as a general rule, that there is far more of the picturesque, more truth to native and characteristic tendencies, and vastly greater suggestiveness, in the back view of a residence, whether in town or country, than in its front. The latter is always artificial; it is meant for the world's eye,

---

[4]*Malta or Madeira:* The island of Malta in the Mediterranean and the Madeira islands in the eastern Atlantic off the coast of Africa were noted for their fine wines.
[5]*buttonwood-tree:* Sycamore.

and is therefore a veil and a concealment. Realities keep in the rear, and put forward an advance-guard of show and humbug. The posterior aspect of any old farm-house, behind which a railroad has unexpectedly been opened, is so different from that looking upon the immemorial highway, that the spectator gets new ideas of rural life and individuality, in the puff or two of steam-breath which shoots him past the premises. In a city, the distinction between what is offered to the public, and what is kept for the family, is certainly not less striking.

But, to return to my window, at the back of the hotel. Together with a due contemplation of the fruit-trees, the grape-vines, the buttonwood-tree, the cat, the birds, and many other particulars, I failed not to study the row of fashionable dwellings to which all these appertained. Here, it must be confessed, there was a general sameness. From the upper-story to the first floor, they were so much alike that I could only conceive of the inhabitants as cut out on one identical pattern, like little wooden toy-people of German manufacture. One long, united roof, with its thousands of slates glittering in the rain, extended over the whole. After the distinctness of separate characters, to which I had recently been accustomed, it perplexed and annoyed me not to be able to resolve this combination of human interests into well-defined elements. It seemed hardly worth while for more than one of those families to be in existence; since they all had the same glimpse of the sky, all looked into the same area, all received just their equal share of sunshine through the front windows, and all listened to precisely the same noises of the street on which they bordered. Men are so much alike, in their nature, that they grow intolerable unless varied by their circumstances.

Just about this time, a waiter entered my room. The truth was, I had rung the bell and ordered a sherry-cobbler.[6]

"Can you tell me," I inquired, "what families reside in any of those houses opposite?"

"The one right opposite is a rather stylish boarding-house," said the waiter. "Two of the gentlemen-boarders keep horses at the stable of our establishment. They do things in very good style, sir, the people that live there."

I might have found out nearly as much for myself, on examining the house a little more closely. In one of the upper chambers, I saw a young man in a dressing gown, standing before the glass and brush-

---

[6]*sherry-cobbler:* A sweet and sour drink made with sherry, lemon juice, and sugar.

ing his hair, for a quarter-of-an-hour together. He then spent an equal space of time in the elaborate arrangement of his cravat, and finally made his appearance in a dress-coat, which I suspected to be newly come from the tailor's, and now first put on for a dinner-party. At a window of the next story below, two children, prettily dressed, were looking out. By-and-by, a middle-aged gentleman came softly behind them, kissed the little girl, and playfully pulled the little boy's ear. It was a papa, no doubt, just come in from his counting-room or office; and anon appeared mamma, stealing as softly behind papa, as he had stolen behind the children, and laying her hand on his shoulder to surprise him. Then followed a kiss between papa and mamma, but a noiseless one; for the children did not turn their heads.

"I bless God for these good folks!" thought I to myself. "I have not seen a prettier bit of nature, in all my summer in the country, than they have shown me here in a rather stylish boarding-house. I will pay them a little more attention, by-and-by."

On the first floor, an iron balustrade ran along in front of the tall, and spacious windows, evidently belonging to a back drawing-room; and, far into the interior, through the arch of the sliding-doors, I could discern a gleam from the windows of the front apartment. There were no signs of present occupancy in this suite of rooms; the curtains being enveloped in a protective covering, which allowed but a small portion of their crimson material to be seen. But two house-maids were industriously at work; so that there was good prospect that the boarding-house might not long suffer from the absence of its most expensive and profitable guests. Meanwhile, until they should appear, I cast my eyes downward to the lower regions. There, in the dusk that so early settles into such places, I saw the red glow of the kitchen-range; the hot cook, or one of her subordinates, with a ladle in her hand, came to draw a cool breath at the back-door; as soon as she disappeared, an Irish man-servant, in a white jacket, crept slily forth and threw away the fragments of a china-dish, which unquestionably he had just broken. Soon afterwards, a lady, showily dressed, with a curling front of what must have been false hair, and reddish brown, I suppose, in hue — though my remoteness allowed me only to guess at such particulars — this respectable mistress of the boarding-house made a momentary transit across the kitchen-window, and appeared no more. It was her final, comprehensive glance, in order to make sure that soup, fish, and flesh, were in a proper state of readiness, before the serving up of dinner.

There was nothing else worth noticing about the house; unless it be, that, on the peak of one of the dormer-windows, which opened out of the roof, sat a dove, looking very dreary and forlorn; insomuch that I wondered why she chose to sit there, in the chilly rain, while her kindred were doubtless nestling in a warm and comfortable dove-cote. All at once, this dove spread her wings, and launching herself in the air, came flying so straight across the intervening space, that I fully expected her to alight directly on my window-sill. In the latter part of her course, however, she swerved aside, flew upward, and vanished, as did likewise the slight, fantastic pathos with which I had invested her.

XVIII. THE BOARDING-HOUSE

The next day, as soon as I thought of looking again towards the opposite house, there sat the dove again, on the peak of the same dormer-window!

It was by no means an early hour; for, the preceding evening, I had ultimately mustered enterprise enough to visit the theatre, had gone late to bed, and slept beyond all limit, in my remoteness from Silas Foster's awakening horn. Dreams had tormented me, throughout the night. The train of thoughts which, for months past, had worn a track through my mind, and to escape which was one of my chief objects in leaving Blithedale, kept treading remorselessly to-and-fro, in their old footsteps, while slumber left me impotent to regulate them. It was not till I had quitted my three friends that they first began to encroach upon my dreams. In those of the last night, Hollingsworth and Zenobia, standing on either side of my bed, had bent across it to exchange a kiss of passion. Priscilla, beholding this — for she seemed to be peeping in at the chamber-window — had melted gradually away, and left only the sadness of her expression in my heart. There it still lingered, after I awoke; one of those unreasonable sadnesses that you know not how to deal with, because it involves nothing for common-sense to clutch.

It was a gray and dripping forenoon; gloomy enough in town, and still gloomier in the haunts to which my recollections persisted in transporting me. For, in spite of my efforts to think of something else, I thought how the gusty rain was drifting over the slopes and valleys of our farm; how wet must be the foliage that overshadowed the pulpit-rock; how cheerless, in such a day, my hermitage — the tree-solitude of my owl-like humors — in the vine-encircled heart of the tall pine! It was a phase of home-sickness. I had wrenched myself too suddenly out of an accustomed sphere. There was no choice now, but to bear the pang of whatever heart-strings were snapt asunder, and that illusive torment (like the ache of a limb long ago cut off) by which a past mode of life prolongs itself into the succeeding one. I was full of idle and shapeless regrets. The thought impressed itself upon me, that I had left duties unperformed. With the power, perhaps, to act in the place of destiny, and avert misfortune from my friends, I had resigned them to their fate. That cold tendency, between instinct and intellect, which made me pry with a speculative interest into people's passions and impulses, appeared to have gone far towards unhumanizing my heart.

But a man cannot always decide for himself whether his own heart is cold or warm. It now impresses me, that, if I erred at all, in regard to Hollingsworth, Zenobia, and Priscilla, it was through too much sympathy, rather than too little.

To escape the irksomeness of these meditations, I resumed my post at the window. At first sight, there was nothing new to be noticed. The general aspect of affairs was the same as yesterday, except that the more decided inclemency of to-day had driven the sparrows to shelter, and kept the cat within doors, whence, however, she soon emerged, pursued by the cook, and with what looked like the better half of a roast chicken in her mouth. The young man in the dress-coat was invisible; the two children, in the story below, seemed to be romping about the room, under the superintendence of a nursery-maid. The damask curtains of the drawing-room, on the first floor, were now fully displayed, festooned gracefully from top to bottom of the windows, which extended from the ceiling to the carpet. A narrower window, at the left of the drawing-room, gave light to what was probably a small boudoir, within which I caught the faintest imaginable glimpse of a girl's figure, in airy drapery. Her arm was in regular movement, as if she were busy with her German worsted, or some other such pretty and unprofitable handiwork.

While intent upon making out this girlish shape, I became sensible that a figure had appeared at one of the windows of the drawing-room. There was a presentiment in my mind; or perhaps my first glance, imperfect and sidelong as it was, had sufficed to convey subtle information of the truth. At any rate, it was with no positive surprise, but as if I had all along expected the incident, that, directing my eyes thitherward, I beheld — like a full-length picture, in the space between the heavy festoons of the window-curtains — no other than

Zenobia! At the same instant, my thoughts made sure of the identity of the figure in the boudoir. It could only be Priscilla.

Zenobia was attired, not in the almost rustic costume which she had heretofore worn, but in a fashionable morning-dress. There was, nevertheless, one familiar point. She had, as usual, a flower in her hair, brilliant, and of a rare variety, else it had not been Zenobia. After a brief pause at the window, she turned away, exemplifying, in the few steps that removed her out of sight, that noble and beautiful motion which characterized her as much as any other personal charm. Not one woman in a thousand could move so admirably as Zenobia. Many women can sit gracefully; some can stand gracefully; and a few, perhaps, can assume a series of graceful positions. But natural movement is the result and expression of the whole being, and cannot be well and nobly performed, unless responsive to something in the character. I often used to think that music — light and airy, wild and passionate, or the full harmony of stately marches, in accordance with her varying mood — should have attended Zenobia's footsteps.

I waited for her re-appearance. It was one peculiarity, distinguishing Zenobia from most of her sex, that she needed for her moral well-being, and never would forego, a large amount of physical exercise. At Blithedale, no inclemency of sky or muddiness of earth had ever impeded her daily walks. Here, in town, she probably preferred to tread the extent of the two drawing-rooms, and measure out the miles by spaces of forty feet, rather than bedraggle her skirts over the sloppy pavements. Accordingly, in about the time requisite to pass through the arch of the sliding-doors to the front window, and to return upon her steps, there she stood again, between the festoons of the crimson curtains. But another personage was now added to the scene. Behind Zenobia appeared that face which I had first encountered in the wood-path; the man who had passed, side by side with her, in such mysterious familiarity and estrangement, beneath my vine-curtained hermitage in the tall pine-tree. It was Westervelt. And though he was looking closely over her shoulder, it still seemed to me, as on the former occasion, that Zenobia repelled him — that, perchance, they mutually repelled each other — by some incompatibility of their spheres.

This impression, however, might have been altogether the result of fancy and prejudice, in me. The distance was so great as to obliterate any play of feature, by which I might otherwise have been made a partaker of their counsels.

There now needed only Hollingsworth and old Moodie to complete the knot of characters, whom a real intricacy of events, greatly assisted by my method of insulating them from other relations, had kept so long upon my mental stage, as actors in a drama. In itself, perhaps, it was no very remarkable event, that they should thus come across me, at the moment when I imagined myself free. Zenobia, as I well knew, had retained an establishment in town, and had not unfrequently withdrawn herself from Blithedale, during brief intervals, on one of which occasions she had taken Priscilla along with her. Nevertheless, there seemed something fatal in the coincidence that had borne me to this one spot, of all others in a great city, and transfixed me there, and compelled me again to waste my already wearied sympathies on affairs which were none of mine, and persons who cared little for me. It irritated my nerves; it affected me with a kind of heart-sickness. After the effort which it cost me to fling them off — after consummating my escape, as I thought, from these goblins of flesh and blood, and pausing to revive myself with a breath or two of an atmosphere in which they should have no share — it was a positive despair, to find the same figures arraying themselves before me, and presenting their old problem in a shape that made it more insoluble than ever.

I began to long for a catastrophe. If the noble temper of Hollingsworth's soul were doomed to be utterly corrupted by the too powerful purpose, which had grown out of what was noblest in him; if the rich and generous qualities of Zenobia's womanhood might not save her; if Priscilla must perish by her tenderness and faith, so simple and so devout; — then be it so! Let it all come! As for me, I would look on, as it seemed my part to do, understandingly, if my intellect could fathom the meaning and the moral, and, at all events, reverently and sadly. The curtain fallen, I would pass onward with my poor individual life, which was now attenuated of much of its proper substance, and diffused among many alien interests.

Meanwhile, Zenobia and her companion had retreated from the window. Then followed an interval, during which I directed my eyes towards the figure in the boudoir. Most certainly it was Priscilla, although dressed with a novel and fanciful elegance. The vague perception of it, as viewed so far off, impressed me as if she had suddenly passed out of a chrysalis state and put forth wings. Her hands were not now in motion. She had dropt her work and sat with her head thrown back, in the same attitude that I had seen several times

before, when she seemed to be listening to an imperfectly distinguished sound.

Again the two figures in the drawing-room became visible. They
were now a little withdrawn from the window, face to face, and, as I
could see by Zenobia's emphatic gestures, were discussing some subject in which she, at least, felt a passionate concern. By-and-by, she
broke away, and vanished beyond my ken. Westervelt approached
the window, and leaned his forehead against a pane of glass, displaying the sort of smile on his handsome features which, when I before
met him, had let me into the secret of his gold-bordered teeth. Every
human being, when given over to the Devil, is sure to have the wizard
mark upon him, in one form or another. I fancied that this smile,
with its peculiar revelation, was the Devil's signet on the Professor.

This man, as I had soon reason to know, was endowed with a cat-
like circumspection; and though precisely the most unspiritual quality
in the world, it was almost as effective as spiritual insight, in making
him acquainted with whatever it suited him to discover. He now
proved it, considerably to my discomfiture, by detecting and recognizing me, at my post of observation. Perhaps I ought to have blushed
at being caught in such an evident scrutiny of Professor Westervelt
and his affairs. Perhaps I did blush. Be that as it might, I retained
presence of mind enough not to make my position yet more irksome,
by the poltroonery[1] of drawing back.

Westervelt looked into the depths of the drawing-room, and beckoned. Immediately afterwards, Zenobia appeared at the window,
with color much heightened, and eyes which, as my conscience whispered me, were shooting bright arrows, barbed with scorn, across the
intervening space, directed full at my sensibilities as a gentleman. If
the truth must be told, far as her flight-shot was, those arrows hit the
mark. She signified her recognition of me by a gesture with her head
and hand, comprising at once a salutation and dismissal. The next
moment, she administered one of those pitiless rebukes which a
woman always has at hand, ready for an offence, (and which she so
seldom spares, on due occasion,) by letting down a white linen curtain between the festoons of the damask ones. It fell like the drop-
curtain of a theatre, in the interval between the acts.

Priscilla had disappeared from the boudoir. But the dove still kept
her desolate perch, on the peak of the attic-window.

---

[1]*poltroonery:* Lack of spirit; cowardice.

XIX. ZENOBIA'S DRAWING-ROOM

The remainder of the day, so far as I was concerned, was spent in meditating on these recent incidents. I contrived, and alternately rejected, innumerable methods of accounting for the presence of Zenobia and Priscilla, and the connection of Westervelt with both. It must be owned, too, that I had a keen, revengeful sense of the insult inflicted by Zenobia's scornful recognition, and more particularly by her letting down the curtain; as if such were the proper barrier to be interposed between a character like hers, and a perceptive faculty like mine. For, was mine a mere vulgar curiosity? Zenobia should have known me better than to suppose it. She should have been able to appreciate that quality of the intellect and the heart, which impelled me (often against my own will, and to the detriment of my own comfort) to live in other lives, and to endeavor — by generous sympathies, by delicate intuitions, by taking note of things too slight for record, and by bringing my human spirit into manifold accordance with the companions whom God assigned me — to learn the secret which was hidden even from themselves.

Of all possible observers, methought, a woman, like Zenobia, and a man, like Hollingsworth, should have selected me. And, now, when the event has long been past, I retain the same opinion of my fitness for the office. True; I might have condemned them. Had I been judge, as well as witness, my sentence might have been stern as that of Destiny itself. But, still, no trait of original nobility of character; no struggle against temptation; no iron necessity of will, on the one hand, nor extenuating circumstance to be derived from passion and despair, on the other; no remorse that might co-exist with error, even if powerless to prevent it; no proud repentance, that should claim retribution as a meed — would go unappreciated. True, again, I might give my full assent to the punishment which was sure to follow. But it would be given mournfully, and with undiminished love. And, after all was finished, I would come, as if to gather up the white ashes of those who had perished at the stake, and to tell the world — the wrong being now atoned for — how much had perished there, which it had never yet known how to praise.

I sat in my rocking-chair, too far withdrawn from the window to expose myself to another rebuke, like that already inflicted. My eyes still wandered towards the opposite house, but without effecting any new discoveries. Late in the afternoon, the weathercock on the church-spire indicated a change of wind; the sun shone dimly out, as if the golden wine of its beams were mingled half-and-half with water. Nevertheless, they kindled up the whole range of edifices, threw a glow over the windows, glistened on the wet roofs, and, slowly withdrawing upward, perched upon the chimney-tops; thence they took a higher flight, and lingered an instant on the tip of the spire, making it the final point of more cheerful light in the whole sombre scene. The next moment, it was all gone. The twilight fell into the area like a shower of dusky snow; and before it was quite dark, the gong of the hotel summoned me to tea.

When I returned to my chamber, the glow of an astral lamp[1] was penetrating mistily through the white curtain of Zenobia's drawing-room. The shadow of a passing figure was now-and-then cast upon this medium, but with too vague an outline for even my adventurous conjectures to read the hieroglyphic that it presented.

All at once, it occurred to me how very absurd was my behavior, in thus tormenting myself with crazy hypotheses as to what was going on within that drawing-room, when it was at my option to be personally present there. My relations with Zenobia, as yet un-changed — as a familiar friend, and associated in the same life-long enterprise — gave me the right, and made it no more than kindly courtesy demanded, to call on her. Nothing, except our habitual in-dependence of conventional rules, at Blithedale, could have kept me from sooner recognizing this duty. At all events, it should now be performed.

In compliance with this sudden impulse, I soon found myself actu-ally within the house, the rear of which, for two days past, I had been so sedulously watching. A servant took my card, and immediately re-turning, ushered me up-stairs. On the way, I heard a rich, and, as it were, triumphant burst of music from a piano, in which I felt Zeno-bia's character, although heretofore I had known nothing of her skill upon the instrument. Two or three canary-birds, excited by this gush of sound, sang piercingly, and did their utmost to produce a kindred melody. A bright illumination streamed through the door of the front drawing-room; and I had barely stept across the threshold before Zenobia came forward to meet me, laughing, and with an extended hand.

"Ah, Mr. Coverdale," said she, still smiling, but, as I thought, with a good deal of scornful anger underneath, "it has gratified me to see

---

[1]*astral lamp:* A kind of oil lamp in which the fall of the light is not broken by shadow.

the interest which you continue to take in my affairs! I have long recognized you as a sort of transcendental Yankee, with all the native
propensity of your countrymen to investigate matters that come
within their range, but rendered almost poetical, in your case, by the
refined methods which you adopt for its gratification. After all, it was
an unjustifiable stroke, on my part — was it not? — to let down the
window-curtain!"

"I cannot call it a very wise one," returned I, with a secret bitterness which, no doubt, Zenobia appreciated. "It is really impossible to
hide anything, in this world, to say nothing of the next. All that we
ought to ask, therefore, is, that the witnesses of our conduct, and the
speculators on our motives, should be capable of taking the highest
view which the circumstances of the case may admit. So much being
secured, I, for one, would be most happy in feeling myself followed,
everywhere, by an indefatigable human sympathy."

"We must trust for intelligent sympathy to our guardian angels, if
any there be," said Zenobia. "As long as the only spectator of my
poor tragedy is a young man, at the window of his hotel, I must still
claim the liberty to drop the curtain."

While this passed, as Zenobia's hand was extended, I had applied
the very slightest touch of my fingers to her own. In spite of an external freedom, her manner made me sensible that we stood upon no
real terms of confidence. The thought came sadly across me, how
great was the contrast betwixt this interview and our first meeting.
Then, in the warm light of the country fireside, Zenobia had greeted
me cheerily and hopefully, with a full sisterly grasp of the hand, conveying as much kindness in it as other women could have evinced by
the pressure of both arms around my neck, or by yielding a cheek to
the brotherly salute. The difference was as complete as between her
appearance, at that time — so simply attired, and with only the one
superb flower in her hair — and now, when her beauty was set off by
all that dress and ornament could do for it. And they did much. Not,
indeed, that they created, or added anything to what Nature had lavishly done for Zenobia. But, those costly robes which she had on,
those flaming jewels on her neck, served as lamps to display the personal advantages which required nothing less than such an illumination, to be fully seen. Even her characteristic flower, though it seemed
to be still there, had undergone a cold and bright transfiguration; it
was a flower exquisitely imitated in jeweller's work, and imparting
the last touch that transformed Zenobia into a work of art.

"I scarcely feel," I could not forbear saying, "as if we had ever met before. How many years ago it seems, since we last sat beneath Eliot's pulpit, with Hollingsworth extended on the fallen leaves, and Priscilla at his feet! Can it be, Zenobia, that you ever really numbered yourself with our little band of earnest, thoughtful, philanthropic laborers?"

"Those ideas have their time and place," she answered, coldly. "But, I fancy, it must be a very circumscribed mind that can find room for no others."

Her manner bewildered me. Literally, moreover, I was dazzled by the brilliancy of the room. A chandelier hung down in the centre, glowing with I know not how many lights; there were separate lamps, also, on two or three tables, and on marble brackets, adding their white radiance to that of the chandelier. The furniture was exceedingly rich. Fresh from our old farm-house, with its homely board and benches in the dining-room, and a few wicker-chairs in the best parlor, it struck me that here was the fulfilment of every fantasy of an imagination, revelling in various methods of costly self-indulgence and splendid ease. Pictures, marbles, vases; in brief, more shapes of luxury than there could be any object in enumerating, except for an auctioneer's advertisement — and the whole repeated and doubled by the reflection of a great mirror, which showed me Zenobia's proud figure, likewise, and my own. It cost me, I acknowledge, a bitter sense of shame, to perceive in myself a positive effort to bear up against the effect which Zenobia sought to impose on me. I reasoned against her, in my secret mind, and strove so to keep my footing. In the gorgeousness with which she had surrounded herself — in the redundance of personal ornament, which the largeness of her physical nature and the rich type of her beauty caused to seem so suitable — I malevolently beheld the true character of the woman, passionate, luxurious, lacking simplicity, not deeply refined, incapable of pure and perfect taste.

But, the next instant, she was too powerful for all my opposing struggles. I saw how fit it was that she should make herself as gorgeous as she pleased, and should do a thousand things that would have been ridiculous in the poor, thin, weakly characters of other women. To this day, however, I hardly know whether I then beheld Zenobia in her truest attitude, or whether that were the truer one in which she had presented herself at Blithedale. In both, there was something like the illusion which a great actress flings around her.

"Have you given up Blithedale forever?" I inquired.

"Why should you think so?" asked she.

"I cannot tell," answered I; "except that it appears all like a dream that we were ever there together."

"It is not so to me," said Zenobia. "I should think it a poor and meagre nature, that is capable of but one set of forms, and must convert all the past into a dream, merely because the present happens to be unlike it. Why should we be content with our homely life of a few months past, to the exclusion of all other modes? It was good; but there are other lives as good or better. Not, you will understand, that I condemn those who give themselves up to it more entirely than I, for myself, should deem it wise to do."

It irritated me, this self-complacent, condescending, qualified approval and criticism of a system to which many individuals — perhaps as highly endowed as our gorgeous Zenobia — had contributed their all of earthly endeavor, and their loftiest aspirations. I determined to make proof if there were any spell that would exorcise her out of the part which she seemed to be acting. She should be compelled to give me a glimpse of something true; some nature, some passion, no matter whether right or wrong, provided it were real.

"Your allusion to that class of circumscribed characters, who can live only in one mode of life," remarked I, coolly, "reminds me of our poor friend Hollingsworth. Possibly, he was in your thoughts, when you spoke thus. Poor fellow! It is a pity that, by the fault of a narrow education, he should have so completely immolated himself to that one idea of his; especially as the slightest modicum of common-sense would teach him its utter impracticability. Now that I have returned into the world, and can look at his project from a distance, it requires quite all my real regard for this respectable and well-intentioned man to prevent me laughing at him — as, I find, society at large does!"

Zenobia's eyes darted lightning; her cheeks flushed; the vividness of her expression was like the effect of a powerful light, flaming up suddenly within her. My experiment had fully succeeded. She had shown me the true flesh and blood of her heart, by thus involuntarily resenting my slight, pitying, half-kind, half-scornful mention of the man who was all in all with her. She herself, probably, felt this; for it was hardly a moment before she tranquillized her uneven breath, and seemed as proud and self-possessed as ever.

"I rather imagine," said she, quietly, "that your appreciation falls short of Mr. Hollingsworth's just claims. Blind enthusiasm, absorption in one idea, I grant, is generally ridiculous, and must be fatal to the respectability of an ordinary man; it requires a very high and powerful character, to make it otherwise. But a great man — as, perhaps, you do not know — attains his normal condition only through the inspiration of one great idea. As a friend of Mr. Hollingsworth, and, at the same time, a calm observer, I must tell you that he seems to me such a man. But you are very pardonable for fancying him ridiculous. Doubtless, he is so — to you! There can be no truer test of the noble and heroic, in any individual, than the degree in which he possesses the faculty of distinguishing heroism from absurdity."

I dared make no retort to Zenobia's concluding apothegm. In truth, I admired her fidelity. It gave me a new sense of Hollingsworth's native power, to discover that his influence was no less potent with this beautiful woman, here, in the midst of artificial life, than it had been, at the foot of the gray rock, and among the wild birch-trees of the wood-path, when she so passionately pressed his hand against her heart. The great, rude, shaggy, swarthy man! And Zenobia loved him!

"Did you bring Priscilla with you?" I resumed. "Do you know, I have sometimes fancied it not quite safe, considering the susceptibility of her temperament, that she should be so constantly within the sphere of a man like Hollingsworth? Such tender and delicate natures, among your sex, have often, I believe, a very adequate appreciation of the heroic element in men. But, then, again, I should suppose them as likely as any other women to make a reciprocal impression. Hollingsworth could hardly give his affections to a person capable of taking an independent stand, but only to one whom he might absorb into himself. He has certainly shown great tenderness for Priscilla."

Zenobia had turned aside. But I caught the reflection of her face in the mirror, and saw that it was very pale; — as pale, in her rich attire, as if a shroud were round her.

"Priscilla is here," said she, her voice a little lower than usual. "Have not you learnt as much, from your chamber-window? Would you like to see her?"

She made a step or two into the back drawing-room, and called: — "Priscilla! Dear Priscilla!"

XX. THEY VANISH

Priscilla immediately answered the summons, and made her appearance through the door of the boudoir. I had conceived the idea — which I now recognized as a very foolish one — that Zenobia would have taken measures to debar me from an interview with this girl, between whom and herself there was so utter an opposition of their dearest interests, that, on one part or the other, a great grief, if not likewise a great wrong, seemed a matter of necessity. But, as Priscilla was only a leaf, floating on the dark current of events, without influencing them by her own choice or plan — as she probably guessed not whither the stream was bearing her, nor perhaps even felt its inevitable movement — there could be no peril of her communicating to me any intelligence with regard to Zenobia's purposes.

On perceiving me, she came forward with great quietude of manner; and when I held out my hand, her own moved slightly towards it, as if attracted by a feeble degree of magnetism.

"I am glad to see you, my dear Priscilla," said I, still holding her hand. "But everything that I meet with, now-a-days, makes me wonder whether I am awake. You, especially, have always seemed like a figure in a dream — and now more than ever."

"Oh, there is substance in these fingers of mine!" she answered, giving my hand the faintest possible pressure, and then taking away her own. "Why do you call me a dream? Zenobia is much more like one than I; she is so very, very beautiful! And, I suppose," added Priscilla, as if thinking aloud, "everybody sees it, as I do."

But, for my part, it was Priscilla's beauty, not Zenobia's, of which I was thinking, at that moment. She was a person who could be quite obliterated, so far as beauty went, by anything unsuitable in her attire; her charm was not positive and material enough to bear up against a mistaken choice of color, for instance, or fashion. It was safest, in her case, to attempt no art of dress; for it demanded the most perfect taste, or else the happiest accident in the world, to give her precisely the adornment which she needed. She was now dressed in pure white, set off with some kind of gauzy fabric, which — as I bring up her figure in my memory, with a faint gleam on her shadowy hair, and her dark eyes bent shyly on mine, through all the vanished years — seems to be floating about her like a mist. I wondered what Zenobia meant by evolving so much loveliness out of this poor girl. It was what few women could afford to do; for, as I looked from one to the other, the sheen and splendor of Zenobia's presence took nothing from Priscilla's softer spell, if it might not rather be thought to add to it.

"What do you think of her?" asked Zenobia.

I could not understand the look of melancholy kindness with which Zenobia regarded her. She advanced a step, and beckoning Priscilla near her, kissed her cheek; then, with a slight gesture of repulse, she moved to the other side of the room. I followed.

"She is a wonderful creature," I said. "Ever since she came among us, I have been dimly sensible of just this charm which you have brought out. But it was never absolutely visible till now. She is as lovely as a flower!"

"Well; say so, if you like," answered Zenobia. "You are a poet — at least, as poets go, now-a-days — and must be allowed to make an opera-glass of your imagination, when you look at women. I wonder, in such Arcadian freedom of falling in love as we have lately enjoyed, it never occurred to you to fall in love with Priscilla! In society, indeed, a genuine American never dreams of stepping across the inappreciable air-line which separates one class from another. But what was rank to the colonists of Blithedale?"

"There were other reasons," I replied, "why I should have demonstrated myself an ass, had I fallen in love with Priscilla. By-the-by, has Hollingsworth ever seen her in this dress?"

"Why do you bring up his name, at every turn?" asked Zenobia, in an undertone, and with a malign look which wandered from my face to Priscilla's. "You know not what you do! It is dangerous, sir, believe me, to tamper thus with earnest human passions, out of your own mere idleness, and for your sport. I will endure it no longer! Take care that it does not happen again! I warn you!"

"You partly wrong me, if not wholly," I responded. "It is an uncertain sense of some duty to perform, that brings my thoughts, and therefore my words, continually to that one point."

"Oh, this stale excuse of duty!" said Zenobia, in a whisper so full of scorn that it penetrated me like the hiss of a serpent. "I have often heard it before, from those who sought to interfere with me, and I know precisely what it signifies. Bigotry; self-conceit; an insolent curiosity; a meddlesome temper; a cold-blooded criticism, founded on a shallow interpretation of half-perceptions; a monstrous scepticism in regard to any conscience or any wisdom, except one's own; a most irreverent propensity to thrust Providence aside, and substitute one's self in its awful place — out of these, and other motives as miserable as these, comes your idea of duty! But beware, sir! With all your fancied acuteness, you step blindfold into these affairs. For any mischief that may follow your interference, I hold you responsible!"

It was evident, that, with but a little further provocation, the lioness would turn to bay; if, indeed, such were not her attitude, already. I bowed, and, not very well knowing what else to do, was about to withdraw. But, glancing again towards Priscilla, who had retreated into a corner, there fell upon my heart an intolerable burthen of despondency, the purport of which I could not tell, but only felt it to bear reference to her. I approached her, and held out my hand; a gesture, however, to which she made no response. It was always one of her peculiarities that she seemed to shrink from even the most friendly touch, unless it were Zenobia's or Hollingsworth's. Zenobia, all this while, stood watching us, but with a careless expression, as if it mattered very little what might pass.

"Priscilla," I inquired, lowering my voice, "when do you go back to Blithedale?"

"Whenever they please to take me," she said.

"Did you come away of your own free-will?" I asked.

"I am blown about like a leaf," she replied. "I never have any free-will."

"Does Hollingsworth know that you are here?" said I.

"He bade me come," answered Priscilla.

She looked at me, I thought, with an air of surprise, as if the idea were incomprehensible, that she should have taken this step without his agency.

"What a gripe[1] this man has laid upon her whole being!" muttered I, between my teeth. "Well; as Zenobia so kindly intimates, I have no more business here. I wash my hands of it all. On Hollingsworth's head be the consequences! Priscilla," I added, aloud, "I know not that ever we may meet again. Farewell!"

As I spoke the word, a carriage had rumbled along the street, and stopt before the house. The door-bell rang, and steps were immediately afterwards heard on the staircase. Zenobia had thrown a shawl over her dress.

"Mr. Coverdale," she said, with cool courtesy, "you will perhaps excuse us. We have an engagement, and are going out."

"Whither?" I demanded.

"Is not that a little more than you are entitled to inquire?" said she, with a smile. "At all events, it does not suit me to tell you."

The door of the drawing-room opened, and Westervelt appeared. I observed that he was elaborately dressed, as if for some grand entertainment. My dislike for this man was infinite. At that moment, it amounted to nothing less than a creeping of the flesh, as when, feeling about in a dark place, one touches something cold and slimy, and questions what the secret hatefulness may be. And, still, I could not but acknowledge, that, for personal beauty, for polish of manner, for all that externally befits a gentleman, there was hardly another like

---

[1]*gripe:* Grip.

him. After bowing to Zenobia, and graciously saluting Priscilla in her corner, he recognized me by a slight, but courteous inclination.

"Come, Priscilla," said Zenobia, "it is time. Mr. Coverdale, good evening!"

As Priscilla moved slowly forward, I met her in the middle of the drawing-room.

"Priscilla," said I, in the hearing of them all, "do you know whither you are going?"

"I do not know," she answered.

"Is it wise to go? — and is it your choice to go?" I asked. "If not — I am your friend, and Hollingsworth's friend — tell me so, at once!"

"Possibly," observed Westervelt, smiling, "Priscilla sees in me an older friend than either Mr. Coverdale or Mr. Hollingsworth. I shall willingly leave the matter at her option."

While thus speaking, he made a gesture of kindly invitation; and Priscilla passed me, with the gliding movement of a sprite, and took his offered arm. He offered the other to Zenobia. But she turned her proud and beautiful face upon him, with a look which — judging from what I caught of it in profile — would undoubtedly have smitten the man dead, had he possessed any heart, or had this glance attained to it. It seemed to rebound, however, from his courteous visage, like an arrow from polished steel. They all three descended the stairs; and when I likewise reached the street-door, the carriage was already rolling away.

XXI. AN OLD ACQUAINTANCE

Thus excluded from everybody's confidence, and attaining no further, by my most earnest study, than to an uncertain sense of something hidden from me, it would appear reasonable that I should have flung off all these alien perplexities. Obviously, my best course was, to betake myself to new scenes. Here, I was only an intruder. Elsewhere, there might be circumstances in which I could establish a personal interest, and people who would respond, with a portion of their sympathies, for so much as I should bestow of mine.

Nevertheless, there occurred to me one other thing to be done. Remembering old Moodie, and his relationship with Priscilla, I determined to seek an interview, for the purpose of ascertaining whether the knot of affairs was as inextricable, on that side, as I found it on all others. Being tolerably well acquainted with the old man's haunts, I went, the next day, to the saloon of a certain establishment about which he often lurked. It was a reputable place enough, affording good entertainment in the way of meat, drink, and fumigation;[1] and there, in my young and idle days and nights, when I was neither nice nor wise, I had often amused myself with watching the staid humors and sober jollities of the thirsty souls around me.

At my first entrance, old Moodie was not there. The more patiently to await him, I lighted a cigar, and establishing myself in a corner, took a quiet, and, by sympathy, a boozy kind of pleasure in the customary life that was going forward. Human nature, in my opinion, has a naughty instinct that approves of wine, at least, if not of stronger liquor. The temperance-men may preach till doom's day; and still this cold and barren world will look warmer, kindlier, mellower, through the medium of a toper's glass;[2] nor can they, with all their efforts, really spill his draught upon the floor, until some hitherto unthought-of discovery shall supply him with a truer element of joy. The general atmosphere of life must first be rendered so inspiriting that he will not need his delirious solace. The custom of tippling has its defensible side, as well as any other question. But these good people snatch at the old, time-honored demijohn, and offer nothing — either sensual or moral — nothing whatever to supply its place; and human life, as it goes with a multitude of men, will not endure so great a vacuum as would be left by the withdrawal of that big-bellied convexity. The space, which it now occupies, must somehow or other be filled up. As for the rich, it would be little matter if a blight fell upon their vineyards; but the poor man — whose only glimpse of a better state is through the muddy medium of his liquor — what is to be done for him? The reformers should make their efforts positive, instead of negative; they must do away with evil by substituting good.

The saloon was fitted up with a good deal of taste. There were pictures on the walls, and among them an oil-painting of a beef-steak, with such an admirable show of juicy tenderness, that the beholder sighed to think it merely visionary, and incapable of ever being put upon a gridiron. Another work of high art was the lifelike representation of a noble sirloin; another, the hind-quarters of a deer, retaining

---

[1]*fumigation:* Pipe and cigar smoking.
[2]*toper's glass:* A "toper" is a heavy drinker. The section from "Human nature" to the end of the paragraph was cut from the manuscript and hence from earlier editions but was restored for the Centenary edition.

the hoofs and tawny fur; another, the head and shoulders of a salmon; and, still more exquisitely finished, a brace of canvass-back ducks, in which the mottled feathers were depicted with the accuracy of a daguerreotype.[3] Some very hungry painter, I suppose, had wrought these subjects of still life, heightening his imagination with his appetite, and earning, it is to be hoped, the privilege of a daily dinner off whichever of his pictorial viands he liked best. Then there was a fine old cheese, in which you could almost discern the mites; and some sardines, on a small plate, very richly done, and looking as if oozy with the oil in which they had been smothered. All these things were so perfectly imitated, that you seemed to have the genuine article before you, and yet with an indescribable, ideal charm; it took away the grossness from what was fleshiest and fattest, and thus helped the life of man, even in its earthliest relations, to appear rich and noble, as well as warm, cheerful, and substantial. There were pictures, too, of gallant revellers, those of the old time, Flemish, apparently, with doublets and slashed sleeves, drinking their wine out of fantastic, long-stemmed glasses; quaffing joyously, quaffing forever, with inaudible laughter and song; while the champagne bubbled immortally against their moustaches, or the purple tide of Burgundy ran inexhaustibly down their throats.

But, in an obscure corner of the saloon, there was a little picture — excellently done, moreover — of a ragged, bloated, New England toper, stretched out on a bench, in the heavy, apoplectic sleep of drunkenness. The death-in-life was too well portrayed. You smelt the fumy liquor that had brought on this syncope.[4] Your only comfort lay in the forced reflection, that, real as he looked, the poor caitiff[5] was but imaginary, a bit of painted canvass, whom no delirium tremens, nor so much as a retributive headache, awaited, on the morrow.

By this time, it being past eleven o'clock, the two barkeepers of the saloon were in pretty constant activity. One of these young men had a rare faculty in the concoction of gin-cocktails. It was a spectacle to behold, how, with a tumbler in each hand, he tossed the contents

---

[3]*daguerreotype:* A photograph reproduced through a chemical process on a silver or silver-covered copper plate. Invented and displayed to the public in 1839 by Louis Daguerre (1789–1851). See *The House of the Seven Gables,* especially ch. 12.

[4]*syncope:* Partial or complete loss of consciousness.

[5]*caitiff:* Mean or wicked or simply unfortunate and wretched man.

from one to the other. Never conveying it awry, nor spilling the least drop, he compelled the frothy liquor, as it seemed to me, to spout forth from one glass and descend into the other, in a great parabolic curve, as well-defined and calculable as a planet's orbit. He had a good forehead, with a particularly large development just above the eyebrows; fine intellectual gifts, no doubt, which he had educated to this profitable end; being famous for nothing but gin-cocktails, and commanding a fair salary by his one accomplishment. These cock-tails, and other artificial combinations of liquor (of which there were at least a score, though mostly, I suspect, fantastic in their differ-ences,) were much in favor with the younger class of customers, who, at farthest, had only reached the second stage of potatory life. The staunch, old soakers, on the other hand — men who, if put on tap, would have yielded a red alcoholic liquor, by way of blood — usually confined themselves to plain brandy-and-water, gin, or West India rum; and, oftentimes, they prefaced their dram with some medicinal remark as to the wholesomeness and stomachic qualities of that par-ticular drink. Two or three appeared to have bottles of their own, be-hind the counter; and winking one red eye to the barkeeper, he forth-with produced these choicest and peculiar cordials, which it was a matter of great interest and favor, among their acquaintances, to ob-tain a sip of.

Agreeably to the Yankee habit, under whatever circumstances, the deportment of all these good fellows, old or young, was decorous and thoroughly correct. They grew only the more sober in their cups; there was no confused babble, nor boisterous laughter. They sucked in the joyous fire of the decanters, and kept it smouldering in their in-most recesses, with a bliss known only to the heart which it warmed and comforted. Their eyes twinkled a little, to be sure; they hemmed vigorously, after each glass, and laid a hand upon the pit of the stom-ach, as if the pleasant titillation, there, was what constituted the tan-gible part of their enjoyment. In that spot, unquestionably, and not in the brain, was the acme of the whole affair. But the true purpose of their drinking — and one that will induce men to drink, or do some-thing equivalent, as long as this weary world shall endure — was the renewed youth and vigor, the brisk, cheerful sense of things present and to come, with which, for about a quarter-of-an-hour, the dram permeated their systems. And when such quarters-of-an-hour can be obtained in some mode less baneful to the great sum of a man's life — but, nevertheless, with a little spice of impropriety, to give it a wild flavor — we temperance-people may ring out our bells for victory!

The prettiest object in the saloon was a tiny fountain, which threw up its feathery jet, through the counter, and sparkled down again into an oval basin, or lakelet, containing several gold-fishes. There was a bed of bright sand, at the bottom, strewn with coral and rock-work; and the fishes went gleaming about, now turning up the sheen of a golden side, and now vanishing into the shadows of the water, like the fanciful thoughts that coquet with a poet in his dream. Never before, I imagine, did a company of water-drinkers remain so entirely uncontaminated by the bad example around them; nor could I help wondering that it had not occurred to any freakish inebriate, to empty a glass of liquor into their lakelet. What a delightful idea! Who would not be a fish, if he could inhale jollity with the essential element of his existence!

I had begun to despair of meeting old Moodie, when, all at once, I recognized his hand and arm, protruding from behind a screen that was set up for the accommodation of bashful topers. As a matter of course, he had one of Priscilla's little purses, and was quietly insinuating it under the notice of a person who stood near. This was always old Moodie's way. You hardly ever saw him advancing towards you, but became aware of his proximity without being able to guess how he had come thither. He glided about like a spirit, assuming visibility close to your elbow, offering his petty trifles of merchandise, remaining long enough for you to purchase, if so disposed, and then taking himself off, between two breaths, while you happened to be thinking of something else.

By a sort of sympathetic impulse that often controlled me, in those more impressible days of my life, I was induced to approach this old man in a mode as undemonstrative as his own. Thus, when, according to his custom, he was probably just about to vanish, he found me at his elbow.

"Ah!" said he, with more emphasis than was usual with him. "It is Mr. Coverdale!"

"Yes, Mr. Moodie, your old acquaintance," answered I. "It is some time now since we ate our luncheon together, at Blithedale, and a good deal longer since our little talk together, at the street-corner."

"That was a good while ago," said the old man.

And he seemed inclined to say not a word more. His existence looked so colorless and torpid — so very faintly shadowed on the canvass of reality — that I was half afraid lest he should altogether disappear, even while my eyes were fixed full upon his figure. He was certainly the wretchedest old ghost in the world, with his crazy hat, the dingy handkerchief about his throat, his suit of threadbare gray, and especially that patch over his right eye,[6] behind which he always seemed to be hiding himself. There was one method, however, of bringing him out into somewhat stronger relief. A glass of brandy would effect it. Perhaps the gentler influence of a bottle of claret might do the same. Nor could I think it a matter for the recording angel to write down against me, if — with my painful consciousness of the frost in this old man's blood, and the positive ice that had congealed about his heart — I should thaw him out, were it only for an hour, with the summer warmth of a little wine. What else could possibly be done for him? How else could he be imbued with energy enough to hope for a happier state, hereafter? How else be inspirited[7] to say his prayers? For there are states of our spiritual system, when the throb of the soul's life is too faint and weak to render us capable of religious aspiration.

"Mr. Moodie," said I, "shall we lunch together? And would you like to drink a glass of wine?"

His one eye gleamed. He bowed; and it impressed me that he grew to be more of a man at once, either in anticipation of the wine, or as a grateful response to my good-fellowship in offering it.

"With pleasure," he replied.

The barkeeper, at my request, showed us into a private room, and, soon afterwards, set some fried oysters and a bottle of claret on the table; and I saw the old man glance curiously at the label of the bottle, as if to learn the brand.

"It should be good wine," I remarked, "if it have any right to its label."

"You cannot suppose, sir," said Moodie, with a sigh, "that a poor old fellow, like me, knows any difference in wines."

And yet, in his way of handling the glass, in his preliminary snuff at the aroma, in his first cautious sip of the wine, and the gustatory skill with which he gave his palate the full advantage of it, it was impossible not to recognize the connoisseur.

---

[6]*patch over his right eye:* On p. 98, the patch is over his left eye.
[7]*inspirited:* The Centenary edition uses this word from the manuscript, rather than *inspired,* which was used in the first edition.

"I fancy, Mr. Moodie," said I, "you are a much better judge of wines than I have yet learned to be. Tell me fairly — did you never drink it where the grape grows?"

"How should that have been, Mr. Coverdale?" answered old Moodie, shyly; but then he took courage, as it were, and uttered a feeble little laugh. "The flavor of this wine," added he, "and its perfume, still more than its taste, makes me remember that I was once a young man!"

"I wish, Mr. Moodie," suggested I — not that I greatly cared about it, however, but was only anxious to draw him into some talk about Priscilla and Zenobia — "I wish, while we sit over our wine, you would favor me with a few of those youthful reminiscences."

"Ah," said he, shaking his head, "they might interest you more than you suppose. But I had better be silent, Mr. Coverdale. If this good wine — though claret, I suppose, is not apt to play such a trick — but if it should make my tongue run too freely, I could never look you in the face again."

"You never did look me in the face, Mr. Moodie," I replied, "until this very moment."

"Ah!" sighed old Moodie.

It was wonderful, however, what an effect the mild grape-juice wrought upon him. It was not in the wine, but in the associations which it seemed to bring up. Instead of the mean, slouching, furtive, painfully depressed air of an old city-vagabond, more like a gray kennel-rat[8] than any other living thing, he began to take the aspect of a decayed gentleman. Even his garments — especially after I had myself quaffed a glass or two — looked less shabby than when we first sat down. There was, by-and-by, a certain exuberance and elaborateness of gesture, and manner, oddly in contrast with all that I had hitherto seen of him. Anon, with hardly any impulse from me, old Moodie began to talk. His communications referred exclusively to a long past and more fortunate period of his life, with only a few unavoidable allusions to the circumstances that had reduced him to his present state. But, having once got the clue, my subsequent researches acquainted me with the main facts of the following narrative; although, in writing it out, my pen has perhaps allowed itself a trifle of romantic and legendary license, worthier of a small poet than of a grave biographer.

---

[8]*kennel-rat:* Rat living in the gutter of a street (from *canel* or *kennel,* meaning street or drainage gutter).

XXII. FAUNTLEROY

Five-and-twenty years ago, at the epoch of this story, there dwelt, in one of the middle states, a man whom we shall call Fauntleroy;[1] a man of wealth, and magnificent tastes, and prodigal expenditure. His home might almost be styled a palace; his habits, in the ordinary sense, princely. His whole being seemed to have crystallized itself into an external splendor, wherewith he glittered in the eyes of the world, and had no other life than upon this gaudy surface. He had married a lovely woman, whose nature was deeper than his own. But his affection for her, though it showed largely, was superficial, like all his other manifestations and developments; he did not so truly keep this noble creature in his heart, as wear her beauty for the most brilliant ornament of his outward state. And there was born to him a child, a beautiful daughter, whom he took from the beneficent hand of God with no just sense of her immortal value, but as a man, already rich in gems, would receive another jewel. If he loved her, it was because she shone.

After Fauntleroy had thus spent a few empty years, corruscating[2] continually an unnatural light, the source of it — which was merely his gold — began to grow more shallow, and finally became exhausted. He saw himself in imminent peril of losing all that had heretofore distinguished him; and, conscious of no innate worth to fall back upon, he recoiled from this calamity, with the instinct of a soul shrinking from annihilation. To avoid it — wretched man! — or, rather, to defer it, if but for a month, a day, or only to procure himself the life of a few breaths more, amid the false glitter which was now less his own than ever — he made himself guilty of a crime. It was just the sort of crime, growing out of its artificial state, which society (unless it should change its entire constitution for this man's unworthy sake) neither could nor ought to pardon. More safely might it pardon murder. Fauntleroy's guilt was discovered. He fled; his wife perished by the necessity of her innate nobleness, in its alliance with a being so ignoble; and betwixt her mother's death and her father's ignominy, his daughter was left worse than orphaned.

There was no pursuit after Fauntleroy. His family-connections,

---

[1] *Fauntleroy:* Perhaps derives from Henry Fauntleroy (1785–1824), London banker convicted and hanged for forgery.

[2] *corruscating:* Not in *The Oxford English Dictionary* or *Webster's Third New International Dictionary;* probably from the Latin, *corusco,* meaning to gleam, glitter, flash.

who had great wealth, made such arrangements with those whom he had attempted to wrong, as secured him from the retribution that would have overtaken an unfriended criminal. The wreck of his estate was divided among his creditors. His name, in a very brief space, was forgotten by the multitude who had passed it so diligently from mouth to mouth. Seldom, indeed, was it recalled, even by his closest former intimates. Nor could it have been otherwise. The man had laid no real touch on any mortal's heart. Being a mere image, an optical delusion, created by the sunshine of prosperity, it was his law to vanish into the shadow of the first intervening cloud. He seemed to leave no vacancy; a phenomenon which, like many others that attended his brief career, went far to prove the illusiveness of his existence.

Not, however, that the physical substance of Fauntleroy had literally melted into vapor. He had fled northward, to the New England metropolis,[3] and had taken up his abode, under another name, in a squalid street, or court, of the older portion of the city. There he dwelt among poverty-stricken wretches, sinners, and forlorn, good people, Irish, and whomsoever else were neediest. Many families were clustered in each house together, above stairs and below, in the little peaked garrets, and even in the dusky cellars. The house, where Fauntleroy paid weekly rent for a chamber and a closet, had been a stately habitation, in its day. An old colonial Governor had built it, and lived there, long ago, and held his levees[4] in a great room where now slept twenty Irish bedfellows, and died in Fauntleroy's chamber, which his embroidered and white-wigged ghost still haunted. Tattered hangings, a marble hearth, traversed with many cracks and fissures, a richly-carved oaken mantel-piece, partly hacked-away for kindling-stuff, a stuccoed ceiling, defaced with great, unsightly patches of the naked laths; — such was the chamber's aspect, as if, with its splinters and rags of dirty splendor, it were a kind of practical gibe at this poor, ruined man of show.

At first, and at irregular intervals, his relatives allowed Fauntleroy a little pittance to sustain life; not from any love, perhaps, but lest poverty should compel him, by new offences, to add more shame to that with which he had already stained them. But he showed no tendency to further guilt. His character appeared to have been radically changed (as, indeed, from its shallowness, it well might) by his miser-

---

[3]*New England metropolis:* Boston.
[4]*levees:* Reception held by a person of distinction or rank on rising from bed. From the French *lever,* to lift up, to raise; (*se*) *lever,* to get up.

able fate; or, it may be, the traits now seen in him were portions of the same character, presenting itself in another phase. Instead of any longer seeking to live in the sight of the world, his impulse was to shrink into the nearest obscurity, and to be unseen of men, were it possible, even while standing before their eyes. He had no pride; it was all trodden in the dust. No ostentation; for how could it survive, when there was nothing left of Fauntleroy, save penury and shame! His very gait demonstrated that he would gladly have faded out of view, and have crept about invisibly, for the sake of sheltering himself from the irksomeness of a human glance. Hardly, it was averred, within the memory of those who knew him now, had he the hardihood to show his full front to the world. He skulked in corners, and crept about in a sort of noonday twilight, making himself gray and misty, at all hours, with his morbid intolerance of sunshine.

In his torpid despair, however, he had done an act which that condition of the spirit seems to prompt, almost as often as prosperity and hope. Fauntleroy was again married. He had taken to wife a forlorn, meek-spirited, feeble young woman, a seamstress, whom he found dwelling with her mother in a contiguous chamber of the old gubernatorial residence. This poor phantom — as the beautiful and noble companion of his former life had done — brought him a daughter. And sometimes, as from one dream into another, Fauntleroy looked forth out of his present grimy environment, into that past magnificence, and wondered whether the grandee of yesterday or the pauper of to-day were real. But, in my mind, the one and the other were alike impalpable. In truth, it was Fauntleroy's fatality to behold whatever he touched dissolve. After a few years, his second wife (dim shadow that she had always been) faded finally out of the world, and left Fauntleroy to deal as he might with their pale and nervous child. And, by this time, among his distant relatives — with whom he had grown a weary thought, linked with contagious infamy, and which they were only too willing to get rid of — he was himself supposed to be no more.

The younger child, like his elder one, might be considered as the true offspring of both parents, and as the reflection of their state. She was a tremulous little creature, shrinking involuntarily from all mankind, but in timidity, and no sour repugnance. There was a lack of human substance in her; it seemed as if, were she to stand up in a sunbeam, it would pass right through her figure, and trace out the cracked and dusty window-panes upon the naked floor. But, nevertheless, the poor child had a heart; and from her mother's gentle character, she had inherited a profound and still capacity of affection. And so her life was one of love. She bestowed it partly on her father, but, in greater part, on an idea.

For Fauntleroy, as they sat by their cheerless fireside — which was no fireside, in truth, but only a rusty stove — had often talked to the little girl about his former wealth, the noble loveliness of his first wife, and the beautiful child whom she had given him. Instead of the fairy tales, which other parents tell, he told Priscilla this. And, out of the loneliness of her sad little existence, Priscilla's love grew, and tended upward, and twined itself perseveringly around this unseen sister; as a grape-vine might strive to clamber out of a gloomy hollow among the rocks, and embrace a young tree, standing in the sunny warmth above. It was almost like worship, both in its earnestness and its humility; nor was it the less humble, though the more earnest, because Priscilla could claim human kindred with the being whom she so devoutly loved. As with worship, too, it gave her soul the refreshment of a purer atmosphere. Save for this singular, this melancholy, and yet beautiful affection, the child could hardly have lived; or, had she lived, with a heart shrunken for lack of any sentiment to fill it, she must have yielded to the barren miseries of her position, and have grown to womanhood, characterless and worthless. But, now, amid all the sombre coarseness of her father's outward life, and of her own, Priscilla had a higher and imaginative life within. Some faint gleam thereof was often visible upon her face. It was as if, in her spiritual visits to her brilliant sister, a portion of the latter's brightness had permeated our dim Priscilla, and still lingered, shedding a faint illumination through the cheerless chamber, after she came back.

As the child grew up, so pallid and so slender, and with much unaccountable nervousness, and all the weaknesses of neglected infancy still haunting her, the gross and simple neighbors whispered strange things about Priscilla. The big, red, Irish matrons, whose innumerable progeny swarmed out of the adjacent doors, used to mock at the pale Western child. They fancied — or, at least, affirmed it, between jest and earnest — that she was not so solid flesh and blood as other children, but mixed largely with a thinner element. They called her ghost-child, and said that she could indeed vanish, when she pleased, but could never, in her densest moments, make herself quite visible. The sun, at mid-day, would shine through her; in the first gray of the twilight, she lost all the distinctness of her outline; and, if you followed the dim thing into a dark corner, behold! she was not there.

And it was true, that Priscilla had strange ways; strange ways, and stranger words, when she uttered any words at all. Never stirring out of the old Governor's dusky house, she sometimes talked of distant places and splendid rooms, as if she had just left them. Hidden things were visible to her, (at least, so the people inferred from obscure hints, escaping unawares out of her mouth,) and silence was audible. And, in all the world, there was nothing so difficult to be endured, by those who had any dark secret to conceal, as the glance of Priscilla's timid and melancholy eyes.

Her peculiarities were the theme of continual gossip among the other inhabitants of the gubernatorial mansion. The rumor spread thence into a wider circle. Those who knew old Moodie — as he was now called — used often to jeer him, at the very street-corners, about his daughter's gift of second-sight and prophecy. It was a period when science (though mostly through its empirical professors) was bringing forward, anew, a hoard of facts and imperfect theories, that had partially won credence, in elder times, but which modern scepticism had swept away as rubbish. These things were now tossed up again, out of the surging ocean of human thought and experience. The story of Priscilla's preternatural manifestations, therefore, attracted a kind of notice of which it would have been deemed wholly unworthy, a few years earlier. One day, a gentleman ascended the creaking staircase, and inquired which was old Moodie's chamber-door. And, several times, he came again. He was a marvellously handsome man, still youthful, too, and fashionably dressed. Except that Priscilla, in those days, had no beauty, and, in the languor of her existence, had not yet blossomed into womanhood, there would have been rich food for scandal in these visits; for the girl was unquestionably their sole object, although her father was supposed always to be present. But, it must likewise be added, there was something about Priscilla that calumny could not meddle with; and thus far was she privileged, either by the preponderance of what was spiritual, or the thin and watery blood that left her cheek so pallid.

Yet, if the busy tongues of the neighborhood spared Priscilla, in one way, they made themselves amends by renewed and wilder babble, on another score. They averred that the strange gentleman was a wizard, and that he had taken advantage of Priscilla's lack of earthly substance to subject her to himself, as his familiar spirit, through whose medium he gained cognizance of whatever happened, in regions near or remote. The boundaries of his power were defined by the verge of the pit of Tartarus, on the one hand, and the third sphere[5] of the celestial world, on the other. Again, they declared their suspicion that the wizard, with all his show of manly beauty, was really an aged and wizened figure, or else that his semblance of a human body was only a necromantic, or perhaps a mechanical contrivance, in which a demon walked about. In proof of it, however, they could merely instance a gold band around his upper teeth, which had once been visible to several old women, when he smiled at them from the top of the Governor's staircase. Of course, this was all absurdity, or mostly so. But, after every possible deduction, there remained certain very mysterious points about the stranger's character, as well as the connection that he established with Priscilla. Its nature, at that period, was even less understood than now, when miracles of this kind have grown so absolutely stale, that I would gladly, if the truth allowed, dismiss the whole matter from my narrative.

We must now glance backward, in quest of the beautiful daughter of Fauntleroy's prosperity. What had become of her? Fauntleroy's only brother, a bachelor, and with no other relative so near, had adopted the forsaken child. She grew up in affluence, with native graces clustering luxuriantly about her. In her triumphant progress towards womanhood, she was adorned with every variety of feminine accomplishment. But she lacked a mother's care. With no adequate control, on any hand, (for a man, however stern, however wise, can never sway and guide a female child,) her character was left to shape itself. There was good in it, and evil. Passionate, self-willed, and imperious, she had a warm and generous nature; showing the richness of the soil, however, chiefly by the weeds that flourished in it, and choked up the herbs of grace. In her girlhood, her uncle died. As Fauntleroy was supposed to be likewise dead, and no other heir was known to exist, his wealth devolved on her, although, dying suddenly, the uncle left no will. After his death, there were obscure passages in Zenobia's history. There were whispers of an attachment, and even a secret marriage, with a fascinating and accomplished, but unprincipled young man. The incidents and appearances, however, which led to this surmise, soon passed away and were forgotten.

Nor was her reputation seriously affected by the report. In fact, so

[5]*the pit of Tartarus* and *the third sphere:* In classical mythology, Tartarus, the infernal region, was sometimes equated with (though often placed beneath) Hades; the third sphere in the Ptolemaic system was the sphere of Venus. See Homer, *Odyssey,* 4:561–69, 10:513–15, 11; Hesiod, *Theogony,* and *Works and Days,* 167–73.

great was her native power and influence, and such seemed the careless purity of her nature, that whatever Zenobia did was generally acknowledged as right for her to do. The world never criticized her so harshly as it does most women who transcend its rules. It almost yielded its assent, when it beheld her stepping out of the common path, and asserting the more extensive privileges of her sex, both theoretically and by her practice. The sphere of ordinary womanhood was felt to be narrower than her development required.

A portion of Zenobia's more recent life is told in the foregoing pages. Partly in earnest — and, I imagine, as was her disposition, half in a proud jest, or in a kind of recklessness that had grown upon her, out of some hidden grief — she had given her countenance, and promised liberal pecuniary aid, to our experiment of a better social state. And Priscilla followed her to Blithedale. The sole bliss of her life had been a dream of this beautiful sister, who had never so much as known of her existence. By this time, too, the poor girl was enthralled in an intolerable bondage, from which she must either free herself or perish. She deemed herself safest near Zenobia, into whose large heart she hoped to nestle.

One evening, months after Priscilla's departure, when Moodie (or shall we call him Fauntleroy?) was sitting alone in the state-chamber of the old Governor, there came footsteps up the staircase. There was a pause on the landing-place. A lady's musical, yet haughty accents were heard making an inquiry from some denizen of the house, who had thrust a head out of a contiguous chamber. There was then a knock at Moodie's door.

"Come in!" said he.

And Zenobia entered. The details of the interview that followed, being unknown to me — while, notwithstanding, it would be a pity quite to lose the picturesqueness of the situation — I shall attempt to sketch it, mainly from fancy, although with some general grounds of surmise in regard to the old man's feelings.

She gazed, wonderingly, at the dismal chamber. Dismal to her, who beheld it only for an instant, and how much more so to him, into whose brain each bare spot on the ceiling, every tatter of the paper-hangings, and all the splintered carvings of the mantel-piece, seen wearily through long years, had worn their several prints! Inexpressibly miserable is this familiarity with objects that have been, from the first, disgustful.

"I have received a strange message," said Zenobia, after a moment's silence, "requesting, or rather enjoining it upon me, to come hither. Rather from curiosity than any other motive — and because, though a woman, I have not all the timidity of one — I have complied. Can it be you, sir, who thus summoned me?"

"It was," answered Moodie.

"And what was your purpose?"she continued. "You require charity, perhaps? In that case, the message might have been more fitly worded. But you are old and poor; and age and poverty should be allowed their privileges. Tell me, therefore, to what extent you need my aid."

"Put up your purse," said the supposed mendicant, with an inexplicable smile. "Keep it — keep all your wealth — until I demand it all, or none! My message had no such end in view. You are beautiful, they tell me; and I desired to look at you!"

He took the one lamp that showed the discomfort and sordidness of his abode, and approaching Zenobia, held it up, so as to gain the more perfect view of her, from top to toe. So obscure was the chamber, that you could see the reflection of her diamonds thrown upon the dingy wall, and flickering with the rise and fall of Zenobia's breath. It was the splendor of those jewels on her neck, like lamps that burn before some fair temple, and the jewelled flower in her hair, more than the murky yellow light, that helped him to see her beauty. But he beheld it, and grew proud at heart; his own figure, in spite of his mean habiliments, assumed an air of state and grandeur.

"It is well!" cried old Moodie. "Keep your wealth. You are right worthy of it. Keep it, therefore, but with one condition, only!"

Zenobia thought the old man beside himself, and was moved with pity.

"Have you none to care for you?" asked she. "No daughter? — no kind-hearted neighbor? — no means of procuring the attendance which you need? Tell me, once again, can I do nothing for you?"

"Nothing," he replied. "I have beheld what I wished. Now, leave me! Linger not a moment longer; or I may be tempted to say what would bring a cloud over that queenly brow. Keep all your wealth, but with only this one condition. Be kind — be no less kind than sisters are — to my poor Priscilla!"

And, it may be, after Zenobia withdrew, Fauntleroy paced his gloomy chamber, and communed with himself, as follows: — or, at all events, it is the only solution, which I can offer, of the enigma presented in his character.

"I am unchanged — the same man as of yore!" said he. "True; my brother's wealth, he dying intestate, is legally my own. I know it; yet, of my own choice, I live a beggar, and go meanly clad, and hide my-self behind a forgotten ignominy. Looks this like ostentation? Ah, but, in Zenobia, I live again! Beholding her so beautiful — so fit to be adorned with all imaginable splendor of outward state — the cursed vanity, which, half-a-lifetime since, dropt off like tatters of once gaudy apparel from my debased and ruined person, is all re-newed for her sake! Were I to re-appear, my shame would go with me from darkness into daylight. Zenobia has the splendor, and not the shame. Let the world admire her, and be dazzled by her, the bril-liant child of my prosperity! It is Fauntleroy that still shines through her!"

But, then, perhaps, another thought occurred to him.

"My poor Priscilla! And am I just, to her, in surrendering all to this beautiful Zenobia? Priscilla! I love her best — I love her only! — but with shame, not pride. So dim, so pallid, so shrinking — the daughter of my long calamity! Wealth were but a mockery in Priscilla's hands. What is its use, except to fling a golden radiance around those who grasp it? Yet, let Zenobia take heed! Priscilla shall have no wrong!"

But, while the man of show thus meditated — that very evening, so far as I can adjust the dates of these strange incidents — Priscilla — poor, pallid flower! — was either snatched from Zeno-bia's hand, or flung wilfully away!

XXIII. A VILLAGE-HALL

Well! I betook myself away, and wandered up and down, like an exorcised spirit that had been driven from its old haunts, after a mighty struggle. It takes down the solitary pride of man, beyond most other things, to find the impracticability of flinging aside affec-tions that have grown irksome. The bands, that were silken once, are apt to become iron fetters, when we desire to shake them off. Our souls, after all, are not our own. We convey a property in them to those with whom we associate, but to what extent can never be known, until we feel the tug, the agony, of our abortive effort to re-sume an exclusive sway over ourselves. Thus, in all the weeks of my absence, my thoughts continually reverted back, brooding over the by-gone months, and bringing up incidents that seemed hardly to have left a trace of themselves, in their passage. I spent painful hours in recalling these trifles, and rendering them more misty and unsub-stantial than at first, by the quantity of speculative musing, thus kneaded in with them. Hollingsworth, Zenobia, Priscilla! These three had absorbed my life into themselves. Together with an inexpressible longing to know their fortunes, there was likewise a morbid resentment of my own pain, and a stubborn reluctance to come again within their sphere.

All that I learned of them, therefore, was comprised in a few brief and pungent squibs, such as the newspapers were then in the habit of bestowing on our socialist enterprise. There was one paragraph which, if I rightly guessed its purport, bore reference to Zenobia, but was too darkly hinted to convey even thus much of certainty. Hollingsworth, too, with his philanthropic project, afforded the penny-a-liners[1] a theme for some savage and bloody-minded jokes; and, considerably to my surprise, they affected me with as much indignation as if we had still been friends.

Thus passed several weeks; time long enough for my brown and toil-hardened hands to re-accustom themselves to gloves. Old habits, such as were merely external, returned upon me with wonderful promptitude. My superficial talk, too, assumed altogether a worldly tone. Meeting former acquaintances, who showed themselves inclined to ridicule my heroic devotion to the cause of human welfare, I spoke of the recent phase of my life as indeed fair matter for a jest. But I also gave them to understand that it was, at most, only an experiment, on which I had staked no valuable amount of hope or fear; it had enabled me to pass the summer in a novel and agreeable way, had afforded me some grotesque specimens of artificial simplicity, and could not, therefore, so far as I was concerned, be reckoned a failure. In no one instance, however, did I voluntarily speak of my three friends. They dwelt in a profounder region. The more I consider myself, as I then was, the more do I recognize how deeply my connection with those three had affected all my being.

As it was already the epoch of annihilated space, I might, in the time I was away from Blithedale, have snatched a glimpse at England, and been back again. But my wanderings were confined within a very limited sphere. I hopped and fluttered, like a bird with a string about its leg, gyrating round a small circumference, and keeping up a restless activity to no purpose. Thus, it was still in our familiar Massachusetts — in one of its white country-villages — that I must next particularize an incident.

---

[1]*penny-a-liners:* A hack writer, a journalist paid one penny per line.

The scene was one of those Lyceum-halls,[2] of which almost every village has now its own, dedicated to that sober and pallid, or, rather, drab-colored, mode of winter-evening entertainment, the Lecture. Of late years, this has come strangely into vogue, when the natural tendency of things would seem to be, to substitute lettered for oral methods of addressing the public. But, in halls like this, besides the winter course of lectures, there is a rich and varied series of other exhibitions. Hither comes the ventriloquist, with all his mysterious tongues; the thaumaturgist,[3] too, with his miraculous transformations of plates, doves, and rings, his pancakes smoking in your hat, and his cellar of choice liquors, represented in one small bottle. Here, also, the itinerant professor instructs separate classes of ladies and gentlemen in physiology, and demonstrates his lessons by the aid of real skeletons, and mannikins in wax, from Paris. Here is to be heard the choir of Ethiopian melodists, and to be seen, the diorama of Moscow or Bunker Hill, or the moving panorama of the Chinese wall. Here is displayed the museum of wax figures, illustrating the wide catholicism of earthly renown by mixing up heroes and statesmen, the Pope and the Mormon Prophet,[4] kings, queens, murderers, and beautiful ladies; every sort of person, in short, except authors, of whom I never beheld even the most famous, done in wax. And here, in this many-purposed hall, (unless the selectmen of the village chance to have more than their share of the puritanism, which, however diversified with later patchwork, still gives its prevailing tint to New England character,) here the company of strolling players sets up its little stage, and claims patronage for the legitimate drama.

But, on the autumnal evening which I speak of, a number of printed handbills — stuck up in the bar-room and on the sign-post of the hotel, and on the meeting-house porch, and distributed largely through the village — had promised the inhabitants an interview with that celebrated and hitherto inexplicable phenomenon, the Veiled Lady!

The hall was fitted up with an amphitheatrical descent of seats towards a platform, on which stood a desk, two lights, a stool, and a

---

[2]*Lyceum-halls:* The first American lyceums, societies for literary, cultural, and scientific education, were launched in the late 1820s and 1830s. Emerson was one of the most popular speakers. See Carl Bode, *The American Lyceum: Town Meeting of the Mind* (New York: Oxford UP, 1956).

[3]*thaumaturgist:* Magician, performer of miracles.

[4]*the Mormon prophet:* Joseph Smith (1805–1844), prophet, visionary, translator/publisher of *The Book of Mormon*, and founder of the Mormon Church in 1830.

capacious, antique chair. The audience was of a generally decent and respectable character; old farmers, in their Sunday black coats, with shrewd, hard, sun-dried faces, and a cynical humor, oftener than any other expression, in their eyes; pretty girls, in many-colored attire; pretty young men — the schoolmaster, the lawyer, or student-at-law, the shopkeeper — all looking rather suburban than rural. In these days, there is absolutely no rusticity, except when the actual labor of the soil leaves its earth-mould on the person. There was likewise a considerable proportion of young and middle-aged women, many of them stern in feature, with marked foreheads, and a very definite line of eyebrow; a type of womanhood in which a bold intellectual development seems to be keeping pace with the progressive delicacy of the physical constitution. Of all these people I took note, at first, according to my custom. But I ceased to do so, the moment that my eyes fell on an individual who sat two or three seats below me, immoveable, apparently deep in thought, with his back, of course, towards me, and his face turned steadfastly upon the platform.

After sitting awhile, in contemplation of this person's familiar contour, I was irresistibly moved to step over the intervening benches, lay my hand on his shoulder, put my mouth close to his ear, and address him in a sepulchral, melodramatic whisper: —

"Hollingsworth! Where have you left Zenobia!"

His nerves, however, were proof against my attack. He turned half around, and looked me in the face, with great, sad eyes, in which there was neither kindness nor resentment, nor any perceptible surprise.

"Zenobia, when I last saw her," he answered, "was at Blithedale."

He said no more. But there was a great deal of talk going on, near me, among a knot of people who might be considered as representing the mysticism, or, rather, the mystic sensuality, of this singular age. The nature of the exhibition, that was about to take place, had probably given the turn to their conversation.

I heard, from a pale man in blue spectacles, some stranger stories than ever were written in a romance; told, too, with a simple, unimaginative steadfastness, which was terribly efficacious in compelling the auditor to receive them into the category of established facts. He cited instances of the miraculous power of one human being over the will and passions of another; insomuch that settled grief was but a shadow, beneath the influence of a man possessing this potency, and the strong love of years melted away like a vapor. At the bidding of one of these wizards, the maiden, with her lover's kiss still burning on her lips, would turn from him with icy indifference; the newly made widow would dig up her buried heart out of her young husband's grave, before the sods had taken root upon it; a mother, with her babe's milk in her bosom, would thrust away her child. Human character was but soft wax in his hands; and guilt, or virtue, only the forms into which he should see fit to mould it. The religious sentiment was a flame which he could blow up with his breath, or a spark that he could utterly extinguish. It is unutterable, the horror and disgust with which I listened, and saw, that, if these things were to be believed, the individual soul was virtually annihilated, and all that is sweet and pure, in our present life, debased, and that the idea of man's eternal responsibility was made ridiculous, and immortality rendered, at once, impossible, and not worth acceptance. But I would have perished on the spot, sooner than believe it.

The epoch of rapping spirits,[5] and all the wonders that have followed in their train — such as tables, upset by invisible agencies, bells, self-tolled at funerals, and ghostly music, performed on jews-harps — had not yet arrived. Alas, my countrymen, methinks we have fallen on an evil age! If these phenomena have not humbug at the bottom, so much the worse for us. What can they indicate, in a spiritual way, except that the soul of man is descending to a lower point than it has ever before reached, while incarnate? We are pursuing a downward course, in the eternal march, and thus bring ourselves into the same range with beings whom death, in requital of their gross and evil lives, has degraded below humanity. To hold intercourse with spirits of this order, we must stoop, and grovel in some element more vile than earthly dust. These goblins, if they exist at all, are but the shadows of past mortality, outcasts, mere refuse-stuff, adjudged unworthy of the eternal world, and, on the most favorable supposition, dwindling gradually into nothingness. The less we have to say to them, the better; lest we share their fate!

The audience now began to be impatient; they signified their desire for the entertainment to commence, by thump of sticks and stamp of boot-heels. Nor was it a great while longer, before, in response to their call, there appeared a bearded personage in Oriental robes, looking like one of the enchanters of the Arabian Nights.[6] He came

---

[5]*rapping spirits:* "Spirit-rapping" which became popular in the 1840s and 1850s, was an attempt to communicate with the dead through knocks or raps.

[6]*Arabian Nights:* Collection of Persian-Indian-Arabian tales, dating in their present form from the mid-fifteenth century.

upon the platform from a side-door — saluted the spectators, not with a salaam, but a bow — took his station at the desk — and first blowing his nose with a white handkerchief, prepared to speak. The environment of the homely village-hall, and the absence of many ingenious contrivances of stage-effect, with which the exhibition had heretofore been set off, seemed to bring the artifice of this character more openly upon the surface. No sooner did I behold the bearded enchanter, than laying my hand again on Hollingsworth's shoulder, I whispered in his ear: —

"Do you know him?"

"I never saw the man before," he muttered, without turning his head.

But I had seen him, three times, already. Once, on occasion of my first visit to the Veiled Lady; a second time, in the wood-path at Blithedale; and, lastly, in Zenobia's drawing-room. It was Westervelt. A quick association of ideas made me shudder, from head to foot; and, again, like an evil spirit, bringing up reminiscences of a man's sins, I whispered a question in Hollingsworth's ear.

"What have you done with Priscilla?"

He gave a convulsive start, as if I had thrust a knife into him, writhed himself round on his seat, glared fiercely into my eyes, but answered not a word.

The Professor began his discourse, explanatory of the psychological phenomena, as he termed them, which it was his purpose to exhibit to the spectators. There remains no very distinct impression of it on my memory. It was eloquent, ingenious, plausible, with a delusive show of spirituality, yet really imbued throughout with a cold and dead materialism. I shivered, as at a current of chill air, issuing out of a sepulchral vault and bringing the smell of corruption along with it. He spoke of a new era that was dawning upon the world; an era that would link soul to soul, and the present life to what we call futurity, with a closeness that should finally convert both worlds into one great, mutually conscious brotherhood. He described (in a strange, philosophical guise, with terms of art, as if it were a matter of chemical discovery) the agency by which this mighty result was to be effected; nor would it have surprised me, had he pretended to hold up a portion of his univerally pervasive fluid, as he affirmed it to be, in a glass phial.

At the close of his exordium, the Professor beckoned with his hand — one, twice, thrice — and a figure came gliding upon the platform, enveloped in a long veil of silvery whiteness. It fell about her, like the texture of a summer cloud, with a kind of vagueness, so that the outline of the form, beneath it, could not be accurately discerned. But the movement of the Veiled Lady was graceful, free, and unembarrassed, like that of a person accustomed to be the spectacle of thousands. Or, possibly, a blindfold prisoner within the sphere with which this dark, earthly magician had surrounded her, she was wholly unconscious of being the central object to all those straining eyes.

Pliant to his gesture, (which had even an obsequious courtesy, but, at the same time, a remarkable decisiveness,) the figure placed itself in the great chair. Sitting there, in such visible obscurity, it was perhaps as much like the actual presence of a disembodied spirit as anything that stage-trickery could devise. The hushed breathing of the spectators proved how high-wrought were their anticipations of the wonders to be performed, through the medium of this incomprehensible creature. I, too, was in breathless suspense, but with a far different presentiment of some strange event at hand.

"You see before you the Veiled Lady," said the bearded Professor, advancing to the verge of the platform. "By the agency of which I have just spoken, she is, at this moment, in communion with the spiritual world. That silvery veil is, in one sense, an enchantment, having been dipt, as it were, and essentially imbued, through the potency of my art, with the fluid medium of spirits. Slight and ethereal as it seems, the limitations of time and space have no existence within its folds. This hall — these hundreds of faces, encompassing her within so narrow an amphitheatre — are of thinner substance, in her view, than the airiest vapor that the clouds are made of. She beholds the Absolute!"

As preliminary to other, and far more wonderful psychological experiments, the exhibitor suggested that some of his auditors should endeavor to make the Veiled Lady sensible of their presence by such methods — provided, only, no touch were laid upon her person — as they might deem best adapted to that end. Accordingly, several deep-lunged country-fellows, who looked as if they might have blown the apparition away with a breath, ascended the platform. Mutually encouraging one another, they shouted so close to her ear, that the veil stirred like a wreath of vanishing mist; they smote upon the floor with bludgeons; they perpetrated so hideous a clamor, that methought it might have reached, at least a little way, into the eternal sphere. Finally, with the assent of the Professor, they laid hold of the great chair, and were startled, apparently, to find it soar upward, as if lighter than the air through which it rose. But the Veiled Lady remained seated and motionless, with a composure that was hardly less than awful, because implying so immeasurable a distance betwixt her and these rude persecutors.

"These efforts are wholly without avail," observed the Professor, who had been looking on with an aspect of serene indifference. "The roar of a battery of cannon would be inaudible to the Veiled Lady. And yet, were I to will it, sitting in this very hall, she could hear the desert-wind sweeping over the sands, as far off as Arabia; the icebergs grinding one against the other, in the polar seas; the rustle of a leaf in an East Indian forest; the lowest whispered breath of the bashfullest maiden in the world, uttering the first confession of her love! Nor does there exist the moral inducement, apart from my own behest, that could persuade her to lift the silvery veil, or arise out of that chair!"

Greatly to the Professor's discomposure, however, just as he spoke these words, the Veiled Lady arose. There was a mysterious tremor that shook the magic veil. The spectators, it may be, imagined that she was about to take flight into that invisible sphere, and to the society of those purely spiritual beings, with whom they reckoned her so near akin. Hollingsworth, a moment ago, had mounted the platform, and now stood gazing at the figure, with a sad intentness that brought the whole power of his great, stern, yet tender soul, into his glance.

"Come!" said he, waving his hand towards her. "You are safe!"

She threw off the veil, and stood before that multitude of people, pale, tremulous, shrinking, as if only then had she discovered that a thousand eyes were gazing at her. Poor maiden! How strangely had she been betrayed! Blazoned abroad as a wonder of the world, and performing what were adjudged as miracles — in the faith of many, a seeress and a prophetess — in the harsher judgment of others, a mountebank — she had kept, as I religiously believe, her virgin reserve and sanctity of soul, throughout it all. Within that encircling veil, though an evil hand had flung it over her, there was as deep a seclusion as if this forsaken girl had, all the while, been sitting under the shadow of Eliot's pulpit, in the Blithedale woods, at the feet of him who now summoned her to the shelter of his arms. And the true heart-throb of a woman's affection was too powerful for the jugglery that had hitherto environed her. She uttered a shriek and fled to Hollingsworth, like one escaping from her deadliest enemy, and was safe forever!

XXIV. THE MASQUERADERS

Two nights had passed since the foregoing occurrences, when, in a breezy September forenoon, I set forth from town, on foot, towards Blithedale.

It was the most delightful of all days for a walk, with a dash of invigorating ice-temper in the air, but a coolness that soon gave place to the brisk glow of exercise, while the vigor remained as elastic as before. The atmosphere had a spirit and sparkle in it. Each breath was like a sip of ethereal wine, tempered, as I said, with a crystal lump of ice. I had started on this expedition in an exceedingly sombre mood, as well befitted one who found himself tending towards home, but was conscious that nobody would be quite overjoyed to greet him there. My feet were hardly off the pavement, however, when this morbid sensation began to yield to the lively influences of air and motion. Nor had I gone far, with fields yet green on either side, before my step became as swift and light as if Hollingsworth were waiting to exchange a friendly hand-grip, and Zenobia's and Priscilla's open arms would welcome the wanderer's re-appearance. It has happened to me, on other occasions, as well as this, to prove how a state of physical well-being can create a kind of joy, in spite of the profoundest anxiety of mind.

The pathway of that walk still runs along, with sunny freshness, through my memory. I know not why it should be so. But my mental eye can even now discern the September grass, bordering the pleasant roadside with a brighter verdure than while the summer-heats were scorching it; the trees, too, mostly green, although, here and there, a branch or shrub has donned its vesture of crimson and gold, a week or two before its fellows. I see the tufted barberry bushes, with their small clusters of scarlet fruit; the toadstools, likewise, some spotlessly white, others yellow or red — mysterious growths, springing suddenly from no root or seed, and growing nobody can tell how or wherefore. In this respect, they resembled many of the emotions in my breast. And I still see the little rivulets, chill, clear, and bright, that murmured beneath the road, through subterranean rocks, and deepened into mossy pools where tiny fish were darting to-and-fro, and within which lurked the hermit-frog. But, no — I never can account for it — that, with a yearning interest to learn the upshot of all my story, and returning to Blithedale for that sole purpose, I should examine these things so like a peaceful-bosomed naturalist. Nor why, amid all my sympathies and fears, there shot, at times, a wild exhilaration through my frame!

Thus I pursued my way, along the line of the ancient stone-wall that Paul Dudley[1] built, and through white villages, and past orchards of ruddy apples, and fields of ripening maize, and patches of woodland, and all such sweet rural scenery as looks the fairest, a little beyond the suburbs of a town. Hollingsworth, Zenobia, Priscilla! They glided mistily before me, as I walked. Sometimes, in my solitude, I laughed with the bitterness of self-scorn, remembering how unreservedly I had given up my heart and soul to interests that were not mine. What had I ever had to do with them? And why, being now free, should I take this thraldom on me, once again? It was both sad and dangerous, I whispered to myself, to be in too close affinity with the passions, the errors, and the misfortunes, of individuals who stood within a circle of their own, into which, if I stept at all, it must be as an intruder, and at a peril that I could not estimate.

Drawing nearer to Blithedale, a sickness of the spirits kept alternating with my flights of causeless buoyancy. I indulged in a hundred odd and extravagant conjectures. Either there was no such place as Blithedale, nor ever had been, nor any brotherhood of thoughtful laborers, like what I seemed to recollect there; or else it was all changed, during my absence. It had been nothing but dream-work and enchantment. I should seek in vain for the old farm-house, and for the greensward, the potatoe-fields, the root-crops, and acres of Indian corn, and for all that configuration of the land which I had imagined. It would be another spot, and an utter strangeness.

These vagaries were of the spectral throng, so apt to steal out of an unquiet heart. They partly ceased to haunt me, on my arriving at a point whence, through the trees, I began to catch glimpses of the Blithedale farm. That, surely, was something real. There was hardly a square foot of all those acres, on which I had not trodden heavily in one or another kind of toil. The curse of Adam's posterity — and, curse or blessing be it, it gives substance to the life around us — had first come upon me there. In the sweat of my brow, I had there earned bread and eaten it, and so established my claim to be on earth, and my fellowship with all the sons of labor. I could have knelt down, and have laid my breast against that soil. The red clay, of which my frame was moulded, seemed nearer akin to those crumbling furrows than to any other portion of the world's dust. There was my home; and there might be my grave.

[1]*Paul Dudley*: Dudley (1675–1751) was a Massachusetts jurist, legislator, and landholder.

I felt an invincible reluctance, nevertheless, at the idea of presenting myself before my old associates, without first ascertaining the
state in which they were. A nameless foreboding weighed upon me.
Perhaps, should I know all the circumstances that had occurred, I
might find it my wisest course to turn back, unrecognized, unseen,
and never look at Blithedale more. Had it been evening, I would have
stolen softly to some lighted window of the old farm-house, and
peeped darkling in, to see all their well-known faces round the
supper-board. Then, were there a vacant seat, I might noiselessly un-
close the door, glide in, and take my place among them, without a
word. My entrance might be so quiet, my aspect so familiar, that they
would forget how long I had been away, and suffer me to melt into
the scene, as a wreath of vapor melts into a larger cloud. I dreaded a
boisterous greeting. Beholding me at table, Zenobia, as a matter of
course, would send me a cup of tea, and Hollingsworth fill my plate
from the great dish of pan-dowdy, and Priscilla, in her quiet way,
would hand the cream, and others help me to the bread and butter.
Being one of them again, the knowledge of what had happened
would come to me, without a shock. For, still, at every turn of my
shifting fantasies, the thought stared me in the face, that some evil
thing had befallen us, or was ready to befall.

Yielding to this ominous impression, I now turned aside into the
woods, resolving to spy out the posture of the Community, as craftily
as the wild Indian before he makes his onset. I would go wandering
about the outskirts of the farm, and, perhaps catching sight of a solitary acquaintance, would approach him amid the brown shadows of
the trees, (a kind of medium fit for spirits departed and revisitant, like
myself,) and entreat him to tell me how all things were.

The first living creature that I met, was a partridge, which sprung
up beneath my feet, and whirred away; the next was a squirrel, who
chattered angrily at me, from an overhanging bough. I trod along by
the dark, sluggish river, and remember pausing on the bank, above
one of its blackest and most placid pools — (the very spot, with the
barkless stump of a tree aslantwise over the water, is depicting itself
to my fancy, at this instant) — and wondering how deep it was, and
if any overladen soul had ever flung its weight of mortality in thither,
and if it thus escaped the burthen, or only made it heavier. And perhaps the skeleton of the drowned wretch still lay beneath the inscrutable depth, clinging to some sunken log at the bottom with the
gripe of its old despair. So slight, however, was the track of these
gloomy ideas, that I soon forgot them in the contemplation of a

brood of wild ducks, which were floating on the river, and anon took flight, leaving each a bright streak over the black surface. By-and-by, I came to my hermitage, in the heart of the white-pine tree, and clambering up into it, sat down to rest. The grapes, which I had watched throughout the summer, now dangled around me in abundant clusters of the deepest purple, deliciously sweet to the taste, and though wild, yet free from that ungentle flavor which distinguishes nearly all our native and uncultivated grapes. Methought a wine might be pressed out of them, possessing a passionate zest, and endowed with a new kind of intoxicating quality, attended with such bacchanalian ecstasies as the tamer grapes of Madeira, France, and the Rhine, are inadequate to produce. And I longed to quaff a great goblet of it, at that moment!

While devouring the grapes, I looked on all sides out of the peep-holes of my hermitage, and saw the farm-house, the fields, and almost every part of our domain, but not a single human figure in the landscape. Some of the windows of the house were open, but with no more signs of life than in a dead man's unshut eyes. The barn-door was ajar, and swinging in the breeze. The big, old dog — he was a relic of the former dynasty of the farm — that hardly ever stirred out of the yard, was nowhere to be seen. What, then, had become of all the fraternity and sisterhood? Curious to ascertain this point, I let myself down out of the tree, and going to the edge of the wood, was glad to perceive our herd of cows, chewing the cud, or grazing, not far off. I fancied, by their manner, that two or three of them recognized me, (as, indeed, they ought, for I had milked them, and been their chamberlain, times without number;) but, after staring me in the face, a little while, they phlegmatically began grazing and chewing their cuds again. Then I grew foolishly angry at so cold a reception, and flung some rotten fragments of an old stump at these unsentimental cows.

Skirting farther round the pasture, I heard voices and much laughter proceeding from the interior of the wood. Voices, male and feminine; laughter, not only of fresh young throats, but the bass of grown people, as if solemn organ-pipes should pour out airs of merriment. Not a voice spoke, but I knew it better than my own; not a laugh, but its cadences were familiar. The wood, in this portion of it, seemed as full of jollity as if Comus and his crew[2] were holding their revels, in one of its usually lonesome glades. Stealing onward as far as I durst, without hazard of discovery, I saw a concourse of strange figures be-

[2]*Comus and his crew*: Name of the evil tempter in Milton's *Comus*.

neath the overshadowing branches; they appeared, and vanished, and came again, confusedly, with the streaks of sunlight glimmering down upon them.

Among them was an Indian chief, with blanket, feathers and war-paint, and uplifted tomahawk; and near him, looking fit to be his woodland-bride, the goddess Diana, with the crescent on her head, and attended by our big, lazy dog, in lack of any fleeter hound. Drawing an arrow from her quiver, she let it fly, at a venture, and hit the very tree behind which I happened to be lurking. Another group consisted of a Bavarian broom-girl, a negro of the Jim Crow order,[3] one or two foresters of the middle-ages, a Kentucky woodsman in his trimmed hunting-shirt and deerskin leggings, and a Shaker elder,[4] quaint, demure, broad-brimmed, and square-skirted. Shepherds of Arcadia, and allegoric figures from the Faerie Queen,[5] were oddly mixed up with these. Arm in arm, or otherwise huddled together, in strange discrepancy, stood grim Puritans, gay Cavaliers,[6] and Revolutionary officers, with three-cornered cocked-hats, and queues longer than their swords. A bright-complexioned, dark-haired, vivacious little gipsy, with a red shawl over her head, went from one group to another, telling fortunes by palmistry; and Moll Pitcher,[7] the renowned old witch of Lynn, broomstick in hand, showed herself prominently in the midst, as if announcing all these apparitions to be the offspring of her necromantic art. But Silas Foster, who leaned against a tree near by, in his customary blue frock, and smoking a short pipe, did more to disenchant the scene, with his look of shrewd, acrid, Yankee observation, than twenty witches and necromancers could have done, in the way of rendering it weird and fantastic.

A little further off, some old-fashioned skinkers and drawers,[8] all with portentously red noses, were spreading a banquet on the leaf-strewn earth; while a horned and long-tailed gentleman (in whom I

[3]*the Jim Crow order*: White person in blackface, from the name of a stock character in nineteenth-century minstrel shows.

[4]*Shaker elder*: A prominent member of an American religious community, known for their skill at farming and woodcraft, whose religious rites involved "shaking" off sin. See Hawthorne's stories "The Canterbury Pilgrims" (1833) and "The Shaker Bridal" (1838).

[5]*the Faerie Queen*: Allegorical epic (1590, 1596) by Edmund Spenser (1552–1599).

[6]*Puritans, gay Cavaliers*: The English Puritans, in control of Parliament from 1642 to 1649, were opposed by the Cavaliers, supporters of King Charles I.

[7]*Moll Pitcher*: Fortune-teller who practiced in Lynn, Massachusetts, in the late eighteenth and early nineteenth centuries; also mentioned in *The House of the Seven Gables*, ch. 18.

[8]*skinkers and drawers*: Servers of liquor.

recognized the fiendish musician, erst seen by Tam O'Shanter)[9] tuned his fiddle, and summoned the whole motley rout to a dance, before partaking of the festal cheer. So they joined hands in a circle, whirling round so swiftly, so madly, and so merrily, in time and tune with the Satanic music, that their separate incongruities were blended all together; and they became a kind of entanglement that went nigh to turn one's brain, with merely looking at it. Anon, they stopt, all of a sudden, and staring at one another's figures, set up a roar of laughter; whereat, a shower of the September leaves (which, all day long, had been hesitating whether to fall or no) were shaken off by the movement of the air, and came eddying down upon the revellers.

Then, for lack of breath, ensued a silence; at the deepest point of which, tickled by the oddity of surprising my grave associates in this masquerading trim, I could not possibly refrain from a burst of laughter, on my own separate account.

"Hush!" I heard the pretty gipsy fortuneteller say. "Who is that laughing?"

"Some profane intruder!" said the goddess Diana. "I shall send an arrow through his heart, or change him into a stag, as I did Actaeon,[10] if he peeps from behind the trees!"

"Me take his scalp!" cried the Indian chief, brandishing his tomahawk, and cutting a great caper in the air.

"I'll root him in the earth, with a spell that I have at my tongue's end!" squeaked Moll Pitcher. "And the green moss shall grow all over him, before he gets free again!"

"The voice was Miles Coverdale's," said the fiendish fiddler, with a whisk of his tail and a toss of his horns. "My music has brought him hither. He is always ready to dance to the devil's tune!"

Thus put on the right track, they all recognized the voice at once, and set up a simultaneous shout.

"Miles! Miles! Miles Coverdale, where are you?" they cried. "Zenobia! Queen Zenobia! Here is one of your vassals lurking in the wood. Command him to approach, and pay his duty!"

The whole fantastic rabble forthwith streamed off in pursuit of me, so that I was like a mad poet hunted by chimaeras.[11] Having

---

[9]*Tam O'Shanter*: The drunken title character of a poem (1791), by the Scottish poet Robert Burns, encounters Old Nick, the Devil.

[10]*Actaeon*: In classical mythology, a hunter turned into a stag by the goddess Diana (he had watched her bathing) and torn to pieces by his own dogs. See Ovid, *Metamorphoses*, 3:138–252.

[11]*chimaeras*: Illusions, fabrications of the mind, often horrible and frightening.

fairly the start of them, however, I succeeded in making my escape, and soon left their merriment and riot at a good distance in the rear. Its fainter tones assumed a kind of mournfulness, and were finally lost in the hush and solemnity of the wood. In my haste, I stumbled over a heap of logs and sticks that had been cut for firewood, a great while ago, by some former possessor of the soil, and piled up square, in order to be carted or sledded away to the farm-house. But, being forgotten, they had lain there, perhaps fifty years, and possibly much longer; until, by the accumulation of moss, and the leaves falling over them and decaying there, from autumn to autumn, a green mound was formed, in which the softened outline of the wood-pile was still perceptible. In the fitful mood that then swayed my mind, I found something strangely affecting in this simple circumstance. I imagined the long-dead woodman, and his long-dead wife and children, coming out of their chill graves, and essaying to make a fire with this heap of mossy fuel!

From this spot I strayed onward, quite lost in reverie, and neither knew nor cared whither I was going, until a low, soft, well-remembered voice spoke, at a little distance.

"There is Mr. Coverdale!"

"Miles Coverdale!" said another voice — and its tones were very stern — "Let him come forward, then!"

"Yes, Mr. Coverdale," cried a woman's voice — clear and melodious, but, just then, with something unnatural in its chord — "You are welcome! But you come half-an-hour too late, and have missed a scene which you would have enjoyed!"

I looked up, and found myself nigh Eliot's pulpit, at the base of which sat Hollingsworth, with Priscilla at his feet, and Zenobia standing before them.

XXV. THE THREE TOGETHER

Hollingsworth was in his ordinary working-dress. Priscilla wore a pretty and simple gown, with a kerchief about her neck, and a calash,[1] which she had flung back from her head, leaving it suspended by the strings. But Zenobia (whose part among the masquers, as may be supposed, was no inferior one) appeared in a costume of

---

[1]*calash:* A large hood or bonnet arranged so that it could be folded far back on the head.

fanciful magnificence, with her jewelled flower as the central ornament of what resembled a leafy crown, or coronet. She represented
the Oriental princess, by whose name we were accustomed to know
her. Her attitude was free and noble, yet, if a queen's, it was not that
of a queen triumphant, but dethroned, on trial for her life, or perchance condemned, already. The spirit of the conflict seemed, nevertheless, to be alive in her. Her eyes were on fire; her cheeks had each
a crimson spot, so exceedingly vivid, and marked with so definite an
outline, that I at first doubted whether it were not artificial. In a very
brief space, however, this idea was shamed by the paleness that ensued, as the blood sank suddenly away. Zenobia now looked like
marble.

One always feels the fact, in an instant, when he has intruded on
those who love, or those who hate, at some acme of their passion that
puts them into a sphere of their own, where no other spirit can pretend to stand on equal ground with them. I was confused — affected
even with a species of terror — and wished myself away. The intentness of their feelings gave them the exclusive property of the soil and
atmosphere, and left me no right to be or breathe there.

"Hollingsworth — Zenobia — I have just returned to Blithedale,"
said I, "and had no thought of finding you here. We shall meet again
at the house. I will retire."

"This place is free to you," answered Hollingsworth.

"As free as to ourselves," added Zenobia. "This long while past,
you have been following up your game, groping for human emotions
in the dark corners of the heart. Had you been here a little sooner,
you might have seen them dragged into the daylight. I could even
wish to have my trial over again, with you standing by, to see fair-
play! Do you know, Mr. Coverdale, I have been on trial for my life?"

She laughed, while speaking thus. But, in truth, as my eyes wandered from one of the group to another, I saw in Hollingsworth all
that an artist could desire for the grim portrait of a Puritan magistrate, holding inquest of life and death in a case of witchcraft;[2] — in
Zenobia, the sorceress herself, not aged, wrinkled, and decrepit, but
fair enough to tempt Satan with a force reciprocal to his own; — and,
in Priscilla, the pale victim, whose soul and body had been wasted by

---

[2]*Puritan magistrate ... case of witchcraft:* One of Hawthorne's ancestors was
John Hathorne (1641–1717), a magistrate who took part in the Salem witch trials of
1692. See "The Custom-House" (the introduction to *The Scarlet Letter*) and
Hawthorne's story "Young Goodman Brown" (1835).

her spells. Had a pile of faggots been heaped against the rock, this hint of impending doom would have completed the suggestive picture.

"It was too hard upon me," continued Zenobia, addressing Hollingsworth, "that judge, jury, and accuser, should all be comprehended in one man! I demur, as I think the lawyers say, to the jurisdiction. But let the learned Judge Coverdale seat himself on the top of the rock, and you and me stand at its base, side by side, pleading our cause before him! There might, at least, be two criminals, instead of one."

"You forced this on me," replied Hollingsworth, looking her sternly in the face. "Did I call you hither from among the masqueraders yonder? Do I assume to be your judge? No; except so far as I have an unquestionable right of judgment, in order to settle my own line of behavior towards those, with whom the events of life bring me in contact. True; I have already judged you, but not on the world's part — neither do I pretend to pass a sentence!"

"Ah, this is very good!" said Zenobia, with a smile. "What strange beings you men are, Mr. Coverdale! — is it not so? It is the simplest thing in the world, with you, to bring a woman before your secret tribunals, and judge and condemn her, unheard, and then tell her to go free without a sentence. The misfortune is, that this same secret tribunal chances to be the only judgment-seat that a true woman stands in awe of, and that any verdict short of acquittal is equivalent to a death-sentence!"

The more I looked at them, and the more I heard, the stronger grew my impression that a crisis had just come and gone. On Hollingsworth's brow, it had left a stamp like that of irrevocable doom, of which his own will was the instrument. In Zenobia's whole person, beholding her more closely, I saw a riotous agitation; the almost delirious disquietude of a great struggle, at the close of which, the vanquished one felt her strength and courage still mighty within her, and longed to renew the contest. My sensations were as if I had come upon a battle-field, before the smoke was as yet cleared away.

And what subjects had been discussed here? All, no doubt, that, for so many months past, had kept my heart and my imagination idly feverish. Zenobia's whole character and history; the true nature of her mysterious connection with Westervelt; her later purposes towards Hollingsworth, and, reciprocally, his in reference to her; and, finally, the degree in which Zenobia had been cognizant of the plot against Priscilla, and what, at last, had been the real object of that scheme. On these points, as before, I was left to my own conjectures. One thing, only, was certain. Zenobia and Hollingsworth were friends no longer. If their heart-strings were ever intertwined, the knot had been adjudged an entanglement, and was now violently broken.

But Zenobia seemed unable to rest content with the matter, in the posture which it had assumed.

"Ah! Do we part so?" exclaimed she, seeing Hollingsworth about to retire.

"And why not?" said he, with almost rude abruptness. "What is there further to be said between us?"

"Well; perhaps nothing!" answered Zenobia, looking him in the face, and smiling. "But we have come, many times before, to this gray rock, and we have talked very softly, among the whisperings of the birch-trees. They were pleasant hours! I love to make the latest of them, though not altogether so delightful, loiter away as slowly as may be. And, besides, you have put many queries to me, at this, which you design to be our last interview; and being driven, as I must acknowledge, into a corner, I have responded with reasonable frankness. But, now, with your free consent, I desire the privilege of asking a few questions in my turn."

"I have no concealments," said Hollingsworth.

"We shall see!" answered Zenobia. "I would first inquire, whether you have supposed me to be wealthy?"

"On that point," observed Hollingsworth, "I have had the opinion which the world holds."

"And I held it, likewise," said Zenobia. "Had I not, Heaven is my witness, the knowledge should have been as free to you as me. It is only three days since I knew the strange fact that threatens to make me poor; and your own acquaintance with it, I suspect, is of at least as old a date. I fancied myself affluent. You are aware, too, of the disposition which I purposed making of the larger portion of my imaginary opulence; — nay, were it all, I had not hesitated. Let me ask you further, did I ever propose or intimate any terms of compact, on which depended this — as the world would consider it — so important sacrifice?"

"You certainly spoke of none," said Hollingsworth.

"Nor meant any," she responded. "I was willing to realize your dream, freely — generously, as some might think — but, at all events, fully — and heedless though it should prove the ruin of my fortune. If, in your own thoughts, you have imposed any conditions of this expenditure, it is you that must be held responsible for whatever is sordid and unworthy in them. And, now, one other question! Do you love this girl?"

"Oh, Zenobia!" exclaimed Priscilla, shrinking back, as if longing for the rock to topple over, and hide her.

"Do you love her?" repeated Zenobia.

"Had you asked me that question, a short time since," replied Hollingsworth, after a pause, during which, it seemed to me, even the birch-trees held their whispering breath, "I should have told you — 'No!' My feelings for Priscilla differed little from those of an elder brother, watching tenderly over the gentle sister whom God has given him to protect."

"And what is your answer, now?" persisted Zenobia.

"I do love her!" said Hollingsworth, uttering the words with a deep, inward breath, instead of speaking them outright. "As well declare it thus, as in any other way. I do love her!"

"Now, God be judge between us," cried Zenobia, breaking into sudden passion, "which of us two has most mortally offended Him! At least, I am a woman — with every fault, it may be, that a woman ever had, weak, vain, unprincipled, (like most of my sex; for our virtues, when we have any, are merely impulsive and intuitive,) passionate, too, and pursuing my foolish and unattainable ends, by indirect and cunning, though absurdly chosen means, as an hereditary bond-slave must — false, moreover, to the whole circle of good, in my reckless truth to the little good I saw before me — but still a woman! A creature, whom only a little change of earthly fortune, a little kinder smile of Him who sent me hither, and one true heart to encourage and direct me, might have made all that a woman can be! But how is it with you? Are you a man? No; but a monster! A cold, heartless, self-beginning and self-ending piece of mechanism!"

"With what, then, do you charge me?" asked Hollingsworth, aghast, and greatly disturbed at this attack. "Show me one selfish end in all I ever aimed at, and you may cut it out of my bosom with a knife!"

"It is all self!" answered Zenobia, with still intenser bitterness. "Nothing else; nothing but self, self, self! The fiend, I doubt not, has made his choicest mirth of you, these seven years past, and especially in the mad summer which we have spent together. I see it now! I am awake, disenchanted, disenthralled! Self, self, self! You have embodied yourself in a project. You are a better masquerader than the witches and gipsies yonder; for your disguise is a self-deception. See whither it has brought you! First, you aimed a death-blow, and a treacherous one, at this scheme of a purer and higher life, which so many noble spirits had wrought out. Then, because Coverdale could not be quite your slave, you threw him ruthlessly away. And you took me, too, into your plan, as long as there was hope of my being available, and now fling me aside again, a broken tool! But, foremost, and blackest of your sins, you stifled down your inmost consciousness! — you did a deadly wrong to your own heart! — you were ready to sacrifice this girl, whom, if God ever visibly showed a purpose, He put into your charge, and through whom He was striving to redeem you!"

"This is a woman's view," said Hollingsworth, growing deadly pale — "a woman's, whose whole sphere of action is in the heart, and who can conceive of no higher nor wider one!"

"Be silent!" cried Zenobia, imperiously. "You know neither man nor woman! The utmost that can be said in your behalf — and because I would not be wholly despicable in my own eyes, but would fain excuse my wasted feelings, nor own it wholly a delusion, therefore I say it — is, that a great and rich heart has been ruined in your breast. Leave me, now! You have done with me, and I with you. Farewell!"

"Priscilla," said Hollingsworth, "come!"

Zenobia smiled; possibly, I did so too. Not often, in human life, has a gnawing sense of injury found a sweeter morsel of revenge, than was conveyed in the tone with which Hollingsworth spoke those two words. It was the abased and tremulous tone of a man, whose faith in himself was shaken, and who sought, at last, to lean on an affection. Yes; the strong man bowed himself, and rested on this poor Priscilla. Oh, could she have failed him, what a triumph for the lookers-on!

And, at first, I half imagined that she was about to fail him. She rose up, stood shivering, like the birch-leaves that trembled over her head, and then slowly tottered, rather than walked, towards Zenobia. Arriving at her feet, she sank down there, in the very same attitude which she had assumed on their first meeting, in the kitchen of the old farm-house. Zenobia remembered it.

"Ah, Priscilla," said she, shaking her head, "how much is changed since then! You kneel to a dethroned princess. You, the victorious one! But he is waiting for you. Say what you wish, and leave me."

"We are sisters!" gasped Priscilla.

I fancied that I understood the word and action; it meant the offering of herself, and all she had, to be at Zenobia's disposal. But the latter would not take it thus.

"True; we are sisters!" she replied; and, moved by the sweet word, she stooped down and kissed Priscilla — but not lovingly; for a sense of fatal harm, received through her, seemed to be lurking in Zenobia's heart — "We had one father! You knew it from the first; I, but a little while — else some things, that have chanced, might have been spared you. But I never wished you harm. You stood between me and an end which I desired. I wanted a clear path. No matter what I meant. It is over now. Do you forgive me?"

"Oh, Zenobia," sobbed Priscilla, "it is I that feel like the guilty one!"

"No, no, poor little thing!" said Zenobia, with a sort of contempt. "You have been my evil fate; but there never was a babe with less strength or will to do an injury. Poor child! Methinks you have but a melancholy lot before you, sitting all alone in that wide, cheerless heart, where, for aught you know — and as I, alas! believe — the fire which you have kindled may soon go out. Ah, the thought makes me shiver for you! What will you do, Priscilla, when you find no spark among the ashes?"

"Die!" she answered.

"That was well said!" responded Zenobia, with an approving smile. "There is all a woman in your little compass, my poor sister. Meanwhile, go with him, and live!"

She waved her away, with a queenly gesture, and turned her own face to the rock. I watched Priscilla, wondering what judgment she would pass, between Zenobia and Hollingsworth; how interpret his behavior, so as to reconcile it with true faith both towards her sister and herself; how compel her love for him to keep any terms whatever with her sisterly affection! But, in truth, there was no such difficulty as I imagined. Her engrossing love made it all clear. Hollingsworth could have no fault. That was the one principle at the centre of the universe. And the doubtful guilt or possible integrity of other people, appearances, self-evident facts, the testimony of her own senses — even Hollingsworth's self-accusation, had he volunteered it — would have weighed not the value of a mote of thistle-down, on the other side. So secure was she of his right, that she never thought of comparing it with another's wrong, but left the latter to itself.

Hollingsworth drew her arm within his, and soon disappeared with her among the trees. I cannot imagine how Zenobia knew when they were out of sight; she never glanced again towards them. But, retaining a proud attitude, so long as they might have thrown back a retiring look, they were no sooner departed — utterly departed —

than she began slowly to sink down. It was as if a great, invisible, irresistible weight were pressing her to the earth. Settling upon her
knees, she leaned her forehead against the rock, and sobbed convul-
sively; dry sobs, they seemed to be, such as having nothing to do with
tears.

XXVI. ZENOBIA AND COVERDALE

Zenobia had entirely forgotten me. She fancied herself alone with
her great grief. And had it been only a common pity that I felt for
her — the pity that her proud nature would have repelled, as the one
worst wrong which the world yet held in reserve — the sacredness
and awfulness of the crisis might have impelled me to steal away,
silently, so that not a dry leaf should rustle under my feet. I would
have left her to struggle, in that solitude, with only the eye of God
upon her. But, so it happened, I never once dreamed of questioning
my right to be there, now, as I had questioned it, just before, when I
came so suddenly upon Hollingsworth and herself, in the passion of
their recent debate. It suits me not to explain what was the analogy
that I saw, or imagined, between Zenobia's situation and mine; nor, I
believe, will the reader detect this one secret, hidden beneath many a
revelation which perhaps concerned me less. In simple truth, however, as Zenobia leaned her forehead against the rock, shaken with
that tearless agony, it seemed to me that the self-same pang, with
hardly mitigated torment, leaped thrilling from her heart-strings to
my own. Was it wrong, therefore, if I felt myself consecrated to the
priesthood, by sympathy like this, and called upon to minister to this
woman's affliction, so far as mortal could?

But, indeed, what could mortal do for her? Nothing! The attempt
would be a mockery and an anguish. Time, it is true, would steal
away her grief, and bury it, and the best of her heart in the same
grave. But Destiny itself, methought, in its kindliest mood, could do
no better for Zenobia, in the way of quick relief, than to cause the
impending rock to impend a little further, and fall upon her head. So
I leaned against a tree, and listened to her sobs, in unbroken silence.
She was half prostrate, half kneeling, with her forehead still pressed
against the rock. Her sobs were the only sound; she did not groan,
nor give any other utterance to her distress. It was all involuntary.

At length, she sat up, put back her hair, and stared about her with
a bewildered aspect, as if not distinctly recollecting the scene through

which she had passed, nor cognizant of the situation in which it left her. Her face and brow were almost purple with the rush of blood. They whitened, however, by-and-by, and, for some time, retained this deathlike hue. She put her hand to her forehead, with a gesture that made me forcibly conscious of an intense and living pain there.

Her glance, wandering wildly to-and-fro, passed over me, several times, without appearing to inform her of my presence. But, finally, a look of recognition gleamed from her eyes into mine.

"Is it you, Miles Coverdale?" said she, smiling. "Ah, I perceive what you are about! You are turning this whole affair into a ballad. Pray let me hear as many stanzas as you happen to have ready!"

"Oh, hush, Zenobia!" I answered. "Heaven knows what an ache is in my soul!"

"It is genuine tragedy, is it not?" rejoined Zenobia, with a sharp, light laugh. "And you are willing to allow, perhaps, that I have had hard measure. But it is a woman's doom, and I have deserved it like a woman; so let there be no pity, as, on my part, there shall be no complaint. It is all right now, or will shortly be so. But, Mr. Coverdale, by all means, write this ballad, and put your soul's ache into it, and turn your sympathy to good account, as other poets do, and as poets must, unless they choose to give us glittering icicles instead of lines of fire. As for the moral, it shall be distilled into the final stanza, in a drop of bitter honey."

"What shall it be, Zenobia?" I inquired, endeavoring to fall in with her mood.

"Oh, a very old one will serve the purpose," she replied. "There are no new truths, much as we have prided ourselves on finding some. A moral? Why, this: — that, in the battle-field of life, the downright stroke, that would fall only on a man's steel head-piece, is sure to light on a woman's heart, over which she wears no breastplate, and whose wisdom it is, therefore, to keep out of the conflict. Or this: — that the whole universe, her own sex and yours, and Providence, or Destiny, to boot, make common cause against the woman who swerves one hair's breadth out of the beaten track. Yes; and add, (for I may as well own it, now,) that, with that one hair's breadth, she goes all astray, and never sees the world in its true aspect, afterwards!"

"This last is too stern a moral," I observed. "Cannot we soften it a little?"

"Do it, if you like, at your own peril, not on my responsibility," she answered; then, with a sudden change of subject, she went on: —

"After all, he has flung away what would have served him better than the poor, pale flower he kept. What can Priscilla do for him? Put passionate warmth into his heart, when it shall be chilled with frozen hopes? Strengthen his hands, when they are weary with much doing and no performance? No; but only tend towards him with a blind, instinctive love, and hang her little, puny weakness for a clog upon his arm! She cannot even give him such sympathy as is worth the name. For will he never, in many an hour of darkness, need that proud, intellectual sympathy which he might have had from me? — the sympathy that would flash light along his course, and guide as well as cheer him? Poor Hollingsworth! Where will he find it now?

"Hollingsworth has a heart of ice!" said I, bitterly. "He is a wretch!"

"Do him no wrong!" interrupted Zenobia, turning haughtily upon me. "Presume not to estimate a man like Hollingsworth! It was my fault, all along, and none of his. I see it now! He never sought me. Why should he seek me? What had I to offer him? A miserable, bruised, and battered heart, spoilt long before he met me! A life, too, hopelessly entangled with a villain's! He did well to cast me off. God be praised, he did it! And yet, had he trusted me, and borne with me a little longer, I would have saved him all this trouble."

She was silent, for a time, and stood with her eyes fixed on the ground. Again raising them, her look was more mild and calm.

"Miles Coverdale!" said she.

"Well, Zenobia!" I responded. "Can I do you any service?"

"Very little," she replied. "But it is my purpose, as you may well imagine, to remove from Blithedale; and, most likely, I may not see Hollingsworth again. A woman in my position, you understand, feels scarcely at her ease among former friends. New faces — unaccustomed looks — those only can she tolerate. She would pine, among familiar scenes; she would be apt to blush, too, under the eyes that knew her secret; her heart might throb uncomfortably; she would mortify herself, I suppose, with foolish notions of having sacrificed the honor of her sex, at the foot of proud, contumacious man. Poor womanhood, with its rights and wrongs! Here will be new matter for my course of lectures, at the idea of which you smiled, Mr. Coverdale, a month or two ago. But, as you have really a heart and sympathies, as far as they go, and as I shall depart without seeing Hollingsworth, I must entreat you to be a messenger between him and me."

"Willingly," said I, wondering at the strange way in which her mind seemed to vibrate from the deepest earnest to mere levity. "What is the message?"

"True; — what is it?" exclaimed Zenobia. "After all, I hardly know. On better consideration, I have no message. Tell him — tell him something pretty and pathetic, that will come nicely and sweetly into your ballad — anything you please, so it be tender and submissive enough. Tell him he has murdered me! Tell him that I'll haunt him!" — she spoke these words with the wildest energy — "And give him — no, give Priscilla — this!"

Thus saying, she took the jewelled flower out of her hair; and it struck me as the act of a queen, when worsted in a combat, discrowning herself, as if she found a sort of relief in abasing all her pride.

"Bid her wear this for Zenobia's sake," she continued. "She is a pretty little creature, and will make as soft and gentle a wife as the veriest Bluebeard[1] could desire. Pity that she must fade so soon! These delicate and puny maidens always do. Ten years hence, let Hollingsworth look at my face and Priscilla's, and then choose betwixt them. Or, if he pleases, let him do it now!"

How magnificently Zenobia looked, as she said this! The effect of her beauty was even heightened by the overconsciousness and self-recognition of it, into which, I suppose, Hollingsworth's scorn had driven her. She understood the look of admiration in my face; and — Zenobia to the last — it gave her pleasure.

"It is an endless pity," said she, "that I had not bethought myself of winning your heart, Mr. Coverdale, instead of Hollingsworth's. I think I should have succeeded; and many women would have deemed you the worthier conquest of the two. You are certainly much the handsomest man. But there is a fate in these things. And beauty, in a man, has been of little account with me, since my earliest girlhood, when, for once, it turned my head. Now, farewell!"

"Zenobia, whither are you going?" I asked.

"No matter where," said she. "But I am weary of this place, and sick to death of playing at philanthropy and progress. Of all varieties of mock-life, we have surely blundered into the very emptiest mockery, in our effort to establish the one true system. I have done with it; and Blithedale must find another woman to superintend the laundry, and you, Mr. Coverdale, another nurse to make your gruel, the next time you fall ill. It was, indeed, a foolish dream! Yet it gave us some

---

[1]*Bluebeard:* Murderous tyrant in *Contes du Temps* (1697) by Charles Perrault (1628–1703), who killed six wives and attempts to murder the seventh.

pleasant summer days, and bright hopes, while they lasted. It can do no more; nor will it avail us to shed tears over a broken bubble. Here is my hand! Adieu!"

She gave me her hand, with the same free, whole-souled gesture as on the first afternoon of our acquaintance; and being greatly moved, I bethought me of no better method of expressing my deep sympathy than to carry it to my lips. In so doing, I perceived that this white hand — so hospitably warm when I first touched it, five months since — was now cold as a veritable piece of snow.

"How very cold!" I exclaimed, holding it between both my own, with the vain idea of warming it. "What can be the reason? It is really deathlike!"

"The extremities die first, they say," answered Zenobia, laughing. "And so you kiss this poor, despised, rejected hand! Well, my dear friend, I thank you! You have reserved your homage for the fallen. Lip of man will never touch my hand again. I intend to become a Catholic, for the sake of going into a nunnery. When you next hear of Zenobia, her face will be behind the black-veil; so look your last at it now — for all is over! Once more, farewell!"

She withdrew her hand, yet left a lingering pressure, which I felt long afterwards. So intimately connected, as I had been, with perhaps the only man in whom she was ever truly interested, Zenobia looked on me as the representative of all the past, and was conscious that, in bidding me adieu, she likewise took final leave of Hollingsworth, and of this whole epoch of her life. Never did her beauty shine out more lustrously, than in the last glimpse that I had of her. She departed, and was soon hidden among the trees.

But, whether it was the strong impression of the foregoing scene, or whatever else the cause, I was affected with a fantasy that Zenobia had not actually gone, but was still hovering about the spot, and haunting it. I seemed to feel her eyes upon me. It was as if the vivid coloring of her character had left a brilliant stain upon the air. By degrees, however, the impression grew less distinct. I flung myself upon the fallen leaves, at the base of Eliot's pulpit. The sunshine withdrew up the tree-trunks, and flickered on the topmost boughs; gray twilight made the wood obscure; the stars brightened out; the pendent boughs became wet with chill autumnal dews. But I was listless, worn-out with emotion on my own behalf, and sympathy for others, and had no heart to leave my comfortless lair, beneath the rock.

I must have fallen asleep, and had a dream, all the circumstances of which utterly vanished at the moment when they converged to some tragical catastrophe, and thus grew too powerful for the thin sphere of slumber that enveloped them. Starting from the ground, I found the risen moon shining upon the rugged face of the rock, and myself all in a tremble.

XXVII. MIDNIGHT

It could not have been far from midnight, when I came beneath Hollingsworth's window, and finding it open, flung in a tuft of grass, with earth at the roots, and heard it fall upon the floor. He was either awake, or sleeping very lightly; for scarcely a moment had gone by, before he looked out and discerned me standing in the moonlight.

"Is it you, Coverdale?" he asked. "What is the matter?"

"Come down to me, Hollingsworth!" I answered. "I am anxious to speak with you."

The strange tone of my own voice startled me, and him, probably, no less. He lost no time, and soon issued from the house-door, with his dress half-arranged.

"Again, what is the matter?" he asked, impatiently.

"Have you seen Zenobia," said I, "since you parted from her, at Eliot's pulpit?"

"No," answered Hollingsworth; "nor did I expect it."

His voice was deep, but had a tremor in it. Hardly had he spoken, when Silas Foster thrust his head, done up in a cotton handkerchief, out of another window, and took what he called — as it literally was — a squint at us.

"Well, folks, what are ye about here?" he demanded. "Aha, are you there, Miles Coverdale? You have been turning night into day, since you left us, I reckon; and so you find it quite natural to come prowling about the house, at this time o' night, frightening my old woman out of her wits, and making her disturb a tired man out of his best nap. In with you, you vagabond, and to bed!"

"Dress yourself quietly, Foster," said I. "We want your assistance."

I could not, for the life of me, keep that strange tone out of my voice. Silas Foster, obtuse as were his sensibilities, seemed to feel the ghastly earnestness that was conveyed in it, as well as Hollingsworth did. He immediately withdrew his head, and I heard him yawning, muttering to his wife, and again yawning heavily, while he hurried on his clothes. Meanwhile, I showed Hollingsworth a delicate handkerchief, marked with a well-known cypher, and told where I had found it, and other circumstances which had filled me with a suspicion so terrible, that I left him, if he dared, to shape it out for himself. By the time my brief explanation was finished, we were joined by Silas Foster, in his blue woollen frock.

"Well, boys," cried he, peevishly, "what is to pay now?"

"Tell him, Hollingsworth!" said I.

Hollingsworth shivered, perceptibly, and drew in a hard breath betwixt his teeth. He steadied himself, however, and looking the matter more firmly in the face than I had done, explained to Foster my suspicions and the grounds of them, with a distinctness from which, in spite of my utmost efforts, my words had swerved aside. The toughnerved yeoman, in his comment, put a finish on the business, and brought out the hideous idea in its full terror, as if he were removing the napkin from the face of a corpse.

"And so you think she's drowned herself!" he cried.

I turned away my face.

"What on earth should the young woman do that for?" exclaimed Silas, his eyes half out of his head with mere surprise. "Why, she has more means than she can use or waste, and lacks nothing to make her comfortable, but a husband — and that's an article she could have, any day! There's some mistake about this, I tell you!"

"Come," said I, shuddering. "Let us go and ascertain the truth."

"Well, well," answered Silas Foster, "just as you say. We'll take the long pole, with the hook at the end, that serves to get the bucket out of the draw-well, when the rope is broken. With that, and a couple of long-handled hay-rakes, I'll answer for finding her, if she's anywhere to be found. Strange enough! Zenobia drown herself! No, no, I don't believe it. She had too much sense, and too much means, and enjoyed life a great deal too well."

When our few preparations were completed, we hastened, by a shorter than the customary route, through fields and pastures, and across a portion of the meadow, to the particular spot, on the riverbank, which I had paused to contemplate, in the course of my afternoon's ramble. A nameless presentiment had again drawn me thither, after leaving Eliot's pulpit. I showed my companions where I had found the handkerchief, and pointed to two or three footsteps, impressed into the clayey margin, and tending towards the water. Beneath its shallow verge, among the water-weeds, there were further traces, as yet unobliterated by the sluggish current, which was there almost at a stand-still. Silas Foster thrust his face down close to these footsteps, and picked up a shoe, that had escaped my observation, being half imbedded in the mud.

"There's a kid-shoe that never was made on a Yankee last," observed he. "I know enough of shoemaker's craft to tell that. French manufacture; and see what a high instep! — and how evenly she trod in it! There never was a woman that stept handsomer in her shoes than Zenobia did. Here," he added, addressing Hollingsworth, "would you like to keep the shoe?"

Hollingsworth started back.

"Give it to me, Foster," said I.

I dabbled it in the water, to rinse off the mud, and have kept it ever since. Not far from this spot, lay an old, leaky punt, drawn up on the oozy river-side, and generally half-full of water. It served the angler to go in quest of pickerel, or the sportsman to pick up his wild-ducks. Setting this crazy barque afloat, I seated myself in the stern, with the paddle, while Hollingsworth sat in the bows, with the hooked pole, and Silas Foster amidships, with a hay-rake.

"It puts me in mind of my young days," remarked Silas, "when I used to steal out of bed to go bobbing for horn-pouts[1] and eels. Heigh-ho! — well! — life and death together make sad work for us all. Then, I was a boy, bobbing for fish; and now I am getting to be an old fellow, and here I be, groping for a dead body! I tell you what, lads, if I thought anything had really happened to Zenobia, I should feel kind o' sorrowful."

"I wish, at least, you would hold your tongue!" muttered I.

The moon, that night, though past the full, was still large and oval, and having risen between eight and nine o'clock, now shone aslant-wise over the river, throwing the high, opposite bank, with its woods, into deep shadow, but lighting up the hither shore pretty effectually. Not a ray appeared to fall on the river itself. It lapsed imperceptibly away, a broad, black, inscrutable depth, keeping its own secrets from the eye of man, as impenetrably as mid-ocean could.

"Well, Miles Coverdale," said Foster, "you are the helmsman. How do you mean to manage this business?"

"I shall let the boat drift, broadside foremost, past that stump," I replied. "I know the bottom, having sounded it in fishing. The shore, on this side, after the first step or two, goes off very abruptly; and there is a pool, just by the stump, twelve or fifteen feet deep. The

---

[1]*horn-pouts:* Common variety of large-headed fish.

current could not have force enough to sweep any sunken object — even if partially buoyant — out of that hollow."

"Come, then," said Silas. "But I doubt whether I can touch bottom with this hay-rake, if it's as deep as you say. Mr. Hollingsworth, I think you'll be the lucky man, to-night, such luck as it is!"

We floated past the stump. Silas Foster plied his rake manfully, poking it as far as he could into the water, and immersing the whole length of his arm besides. Hollingsworth at first sat motionless, with the hooked-pole elevated in the air. But, by-and-by, with a nervous and jerky movement, he began to plunge it into the blackness that up-bore us, setting his teeth, and making precisely such thrusts, methought, as if he were stabbing at a deadly enemy. I bent over the side of the boat. So obscure, however, so awfully mysterious, was that dark stream, that — and the thought made me shiver like a leaf — I might as well have tried to look into the enigma of the eternal world, to discover what had become of Zenobia's soul, as into the river's depths, to find her body. And there, perhaps, she lay, with her face upward, while the shadow of the boat, and my own pale face peering downward, passed slowly betwixt her and the sky.

Once, twice, thrice, I paddled the boat up stream, and again suffered it to glide, with the river's slow, funereal motion, downward. Silas Foster had raked up a large mass of stuff, which, as it came towards the surface, looked somewhat like a flowing garment, but proved to be a monstrous tuft of water-weeds. Hollingsworth, with a gigantic effort, upheaved a sunken log. When once free of the bottom, it rose partly out of water — all weedy and slimy, a devilish-looking object, which the moon had not shone upon for half a hundred years — then plunged again, and sullenly returned to its old resting-place, for the remnant of the century.

"That looked ugly!" quoth Silas. "I half thought it was the Evil One on the same errand as ourselves — searching for Zenobia!"

"He shall never get her!" said I, giving the boat a strong impulse.

"That's not for you to say, my boy!" retorted the yeoman. "Pray God he never has, and never may! Slow work this, however! I should really be glad to find something. Pshaw! What a notion that is, when the only good-luck would be, to paddle, and drift and poke, and grope, hereabouts, till morning, and have our labor for our pains! For my part, I shouldn't wonder if the creature had only lost her shoe in the mud, and saved her soul alive, after all. My stars, how she will laugh at us, tomorrow morning!"

It is indescribable what an image of Zenobia — at the breakfast-table, full of warm and mirthful life — this surmise of Silas Foster's brought before my mind. The terrible phantasm of her death was thrown by it into the remotest and dimmest back-ground, where it seemed to grow as improbable as a myth.

"Yes, Silas; it may be as you say!" cried I.

The drift of the stream had again borne us a little below the stump, when I felt — yes, felt, for it was as if the iron hook had smote my breast — felt Hollingsworth's pole strike some object at the bottom of the river. He started up, and almost overset the boat.

"Hold on!" cried Foster. "You have her!"

Putting a fury of strength into the effort, Hollingsworth heaved amain, and up came a white swash to the surface of the river. It was the flow of a woman's garments. A little higher, and we saw her dark hair, streaming down the current. Black River of Death, thou hadst yielded up thy victim! Zenobia was found!

Silas Foster laid hold of the body — Hollingsworth, likewise, grappled with it — and I steered towards the bank, gazing, all the while, at Zenobia, whose limbs were swaying in the current, close at the boat's side. Arriving near the shore, we all three stept into the water, bore her out, and laid her on the ground, beneath a tree.

"Poor child!" said Foster — and his dry old heart, I verily believe, vouchsafed a tear — "I'm sorry for her!"

Were I to describe the perfect horror of the spectacle, the reader might justly reckon it to me for a sin and shame. For more than twelve long years I have borne it in my memory, and could now reproduce it as freshly as if it were still before my eyes. Of all modes of death, methinks it is the ugliest. Her wet garments swathed limbs of terrible inflexibility. She was the marble image of a death-agony. Her arms had grown rigid in the act of struggling, and were bent before her, with clenched hands; her knees, too, were bent, and — thank God for it! — in the attitude of prayer. Ah, that rigidity! It is impossible to bear the terror of it. It seemed — I must needs impart so much of my own miserable idea — it seemed as if her body must keep the same position in the coffin, and that her skeleton would keep it in the grave, and that when Zenobia rose, at the Day of Judgment, it would be in just the same attitude as now!

One hope I had; and that, too, was mingled half with fear. She knelt, as if in prayer. With the last, choking consciousness, her soul, bubbling out through her lips, it may be, had given itself up to the Father, reconciled and penitent. But her arms! They were bent before her, as if she struggled against Providence in never-ending hostility.

Her hands! They were clenched in immitigable defiance. Away with the hideous thought! The flitting moment, after Zenobia sank into the dark pool — when her breath was gone, and her soul at her lips — was as long, in its capacity of God's infinite forgiveness, as the lifetime of the world.

Foster bent over the body, and carefully examined it.

"You have wounded the poor thing's breast," said he to Hollingsworth. "Close by her heart, too!"

"Ha!" cried Hollingsworth, with a start.

And so he had, indeed, both before and after death.

"See!" said Foster. "That's the place where the iron struck her. It looks cruelly, but she never felt it!"

He endeavored to arrange the arms of the corpse decently by its side. His utmost strength, however, scarcely sufficed to bring them down; and rising again, the next instant, they bade him defiance, exactly as before. He made another effort, with the same result.

"In God's name, Silas Foster," cried I, with bitter indignation, "let that dead woman alone!"

"Why, man, it's not decent!" answered he, staring at me in amazement. "I can't bear to see her looking so! Well, well," added he, after a third effort, "'tis of no use, sure enough; and we must leave the women to do their best with her, after we get to the house. The sooner that's done, the better."

We took two rails from a neighboring fence, and formed a bier by laying across some boards from the bottom of the boat. And thus we bore Zenobia homeward. Six hours before, how beautiful! At midnight, what a horror! A reflection occurs to me, that will show ludicrously, I doubt not, on my page, but must come in, for its sterling truth. Being the woman that she was, could Zenobia have foreseen all these ugly circumstances of death, how ill it would become her, the altogether unseemly aspect which she must put on, and, especially, old Silas Foster's efforts to improve the matter, she would no more have committed the dreadful act, than have exhibited herself to a public assembly in a badly-fitting garment! Zenobia, I have often thought, was not quite simple in her death. She had seen pictures, I suppose, of drowned persons, in lithe and graceful attitudes. And she deemed it well and decorous to die as so many village-maidens have, wronged in their first-love, and seeking peace in the bosom of the old, familiar stream — so familiar that they could not dread it — where, in childhood, they used to bathe their little feet, wading mid-leg deep, unmindful of wet skirts. But, in Zenobia's case, there was some tint of the Arcadian affectation that had been visible enough in all our lives, for a few months past.

This, however, to my conception, takes nothing from the tragedy. For, has not the world come to an awfully sophisticated pass, when, after a certain degree of acquaintance with it, we cannot even put ourselves to death in whole-hearted simplicity?

Slowly, slowly, with many a dreary pause — resting the bier often on some rock, or balancing it across a mossy log, to take fresh hold — we bore our burthen onward, through the moonlight, and, at last, laid Zenobia on the floor of the old farm-house. By-and-by, came three or four withered women, and stood whispering around the corpse, peering at it through their spectacles, holding up their skinny hands, shaking their night-capt heads, and taking counsel of one another's experience what was to be done.

With those tire-women,[2] we left Zenobia!

XXVIII. BLITHEDALE-PASTURE

Blithedale, thus far in its progress, had never found the necessity of a burial-ground. There was some consultation among us, in what spot Zenobia might most fitly be laid. It was my own wish, that she should sleep at the base of Eliot's pulpit, and that, on the rugged front of the rock, the name by which we familiarly knew her — ZENOBIA — and not another word, should be deeply cut, and left for the moss and lichens to fill up, at their long leisure. But Hollingsworth (to whose ideas, on this point, great deference was due) made it his request that her grave might be dug on the gently sloping hill-side, in the wide pasture, where, as we once supposed, Zenobia and he had planned to build their cottage. And thus it was done, accordingly.

She was buried very much as other people have been, for hundreds of years gone by. In anticipation of a death, we Blithedale colonists had sometimes set our fancies at work to arrange a funereal cere-mony, which should be the proper symbolic expression of our spiri-tual faith and eternal hopes; and this we meant to substitute for those customary rites, which were moulded originally out of the Gothic gloom, and, by long use, like an old velvet-pall, have so much more

[2]*tire-women:* Lady's maid (from *attire*); here refers to women who prepare and dress a body for burial.

than their first death-smell in them. But, when the occasion came, we found it the simplest and truest thing, after all, to content ourselves with the old fashion, taking away what we could, but interpolating no novelties, and particularly avoiding all frippery of flowers and cheerful emblems. The procession moved from the farm-house. Nearest the dead walked an old man in deep mourning, his face mostly concealed in a white handkerchief, and with Priscilla leaning on his arm. Hollingsworth and myself came next. We all stood around the narrow niche in the cold earth; all saw the coffin lowered in; all heard the rattle of the crumbly soil upon its lid — that final sound, which mortality awakens on the utmost verge of sense, as if in the vain hope of bringing an echo from the spiritual world.

I noticed a stranger — a stranger to most of those present, though known to me — who, after the coffin had descended, took up a handful of earth, and flung it first into the grave. I had given up Hollingsworth's arm, and now found myself near this man.

"It was an idle thing — a foolish thing — for Zenobia to do!" said he. "She was the last woman in the world to whom death could have been necessary. It was too absurd! I have no patience with her."

"Why so?" I inquired, smothering my horror at his cold comment in my eager curiosity to discover some tangible truth, as to his relation with Zenobia. "If any crisis could justify the sad wrong she offered to herself, it was surely that in which she stood. Everything had failed her — prosperity, in the world's sense, for her opulence was gone — the heart's prosperity, in love. And there was a secret burthen on her, the nature of which is best known to you. Young as she was, she had tried life fully, had no more to hope, and something, perhaps, to fear. Had Providence taken her away in its own holy hand, I should have thought it the kindest dispensation that could be awarded to one so wrecked."

"You mistake the matter completely," rejoined Westervelt.

"What, then, is your own view of it?" I asked.

"Her mind was active, and various in its powers," said he; "her heart had a manifold adaptation; her constitution an infinite buoyancy, which (had she possessed only a little patience to await the reflux of her troubles) would have borne her upward, triumphantly, for twenty years to come. Her beauty would not have waned — or scarcely so, and surely not beyond the reach of art to restore it — in all that time. She had life's summer all before her, and a hundred varieties of brilliant success. What an actress Zenobia might have been! It was one of her least valuable capabilities. How forcibly she might

have wrought upon the world, either directly in her own person, or
by her influence upon some man, or a series of men, of controlling
genius! Every prize that could be worth a woman's having — and
many prizes which other women are too timid to desire — lay within
Zenobia's reach."

"In all this," I observed, "there would have been nothing to satisfy
her heart."

"Her heart!" answered Westervelt, contemptuously. "That troublesome organ (as she had hitherto found it) would have been kept in
its due place and degree, and have had all the gratification it could
fairly claim. She would soon have established a control over it. Love
had failed her, you say! Had it never failed her before? Yet she survived it, and loved again — possibly, not once alone, nor twice either.
And now to drown herself for yonder dreamy philanthropist!"

"Who are you," I exclaimed, indignantly, "that dare to speak thus
of the dead? You seem to intend a eulogy, yet leave out whatever was
noblest in her, and blacken, while you mean to praise. I have long
considered you as Zenobia's evil fate. Your sentiments confirm me in
the idea, but leave me still ignorant as to the mode in which you have
influenced her life. The connection may have been indissoluble, except by death. Then, indeed — always in the hope of God's infinite
mercy — I cannot deem it a misfortune that she sleeps in yonder
grave!"

"No matter what I was to her," he answered, gloomily, yet without actual emotion. "She is now beyond my reach. Had she lived, and
hearkened to my counsels, we might have served each other well. But
there Zenobia lies, in yonder pit, with the dull earth over her. Twenty
years of a brilliant lifetime thrown away for a mere woman's whim!"

Heaven deal with Westervelt according to his nature and
deserts! — that is to say, annihilate him. He was altogether earthy,
worldly, made for time and its gross objects, and incapable — except
by a sort of dim reflection, caught from other minds — of so much as
one spiritual idea. Whatever stain Zenobia had, was caught from
him; nor does it seldom happen that a character of admirable qualities loses its better life, because the atmosphere, that should sustain it,
is rendered poisonous by such breath as this man mingled with Zenobia's. Yet his reflections possessed their share of truth. It was a woful
thought, that a woman of Zenobia's diversified capacity should have
fancied herself irretrievably defeated on the broad battle-field of
life, and with no refuge, save to fall on her own sword, merely because Love had gone against her. It is nonsense, and a miserable

wrong — the result, like so many others, of masculine egotism — that the success or failure of woman's existence should be made to depend wholly on the affections, and on one species of affection; while man has such a multitude of other chances, that this seems but an incident. For its own sake, if it will do no more, the world should throw open all its avenues to the passport of a woman's bleeding heart.

As we stood around the grave, I looked often towards Priscilla, dreading to see her wholly overcome with grief. And deeply grieved, in truth, she was. But a character, so simply constituted as hers, has room only for a single predominant affection. No other feeling can touch the heart's inmost core, nor do it any deadly mischief. Thus, while we see that such a being responds to every breeze, with tremulous vibration, and imagine that she must be shattered by the first rude blast, we find her retaining her equilibrium amid shocks that might have overthrown many a sturdier frame. So with Priscilla! Her one possible misfortune was Hollingsworth's unkindness; and that was destined never to befall her — never yet, at least — for Priscilla has not died.

But, Hollingsworth! After all the evil that he did, are we to leave him thus, blest with the entire devotion of this one true heart, and with wealth at his disposal, to execute the long contemplated project that had led him so far astray? What retribution is there here? My mind being vexed with precisely this query, I made a journey, some years since, for the sole purpose of catching a last glimpse at Hollingsworth, and judging for myself whether he were a happy man or no. I learned that he inhabited a small cottage, that his way of life was exceedingly retired, and that my only chance of encountering him or Priscilla was, to meet them in a secluded lane, where, in the latter part of the afternoon, they were accustomed to walk. I did meet them, accordingly. As they approached me, I observed in Hollingsworth's face a depressed and melancholy look, that seemed habitual; the powerfully built man showed a self-distrustful weakness, and a childlike, or childish, tendency to press close, and closer still, to the side of the slender woman whose arm was within his. In Priscilla's manner, there was a protective and watchful quality, as if she felt herself the guardian of her companion, but, likewise, a deep, submissive, unquestioning reverence, and also a veiled happiness in her fair and quiet countenance.

Drawing nearer, Priscilla recognized me, and gave me a kind and friendly smile, but with a slight gesture which I could not help interpreting as an entreaty not to make myself known to Hollingsworth.

Nevertheless, an impulse took possession of me, and compelled me to address him.

"I have come, Hollingsworth," said I, "to view your grand edifice for the reformation of criminals. Is it finished yet?"

"No — nor begun!" answered he, without raising his eyes. "A very small one answers all my purposes."

Priscilla threw me an upbraiding glance. But I spoke again, with a bitter and revengeful emotion, as if flinging a poisoned arrow at Hollingsworth's heart.

"Up to this moment," I inquired, "how many criminals have you reformed?"

"Not one!" said Hollingsworth, with his eyes still fixed on the ground. "Ever since we parted, I have been busy with a single murderer!"

Then the tears gushed into my eyes, and I forgave him. For I remembered the wild energy, the passionate shriek, with which Zenobia had spoken those words — 'Tell him he has murdered me! Tell him that I'll haunt him!' — and I knew what murderer he meant, and whose vindictive shadow dogged the side where Priscilla was not.

The moral which presents itself to my reflections, as drawn from Hollingsworth's character and errors, is simply this: — that, admitting what is called Philanthropy, when adopted as a profession, to be often useful by its energetic impulse to society at large, it is perilous to the individual, whose ruling passion, in one exclusive channel, it thus becomes. It ruins, or is fearfully apt to ruin, the heart; the rich juices of which God never meant should be pressed violently out, and distilled into alcoholic liquor, by an unnatural process; but should render life sweet, bland, and gently beneficent, and insensibly influence other hearts and other lives to the same blessed end. I see in Hollingsworth an exemplification of the most awful truth in Bunyan's book[1] of such; — from the very gate of Heaven, there is a byway to the pit!

But, all this while, we have been standing by Zenobia's grave. I have never since beheld it, but make no question that the grass grew all the better, on that little parallelogram of pasture-land, for the decay of the beautiful woman who slept beneath. How much Nature seems to love us! And how readily, nevertheless, without a sigh or a

---

[1]*Bunyan's book:* That is, *The Pilgrim's Progress* (1678, 1684), a spiritual allegory by John Bunyan (1628–1688). See Hawthorne's story "The Celestial Rail-road" (1843) and the reference to Bunyan's depiction of hell in *The Scarlet Letter* (1850), ch. 10.

complaint, she converts us to a meaner purpose, when her highest one — that of conscious, intellectual life, and sensibility — has been untimely baulked! While Zenobia lived, Nature was proud of her, and directed all eyes upon that radiant presence, as her fairest handi-work. Zenobia perished. Will not Nature shed a tear? Ah, no! She adopts the calamity at once into her system, and is just as well pleased, for aught we can see, with the tuft of ranker vegetation that grew out of Zenobia's heart, as with all the beauty which has be-queathed us no earthly representative, except in this crop of weeds. It is because the spirit is inestimable, that the lifeless body is so little valued.

XXIX. MILES COVERDALE'S CONFESSION

It remains only to say a few words about myself. Not improbably, the reader might be willing to spare me the trouble; for I have made but a poor and dim figure in my own narrative, establishing no sepa-rate interest, and suffering my colorless life to take its hue from other lives. But one still retains some little consideration for one's self; so I keep these last two or three pages for my individual and sole behoof.

But what, after all, have I to tell? Nothing, nothing, nothing! I left Blithedale within the week after Zenobia's death, and went back thither no more. The whole soil of our farm, for a long time after-wards, seemed but the sodded earth over her grave. I could not toil there, nor live upon its products. Often, however, in these years that are darkening around me, I remember our beautiful scheme of a noble and unselfish life, and how fair, in that first summer, appeared the prospect that it might endure for generations, and be perfected, as the ages rolled away, into the system of a people, and a world. Were my former associates now there — were there only three or four of those true-hearted men, still laboring in the sun — I sometimes fancy that I should direct my world-weary footsteps thitherward, and en-treat them to receive me, for old friendship's sake. More and more, I feel that we had struck upon what ought to be a truth. Posterity may dig it up, and profit by it. The experiment, so far as its original pro-jectors were concerned, proved long ago a failure, first lapsing into Fourierism, and dying, as it well deserved, for this infidelity to its own higher spirit. Where once we toiled with our whole hopeful hearts, the town-paupers, aged, nerveless, and disconsolate, creep sluggishly a-field. Alas, what faith is requisite to bear up against such results of generous effort!

My subsequent life has passed — I was going to say, happily — but, at all events, tolerably enough. I am now at middle-age — well, well, a step or two beyond the midmost point, and I care not a fig who knows it! — a bachelor, with no very decided purpose of ever being otherwise. I have been twice to Europe, and spent a year or two, rather agreeably, at each visit. Being well to do in the world, and having nobody but myself to care for, I live very much at my ease, and fare sumptuously every day. As for poetry, I have given it up, notwithstanding that Doctor Griswold[1] — as the reader, of course, knows — has placed me at a fair elevation among our minor minstrelsy, on the strength of my pretty little volume, published ten years ago. As regards human progress, (in spite of my irrepressible yearnings over the Blithedale reminiscences,) let them believe in it who can, and aid in it who choose! If I could earnestly do either, it might be all the better for my comfort. As Hollingsworth once told me, I lack a purpose. How strange! He was ruined, morally, by an overplus of the very same ingredient, the want of which, I occasionally suspect, has rendered my own life all an emptiness. I by no means wish to die. Yet, were there any cause, in this whole chaos of human struggle, worth a sane man's dying for, and which my death would benefit, then — provided, however, the effort did not involve an unreasonable amount of trouble — methinks I might be bold to offer up my life. If Kossuth,[2] for example, would pitch the battle-field of Hungarian rights within an easy ride of my abode, and choose a mild, sunny morning, after breakfast, for the conflict, Miles Coverdale would gladly be his man, for one brave rush upon the levelled bayonets. Farther than that, I should be loth to pledge myself.

I exaggerate my own defects. The reader must not take my own word for it, nor believe me altogether changed from the young man, who once hoped strenuously, and struggled, not so much amiss. Frostier heads than mine have gained honor in the world; frostier hearts have imbibed new warmth, and been newly happy. Life,

<hr>

[1]*Doctor Griswold:* Rufus Griswold (1815–1857) was a prominent journalist, critic, and editor in Philadelphia and New York and the compiler of *The Poets and Poetry of America* (1842) and *Prose Writers of America* (1847).

[2]*Kossuth:* Lajos [Louis] Kossuth (1802–1894), leader in the Hungarian revolution (1848–49), toured the United States in 1851–52 after the failure of the Hungarian republic; he gave a lecture in Boston attended by Hawthorne. See also Donald S. Spencer, *Louis Kossuth and Young America: A Study of Sectionalism and Foreign Policy, 1848–1852* (Columbia: University of Missouri Press, 1977).

however, it must be owned, has come to rather an idle pass with me. Would my friends like to know what brought it thither? There is one secret — I have concealed it all along, and never meant to let the least whisper of it escape — one foolish little secret, which possibly may have had something to do with these inactive years of meridian manhood, with my bachelorship, with the unsatisfied retrospect that I fling back on life, and my listless glance towards the future. Shall I reveal it? It is an absurd thing for a man in his afternoon — a man of the world, moreover, with these three white hairs in his brown moustache, and that deepening track of a crow's foot on each temple — an absurd thing ever to have happened, and quite the absurdest for an old bachelor, like me, to talk about. But it rises in my throat; so let it come.

I perceive, moreover, that the confession, brief as it shall be, will throw a gleam of light over my behavior throughout the foregoing incidents, and is, indeed, essential to the full understanding of my story. The reader, therefore, since I have disclosed so much, is entitled to this one word more. As I write it, he will charitably suppose me to blush, and turn away my face: — [3]

I — I myself — was in love — with — PRISCILLA!

THE END.

---

[3]This paragraph appears in the first edition but not in the manuscript. Compare the "Postscript" Hawthorne added to later printings of *The Marble Faun.*

Part Two

The Blithedale Romance
Cultural Contexts

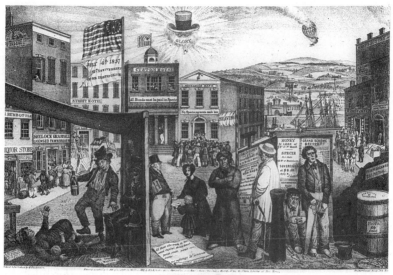

THE TIMES.

"The Times," lithograph by Edward W. Clay, 1837. A financial crisis broke out in 1837 that led to severe unemployment and poverty for many Americans. Its effects persisted throughout the late 1830s and into the 1840s, leading a number of social critics and theorists, such as George Ripley, founder of Brook Farm, to propose utopian communities as an alternative to a capitalist order that appeared to have failed. J. Clarence Davies Collection. Reproduced by permission of the Museum of the City of New York.

1

Prospects for Change

When Hawthorne examined reformers, he saw in them the threat of monomania and fanaticism, and in his short stories of the 1840s, he warned against the distortions of self that the fixation on reform could engender. In "The Procession of Life" (1843), he observed:

> When a good man has long devoted himself to a particular kind of beneficence — to one species of reform — he is apt to become narrowed into the limits of the path wherein he treads, and to fancy that there is no other good to be done on earth but that self-same good to which he has put his hand, and in the very mode that best suits his own conceptions.

This same point is evident in even more powerfully sustained detail in the story "Earth's Holocaust" (reprinted in this chapter). Here Hawthorne shows the terrible momentum of destruction that the reform impulse triggers when reformers concentrate on external conditions, forms, and institutions and forget the primacy of "the Heart."

Perhaps the most controversial reformer of the period was the abolitionist William Lloyd Garrison, editor of *The Liberator,* who declared in his first editorial, "I *will be* as harsh as truth, and as uncompromising as justice." Because Garrison was so uncompromising, he was often charged with the negative qualities, such as fanaticism and intolerance, that Hawthorne associated with reformers.

The movement that Garrison helped to lead now strikes us as the most significant of the reform movements, since it prepared the way for the eventual outbreak of civil war and the end of American slavery. But there were many other movements, some of them closely tied to the economic depression, financial panic, and widespread unemployment of the late 1830s. These included the struggle for workers' rights, land reform, prison reform, and women's rights, and also the campaign for temperance and the development of religious and secular utopias. In addition, there were countless trends, fads, and tendencies, such as the "mesmerism" that intrigued the English woman of letters Harriet Martineau and Margaret Fuller, as the selections below attest. Many persons clung to their favorite reforms and innovative practices as steadfastly as Garrison did to his.

The reformers were a contentious bunch, and they fought frequently among themselves. In the documents included here on economic conditions, for example, George Henry Evans and Orestes A. Brownson highlight the theme of inequality yet differ on the type of change needed. Evans decries the suffering of "poor men" and their families, and proposes changes in laws affecting business, trade, and finance. Similarly, Brownson emphasizes the plight of workers and favors changes in legislation. Brownson differs from Evans, however, in approaching the revolutionary thrust of the arguments that Karl Marx and Friedrich Engels articulated abroad and that became part of the discourse of the European revolutions of 1848. In his view, the ultimate remedy for social injustice in America was "physical force," which, he said, "will come, if it ever come at all, only at the conclusion of war." This essay was assailed as yet another instance of a reformer's fanaticism, and soon Brownson backed away from the vision of class warfare that he had expressed.

Dispute and disagreement also figured in the campaign for temperance, in education and prison reform, and in the anti-slavery movement, and readers need to bear this point in mind when examining the following documents. Some reformers, including Brownson and Evans, stated that while they were opposed to slavery, they judged that in fact the conditions of working men and women in the North were even more intolerable than were those faced by slaves in the South, and that the labor problem therefore needed to be addressed before slavery. Some reformers endorsed Abraham Lincoln's position on temperance, but others concluded that it was too moderate and did not share Lincoln's faith in the power of "persuasion" and "moral influence" to make change.

Differences within the ranks of reformers are evident in prison reform and abolitionism as well. Samuel Gridley Howe laid out his program for reform of the prison in opposition to another plan that competed with it; and for his part, the transcendentalist minister Theodore Parker was less concerned about the prison system itself than about the Christian love that should inform it. The African American abolitionist Frederick Douglass was a relentless foe of slavery, but he also denounced the racism and discrimination he saw in the North and experienced even among his white anti-slavery colleagues. He also dissented from the view that Northern workers were "free" in name only and thus suffered more than did blacks held in bondage.

In his campaign biography of Franklin Pierce, published in 1852, Hawthorne concluded that reformers never achieved the goals that they aimed for. He overstated his case, but his belief in it came from serious reflection on the range of reforms that crisscrossed the United States in the 1830s, 1840s, and 1850s. Hawthorne did not doubt that the nation could be made better, but he balked at the notion that everything could be made better quickly. He perceived reformers turning narrow-minded, hard-hearted, and intolerant, and thereby causing harm as they took away other persons' liberty in the attempt to gain an immediate moral good.

This critique of reform appears in *The Blithedale Romance* in both implicit and explicit ways. Perhaps the clearest case in point is Hawthorne's exposure of Hollingsworth's extreme, unnatural commitment to prison reform. This was an important cause during the antebellum period, in part because of the shocking conditions of America's prisons, but also because criminals posed an especially stark challenge to advocates for change: *Could* criminals change? Were they evil at heart, unable to reform themselves, or, instead, had their natures been skewed and propelled toward evil by rampant injustices in the social system? Hawthorne fastens on the issue in order to show the hazards of being a reformer: Hollingsworth, the reformer of criminals, cruelly disregards others and drives himself into committing moral crimes.

Howe's report on prison reform, which accents the need for "the saving of human souls," is among the best-known writings on the subject. But Parker's "Sermon of the Dangerous Classes," though less familiar, is provocative as well, and it offers a cogent example of how social-reform contexts enrich the reading and interpretation of *The Blithedale Romance*. Parker's tone is determined, forthright, and full of intense conviction as he describes the ways in which "our present mode of treating criminals does no good to this class of men, these victims of circumstances," and argues for their "reformation."

It is possible that Hawthorne intended for Hollingsworth to mirror Parker. In an April 6, 1845, letter, Sophia Hawthorne referred to Parker as "bold and unscrupulous" and complained that "the moment any person thinks he is particularly original, and the private possessor of truth, he becomes one-sided and a monomaniac." She felt that Parker was willful and monomaniacal, and it is likely that Hawthorne concurred with her judgment.

But the key point is less the possible or probable relation between Parker and Hollingsworth than the function that Hawthorne's character serves in the novel. Hawthorne makes Hollingsworth a monomaniac in the destructiveness of his fidelity to reform and, further, in his effort to convert others to his scheme. Eventually Hollingsworth becomes a prisoner of his own guilt, carrying within himself the disfigured soul he had aimed to repair in criminals. The disfigurement of Hollingsworth's nature, and the price that he and others pay for his fanaticism, are powerful evidence of Hawthorne's grave suspicions about reform movements and reformers of the era.

KARL MARX

On Alienated Labor

From The Communist Manifesto

Karl Marx (1818–1883) is the most influential critic of industrial capitalism, the chief theorist of modern socialism, and the founder of international communism. He was born in Trier, Germany; attended the universities of Bonn, Berlin, and Jena; and became an expert scholar of law, philosophy, and history. After editing radical newspapers in Paris and Brussels, he, with his friend and collaborator, Friedrich Engels, reorganized the Communist League in London in 1847. Marx collaborated with Engels to write a militant polemic, *The Communist Manifesto*, published in 1848, the year of widespread revolutions in Europe. It is his best-known text, with the possible exception of the immense *Das Kapital* (1867). But the *Economic and Philosophical Manuscripts* (1844), from which the first excerpt is taken, are highly significant for their description of the industrialized worker's lack of meaningful relation to the product of his labor.

The texts of these selections are from *Karl Marx: Selected Writings,* ed. David McLellan (New York: Oxford UP, 1977), 78–80, 237–38.

On Alienated Labor

We start with a contemporary fact of political economy:

The worker becomes poorer the richer is his production, the more it increases in power and scope. The worker becomes a commodity that is all the cheaper the more commodities he creates. The depreciation of the human world progresses in direct proportion to the increase in value of the world of things. Labour does not only produce commodities; it produces itself and the labourer as a commodity and that to the extent to which it produces commodities in general.

What this fact expresses is merely this: the object that labour produces, its product, confronts it as an alien being, as a power independent of the producer. The product of labour is labour that has solidified itself into an object, made itself into a thing, the objectification of labour. The realization of labour is its objectification. In political economy this realization of labour appears as a loss of reality for the worker, objectification as a loss of the object or slavery to it, and appropriation as alienation, as externalization.

The realization of labour appears as a loss of reality to an extent that the worker loses his reality by dying of starvation. Objectification appears as a loss of the object to such an extent that the worker is robbed not only of the objects necessary for his life but also of the objects of his work. Indeed, labour itself becomes an object he can only have in his power with the greatest of efforts and at irregular intervals. The appropriation of the object appears as alienation to such an extent that the more objects the worker produces, the less he can possess and the more he falls under the domination of his product, capital.

All these consequences follow from the fact that the worker relates to the product of his labour as to an alien object. For it is evident from this presupposition that the more the worker externalizes himself in his work, the more powerful becomes the alien, objective world that he creates opposite himself, the poorer he becomes himself in his inner life and the less he can call his own. It is just the same in religion. The more man puts into God, the less he retains in himself. The worker puts his life into the object and this means that it no longer belongs to him but to the object. So the greater this activity, the more the worker is without an object. What the product of his labour is, that he is not. So the greater this product the less he is himself. The externalization of the worker in his product implies not only that his labour becomes an object, an exterior existence but also that it exists outside him, independent and alien, and becomes a self-sufficient power opposite him, that the life that he has lent to the object affronts him, hostile and alien.

Let us now deal in more detail with objectification, the production of the worker, and the alienation, the loss of the object, his product, which is involved in it.

The worker can create nothing without nature, the sensuous exterior world. It is the matter in which his labour realizes itself, in which it is active, out of which and through which it produces.

But as nature affords the means of life for labour in the sense that labour cannot live without objects on which it exercises itself, so it affords a means of life in the narrower sense, namely the means for the physical subsistence of the worker himself.

Thus the more the worker appropriates the exterior world of sensuous nature by his labour, the more he doubly deprives himself of the means of subsistence, firstly since the exterior sensuous world increasingly ceases to be an object belonging to his work, a means of subsistence for his labour; secondly, since it increasingly ceases to be a means of subsistence in the direct sense, a means for the physical subsistence of the worker.

Thus in these two ways the worker becomes a slave to his object: firstly he receives an object of labour, that is he receives labour, and secondly, he receives the means of subsistence. Thus it is his object that permits him to exist first as a worker and secondly as a physical subject. The climax of this slavery is that only as a worker can he maintain himself as a physical subject and it is only as a physical subject that he is a worker.

(According to the laws of political economy[1] the alienation of the worker in his object is expressed as follows: the more the worker produces the less he has to consume, the more values he creates the more valueless and worthless he becomes, the more formed the product the

---

[1]*political economy:* A branch of social science that studies political and governmental institutions, especially as they affect economic policies and conditions.

more deformed the worker, the more civilized the product, the more barbaric the worker, the more powerful the work the more powerless becomes the worker, the more cultured the work the more philistine the worker becomes and more of a slave to nature.)

Political economy hides the alienation in the essence of labour by not considering the immediate relationship between the worker (labour) and production. Labour produces works of wonder for the rich, but nakedness for the worker. It produces palaces, but only hovels for the worker; it produces beauty, but cripples the worker; it replaces labour by machines but throws a part of the workers back to a barbaric labour and turns the other part into machines. It produces culture, but also imbecility and cretinism for the worker.

The immediate relationship of labour to its products is the relationship of the worker to the objects of his production. The relationship of the man of means to the objects of production and to production itself is only a consequence of this first relationship. And it confirms it. . . .

So when we ask the question: what relationship is essential to labour, we are asking about the relationship of the worker to production.

Up to now we have considered only one aspect of the alienation or externalization of the worker, his relationship to the products of his labour. But alienation shows itself not only in the result, but also in the act of production, inside productive activity itself. How would the worker be able to affront the product of his work as an alien being if he did not alienate himself in the act of production itself? For the product is merely the summary of the activity of production. So if the product of labour is externalization, production itself must be active externalization, the externalization of activity, the activity of externalization. The alienation of the object of labour is only the résumé of the alienation, the externalization in the activity of labour itself.

What does the externalization of labour consist of then?

Firstly, that labour is exterior to the worker, that is, it does not belong to his essence. Therefore he does not confirm himself in his work, he denies himself, feels miserable instead of happy, deploys no free physical and intellectual energy, but mortifies his body and ruins his mind. Thus the worker only feels a stranger. He is at home when he is not working and when he works he is not at home. His labour is therefore not voluntary but compulsory, forced labour. It is therefore not the satisfaction of a need but only a means to satisfy needs outside itself. How alien it really is is very evident from the fact that when there is no physical or other compulsion, labour is avoided like the plague. External labour, labour in which man externalizes himself, is a labour of self-sacrifice and mortification. Finally, the external character of labour for the worker shows itself in the fact that it is not his own but someone else's, that it does not belong to him, that he does not belong to himself in his labour but to someone else. As in religion the human imagination's own activity, the activity of man's head and his heart, reacts independently on the individual as an alien activity of gods or devils, so the activity of the worker is not his own spontaneous activity. It belongs to another and is the loss of himself.

From The Communist Manifesto

The Communist revolution is the most radical rupture with traditional property relations; no wonder that its development involves the most radical rupture with traditional ideas.

But let us have done with the bourgeois objections to Communism.

We have seen. . . , that the first step in the revolution by the working class is to raise the proletariat[2] to the position of ruling class, to win the battle of democracy.

The proletariat will use its political supremacy to wrest, by degrees, all capital from the bourgeoisie, to centralize all instruments of production in the hands of the State, i.e., of the proletariat organized as the ruling class; and to increase the total of productive forces as rapidly as possible.

Of course, in the beginning this cannot be effected except by means of despotic inroads on the rights of property, and on the conditions of bourgeois production; by means of measures, therefore, which appear economically insufficient and untenable, but which, in the course of the movement, outstrip themselves, necessitate further inroads upon the old social order, and are unavoidable as a means of entirely revolutionizing the mode of production.

These measures will of course be different in different countries.

Nevertheless, in the most advanced countries, the following will be pretty generally applicable.

---

[2]*proletariat:* In Marxist doctrine, the class of wage earners who lack their own means of production and hence must sell their labor to survive.

1. Abolition of property in land and application of all rents of land to public purposes.

2. A heavy progressive or graduated income tax.

3. Abolition of all right of inheritance.

4. Confiscation of the property of all emigrants and rebels.

5. Centralization of credit in the hands of the State, by means of a national bank with State capital and an exclusive monopoly.

6. Centralization of the means of communication and transport in the hands of the State.

7. Extension of factories and instruments of production owned by the State; the bringing into cultivation of wastelands, and the improvement of the soil generally in accordance with a common plan.

8. Equal liability of all to labour. Establishment of industrial armies, especially for agriculture.

9. Combination of agriculture with manufacturing industries; gradual abolition of the distinction between town and country, by a more equable distribution of the population over the country.

10. Free education for all children in public schools. Abolition of children's factory labour in its present form. Combination of education with industrial production, etc., etc.

When, in the course of development, class distinctions have disappeared, and all production has been concentrated in the hands of associated individuals, the public power will lose its political character. Political power, properly so called, is merely the organized power of one class for oppressing another. If the proletariat during its contest with the bourgeoisie is compelled, by the force of circumstances, to organize itself as a class, if, by means of a revolution, it makes itself the ruling class, and, as such, sweeps away by force the old conditions of production, then it will, along with these conditions, have swept away the conditions for the existence of class antagonisms and of classes generally, and will thereby have abolished its own supremacy as a class.

In place of the old bourgeois society, with its classes and class antagonisms, we shall have an association, in which the free development of each is the condition for the free development of all.

FRIEDRICH ENGELS

From The Condition of the Working Class in England in 1844

Friedrich Engels (1820–1895) took a position in a cotton factory (partly owned by his father) in Manchester, England, in 1842, and lived mostly in England. In 1844, he met Karl Marx in Paris, and by the middle of the decade, he was active in European revolutionary movements and was collaborating with Marx on writing projects, including *The Communist Manifesto*. He edited or wrote a number of important Marxist texts, including *Anti-Duhring* (1878; trans. 1934) and *The Origin of the Family, Private Property, and the State* (1884; trans. 1902). His most significant early book is *The Condition of the Working Class in England in 1844* (1845). It is filled with vivid descriptions of the harrowing conditions in which workers and their families lived, as in the account below of the city of London, which for many reformers was the archetype of the bad city that industrialism had spawned. Engels identifies here the principles and forces that he deemed central to industrial capitalism and the oppression it imposed. The text is from *The Condition of the Working Class in England in 1844*, trans. W. O. Henderson and W. H. Chaloner (1958; reprint, Stanford: Stanford UP, 1968), 30–31, 88–89.

The Great Towns

London is unique, because it is a city in which one can roam for hours without leaving the built-up area and without seeing the slightest sign of the approach of open country. This enormous agglomeration of population on a single spot has multiplied a hundredfold the economic strength of the two and a half million inhabitants concentrated there. This great population has made London the commercial capital of the world and has created the gigantic docks in which are assembled the thousands of ships which always cover the River Thames. I know nothing more imposing than the view one obtains of the river when sailing from the sea up to London Bridge. Especially above Woolwich the houses and docks are packed tightly together on both banks of the river. The further one goes up the river the thicker becomes the concentration of ships lying at anchor, so that eventually only a narrow shipping lane is left free in mid-stream. Here hundreds of steamships dart rapidly to and fro. All this is so magnificent and impressive that one is lost in admiration. The traveller has good reason to marvel at England's greatness even before he steps on English soil.

It is only later that the traveller appreciates the human suffering which has made all this possible. He can only realise the price that has been paid for all this magnificence after he has tramped the pavements of the main streets of London for some days and has tired himself out by jostling his way through the crowds and by dodging the endless stream of coaches and carts which fills the streets. It is only when he has visited the slums of this great city that it dawns upon him that the inhabitants of modern London have had to sacrifice so much that is best in human nature in order to create those wonders of civilisation with which their city teems. The vast majority of Londoners have had to let so many of their potential creative faculties lie dormant, stunted and unused in order that a small, closely-knit group of their fellow citizens could develop to the full the qualities with which nature has endowed them. The restless and noisy activity of the crowded streets is highly distasteful, and it is surely abhorrent to human nature itself. Hundreds of thousands of men and women drawn from all classes and ranks of society pack the streets of London. Are they not all human beings with the same innate characteristics and potentialities? Are they not all equally interested in the pursuit of happiness? And do they not all aim at happiness by following similar methods? Yet they rush past each other as if they had nothing in common. They are tacitly agreed on one thing only — that everyone should keep to the right of the pavement so as not to collide with the stream of people moving in the opposite direction. No one even thinks of sparing a glance for his neighbour in the streets. The more that Londoners are packed into a tiny space, the more repulsive and disgraceful becomes the brutal indifference with which they ignore their neighbours and selfishly concentrate upon their private affairs. We know well enough that this isolation of the individual — this narrow-minded egotism — is everywhere the fundamental principle of modern society. But nowhere is this selfish egotism so blatantly evident as in the frantic bustle of the great city. The disintegration of society into individuals, each guided by his private principles and each pursuing his own aims, has been pushed to its furthest limits in London. Here indeed human society has been split into its component atoms.

From this it follows that the social conflict — the war of all against all — is fought in the open. The type of society depicted by Stirner[1] actually exists in the great towns of England. Here men regard their fellows not as human beings, but as pawns in the struggle for existence. Everyone exploits his neighbour with the result that the stronger tramples the weaker under foot. The strongest of all, a tiny group of capitalists, monopolise everything, while the weakest, who are in the vast majority, succumb to the most abject poverty.

What is true of London, is true also of all the great towns, such as Manchester, Birmingham and Leeds. Everywhere one finds on the one hand the most barbarous indifference and selfish egotism and on the other the most distressing scenes of misery and poverty. Signs of social conflict are to be found everywhere. Everyone turns his house into a fortress to defend himself — under the protection of the law — from the depredations of his neighbours. Class warfare is so open and shameless that it has to be seen to be believed. The observer of such an appalling state of affairs must shudder at the consequences of such feverish activity and can only marvel that so crazy a social and economic structure should survive at all.

Competition

We have shown in our introduction how, at the very beginning of the Industrial Revolution, it was competition that called the working classes into existence. The increased demand for cloth raised the wages of the weavers and so led the peasants who had worked at the loom in their spare time to give up their work on the land in order to earn more by weaving. We have seen how the growth of large farms forced the peasants off their holdings, turned them into wage-earners and then in some cases drove them into the towns. We saw, too, how the lower middle-classes were also to a great extent ruined and depressed to the condition of wage-earners. We have seen capital becoming concentrated into the hands of a small group of people, while the population has been concentrated in the great towns. Those are the various ways and means by which competition both created the working classes and increased their numbers. It is in modern industry that competition first becomes a factor of major importance and has been given free rein to develop unchecked to its furthest limits. We

---

[1]*Stirner:* Max Stirner was the pseudonym of Johann Kaspar Schmidt (1806–1856), a German anarchist writer.

propose to examine the influence of competition on the working-classes of to-day. The effects of competition between the workers themselves and the consequences of such competition may be considered first.

Competition is the most extreme expression of that war of all against all which dominates modern middle-class society. This struggle for existence — which in extreme cases is a life and death struggle — is waged not only between different classes of society but also between individuals within these social groups. Everybody competes in some way against everyone else and consequently each individual tries to push aside anyone whose existence is a barrier to his own advancement. The workers compete among themselves, and so do the middle classes. The powerloom weaver competes with the handloom weaver. Among the handloom weavers themselves there is continual rivalry. Those who are unemployed or poorly paid try to undercut and so destroy the livelihood of those who have work and are earning better wages. This competition of workers among themselves is the worst aspect of the present situation as far as the proletariat is concerned. This is the sharpest weapon which the middle classes wield against the working classes. This explains the rise of trade unions, which represent an attempt to eliminate such fratricidal conflict between the workers themselves. It explains, too, the fury of the middle classes against trade unions, and their ill-concealed delight at any setback which the unions suffer.

The worker is helpless; left to himself he cannot survive a single day. The middle classes have secured a monopoly of all the necessities of life. What the worker needs he can secure only from the middle classes, whose monopoly is protected by the authority of the State. In law and in fact the worker is the slave of the middle classes, who hold the power of life and death over him. The middle classes offer food and shelter to the worker, but only in return for an 'equivalent,' i.e. for his labour. They even disguise the true state of affairs by making it appear that the worker is acting of his own free will, as a truly free agent and as a responsible adult, when he makes his bargain with the middle classes. A fine freedom indeed, when the worker has no choice but to accept the terms offered by the middle classes or go hungry and naked like the wild beasts. A fine 'equivalent,' when it is the bourgeoisie alone which decides the terms of the bargain. And if a worker is such a fool as to prefer to go hungry rather than accept the 'fair' terms of the middle classes who are his 'natural superiors' — well, then it is easy enough to find another worker. The working classes are numerous enough in all conscience and not all of them are so stupid as to prefer death to life.

This illustrates the effect of competition among the workers themselves. If only all the workers would firmly announce their intention of starving rather than working for the middle classes, then the employers would soon have to surrender their monopoly. Such unity among the workers does not exist and is indeed unlikely to occur. As a result the middle classes are in clover.

ORESTES A. BROWNSON

From "The Laboring Classes"

Orestes A. Brownson (1802–1876), a prolific essayist, author, and editor, made a long spiritual journey from Presbyterian to Universalist to Unitarian minister and, finally, to Roman Catholic. His social thought led him from socialism to membership in the Workingmen's party, then to the Democratic party, and in the end, to a tough-minded, principled conservatism.

Brownson's books include *New Views of Christianity, Society, and the Church* (1836) and *Charles Elwood; or, The Infidel Converted* (1840), a novel shaped by his own experiences. But much of his best writing was for the *United States Magazine and Democratic Review* and the two journals he edited — *The Boston Quarterly Review* (1838–44) and *Brownson's Quarterly Review* (1844–65, 1872–75).

The essay excerpted here was published in two parts in *The Boston Quarterly Review*, 3 (July 1840), 358–95, and (October 1840), 420–512. Part 1 begins with a commentary on the Scottish historian and social critic Thomas Carlyle's *Chartism* (1840), a book that examines the Chartist movement in England, which in the late 1830s and 1840s agitated for working-class reforms (e.g., universal manhood suffrage and the abolition of property qualification for the ballot). Brownson then turns to a general consideration of the "laboring classes," maintaining that their plight is worse than Carlyle believes, and, furthermore, that the reforms that Carlyle and others have proposed are inadequate and naive. Brownson predicts that change will one day occur — the brutalization of the workers and their families cannot continue forever — and that it will be propelled by class warfare, "the like of which the world as yet has never witnessed."

What we would ask is, throughout the Christian world, the actual condition of the laboring classes, viewed simply and exclusively in their capacity of laborers? They constitute at least a moiety[1] of the human race. We exclude the nobility, we exclude also the middle class, and include only actual laborers, who are laborers and not proprietors, owners of none of the funds of production, neither houses, shops, nor lands, nor implements of labor, being therefore solely dependent on their hands. We have no means of ascertaining their precise proportion to the whole number of the race; but we think we may estimate them at one half. In any contest they will be as two to one, because the large class of proprietors who are not employers, but laborers on their own lands or in their own shops will make common cause with them.

Now we will not so belie our acquaintance with political economy, as to allege that these alone perform all that is necessary to the production of wealth. We are not ignorant of the fact, that the merchant, who is literally the common carrier and exchange dealer, performs a useful service, and is therefore entitled to a portion of the proceeds of labor. But make all necessary deductions on his account, and then ask what portion of the remainder is retained, either in kind or in its equivalent, in the hands of the original producer, the workingman? All over the world this fact stares us in the face, the workingman is poor and depressed, while a large portion of the non-workingmen, in the sense we now use the term, are wealthy. It may be laid down as a general rule, with but few exceptions, that men are rewarded in an inverse ratio to the amount of actual service they perform. Under every government on earth the largest salaries are annexed to those offices, which demand of their incumbents the least amount of actual labor either mental or manual. And this is in perfect harmony with the whole system of repartition of the fruits of industry, which obtains in every department of society. Now here is the system which prevails, and here is its result. The whole class of simple laborers are poor, and in general unable to procure anything beyond the bare necessaries of life.

In regard to labor two systems obtain; one that of slave labor, the other that of free labor. Of the two, the first is, in our judgment, except so far as the feelings are concerned, decidedly the least oppressive. If the slave has never been a free man, we think, as a general rule, his sufferings are less than those of the free laborer at wages. As

---

[1]*moiety:* One of the portions, usually one-half, into which something is divided.

to actual freedom one has just about as much as the other. The laborer at wages has all the disadvantages of freedom and none of its blessings, while the slave, if denied the blessings, is freed from the disadvantages. We are no advocates of slavery, we are as heartily opposed to it as any modern abolitionist can be; but we say frankly that, if there must always be a laboring population distinct from proprietors and employers, we regard the slave system as decidedly preferable to the system at wages. It is no pleasant thing to go days without food, to lie idle for weeks, seeking work and finding none, to rise in the morning with a wife and children you love, and know not where to procure them a breakfast, and to see constantly before you no brighter prospect than the alms-house.[2] Yet these are no unfrequent incidents in the lives of our laboring population. Even in seasons of general prosperity, when there was only the ordinary cry of "hard times," we have seen hundreds of people in a no very populous village, in a wealthy portion of our common country, suffering for the want of the necessaries of life, willing to work, and yet finding no work to do. Many and many is the application of a poor man for work, merely for his food, we have seen rejected. These things are little thought of, for the applicants are poor; they fill no conspicuous place in society, and they have no biographers. But their wrongs are chronicled in heaven. It is said there is no want in this country. There may be less than in some other countries. But death by actual starvation in this country is, we apprehend, no uncommon occurrence. The sufferings of a quiet, unassuming but useful class of females in our cities, in general sempstresses, too proud to beg or to apply to the alms-house, are not easily told. They are industrious; they do all that they can find to do; but yet the little there is for them to do, and the miserable pittance they receive for it, is hardly sufficient to keep soul and body together. And yet there is a man who employs them to make shirts, trousers, &c., and grows rich on their labors. He is one of our respectable citizens, perhaps is praised in the newspapers for his liberal donations to some charitable institution. He passes among us as a pattern of morality, and is honored as a worthy Christian. And why should he not be, since our *Christian* community is made up of such as he, and since our clergy would not dare question his piety, lest they should incur the reproach of infidelity, and lose their standing, and their salaries? Nay, since our clergy are raised up, edu-

---

[2]*alms-house:* A privately financed home for the poor.

cated, fashioned, and sustained by such as he? Not a few of our churches rest on Mammon[3] for their foundation. The basement is a trader's shop.

We pass through our manufacturing villages, most of them appear neat and flourishing. The operatives are well dressed, and we are told, well paid. They are said to be healthy, contented, and happy. This is the fair side of the picture; the side exhibited to distinguished visitors. There is a dark side, moral as well as physical. Of the common operatives, few, if any, by their wages, acquire a competence. A few of what Carlyle terms not inaptly the *body-servants* are well paid, and now and then an agent or an overseer rides in his coach. But the great mass wear out their health, spirits, and morals, without becoming one whit better off than when they commenced labor. The bills of mortality in these factory villages are not striking, we admit, for the poor girls when they can toil no longer go home to die. The average life, working life we mean, of the girls that come to Lowell, for instance, from Maine, New Hampshire, and Vermont, we have been assured, is only about three years. What becomes of them then? Few of them ever marry; fewer still ever return to their native places with reputations unimpaired. "She has worked in a Factory," is almost enough to damn to infamy the most worthy and virtuous girl. We know no sadder sight on earth than one of our factory villages presents, when the bell at break of day, or at the hour of breakfast, or dinner, calls out its hundreds or thousands of operatives. We stand and look at these hard working men and women hurrying in all directions, and ask ourselves, where go the proceeds of their labors? The man who employs them, and for whom they are toiling as so many slaves, is one of our city nabobs, revelling in luxury; or he is a member of our legislature, enacting laws to put money in his own pocket; or he is a member of Congress, contending for a high Tariff to tax the poor for the benefit of the rich; or in these times he is shedding crocodile tears over the deplorable condition of the poor laborer, while he docks his wages twenty-five per cent.; building miniature log cabins, shouting Harrison and "hard cider."[4] And this man

[3]*Mammon:* The desire for wealth and material possessions. See Christ's words in Matthew 6:24: "No man can serve two masters. . . . Ye cannot serve God and Mammon."

[4]*Harrison and "hard cider":* William Henry Harrison (1773–1841) was the Whig party's nominee for the presidency in 1840. Portrayed as the epitome of the Midwest common man and known as the "log cabin and hard cider" candidate, he ran a successful campaign that emphasized songs and slogans and torchlight parades.

too would fain pass for a Christian and a republican.[5] He shouts for liberty, stickles for equality, and is horrified at a Southern planter who keeps slaves.

One thing is certain; that of the amount actually produced by the operative, he retains a less proportion than it costs the master to feed, clothe, and lodge his slave. Wages is a cunning device of the devil, for the benefit of tender consciences, who would retain all the advantages of the slave system, without the expense, trouble, and odium of being slave-holders.

Messrs. Thome and Kimball,[6] in their account of emancipation in the West Indies, establish the fact that the employer may have the same amount of labor done, twenty-five per cent. cheaper than the master. What does this fact prove, if not that wages is a more successful method of taxing labor than slavery? We really believe our Northern system of labor is more oppressive, and even more mischievous to morals, than the Southern. We, however, war against both. We have no toleration for either system. We would see the slave a man, but a free man, not a mere operative at wages. This he would not be were he now emancipated. Could the abolitionists effect all they propose, they would do the slave no service. Should emancipation work as well as they say, still it would do the slave no good. He would be a slave still, although with the title and cares of a freeman. If then we had no constitutional objections to abolitionism, we could not, for the reason here implied, be abolitionists.

The slave system, however, in name and form, is gradually disappearing from Christendom. It will not subsist much longer. But its place is taken by the system of labor at wages, and this system, we hold, is no improvement upon the one it supplants. Nevertheless the system of wages will triumph. It is the system which in name sounds honester than slavery, and in substance is more profitable to the master. It yields the wages of iniquity, without its opprobrium. It will therefore supplant slavery, and be sustained — for a time.

Now, what is the prospect of those who fall under the operation of this system? We ask, is there a reasonable chance that any consider-

[5]*republican:* In this context, someone who believes in a government in which the supreme power resides in the body of citizens entitled to vote; someone who favors a representative democracy.
[6]*Messrs. Thome and Kimball:* James Anthony Thome and J. Horace Kimball presented their positive account of West Indian emancipation in *Emancipation in the West Indies: A Six Months' Tour in Antigua, Barbadoes, and Jamaica, in the year 1837,* published in 1838 by the American Anti-Slavery Society.

able portion of the present generation of laborers, shall ever become owners of a sufficient portion of the funds of production to be able to sustain themselves by laboring on their own capital, that is, as independent laborers? We need not ask this question, for everybody knows there is not. Well, is the condition of a laborer at wages the best that the great mass of the working people ought to be able to aspire to? Is it a condition, — nay can it be made a condition, — with which a man should be satisfied; in which he should be contented to live and die?

In our own country this condition has existed under its most favorable aspects, and has been made as good as it can be. It has reached all the excellence of which it is susceptible. It is now not improving but growing worse. The actual condition of the workingman to-day, viewed in all its bearings, is not so good as it was fifty years ago. If we have not been altogether misinformed, fifty years ago, health and industrious habits, constituted no mean stock in trade, and with them almost any man might aspire to competence and independence. But it is so no longer. The wilderness has receded, and already the new lands are beyond the reach of the mere laborer, and the employer has him at his mercy. If the present relation subsist, we see nothing better for him in reserve than what he now possesses, but something altogether worse.

We are not ignorant of the fact that men born poor become wealthy, and that men born to wealth become poor; but this fact does not necessarily diminish the numbers of the poor, nor augment the numbers of the rich. The relative numbers of the two classes remain, or may remain, the same. But be this as it may; one fact is certain, no man born poor has ever, by his wages, as a simple operative, risen to the class of the wealthy. Rich he may have become, but it has not been by his own manual labor. He has in some way contrived to tax for his benefit the labor of others. He may have accumulated a few dollars which he has placed at usury, or invested in trade; or he may, as a master workman, obtain a premium on his journeymen;[7] or he may have from a clerk passed to a partner, or from a workman to an overseer. The simple market wages for ordinary labor, has never been adequate to raise him from poverty to wealth. This fact is decisive of the whole controversy, and proves that the system of wages must be supplanted by some other system, or else one half of the human race must forever be the virtual slaves of the other.

---

[7]*journeymen:* Workers who have learned a trade or craft and who usually work by the day for someone else.

Now the great work for this age and the coming, is to raise up the laborer, and to realize in our own social arrangements and in the actual condition of all men, that equality between man and man, which God has established between the rights of one and those of another. In other words, our business is to emancipate the proletaries, as the past has emancipated the slaves. This is our work. There must be no class of our fellow men doomed to toil through life as mere workmen at wages. If wages are tolerated, it must be, in the case of the individual operative, only under such conditions that by the time he is of a proper age to settle in life, he shall have accumulated enough to be an independent laborer on his own capital, — on his own farm or in his own shop. Here is our work. How is it to be done?

Reformers in general answer this question, or what they deem its equivalent, in a manner which we cannot but regard as very unsatisfactory. They would have all men wise, good, and happy; but in order to make them so, they tell us that we want not external changes, but internal; and therefore instead of declaiming against society and seeking to disturb existing social arrangements, we should confine ourselves to the individual reason and conscience; seek merely to lead the individual to repentance, and to reformation of life; make the individual a practical, a truly religious man, and all evils will either disappear, or be sanctified to the spiritual growth of the soul.

This is doubtless a capital theory, and has the advantage that kings, hierarchies, nobilities, — in a word, all who fatten on the toil and blood of their fellows, will feel no difficulty in supporting it. Nicholas of Russia, the Grand Turk, his Holiness the Pope, will hold us their especial friends for advocating a theory, which secures to them the odor of sanctity even while they are sustaining by their anathemas or their armed legions, a system of things of which the great mass are and must be the victims. If you will only allow me to keep thousands toiling for my pleasure or my profit, I will even aid you in your pious efforts to convert their souls. I am not cruel; I do not wish either to cause, or to see suffering; I am therefore disposed to encourage your labors for the souls of the workingman, providing you will secure to me the products of his bodily toil. So far as the salvation of his soul will not interfere with my income, I hold it worthy of being sought; and if a few thousand dollars will aid you, Mr. Priest, in reconciling him to God, and making fair weather for him hereafter, they are at your service. I shall not want him to work for me in the world to come, and I can indemnify myself for what your salary costs me, by paying him less wages. A capital theory this, which one may advocate without incurring the reproach of a disorganizer, a jacobin,[8] a leveller,[9] and without losing the friendship of the rankest aristocrat in the land.

This theory, however, is exposed to one slight objection, that of being condemned by something like six thousand years' experience. For six thousand years its beauty has been extolled, its praises sung, and its blessings sought, under every advantage which learning, fashion, wealth, and power can secure; and yet under its practical operations, we are assured, that mankind, though totally depraved at first, have been growing worse and worse ever since.

For our part, we yield to none in our reverence for science and religion; but we confess that we look not for the regeneration of the race from priests and pedagogues. They have had a fair trial. They cannot construct the temple of God. They cannot conceive its plan, and they know not how to build. They daub with untempered mortar, and the walls they erect tumble down if so much as a fox attempt to go up thereon. In a word they always league with the people's masters, and seek to reform without disturbing the social arrangements which render reform necessary. They would change the consequents without changing the antecedents, secure to men the rewards of holiness, while they continue their allegiance to the devil. We have no faith in priests and pedagogues. They merely cry peace, peace, and that too when there is no peace, and can be none.

We admit the importance of what Dr. Channing[10] in his lectures on the subject we are treating recommends as "self-culture." Self-culture is a good thing, but it cannot abolish inequality, nor restore men to their rights. As a means of quickening moral and intellectual energy, exalting the sentiments, and preparing the laborer to contend manfully for his rights, we admit its importance, and insist as strenuously as any one on making it as universal as possible; but as constituting in itself a remedy for the vices of the social state, we have no faith in it. As a means it is well, as the end it is nothing.

The truth is, the evil we have pointed out is not merely individual

[8]*jacobin:* A political extremist or radical; derives from the Jacobin political group of the French Revolution in the 1790s, associated with terrorism and violence.

[9]*leveller:* Someone who favors equality before the law and political and economic rights and religious toleration; the term comes from the Levellers, a radical group in the Parliamentary army during the English civil war of the mid-seventeenth century.

[10]*Dr. Channing:* William Ellery Channing (1780–1842) was a Unitarian clergyman and author.

in its character. It is not, in the case of any single individual, of any one man's procuring, nor can the efforts of any one man, directed solely to his own moral and religious perfection, do aught to remove it. What is purely individual in its nature, efforts of individuals to perfect themselves, may remove. But the evil we speak of is inherent in all our social arrangements, and cannot be cured without a radical change of those arrangements. Could we convert all men to Christianity in both theory and practice, as held by the most enlightened sect of Christians among us, the evils of the social state would remain untouched. Continue our present system of trade, and all its present evil consequences will follow, whether it be carried on by your best men or your worst. Put your best men, your wisest, most moral, and most religious men, at the head of your paper money banks, and the evils of the present banking system will remain scarcely diminished. The only way to get rid of its evils is to change the system, not its managers. The evils of slavery do not result from the personal characters of slave masters. They are inseparable from the system, let who will be masters. Make all your rich men good Christians, and you have lessened not the evils of existing inequality in wealth. The mischievous effects of this inequality do not result from the personal characters of either rich or poor, but from itself, and they will continue, just so long as there are rich men and poor men in the same community. You must abolish the system or accept its consequences. No man can serve both God and Mammon. If you will serve the devil, you must look to the devil for your wages; we know no other way.

Let us not be misinterpreted. We deny not the power of Christianity. Should all men become good Christians, we deny not that all social evils would be cured. But we deny in the outset that a man, who seeks merely to save his own soul, merely to perfect his own individual nature, can be a good Christian. The Christian forgets himself, buckles on his armor, and goes forth to war against principalities and powers, and against spiritual wickedness in high places. No man can be a Christian who does not begin his career by making war on the mischievous social arrangements from which his brethren suffer. He who thinks he can be a Christian and save his soul, without seeking their radical change, has no reason to applaud himself for his proficiency in Christian science, nor for his progress towards the kingdom of God. Understand Christianity, and we will admit, that should all men become good Christians, there would be nothing to complain of. But one might as well undertake to dip the ocean dry with a clamshell, as to undertake to cure the evils of the social state by converting men to the Christianity of the Church. . . .

According to the Christianity of Christ no man can enter the kingdom of God, who does not labor with all zeal and diligence to establish the kingdom of God on the earth; who does not labor to bring down the high, and bring up the low; to break the fetters of the bound and set the captive free; to destroy all oppression, establish the reign of justice, which is the reign of equality, between man and man; to introduce new heavens and a new earth, wherein dwelleth righteousness, wherein all shall be as brothers, loving one another, and no one possessing what another lacketh. No man can be a Christian who does not labor to reform society, to mould it according to the will of God and the nature of man; so that free scope shall be given to every man to unfold himself in all beauty and power, and to grow up into the stature of a perfect man in Christ Jesus. No man can be a Christian who does not refrain from all practices by which the rich grow richer and the poor poorer, and who does not do all in his power to elevate the laboring classes, so that one man shall not be doomed to toil while another enjoys the fruits; so that each man shall be free and independent, sitting under "his own vine and figtree with none to molest or to make afraid." We grant the power of Christianity in working out the reform we demand; we agree that one of the most efficient means of elevating the workingmen is to christianize the community. But you must christianize it. It is the Gospel of Jesus you must preach, and not the gospel of the priests. Preach the Gospel of Jesus, and that will turn every man's attention to the crying evil we have designated, and will arm every Christian with power to effect those changes in social arrangements, which shall secure to all men the equality of position and condition, which it is already acknowledged they possess in relation to their rights. But let it be the genuine Gospel that you preach, and not that pseudo-gospel, which lulls the conscience asleep, and permits men to feel that they may be servants of God while they are slaves to the world, the flesh, and the devil; and while they ride roughshod over the hearts of their prostrate brethren. We must preach no Gospel that permits men to feel that they are honorable men and good Christians, although rich and with eyes standing out with fatness, while the great mass of their brethren are suffering from iniquitous laws, from mischievous social arrangements, and pining away for the want of the refinements and even the necessaries of life. . . .

Now the evils of which we have complained are of a social nature.

That is, they have their root in the constitution of society as it is, and they have attained to their present growth by means of social influences, the action of government, of laws, and of systems and institutions upheld by society, and of which individuals are the slaves. This being the case, it is evident that they are to be removed only by the action of society, that is, by government, for the action of society is government.

But what shall government do? Its first doing must be an *un*doing. There has been thus far quite too much government, as well as government of the wrong kind. The first act of government we want, is a still further limitation of itself. It must begin by circumscribing within narrower limits its powers. And then it must proceed to repeal all laws which bear against the laboring classes, and then to enact such laws as are necessary to enable them to maintain their equality. We have no faith in those systems of elevating the working classes, which propose to elevate them without calling in the aid of the government. We must have government, and legislation expressly directed to this end.

But again what legislation do we want so far as this country is concerned? We want first the legislation which shall free the government, whether State or Federal, from the control of the Banks. The Banks represent the interest of the employer, and therefore of necessity interests adverse to those of the employed; that is, they represent the interests of the business community in opposition to the laboring community. So long as the government remains under the control of the Banks, so long it must be in the hands of the natural enemies of the laboring classes, and may be made, nay, will be made, an instrument of depressing them yet lower. It is obvious then that, if our object be the elevation of the laboring classes, we must destroy the power of the Banks over the government, and place the government in the hands of the laboring classes themselves, or in the hands of those, if such there be, who have an identity of interest with them. But this cannot be done so long as the Banks exist. Such is the subtle influence of credit, and such the power of capital, that a banking system like ours, if sustained, necessarily and inevitably becomes the real and efficient government of the country. We have been struggling for ten years in this country against the power of the banks, struggling to free merely the Federal government from their grasp, but with humiliating success. At this moment, the contest is almost doubtful, — not indeed in our mind, but in the minds of a no small portion of our countrymen. The partizans of the Banks count on certain victory. The Banks discount freely to build "log cabins," to purchase "hard cider," and to defray the expense of manufacturing enthusiasm for a cause which is at war with the interests of the people. That they will succeed, we do not for one moment believe; but that they could maintain the struggle so long, and be as strong as they now are, at the end of ten years' constant hostility, proves but all too well the power of the Banks, and their fatal influence on the political action of the community. The present character, standing, and resources of the Bank party, prove to a demonstration that the Banks must be destroyed, or the laborer not elevated. Uncompromising hostility to the whole banking system should therefore be the motto of every working man, and of every friend of Humanity. The system must be destroyed. On this point there must be no misgiving, no subterfuge, no palliation. The system is at war with the rights and interest of labor, and it must go. Every friend of the system must be marked as an enemy to his race, to his country, and especially to the laborer. No matter who he is, in what party he is found, or what name he bears, he is, in our judgment, no true democrat, as he can be no true Christian.

Following the distruction of the Banks, must come that of all monopolies, of all PRIVILEGE. There are many of these. We cannot specify them all; we therefore select only one, the greatest of them all, the privilege which some have of being born rich while others are born poor. It will be seen at once that we allude to the hereditary descent of property, an anomaly in our American system, which must be removed, or the system itself will be destroyed. We cannot now go into a discussion of this subject, but we promise to resume it at our earliest opportunity. We only say now, that as we have abolished hereditary monarchy and hereditary nobility, we must complete the work by abolishing hereditary property.[11] A man shall have all he

[11]I am aware that I broach in this place a delicate subject, though I by no means advance a novel doctrine. In justice to those friends with whom I am in the habit of thinking and acting on most subjects, as well as to the political party with which I am publicly connected, I feel bound to say, that my doctrine, on the hereditary descent of property, is put forth by myself alone, and on my own responsibility. There are to my knowledge, none of my friends who entertain the doctrine, and who would not, had I consulted them, have labored to convince me of its unsoundness. Whatever then may be the measure of condemnation the community in its wisdom may judge it proper to mete out for its promulgation, that condemnation should fall on my head alone. I hold not myself responsible for others' opinions, and I wish not others to be held responsible for mine.

I cannot be supposed to be ignorant of the startling nature of the proposition I have

honestly acquires, so long as he himself belongs to the world in which he acquires it. But his power over his property must cease with his life, and his property must then become the property of the state, to be disposed of by some equitable law for the use of the generation which takes his place. Here is the principle without any of its details, and this is the grand legislative measure to which we look forward. We see no means of elevating the laboring classes which can be effectual without this. And is this a measure to be easily carried? Not at all. It will cost infinitely more than it cost to abolish either hereditary monarchy or hereditary nobility. It is a great measure, and a startling. The rich, the business community, will never voluntarily consent to it, and we think we know too much of human nature to believe that it will ever be effected peaceably. It will be effected only by the strong arm of physical force. It will come, if it ever come at all, only at the conclusion of war, the like of which the world as yet has never witnessed, and from which, however inevitable it may seem to the eye of philosophy, the heart of Humanity recoils with horror.

We are not ready for this measure yet. There is much previous work to be done, and we should be the last to bring it before the legislature. The time, however, has come for its free and full discussion. It must be canvassed in the public mind, and society prepared for acting on it. No doubt they who broach it, and especially they who support it, will experience a due share of contumely and abuse. They will be regarded by the part of the community they oppose, or may be

---

made, nor can I, if I regard myself of the least note in the commonwealth, expect to be able to put forth such propositions, and go scathless. Because I advance singular doctrines, it is not necessary to suppose that I am ignorant of public opinion, or that I need to be informed as to the manner in which my doctrines are likely to be received. I have made the proposition, which I have, deliberately, with what I regard a tolerably clear view of its essential bearings, and after having meditated it, and been satisfied of its soundness, for many years. I make it then with my eyes open, if the reader please, "with malice prepense." I am then entitled to no favor, and I ask as I expect none. But I am not quite so unfortunate as to be wholly without friends in this world. There are those to whom I am linked by the closest ties of affection, and whose approbation and encouragement, I have ever found an ample reward for all the labors I could perform. Their reputations are dear to me. For their sake I add this note, that they may not be in the least censured for the fact, that one whom they have honored with their friendship, and in a journal which, in its general character, they have not hesitated to commend, has seen proper to put forth a doctrine, which, to say the least, for long years to come must be condemned almost unanimously. [Brownson's note]

thought to oppose, as "graceless varlets," against whom every man of substance should set his face. But this is not, after all, a thing to disturb a wise man, nor to deter a true man from telling his whole thought. He who is worthy of the name of man, speaks what he honestly believes the interests of his race demand, and seldom disquiets himself about what may be the consequences to himself. Men have, for what they believed the cause of God or man, endured the dungeon, the scaffold, the stake, the cross, and they can do it again, if need be. This subject must be freely, boldly, and fully discussed, whatever may be the fate of those who discuss it.

GEORGE H. EVANS

On Land Reform

"Vote Yourself a Farm"

George Henry Evans (1805–1856), born in England, came to the United States in 1820. Influenced by the writings of Thomas Paine and Thomas Jefferson, he was a newspaper editor and writer who called for labor reform, workingmen's parties, the end of imprisonment for debt, and, especially, land reform that would ensure each family be provided with its own homestead. His *Working Man's Advocate* was one of the first newspapers in America devoted to the cause of workers' rights.

In the first selection here — two public letters written to the abolitionist and wealthy New York state landowner Gerrit Smith (1797–1874) — Evans observes that the "slavery" experienced by workers in the North is more grievous than that endured by blacks in the South, and thus that their plight requires attention first. This emphasis on the enslavement of white workers, not only in the United States but in England as well (see "Black and White Slaves in America and England," pp. 282–83), was common among labor reformers, though Garrison, Smith, and other abolitionists denounced it as inaccurate and misleading. It is also suggested in Evans's editorial "Vote Yourself a Farm," which was published in the *True Workingman*, January 24, 1846, and many thousands of copies of which were distributed as a circular.

The text used here is from *A Documentary History of American Industrial Society,* ed. John R. Commons, vol. 7 (Cleveland: Arthur H. Clark, 1910) 360–62, 362–64, 305–07.

On Land Reform

From a Letter to Gerrit Smith, *Working Man's Advocate,* July 27, 1844

My object was to show you, that a man cannot be free, as he ought to be, while living on land claimed by other men, without the right to the use of land for his own subsistence. This seems quite clear to me, and yet I can easily imagine why it is not yet clear to you. You have, probably, always lived on land that you considered yours, without the fear of want. I have been very differently situated. You have not known what it was to be behind hand with your rent, notwithstanding your utmost exertions to meet the demand: I have. You have not known what it was to have the officers of the law seize upon your little stock of household goods, and threaten to sell them if the rent was not paid by a certain time: I have. You have not known what it was, under such circumstances, to be compelled to submit to the sacrifice, or, with almost equal repugnance to your feelings, borrow of your friend to satisfy the claim. You have not known what it was to want bread for your family after having been drained of your last cent by the landlord: I have. These things occurred many years ago, but the impressions they made are still vivid on my mind, and frequently recur when I see others similarly situated; and I beg you to bear in mind that thousands in the cities are continually tortured by the same agonizing system. This is an evil of the first magnitude, about which the black slave knows nothing; and this can afford you but a faint idea of the miseries of a city tenantry, which the black has never dreamed of. This, however, may lead you to understand why I have contended that the landless white is in a state of slavery quite as galling as that of the black. I know that families cannot be separated by force among the whites, as they are among the blacks, and I say this is an abuse that ought to be speedily abated at the South; but does not the white poor man suffer even in this respect almost as much as the black? See how families are separated even under the present system; not, indeed, by brute force, but, with equal effect, by the lash of want.

I am decidedly of opinion, sir, that there is more real suffering among the landless whites of the north, than among the blacks of the south; and if the question was, whether the landholders of the United States should have control of labor for ever under the northern or the southern system of slavery, I would hold up my hands for the latter; but does it follow, that because I see greater slavery here than at the south, and would first abolish slavery here, that, therefore, I justify negro slavery? I think not. . . .

We have made "the experiment" of speaking out against slavery. We believe the black has as good a right to be free as the white; that "all men are created equal"; and I have frequently asserted this right, in print, years ago. I believe that all men have equal natural and political rights; and I harbor no prejudice against color; still, there is a prejudice against color, which it would take ages to remove; and for their sakes, and not from any prejudice of my own, did I suggest, that, if the public lands were made free, a portion should be set apart for their voluntary settlement. Although I know thousands of whites who contend that the blacks have equal political rights, I have yet to be acquainted with one who would like to be placed on terms of social equality with them. There is a general repugnance against this, which arises from the ignorance engendered by the long continued oppression of the colored race; and this repugnance can only be overcome, if it can be overcome at all, by the improvement that would follow their political emancipation. . . .

I think you err in wishing to transfer the black from the one form of slavery to the other and worse one. What particular means you propose to abolish slavery, I am not informed of; but suppose that you had the power, tomorrow, to place the black laborers of the south in the same position as the white laborers of the north; as "cash produces more labor than the lash," is it not probable that the slaveholders would get as much labor performed by two-thirds or three-fourths of the number of their laborers as they now do by the whole? If we may judge from the effects of the cash or wages system here, (which, for instance, compels a poor seamstress to make three pair of light pantaloons a day for twenty-four cents, and this is in a city where rent is a dollar a week!) such would inevitably be the result at the south. Then what would become of the surplus? Is it not probable that some of it would find its way to the North, where there is already so great a surplus that the working men are frequently striking against a reduction of their wages? The condition of the labouring classes everywhere would be made worse by such a change; the few would, still easier than at present, amass wealth out of the proceeds of their toil, and the wealth thus amassed would be expended in a still further monopoly of the soil.

From a Letter to Gerrit Smith,
Working Man's Advocate, August 17, 1844

The main difference between us now is, if I understand you, not about the objects to be obtained; but about the order and means of attaining them. There is yet another difference, however. You do not yet see that there is white slavery: you call it poverty. I must still, until further enlightened, maintain that the landless poor man is a slave; if not quite so degraded a slave as the black, still so near it that the difference is hardly worth talking about. The one is a slave to a single master; the other to a master-class. The one has not the power of changing his taskmaster, but he is assured a support in sickness and old age; the other may change his taskmaster, but has no security for sickness and old age. The one labors under the fear of the whip; the other under the fear of want. The one may labor, for aught that we know, from sunrise to sunset; the other is frequently obliged to do more than that. The one is sometimes forcibly separated from his family, and his family from one another; the other is frequently, by force of poverty, compelled to submit to the same deprivations. I am not drawing this parallel to extenuate black slavery; far from it. I probably consider it as heinous as you do. My object is to show you that there are white slaves as well as black ones, and if I do not convince you, it will be for the want of the powers of language. I do not assert that poverty makes a man a slave; for a man might be poor, and yet be independent, if he had his land to work upon, from which he could not be ejected. The man who has no land and therefore must work for others, is the slave, whether he has one master or the choice of many. . . . I wish, sir, that you could see the true position of the free blacks in New York; the servants in cellars, for instance, whose highest ambition it is to imitate the follies and foibles of their masters and mistresses; then again, those who reside in the back streets and alleys, living, no one can tell how, in dirt, depravity, and ignorance; seeing, perhaps, that something is wrong in the system to which they are attached, but knowing of no better remedy than to help themselves to what they conveniently can of the wealth they see around them. If you could see these poor wretches in their dirty, crowded, comfortless dwellings, you would involuntarily exclaim that they would be better off even on a southern plantation. But they ought to be on their own plantation.

"Vote Yourself a Farm"

Are you an American citizen? Then you are a joint-owner of the public lands. Why not take enough of your property to provide yourself a home? Why not vote yourself a farm?

Remember poor Richard's[1] saying: "Now I have a sheep and a cow, every one bids me 'good morrow.'" If a man have a house and a home of his own, though it be a thousand miles off, he is well received in other people's houses; while the homeless wretch is turned away. The bare right to a farm, though you should never go near it, would save you from many an insult. Therefore, Vote yourself a farm.

Are you a party follower? Then you have long enough employed your vote to benefit scheming officeseekers; use it for once to benefit yourself — Vote yourself a farm.

Are you tired of slavery — of drudging for others — of poverty and its attendant miseries? Then, Vote yourself a farm.

Are you endowed with reason? Then you must know that your right to life hereby includes the right to a place to live in — the right to a home. Assert this right, so long denied mankind by feudal robbers and their attorneys. Vote yourself a farm.

Are you a believer in the scriptures? Then assert that the land is the Lord's, because He made it. Resist then the blasphemers who exact money for His work, even as you would resist them should they claim to be worshipped for His holiness. Emancipate the poor from the necessity of encouraging such blasphemy — Vote the freedom of the public lands.

Are you a man? Then assert the sacred rights of man — especially your right to stand upon God's earth, and to till it for your own profit. Vote yourself a farm.

---

[1] *poor Richard's:* Refers to *Poor Richard's Almanack,* an annual compilation of common-sense maxims and sayings published by Benjamin Franklin (1706–1790) from 1732 to 1737.

Would you free your country, and the sons of toil everywhere, from the heartless, irresponsible mastery of the aristocracy of avarice? Would you disarm this aristocracy of its chief weapon, the fearful power of banishment from God's earth? Then join with your neighbors to form a true American party, having for its guidance the principles of the American revolution, and whose chief measures shall be — 1. To limit the quantity of land that any one man may henceforth monopolize or inherit; and 2. To make the public lands free to actual settlers only, each having the right to sell his improvements to any man not possessed of other land. These great measures once carried, wealth would become a changed social element; it would then consist of the accumulated products of human labor, instead of a hoggish monopoly of the products of God's labor; and the antagonism of capital and labor would forever cease. Capital could no longer grasp the largest share of the laborer's earnings, as a reward for not doing him all the injury the laws of the feudal aristocracy authorize, viz: the denial of all stock to work upon and all place to live in. To derive any profit from the laborer, it must first give him work; for it could no longer wax fat by levying a dead tax upon his existence. The hoary iniquities of Norman land pirates[2] would cease to pass current as American law. Capital, with its power for good undiminished, would lose the power to oppress; and a new era would dawn upon the earth, and rejoice the souls of a thousand generations. Therefore forget not to Vote yourself a farm.

[2]*Norman land pirates:* Led by Duke William ("William the Conqueror," ca. 1028–1087), the Normans, from Normandy in northern France, conquered England and a large part of Wales in the eleventh century. Evans suggests that American law should not reflect the tradition of English law, with its origin in war, conquest, and unjust seizure of land. Compare Thomas Paine's reference in *Common Sense* (1776) to William the Conqueror as "a French bastard landing with an armed banditti."

SOLOMON NORTHRUP

The Slave's Work Day

Solomon Northrup (1808?–1863) was born in freedom and lived until his early thirties in upstate New York with his wife and three children, working as a farmer, laborer, and musician. In March 1841, he was kidnapped and sold to slave traders in Washington, D.C. He and other slaves were sent by ship to New Orleans, where he was bought by a planter. For the next twelve years, Northrup was a slave under several different masters in the Red River area of Louisiana. In 1852, with the help of a Canadian abolitionist and agents acting for the state of New York, Northrup was finally rescued, and in the following year, he published a narrative of his period in slavery, *Twelve Years a Slave: Narrative of Solomon Northrup*. It was widely read, and often linked to *Uncle Tom's Cabin*, which had appeared the year before. This excerpt shows the harsh, brutalizing conditions of life and labor that Northrup and his fellow slaves endured as they grew cotton under the supervision of master Edwin Epps.

The ground is prepared by throwing up beds or ridges, with the plough — back-furrowing, it is called. Oxen and mules, the latter almost exclusively, are used in ploughing. The women as frequently as the men perform this labor, feeding, currying, and taking care of their teams, and in all respects doing the field and stable work, precisely as do the ploughboys of the North.

The beds, or ridges, are six feet wide, that is, from water furrow to water furrow. A plough drawn by one mule is then run along the top of the ridge or center of the bed, making the drill, into which a girl usually drops the seed, which she carries in a bag hung round her neck. Behind her comes a mule and harrow, covering up the seed, so that two mules, three slaves, a plough and harrow, are employed in planting a row of cotton. This is done in the months of March and April. Corn is planted in February. When there are no cold rains, the cotton usually makes its appearance in a week. In the course of eight or ten days afterwards the first hoeing is commenced. This is performed in part, also, by the aid of the plough and mule. The plough passes as near as possible to the cotton on both sides, throwing the furrow from it. Slaves follow with their hoes, cutting up the grass and cotton, leaving hills two feet and a half apart. This is called scraping cotton. In two weeks more commences the second hoeing. This time the furrow is thrown towards the cotton. Only one stalk, the largest, is now left standing in each hill. In another fortnight it is hoed the third time, throwing the furrow towards the cotton in the same manner as before, and killing all the grass between the rows. About the first of July, when it is a foot high or thereabouts, it is hoed the fourth and last time. Now the whole space between the rows is ploughed, leaving a deep water furrow in the center. During all these hoeings the overseer or driver follows the slaves on horseback with a whip, such as has been described. The fastest hoer takes the lead row. He is usually about a rod in advance of his companions. If one of them passes him, he is whipped. If one falls behind or is a moment idle, he is whipped. In fact, the lash is flying from morning until night, the whole day long. The hoeing season thus continues from April until July, a field having no sooner been finished once, than it is commenced again.

In the latter part of August begins the cotton picking season. At this time each slave is presented with a sack. A strap is fastened to it, which goes over the neck, holding the mouth of the sack breast high, while the bottom reaches nearly to the ground. Each one is also presented with a large basket that will hold about two barrels. This is to put the cotton in when the sack is filled. The baskets are carried to the field and placed at the beginning of the rows.

When a new hand, one unaccustomed to the business, is sent for the first time into the field, he is whipped up smartly, and made for that day to pick as fast as he can possibly. At night it is weighed, so that his capability in cotton picking is known. He must bring in the same weight each night following. If it falls short, it is considered evidence that he has been laggard, and a greater or less number of lashes is the penalty.

An ordinary day's work is two hundred pounds. A slave who is accustomed to picking, is punished, if he or she brings in a less quantity than that. There is a great difference among them as regards this kind of labor. Some of them seem to have a natural knack, or quickness, which enables them to pick with great celerity, and with both hands, while others, with whatever practice or industry, are utterly unable to come up to the ordinary standard. Such hands are taken from the cotton field and employed in other business. Patsey, of whom I shall have more to say, was known as the most remarkable cotton picker on Bayou Bœuf. She picked with both hands and with such surprising rapidity, that five hundred pounds a day was not unusual for her.

Each one is tasked, therefore, according to his picking abilities, none, however, to come short of two hundred weight. I, being unskillful always in that business, would have satisfied my master by bringing in the latter quantity, while on the other hand, Patsey would surely have been beaten if she failed to produce twice as much.

The cotton grows from five to seven feet high, each stalk having a great many branches, shooting out in all directions, and lapping each other above the water furrow.

There are few sights more pleasant to the eye, than a wide cotton field when it is in the bloom. It presents an appearance of purity, like an immaculate expanse of light, new-fallen snow.

Sometimes the slave picks down one side of a row, and back upon the other, but more usually, there is one on either side, gathering all that has blossomed, leaving the unopened bolls for a succeeding picking. When the sack is filled, it is emptied into the basket and trodden down. It is necessary to be extremely careful the first time going through the field, in order not to break the branches off the stalks. The cotton will not bloom upon a broken branch. Epps never failed to inflict the severest chastisement on the unlucky servant who, either carelessly or unavoidably, was guilty in the least degree in this respect.

The hands are required to be in the cotton field as soon as it is light in the morning, and, with the exception of ten or fifteen minutes, which is given them at noon to swallow their allowance of cold bacon, they are not permitted to be a moment idle until it is too dark to see, and when the moon is full, they often times labor till the middle of the night. They do not dare to stop even at dinner time, nor return to the quarters, however late it be, until the order to halt is given by the driver.

The day's work over in the field, the baskets are "toted," or in other words, carried to the gin-house, where the cotton is weighed. No matter how fatigued and weary he may be — no matter how much he longs for sleep and rest — a slave never approaches the gin-house with his basket of cotton but with fear. If it falls short in weight — if he has not performed the full task appointed him, he knows that he must suffer. And if he has exceeded it by ten or twenty pounds, in all probability his master will measure the next day's task accordingly. So, whether he has too little or too much, his approach to the gin-house is always with fear and trembling. Most frequently they have too little, and therefore it is they are not anxious to leave the field. After weighing, follow the whippings; and then the baskets are carried to the cotton house, and their contents stored away like hay, all hands being sent in to tramp it down. If the cotton is not dry, instead of taking it to the gin-house at once, it is laid upon platforms, two feet high, and some three times as wide, covered with boards or plank, with narrow walks running between them.

This done, the labor of the day is not yet ended, by any means. Each one must then attend to his respective chores. One feeds the mules, another the swine — another cuts the wood, and so forth; besides, the packing is all done by candle light. Finally, at a late hour, they reach the quarters, sleepy and overcome with the long day's toil. Then a fire must be kindled in the cabin, the corn ground in the small hand-mill, and supper, and dinner for the next day in the field, prepared. All that is allowed them is corn and bacon, which is given out at the corncrib and smoke-house every Sunday morning. Each one receives, as his weekly allowance, three and a half pounds of bacon, and corn enough to make a peck of meal. That is all — no tea, coffee, sugar, and with the exception of a very scanty sprinkling now and then, no salt. I can say, from a ten years' residence with Master Epps, that no slave of his is ever likely to suffer from the gout, superinduced by excessive high living. Master Epps' hogs were fed on *shelled* corn — it was thrown out to his "niggers" in the ear. The former, he thought, would fatten faster by shelling, and soaking it in the water — the latter, perhaps, if treated in the same manner, might grow too fat to labor. Master Epps was a shrewd calculator and knew how to manage his own animals, drunk or sober.

The corn mill stands in the yard beneath a shelter. It is like a common coffee mill, the hopper holding about six quarts. There was one privilege which Master Epps granted freely to every slave he had. They might grind their corn nightly, in such small quantities as their daily wants required, or they might grind the whole week's allowance at one time, on Sundays, just as they preferred. A very generous man was Master Epps!

I kept my corn in a small wooden box, the meal in a gourd; and, by the way, the gourd is one of the most convenient and necessary utensils on a plantation. Besides supplying the place of all kinds of crockery in a slave cabin, it is used for carrying water to the fields. Another, also, contains the dinner. It dispenses with the necessity of pails, dippers, basins, and such tin and wooden superfluities altogether.

When the corn is ground, and fire is made, the bacon is taken down from the nail on which it hangs, a slice cut off and thrown upon the coals to broil. The majority of slaves have no knife, much less a fork. They cut their bacon with the axe at the woodpile. The corn meal is mixed with a little water, placed in the fire, and baked. When it is "done brown," the ashes are scraped off, and being placed upon a chip, which answers for a table, the tenant of the slave hut is ready to sit down upon the ground to supper. By this time it is usually midnight. The same fear of punishment with which they approach the gin-house, possesses them again on lying down to get a snatch of rest. It is the fear of oversleeping in the morning. Such an offence would certainly be attended with not less than twenty lashes. With a prayer that he may be on his feet and wide awake at the first sound of the horn, he sinks to his slumbers nightly.

The softest couches in the world are not to be found in the log mansion of the slave. The one whereon I reclined year after year, was a plank twelve inches wide and ten feet long. My pillow was a stick of wood. The bedding was a coarse blanket, and not a rag or shred beside. Moss might be used, were it not that it directly breeds a swarm of fleas.

The cabin is constructed of logs, without floor or window. The latter is altogether unnecessary, the crevices between the logs admitting sufficient light. In stormy weather the rain drives through them, rendering it comfortless and extremely disagreeable. The rude door hangs on great wooden hinges. In one end is constructed an awkward fire-place.

An hour before day light the horn is blown. Then the slaves arouse, prepare their breakfast, fill a gourd with water, in another deposit their dinner of cold bacon and corn cake, and hurry to the field again. It is an offence invariably followed by a flogging, to be found at the quarters after daybreak. Then the fears and labors of another day begin; and until its close there is no such thing as rest. He fears he will be caught lagging through the day; he fears to approach the gin-house with his basket-load of cotton at night; he fears, when he lies down, that he will oversleep himself in the morning. Such is a true, faithful, unexaggerated picture and description of the slave's daily life, during the time of cotton-picking, on the shores of Bayou Bœuf. . . .

It was rarely that a day passed by without one or more whippings. This occurred at the time the cotton was weighed. The delinquent, whose weight had fallen short, was taken out, stripped, made to lie upon the ground, face downwards, when he received a punishment proportioned to his offence. It is the literal, unvarnished truth, that the crack of the lash, and the shrieking of the slaves, can be heard from dark till bed time, on Epps' plantation, any day almost during the entire period of the cotton-picking season.

The number of lashes is graduated according to the nature of the case. Twenty-five are deemed a mere brush, inflicted, for instance, when a dry leaf or piece of boll is found in the cotton, or when a branch is broken in the field; fifty is the ordinary penalty following all delinquencies of the next higher grade; one hundred is called severe: it is the punishment inflicted for the serious offence of standing idle in the field; from one hundred and fifty to two hundred is bestowed upon him who quarrels with his cabin-mates, and five hundred, well laid on, besides the mangling of the dogs, perhaps, is certain to consign the poor, unpitied runaway to weeks of pain and agony.

During the two years Epps remained on the plantation at Bayou Huff Power, he was in the habit, as often as once in a fortnight at least, of coming home intoxicated from Holmesville. The shooting-matches almost invariably concluded with a debauch. At such times he was boisterous and half-crazy. Often he would break the dishes, chairs, and whatever furniture he could lay his hands on. When satisfied with his amusement in the house, he would seize the whip and walk forth into the yard. Then it behooved the slaves to be watchful and exceeding wary. The first one who came within reach felt the smart of his lash. Sometimes for hours he would keep them running in all directions, dodging around the corners of the cabins. Occasionally he would come upon one unawares, and if he succeeded in inflicting a fair, round blow, it was a feat that much delighted him. The younger children, and the aged, who had become inactive, suffered then. In the midst of the confusion he would slily take his stand behind a cabin, waiting with raised whip, to dash it into the first black face that peeped cautiously around the corner.

At other times he would come home in a less brutal humor. Then there must be a merry-making. Then all must move to the measure of a tune. Then Master Epps must needs regale his melodious ears with the music of a fiddle. Then did he become buoyant, elastic, gaily "tripping the light fantastic toe" around the piazza and all through the house.

Tibeats, at the time of my sale, had informed him I could play on the violin. He had received his information from Ford. Through the importunities of Mistress Epps, her husband had been induced to purchase me one during a visit to New-Orleans. Frequently I was called into the house to play before the family, mistress being passionately fond of music.

All of us would be assembled in the large room of the great house, whenever Epps came home in one of his dancing moods. No matter how worn out and tired we were, there must be a general dance. When properly stationed on the floor, I would strike up a tune.

"Dance, you d —— d niggers, dance," Epps would shout.

Then there must be no halting or delay, no slow or languid movements; all must be brisk, and lively, and alert. "Up and down, heel and toe, and away we go," was the order of the hour. Epps' portly form mingled with those of his dusky slaves, moving rapidly through all the mazes of the dance.

Usually his whip was in his hand, ready to fall about the ears of the presumptuous thrall, who dared to rest a moment, or even stop to catch his breath. When he was himself exhausted, there would be a brief cessation, but it would be very brief. With a slash, and crack, and flourish of the whip, he would shout again, "Dance, niggers, dance," and away they would go once more, pell-mell, while I, spurred by an occasional sharp touch of the lash, sat in a corner, extracting from my violin a marvelous quick-stepping tune. The mistress often upbraided him, declaring she would return to her father's house at Cheneyville; nevertheless, there were times she could not restrain a burst of laughter, on witnessing his uproarious pranks. Frequently, we were thus detained until almost morning. Bent with excessive toil — actually suffering for a little refreshing rest, and feeling rather as if we could cast ourselves upon the earth and weep, many a night in the house of Edwin Epps have his unhappy slaves been made to dance and laugh.

Notwithstanding these deprivations in order to gratify the whim of an unreasonable master, we had to be in the field as soon as it was light, and during the day perform the ordinary and accustomed task. Such deprivations could not be urged at the scales in extenuation of any lack of weight, or in the cornfield for not hoeing with the usual rapidity. The whippings were just as severe as if we had gone forth in the morning, strengthened and invigorated by a night's repose. Indeed, after such frantic revels, he was always more sour and savage than before, punishing for slighter causes, and using the whip with increased and more vindictive energy.

Ten years I toiled for that man without reward. Ten years of my incessant labor has contributed to increase the bulk of his possessions.

Ten years I was compelled to address him with down-cast eyes and uncovered head — in the attitude and language of a slave. I am indebted to him for nothing, save undeserved abuse and stripes.

WILLIAM LLOYD GARRISON

"To the Public"

William Lloyd Garrison (1805–1879) battled for many reforms, but he is best known for founding and editing the radical abolitionist paper *The Liberator,* published weekly in Boston from January 1831 to December 1865. His fiery rhetoric testified to his commitment to the anti-slavery cause and won him loyal supporters. But his extreme adherence to principle, refusal to compromise, and tendency to regard disagreement as disloyalty made him a very controversial figure in the ranks of nineteenth-century reformers. "To the Public" was the editorial in the first issue of *The Liberator,* January 1, 1831.

In the month of August, I issued proposals for publishing "THE LIBERATOR" in Washington city; but the enterprise, though hailed in different sections of the country, was palsied by public indifference. Since that time, the removal of the Genius of Universal Emancipation[1] to the Seat of Government has rendered less imperious the establishment of a similar periodical in that quarter.

During my recent tour for the purpose of exciting the minds of the people by a series of discourses on the subject of slavery, every place that I visited gave fresh evidence of the fact, that a greater revolution in public sentiment was to be effected in the free states — *and particularly in New-England* — than at the south. I found contempt more bitter, opposition more active, detraction more relentless, prejudice more stubborn, and apathy more frozen, than among slave owners themselves. Of course, there were individual exceptions to the contrary. This state of things afflicted, but did not dishearten me. I determined, at every hazard, to lift up the standard of emancipation in the eyes of the

---

[1]*the Genius of Universal Emancipation:* This was an anti-slavery paper, edited by Benjamin Lundy (1789–1839), with which Garrison had been associated in Baltimore.

nation, *within sight of Bunker Hill*[2] *and in the birth place of liberty.* That standard is now unfurled; and long may it float, unhurt by the spoliations of time or the missiles of a desperate foe — yea, till every chain be broken, and every bondman set free! Let southern oppressors tremble — let their secret abettors tremble — let their northern apologists tremble — let all the enemies of the persecuted blacks tremble.

I deem the publication of my original Prospectus unnecessary, as it has obtained a wide circulation. The principles therein inculcated will be steadily pursued in this paper, excepting that I shall not array myself as the political partisan of any man. In defending the great cause of human rights, I wish to derive the assistance of all religions and of all parties.

Assenting to the "self-evident truth" maintained in the American Declaration of Independence, "that all men are created equal, and endowed by their Creator with certain inalienable rights — among which are life, liberty and the pursuit of happiness," I shall strenuously contend for the immediate enfranchisement of our slave population. In Park-street Church, on the Fourth of July, 1829, in an address on slavery, I unreflectingly assented to the popular but pernicious doctrine of *gradual* abolition. I seize this opportunity to make a full and unequivocal recantation, and thus publicly to ask pardon of my God, of my country, and of my brethren the poor slaves, for having uttered a sentiment so full of timidity, injustice and absurdity. A similar recantation, from my pen, was published in the Genius of Universal Emancipation at Baltimore, in September, 1829. My conscience is now satisfied.

I am aware, that many object to the severity of my language; but is there not cause for severity? I *will be* as harsh as truth, and as uncompromising as justice. On this subject, I do not wish to think, or speak, or write, with moderation. No! no! Tell a man whose house is on fire, to give a moderate alarm; tell him to moderately rescue his wife from the hands of the ravisher; tell the mother to gradually extricate her babe from the fire into which it has fallen; — but urge me not to use moderation in a cause like the present. I am in earnest — I will not equivocate — I will not excuse — I will not retreat a single inch — AND I WILL BE HEARD. The apathy of the people is enough to make every statue leap from its pedestal, and to hasten the resurrection of the dead.

[2]*Bunker Hill:* Site of an important early battle (in fact, however, the battle took place on Breed's Hill) in the American Revolution, fought in Boston on June 17, 1775.

It is pretended, that I am retarding the cause of emancipation by the coarseness of my invective, and the precipitancy of my measures. *The charge is not true.* On this question my influence, — humble as it is, — is felt at this moment to a considerable extent, and shall be felt in coming years — not perniciously, but beneficially — not as a curse, but as a blessing; and posterity will bear testimony that I was right. I desire to thank God, that he enables me to disregard "the fear of man which bringeth a snare," and to speak his truth in its simplicity and power. And here I close with this fresh dedication:

> Oppression! I have seen thee, face to face,
> And met thy cruel eye and cloudy brow;
> But thy soul-withering glance I fear not now —
> For dread to prouder feelings doth give place
> Of deep abhorrence! Scorning the disgrace
> Of slavish knees that at thy footstool bow,
> I also kneel — but with far other vow
> Do hail thee and thy hord of hirelings base: —
> I swear, while life-blood warms my throbbing veins,
> Still to oppose and thwart, with heart and hand,
> Thy brutalising sway — till Afric's chains
> Are burst, and Freedom rules the rescued land, —
> Trampling Oppression and his iron rod:
> *Such is the vow I take* — SO HELP ME GOD!

FREDERICK DOUGLASS

Letter to William Lloyd Garrison, January 1, 1846

Frederick Douglass (1818–1895) escaped from slavery in Maryland in September 1838 and soon became an avid reader of William Lloyd Garrison's abolitionist newspaper, *The Liberator*. He met Garrison and heard him speak at the annual meeting of the Bristol Anti-Slavery Society, held in New Bedford, Massachusetts, on August 9, 1841. The next day, Douglass joined Garrison and forty others on a boat trip to Nantucket, where another anti-slavery meeting was to take place. During the trip itself, Douglass was heartened by the protest that Garrison mounted against segregation aboard the vessel. At the Nantucket meeting, Douglass spoke for the first time in public, with Garrison following him.

It was at this same meeting that Douglass was invited to become an anti-slavery lecturer for the Massachusetts Anti-Slavery Society. During the next four years, Douglass was a speaker for the society, often traveling with the Boston abolitionist Wendell Phillips (1811–1884). Both Phillips and Garrison wrote prefatory remarks for Douglass's autobiographical *Narrative,* published in May 1845, by the Anti-Slavery Office in Boston.

Douglass never accepted the argument that slavery was only one part of a larger labor problem and that the white "wage slaves" of the North suffered more than enslaved African Americans. White workers, he replied, were legally free and enjoyed protections under the law that were denied to black slaves and that were not even extended to free blacks in the Northern states. The most pressing issues on the national scene, for Douglass, were slavery in the South and prejudice and discrimination against African Americans everywhere.

Douglass toured and lectured in the British Isles from August 1845 to April 1847. This letter to Garrison, written while Douglass was in Ireland, was published in *The Liberator* on January 30, 1846.

Victoria Hotel, Belfast,
January 1, 1846

My Dear Friend Garrison:

I am now about to take leave of the Emerald Isle, for Glasgow, Scotland. I have been here a little more than four months. Up to this time, I have given no direct expression of the views, feelings and opinions which I have formed, respecting the character and condition of the people in this land. I have refrained thus purposely. I wish to speak advisedly, and in order to do this, I have waited till I trust experience has brought my opinions to an intelligent maturity. I have been thus careful, not because I think what I may say will have much effect in shaping the opinions of the world, but because whatever of influence I may possess, whether little or much, I wish it to go in the right direction, and according to truth. I hardly need say that, in speaking of Ireland, I shall be influenced by prejudices in favor of America. I think my circumstances all forbid that. I have no end to serve, no creed to uphold, no government to defend; and as to nation, I belong to none. I have no protection at home, or resting-place abroad. The land of my birth welcomes me to her shores only as a slave, and spurns with contempt the idea of treating me differently. So that I am an outcast from the society of my childhood, and an

outlaw in the land of my birth. "I am a stranger with thee, and a so-
journer as all my fathers were."[1] That men should be patriotic is to
me perfectly natural; and as a philosophical fact, I am able to give it
an *intellectual* recognition. But no further can I go. If ever I had any
patriotism, or any capacity for the feeling, it was whipt out of me
long since by the lash of the American soul-drivers.

In thinking of America, I sometimes find myself admiring her
bright blue sky — her grand old woods — her fertile fields — her
beautiful rivers — her mighty lakes, and star-crowned mountains.
But my rapture is soon checked, my joy is soon turned to mourning.
When I remember that all is cursed with the infernal spirit of slave-
holding, robbery and wrong, — when I remember that with the waters of her noblest rivers, the tears of my brethren are borne to the
ocean, disregarded and forgotten, and that her most fertile fields
drink daily of the warm blood of my outraged sisters, I am filled with
unutterable loathing, and led to reproach myself that any thing could
fall from my lips in praise of such a land. America will not allow her
children to love her. She seems bent on compelling those who would
be her warmest friends, to be her worst enemies. May God give her
repentance before it is too late, is the ardent prayer of my heart. I will
continue to pray, labor and wait, believing that she cannot always be
insensible to the dictates of justice, or deaf to the voice of humanity.

My opportunities for learning the character and condition of the
people of this land have been very great. I have travelled almost from
the hill of "Howth" to the Giant's Causeway, and from the Giant's
Causeway to Cape Clear. During these travels, I have met with much
in the character and condition of the people to approve, and much to
condemn — much that has thrilled me with pleasure — and very
much that has filled me with pain. I will not, in this letter, attempt to
give any description of those scenes which have given me pain. This I
will do hereafter. I have enough, and more than your subscribers will
be disposed to read at one time, of the bright side of the picture. I can
truly say, I have spent some of the happiest moments of my life since
landing in this country. I seem to have undergone a transformation. I
live a new life. The warm and generous co-operation extended to me
by the friends of my despised race — the prompt and liberal manner
with which the press has rendered me its aid — the glorious enthusiasm with which thousands have flocked to hear the cruel wrongs of
my down-trodden and long-enslaved fellow-countrymen portrayed —

[1]*I am a stranger . . . were:* Psalms 39:12.

the deep sympathy for the slave, and the strong abhorrence of the slaveholder, everywhere evinced — the cordiality with which members and ministers of various religious bodies, and of various shades of religious opinion, have embraced me, and lent me their aid — the kind hospitality constantly proffered to me by persons of the highest rank in society — the spirit of freedom that seems to animate all with whom I come in contact — and the entire absence of every thing that looked like prejudice against me, on account of the color of my skin — contrasted so strongly with my long and bitter experience in the United States, that I look with wonder and amazement on the transition. In the Southern part of the United States, I was a slave, thought of and spoken of as property. In the language of the LAW, *"held, taken, reputed and adjudged to be a chattel in the hands of my owners and possessors, and their executors, administrators, and assigns, to all intents, constructions, and purposes whatsoever."* — Brev. Digest, 224. In the Northern States, a fugitive slave, liable to be hunted at any moment like a felon, and to be hurled into the terrible jaws of slavery — doomed by an inveterate prejudice against color to insult and outrage on every hand, (Massachusetts out of the question) — denied the privileges and courtesies common to others in the use of the most humble means of conveyance — shut out from the cabins on steamboats — refused admission to respectable hotels — caricatured, scorned, scoffed, mocked and maltreated with impunity by any one, (no matter how black his heart,) so he has a white skin. But now behold the change! Eleven days and a half gone, and I have crossed three thousand miles of the perilous deep. Instead of a democratic government, I am under a monarchical government. Instead of the bright blue sky of America, I am covered with the soft grey fog of the Emerald Isle. I breathe, and lo! the chattel becomes a man. I gaze around in vain for one who will question my equal humanity, claim me as his slave, or offer me an insult. I employ a cab — I am seated beside white people — I reach the hotel — I enter the same door — I am shown into the same parlor — I dine at the same table — and no one is offended. No delicate nose grows deformed in my presence. I find no difficulty here in obtaining admission into any place of worship, instruction or amusement, on equal terms with people as white as any I ever saw in the United States. I meet nothing to remind me of my complexion. I find myself regarded and treated at every turn with the kindness and deference paid to white people. When I go to church, I am met by no upturned nose and scornful lip to tell me, *"We don't allow n——rs in here"!*

I remember, about two years ago, there was in Boston, near the southwest corner of Boston Common, a menagerie. I had long desired to see such a collection as I understood were being exhibited there. Never having had an opportunity while a slave, I resolved to seize this, my first, since my escape. I went, and as I approached the entrance to gain admission, I was met and told by the door-keeper, in a harsh and contemptuous tone, *"We don't allow n——rs in here."* I also remember attending a revival meeting in the Rev. Henry Jackson's meeting-house, at New-Bedford, and going up the broad aisle to find a seat. I was met by a good deacon, who told me, in a pious tone, *"We don't allow n——rs in here"!* Soon after my arrival in New-Bedford from the South, I had a strong desire to attend the Lyceum, but was told, *"They don't allow n——rs in here"!* While passing from New York to Boston on the steamer Massachusetts, on the night of 9th Dec. 1843, when chilled almost through with the cold, I went into the cabin to get a little warm. I was soon touched upon the shoulder, and told, *"We don't allow n——rs in here"!* On arriving in Boston from an anti-slavery tour, hungry and tired, I went into an eating-house near my friend Mr. Campbell's, to get some refreshments. I was met by a lad in a white apron, *"We don't allow n——rs in here"!* A week or two before leaving the United States, I had a meeting appointed at Weymouth, the home of that glorious band of true abolitionists, the Weston family, and others. On attempting to take a seat in the Omnibus to that place, I was told by the driver, (and I never shall forget his fiendish hate,) *"I don't allow n——rs in here"!* Thank heaven for the respite I now enjoy! I had been in Dublin but a few days, when a gentleman of great respectability kindly offered to conduct me through all the public buildings of that beautiful city; and a little afterwards, I found myself dining with the Lord Mayor of Dublin. What a pity there was not some American democratic Christian at the door of his splendid mansion, to bark out at my approach, *"They don't allow n——rs in here"!* The truth is, the people here know nothing of the republican Negro hate prevalent in our glorious land. They measure and esteem men according to their moral and intellectual worth, and not according to the color of their skin. Whatever may be said of the aristocracies here, there is none based on the color of a man's skin. This species of aristocracy belongs pre-eminently to "the land of the free, and the home of the brave." I have never found it abroad, in any but Americans. It sticks to them wherever they go. They find it almost as hard to get rid of it as to get rid of their skins.

The second day after my arrival at Liverpool, in company with my friend Buffum, and several other friends, I went to Eaton Hall, the residence of the Marquis of Westminster, one of the most splendid buildings in England. On approaching the door, I found several of our American passengers, who came out with us in [the ship] the Cambria, waiting at the door for admission, as but one party was allowed in the house at a time. We all had to wait till the company within came out. And of all the faces, expressive of chagrin, those of the Americans were pre-eminent. They looked as sour as vinegar, and bitter as gall, when they found I was to be admitted on equal terms with themselves. When the door was opened, I walked in, on an equal footing with my white fellow-citizens, and from all I could see, I had as much attention paid me by the servants that showed us through the house, as any with a paler skin. As I walked through the building, the statuary did not fall down, the pictures did not leap from their places, the doors did not refuse to open, and the servants did not say, *"We don't allow n——rs in here"!*

A happy new year to you, and all the friends of freedom.

Excuse this imperfect scrawl, and believe me to be ever and always yours,

FREDERICK DOUGLASS

ABRAHAM LINCOLN

"Address to the Washingtonian Temperance Society of Springfield, Illinois"

The temperance movement in the antebellum period was a mighty engine for reform and social change. By 1835, the American Temperance Society, begun by evangelicals in Boston a decade earlier, claimed 1.5 million members — more than 10 percent of the free population of the country.

Many persons across the political and religious spectrum were involved in temperance, including the lawyer and Illinois legislator Abraham Lincoln (1809–1865). He gave the speech reprinted here on February 22 (Washington's birthday), 1842, before the Washingtonian Temperance Society, in Springfield, Illinois. The Washingtonian movement, which started in the late 1830s, concentrated on reforming drunkards and persuading them to take an abstinence pledge. It was a mass movement that involved many skilled and unskilled workers and artisans. After delivering his speech to the local Washingtonian branch in the Presbyterian Church at midday, Lincoln joined them in a grand parade. Not all, however, were pleased with his views on the temperance issue, for his tone seemed more sympathetic to drunkards than true believers found acceptable.

Hawthorne's writing and publication of *The Blithedale Romance* coincided with the mid-century climax of the temperance cause — the passage in 1851 of the "Maine law," which prohibited in that state the manufacture and sale of intoxicating liquors. The prohibitionist and Portland mayor Neal Dow (1804–1897), who drew support from Washingtonians in Maine, was the force behind this campaign. By 1855, thirteen states (nearly one-third of the nation) had passed similar laws; Massachusetts instituted such a law in July, 1852.

The night before his departure for Blithedale, Miles Coverdale enjoys a "last bottle" of sherry with a friend. The next morning, as he prepares to leave his apartment, he bids good-bye to his wine and whiskey — a change for the better that temperance advocates would have noticed (ch. 2). They would have been less pleased about the "sherry-cobbler" he orders in his hotel room and his complaints about "temperance-men" when he visits a saloon (chs. 17, 21). There is no drinking at Blithedale, but Coverdale's narration turns a number of times to images of and allusions to alcohol, spirits, and intoxication.

Not long after *The Blithedale Romance* appeared, the prolific author and temperance advocate, T. S. Arthur (1809–1885) published *Ten Nights in A Bar-Room: And What I Saw There* (1854), a novel on the disasters of drinking that by 1860 had become a popular classic. (See the illustrations on pp. 284–85.)

The text for this selection is from *Abraham Lincoln: His Speeches and Writings*, ed. Roy P. Basler (Cleveland: World, 1946), 131–41.

Although the Temperance cause has been in progress for near twenty years, it is apparent to all, that it is, *just now*, being crowned with a degree of success, hitherto unparalleled.

The list of its friends is daily swelled by the additions of fifties, of hundreds, and of thousands. The cause itself seems suddenly transformed from a cold abstract theory, to a living, breathing, active, and powerful chieftain, going forth "conquering and to conquer." The citadels of his great adversary are daily being stormed and dismantled; his temples and his altars, where the rites of his idolatrous worship have long been performed, and where human sacrifices have long been wont to be made, are daily desecrated and deserted. The trump of the conqueror's fame is sounding from hill to hill, from sea to sea, and from land to land, and calling millions to his standard at a blast.

For this new and splendid success, we heartily rejoice. That that success is so much greater *now* than *heretofore,* is doubtless owing to rational causes; and if we would have it to continue, we shall do well to enquire what those causes are. The warfare heretofore waged against the demon of Intemperance, has, some how or other, been erroneous. Either the champions engaged, or the tactics they adopted, have not been the most proper. These champions for the most part, have been Preachers, Lawyers, and hired agents. Between these and the mass of mankind, there is a want of *approachability,* if the term be admissible, partially at least, fatal to their success. They are supposed to have no sympathy of feeling or interest, with those very persons whom it is their object to convince and persuade.

And again, it is so easy and so common to ascribe motives to men of these classes, other than those they profess to act upon. The *preacher,* it is said, advocates temperance because he is a fanatic, and desires a union of Church and State; the *lawyer,* from his pride and vanity of hearing himself speak; and the *hired agent,* for his salary. But when one, who has long been known as a victim of intemperance, bursts the fetters that have bound him, and appears before his neighbors "clothed, and in his right mind," a redeemed specimen of long lost humanity, and stands up with tears of joy trembling in eyes, to tell of the miseries *once* endured, *now* to be endured no more forever; of his once naked and starving children, now clad and fed comfortably; of a wife long weighed down with woe, weeping, and a broken heart, now restored to health, happiness, and renewed affection; and how easily it all is done, once it is resolved to be done; however simple his language, there is a logic, and an eloquence in it, that few, with human feelings, can resist. They cannot say that *he* desires a union of church and state, for he is not a church member; they cannot say *he* is vain of hearing himself speak, for his whole demeanor shows, he would gladly avoid speaking at all; they cannot say *he* speaks for pay for he receives none, and asks for none. Nor can his sincerity in any way be doubted; or his sympathy for those he would persuade to imitate his example, be denied.

In my judgment, it is to the battles of this new class of champions that our late success is greatly, perhaps chiefly, owing. But, had the old school champions themselves, been of the most wise selecting, was their *system* of tactics, the most judicious? It seems to me, it was not. Too much denunciation against dram[1] sellers and dram-drinkers was indulged in. This, I think, was both impolitic and unjust. It was *impolitic,* because, it is not much in the nature of man to be driven to any thing; still less to be driven about that which is exclusively his own business; and least of all, where such driving is to be submitted to, at the expense of pecuniary interest, or burning appetite. When the dram-seller and drinker, were incessantly told, not in the accents of entreaty and persuasion, diffidently addressed by erring man to an erring brother; but in the thundering tones of anathema and denunci-ation, with which the lordly Judge often groups together all the crimes of the felon's life, and thrusts them in his face just ere he passes sentence of death upon him, that *they* were the authors of all the vice and misery and crime in the land; that *they* were the manu-facturers and material of all the thieves and robbers and murderers that infested the earth; that *their* houses were the workshops of the devil; and that *their persons* should be shunned by all the good and virtuous, as moral pestilences — I say, when they were told all this, and in this way, it is not wonderful that they were slow, *very slow,* to acknowledge the truth of such denunciations, and to join the ranks of their denouncers, in a hue and cry against themselves.

To have expected them to do otherwise than as they did — to have expected them not to meet denunciation with denunciation, crimina-tion with crimination, and anathema with anathema, was to expect a reversal of human nature, which is God's decree, and never can be re-versed. When the conduct of men is designed to be influenced, *per-suasion,* kind, unassuming persuasion, should ever be adopted. It is an old and a true maxim, that a "drop of honey catches more flies than a gallon of gall." So with men. If you would win a man to your cause, *first* convince him that you are his sincere friend. Therein is a drop of honey that catches his heart, which, say what he will, is the great high road to his reason, and which, when once gained, you will find but little trouble in convincing his judgment of the justice of your cause, if indeed that cause really be a just one. On the contrary, as-sume to dictate to his judgment, or to command his action, or to mark him as one to be shunned and despised, and he will retreat within himself, close all the avenues to his head and his heart; and tho' your cause be naked truth itself, transformed to the heaviest

---

[1]*dram:* A small quantity of something to drink, usually of liquor.

lance, harder than steel, and sharper than steel can be made, and tho' you throw it with more than Herculean force and precision, you shall no more be able to pierce him, than to penetrate the hard shell of a tortoise with a rye straw.

Such is man, and so *must* he be understood by those who would lead him, even to his own best interest.

On this point, the Washingtonians greatly excel the temperance advocates of former times. Those whom *they* desire to convince and persuade, are their old friends and companions. They know they are not demons, nor even the worst of men. *They* know that generally, they are kind, generous and charitable, even beyond the example of their more staid and sober neighbors. *They* are practical philanthropists; and *they* glow with a generous and brotherly zeal, that mere theorizers are incapable of feeling. Benevolence and charity possess *their* hearts entirely; and out of the abundance of their hearts, their tongues give utterance. "Love through all their actions runs, and all their words are mild." In this spirit they speak and act, and in the same, they are heard and regarded. And when such is the temper of the advocate, and such of the audience, no good cause can be unsuccessful.

But I have said that denunciations against dram-sellers and dram-drinkers, are *unjust* as well as impolitic. Let us see.

I have not enquired at what period of time the use of intoxicating drinks commenced; nor is it important to know. It is sufficient that to all of us who now inhabit the world, the practice of drinking them, is just as old as the world itself, — that is, we have seen the one, just as long as we have seen the other. When all such of us, as have now reached the years of maturity, first opened our eyes upon the stage of existence, we found intoxicating liquor, recognized by every body, used by every body, and repudiated by nobody. It commonly entered into the first draught of the infant, and the last draught of the dying man. From the sideboard of the parson, down to the ragged pocket of the houseless loafer, it was constantly found. Physicians prescribed it in this, that, and the other disease. Government provided it for its soldiers and sailors; and to have a rolling or raising, a husking or hoe-down, any where without it, was *positively insufferable.*

So too, it was every where a respectable article of manufacture and of merchandize. The making of it was regarded as an honorable livelihood; and he who could make most, was the most enterprising and respectable. Large and small manufactories of it were every where erected, in which all the earthly goods of their owners were invested. Wagons drew it from town to town — boats bore it from clime to clime, and the winds wafted it from nation to nation; and merchants bought and sold it, by wholesale and by retail, with precisely the same feelings, on the part of seller, buyer, and bystander, as are felt at the selling and buying of flour, beef, bacon, or any other of the real necessaries of life. Universal public opinion not only tolerated, but recognized and adopted its use.

It is true, that even *then,* it was known and acknowledged, that many were greatly injured by it; but none seemed to think the injury arose from the *use* of a *bad thing,* but from the *abuse* of a *very good thing.* The victims to it were pitied, and compassionated, just as now are, the heirs of consumptions, and other hereditary diseases. Their failing was treated as a *misfortune,* and not as a *crime,* or even as a *disgrace.*

If, then, what I have been saying be true, is it wonderful, that *some* should think and act *now,* as *all* thought and acted *twenty years ago?* And is it *just* to assail, *contemn,* or despise them, for doing so? The universal *sense* of mankind, on any subject, is an argument, or at least an *influence* not easily overcome. The success of the argument in favor of the existence of an over-ruling Providence, mainly depends upon that sense; and men ought not, in justice, to be denounced for yielding to it, in any case, or for giving it up slowly, *especially,* where they are backed by interest, fixed habits, or burning appetites.

Another error, as it seems to me, into which the old reformers fell, was, the position that all habitual drunkards were utterly incorrigible, and therefore, must be turned adrift, and damned without remedy, in order that the grace of temperance might abound to the temperate *then,* and to all mankind some hundred years *thereafter.* There is in this something so repugnant to humanity, so uncharitable, so cold-blooded and feelingless, that it never did, nor ever can enlist the enthusiasm of a popular cause. We could not love the man who taught it — we could not hear him with patience. The heart could not throw open its portals to it. The generous man could not adopt it. It could not mix with his blood. It looked so fiendishly selfish, so like throwing fathers and brothers overboard, to lighten the boat for our security — that the noble minded shrank from the manifest meanness of the thing.

And besides this, the benefits of a reformation to be effected by such a system, were too remote in point of time, to warmly engage many in its behalf. Few can be induced to labor exclusively for posterity; and none will do it enthusiastically. Posterity has done nothing for us; and theorise on it as we may, practically we shall do very little for it, unless we are made to think, we are, at the same time, doing something for ourselves. What an ignorance of human nature does it exhibit, to ask or expect a whole community to rise up and labor for the *temporal* happiness of *others* after *themselves* shall be consigned to the dust, a majority of which community take no pains whatever to secure their own eternal welfare, at a no greater distant day? Great distance, in either time or space, has wonderful power to lull and render quiescent the human mind. Pleasures to be enjoyed, or pains to be endured, *after* we shall be dead and gone, are but little regarded, even in our *own* cases, and much less in the cases of others.

Still, in addition to this, there is something so ludicrous in *promises* of good, or *threats* of evil, a great way off, as to render the whole subject with which they are connected, easily turned into ridicule. "Better lay down that spade you're stealing, Paddy, — if you don't you'll pay for it at the day of judgment." "By the powers, if ye'll credit me so long, I'll take another, jist."

By the Washingtonians, this system of consigning the habitual drunkard to hopeless ruin, is repudiated. *They* adopt a more enlarged philanthropy. *They* go for present as well as future good. *They* labor for all *now* living, as well as all *hereafter* to live. *They* teach *hope* to all — *despair* to none. As applying to *their* cause, *they* deny the doctrine of unpardonable sin. As in Christianity it is taught, so in this *they* teach, that

> "While the lamp holds out to burn,
> The vilest sinner may return."

And, what is matter of the most profound gratulation, they, by experiment upon experiment, and example upon example, prove the maxim to be no less true in the one case than in the other. On every hand we behold those, who but yesterday, were the chief of sinners, now the chief apostles of the cause. Drunken devils are cast out by ones, by sevens, and by legions; and their unfortunate victims, like the poor possessed, who was redeemed from his long and lonely wanderings in the tombs, are publishing to the ends of the earth, how great things have been done for them.

To these *new champions*, and this *new* system of tactics, our late success is mainly owing; and to *them* we must chiefly look for the final consummation. The ball is now rolling gloriously on, and none are so able as *they* to increase its speed, and its bulk — to add to its momentum, and its magnitude. Even though unlearned in letters, for this task, none others are so well educated. To fit them for this work, they have been taught in the true school. *They* have been in *that* gulf, from which they would teach others the means of escape. *They* have passed that prison wall, which others have long declared impassable; and who that has not, shall dare to weigh opinions with *them,* as to the mode of passing.

But if it be true, as I have insisted, that those who have suffered by intemperance *personally,* and have reformed, are the most powerful and efficient instruments to push the reformation to ultimate success, it does not follow, that those who have not suffered, have no part left them to perform. Whether or not the world would be vastly benefitted by a total and final banishment from it of all intoxicating drinks, seems to me not *now* to be an open question. Three-fourths of mankind confess the affirmative with their *tongues,* and, I believe, all the rest acknowledge it in their *hearts.*

Ought *any,* then, to refuse their aid in doing what the good of the *whole* demands? Shall he, who cannot do *much,* be, for that reason, excused if he do *nothing?* "But," says one, "what good can I do by signing the pledge? I never drink even without signing." This question has already been asked and answered more than millions of times. Let it be answered once more. For the man to suddenly, or in any other way, to break off from the use of drams, who has indulged in them for a long course of years, and until his appetite for them has become ten or a hundred fold stronger, and more craving, than any natural appetite can be, requires a most powerful moral effort. In such an undertaking, he needs every moral support and influence, that can possibly be brought to his aid, and thrown around him. And not only so; but every moral prop, should be taken *from* whatever argument might rise in his mind to lure him to his backsliding. When he casts his eyes around him, he should be able to see, all that he respects, all that he admires, and all that he loves, kindly and anxiously pointing him onward; and none beckoning him back, to his former miserable "wallowing in the mire."

But it is said by some, that men will *think* and *act* for themselves; that none will disuse spirits or any thing else, merely because his neighbors do; and that *moral influence* is not that powerful engine contended for. Let us examine this. Let me ask the man who would maintain this position most stiffly, what compensation he will accept to go to church some Sunday and sit during the sermon with his wife's bonnet upon his head? Not a trifle, I'll venture. And why not? There would be nothing irreligious in it: nothing immoral, nothing uncomfortable. Then why not? Is it not because there would be something egregiously unfashionable in it? Then it is the influence of *fashion;* and what is the influence of fashion, but the influence that *other* people's actions have on our own actions, the strong inclination each of us feels to do as we see all our neighbors do? Nor is the influence of fashion confined to any particular thing or class of things. It is just as strong on one subject as another. Let us make it as unfashionable to withhold our names from the temperance pledge as for husbands to wear their wives bonnets to church, and instances will be just as rare in the one case as the other.

"But," say some, "we are no drunkards; and we shall not acknowledge ourselves such by joining a reformed drunkard's society, whatever our influence might be." Surely no Christian will adhere to this objection. If they believe, as they profess, that Omnipotence condescended to take on himself the form of sinful man, and, as such, to die an ignominious death for their sakes, surely they will not refuse submission to the infinitely lesser condescension, for the temporal, and perhaps eternal salvation, of a large, erring, and unfortunate class of their own fellow creatures. Nor is the condescension very great.

In my judgment, such of us as have never fallen victims, have been spared more from the absence of appetite, than from any mental or moral superiority over those who have. Indeed, I believe, if we take habitual drunkards as a class, their heads and their hearts will bear an advantageous comparison with those of any other class. There seems ever to have been a proneness in the brilliant, and the warm-blooded, to fall into this vice. The demon of intemperance ever seems to have delighted in sucking the blood of genius and of generosity. What one of us but can call to mind some dear relative, more promising in youth than all his fellows, who has fallen a sacrifice to his rapacity? He ever seems to have gone forth, like the Egyptian angel of death, commissioned to slay if not the first, the fairest born of every family. Shall he now be arrested in his desolating career? In that arrest, all can give aid that will; and who shall be excused that *can,* and will not? Far around as human breath has ever blown, he keeps our fathers, our brothers, our sons, and our friends, prostrate in the chains of moral death. To all the living every where, we cry, "come sound the moral resurrection trump, that these may rise and stand up, an exceeding great army" — "Come from the four winds, O breath! and breathe upon these slain, that they may live."

If the relative grandeur of revolutions shall be estimated by the great amount of human misery they alleviate, and the small amount they inflict, then, indeed, will this be the grandest the world shall ever have seen. Of our political revolution of '76, we all are justly proud. It has given us a degree of political freedom, far exceeding that of any other of the nations of the earth. In it the world has found a solution of that long mooted problem, as to the capability of man to govern himself. In it was the germ which has vegetated, and still is to grow and expand into the universal liberty of mankind.

But with all these glorious results, past, present, and to come, it had its evils too. It breathed forth famine, swam in blood and rode on fire; and long, long after, the orphan's cry, and the widow's wail, continued to break the sad silence that ensued. These were the price, the inevitable price, paid for the blessings it bought.

Turn now, to the temperance revolution. In *it,* we shall find a stronger bondage broken; a viler slavery, manumitted; a greater tyrant deposed. In *it,* more of want supplied, more disease healed, more sorrow assuaged. By *it* no orphans starving, no widows weeping. By *it,* none wounded in feeling, none injured in interest. Even the dram-maker, and dram seller, will have glided into other occupations *so* gradually, as never to have felt the shock of change; and will stand ready to join all others in the universal song of gladness.

And what a noble ally this, to the cause of political freedom. With such an aid, its march cannot fail to be on and on, till every son of earth shall drink in rich fruition, the sorrow quenching draughts of perfect liberty. Happy day, when, all appetites controled, all passions subdued, all matters subjected, *mind,* all conquering *mind,* shall live and move the monarch of the world. Glorious consummation! Hail fall of Fury! Reign of Reason, all hail!

And when the victory shall be complete — when there shall be neither a slave nor a drunkard on the earth — how proud the title of that *Land,* which may truly claim to be the birthplace and the cradle of both those revolutions, that shall have ended in that victory. How nobly distinguished that People, who shall have planted, and nurtured to maturity, both the political and moral freedom of their species.

This is the one hundred and tenth anniversary of the birthday of Washington. We are met to celebrate this day. Washington is the mightiest name of earth — *long since* mightiest in the cause of civil liberty; *still* mightiest in moral reformation. On that name, an eulogy is expected. It cannot be. To add brightness to the sun, or glory to the name of Washington, is alike impossible. Let none attempt it. In solemn awe pronounce the name, and in its naked deathless splendor, leave it shining on.

SAMUEL GRIDLEY HOWE

From Report of the Minority of the Special Committee of the Boston Prison Discipline Society

Prison reform was one of the most urgent issues of the era, and two new systems — organized and orderly but extremely rigid — competed for acceptance. The first, the "Pennsylvania" or "separate" system, stressed the total isolation of prisoners, who lived in windowless cells, could not speak with other prisoners (indeed, they were prevented even from knowing the identities of other inmates), and were denied outside visitors. A model institution of this type was the Eastern Penitentiary in Philadelphia, which opened in 1829. The second, the "Auburn" or "congregate" system, begun at the Auburn and Ossining (Sing Sing) prisons in New York State in the early 1820s, enforced isolation at night and forbade conversation but allowed prisoners to work together, under strict supervision, during the day. (See the illustrations on p. 286.)

In a lengthy report written for the Boston Prison Discipline Society in 1846, the educator, philanthropist, and reformer Samuel Gridley Howe (1801–1876) argued in favor of the stricter Pennsylvania system, which, in his view, carried out fully the principle that the Auburn system acknowledged but only partially implemented. It was necessary, he maintained, to "separate" the criminal so that he could serve his time free from evil influences and hence return to society more virtuous and reflective. Howe was involved in a number of other reforms and played a crucial role in establishing Boston's Perkins Institute for the Blind.

What is necessary for reformation is daily and regular opportunity for reflection, aided by the company and example of the virtuous, and undisturbed by the influence of the bad. It is impossible for ordinary mortals to resist the silent influence of those in whose society they live. This is true of vicious and of virtuous influences. Criminals in masses support and encourage each other. Even if they do not speak, the sight of each other in such great numbers confirms and hardens them in their evil thoughts. A sixpence held close to the eye will darken the disk of a distant planet; and the three or four hundred convicts present to the eye of each inmate of a Congregate prison shut out from him the great public beyond; indeed, they form to him the public whose good opinion he would gain, *by excelling in those things which they admire;* whose ridicule he would fain avoid, and with whose tone of mind he would always keep his own in concert-pitch.

The tendency to imitate, and the desire of approbation by excelling in what others think excellent, are in society what attraction is among the particles of matter; and they act, too, in the same way, inversely as the square of the distance. To the child, it is glory enough to imitate sounds and movements, and be applauded therefor; to the savage, it is glory enough to excel his tribe in feats of strength; to the peasant, his village in skill; the petty politician is gratified by the huzzas and votes of his immediate neighbours and countrymen; and it is only a higher and wider range of the same feeling which makes the great man look for the world's applause, or, looking forward, sigh for a continuance of the approval of unborn generations.

Now, the ordinary inmates of our prisons are like children and peasants; they imitate only those immediately about them, and regard only the public opinion of the little society in which they move. That society, in a Congregate prison, is *the mass of convicts* by whom they are surrounded; the officers and the chaplains are only three or four individuals; while the criminals are the public, — they are the public, held close to the eye, which hides from the feeble vision the great public beyond the walls. But in a prison on the Separate system, the only persons with whom the convict comes in contact are the officers, teachers, and visiters; and the principles of the human mind to which we have just alluded will force him to try to imitate them, and to gain their approval.

It is a great mistake to regard convicts as forming a class apart; it is a worse one to treat them as such. It is not for man to draw the exact line between degrees of guilt; and many whom the law calls guilty are better than some whom it considers innocent. The convict class is a conventional, and not a natural division, and it has no precise boundaries. As human virtue has never soared so high that the good may not aspire to mount above those who have gone before them, so vice has never sunk so low but the vicious may go yet lower; in the lowest depth of degradation, there is yet a lower deep. The convict is still a man, and, like the rest of men, subject to all those influences, for good or for evil, which make the rest of us what we are. He has forfeited his liberty to society, but nothing more; he must stoop to pass the prison portal, but then he has a right to stand erect and say, *In the name of justice, do not surround me with bad associates and with evil influences, do not subject me to unnecessary temptation, do not expose me to further degradation; — but, for human-*

ity's sake, help me to form good resolutions; remove me from my old
companions, and surround me with virtuous associates.

The prison should not be the place where the guilty man sees and
knows others as guilty as himself, nor the pillory in which he is exposed to the public gaze; but it should be like the dark valley of the
shadow of death, through which he can walk safely, leaning on the
kindly arm of humanity.

The Separate system secludes the convict, not only from the world,
but from the influence of the presence of other convicts; it removes
him from temptation, and surrounds him with virtuous associates.

But the Congregate system offers no such seclusion to the unfortunate inmate; he must march, and sit, and work with other convicts.
Now, we appeal to every humane person, whose sensibilities have not
been blunted by the frequency of the spectacle, to say whether the
sight of the long lines of convicts, paraded in the prison-yard, —
marched up and down in silence like "dumb driven cattle," — taking
in their hands their night-tubs, or their supper-cans, as the case may
be, — wheeled into their cells by word of command, — treated in
every way as a Russian corporal treats his slaughtering-machines
called soldiers, — whether such a sight is not most painful to him.
There are, in those closely serried ranks, men of all ages, of all capacities, and of all degrees of degradation; — the beardless boy, a novi-
tiate in crime, who scans with timid glance the group of spectators,
fearful of recognizing in it a brother, sister, or friend; he has his hand,
perhaps, on the shoulder of the hoary-headed lecher, who whispers to
him words of pollution; — the man of education, who has committed
forgery, is in lock-step with the poor wretch whose only teacher was
his animal appetites, and who is a brute in human form.

Now, what is most painful to the spectator, — what is and ever
must be an objection to the Congregate system, — what is and ever
must be unfavorable to the reformation of the convict, — is, first, the
exposure of the men to each other (and to spectators), and, second,
the necessity of treating them as irresponsible machines. Such discipline may be borne by boys, and by soldiers who voluntarily incur it,
and who are at times relieved from it; but for grown men, for moral
agents, for men whom we intend to reform, whose feeble moral nature should have some exercise, that it may be strengthened, it must
be humiliating, and end by breaking down all self-respect, or engen-
dering feelings of ill-will or hatred to those who subject them to it.

We know that it will be said, we do not understand the convict,
that we ascribe to him a feeling of shame which he does not possess;
but we are sure, not only from a knowledge of human nature, but

from acquaintance with convicts, that *some* do commence their prison life with a painful sense of their shameful degradation, that they would fain shun every eye, — and that they finish by holding up a brazen front, and almost exulting in the convict garb. It is true that such cases may be rare; but it is a principle in law that it is better for ninety-and-nine guilty to escape, rather than that one innocent man should suffer; so let it be in prison; let us adopt a system, which, while it cannot injure the hardened and shameless offender, shall give to the novice, to him whose sense of shame is still vivid, the means of avoiding acquaintance and familiarity with other convicts; where he may not lose all his self-respect, and not feel that he has lost all hope of enjoying the respect of the world.

It will be said that this exposure forms a necessary part of the punishment, and that the system contemplates it as such. We know it does, and therefore do we protest against it as unwise, ineffectual, and unfavorable to reform. We believe that this system of exposure, aggravated as it is, by forcing the men to wear a *uniform* which is purposely contrived to be so grotesque as to be an unmistakable badge of degradation, is founded upon the same error which once made us work convicts in chain-gangs about the streets, and which we now abandon to the nations behind us in civilization, because it is unkind, unjust, and pernicious.

It is unkind, because it is an unnecessary aggravation of the legal sentence. It is unjust, because it falls with the greatest severity upon the best prisoners. The old convict or the shameless wretch may don his prison dress, and march out with defiant exultation; but to a sensitive novice in crime, that dress must be the poisoned shirt of Nessus,[1] which he can never strip off until his pride and all his self-respect have been torn away by it. It is pernicious, because, while it destroys the self-respect of the convict, it seems to go upon the principle that degradation is a part of the system of punishment. This, indeed, is assumed by many who advocate the exposure of the prisoners in the Congregate prisons; but this doctrine is as unsound as its effects are injurious. The prisoner *degraded himself* by his vices and crimes, and it should be the object of his prison discipline to elevate and purify, not to shame and degrade him more. It is a fatal error to connect any unnecessary degradation with punishment; the righteous God will not break the bruised reed, and shall unrighteous man? It is said that the degradation of exposure is inflicted as a means of deter-

---

[1]*poisoned shirt of Nessus:* Hercules's death was caused by a poisoned robe that had belonged to the centaur Nessus. It clung to Hercules's flesh and gave him grievous pain.

ring others from crime; but we have no right to do evil that good may come out of it; we have no right to degrade one man that another may be elevated, much less have we a right to injure one man's moral nature that other men's goods and chattels may be safe.

Make the prison and its discipline so painful as to be dreaded and shunned, as God makes sickness and suffering; but make them, as He does, curative in their operation, and not destructive. To suffer punishment as the natural consequence of sin or crime is not in itself degrading; and though we may not expect to make convicts look upon it, as did Socrates,[2] as a thing to be sought rather than shunned, still we ourselves, and all who have any thing to do with the administration of penal justice, ought to be ashamed if we view it less wisely than did the noble old heathen.

But a great change is to be wrought in society, before the public, or even legislators, will look upon prisons with sufficient interest to understand their importance, and to establish them in wisdom. The confession of the Directors of the Congregate prison at Sing Sing, in their Report of 1844, may be applied to most prisons upon that system: — "One object of a Penitentiary, that of punishment, is well provided for here; the other object, and one equally important, that of reformation, is not."[3]

We look with interest upon the reformed drunkard and the reformed gambler; and he who in his religious reformation confesses to a multitude of sins gains our respect; but the poor convict, the prison-bird, is a Pariah for life. Now, when we reflect upon the multitude of sins that go unwhipped of justice, and the multitude of men who go at large, though they violate all the laws of morality, it seems strange to find how certainly and swiftly the arm of the law arrests those who sin against our property. It may be right that nine tenths of penal legislation should be for the protection of property, and we would not weaken the barriers of stone and iron by which society protects its material interests. But we would not stop there: the prison should be sanctified by the high ends which it proposes, the saving of human souls; and every one of its regulations should have in view the reformation of the prisoner, as far as is consistent with his safe keeping. Like our lunatic asylums, they should be considered places of cure for all the curable, and of safe keeping for the incurable.

---

[2]*Socrates:* A Greek philosopher (469–399 B.C.) accused of impiety, corrupting youth, and neglecting the gods, Socrates was sentenced to death by drinking hemlock.

[3]Report of the Directors of Sing Sing Prison, 1844, p. 23. [Howe's note]

AMERICA.

God bless you massa! you feed and clothe us. When we are sick you nurse us, and when too old to work, you provide for us!

These poor creatures are a sacred legacy from my ancestors and while a dollar is left me, nothing shall be spared to increase their comfort and happiness.

Published by A. Donnelly No 19½ Courtland St N.Y.

BLACK AND W

"Caricature — Black and White Slaves in America and England," published by A. Donnelly, 1841. It was a common claim by pro-slavery advocates that the conditions of life for black slaves were superior to those that faced "free" white workers in the northern United States and in England. Even some of those who were opposed to slavery on moral grounds conceded this point. Collection of The New-York Historical Society; reproduced by permission.

T. S. Arthur's best-seller, *Ten Nights in A Bar-Room: And What I Saw There* (1854), dramatized the squalor and degradation that drinking liquor caused, and his argument for temperance was reinforced by the illustrations that his book included.

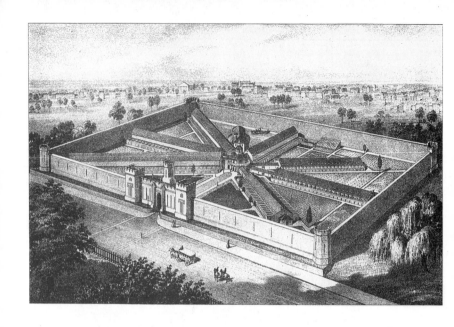

(Above): "The State Penitentiary for the Eastern District of Pennsylvania," 1855. Print and Picture Collection, The Free Library of Philadelphia. (Below): "Dining Room at Sing Sing Prison — The Prisoners Piling in for Dinner," woodcut, 1876. The Bettmann Archive.

THEODORE PARKER

From "A Sermon of the Dangerous Classes in Society"

Theodore Parker (1810–1860) was an important minister, reformer, and author. He was born in Lexington, Massachusetts, and, after attending Harvard Divinity School, became the pastor of the Unitarian church in West Roxbury, Massachusetts — which meant that he was near the Brook Farm community that his good friend George Ripley had launched.

During the 1840s, Parker grew interested in prison reform, and in his sermon on "the dangerous classes in society," delivered in Boston, January 31, 1847, he addressed the issue in detail. Parker conceded that some men were "born criminals," afflicted with a "bad nature," but he insisted that the vast majority of criminals were the product of harmful social conditions, particularly in cities. Criminals, he maintained, should receive Christian teaching and training, not punishment and incarceration — "love," rather than "force."

The text for this selection is from Theodore Parker, *Speeches, Addresses, and Occasional Sermons*, 2 vols. (Boston: Crosby & Nichols, 1852), 1:201–38.

What shall be done for Criminals, the backward children of society, who refuse to keep up with the moral or legal advance of mankind? They are a dangerous class. There are three things which are sometimes confounded: there is Error, an unintentional violation of a natural law. Sometimes this comes from abundance of life and energy; sometimes from ignorance, general or special; sometimes from heedlessness, which is ignorance for the time. Next there is Crime, the violation of a human statute. Suppose the statute also represents a law of God — the violation thereof may be the result of ignorance, or of design, it may come from a bad heart. Then it becomes a Sin — the wilful violation of a known law of God. There are many errors which are not crimes; and the best men often commit them innocently, but not without harm, violating laws of the body or the soul, which they have not grown up to understand. There have been many crimes; yes, conscious violations of man's law which were not sins, but rather a keeping of God's law. There are still a great many sins not forbidden by any human statute, not considered as crimes. It is no crime to go and fight in a wicked war; nay, it is thought a virtue. It was a crime in the heroes of the American Revolution to demand the unalienable rights of man — they were "traitors" who did it; a crime in Jesus to sum up the "Law and the Prophets," in one word, Love; he was reckoned an "infidel," guilty of blasphemy against Moses! Now to punish an error as a crime, a crime as a sin, leads to confusion at the first, and to much worse than confusion in the end.

But there are crimes which are a violation of the eternal principles of justice. It is of such, and the men who commit them, that I am now to speak. What shall be done for the dangerous classes, the criminals?

The first question is, What end shall we aim at in dealing with them? The means must be suited to accomplish that end. We may desire vengeance; then the hurt inflicted on the criminal will be proportioned to the loss or hurt sustained by society. A man has stolen my goods, injured my person, traduced my good name, sought to take my life. I will not ask for the motive of his deeds, or the cause of that motive. I will only consider my own damage, and will make him smart for that. I will use violence — having an eye for an eye and a tooth for a tooth. I will deliver him over to the tormenters till my vengeance is satisfied. If he slew my friend, or sought to slay but lacked the power, as I have the ability I will kill him! This desire of vengeance, of paying a hurt with a hurt, has still very much influence on our treatment of criminals. I fear it is still the chief aim of our penal jurisprudence. When vengeance is the aim, violence is the most suitable method; jails and the gallows most appropriate instruments! But is it right to take vengeance; for one to hurt a man to-day solely because he hurt me yesterday? If so, the proof of that right must be found in my nature, in the law of God; a man can make a statute, God only a right. As I study my nature, I find no such right; reason gives me none; conscience none; religion quite as little. Doubtless I have a right to defend myself by all manly means; to protect myself for the future no less than for the present. In doing that, it may be needful that I should restrain, and in restraining seize and hold, and in holding incidentally hurt my opponent. But I cannot see what right I have in cold blood wilfully to hurt a man because he once hurt me, and does not intend to repeat the wrong. Do I look to the authority of the greatest Son of man? I find no allusion to such a right. I find no law of God which allows vengeance. In his providence I find justice everywhere as beautiful as certain; but vengeance nowhere. I know this is not the common notion entertained of God and his providence.

I shudder to think at the barbarism which yet prevails under the guise of Christianity; the vengeance which is sought for in the name of God!

The aim may be not to revenge a crime, but to prevent it; to deter the offender from repeating the deed, and others from the beginning thereof. In all modern legislation the vindictive spirit is slowly yielding to the design of preventing crime. The method is to inflict certain uniform and specific penalties for each offence, proportionate to the damage which the criminal has done; to make the punishment so certain, so severe, or so infamous, that the offender shall forbear for the future, and innocent men be deterred from crime. But have we a right to punish a man for the example's sake? I may give up my life to save a thousand lives, or one if I will. But society has no right to take it, without my consent, to save the whole human race! I admit that society has the right of eminent domain over my property, and may take my land for a street; may destroy my house to save the town; perhaps seize on my store of provisions in time of famine. It can render me an equivalent for those things. I have not the same lien on any portion of the universe as on my life, my person. To these I have rights which none can alienate except myself, which no man has given, which all men can never justly take away. For any injustice wilfully done to me, the human race can render me no equivalent.

I know society claims the right of eminent domain over person and life not less than over house and land — to take both for the Commonwealth. I deny the right — certainly it has never been shown. Hence to me, resting on the broad ground of natural justice, the law of God, capital punishment seems wholly inadmissible, homicide with the pomp and formality of law. It is a relic of the old barbarism — paying hurt for hurt. No one will contend that it is inflicted for the offender's good. For the good of others I contend we have no right to inflict it without the sufferer's consent. To put a criminal to death seems to me as foolish as for the child to beat the stool it has stumbled over, and as useless too. I am astonished that nations with the name of Christian ever on their lips, continue to disgrace themselves by killing men, formally and in cold blood; to do this with prayers — "Forgive us as we forgive;" doing it in the name of God! I do not wonder that in the codes of nations, Hebrew or heathen, far lower than ourselves in civilization, we should find laws enforcing this punishment; laws too enacted in the name of God. But it fills me with amazement that worthy men in these days should go back to such sources for their wisdom; should walk dry-shod through the Gospels and seek in records of a barbarous people to justify this atrocious act! Famine, pestilence, war are terrible evils, but no one is so dreadful in its effects as the general prevalence of a great theological idea that is false.

It makes me shudder to recollect that out of the twenty-eight States of this Union twenty-seven should still continue the gallows as a part of the furniture of a Christian Government. I hope our own State, dignified already by so many noble acts, will soon rid herself of the stain. Let us try the experiment of abolishing this penalty, if we will for twenty years, or but ten, and I am confident we shall never return to that punishment. If a man be incapable of living in society, so ill-born or ill-bred that you cannot cure or mend him, why, hide him away out of society. Let him do no harm, but treat him kindly, not like a wolf but a man. Make him work, to be useful to himself, to society, but do not kill him. Or if you do, never say again, "Forgive us our trespasses as we forgive those that trespass against us." What if He should take you at your word! What would you think of a father who to-morrow should take the Old Testament for his legal warrant, and bring his son before your Mayor and Aldermen because he was "stubborn and rebellious, a drunkard and a glutton," and they should stone him to death in front of the City Hall! But there is quite as good a warrant in the Old Testament for that as for hanging a man. The law is referred to Jehovah as its author. How much better is it to choke the life out of a man behind the prison wall? Is not society the father of us all, our protector and defender? Hanging is vengeance; nothing but vengeance. I can readily conceive of that great Son of man, whom the loyal world so readily adores, performing all needful human works with manly dignity. Artists once loved to paint the Saviour in the lowly toil of lowly men, his garments covered with the dust of common life; his soul sullied by no pollution. But paint him to your fancy as an executioner; legally killing a man; the halter in his hands, hanging Judas for high treason! You see the relation which that punishment bears to Christianity. Yet what was unchristian in Jesus does not become Christian in the sheriff. We call ourselves Christians; we often repeat the name, the words of Christ, — but his prayer? oh no — not that.

There are now in this land I think sixteen men under sentence of death; sixteen men to be hanged till they are dead! Is there not in the nation skill to heal these men? Perhaps it is so. I have known hearts which seemed to me cold stones, so hard, so dry. No kindly steel had alchemy to win a spark from them. Yet their owners went about the streets and smiled their hollow smiles; the ghastly brother cast his shadow in the sun, or wrapped his cloak about him in the wintry hour, and still the world went on though the worst of men remained unhanged. Perhaps you cannot cure these men! — is there not power enough to keep them from doing harm; to make them useful? Shame on us that we know no better than thus to pour out life upon the dust, and then with reeking hands turn to the poor and weak and say, "Ye shall not kill."

But if the prevention of crime be the design of the punishment, then we must not only seek to hinder the innocent from vice, but we must reform the criminal. Do our methods of punishment effect that object? During the past year we have committed to the various prisons in Massachusetts five thousand six hundred sixty-nine persons for crime. How many of them will be reformed and cured by this treatment, and so live honest and useful lives hereafter? I think very few. The facts show that a great many criminals are never reformed by their punishment. Thus in France, taking the average of four years, it seems that twenty-two out of each hundred criminals were punished oftener than once; in Scotland thirty-six out of the hundred. Of the seventy-eight received at your State's prison the last year — seventeen have been sent to that very prison before. How many of them have been tenants of other institutions I know not, but as only twenty-three of the seventy-eight are natives of this State, it is plain that many, under other names, may have been confined in jail before. Yet of these seventy-eight, ten are less than twenty years old. Of thirty-five men sent from Boston to the State's prison in one year, fourteen had been there before. More than half the inmates of the House of Correction in this city are punished oftener than once! These facts show that if we aim at the reformation of the offender we fail most signally. Yet every criminal not reformed lives mainly at the charge of society; and lives too in the most costly way, for the articles he steals have seldom the same value to him as to the lawful owner.

It seems to me that our whole method of punishing crimes is a false one; that but little good comes of it, or can come. We beat the stool which we have stumbled over. We punish a man in proportion to the loss or the fear of society; not in proportion to the offender's state of mind; not with a careful desire to improve that state of mind. This is wise if vengeance be the aim; if reformation, it seems sheer folly. I know our present method is the result of six thousand years' experience of mankind; I know how easy it is to find fault — how difficult to devise a better mode. Still the facts are so plain that one with half an eye cannot fail to see the falseness of the present methods. To remove the evil, we must remove its cause, — so let us look a little into this matter, and see from what quarter our criminals proceed.

Here are two classes.

I. There are the foes of society; men that are criminals in soul, born criminals, who have a bad nature. The cause of their crime therefore is to be found in their nature itself, in their organization if you will. All experience shows that some men are born with a depraved organization, an excess of animal passions, or a deficiency of other powers to balance them.

II. There are the victims of society; men that become criminals by circumstances, made criminals, not born; men who become criminals, not so much from strength of evil in their soul, or excess of evil propensities in their organization, as from strength of evil in their circumstances. I do not say that a man's character is wholly determined by the circumstances in which he is placed, but all experience shows that circumstances, such as exposure in youth to good men or bad men, education, intellectual, moral, and religious, or neglect thereof entire or partial, have a vast influence in forming the character of men, especially of men not well endowed by nature.

Now the criminals in soul are the most dangerous of men, the born foes of society. I will not at this moment undertake to go behind their organization and ask, "How comes it that they are so ill-born?" I stop now at that fact. The cause of their crime is in their bodily constitution itself. This is always a small class. There are in New England perhaps five hundred men born blind or deaf. Apart from the idiots, I think there are not half so many who by nature and bodily constitution are incapable of attaining the average morality of the race at this day; not so many born foes of society as are born blind or deaf.

The criminals from circumstances become what they are by the action of causes which may be ascertained, guarded against, mitigated, and at last overcome and removed. These men are born of poor parents, and find it difficult to satisfy the natural wants of food, clothing, and shelter. They get little culture, intellectual or moral. The schoolhouse is open, but the parent does not send the children, he wants their services, to beg for him, perhaps to steal, it may be to do little services which lie within their power. Besides, the child must be ill-clad, and so a mark is set on him. The boy of the perishing classes, with but common endowments, cannot learn at school as one of the thrifty or abounding class. Then he receives no stimulus at home;

there everything discourages his attempts. He cannot share the pleasure and sport of his youthful fellows. His dress, his uncleanly habits,
the result of misery, forbid all that. So the children of the perishing
herd together, ignorant, ill-fed, and miserably clad. You do not find
the sons of this class in your colleges, in your high schools where all
is free for the people; few even in the grammer schools; few in the
churches. Though born into the nineteenth century after Christ, they
grow up almost in the barbarism of the nineteenth century before
him. Children that are blind and deaf, though born with a superior
organization, if left to themselves become only savages, little more
than animals. What are we to expect of children, born indeed with
eyes and ears, but yet shut out from the culture of the age they live
in? In the corruption of a city, in the midst of its intenser life, what
wonder that they associate with crime, that the moral instinct, baffled
and cheated of its due, becomes so powerless in the boy or girl; what
wonder that reason never gets developed there, nor conscience nor
that blessed religious sense learns ever to assert its power? Think of
the temptations that beset the boy; those yet more revolting which
address the other sex. Opportunities for crime continually offer.
Want impels, desire leagues with opportunity, and the result we
know. Add to all this the curse that creates so much disease, poverty,
wretchedness and so perpetually begets crime; I mean intemperance!
That is almost the only pleasure of the perishing class. What recognized amusement have they but this, of drinking themselves drunk?
Do you wonder at this? with no air, nor light, nor water, with scanty
food and a miserable dress, with no culture, living in a cellar or a gar-
ret, crowded, stifling, and offensive even to the rudest sense, do you
wonder that man or woman seeks a brief vacation of misery in the
dram-shop and in its drunkenness? I wonder not. Under such circumstances how many of you would have done better? To suffer continually from lack of what is needful for the natural bodily wants of food,
of shelter, of warmth, that suffering is misery. It is not too much to
say, there are always in this city thousands of persons who smart
under that misery. They are indeed a perishing class.

Almost all our criminals, victims and foes, come from this portion
of society. Most of those born with an organization that is predis-
posed to crime are born there. The laws of nature are unavoidably violated from generation to generation. Unnatural results must follow.
The misfortunes of the father are visited on his miserable child. Cows
and sheep degenerate when the demands of nature are not met, and
men degenerate not less. Only the low, animal instincts, those of

self-defence and self-perpetuation get developed; these with preternatural force. The animal man wakes, becomes brutish, while the
spiritual element sleeps within him. Unavoidably then the perishing is
mother of the dangerous class.

I deny not that a portion of criminals come from other sources,
but at least nine tenths thereof proceed from this quarter. Of two
hundred and seventy-three thousand, eight hundred and eighteen
criminals punished in France from 1825 to 1839, more than half
were wholly unable even to read, and had been brought up subject to
no family affections. Out of seventy criminals in one prison at Glasgow who were under eighteen, fifty were orphans having lost one or
both parents, and nearly all the rest had parents of bad character and
reputation. Taking all the criminals in England and Wales in 1841,
there were not eight in a hundred that could read and write well. In
our country, where everybody gets a mouthful of education, though
scarce any one a full meal, the result is a little different. Thus of the
seven hundred and ninety prisoners in the Mount Pleasant State's
Prison in New York, one hundred it is said could read and understand. Yet of all our criminals only a very small proportion have been
in a condition to obtain the average intellectual and moral culture of
our times.

Our present mode of treating criminals does no good to this class
of men, these victims of circumstances. I do not know that their improvement is even contemplated. We do not ask what causes made
this man a criminal, and then set ourselves to remove those causes.
We look only at the crime; so we punish practically a man because he
had a wicked father; because his education was neglected, and he exposed to the baneful influence of unholy men. In the main we treat all
criminals alike if guilty of the same offence, though the same act de-
notes very different degrees of culpability in the different men, and
the same punishment is attended with quite opposite results. Two
men commit similar crimes, we sentence them both to the State
Prison for ten years. At the expiration of one year let us suppose one
man has thoroughly reformed, and has made strict and solemn resolutions to pursue an honest and useful life. I do not say such a result
is to be expected from such treatment; still it is possible, and I think
has happened, perhaps many times. We do not discharge the man; we
care nothing for his penitence; nothing for his improvement; we keep
him nine years more. That is an injustice to him; we have robbed him
of nine years of time which he might have converted into life. It is unjust also to society, which needs the presence and the labor of all that

can serve. The man has been a burthen to himself and to us. Suppose at the expiration of his ten years the other man is not reformed at all; this result, I fear, happens in the great majority of cases. He is no better for what he has suffered; we know that he will return to his career of crime, with new energy and with even malice. Still he is discharged. This is unjust to him, for he cannot bear the fresh exposure to circumstances which corrupted him at first, and he will fall lower still. It is unjust to society, for the property and the persons of all are exposed to his passions just as much as before. He feels indignant as if he had suffered a wrong. He says, "Society has taken vengeance on me, when I was to be pitied more than blamed. Now I will have my turn. They will not allow me to live by honest toil. I will learn their lesson. I will plunder their wealth, their roof shall blaze!" He will live at the expense of society, and in the way least profitable and most costly to mankind. This idle savage will levy destructive contributions on the rich, the thrifty, and the industrious. Yes, he will help teach others the wickedness which himself once, and perhaps unavoidably learned. So in the very bosom of society there is a horde of marauders waging perpetual war against mankind.

Do not say my sympathies are with the wicked, not the industrious and good. It is not so. My sympathies are not confined to one class, honorable or despised. But it seems to me this whole method of keeping a criminal a definite time and then discharging him, whether made better or worse, is a mistake. Certainly it is so if we aim at his reformation. What if a shepherd made it a rule to look one hour for each lost sheep, and then return with or without the wanderer? What if a smith decreed that one hour and no more should be spent in shoeing a horse, and so worked that time on each, though half that time were enough — or sent home the beast with but three shoes, or two, or one, because the hour passed by? What if the physicians decreed, that all men sick of some contagious disease, should spend six weeks in the hospital, then, if the patient were found well the next day after admission, still kept him the other forty; or, if not mended at the last day, sent him out sick to the world? Such a course would be less unjust, less inhuman, only the wrong is more obvious.

To aggravate the matter still more, we have made the punishment more infamous than the crime. A man may commit great crimes which indicate deep depravity; may escape the legal punishment thereof by gold, by flight, by further crimes, and yet hold up his head unblushing and unrepentant amongst mankind. Let him commit a small crime, which shall involve no moral guilt, and be legally punished — who respects him again? What years of noble life are deemed enough to wipe the stain out of his reputation? Nay, his children after him, to the third generation, must bear the curse!

The evil does not stop with the infamy. A guilty man has served out his time. He is thoroughly resolved on industry and a moral life. Perhaps he has not learned that crime is wrong, but found it unprofitable. He will live away from the circumstances which before led him to crime. He comes out of prison, and the jail-mark is on him. He now suffers the severest part of his punishment. Friends and relations shun him. He is doomed and solitary in the midst of the crowd. Honest men will seldom employ him. The thriving class look on him with shuddering pity; the abounding loathe the convict's touch. He is driven among the dangerous and the perishing; they open their arms and offer him their destructive sympathy. They minister to his wants; they exaggerate his wrongs; they nourish his indignation. His direction is no longer in his own hands. His good resolutions — he knows they were good, but only impossible. He looks back, and sees nothing but crime and the vengeance society takes for the crime. He looks around, and the world seems thrusting at him from all quarters. He looks forward, and what prospect is there? "Hope never comes that comes to all."[1] He must plunge afresh into that miry pit, which at last is sure to swallow him up. He plunges anew, and the jail awaits him; again; deeper yet; the gallows alone can swing him clear from that pestilent ditch. But he is a man and a brother, our companion in weakness. With his education, exposure, temptation, outward and from within, how much better would the best of you become?

No better result is to be looked for from such a course. Of the one thousand five hundred and ninety-two persons in the State's prison of New York, four hundred have been there more than once. In five years, from 1841 to 1847, there were punished in the House of Correction in this city, five thousand seven hundred and forty-eight persons; of these three thousand one hundred and forty-six received such a sentence oftener than once. Yes, in five years three hundred and thirteen were sent thither, each ten times or more! How many found a place in other jails I know not.

What if fathers treated dull or vicious boys in this manner at home — making them infamous for the first offence, or the first dullness, and then refusing to receive them back again? What if the father sent out his son with bad boys, and when he erred and fell said: "You

---

[1] *"Hope never comes . . . to all"*: John Milton, *Paradise Lost*, book 1, lines 66–67.

did mischief with bad boys once; I know they enticed you. I knew you were feeble and could not resist their seductions. But I shall punish you. Do as well as you please, I will not forgive you. If you err again, I will punish you afresh. If you do never so well, you shall be infamous for ever!" What if a public teacher never took back to college a boy who once had broke the academic law — but made him infamous for ever? What if the physicians had kept a patient the requisite time in the hospital, and discharged him as wholly cured, but bid men beware of him and shun him for ever? That is just what we are doing with this class of criminals; not intentionally, not consciously — but doing none the less! . . .

I know how easy it is to find fault, and how difficult to propose a better way; how easy to misunderstand all that I have said, how easy to misrepresent it all. But it seems to me that hitherto we have set out wrong in this undertaking; have gone on wrong, and, by the present means, can never remove the causes of crime nor much improve the criminals as a class. Let me modestly set down my thoughts on this subject, in hopes that other men, wiser and more practical, will find out a way yet better still. A jail, as a mere house of punishment for offenders, ought to have no place in an enlightened people. It ought to be a moral hospital where the offender is kept till he is cured. That his crime is great or little, is comparatively of but small concern. It is wrong to detain a man against his will after he is cured; wrong to send him out before he is cured, for he will rob and corrupt society, and at last miserably perish. We shall find curable cases and incurable.

I would treat the small class of born criminals, the foes of society, as maniacs. I would not kill them more than madmen; I would not inflict needless pain on them. I would not try to shame, to whip, or to starve into virtue men morally insane. I would not torture a man because born with a defective organization. Since he could not live amongst men, I would shut him out from society; would make him work for his own good and the good of society. The thought of punishment for its own sake, or as a compensation for the evil which a man has done, I would not harbor for a moment. If a man has done me a wrong, calumniated, insulted, abused me with all his power, it renders the matter no better that I turn round and make him smart for it. If he has burned my house over my head, and I kill him in return, it does not rebuild my house. I cannot leave him at large to burn other men's houses. He must be restrained. But if I cure the man perhaps he will rebuild it, at any rate, will be of some service to the world, and others gain much while I lose nothing.

When the victims of society violated its laws, I would not torture a man for his misfortune, because his father was poor, his mother a brute; because his education was neglected. I would shut him out from society for a time. I would make him work for his own good and the good of others. The evil he had caught from the world I would overcome by the good that I would present to him. I would not clothe him with an infamous dress, crowd him with other men whom society had made infamous, leaving them to ferment and rot together. I would not set him up as a show to the public, for his enemy, or his rival, or some miserable fop to come and stare at with merciless and tormenting eye. I would not load him with chains, nor tear his flesh with a whip. I would not set soldiers with loaded gun to keep watch over him, insulting their brother by mocking and threats. I would treat the man with firmness, but with justice, with pity, with love. I would teach the man; what his family could not do for him, what society and the church had failed of, the jail should do, for the jail should be a manual labor school, not a dungeon of torture. I would take the most gifted, the most cultivated, the wisest and most benevolent, yes, the most Christian man in the State, and set him to train up these poor savages of civilization. The best man is the natural physician of the wicked. A violent man, angry, cruel, remorseless, should never enter the jail except as a criminal. You have already taken one of the greatest, wisest, and best men of this Commonwealth,[2] and set him to watch over the public education of the people. True, you give him little money, and no honor; he brings the honor to you, not asking but giving that. You begin to see the result of setting such a man to such a work, though unhonored and ill paid. Soon you will see it more plainly in the increase of temperance, industry, thrift, of good morals and sound religion! I would set such a man, if I could find such another, to look after the dangerous classes of society. I would pay him for it; honor him for it. I would have a Board of Public Morals to look after this matter of crime, a Secretary of Public Morals, a Christian Censor, whose business it should be to attend to this class, to look after the jails and make them houses of refuge, of instruction, which should do for the perishing class what the school-house and the church do for others. I would send missionaries amongst the most exposed portions of mankind as well as

[2]*one of the greatest . . . of this Commonwealth:* Horace Mann (1796–1859), Massachusetts lawyer, legislator, educator. He was an important reformer of the teaching profession and an advocate for public education. Mann served as secretary of the state board of education from 1837 to 1848.

amongst the savages of New Holland.[3] I would send wise men, good men. There are already some such engaged in this work. I would strengthen their hands. I would make crime infamous. If there are men whose crime is to be traced not to a defective organization of body, not to the influence of circumstances, but only to voluntary and self-conscious wickedness, — I would make these men infamous. It should be impossible for such a man, a voluntary foe of mankind, to live in society. I would have the jail such a place that the friends of a criminal of either class should take him as now they take a lunatic or a sick man, and bring him to the Court that he might be healed if curable, or if not might be kept from harm and hid away out of sight. Crime and sin should be infamous; not its correction, least of all its cure. I would not loathe and abhor a man who had been corrected and reformed by the jail more than a boy who had been reformed by his teacher, or a man cured of lunacy. I would have society a father who goes out to meet the prodigal while yet a great way off; yes, goes and brings him away from his riotous living, washes him, clothes him, and restores him to a right mind. There is a prosecuting attorney for the State; I would have also a defending attorney for the accused, that justice might be done all round. Is the State only a step-mother? Then is she not a Christian Commonwealth but a barbarous despotism, fitly represented by that uplifted sword on her public seal, and that motto of barbarous and bloody Latin.[4] I would have the State aid men and direct them after they have been discharged from the jail, not leave them to perish; not force them to perish. Society is the natural guardian of the weak.

I cannot think the method here suggested would be so costly as the present. It seems to me that institutions of this character might be made not only to support themselves, but be so managed as to leave a balance of income considerably beyond the expense. This might be made use of for the advantage of the criminal when he returned to society; or with it he might help make restitution of what he had once stolen. Besides being less costly, it would cure the offender and send back valuable men into society.

It seems to me that our whole criminal legislation is based on a false principle — force and not love; that it is eminently well adapted

---

[3]*New Holland:* Refers to the Netherlands East Indies but often was used broadly to suggest India, Southeast Asia, and the Malay archipelago.

[4]*motto of barbarous and bloody Latin:* The state motto of Massachusetts is *Ense petit placidam sub libertate quitem* (By the sword we seek peace, but peace only under liberty).

to revenge, not at all to correct, to teach, to cure. The whole apparatus for the punishment of offenders, from the gallows down to the
House of Correction, seems to me wrong; wholly wrong, unchristian,
and even inhuman. We teach crime while we punish it. Is it consistent
for the State to take vengeance when I may not? Is it better for the
State to kill a man in cold blood, than for me to kill my brother when
in a rage? I cannot help thinking that the gallows and even the jail, as
now administered, are practical teachers of violence and wrong! I
cannot think it will always be so. Hitherto we have looked on criminals as voluntary enemies of mankind. We have treated them as wild
beasts, not as dull or loitering boys. We have sought to destroy by
death, to disable by mutilation or imprisonment, to terrify and sub-
due, not to convince, to reform, encourage, and bless.

HARRIET MARTINEAU

From "Miss Martineau on Mesmerism"

The belief in mesmerism, or "animal magnetism," is merely one di-
mension of the extraordinary interest in spiritualism in the 1840s, 1850s,
and later decades. Many reformers, writers, and intellectuals — among
them William Lloyd Garrison, the newspaper editor Horace Greeley, the
abolitionist minister and author Thomas Wentworth Higginson, and the
historian George Bancroft — took spiritualism seriously and observed or
even participated in such practices as séances, spirit-rappings, and com-
munions with the dead.

Hawthorne was skeptical and, as his letter of October 18, 1841, to
Sophia attests (see Chapter 3, p. 423), he feared that mesmerism violated
the privacy and sanctity of the individual. But while it is easy enough
today to share his concern, it needs to be emphasized that mesmerism
and other forms of spiritualist theory and practice appealed to respectable men and women intent on communicating with forces in nature
beyond or higher than themselves. What looks like a fad or fraud from
one vantage point appears, from another, as akin to transcendentalism,
with its fervent belief in the spark of divinity that all persons carry within
them and with which they must make contact.

Harriet Martineau (1802–1876) was an accomplished English woman
of letters, novelist, intellectual, and reformer. She traveled to the United
States in 1834 and reported on her findings in *Society in America*

(1837). Her detailed, personalized account of mesmerism appeared in *The Phalanx*, the Fourierist monthly published in New York City, on February 8, 1845.

It is important to society to know whether Mesmerism is true. The revival of its pretensions from age to age makes the negative of this question appear so improbable, and the affirmative involves anticipations so vast, that no testimony of a conscientious witness can be unworthy of attention. I am now capable of affording testimony; and all personal considerations must give way before the social duty of imparting the facts of which I am in possession.

Those who know Mesmerism to be true from their own experience are now a large number; many more, I believe, than is at first supposed by those who have not attended to the subject. Another considerable class consists of those who believe upon testimony; who find it impossible not to yield credit to the long array of cases in many books, and to the attestation of friends whose judgment and veracity they are in the habit of respecting. After these there remain a good many who amuse themselves with observing some of the effects of Mesmerism, calling them strange and unaccountable, and then going away and thinking no more about them; and lastly, the great majority who know nothing of the matter, and are so little aware of its seriousness as to call it "a bore," or to laugh at it as a nonsense or a cheat.

If nonsense, it is remarkable that those who have most patiently and deeply examined it, should be the most firmly and invariably convinced of its truth. If it is a cheat, it is no laughing matter. If large numbers of men can, age after age, be helplessly prostrated under such a delusion as this, under a wicked influence, so potential over mind and body, it is one of the most mournful facts in the history of man.

For some years before June last, I was in the class of believers upon testimony. I had witnessed no mesmeric facts whatever; but I could not doubt the existence of many which were related to me, without distrusting the understanding, or the integrity, of some of the wisest and best people I knew. Nor did I find it possible to resist the evidence of books, of details of many cases of bodily and mental effects. Nor if it had been possible, could I have thought it desirable or philosophical to set up my negative ignorance of the functions of the nerves and the powers of the mind, against the positive evidence of observers and recorders of new phenomena. People do not, or ought not, to reach my years without learning that the strangeness and absolute novelty of facts attested by more than one mind, is rather a presumption of their truth than the contrary, as there would be something more familiar in any devices or conceptions of men; that our researches into the powers of nature, of human nature with the rest, have as yet gone such a little way that many discoveries are yet to be looked for; and that while we have hardly recovered from the surprise of the new lights thrown upon the functions and texture of the human frame by Harvey, Bell, and others,[1] it is too soon to decide that there shall be no more as wonderful, and presumptuous in the extreme to predetermine what they shall or shall not be.

Such was the state of my mind on the subject of Mesmerism six years ago, when I related a series of facts, on the testimony of five persons whom I could trust, to one whose intellect I was accustomed to look up to, though I had occasion to see that great discoveries were received or rejected by him on other grounds than the evidence on which their pretensions rested. He threw himself back in his chair when I began my story, exclaiming, "Is it possible that you are bit by that nonsense?" On my detailing the amount of testimony on which I believed what I was telling, he declared, as he frequently did afterward, that if he saw the incidents himself, he would not believe them; he would sooner think himself and the whole company mad than admit them. This declaration did me good; though, of course, it gave me concern. It showed me that I must keep my mind free, and observe and decide independently, as there could be neither help nor hindrance from minds self-exiled in this way from the region of evidence. From that time till June last, I was, as I have said, a believer in Mesmerism on testimony.

The reason why I did not qualify myself for belief or disbelief on evidence was a substantial one. From the early summer of 1839, I was a prisoner from illness. My recovery now, by means of mesmeric treatment alone, has given me the most thorough knowledge possible that Mesmerism is true.

This [is] not the place in which to give any details of disease. It will be sufficient to explain in order to render my story intelligible, that

---

[1]*Harvey, Bell, and others:* William Harvey (1578–1657) was an English physician and discoverer of the circulation of the blood; Sir Charles Bell (1774–1842) was a Scottish anatomist and surgeon.

the internal disease, under which I have suffered, appears to have been coming on for many years; that after warnings of failing health, which I carelessly overlooked, I broke down, while travelling abroad in June 1839; — that I sank lower and lower for three years after my return, and remained nearly stationary for two more, preceding last June. During these five years, I never felt wholly at ease for one single hour. I seldom had severe pain; but never entire comfort. A besetting sickness, almost disabling me from taking food for two years, brought me very low; and, together with other evils, it confined me to a position of almost entire stillness, — to a life passed between my bed and sofa. It was not till after many attempts at gentle exercise, that my friends agreed with me that the cost was too great for any advantage gained; and at length it was clear that even going down one flight of stairs was imprudent. From that time, I lay still; and by means of this undisturbed quiet, and such an increase of opiates as kept down my most urgent discomforts, I passed the last two years with less suffering than the three preceding. There was, however, no favorable change in the disease. Everything was done for me that the best medical skill and science could suggest, and the most indefatigable humanity and family affection devise; but nothing could avail beyond mere alleviation. My dependence on opiates was desperate. My kind and vigilant medical friend, — the most sanguine man I know, and the most bent upon keeping his patients hopeful, — avowed to me last Christmas, and twice afterward, that he found himself compelled to give up all hope of affecting the disease, — of doing more than keeping me up, in collateral respects, to the highest practicable point. This was no surprise to me; for when any specific medicine is taken for above two years without affecting the disease, there is no more ground for hope in reason than in feeling. In June last, I suffered more than usual, and new measures of alleviation were resorted to. As to all the essential points of the disease, I was never lower than immediately before I made trial of Mesmerism.

If, at any time during my illness, I had been asked, with serious purpose, whether I believed there was no resource for me, I should have replied that Mesmerism might perhaps give me partial relief. I thought it right — and still think it was right — to wear out all other means first. It was not, however, for the reason that the testimony might be thus rendered wholly unquestionable, though I now feel my years of suffering but a light cost for such result; — it was for a more personal reason that I waited. Surrounded as I was by relations and friends, who, knowing nothing of Mesmerism, regarded it as a delusion or an imposture — tenderly guarded and cared for as I was by those who so thought, and who went even further than myself in deference for the ordinary medical skill and practice, it was morally impossible for me to entertain the idea of trying Mesmerism while any hope was cherished from other means.

If it had not been so, there was the difficulty that I could not move, to go in search of aid from Mesmerists; and to bring it hither while other means were in course of trial was out of the question. After my medical friend's avowal of his hopelessness, however, I felt myself not only at liberty but in duty bound, to try, if possible, the only remaining resource for alleviation. I felt then, and I feel now, that through all mortification of old prejudices, and all springing up of new, nobody in the world would undertake to say I was wrong in seeking even recovery by any harmless means, when every hope was given up by all: and it was not recovery that was in my thoughts, but only solace. It never presented itself to me as possible that disease so long and deeply fixed could be removed; and I was perfectly sincere in saying, that the utmost I looked for was release from my miserable dependence on opiates. Deep as are my obligations to my faithful and skillful medical friend, for a long course of humane effort on his part, no one kindness of his has touched me so sensibly as the grace with which he met my desire to try a means of which he had no knowledge or opinion, and himself brought over the Mesmerist under whom the first trial of my susceptibilities was made.

Last winter, I wrote to two friends in London, telling them of my desire to try Mesmerism, and entreating them to be on the watch to let me know if any one came this way of whose aid I might avail myself. They watched for me; and one made it a business to gain all the information she could on my behalf; but nothing was actually done, or seemed likely to be done, when in June a sudden opening for the experiment was made, without any effort of my own, and on the 22d I found myself, for the first time, under the hands of a Mesmerist.

It all came about easily and naturally at last. I had letters, — several in the course of ten days, — one relating a case in which a surgeon, a near relative of mine, had, to his own astonishment, operated on a person in the mesmeric sleep without causing pain; — one from an invalid friend, ignorant of Mesmerism, who suggested it to me as a *pis aller;*[2] — and one from Mr. and Mrs. Basil Montagu, who, supposing me an unbeliever, yet related to me the case of Ann Vials, and

[2]*pis aller:* A last resource or means to cope with a difficulty or problem.

earnestly pressed upon me the expediency of a trial: — and, at the same time, Mr. Spencer T. Hall being at Newcastle lecturing, my medical friend went out of curiosity, was impressed by what he saw, and came to me very full of the subject. I told him what was in my mind; and I have said above with what a grace he met my wishes, and immediately set about gratifying them.

At the end of four months I was, as far as my feelings could be any warrant, quite well. My mesmerist and I are not so precipitate as to conclude my disease yet extirpated, and my health established beyond all danger of relapse; because time only can prove such facts. We have not yet discontinued the mesmeric treatment, and I have not re-entered upon the hurry and bustle of the world. The case is thus not complete enough for a professional statement. But, as I am aware of no ailment, and am restored to the full enjoyment of active days and nights of rest, to the full use of my powers of body and mind; and as many invalids, still languishing in such illness as I have recovered from, are looking to me for guidance in the pursuit of health by the same means, I think it right not to delay giving a precise statement of my own mesmeric experience, and of my observation of some different manifestations in the instance of another patient in the same house. A further reason against delay is, that it would be a pity to omit the record of some of the fresh feeling and immature ideas which attend an early experience of mesmeric influence, and which it may be an aid and comfort to novices to recognize from my record. And again, as there is no saying in regard to a subject so obscure, what is trivial and what is not, the fullest detail is likely to be the wisest; and the earlier the narrative the fuller, while better knowledge will teach us hereafter what are the non-essentials that may be dismissed.

On Saturday, June 22nd, Mr. Spencer Hall and my medical friend came, as arranged, at my worst hour of the day, between the expiration of one opiate and the taking of another. By an accident the gentlemen were rather in a hurry, — a circumstance unfavorable to a first experiment. But result enough was obtained to encourage a further trial, though it was of a nature entirely unanticipated by me. I had no other idea than that I should either drop asleep or feel nothing. I did not drop asleep, and I did feel something very strange. Various passes were tried by Mr. Hall; the first that appeared effectual, and the most so for some time after, were passes over the head, and a little way down the spine. A very short time after these were tried, and twenty minutes from the beginning of the *séance*, I became sensible of an extraordinary appearance, most unexpected, and wholly unlike anything I had ever conceived of. Something seemed to diffuse itself through the atmosphere, — not like smoke, nor steam, nor haze, — but most like a clear twilight, closing in from the windows and down from the ceiling, and in which one object after another melted away, till scarcely anything was left visible before my wide-open eyes. First, the outlines of all objects were blurred; then a bust, standing on a pedestal in a strong light, melted quite away; then the opposite bust; then the floor, and the ceiling, till one small picture, high up on the opposite wall, only remained visible, — like a patch of phosphoric light. I feared to move my eyes, lest the singular appearance should vanish; and I cried out, "O! deepen it! deepen it!" supposing this the precursor of the sleep. It could not be deepened, however; and when I glanced aside from the luminous point, I found that I need not fear the return of objects to their ordinary appearance while the passes were continued. The busts reappeared, ghost-like, in the dim atmosphere, like faint shadows, except that their outlines, and the parts in the highest relief, burned with the same phosphoric light. The features of one, an Isis with bent head, seemed to be illuminated by a fire on the floor, though this bust has its back to the windows. Wherever I glanced, all outlines were dressed in this beautiful light; and so they have been, at every *séance,* without exception, to this day; though the appearance has rather given way to drowsiness since I left off opiates entirely. This appearance continued during the remaining twenty minutes before the gentlemen were obliged to leave me. The other effects were, first, heat, oppression and sickness, and for a few hours after, disordered stomach; followed, in the course of the evening, by a feeling of lightness and relief, in which I thought I could hardly be mistaken.

On occasions of a perfectly new experience, however, scepticism and self-distrust is very strong. I was aware of this beforehand, and also, of course, of the common sneer — that mesmeric effects are "all imagination." When the singular appearances presented themselves, I thought to myself, — "Now, shall I ever believe that this was all fancy? When it is gone, and when people laugh, shall I ever doubt having seen what is now as distinct to my waking eyes as the rolling waves of yonder sea, or the faces round my sofa?" I did a little doubt it in the course of the evening: I had some misgivings even so soon as that; and yet more the next morning, when it appeared like a dream.

Great was the comfort, therefore, of recognizing appearances on the second afternoon. "Now," thought I, "can I again doubt?" I did, more faintly; but, before a week was over, I was certain of the fidelity of my own senses in regard to this, and more.

There was no other agreeable experience on this second afternoon. Mr. Hall was exhausted and unwell, from having mesmerized many patients; and I was more oppressed and disordered than on the preceding day, and the disorder continued for a longer time: but again, towards night, I felt refreshed and relieved. How much of my ease was to be attributed to Mesmerism, and how much to my accustomed opiate, there was no saying, in the then uncertain state of my mind.

The next day, however left no doubt. Mr. Hall was prevented by illness from coming over, too late to let me know. Unwilling to take my opiate while in expectation of his arrival, and too wretched to do without some resource, I rang for my maid, and asked whether she had any objection to attempt what she saw Mr. Hall do the day before. With the greatest alacrity she complied. Within one minute the twilight and phosphoric lights appeared; and in two or three more a delicious sensation of ease spread through me, — a cool comfort, before which all pain and distress gave way, oozing out, as it were, at the soles of my feet. During that hour, and almost the whole evening, I could no more help exclaiming with pleasure than a person in torture crying out with pain. I became hungry, and ate with relish, for the first time for five years. There was no heat, oppression, or sickness during the *séance,* nor any disorder afterwards. During the whole evening, instead of the lazy hot ease of opiates, under which pain is felt to lie in wait, I experienced something of the indescribable sensation of health, which I had quite lost and forgotten. I walked about my rooms, and was gay and talkative. Something of this relief remained till the next morning; and then there was no reaction. I was no worse than usual: and perhaps rather better.

Nothing is to me more unquestionable and more striking about this influence than the absence of all reaction. Its highest exhilaration is followed, not by depression or exhaustion, but by a further renovation. From the first hour to the present, I have never fallen back a single step. Every point gained has been steadily held. Improved composure of nerve and spirits has followed upon every mesmeric exhilaration. I have been spared all the weaknesses of convalescence, and carried through all the usually formidable enterprises of return from deep disease to health, with a steadiness and tranquility astonishing to all witnesses. At this time, before venturing to speak of my health as established, I believe myself more firm in nerve, more calm and steady in mind and spirits, than at any time of my life before. So much, in consideration of the natural and common fear of the mesmeric influence as pernicious excitement — as a kind of intoxication.

When Mr. Hall saw how congenial was the influence of this new Mesmerist, he advised our going on by ourselves, which we did till the 5th of September. I owe much to Mr. Hall for his disinterested zeal and kindness. He did for me all he could; and it was much to make a beginning, and put us in the way of proceeding.

I next procured, for guidance, Deleuze's "Instruction Pratique sur le Magnetisme Animal." Out of this I directed my maid; and for some weeks we went on pretty well. Finding my appetite and digestion sufficiently improved, I left off tonics, and also the medicine which I had taken for two years and four months, in obedience to my doctor's hope of affecting the disease — though the eminent physician who saw me before that time declared that he had "tried it in an infinite number of such cases, and never knew it avail." I never felt the want of these medicines, nor others which I afterward discontinued. From the first week in August, I took no medicines but opiates; and these I was gradually reducing. These particulars are mentioned to show how early in the experiment Mesmerism became my sole reliance.

On four days, scattered through six weeks, our *séance* was prevented by visitors or other accidents. On these four days, the old distress and pain recurred; but never on the days when I was mesmerized.

From the middle of August (after I had discontinued all medicines but opiates,) the departure of the worst pains and oppressions of my disease made me suspect that the complaint itself — the incurable, hopeless disease of so many years — was reached; and now I first began to glance toward the thought of recovery. In two or three weeks more it became certain that I was not deceived; and the radical amendment has since gone on, without intermission.

Another thing, however, was also becoming clear: that more aid was necessary. My maid did for me whatever, under my own instructions, good will and affection could do. But the patient and strenuous purpose required in a case of such long and deep-seated disease can only be looked for in an educated person, so familiar with the practice of Mesmerism as to be able to keep a steady eye on the end, through all delays and doubtful incidents. And it is also important, if not necessary, that the predominance of will should be in the Mesmerist, not the patient. The offices of an untrained servant may avail perfectly in a short case — for the removal of sudden pain, or a brief illness; but, from the subordination being in the wrong party, we found ourselves coming to a stand.

This difficulty was abolished by the kindness and sagacity of Mr. Atkinson, who had been my adviser throughout. He explained my position to a friend of his — a lady, the widow of a clergyman, deeply and practically interested in Mesmerism — possessed of great Mesmeric power, and of those high qualities of mind and heart which fortify and sanctify its influence. In pure zeal and benevolence, this lady came to me, and has been with me ever since. When I found myself able to repose on the knowledge and power (mental and moral) of my Mesmerist, the last impediments to my progress were cleared away, and I improved accordingly.

Under her hands the visual appearance and other immediate sensations were much the same as before; but the experience of recovery was more rapid. I can describe it only by saying, that I felt as if my life were fed from day to day. The vital force infused or induced was as clear and certain as the strength given by food to those who are faint from hunger. I am careful to avoid theorizing at present on a subject which has not yet furnished me with a sufficiency of facts; but it can hardly be called theorizing to say (while silent as to the nature of the agency) that the principle of life itself — that principle which is antagonistic to disease — appears to be fortified by the mesmeric influence; and thus far we may account for Mesmerism being no specific, but successful through the widest range of diseases that are not hereditary, and have not caused disorganization. No mistake about Mesmerism is more prevalent than the supposition that it can avail only in nervous diseases. The numerous cases recorded of cure of rheumatism, dropsy, cancer, and the whole class of tumors — cases as distinct, and almost as numerous as those of cure of paralysis, epilepsy, and other diseases of the brain and nerves, must make any inquirer cautious of limiting his anticipations and experiments by any theory of exclusive action on the nervous system. Whether Mesmerism, and, indeed, any influence whatever, acts exclusively through the nervous system, is another question.

A few days after the arrival of my kind Mesmerist, I had my foot on the grass for the first time for four years and a half. I went down to the little garden under my windows. I never before was in the

open air, after an illness of merely a week or two, without feeling
more or less overpowered; but now, under the open sky, after four
years and a half spent between bed and sofa, I felt no faintness, exhaustion, or nervousness, of any kind. I was somewhat haunted for
a day or two by the stalks of the grass, which I had not seen growing for so long (for, well-supplied as I had been with flowers, rich
and rare, I had seen no grass, except from my windows;) but at the
time, I was as self-possessed as any walker in the place. In a day or
two, I walked round the garden, then down the lane, then to the
haven, and so on, till now, in two months, five miles are no fatigue
to me. At first, the evidences of the extent of the disease were so
clear as to make me think that I had never before fully understood
how ill I had been. They disappeared, one by one; and now I feel
nothing of them.

MARGARET FULLER

From "The New Science; or, The Philosophy of Mesmerism or Animal Magnetism"

Margaret Fuller (1810–1850) was an essayist, editor, translator, poet,
commentator on social and political issues, advocate of women's rights,
and lecturer and leader of "conversations" on philosophical and cultural
topics. She was also a frequent visitor to Brook Farm. Her books include
Summer on the Lakes (1844), *Woman in the Nineteenth Century*
(1845), and *Papers on Literature and Art* (1846). By the mid-1840s,
Fuller had become a regular contributor to the New York *Daily Tribune*,
and the article included here — keyed to a review of J. Stanley Grimes's
Ethnology; or, The Philosophy of Mesmerism and Phrenology — was
published in the *Tribune* on February 17, 1845. It was later included in
Fuller's posthumous *Life Without and Life Within: Reviews, Narratives,
Essays, and Poems* (1859), from which this reprinted text is taken.

Fuller here recalls a meeting with a blind somnambulist (that is, someone who speaks, walks, or acts while in a sleep) who tried to mesmerize
or "magnetize" her. By early 1845, Fuller was seeing a mesmerist regularly, perhaps weekly, and reporting that the treatment helped ease the
pain of her twisted spine and severe headaches.

(For a portrait of Fuller, see p. 476.)

Some years ago I went, unexpectedly, into a house where a blind girl, thought at that time to have attained an extraordinary degree of clairvoyance, lay in a trance of somnambulism. I was not invited there, nor known to the party, but accompanied a gentleman who was.

The somnambulist was in a very happy state. On her lips was the satisfied smile, and her features expressed the gentle elevation incident to the state. At that time I had never seen any one in it, and had formed no image or opinion on the subject. I was agreeably impressed by the somnambulist, but on listening to the details of her observations on a distant place, I thought she had really no vision, but was merely led or impressed by the mind of the person who held her hand.

After a while I was beckoned forward, and my hand given to the blind girl. The latter instantly dropped it with an expression of pain, and complained that she should have been brought in contact with a person so sick, and suffering at that moment under violent nervous headache. This really was the case, but no one present could have been aware of it.

After a while the somnambulist seemed penitent and troubled. She asked again for my hand which she had rejected, and, while holding it, attempted to magnetize the sufferer. She seemed touched by profound pity, spoke most intelligently of the disorder of health and its causes, and gave advice, which, if followed at that time, I have every reason to believe would have remedied the ill.

Not only the persons present, but the person advised also, had no adequate idea then of the extent to which health was affected, nor saw fully, till some time after, the justice of what was said by the somnambulist. There is every reason to believe that neither she, nor the persons who had the care of her, knew even the name of the person whom she so affectionately wished to help.

Several years after, in visiting an asylum for the blind, I saw this same girl seated there. She was no longer a somnambulist, though, from a nervous disease, very susceptible to magnetic influences. I went to her among a crowd of strangers, and shook hands with her as several others had done. I then asked, "Do you not know me?" She answered, "No." "Do you not remember ever to have met me?" She tried to recollect, but still said, "No." I then addressed a few remarks to her about her situation there, but she seemed preoccupied, and, while I turned to speak with some one else, wrote with a pencil these words, which she gave me at parting: —

> "The ills that Heaven decrees
> The brave with courage bear."

Others may explain this as they will; to me it was a token that the same affinity that had acted before, gave the same knowledge; for the writer was at the time ill in the same way as before. It also seemed to indicate that the somnambulic trance was only a form of the higher development, the sensibility to more subtle influences — in the terms of Mr. Grimes, a susceptibility to etherium. The blind girl perhaps never knew who I was, but saw my true state more clearly than any other person did, and I have kept those pencilled lines, written in the stiff, round character proper to the blind, as a talisman of "Credenciveness," as the book before me styles it, Credulity as the world at large does, and, to my own mind, as one of the clews granted, during this earthly life, to the mysteries of future states of being, and more rapid and complete modes of intercourse between mind and mind.

NATHANIEL HAWTHORNE

"Earth's Holocaust"

"Earth's Holocaust," first published in *Graham's Lady's and Gentleman's Magazine* in March 1844, is the best of Hawthorne's mid-1840s stories on the subject of reform and reformers. It presents a satiric indictment of innovators, radicals, and persons captivated by a single idea, and it exposes the wicked deeds done by those claiming benevolent motives. Hawthorne treats the exteriority with which, as he sees it, reform is prosecuted, as men and women look outside themselves for change and hence neglect the need first to purge the heart. "Earth's Holocaust" is compelling in its own right, and it bears noting that Hawthorne reprinted it in both editions of *Mosses from an Old Manse* (1846, 1854). But the story is valuable as well in dramatizing by contrast the greater complexity of *The Blithedale Romance*, which would appear eight years later. The text is from *Mosses from an Old Manse*, in *The Centenary Edition of the Works of Nathaniel Hawthorne*, vol. 10 (Columbus: Ohio State UP, 1974), 381–404.

Once upon a time — but whether in time past or time to come, is a matter of little or no moment — this wide world had become so over-burthened with an accumulation of worn-out trumpery, that the inhabitants determined to rid themselves of it by a general bonfire. The site fixed upon, at the representation of the Insurance Companies, and as being as central a spot as any other on the globe, was one of the broadest prairies of the West, where no human habitation would be endangered by the flames, and where a vast assemblage of spectators might commodiously admire the show. Having a taste for sights of this kind, and imagining, likewise, that the illumination of the bonfire might reveal some profundity of moral truth, heretofore hidden in mist or darkness, I made it convenient to journey thither and be present. At my arrival, although the heap of condemned rubbish was as yet comparatively small, the torch had already been applied. Amid that boundless plain, in the dusk of evening, like a far-off star alone in the firmament, there was merely visible one tremulous gleam, whence none could have anticipated so fierce a blaze as was destined to ensue. With every moment, however, there came foot-travellers, women holding up their aprons, men on horseback, wheel-barrows, lumbering baggage-wagons, and other vehicles great and small, and from far and near, laden with articles that were judged fit for nothing but to be burnt.

"What materials have been used to kindle the flames?" inquired I of a bystander; for I was desirous of knowing the whole process of the affair, from beginning to end.

The person whom I addressed was a grave man, fifty years old or thereabout, who had evidently come thither as a looker-on; he struck me immediately as having weighed for himself the true value of life and its circumstances, and therefore as feeling little personal interest in whatever judgment the world might form of them. Before answering my question, he looked me in the face, by the kindling light of the fire.

"Oh, some very dry combustibles," replied he, "and extremely suitable to the purpose — no other, in fact, than yesterday's newspapers, last month's magazines, and last year's withered leaves. Here, now, comes some antiquated trash, that will take fire like a handfull of shavings."

As he spoke, some rough-looking men advanced to the verge of the bonfire, and threw in, as it appeared, all the rubbish of the Herald's Office; the blazonry of coat-armor; the crests and devices of illustrious families; pedigrees that extended back, like lines of light, into the mist of the dark ages; together with stars, garters, and embroidered collars; each of which, as paltry a bauble as it might appear to the uninstructed eye, had once possessed vast significance, and was still, in truth, reckoned among the most precious of moral or material facts, by the worshippers of the gorgeous past. Mingled with this confused heap, which was tossed into the flames by armsfull at once, were innumerable badges of knighthood; comprising those of all the European sovereignties, and Napoleon's decoration of the Legion of Honor,[1] the ribands of which were entangled with those of the ancient order of St. Louis.[2] There, too, were the medals of our own society of Cincinnati,[3] by means of which, as history tells us, an order of hereditary knights came near being constituted out of the king-quellers of the Revolution. And, besides, there were the patents of nobility of German counts and barons, Spanish grandees, and English peers, from the worm-eaten instrument signed by William the Conqueror,[4] down to the bran-new parchment of the latest lord, who has received his honors from the fair hand of Victoria.[5]

At sight of the dense volumes of smoke, mingled with vivid jets of flame, that gushed and eddied forth from this immense pile of earthly distinctions, the multitude of plebeian spectators set up a joyous shout, and clapt their hands with an emphasis that made the welkin[6] echo. That was their moment of triumph, achieved after long ages, over creatures of the same clay and same spiritual infirmities, who had dared to assume the privileges due only to Heaven's better workmanship. But now there rushed towards the blazing heap a gray-haired man, of stately presence, wearing a coat from the breast of which some star, or other badge of rank, seemed to have been forcibly wrenched away. He had not the tokens of intellectual power in his face; but still there was the demeanor — the habitual, and almost native dignity — of one who had been born to the idea of his

---

[1]*Legion of Honor:* French civilian and military decoration.

[2]*ancient order of St. Louis:* Order of knights founded by the French King Louis IX (1226–1270).

[3]*society of Cincinnati:* Organization founded in 1783 by American Revolutionary army officers.

[4]*William the Conqueror:* William I (c. 1028–1087), crowned king of England after the battle of Hastings in 1066.

[5]*Victoria:* Alexandrina Victoria (1819–1901), queen of the United Kingdom of Great Britain and Ireland from 1838 until her death.

[6]*welkin:* Firmament, sky, the vault of heaven.

own social superiority, and had never felt it questioned, till that moment.

"People," cried he, gazing at the ruin of what was dearest in his eyes, with grief and wonder, but, nevertheless, with a degree of stateliness — "people, what have you done! This fire is consuming all that marked your advance from barbarism, or that could have prevented your relapse thither. We — the men of the privileged orders — were those who kept alive, from age to age, the old chivalrous spirit; the gentle and generous thought; the higher, the purer, the more refined and delicate life! With the nobles, too, you cast off the poet, the painter, the sculptor — all the beautiful arts; — for we were their patrons, and created the atmosphere in which they flourish. In abolishing the majestic distinctions of rank, society loses not only its grace, but its steadfastness — "

More he would doubtless have spoken; but here there arose an outcry, sportive, contemptuous, and indignant, that altogether drowned the appeal of the fallen nobleman; insomuch that, casting one look of despair at his own half-burnt pedigree, he shrunk back into the crowd, glad to shelter himself under his new-found insignificance.

"Let him thank his stars that we have not flung him into the same fire!" shouted a rude figure, spurning the embers with his foot. "And, henceforth, let no man dare to show a piece of musty parchment, as his warrant for lording it over his fellows! If he have strength of arm, well and good; it is one species of superiority. If he have wit, wisdom, courage, force of character, let these attributes do for him what they may. But, from this day forward, no mortal must hope for place and consideration, by reckoning up the mouldy bones of his ancestors! That nonsense is done away."

"And in good time," remarked the grave observer by my side — in a low voice however — "if no worse nonsense come in its place. But at all events, this species of nonsense has fairly lived out its life."

There was little space to muse or moralize over the embers of this time-honored rubbish; for, before it was half burnt out, there came another multitude from beyond the sea, bearing the purple robes of royalty, and the crowns, globes, and sceptres of emperors and kings. All these had been condemned as useless baubles; playthings, at best, fit only for the infancy of the world, or rods to govern and chastise it in its nonage; but with which universal manhood, at its full-grown stature, could no longer brook to be insulted. Into such contempt had these regal insignia now fallen, that the gilded crown and tinselled robes of the player-king, from Drury Lane Theatre, had been thrown in among the rest, doubtless as a mockery of his brother-monarchs, on the great stage of the world. It was a strange sight, to discern the crown-jewels of England, glowing and flashing in the midst of the fire. Some of them had been delivered down from the times of the Saxon princes; others were purchased with vast revenues, or, perchance, ravished from the dead brows of the native potentates of Hindostan; and the whole now blazed with a dazzling lustre, as if a star had fallen in that spot, and been shattered into fragments. The splendor of the ruined monarchy had no reflection, save in those inestimable precious-stones. But, enough on this subject! It were but tedious to describe how the Emperor of Austria's mantle was converted to tinder, and how the posts and pillars of the French throne became a heap of coals, which it was impossible to distinguish from those of any other wood. Let me add, however, that I noticed one of the exiled Poles, stirring up the bonfire with the Czar of Russia's[7] sceptre, which he afterwards flung into the flames.

"The smell of singed garments is quite intolerable here," observed my new acquaintance, as the breeze enveloped us in the smoke of a royal wardrobe. "Let us get to windward, and see what they are doing on the other side of the bonfire."

We accordingly passed round, and were just in time to witness the arrival of a vast procession of Washingtonians — as the votaries of temperance call themselves now-a-days — accompanied by thousands of the Irish disciples of Father Mathew,[8] with that great apostle at their head. They brought a rich contribution to the bonfire; being nothing less than all the hogsheads and barrels of liquor in the world, which they rolled before them across the prairie.

"Now, my children," cried Father Mathew, when they reached the verge of the fire — "one shove more, and the work is done! And now let us stand off, and see Satan deal with his own liquor!"

Accordingly, having placed their wooden vessels within reach of the flames, the procession stood off at a safe distance, and soon beheld them burst into a blaze that reached the clouds, and threatened to set the sky itself on fire. And well it might. For here was the whole world's stock of spirituous liquors, which, instead of kindling a fren-

[7]*Czar of Russia's:* Czar Nicholas I (1796–1855), emperor of Russia, suppressed rebellions by the Polish people in the 1830s.
[8]*Father Mathew:* Theobald Mathew (1790–1856), Irish Catholic priest and advocate of temperance.

zied light in the eyes of individual topers[9] as of yore, soared upward with a bewildering gleam that startled all mankind. It was the aggregate of that fierce fire, which would otherwise have scorched the hearts of millions. Meantime, numberless bottles of precious wine were flung into the blaze; which lapped up the contents as if it loved them, and grew, like other drunkards, the merrier and fiercer for what it quaffed. Never again will the insatiable thirst of the fire-fiend be so pampered! Here were the treasures of famous bon-vivants — liquors that had been tossed on ocean, and mellowed in the sun, and hoarded long in the recesses of the earth — the pale, the gold, the ruddy juice of whatever vineyards were most delicate — the entire vintage of Tokay[10] — all mingling in one stream with the vile fluids of the common pot-house, and contributing to heighten the self-same blaze. And while it rose in a gigantic spire, that seemed to wave against the arch of the firmament, and combine itself with the light of stars, the multitude gave a shout, as if the broad earth were exulting in its deliverance from the curse of ages.

But the joy was not universal. Many deemed that human life would be gloomier than ever, when that brief illumination should sink down. While the reformers were at work, I had overheard muttered expostulations from several respectable gentlemen with red noses, and wearing gouty shoes; and a ragged worthy, whose face looked like a hearth where the fire is burnt out, now expressed his discontent more openly and boldly.

"What is this world good for," said the Last Toper, "now that we can never be jolly any more? What is to comfort the poor man in sorrow and perplexity? — how is he to keep his heart warm against the cold winds of this cheerless earth? — and what do you propose to give him, in exchange for the solace that you take away? How are old friends to sit together by the fireside, without a cheerful glass between them? A plague upon your reformation! It is a sad world, a cold world, a selfish world, a low world, not worth an honest fellow's living in, now that good-fellowship is gone forever!"

This harangue excited great mirth among the bystanders. But, preposterous as was the sentiment, I could not help commiserating the forlorn condition of the Last Toper, whose boon-companions had dwindled away from his side, leaving the poor fellow without a soul to countenance him in sipping his liquor, nor, indeed, any liquor to

[9]*toper:* A heavy drinker.
[10]*Tokay:* Tokay (or Tokaj), Hungary, was known for its wine production.

sip. Not that this was quite the true state of the case; for I had observed him, at a critical moment, filch a bottle of fourth-proof brandy
that fell beside the bonfire, and hide it in his pocket.

The spirituous and fermented liquors being thus disposed of, the
zeal of the reformers next induced them to replenish the fire with all
the boxes of tea and bags of coffee in the world. And now came the
planters of Virginia, bringing their crops of tobacco. These, being cast
upon the heap of inutility, aggregated it to the size of a mountain,
and incensed the atmosphere with such potent fragrance, that
methought we should never draw pure breath again. The present sacrifice seemed to startle the lovers of the weed, more than any that
they had hitherto witnessed.

"Well; — they've put my pipe out," said an old gentleman, flinging it into the flames in a pet. "What is this world coming to? Everything rich and racy — all the spice of life — is to be condemned as
useless. Now that they have kindled the bonfire, if these nonsensical
reformers would fling themselves into it, all would be well enough!"

"Be patient," responded a staunch conservative; — "it will come
to that in the end. They will first fling us in, and finally themselves."

From the general and systematic measures of reform, I now turned
to consider the individual contributions to this memorable bonfire. In
many instances, these were of a very amusing character. One poor
fellow threw in his empty purse, and another, a bundle of counterfeit
or insolvable bank-notes. Fashionable ladies threw in their last season's bonnets, together with heaps of ribbon, yellow lace, and much
other half-worn milliner's ware; all of which proved even more
evanescent in the fire, than it had been in the fashion. A multitude of
lovers, of both sexes — discarded maids or bachelors, and couples,
mutually weary of one another — tossed in bundles of perfumed letters and enamored sonnets. A hack-politician, being deprived of
bread by the loss of office, threw in his teeth, which happened to be
false ones. The Rev. Sydney Smith[11] — having voyaged across the Atlantic for that sole purpose — came up to the bonfire, with a bitter
grin, and threw in certain repudiated bonds, fortified though they
were with the broad seal of a sovereign state. A little boy of five years
old, in the premature manliness of the present epoch, threw in his
playthings; a college-graduate, his diploma; an apothecary, ruined by
the spread of homœopathy, his whole stock of drugs and medicines; a

---

[11]*Sydney Smith:* Smith (1771–1845) was an English clergyman and author who had
criticized the state of Pennsylvania for its repudiation of debts.

physician, his library; a parson, his old sermons; and a fine gentleman of the old school, his code of manners, which he had formerly written down for the benefit of the next generation. A widow, resolving on a second marriage, slily threw in her dead husband's miniature. A young man, jilted by his mistress, would willingly have flung his own desperate heart into the flames, but could find no means to wrench it out of his bosom. An American author, whose works were neglected by the public, threw his pen and paper into the bonfire, and betook himself to some less discouraging occupation. It somewhat startled me to overhear a number of ladies, highly respectable in appearance, proposing to fling their gowns and petticoats into the flames, and assume the garb, together with the manners, duties, offices, and responsibilities, of the opposite sex.

What favor was accorded to this scheme, I am unable to say; my attention being suddenly drawn to a poor, deceived, and half-delirious girl, who, exclaiming that she was the most worthless thing alive or dead, attempted to cast herself into the fire, amid all that wrecked and broken trumpery of the world. A good man, however, ran to her rescue.

"Patience, my poor girl!" said he, as he drew her back from the fierce embrace of the destroying angel. "Be patient, and abide Heaven's will. So long as you possess a living soul, all may be restored to its first freshness. These things of matter, and creations of human fantasy, are fit for nothing but to be burnt, when once they have had their day. But your day is Eternity!"

"Yes," said the wretched girl, whose frenzy seemed now to have sunk down into deep despondency; — "yes; and the sunshine is blotted out of it!"

It was now rumored among the spectators, that all the weapons and munitions of war were to be thrown into the bonfire; with the exception of the world's stock of gunpowder, which, as the safest mode of disposing of it, had already been drowned in the sea. This intelligence seemed to awaken great diversity of opinion. The hopeful philanthropist esteemed it a token that the millenium was already come; while persons of another stamp, in whose view mankind was a breed of bull-dogs, prophesied that all the old stoutness, fervor, nobleness, generosity, and magnanimity of the race, would disappear; these qualities, as they affirmed, requiring blood for their nourishment. They comforted themselves, however, in the belief that the proposed abolition of war was impracticable, for any length of time together.

Be that as it might, numberless great guns, whose thunder had long been the voice of battle — the artillery of the Armada, the battering-trains of Marlborough, and the adverse cannon of Napoleon and Wellington[12] — were trundled into the midst of the fire. By the continual addition of dry combustibles, it had now waxed so intense, that neither brass nor iron could withstand it. It was wonderful to behold, how those terrible instruments of slaughter melted away like playthings of wax. Then the armies of the earth wheeled around the mighty furnace, with their military music playing triumphant marches, and flung in their muskets and swords. The standard-bearers, likewise, cast one look upward at their banners, all tattered with shot-holes, and inscribed with the names of victorious fields; and giving them a last flourish on the breeze, they lowered them into the flame, which snatched them upward in its rush towards the clouds. This ceremony being over, the world was left without a single weapon in its hands, except, possibly, a few old King's arms and rusty swords, and other trophies of the Revolution, in some of our state-armories. And now the drums were beaten and the trumpets brayed all together, as a prelude to the proclamation of universal and eternal peace, and the announcement that glory was no longer to be won by blood; but that it would henceforth be the contention of the human race, to work out the greatest mutual good; and that beneficence, in the future annals of the earth, would claim the praise of valor. The blessed tidings were accordingly promulgated, and caused infinite rejoicings among those who had stood aghast at the horror and absurdity of war.

But I saw a grim smile pass over the scarred visage of a stately old commander — by his war-worn figure and rich military dress, he might have been one of Napoleon's famous marshals — who, with the rest of the world's soldiery, had just flung away the sword, that had been familiar to his right hand for half-a-century.

"Aye, aye!" grumbled he. "Let them proclaim what they please; but, in the end, we shall find that all this foolery has only made more work for the armorers and cannon-founderies."

"Why, Sir," exclaimed I, in astonishment, "do you imagine that the human race will ever so far return on the steps of its past madness, as to weld another sword, or cast another cannon?"

---

[12]*Armada, Marlborough, Napoleon, Wellington:* Fleet of warships (the Spanish Armada was defeated by the English in 1588); Duke of Marlborough (1650–1722), distinguished English general; Duke of Wellington (1769–1852), defeated Napoleon in the battle of Waterloo, June 1815.

"There will be no need," observed, with a sneer, one who neither felt benevolence, nor had faith in it. "When Cain wished to slay his brother, he was at no loss for a weapon."

"We shall see," replied the veteran commander. — "If I am mistaken, so much the better; but, in my opinion — without pretending to philosophize about the matter — the necessity of war lies far deeper than these honest gentlemen suppose. What! Is there a field for all the petty disputes of individuals, and shall there be no great law-court for the settlement of national difficulties? The battle-field is the only court where such suits can be tried!"

"You forget, General," rejoined I, "that, in this advanced stage of civilization, Reason and Philanthropy combined will constitute just such a tribunal as is requisite."

"Ah, I had forgotten that, indeed!" said the old warrior, as he limped away.

The fire was now to be replenished with materials that had hitherto been considered of even greater importance to the well-being of society, than the warlike munitions which we had already seen consumed. A body of reformers had travelled all over the earth, in quest of the machinery by which the different nations were accustomed to inflict the punishment of death. A shudder passed through the multitude, as these ghastly emblems were dragged forward. Even the flames seemed at first to shrink away, displaying the shape and murderous contrivance of each in a full blaze of light, which, of itself, was sufficient to convince mankind of the long and deadly error of human law. Those old implements of cruelty — those horrible monsters of mechanism — those inventions which it seemed to demand something worse than man's natural heart to contrive, and which had lurked in the dusky nooks of ancient prisons, the subject of terror-stricken legends — were now brought forth to view. Headsmen's axes, with the rust of noble and royal blood upon them, and a vast collection of halters that had choked the breath of plebeian victims, were thrown in together. A shout greeted the arrival of the guillotine, which was thrust forward on the same wheels that had borne it from one to another of the blood-stained streets of Paris. But the loudest roar of applause went up, telling the distant sky of the triumph of the earth's redemption, when the gallows made its appearance. An ill-looking fellow, however, rushed forward, and putting himself in the path of the reformers, bellowed hoarsely, and fought with brute fury to stay their progress.

It was little matter of surprise, perhaps, that the executioner should thus do his best to vindicate and uphold the machinery by which he himself had his livelihood, and worthier individuals their death. But it deserved special note, that men of a far different sphere — even of that consecrated class in whose guardianship the world is apt to trust its benevolence — were found to take the hangman's view of the question.

"Stay, my brethren!" cried one of them. "You are misled by a false philanthropy! — you know not what you do. The gallows is a heaven-oriented instrument! Bear it back, then, reverently, and set it up in its old place; else the world will fall to speedy ruin and desolation!"

"Onward, onward!" shouted a leader in the reform. "Into the flames with the accursed instrument of man's bloody policy! How can human law inculcate benevolence and love, while it persists in setting up the gallows as its chief symbol? One heave more, good friends; and the world will be redeemed from its greatest error!"

A thousand hands, that, nevertheless, loathed the touch, now lent their assistance, and thrust the ominous burthen far, far, into the centre of the raging furnace. There its fatal and abhorred image was beheld, first black, then a red coal, then ashes.

"That was well done!" exclaimed I.

"Yes; it was well done," replied — but with less enthusiasm than I expected — the thoughtful observer who was still at my side; "well done, if the world be good enough for the measure. Death, however, is an idea that cannot easily be dispensed with, in any condition between the primal innocence and that other purity and perfection, which, perchance, we are destined to attain, after travelling round the full circle. But, at all events, it is well that the experiment should now be tried."

"Too cold! — too cold!" impatiently exclaimed the young and ardent leader in this triumph. "Let the heart have its voice here, as well as the intellect. And as for ripeness — and as for progress — let mankind always do the highest, kindest, noblest thing, that, at any given period, it has attained to the perception of; and surely that thing cannot be wrong, nor wrongly timed!"

I know not whether it were the excitement of the scene, or whether the good people around the bonfire were really growing more enlightened, every instant; but they now proceeded to measures, in the full length of which I was hardly prepared to keep them company. For instance, some threw their marriage-certificates into the flames, and declared themselves candidates for a higher, holier, and more comprehensive union than that which had subsisted from the birth of time, under the form of the connubial tie. Others hastened to the vaults of banks, and to the coffers of the rich — all of which were open to the first-comer, on this fated occasion — and brought entire bales of paper-money to enliven the blaze, and tons of coin to be melted down by its intensity. Henceforth, they said, universal benevolence, uncoined and exhaustless, was to be the golden currency of the world. At this intelligence, the bankers, and speculators in the stocks, grew pale; and a pick-pocket, who had reaped a rich harvest among the crowd, fell down in a deadly fainting-fit. A few men of business burnt their day-books and legers, the notes and obligations of their creditors, and all other evidences of debts due to themselves; while perhaps a somewhat larger number satisfied their zeal for reform with the sacrifice of any uncomfortable recollection of their own indebtment. There was then a cry, that the period was arrived, when the title-deeds of landed property should be given to the flames, and the whole soil of the earth revert to the public, from whom it had been wrongfully abstracted, and most unequally distributed among individuals. Another party demanded, that all written constitutions, set forms of government, legislative acts, statute-books, and everything else on which human invention had endeavored to stamp its arbitrary laws, should at once be destroyed, leaving the consummated world as free as the man first created.

Whether any ultimate action was taken with regard to these propositions, is beyond my knowledge; for, just then, some matters were in progress that concerned my sympathies more nearly.

"See! — see! — what heaps of books and pamphlets," cried a fellow, who did not seem to be a lover of literature. "Now we shall have a glorious blaze!"

"That's just the thing," said a modern philosopher. "Now we shall get rid of the weight of dead men's thought, which has hitherto pressed so heavily on the living intellect, that it has been incompetent to any effectual self-exertion. Well done, my lads! Into the fire with them! Now you are enlightening the world, indeed!"

"But what is to become of the Trade?" cried a frantic bookseller.

"Oh, by all means, let them accompany their merchandise," coolly observed an author. "It will be a noble funeral-pile!"

The truth was, that the human race had now reached a stage of progress, so far beyond what the wisest and wittiest men of former ages had ever dreamed of, that it would have been a manifest absurdity to allow the earth to be any longer encumbered with their poor achievements in the literary line. Accordingly, a thorough and searching investigation had swept the booksellers' shops, hawkers' stands, public and private libraries, and even the little book-shelf by the country fireside, and had brought the world's entire mass of printed paper, bound or in sheets, to swell the already mountain-bulk of our illustrious bonfire. Thick, heavy folios, containing the labors of lexicographers, commentators, and encyclopediasts, were flung in, and, falling among the embers with a leaden thump, smouldered away to ashes, like rotten wood. The small, richly-gilt, French tomes, of the last age, with the hundred volumes of Voltaire[13] among them, went off in a brilliant shower of sparkles, and little jets of flame; while the current literature of the same nation burnt red and blue, and threw an infernal light over the visages of the spectators, converting them all to the aspect of parti-colored fiends. A collection of German stories emitted a scent of brimstone. The English standard authors made excellent fuel, generally exhibiting the properties of sound oak logs. Milton's works, in particular, sent up a powerful blaze, gradually reddening into a coal, which promised to endure longer than almost any other material of the pile. From Shakspeare there gushed a flame of such marvellous splendor, that men shaded their eyes as against the sun's meridian glory; nor, even when the works of his own elucidators were flung upon him, did he cease to flash forth a dazzling radiance, from beneath the ponderous heap. It is my belief, that he is still blazing as fervidly as ever.

"Could a poet but light a lamp at that glorious flame," remarked I, "he might then consume the midnight oil to some good purpose."

"That is the very thing which modern poets have been too apt to do — or, at least, to attempt," answered a critic. "The chief benefit to be expected from this conflagration of past literature, undoubtedly is, that writers will henceforth be compelled to light their lamps at the sun or stars."

"If they can reach so high," said I. "But that task requires a giant, who may afterwards distribute the light among inferior men. It is not every one that can steal the fire from Heaven, like Prometheus; but when once he had done the deed, a thousand hearths were kindled by it."

---

[13]*Voltaire:* French author and philosopher (1694–1778).

It amazed me much to observe, how indefinite was the proportion between the physical mass of any given author, and the property of brilliant and long-continued combustion. For instance, there was not a quarto volume of the last century — nor, indeed, of the present — that could compete, in that particular, with a child's little gilt-covered book, containing Mother Goose's Melodies. The Life and Death of Tom Thumb outlasted the biography of Marlborough. An epic — indeed, a dozen of them — was converted to white ashes, before the single sheet of an old ballad was half-consumed. In more than one case, too, when volumes of applauded verse proved incapable of anything better than a stifling smoke, an unregarded ditty of some nameless bard — perchance, in the corner of a newspaper — soared up among the stars, with a flame as brilliant as their own. Speaking of the properties of flame, methought Shelley's poetry emitted a purer light than almost any other productions of his day; contrasting beautifully with the fitful and lurid gleams, and gushes of black vapor, that flashed and eddied from the volumes of Lord Byron. As for Tom Moore, some of his songs diffused an odor like a burning pastille.[14]

I felt particular interest in watching the combustion of American authors, and scrupulously noted, by my watch, the precise number of moments that changed most of them from shabbily-printed books to indistinguishable ashes. It would be invidious, however, if not perilous, to betray these awful secrets; so that I shall content myself with observing, that it was not invariably the writer most frequent in the public mouth, that made the most splendid appearance in the bonfire. I especially remember, that a great deal of excellent inflammability was exhibited in a thin volume of poems by Ellery Channing;[15] although, to speak the truth, there were certain portions that hissed and spluttered in a very disagreeable fashion. A curious phenomenon occurred, in reference to several writers, native as well as foreign. Their books, though of highly respectable figure, instead of bursting into a blaze, or even smouldering out their substance in smoke, suddenly melted away, in a manner that proved them to be ice.

[14]Percy Bysshe Shelley (1792–1822) and Lord Byron (1788–1824) were English romantic poets; Tom Moore (1779–1852) was an Irish satirist and poet; *pastille:* A paper tube filled with combustible material.
[15]*Ellery Channing:* William Ellery Channing (1818–1901) was a Concord poet and friend of Hawthorne.

If it be no lack of modesty to mention my own works, it must here be confessed, that I looked for them with fatherly interest, but in vain. Too probably, they were changed to vapor by the first action of the heat; at best, I can only hope, that, in their quiet way, they contributed a glimmering spark or two to the splendor of the evening.

"Alas, and woe is me!" thus bemoaned himself a heavy-looking gentleman in green spectacles. "The world is utterly ruined, and there is nothing to live for any longer! The business of my life is snatched from me. Not a volume to be had for love or money!"

"This," remarked the sedate observer beside me, "is a book-worm — one of those men who are born to gnaw dead thoughts. His clothes, you see, are covered with the dust of libraries. He has no inward fountain of ideas; and, in good earnest, now that the old stock is abolished, I do not see what is to become of the poor fellow. Have you no word of comfort for him?"

"My dear Sir," said I to the desperate book-worm, "is not Nature better than a book? — is not the human heart deeper than any system of philosophy? — is not life replete with more instruction than past observers have found it possible to write down in maxims? Be of good cheer! The great book of Time is still spread wide open before us; and, if we read it aright, it will be to us a volume of eternal Truth."

"Oh, my books, my books, my precious, printed books!" reiterated the forlorn book-worm. "My only reality was a bound volume; and now they will not leave me even a shadowy pamphlet!"

In fact, the last remnant of the literature of all the ages was now descending upon the blazing heap, in the shape of a cloud of pamphlets from the press of the New World. These, likewise, were consumed in the twinkling of an eye, leaving the earth, for the first time since the days of Cadmus,[16] free from the plague of letters — an enviable field for the authors of the next generation!

"Well! — and does anything remain to be done?" inquired I, somewhat anxiously. "Unless we set fire to the earth itself, and then leap boldly off into infinite space, I know not that we can carry reform to any further point."

"You are vastly mistaken, my good friend," said the observer.

---

[16]*Cadmus:* Founder of Thebes, was said to have brought the Phoenician alphabet to Greece.

"Believe me, the fire will not be allowed to settle down, without the addition of fuel that will startle many persons, who have lent a willing hand thus far."

Nevertheless, there appeared to be a relaxation of effort, for a little time, during which, probably, the leaders of the movement were considering what should be done next. In the interval, a philosopher threw his theory into the flames; a sacrifice, which, by those who knew how to estimate it, was pronounced the most remarkable that had yet been made. The combustion, however, was by no means brilliant. Some indefatigable people, scorning to take a moment's ease, now employed themselves in collecting all the withered leaves and fallen boughs of the forest, and thereby recruited the bonfire to a greater height than ever. But this was mere by-play.

"Here comes the fresh fuel that I spoke of," said my companion.

To my astonishment, the persons who now advanced into the vacant space, around the mountain of fire, bore surplices and other priestly garments, mitres, crosiers, and a confusion of popish and protestant emblems, with which it seemed their purpose to consummate this great Act of Faith. Crosses, from the spires of old cathedrals, were cast upon the heap, with as little remorse as if the reverence of centuries, passing in long array beneath the lofty towers, had not looked up to them as the holiest of symbols. The font, in which infants were consecrated to God; the sacramental vessels, whence Piety had received the hallowed draught; were given to the same destruction. Perhaps it most nearly touched my heart, to see, among these devoted relics, fragments of the humble communion-tables and undecorated pulpits, which I recognized as having been torn from the meeting-houses of New-England. Those simple edifices might have been permitted to retain all of sacred embellishment that their Puritan founders had bestowed, even though the mighty structure of St. Peter's[17] had sent its spoils to the fire of this terrible sacrifice. Yet I felt that these were but the externals of religion, and might most safely be relinquished by spirits that best knew their deep significance.

"All is well," said I, cheerfully. "The wood-paths shall be the aisles of our cathedral — the firmament itself shall be its ceiling! What needs an earthly roof between the Deity and his worshipper? Our faith can well afford to lose all the drapery that even the holiest men

[17]*St. Peter's:* In Vatican City, Rome, the largest Catholic church, famous for its immense dome.

have thrown around it, and be only the more sublime in its simplicity."

"True," said my companion. "But will they pause here?"

The doubt, implied in his question, was well-founded. In the general destruction of books, already described, a holy volume — that
stood apart from the catalogue of human literature, and yet, in one
sense, was at its head — had been spared. But the Titan[18] of innova-
tion — angel or fiend, double in his nature, and capable of deeds befitting both characters — at first shaking down only the old and rotten
shapes of things, had now, as it appeared, laid his terrible hand upon
the main pillars, which supported the whole edifice of our moral and
spiritual state. The inhabitants of the earth had grown too enlightened
to define their faith within a form of words, or to limit the spiritual by
any analogy to our material existence. Truths, which the Heavens
trembled at, were now but a fable of the world's infancy. Therefore, as
the final sacrifice of human error, what else remained, to be thrown
upon the embers of that awful pile, except the Book, which, though a
celestial revelation to past ages, was but a voice from a lower sphere,
as regarded the present race of man? It was done! Upon the blazing
heap of falsehood and worn-out truth — things that the earth had
never needed, or had ceased to need, or had grown childishly weary
of — fell the ponderous church-Bible, the great old volume, that had
lain so long on the cushions of the pulpit, and whence the pastor's
solemn voice had given holy utterances, on so many a Sabbath-day.
There, likewise, fell the family-Bible, which the long-buried patriarch
had read to his children — in prosperity or sorrow, by the fireside, and
in the summer-shade of trees — and had bequeathed downward, as
the heirloom of generations. There fell the bosom-Bible, the little volume that had been the soul's friend of some sorely tried Child of Dust,
who thence took courage, whether his trial were for life or death,
steadfastly confronting both, in the strong assurance of Immortality.

All these were flung into the fierce and riotous blaze; and then a
mighty wind came roaring across the plain, with a desolate howl, as
if it were the angry lamentation of the Earth for the loss of Heaven's
sunshine; and it shook the gigantic pyramid of flame, and scattered
the cinders of half-consumed abominations around upon the spectators.

[18]*Titan:* The Titans were the race of giant gods whom Zeus and the Olympian gods
defeated.

"This is terrible!" said I, feeling that my cheek grew pale, and seeing a like change in the visages about me.

"Be of good courage yet," answered the man with whom I had so often spoken. He continued to gaze steadily at the spectacle, with a singular calmness, as if it concerned him merely as an observer. — "Be of good courage — nor yet exult too much; for there is far less both of good and evil, in the effect of this bonfire, than the world might be willing to believe."

"How can that be?" exclaimed I, impatiently. — "Has it not consumed everything? Has it not swallowed up, or melted down, every human or divine appendage of our mortal state, that had substance enough to be acted on by fire? Will there be anything left us, tomorrow morning, better or worse than a heap of embers and ashes?"

"Assuredly there will," said my grave friend. "Come hither tomorrow morning — or whenever the combustible portion of the pile shall be quite burnt out — and you will find among the ashes everything really valuable that you have seen cast into the flames. Trust me; the world of tomorrow will again enrich itself with the gold and diamonds, which have been cast off by the world of to-day. Not a truth is destroyed — nor buried so deep among the ashes, but it will be raked up at last."

This was a strange assurance. Yet I felt inclined to credit it; the more especially as I beheld, among the wallowing flames, a copy of the Holy Scriptures, the pages of which, instead of being blackened into tinder, only assumed a more dazzling whiteness, as the fingermarks of human imperfection were purified away. Certain marginal notes and commentaries, it is true, yielded to the intensity of the fiery test, but without detriment to the smallest syllable that had flamed from the pen of inspiration.

"Yes; — there is the proof of what you say," answered I, turning to the observer. "But, if only what is evil can feel the action of the fire, then, surely, the conflagration has been of inestimable utility. Yet, if I understand aright, you intimate a doubt whether the world's expectation of benefit will be realized by it."

"Listen to the talk of these worthies," said he, pointing to a group in front of the blazing pile. — "Possibly, they may teach you something useful, without intending it."

The persons, whom he indicated, consisted of that brutal and most earthy figure, who had stood forth so furiously in defence of the gallows — the hangman, in short — together with the Last Thief and

the Last Murderer; all three of whom were clustered about the Last
Toper. The latter was liberally passing the brandy-bottle, which he
had rescued from the general destruction of wines and spirits. This
little convivial party seemed at the lowest pitch of despondency; as
considering that the purified world must needs be utterly unlike, the
sphere that they had hitherto known, and therefore but a strange and
desolate abode for gentlemen of their kidney.

"The best counsel for all of us, is," remarked the hangman,
"that — as soon as we have finished the last drop of liquor — I help
you, my three friends, to a comfortable end upon the nearest tree,
and then hang myself on the same bough. This is no world for us, any
longer."

"Poh, poh, my good fellows!" said a dark-complexioned personage, who now joined the group — his complexion was indeed fearfully dark; and his eyes glowed with a redder light than that of the
bonfire — "Be not so cast down, my dear friends; you shall see good
days yet. There is one thing that these wiseacres have forgotten to
throw into the fire, and without which all the rest of the conflagration is just nothing at all — yes; though they had burnt the earth itself
to a cinder!"

"And what may that be?" eagerly demanded the Last Murderer.

"What, but the human heart itself!" said the dark-visaged
stranger, with a portentous grin. "And, unless they hit upon some
method of purifying that foul cavern, forth from it will re-issue all the
shapes of wrong and misery — the same old shapes, or worse ones —
which they have taken such a vast deal of trouble to consume to
ashes. I have stood by, this live-long night, and laughed in my sleeve
at the whole business. Oh, take my word for it, it will be the old
world yet!"

This brief conversation supplied me with a theme for lengthened
thought. How sad a truth — if true it were — that Man's age-long
endeavor for perfection had served only to render him the mockery of
the Evil Principle, from the fatal circumstance of an error at the very
root of the matter! The Heart — the Heart — there was the little, yet
boundless sphere, wherein existed the original wrong, of which the
crime and misery of this outward world were merely types. Purify
that inner sphere; and the many shapes of evil that haunt the outward, and which now seem almost our only realities, will turn to
shadowy phantoms, and vanish of their own accord. But, if we go no
deeper than the Intellect, and strive, with merely that feeble instrument, to discern and rectify what is wrong, our whole accomplish-

ment will be a dream; so unsubstantial, that it matters little whether the bonfire, which I have so faithfully described, were what we choose to call a real event, and a flame that would scorch the finger — or only a phosphoric radiance, and a parable of my own brain!

"View of a Phalanx, a French Village Designed According to the Social Theory of Charles Fourier," by Charles Daubigny, ca. 1848. Charles Fourier was one of the leading utopian theorists of the first half of the nineteenth century, and his ideas were put into practice in a number of American utopian communities, including Brook Farm in its later phase. By permission of the Houghton Library, Harvard University.

2

The Idea of Community

A flawed but admirable effort to construct a Christian community on a new basis, Brook Farm was one manifestation of the general quest for social renewal and regeneration that coincided with (and extended beyond) the emergence of the new nation in the 1770s. Many of the experimental, utopian communities can be traced to, or were influenced by, the religious revivalism of the Second Great Awakening in the 1820s and 1830s. The first Great Awakening occurred in the colonies from the 1730s to the 1760s, and it was marked by intense religious enthusiasm and revivalism, much of it kindled by the powerful preacher and evangelist George Whitefield (1714–1770). The major voice of the second wave was Charles Grandison Finney (1792–1875), who, after experiencing a religious conversion in 1821, conducted revivals in northern New York and elsewhere.

Finney urged men and women to apply to their lives and communities Christ's words in the Gospel: "Be ye therefore perfect, even as your Father which is in heaven is perfect" (Matthew 5:48). This injunction spurred not only individual conversions, but also the formation of benevolent and reform groups, associations, networks, and organizations — including the Bible Society, the American Tract Society, and the Home Missionary Society — that were dedicated to "perfecting" social conditions and establishing God's kingdom (heaven on earth) in the present.

More than a hundred new communities — religious or secular utopias — were founded in the period between the Revolution and the Civil War. The most common were the thirty or more across the country founded on the tenets of the French socialist Charles Fourier and his American translator and disciple/advocate, Albert Brisbane. The largest of these was Red Bank, New Jersey (peak membership was 125–50), with seven others clustered in northern Pennsylvania and still more scattered elsewhere in the East and Midwest.

Earlier communities include the Shaker settlement in Mount Lebanon, New York, organized in 1787, and soon replicated elsewhere; the German pietist George Rapp's Harmony Society in western Pennsylvania, begun in 1805; Robert Owen and his son Robert Dale Owen's New Harmony, Indiana, a cooperative settlement intended to replace the competitive, capitalist order and to do so without formal religion, founded in May 1825; and Frances Wright's Owenite community in Nashoba, Tennessee, that was started in the fall of 1825 for the education of slaves and that included integrated schools.

Later examples, in addition to Brook Farm, include Adin Ballou's Hopedale, launched in Massachusetts in the early 1840s, which emphasized temperance, abolitionism, and other reforms; John Humphrey Noyes's Putney, Vermont, in the 1830s, and Oneida, New York, in the late 1840s, which were based on evangelical Christian principles and were radically perfectionist in spirit and liberated in sexual practices; John A. Collins's no-government/common property community in Skaneateles, New York, January 1844; Josiah Warren's Modern Times, on Long Island, in 1851; and the Icarian community, keyed to the ideas of Étienne Cabet, a French radical and author of the utopian novel *Voyage en Icarie*, first established in Texas in mid-1848 and later relocated in Illinois, Missouri, and Iowa.

Perhaps the most successful of all were the communities of Mormons, whom Joseph Smith led in Ohio, Missouri, and Illinois in the late 1830s and 1840s, and whom Brigham Young, after Smith was killed by a mob in 1844, brought to their permanent home in the Great Salt Lake Valley in the Utah territory.

The selections in this chapter provide insight into the nature of life in several of the above communities, in addition to illustrating the theories and principles that animated America's many utopian experiments. These documents also provide illuminating points of comparison with both the community at Brook Farm and the fictional Blithedale. In addition, the selection by the anti-slavery author Harriet Beecher Stowe, evoking the blissful harmony of a Quaker settlement, recalls for us that the small new communities were under way in a nation increasingly divided over slavery.

A key theme in many of the selections is the relationship between human nature and social systems. Robert Owen, for example, stresses that the "social or cooperative system" he advocates is "founded on a real knowledge of human nature." Frances Wright similarly recommends changes that will liberate the development of the natures of young men and women so that, when they reach adulthood, they will be equipped to "perfect the free institutions of America." In Fourier's and Brisbane's writings, too, the emphasis falls on the barriers that the current social, political, and economic order has erected to frustrate and retard the best capacities of human nature. "In work, as in pleasure," Fourier concludes, "variety is evidently the desire of nature," and he proposes a new scheme for work in his utopia that would satisfy, rather than repress, this desire. Likewise, when Brisbane criticizes the "social mechanism" and proposes how it should be changed, he aims to free men and women from bondage to degrading, antihuman forms of labor and social life and lead them to see the benefits of new modes of "Association" in community and work.

The proponents of these secular and religious utopias — Adin Ballou referred to Hopedale as "a miniature Christian Republic" — sincerely hoped for social betterment and were willing to challenge custom, tradition, and convention. But to Hawthorne, utopias were dangerous — alluring and even admirable to a degree in theory but ultimately misconceived and not at all likely to work well or last long in practice. In *The Blithedale Romance*, neither Hollingsworth nor Zenobia becomes better as a result of membership in the Blithedale community. If anything, they become worse, as the new setting they select for their lives ultimately gives them only a different, more perilous stage upon which to exemplify their basic personalities.

CHARLES FOURIER

The Impact of Industrialism

The Benefits of Association

The Condition of Women

Charles Fourier (1772–1837), born in a French bourgeois family (his father was a wealthy merchant), was imprisoned and nearly executed during the French Revolution. He became an important social philosopher and utopian theorist — and a controversial one for his radical, liberated views on sexual relationships. His central claim was that the natural passions of mankind would lead to peace and harmony if they were properly directed and scientifically planned. The best unit for social development, he argued, was the self-sufficient "phalanx." It would number about sixteen hundred persons, who would live in a main building, the phalanstery. Their work, largely agricultural, would be highly systematized yet made flexible enough to enable each person to follow his or her natural desires: labor thus would be "attractive" rather than tedious and burdensome.

Ripley, Fuller, and Emerson were familiar by 1840 with Fourier's ideas. In an October 18, 1840, letter, Fuller noted that she and Emerson and others had been taking part in "Phalanx talk." But Brook Farm itself did not become a community explicitly based on Fourierist principles until 1844 — several years after Hawthorne's period as one of the original members. In *The Blithedale Romance*, Coverdale and Hollingsworth discuss Fourier (ch. 7), and Hollingsworth condemns him for making "the selfish principle" the "master-workman of his system."

Fourier's theories about sexual liberation proved awkward for his American followers and were frequently omitted from summaries of his work. But his commitment to expanding roles and opportunities for women nonetheless made him an appealing figure to many reformers involved in campaigns for women's rights.

The first and third selections are from *Théorie des Quatres Mouvements* (2nd ed., 1841); the second is from *Théorie de l'Unité Universelle* (2nd ed., 1838). The English translation is by Julia Franklin, in *Selections from the Works of Fourier* (1901; reprint, New York: Gordon, 1972), 83–85, 165–66, 76–77.

The Impact of Industrialism

Industrialism is the latest of our scientific chimeras; it is the mania of producing in confusion, without any system of proportional compensation, without any guarantee to the producer or wage-earner that he will participate in the increase of wealth; accordingly, we find the industrial regions sprinkled with beggars to as great, or, perhaps, a greater extent than those countries which are indifferent to this sort of progress.

Let us judge systems here by their results; it is England that is the point aimed at, the model offered to the nations, the object of their jealousy; in order to estimate the happiness of its people, I shall fortify myself by unexceptionable testimony.

Assembly of master-workmen of Birmingham, March 21, 1827. It declares "that the industry and frugality of the working man are unable to shield him from want, that the mass of wage-earners employed in agriculture are destitute; that they actually die of hunger in a country where there is a superabundance of food." Testimony all the less open to suspicion in that it proceeds from the class of foremen who are interested in justifying the wages of the working-men and disguising their wretchedness.

Here is a second witness, equally interested in concealing the weak side of his nation; it is an economist, an industrialist, who is going to denounce his own science.

London, House of Commons, February 28, 1826.

Mr. Huskisson, Minister of Commerce, says: "Our silk factories employ thousands of children who are held in leash from three o'clock in the morning until ten o'clock at night: how much do they get a week? a shilling and a half, thirty-seven French sous, about *five and a half sous per day,* for being tied down to their work nineteen hours, superintended by foremen provided with whips with which they strike every child that stops for a moment."

This is slavery actually restored: it is evident that the excess of industrial competition leads civilised nations to the same degree of poverty and servitude as the populace of China and Hindustan, most anciently famous by their prodigies in agriculture and manufactures.

Alongside of England let us place Ireland, which, by double excess in extreme cultivation and in sub-division of properties, has arrived at the same condition of destitution which England attains by double excess in manufactures and great estates. This contrast in one and the same empire well demonstrates the vicious circle of civilised industry.

The newspapers of Dublin (1826) say: "There is an epidemic prevailing here among the people: the sick that are taken to the hospital recover as soon as they have been given food." Their sickness, then, is HUNGER: one need not be a sorcerer to divine that, since they are cured as soon as they have something to eat. Have no fear that this epidemic will attack the great: you will not see either the Lord-Lieutenant or the Archbishop of Dublin fall ill from hunger, but rather from indigestion.

And in places where the civilised masses do not die of *pressing* hunger, they die of *slow* hunger through privations, of *speculative* hunger which constrains them to nourish themselves with unwholesome food, of *imminent* hunger through overwork, through engaging in pernicious pursuits, enduring excessive fatigue, which gives birth to fevers, to infirmities.

The Benefits of Association

We know what effect association and ownership have upon one engaged in industrial occupations. He appears sluggish while working for wages, for others' benefit; but the moment commercial association has inoculated him with the spirit of ownership and participation, he becomes a prodigy of diligence, and they say of him: *"He is not the same man; one cannot recognise him."* Why? Because he has become a COMPOSITE owner. His emulation is so much the more valuable in that he works for a whole body of associates and not himself alone, as is the case with the small cultivator, so highly lauded by morality, and who is in reality nothing but an egoist: — poor morality, which in all things has an unlucky hand, can praise only the sources of vice. It was natural enough that it should end by praising free trade or the rule of falsehood. . . .

He ought to love work, say our sages: yes! but how go about it? What is lovable about it in civilisation for nine-tenths of mankind, who reap only weariness from it and no benefits? Consequently, it is generally shunned by the rich, who engage only in the lucrative and agreeable side of it, in direction. How cause it to be liked by the poor, when it cannot be rendered pleasant to the rich?

In order to attain happiness, it is necessary to introduce it into the labours which engage the greater part of our lives. Life is a long torment to one who pursues occupations without attraction. Morality teaches us to love work: let it know, then, how to render work lovable, and, first of all, let it introduce luxury into husbandry[1] and the workshop. If the arrangements are poor, repulsive, how arouse industrial attraction?

In work, as in pleasure, variety is evidently the desire of nature. Any enjoyment prolonged, without interruption, beyond two hours, conduces to satiety, to abuse, blunts our faculties, and exhausts pleasure. A repast of four hours will not pass off without excess; an opera of four hours will end by cloying the spectator. Periodical variety is a necessity of the body and of the soul, a necessity in all nature; even the soil requires alteration of seeds, and seed alteration of soil. The stomach will soon reject the best dish if it be offered every day, and the soul will be blunted in the exercise of any virtue if it be not relieved by some other virtue.

If there is need of variety in pleasure after indulging in it for two hours, so much the more does labour require this diversity, which is continual in the associative state, and is guaranteed to the poor as well as the rich.

The chief source of light-heartedness among Harmonians is the frequent change of sessions. Life is a perpetual torment to our workmen, who are obliged to spend twelve, and frequently fifteen, consecutive hours in some tedious labour. Even ministers are not exempt; we find some of them complain of having passed an entire day in the stupefying task of affixing signatures to thousands of official vouchers. Such wearisome duties are unknown in the associative order; the Harmonians, who devote an hour, an hour and a half, or at most two hours, to the different sessions, and who, in these short sessions, are sustained by cabalistic impulses and by friendly union with selected associates, cannot fail to bring and to find cheerfulness everywhere.

The Condition of Women

If God has endowed amorous customs with such great influence upon the social mechanism and upon the metamorphoses which it is capable of undergoing, this must be a consequence of his horror of oppression and violence; he desired the well-being or the misery of

---

[1]*husbandry:* Domestic management or care of a household but also refers to the cultivation or production of plants and animals.

human societies to be proportional to the constraint or freedom which they would allow. Now God recognises as freedom only that which is extended to both sexes and not to one alone; he desired, likewise, that all the seeds of social abominations such as savagery, barbarism, civilisation, should have as their sole pivot the subjection of women, and that all the seeds of social well-being such as the sixth, seventh, eighth periods[2] should have no pivot but the progressive enfranchisement of the weak sex.

As a general proposition: *Social advances and changes of periods are brought about by virtue of the progress of women towards liberty, and the decadences of the social order are brought about by virtue of the decrease of liberty of women.*

Other events influence these political vicissitudes; but there is no cause which so rapidly produces social progress or decline as a change in the condition of women. I have already said that the adoption of closed harems would of itself soon transform us into barbarians, and the opening of the harems would of itself cause a people to pass from barbarism to civilisation. To sum up, *the extension of privileges to women is the general principle of all social progress.*

ALBERT BRISBANE

From Social Destiny of Man, or Association and Reorganization of Industry

Albert Brisbane (1809–1890), born in Batavia, New York, studied in Europe under such renowned figures as the French philosopher and social theorist Victor Cousin, the French historian François Guizot, and the German philosopher G. W. F. Hegel. His mentor was, above all others, Charles Fourier, and *Social Destiny of Man* was the first important text on Fourier's ideas written for American readers. Morris Hillquit, in his *History of Socialism in the United States* (1903), noted that Brisbane's book was studied "by all classes of persons interested in social problems" and "laid the foundations for the Fourierist movement" in the United States. Brisbane went on to describe and promote Fourierism in addi-

---

[2]*the sixth, seventh, eighth periods:* Stages of social evolution that Fourier describes, with the eighth representing his goal: "Harmonism, complete association."

tional books, essays, lectures, and a newspaper column (1842–44) in the New York *Tribune.*

In this excerpt from *Social Destiny of Man* (1840), Brisbane discusses slavery, abolition, and the need to solve the labor problem by following the guidelines for a new social organization that Fourier had presented.

Our progress is *Political,* not *Social.* Our social mechanism, the fundamental principles of our society, are the same as those of Europe, and *those principles are false.* Having deviated from the general policy of other nations, could we go one step further, and realize a change in the social mechanism itself, we should then accomplish an important part in the history of the world. But notwithstanding our political innovations, no questions unfortunately of a social nature are discussed with us, nor is the public mind in the least directed to new social principles. Our political leaders, aiming at administrative reforms, are not even aware, that the possibility exists in the nature of things of a reform in the mechanism of society. They propose no change of system, such as the substituting of agricultural Association in the place of agricultural incoherence or piece-meal cultivation — the present mode of farming — combination of interests, and unity of industrial relations, in the place of the perpetual conflicts, which now exist. The energies of the people are so absorbed in personal or party interests, that their attention is withdrawn from real, that is social progress. It is believed that the society in which we vegetate, is unchangeable, that the evils we suffer are attached to human nature, inseparable from it, and independent of the social organization. Although four forms of society have existed on the earth, the Savage, Patriarchal, Barbarian, and Civilized, still this does not lead to the apparently simple conclusion, that a fifth or a sixth, perhaps more happy and just, may be organized. As the intellectual activity of the country is not at all directed to social questions, and to a change of system, its highest hopes for the future, its *ideal,* in a political point of view, can only be to pursue the direction it has chosen, continue its present policy, and avoid with the greatest care, violent controversies and sectional quarrels, which may break it up, and the Union also.

So far, none but those of a superficial character have arisen, but the portentous question of abolition comes in another shape. It has wrought in its discussion religious zeal in the North, and is opposed by the spirit of property in the South. These two sentiments are as irreconcilable in the present juncture, as they are inflexible in the human mind.

This question cannot change with parties, nor with men, because it is based on convictions, which are among the fundamental, political and religious dogmas of society. Slavery, it is asserted, is an infringement of two laws — of Divine law which proclaims the equality of human nature before God, and of Human law, which declares an equality of political rights. These convictions, which exist more or less strongly in all minds, but which are tempered and balanced by the thousand other interests of the day, are easily roused in the feelings of men of certain temperaments, and grow to fanaticism, if worked upon constantly. A fanaticism, based on these convictions, is rapidly spreading, and opposition of course will strengthen rather than weaken it. Without doubt slavery is false; it is a character of the third or barbarian society, which has been retained, and engrafted on the civilized social mechanism; but how many things are there which are false in civilization! Its whole mechanism is false; first, in its separate or isolated households, or as many houses as families, producing a complication twenty-times greater than necessary; second, in its incoherent system of industry, causing a perpetual conflict of all interests; thirdly, in the absence of Association, economy and unity in all its relations. Slavery is one of its defects; but it is not the foundation of social evil; it is only an accidental character; it should not therefore be attacked first, and above all not separately.

Nearly the whole agricultural industry of the South is dependent upon slavery, hence the question is so momentous. If you abolish it suddenly, you infringe on a great many other rights, which are among the fundamental ones of the social compact. A conflict of principles without doubt exists, but it only proves that the civilized social mechanism is a labyrinth of contradictions and conflicts throughout. When a reform becomes necessary, we should go to the foundation of evil, before attacking the superstructure. If it be inquired where a fundamental change is to be commenced, we answer, in agriculture, which as the primary branch of industry, as the principal source of riches, is the basis of the social order. The root of evil is in our incoherent system of industry, carried on by isolated individuals with hostile and conflicting interests; replace it by a system of agricultural Association, productive of unity and combination, and the problem is solved. No branch, slavery for example, can be attacked separately without producing commotions; but agricultural Association, which would replace the desultory action of individuals by the combined efforts of masses, distribute judiciously and appropriately the capacity, talent and labor of the different sexes and ages, introduce method and a scientific system of cultivation in the place of waste and ignorance, would conflict with no rights or principles, but, on the contrary, would forward greatly the interests and welfare of all classes, both rich and poor.

On the question of slavery, the South will not of course remain passive; its slaves are its productive property, its active wealth. To suppose that a whole country will sacrifice practical benefits, acquired advantages, to questions of a political or other nature, which do not come home to the feelings of men like the interests of property and a guarantee of a worldly existence, remains to be proved by some other history than that of the past. The principle of property cannot be attacked in the South without jeoparding in an imminent degree our political union; if the Abolitionists can spread their views and strengthen their party, so as to give it a preponderance over the opposing fractions of other parties, and if, when they have obtained this power, they proceed to carry out practically their principles, the South may deem it expedient to secede from the North, — and the Union ceases! After the withdrawal of the South, after securing itself against the spreading of these doctrines, which it considers hostile to its peace and industry, so as to allow them no access under any form, what then has the abolition party of the North to do? Will it remain quiet and abandon its object, or to what means will it resort to carry out its views?

Should a separation take place, and were the Abolitionists to abstain from further action, it is probable that this division would sooner or later result in misunderstandings, quarrels and perhaps even war. It is possible we might fall back in the old track, which has heretofore been pursued by nations, and go so far as to act over even a part of the history of the past, and add one more page to the bloody annals of the human race. Such a fatal result should be guarded against with the greatest care.

The foreboding question of abolition, which arises so portentous on our political horizon, cannot be met and solved by present means; it requires those of Association and Attractive industry. That men are ignorant of their destiny, and of the great work they could accomplish on this earth, is proved, on the one hand, by their trifling political controversies, and by their readiness to embark in strife and bloodshed on the most trivial subjects; and on the other, by their apathetic resignation to evils time has sanctioned, and to the monotony, misery and injustice of our subversive societies. . . .

Why should not the strong philanthropic feeling, which exists for a few negroes of the South, be extended to the white laboring populations of civilized countries, which are so much more numerous? Their constancy in labor, the responsibility and anxiety imposed upon them by the care of families, their respect for property and order under all the poverty and privations they undergo, merit in the highest degree the attention of those, who feel an interest in the amelioration of the social condition of man.

But little can be expected from individual philanthropy; it is the mere germ of social good; it must be extended, universalised to be valuable; if it is not, it degenerates into fanaticism on some one point, and its efforts are wasted in the conflicts of opposing interests. True, that is, collective philanthropy embracing the entire earth, and the interests of all those who are oppressed; applying collective and general, instead of individual measures of relief, would be a valuable lever of social justice; but the philanthropy of the day is decidedly individual, and it will therefore, we fear, exhaust its efforts without aiding essentially the cause of mankind. . . .

If we look at the cities of civilized Europe — and some times at our own — we see the laboring classes wandering from manufactory to manufactory, or shop to shop, inquiring for work and refused it. Without any means of existence while out of employ, pressed by want, often by starvation, they reduce the price of their day's labor, selling fourteen and more hours of monotonous drudgery out of each twenty-four for a miserable pittance. If they manage to avoid actual famine, slow starvation, unhealthy and excessive labor and anxiety, sow the seeds of disease, undermine the constitution, and counteract the healthy influence, which labor should have on the human frame.

To creatures thus situated, what mockery to offer them the right to vote, or the guarantee of not being thrown into prison without a writ of habeas-corpus! Are they free, because they possess these illusory guarantees, when they are at the same time the slaves of labor, the serfs of capitalists? It is true, the whip does not force them to labor, like the real slave; but does not the alternative of want or famine do it as effectually? If their bodies cannot be sold, they have to bargain their liberty and their time, without being able to dispose scarcely of an hour. No: *Civil* liberty is perfectly illusory without *Industrial* liberty; it is a stepstone, a mere means of enabling man to attain to his destiny. Possessing Civil liberty, he is free to discuss all measures of a social reform, and the principles of a true social organization; it should be made use of, and applied to this purpose; if not, it degenerates into party controversy, sows the seeds of violent contentions, and after running its course, sinks into the political tyranny, out of which it emerged.

One of the implied objects of this work in its criticism of the present social organization, is to prove the entire absence of Industrial liberty; in treating later of a reorganization of labor, we will show the means of obtaining it. It is sufficient to say for the present, that it can only exist in a system of Association, based on ATTRACTIVE INDUSTRY, affording every individual the option of a great many branches of work, with varied and frequent changes, guaranteeing him a sufficiency of food, raiment and lodging, and giving to the material organization of labour the greatest elegance and facility possible. When the passions, now reputed our enemies, are directed towards industrial occupations, instead of war and political controversy, we will find them precious springs of action; and when labor is performed by groups of friends, freely united, varying their occupations through the day, to prevent monotony and satiety; and when industry is enobled, as war, the magistracy and science have been, we will see that attractive Industry is not a dream of perfection, but an immense benefit reserved for us by the Creator, and attainable whenever we shall cease abusing the passions, his most perfect work, and proceed to study their nature, and a social mechanism adapted to them.

This mechanism is to be found in the law of Groups and Series of Groups, the law according to which the Creator distributes all harmonies of the universe. The movement of Planets, the creation of different classes of animals, plants and minerals, each class or family forming a group, the harmony of sounds, colors, etc., are all based upon this great principle. Instead of studying and applying it to the passions, moralists, philosophers and legislators have looked upon them as depraved and vicious, and have declared them, through ignorance, incapable of good. Seeing them falsely developed in the civilized social mechanism, and struck with the evils they produce, they have concluded, that repression was the only means of obtaining order and justice; and instead of inquiring whether some social mechanism could not be discovered, which would make use of ALL those passions, as they were created, they have persisted in their conclusion, and directed their efforts to the organization of a vast system of compression, the principle levers of which are scaffolds, prisons, gibbets, exiling, branding and fines, causing an immense expense to society, and resulting only in a social chaos, which under the four different forms of the savage, patriarchal, barbarian and civilized societies, has been a scourge to the earth, and a disgrace to the genius of man!

"A Group of Oneida Perfectionists, John Humphrey Noyes in right foreground," photograph ca. 1863. Courtesy of the Oneida Community Mansion House.

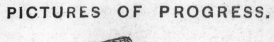

"Pictures of Progress," cartoon from *Yankee Doodle* magazine, December 19, 1846. This cartoon pokes fun at the organization of Fourierist communities into work groups having specific tasks and duties. The cartoonist suggests that in Fourier's utopia some will inevitably seek to benefit from the labor performed by others. By permission of the Houghton Library, Harvard University.

THE CRISIS,

OR THE CHANGE FROM ERROR AND MISERY, TO TRUTH AND HAPPINESS.

1832.

IF WE CANNOT YET   RECONCILE ALL OPINIONS,

LET US ENDEAVOUR   TO UNITE ALL HEARTS.

IT IS OF ALL TRUTHS THE MOST IMPORTANT, THAT THE CHARACTER OF MAN IS FORMED FOR—NOT BY HIMSELF.

Design of a Community of 2,000 Persons, founded upon a principle, commended by Plato, Lord Bacon, Sir T. More, & R. Owen.

EDITED BY
ROBERT OWEN AND ROBERT DALE OWEN.

London:
PRINTED AND PUBLISHED BY J. EAMONSON, 15, CHICHESTER PLACE, GRAY'S INN ROAD.
STRANGE, PATERNOSTER ROW. PURKISS, OLD COMPTON STREET, AND MAY BE HAD OF ALL BOOKSELLERS.
1833.

Title page from *The Crisis, or The Change from Error and Misery, to Truth and Happiness,* edited by Robert Owen and Robert Dale Owen, 1832, London 1833. Robert Owen (1771–1858) was an important reformer, socialist, and philanthropist; his ideas formed the basis for the New Harmony, Indiana, settlement in the mid-1820s, where his son, Robert Dale Owen, was one of the community's members. Reprinted by permission of Rare Books and Manuscripts Division, Collection of the Astor, Lenox, and Tilden Foundations, New York Public Library.

ONEIDA COMMUNITY BEASTLINESS!

THE OBSCENE ORGIES AND PERNICIOUS TEACHINGS OF THE PATRIARCH NOYES AMONG THE NOVICES OF HIS SAINTLY SECT.

"Obscene Orgies and Pernicious Teachings," from the *National Police Gazette*, reprinted in Edward van Every's *Sins of America, as "Exposed" by The "Police Gazette"* (1900). This cartoon is an example of the fear and public protest generated by John Humphrey Noyes's opinions on "free love." Here, the Oneida community is caricatured as licentious and immoral.

ROBERT OWEN

On Individual Society vs. Cooperative Society

The educator, philanthropist, and reformer Robert Owen (1771–1858) was the wealthy owner of cotton-spinning mills in Manchester, England. He purchased the New Lanark mills in Scotland in 1799 and established a model cooperative community there that included a work force of two thousand. Profits increased, even as the workers' living conditions improved. As Owen explained in *A New View of Society* (1816), he believed that better environments made better, more productive persons. In 1821 he traveled to the United States and, with the aid of his son Robert Dale Owen (1801–1877), soon began a cooperative, agricultural-industrial community at New Harmony, Indiana. When New Harmony failed in the late 1820s because of debt, internal dissent, and external criticism of its unorthodox views on religion and private property, Owen returned to pursuing labor reform in England. His son became a journalist in New York and, later, an Indiana legislator and member of Congress.

This selection is from an address that Owen delivered to the New Harmony Community, May 28, 1826, and that was published on June 7, 1826 in the *New-Harmony Gazette.*

The principles and practices of individual society are totally different from those of cooperative society, and are, indeed, directly opposed to it.

Individual society is founded on an error regarding human nature, and is regulated by a mistaken view of self interest. Whether the parties are what is called successful or not, their expectations of happiness are necessarily disappointed; for happiness can not exist where an opposition of feeling and interest towards almost all with whom we have any intercourse, is experienced. The certain and necessary tendency of this state of things, is to produce a compound character throughout society, in which all the worst feelings of our nature are implanted; thus to inflict upon man almost all the suffering and misery we see, and to render it utterly impractible for any one to live in such a society, without being continually compelled to practise hypocrisy, with regard to his thoughts and feelings. Thus has the human race been prevented from attaining happiness in any age, in any country; and the same causes, as long as they shall be permitted to remain, will prevent us from enjoying the happiness which, when this hypocrisy shall be removed, will be discovered to belong to our nature. Thus it is, that ignorance produces the selfish system of competition and opposition; of hypocrisy and deception; and hypocrisy and deception produce every moral evil in society, and almost all the misery that the human race can suffer. So long as society is founded on these notions, those only who are irrational will expect to find even contentment among any of the human family.

Such are the principles on which the individual system is founded, and such as have been described must ever be the evil results of it in practice.

This social or cooperative system, on the contrary, is founded on a real knowledge of human nature, — which knowledge is to be obtained only by discarding all imaginary and contradictory notions on the subject, and by depending wholly on such facts regarding it, as experience has made universally known, and which are admitted by all.

By attending to these facts it will be discovered that our nature cannot enjoy any permanent satisfaction without sincerity — and that sincerity can exist only in a community in which the interest and feelings of all can be united on the broad principle of equality and common property. And again, equality and common property are necessary to produce the unity of interest and good feelings which can alone create and perpetuate the harmony of the community. For a community cannot exist without a community spirit. To produce this spirit — equality and common property are necessary; and these principles require that all the members of the community should be put, as speedily as local circumstances will admit, into the same condition; that they should be on an equality in regard to food, clothes, houses, furniture, and supplies of all kinds; and that all should have the best facilities for acquiring knowledge and becoming intelligent. Without intelligence the principles and the practices of the social system cannot be understood or acted upon. For, as ignorance, or which is precisely the same thing, the want of experience, is the real cause of superstition, of all bad feelings, and of almost all suffering, — so will real intelligence prove to be the source and the only sure foundation of all superior and permanent good feeling, of disinterested union, and of happiness. I therefore, after the most calm and deliberate consideration, conclude this part of what I deem it my duty to state to you, by recommending, in the strongest and most affectionate language I can use, that whatever you get, endeavor, by all the means in your power to get a real knowledge of your own nature.

FRANCES WRIGHT

From "Of Existing Evils, and Their Remedy"

The Scottish-born Frances Wright (1795–1852) was a reformer, agitator for women's rights, and abolitionist who, in December 1825, established a community in Nashoba, west Tennessee, for free blacks and slaves who would purchase their freedom through work. Like New Harmony, Nashoba was a failure, in part because of angry public protest against the "free love" ideas that Wright was said to be championing there. Wright nevertheless kept up and intensified her criticisms of slavery, her blasts against racial discrimination and inequality, and her attacks on religion and the institution of marriage. In this selection — an address delivered in Philadelphia, on June 2, 1829, and included in her *Course of Popular Lectures* (1834) — she contends that a new form of schooling is required to remedy the spread of social evils.

Before entering on the development of the means I have here suggested for paving our way to the reform of those evils which now press upon humanity, and which, carried, perhaps, to their acme in some of the nations of Europe, are gaining ground in these United States with a rapidity alarming to all who know how to read the present, or to calculate the future — I must observe, that I am fully aware of the difficulty of convincing all minds of the urgency of these evils, and of the impossibility of engaging all classes in the application of their remedy.

In the first place, the popular suffering, great as it is, weighs not with a sufficiently equal pressure on all parts of the country; and, in the second, affects not equally all classes of the population, so as to excite to that union of exertion, which once made, the reform is effected and the nation redeemed.

While the evil day is only in prospect, or while it visits our neighbour but spares ourselves, such is the selfishness generated by existing habits, and such the supineness generated by that selfishness, that we are but too prone to shrink from every effort not absolutely and immediately necessary for the supply of our own wants or the increase of our own luxuries. Yet, would the most spoiled child of worldly fortune but look around him on the changes and chances which ofttimes sweep away the best secured treasures, and bring in a moment the capitalist to bankruptcy, and his family to want, he could not feel himself entirely removed in sympathy from the suffering portion of his fellow creatures. But let us take the case of the thriving artizan,[1] or successful merchant — on what security does he hold that pecuniary independence which puts the bread into the mouths of his children, and protects from destitution the companion of his bosom? On sustained industry and unremitting exertions, which sickness may interrupt, a fall in the market reduce to half its value, or a few casualties or one miscalculation in a moment annihilate. Or what if death finally interrupt the father's care or the husband's tenderness — where is the stay for his orphan children? where succour for their widowed mother, now charged alone with all the weight of their provision? I have taken no extreme cases; I have taken such as may, in the course of events, be the case of every man who hears me.

Were it my disposition, which, I think, it is not, to exaggerate evils, or were I even disposed to give a fair picture of those really existing among a large mass of the American population, more especially as crowded into the cities and manufacturing districts, easy it were to harrow the feelings of the least sensitive, and, in the relation, to harrow my own.

But as the measure it is my object this evening to suggest to the people of Philadelphia, and my intention hereafter to submit to the whole American nation, must, at the first sight, win to its support the more oppressed and afflicted, I am rather desirous of addressing my prefatory arguments to that class from whence opposition is most to be apprehended.

I know how difficult it is — reared as we all are in the distinctions of class, to say nothing of sect, to conceive of our interests as associated with those of the whole community. The man possessed of a dollar, feels himself to be, not merely one hundred cents richer, but also one hundred cents *better*, than the man who is pennyless; so on through all the gradations of earthly possessions — the estimate of our own moral and political importance swelling always in a ratio exactly proportionate to the growth of our purse. The rich man who

---

[1]*artizan:* Artisan, someone skilled in a trade.

can leave a clear independence to his children, is given to estimate them as he estimates himself, and to imagine something in their nature distinct from that of the less privileged heirs of hard labour and harder fare.

This might indeed appear too gross for any of us to advance in theory, but in feeling how many must plead guilty to the prejudice! Yet is there a moment when, were their thoughts known to each other, all men must feel themselves on a level. It is when as fathers they look on their children, and picture the possibility which may render them orphans, and then calculate all the casualties which may deprive them, if rich, of their inheritance, or, if poor, grind them down to deeper poverty.

But it is first to the rich, I would speak. Can the man of opulence feel tranquil under the prospect of leaving to such guardianship as existing law or individual integrity may supply, the minds, bodies, morals, or even the fortune of their children? I myself was an orphan: and I know that the very law which was my protector, sucked away a portion of my little inheritance, while that law, insufficient and avaricious as it was, alone shielded me from spoliation by my guardian. I know, too, that my youth was one of tribulation, albeit passed in the envied luxuries of aristocracy. I know that the orphan's bread may be watered with tears, even when the worst evil be not there — *dependence.*

Can, then, the rich be without solicitude, when they leave to the mercy of a heartless world the beings of their creation? Who shall cherish their young sensibilities? Who shall stand between them and oppression? Who shall wisper peace in the hour of affliction? Who shall supply principle in the hour of temptation? Who shall lead the tender mind to distinguish between the good and the evil? Who shall fortify it against the corruptions of wealth, or prepare it for the day of adversity? Such, looking upon life as it is, must be the anxious thoughts even of the wealthy. What must be the thoughts of the poor man, it needs not that we should picture.

But, my friends, however differing in degree may be the anxiety of the rich and the poor, still, in its nature, is it the same. Doubt, uncertainty, apprehension, are before all. We hear of deathbed affliction. My friends, I have been often and long on the bed of mortal sickness: no fear had the threatened last sleep for me, for *I was not a parent.*

We have here, then, found an evil common to all classes, and one that is entailed from generation to generation. The measure I am about to suggest, whenever adopted, will blot this now universal affliction from existence; it will also, in the outset, alleviate those popular distresses whose poignancy and happy increase weigh on the heart of philanthropy, and crush the best hopes of enlightened patriotism. It must further, when carried into full effect, work the radical cure of every disease which now afflicts the body politic, and build up for this nation a sound constitution, embracing at once, public prosperity, individual integrity, and universal happiness.

This measure, my friends, has been long present to my mind, as befitting the adoption of the American people; as alone calculated to form an enlightened, a virtuous, and a happy community; as alone capable of supplying a remedy to the evils under which we groan; as alone commensurate with the interests of the human family, and consistent with the political institutions of this great confederated republic.

I had occasion formerly to observe, in allusion to the efforts already made, and yet making, in the cause of popular instruction, more or less throughout the Union, that, as yet, the true principle has not been hit, and that until it be hit all reform must be slow and inefficient.

The noble example of New-England has been imitated by other states, until all not possessed of common schools blush for the popular remissness. But, after all, how can *common schools*,[2] under their best form, and in fullest supply, effect even the purpose which they have in view?

The object proposed by common schools (if I rightly understand it) is to impart to the whole population those means for the acquirement of knowledge which are in common use: reading and writing. To these are added arithmetic, and occasionally, perhaps, some imperfect lessons in the simpler sciences. But I would ask, supposing these institutions should even be made to embrace all the branches of intellectual knowledge, and, thus, science offered gratis to all the children of the land, how are the children of the very class, for whom we suppose the schools instituted to be supplied with food and raiment, or instructed in the trade necessary to their future subsistence, while they are following these studies? How are they, I ask, to be fed and clothed, when, as all facts show, the labour of the parents is often insufficient for their own sustenance, and, almost universally, inadequate to the provision of the family without the united efforts of all its members? In your manufacturing districts you have children

[2]*common schools:* Free public schools.

worked for twelve hours a day; and in the rapid and certain progress of the existing system, you will soon have them, as in England, *worked to death,* and yet unable, through the period of their miserable existence, to earn a pittance sufficient to satisfy the cravings of hunger. At this present time, what leisure or what spirit, think you, have the children of the miserable widows of Philadelphia, realizing, according to the most favourable estimate of your city and county committee, sixteen dollars per annum, for food and clothing? what leisure or what spirit may their children find for visiting a school, although the same should be open to them from sunrise to sunset? Or what leisure have usually the children of your most thriving mechanics, after their strength is sufficiently developed to spin, sew, weave, or wield a tool? It seems to me, my friends, that to build school houses now-a-days is something like building churches. When you have them, you need some measure to ensure their being occupied.

But, as our time is short, and myself somewhat fatigued by continued exertions, I must hasten to the rapid development of the system of instruction and protection which has occurred to me as capable, and alone, capable, of opening the door to universal reform.

In lieu of all common schools, high schools, colleges, seminaries, houses of refuge, or any other juvenile institution, instructional or protective, I would suggest that the state legislatures be directed (after laying off the whole in townships or hundreds) to organize, at suitable distances, and in convenient and healthy situations, establishments for the general reception of all the children resident within the said school district. These establishments to be devoted, severally, to children between a certain age. Say, the first, infants between two and four, or two and six, according to the density of the population, and such other local circumstances as might render a greater or less number of establishments necessary or practicable. The next to receive children from four to eight, or six to twelve years. The next from twelve to sixteen, or to an older age if found desirable. Each establishment to be furnished with instructors in every branch of knowledge, intellectual and operative, with all the apparatus, land, and conveniences necessary for the best development of all knowledge; the same, whether operative or intellectual, being always calculated to the age and strength of the pupils.

To obviate, in the commencement, every evil result possible from the first mixture of a young population, so variously raised in error or neglect, a due separation should be made in each establishment; by which means those entering with bad habits would be kept apart from the others until corrected. How rapidly reform may be effected on the plastic disposition of childhood, has been sufficiently proved in your houses of refuge, more especially when such establishments have been under *liberal* superintendance, as was formerly the case in New-York. Under their orthodox directors, those asylums of youth have been converted into jails.

It will be understood that, in the proposed establishments, the children would pass from one to the other in regular succession, and that the parents who would necessarily be resident in their close neighbourhood, could visit the children at suitable hours, but, in no case, interfere with or interrupt the rules of the institution.

In the older establishments, the well directed and well protected labour of the pupil would, in time, suffice for, and, then exceed their own support; when the surplus might be devoted to the maintenance of the infant establishments.

In the beginning, and until all debt was cleared off, and so long as the same should be found favourable to the promotion of these best palladiums of a nation's happiness, a double tax might be at once expedient and politic.

First, a moderate tax per head for every child, to be laid upon its parents conjointly, or divided between them, due attention being always paid to the varying strength of the two sexes, and to the undue depreciation which now rests on female labour. The more effectually to correct the latter injustice, as well as to consult the convenience of the industrious classes generally, this parental tax might be rendered payable either in money, or in labour, produce, or domestic manufactures, and should be continued for each child until the age when juvenile labour should be found, on the average, equivalent to the educational expenses, which, I have reason to believe, would be at twelve years.

This first tax on parents to embrace equally the whole population; as, however moderate it would inculcate a certain forethought in all the human family; more especially where it is most wanted — in young persons, who before they assumed the responsibility of parents, would estimate their fitness to meet it.

The second tax to be on property, increasing in per centage with the wealth of the individual. In this manner I conceive the rich would contribute, according to their riches, to the relief of the poor, and to the support of the state, by raising up its best bulwark — an enlightened and united generation.

Preparatory to, or connected with, such measures, a registry should be opened by the state, with offices through all the townships, where on the birth of every child, or within a certain time appointed, the same should be entered, together with the names of its parents. When two years old, the parental tax should be payable, and the juvenile institution open for the child's reception; from which time forward it would be under the protective care and guardianship of the state, while it need never be removed from the daily, weekly, or frequent inspection of the parents.

Orphans, of course, would find here an open asylum. If possessed of property, a contribution would be paid for its revenue to the common educational fund; if unprovided, they would be sustained out of the same.

In these nurseries of a free nation, no inequality must be allowed to enter. Fed at a common board; clothed in a common garb, uniting neatness with simplicity and convenience; raised in the exercise of common duties, in the acquirement of the same knowledge and practice of the same industry, varied only according to individual taste and capabilities; in the exercise of the same virtues, in the enjoyment of the same pleasures; in the study of the same nature; in pursuit of the same object — their own and each other's happiness — say! would not such a race, when arrived at manhood and womanhood, work out the reform of society — perfect the free institutions of America.

JOHN HUMPHREY NOYES
AND THE ONEIDA COMMUNITY

On Marriage

John Humphrey Noyes (1811–1886) was a social and religious reformer who declared in the mid-1830s that he had achieved a state of religious perfectionism (that is, sinlessness). A powerful personality and adroit organizer, he started a community of "Bible Communists" in Putney, Vermont, in 1838, but soon he met a public outcry against his "free love" or "complex marriage" view that sexual activity outside the marital bond was permissible. In 1848, he established in New York State the Oneida community, a utopian enterprise that endured for several decades. (For a photograph of members of the Oneida community, see p. 346; for a cartoon depicting the community as depraved, see p. 349.)

Noyes's and his followers' reflections on, and principles for, utopian reform were presented in two books. The first, *The Berean* (1847), dealing with religious theory and published in Putney, drew from a dozen years of articles that had appeared in the community's periodicals. The second, *Bible Communism* (1848), set out Noyes's social theory and was published shortly after Noyes had relocated to Oneida.

The notions expressed here about the biblically sanctioned rightness of sexual activity outside marriage suggest why Noyes was assailed as immoral, licentious, and anarchical. (Fourier was condemned for sexual libertinism, too.) But they also show yet another version — if an extreme one — of the reformers' critique of institutions and the importance that they attached to new, more equal social and sexual roles.

Despite his radicalism on sexual matters, Noyes was opposed to women who threatened to compete with men or usurp male authority, and he frequently cited his endorsement of Saint Paul's words in the New Testament: "The head of every man is Christ; and the head of the woman is the man; and the head of Christ is God" (1 Corinthians 11:3; see also Ephesians 5: 22–23).

The authorship of *Bible Communism* is credited to the Oneida community. This excerpt from it is included in Noyes's *History of American Socialisms* (Philadelphia: Lippincott, 1870), 624–29.

Chapter II. — Showing that Marriage is not an institution of the Kingdom of Heaven, and must give place to Communism.

Proposition 5. — In the Kingdom of Heaven, the institution of marriage, which assigns the exclusive possession of one woman to one man, does not exist. Matt. 22: 23–30.

6. — In the Kingdom of Heaven the intimate union of life and interest, which in the world is limited to pairs, extends through the whole body of believers; i.e., complex marriage takes the place of simple. John 17: 21. Christ prayed that all believers might be one, even as he and the Father are one. His unity with the Father is defined in the words, "All mine are thine, and all thine are mine." Ver. 10. This perfect community of interests, then, will be the condition of all, when his prayer is answered. The universal unity of the members of Christ, is described in the same terms that are used to describe marriage unity. Compare 1 Cor. 12: 12–27, with Gen. 2: 24. See also 1 Cor. 6: 15–17, and Eph. 5: 30–32.

7. — The effects of the effusion of the Holy Spirit on the day of Pentecost, present a practical commentary on Christ's prayer for the unity of believers, and a sample of the tendency of heavenly influences, which fully confirm the foregoing proposition. "All that believed were together and had all things common; and sold their possessions and goods, and parted them to all, as every man had need." "The multitude of them that believed were of one heart and of one soul; neither said any of them that aught of the things which he possessed was his own; but they had all things common." Acts 2: 44, 45, and 4: 32. Here is unity like that of the Father and the Son: "All mine thine, and all thine mine."

8. — Admitting that the Community principle of the day of Pentecost, in its actual operation at that time, extended only to material goods, yet we affirm that there is no intrinsic difference between property in persons and property in things; and that the same spirit which abolished exclusiveness in regard to money, would abolish, if circumstances allowed full scope to it, exclusiveness in regard to women and children. Paul expressly places property in women and property in goods in the same category, and speaks of them together, as ready to be abolished by the advent of the Kingdom of Heaven. "The time," says he, "is short; it remaineth that they that have wives be as though they had none; and they that buy as though they possessed not; for the fashion of this world passeth away." 1 Cor. 7: 29–31.

9. — The abolishment of appropriation is involved in the very nature of a true relation to Christ in the gospel. This we prove thus: The possessive feeling which expresses itself by the possessive pronoun *mine*, is the same in essence when it relates to persons, as when it relates to money or any other property. Amativeness[1] and acquisitiveness are only different channels of one stream. They converge as we trace them to their source. Grammar will help us to ascertain their common center; for the possessive pronoun *mine*, is derived from the personal pronoun *I*; and so the possessive feeling, whether amative or acquisitive, flows from the personal feeling, that is, it is a branch of egotism. Now egotism is abolished by the gospel relation to Christ. The grand mystery of the gospel is vital union with Christ; the merging of self in his life; the extinguishment of the pronoun *I* at the spiritual center. Thus Paul says, "I live, yet not I, but Christ liveth in me." The grand distinction between the Christian and the unbeliever, be-

---

[1] *Amativeness:* Inclination to love.

tween heaven and the world, is, that in one reigns the We-spirit, and in the other the I-spirit. From *I* comes *mine*, and from the I-spirit comes exclusive appropriation of money, women, etc. From *we* comes *ours*, and from the We-spirit comes universal community of interests.

10. — The abolishment of exclusiveness is involved in the love-relation required between all believers by the express injunction of Christ and the apostles, and by the whole tenor of the New Testament. "The new commandment is, that we love one another," and that, not by pairs, as in the world, but *en masse*. We are required to love one another fervently. The fashion of the world forbids a man and woman who are otherwise appropriated, to love one another fervently. But if they obey Christ they must do this; and whoever would allow them to do this, and yet would forbid them (on any other ground than that of present expediency), to express their unity, would "strain at a gnat and swallow a camel"; for unity of hearts is as much more important than any external expression of it, as a camel is larger than a gnat.

11. — The abolishment of social restrictions is involved in the anti-legality of the gospel. It is incompatible with the state of perfected freedom toward which Paul's gospel of "grace without law" leads, that man should be allowed and required to love in all directions, and yet be forbidden to express love except in one direction. In fact Paul says, with direct reference to sexual intercourse — "All things are lawful for me, but all things are not expedient; all things are lawful for me, but I will not be brought under the power of any"; (1 Cor. 6: 12;) thus placing the restrictions which were necessary in the transition period on the basis, not of law, but of expediency and the demands of spiritual freedom, and leaving it fairly to be inferred that in the final state, when hostile surroundings and powers of bondage cease, all restrictions also will cease.

12. — The abolishment of the marriage system is involved in Paul's doctrine of the end of ordinances. Marriage is one of the "ordinances of the worldly sanctuary." This is proved by the fact that it has no place in the resurrection. Paul expressly limits it to life in the flesh. Rom. 7: 2, 3. The assumption, therefore, that believers are dead to the world by the death of Christ (which authorized the abolishment of Jewish ordinances), legitimately makes an end of marriage. Col. 2: 20.

13. — The law of marriage is the same in kind with the Jewish law concerning meats and drinks and holy days, of which Paul said that

they were "contrary to us, and were taken out of the way, being nailed to the cross." Col. 2: 14. The plea in favor of the worldly social system, that it is not arbitrary, but founded in nature, will not bear investigation. All experience testifies (the theory of the novels to the contrary notwithstanding), that sexual love is not naturally restricted to pairs. Second marriages are contrary to the one-love theory, and yet are often the happiest marriages. Men and women find universally (however the fact may be concealed), that their susceptibility to love is not burnt out by one honey-moon, or satisfied by one lover. On the contrary, the secret history of the human heart will bear out the assertion that it is capable of loving any number of times and any number of persons, and that the more it loves the more it can love. This is the law of nature, thrust out of sight and condemned by common consent, and yet secretly known to all.

14. — The law of marriage "worketh wrath." 1. It provokes to secret adultery, actual or of the heart. 2. It ties together unmatched natures. 3. It sunders matched natures. 4. It gives to sexual appetite only a scanty and monotonous allowance, and so produces the natural vices of poverty, contraction of taste and stinginess or jealousy. 5. It makes no provision for the sexual appetite at the very time when that appetite is the strongest. By the custom of the world, marriage, in the average of cases, takes place at about the age of twenty-four; whereas puberty commences at the age of fourteen. For ten years, therefore, and that in the very flush of life, the sexual appetite is starved. This law of society bears hardest on females, because they have less opportunity of choosing their time of marriage than men. This discrepancy between the marriage system and nature, is one of the principal sources of the peculiar diseases of women, of prostitution, masturbation, and licentiousness in general.

AMOS BRONSON ALCOTT
AND CHARLES LANE

On the Community at Fruitlands

Fruitlands, situated on one hundred acres in Harvard, Massachusetts, is related to Brook Farm in that its founders saw it as an improvement on the venture that George Ripley had begun two years earlier. It was launched by the educational reformer and transcendentalist Amos Bronson Alcott (1799–1888) and his English friend Charles Lane on June 1, 1843. Both were visitors to Brook Farm — Alcott had even been invited to become one of its original members. But both had concluded that Brook Farm was not abstemious and stringent enough (e.g., it allowed dairy products) and was too carefree and frivolous.

Fruitlands' residents, numbering about a dozen, included persons who had joined Brook Farm but had left disenchanted and were searching for something better. It quickly proved a disaster, lasting only until the end of the year, when debts, ruined crops, and sickness forced its dissolution. In December, Alcott and Lane considered moving to Brook Farm but rejected this idea for the same reasons they had turned away from Brook Farm and toward Fruitlands in the first place.

Alcott and Lane stated their goals in the letter excerpted here, which was published in the journal *Herald of Freedom*, September 8, 1843.

Our removal to this estate in humble confidence has drawn to us several practical coadjutors, and opened many inquiries by letter for a statement of our principles and modes of life. We cannot perhaps turn our replies to better account than to transcribe some portions of them for your information, and, we trust, for your sincere satisfaction.

. . . We have not yet drawn out any preordained plan of daily operations, as we are impressed with the conviction that by a faithful reliance on the spirit which actuates us, we are sure of attaining to clear revelations of daily practical duties as they are to be daily done by us. Where the Spirit of Love and Wisdom abounds, literal forms are needless, irksome or hinderative; where the Spirit is lacking, no preconceived rules can compensate. . . .

Hence our perseverance in efforts to attain simplicity in diet, plain garments, pure bathing, unsullied dwellings, open conduct, gentle behavior, kindly sympathies, serene minds. These, and the several other particulars needful to the true end of man's residence on earth, may be designated the Family Life. . . .

Trade we hope entirely to avoid at an early day. As a nursery for many evil propensities it is almost universally felt to be a most undesirable course. Such needful articles as we cannot yet raise by our own hand labor from the soil, thus redeemed from human ownership, we shall endeavor to obtain by friendly exchanges, and, as nearly as possible, without the intervention of money.

Of all the traffic in which civilized society is involved, that of human labor is perhaps the most detrimental. From the state of serfdom to the receipt of wages may be a step in human progress; but it is certainly full time for taking a new step out of the hiring system.

Our outward exertions are in the first instance directed to the soil, and as our ultimate aim is to furnish an instance of self-sustaining cultivation without the subjugation of either men or cattle, or the use of foul animal manures, we have at the outset to encounter struggles and oppositions somewhat formidable. Until the land is restored to its pristine fertility by the annual return of its own green crops, as sweet and animating manures, the human hand and simple implement cannot wholly supersede the employment of machinery and cattle. — So long as cattle are used in agriculture, it is very evident that man will remain a slave, whether he be proprietor or hireling. The driving of cattle beyond their natural and pleasurable exertion; the waiting upon them as cook and chambermaid three parts of the year; the excessive labor of mowing, curing, and housing hay, and of collecting other fodder, and the large extra quantity of land needful to keep up this system, forms a combination of unfavorable circumstances which must depress the humane affections, so long as it continues, and overlay them by the injurious and extravagant development of the animal and bestial natures in man. It is calculated that if no animal food were consumed, one-fourth of the land now used would suffice for human sustenance. And the extensive tracts of country now appropriated to grazing, mowing, and other modes of animal provision, could be cultivated by and for intelligent and affectionate human neighbors. The sty and the stable too often secure more of the farmer's regard than he bestows on the garden and the children. No hope is there for humanity while woman is withdrawn from the tender assiduities which adorn her and her household, to the servitudes of the dairy and the flesh pots. If the beasts were wholly absent from man's neighborhood, the human population might be at least four times as dense as it now is without raising the price of land. This would give to the country all the advantages of concentration without the vices which always spring up in the dense city.

Debauchery of both the earthly soil and the human body is the result of this cattle keeping. The land is scourged for crops to feed the animals, whose filthy ordures are used under the erroneous supposition of restoring lost fertility; disease is thus infused into the human body; stimulants and medicines are resorted to for relief, which end in a precipitation of the original evil to a more disastrous depth. These misfortunes which affect not only the body, but by reaction rise to the sphere of the soul, would be avoided, at least in part, by the disuse of animal food. Our diet is therefore strictly of the pure and bloodless kind. No animal substances, neither flesh, butter, cheese, eggs nor milk, pollute our tables or corrupt our bodies, neither tea, coffee, molasses, nor rice, tempts us beyond the bounds of indigenous productions. Our sole beverage is pure fountain water. The native grains, fruits, herbs and roots, dressed with the utmost cleanliness, and regard to their purpose of edifying a healthful body, furnish the pleasantest refections and in the greatest variety requisite to the supply of the various organs. The field, the orchard, the garden, in their bounteous products of wheat, rye, barley, maize, oats, buckwheat; apples, pears, peaches, plums, cherries, currants, berries; potatoes, peas, beans, beets, carrots, melons, and other vines, yield an ample store for human nutrition, without dependence on foreign climes, or the degradations of shipping and trade. The almost inexhaustible variety which the several stages and sorts of vegetable growth, and the several modes of preparation afford, are a full answer to the question which is often put by those who have never ventured into the region of a pure and chaste diet: "If you give up flesh meat, upon what then can you live?"

Our other domestic habits are in harmony with those of diet. We rise with early dawn, begin the day with cold bathing, succeeded by a music lesson, and then a chaste repast. Each one finds occupation until the meridian meal, when usually some interesting and deep-searching conversation gives rest to the body and development to the mind. Occupation, according to the season and the weather, engages us out of doors or within, until the evening meal, — when we again assemble in social communion, prolonged generally until sunset, when we resort to sweet repose for the next day's activity.

In these steps of reform we do not rely as much on scientific reasoning or physiological skill, as on the Spirit's dictates. The pure soul, by the law in its own nature, adopts a pure diet and cleanly customs; nor needs detailed instruction for daily conduct. On a revision of our proceedings it would seem, that if we were in the right course in our particular instance, the greater part of man's duty consists in leaving alone much that he is in the habit of doing. It is a fasting from the present activity, rather than an increased indulgence in it, which, with patient watchfulness, tends to newness of life.

Shall I sip tea or coffee? the inquiry may be. No. Abstain from *all* ardent, as from alcoholic drinks. Shall I consume pork, beef, or mutton? Not if you value health or life. Shall I stimulate with milk? No. Shall I warm my bathing water? Not if cheerfulness is valuable. Shall I clothe in many garments? Not if purity is aimed at. Shall I prolong my dark hours, consuming animal oil and losing bright daylight in the morning? Not if a clear mind is an object. Shall I teach my children the dogmas inflicted on myself, under the pretense that I am transmitting truth? Nay, if you love them intrude not these between them and the Spirit of all Truth. Shall I subjugate cattle? Shall I trade? Shall I claim property in any created thing? Shall I interest myself in politics? To how many of these questions, could we ask them deeply enough, could they be heard as having relation to our eternal welfare, would the response be "Abstain"? Be not so active to do, as sincere to *be*. Being in preference to doing, is the great aim, and this comes to us rather by a resigned willingness than a wilful activity; which is indeed a check to all divine growth. Outward abstinence is a sign of inward fulness; and the only source of true progress is inward. We may occupy ourselves actively in human improvements; — but these unless inwardly well-impelled, never attain to, but rather hinder, divine progress in man. During the utterance of this narrative it has undergone some change in its personal expression which might offend the hypercritical; but we feel assured that you will kindly accept it as the unartful offering of both your friends in ceaseless aspiration.

LOUISA MAY ALCOTT

"Transcendental Wild Oats"

Louisa May Alcott (1832–1888), best known for the novel *Little Women* (1868), was eleven when she lived at Fruitlands with her family. In this satire on her father's scheme, she portrays Amos Bronson Alcott and his wife, Abigail May, as Abel Lamb and Sister Hope; Timon Lion is Charles Lane. Her story was published in *The Independent* on December 18, 1873, and then was reprinted in *Silver Pitchers; and Independence, A Centennial Love Story* (Boston: Roberts Brothers, 1876). Alcott subtitled her story "A Chapter from an Unwritten Romance," which perhaps plays on the title of Hawthorne's novel about Brook Farm.

On the first day of June, 184–, a large wagon, drawn by a small horse and containing a motley load, went lumbering over certain New England hills, with the pleasing accompaniments of wind, rain, and hail. A serene man with a serene child upon his knee was driving, or rather being driven, for the small horse had it all his own way. A brown boy with a William Penn[1] style of countenance sat beside him, firmly embracing a bust of Socrates.[2] Behind them was an energetic-looking woman, with a benevolent brow, satirical mouth, and eyes brimful of hope and courage. A baby reposed upon her lap, a mirror leaned against her knee, and a basket of provisions danced about at her feet, as she struggled with a large, unruly umbrella. Two blue-eyed little girls, with hands full of childish treasures, sat under one old shawl, chatting happily together.

In front of this lively party stalked a tall, sharp-featured man, in a long blue cloak; and a fourth small girl trudged alone beside him through the mud as if she rather enjoyed it.

The wind whistled over the bleak hills; the rain fell in a despondent drizzle, and twilight began to fall. But the calm man gazed as tranquilly into the fog as if he beheld a radiant bow of promise spanning the gray sky. The cheery woman tried to cover every one but herself with the big umbrella. The brown boy pillowed his head on the bald pate of Socrates and slumbered peacefully. The little girls sang lullabies to their dolls in soft, maternal murmurs. The sharp-nosed pedestrian marched steadily on, with the blue cloak streaming out behind him like a banner; and the lively infant splashed through the puddles with a duck-like satisfaction pleasant to behold.

Thus these modern pilgrims journeyed hopefully out of the old world, to found a new one in the wilderness.

The editors of *The Transcendental Tripod* had received from Messrs. Lion & Lamb (two of the aforesaid pilgrims) a communication from which the following statement is an extract: —

"We have made arrangements with the proprietor of an estate of about a hundred acres which liberates this tract from human ownership.[3] Here we shall prosecute our effort to initiate a Family in harmony with the primitive instincts of man.

---

[1] *William Penn:* Penn (1644–1718) was a Quaker statesman and founder of Pennsylvania.

[2] *Socrates:* Greek philosopher (469–399 B.C.).

[3] "*We have made arrangements . . . .*": Here Alcott closely follows a letter about the founding of Fruitlands that her father and his friend Charles Lane published in *The Dial* in July 1843.

"Ordinary secular farming is not our object. Fruit, grain, pulse, herbs, flax, and other vegetable products, receiving assiduous attention, will afford ample manual occupation, and chaste supplies for the bodily needs. It is intended to adorn the pastures with orchards, and to supersede the labor of cattle by the spade and the pruning-knife.

"Consecrated to human freedom, the land awaits the sober culture of devoted men. Beginning with small pecuniary means, this enterprise must be rooted in a reliance on the succors of an ever-bounteous Providence, whose vital affinities being secured by this union with uncorrupted field and unworldly persons, the cares and injuries of a life of gain are avoided.

"The inner nature of each member of the Family is at no time neglected. Our plan contemplates all such disciplines, cultures, and habits as evidently conduce to the purifying of the inmates.

"Pledged to the spirit alone, the founders anticipate no hasty or numerous addition to their numbers. The kingdom of peace is entered only through the gates of self-denial; and felicity is the test and the reward of loyalty to the unswerving law of Love."

This prospective Eden at present consisted of an old red farmhouse, a dilapidated barn, many acres of meadow-land, and a grove. Ten ancient apple-trees were all the "chaste supply" which the place offered as yet; but, in the firm belief that plenteous orchards were soon to be evoked from their inner consciousness, these sanguine founders had christened their domain Fruitlands.

Here Timon Lion intended to found a colony of Latter Day Saints,[4] who, under his patriarchal sway, should regenerate the world and glorify his name for ever. Here Abel Lamb, with the devoutest faith in the high ideal which was to him a living truth, desired to plant a Paradise, where Beauty, Virtue, Justice, and Love might live happily together, without the possibility of a serpent entering in. And here his wife, unconverted but faithful to the end, hoped, after many wanderings over the face of the earth, to find rest for herself and a home for her children.

"There is our new abode," announced the enthusiast, smiling with a satisfaction quite undamped by the drops dripping from his hat-brim, as they turned at length into a cart-path that wound along a steep hillside into a barren-looking valley.

---

[4]*Latter Day Saints:* The Mormon religious movement was organized by Joseph Smith (1805–1844) as the Church of Jesus Christ of Latter-Day Saints in 1830 in Fayette, New York.

"A little difficult of access," observed his practical wife, as she endeavored to keep her various household gods from going overboard with every lurch of the laden ark.

"Like all good things. But those who earnestly desire and patiently seek will soon find us," placidly responded the philosopher from the mud, through which he was now endeavoring to pilot the much-enduring horse.

"Truth lies at the bottom of a well, Sister Hope," said Brother Timon, pausing to detach his small comrade from a gate, whereon she was perched for a clearer gaze into futurity.

"That's the reason we so seldom get at it, I suppose," replied Mrs. Hope, making a vain clutch at the mirror, which a sudden jolt sent flying out of her hands.

"We want no false reflections here," said Timon, with a grim smile, as he crunched the fragments under foot in his onward march.

Sister Hope held her peace, and looked wistfully through the mist at her promised home. The old red house with a hospitable glimmer at its windows cheered her eyes; and, considering the weather, was a fitter refuge than the sylvan bowers some of the more ardent souls might have preferred.

The new-comers were welcomed by one of the elect precious, — a regenerate farmer, whose idea of reform consisted chiefly in wearing white cotton raiment and shoes of untanned leather. This costume, with a snowy beard, gave him a venerable, and at the same time a somewhat bridal appearance.

The goods and chattels of the Society not having arrived, the weary family reposed before the fire on blocks of wood, while Brother Moses White regaled them with roasted potatoes, brown bread and water, in two plates, a tin pan, and one mug; his table service being limited. But, having cast the forms and vanities of a depraved world behind them, the elders welcomed hardship with the enthusiasm of new pioneers, and the children heartily enjoyed this foretaste of what they believed was to be a sort of perpetual picnic.

During the progress of this frugal meal, two more brothers appeared. One was a dark, melancholy man, clad in homespun, whose peculiar mission was to turn his name hind part before and use as few words as possible. The other was a bland, bearded Englishman, who expected to be saved by eating uncooked food and going without clothes. He had not yet adopted the primitive costume, however; but contented himself with meditatively chewing dry beans out of a basket.

"Every meal should be a sacrament, and the vessels used should be

beautiful and symbolical," observed Brother Lamb, mildly, righting
the tin pan slipping about on his knees. "I priced a silver service when
in town, but it was too costly; so I got some graceful cups and vases
of Britannia ware."

"Hardest things in the world to keep bright. Will whiting be allowed in the community?" inquired Sister Hope, with a housewife's
interest in labor-saving institutions.

"Such trivial questions will be discussed at a more fitting time,"
answered Brother Timon, sharply, as he burnt his fingers with a very
hot potato. "Neither sugar, molasses, milk, butter, cheese, nor flesh
are to be used among us, for nothing is to be admitted which has
caused wrong or death to man or beast."

"Our garments are to be linen till we learn to raise our own cotton
or some substitute for woolen fabrics," added Brother Abel, blissfully
basking in an imaginary future as warm and brilliant as the generous
fire before him.

"Haou abaout shoes?" asked Brother Moses, surveying his own
with interest.

"We must yield that point till we can manufacture an innocent
substitute for leather. Bark, wood, or some durable fabric will be invented in time. Meanwhile, those who desire to carry out our idea to
the fullest extent can go barefooted," said Lion, who liked extreme
measures.

"I never will, nor let my girls," murmured rebellious Sister Hope,
under her breath.

"Haou do you cattle'ate to treat the ten-acre lot? Ef things ain't
'tended to right smart, we shan't hev no crops," observed the practical patriarch in cotton.

"We shall spade it," replied Abel, in such perfect good faith that
Moses said no more, though he indulged in a shake of the head as he
glanced at hands that had held nothing heavier than a pen for years.
He was a paternal old soul and regarded the younger men as promising boys on a new sort of lark.

"What shall we do for lamps, if we cannot use any animal substance? I do hope light of some sort is to be thrown upon the enterprise," said Mrs. Lamb, with anxiety, for in those days kerosene and
camphene were not, and gas unknown in the wilderness.

"We shall go without till we have discovered some vegetable oil or
wax to serve us," replied Brother Timon, in a decided tone, which
caused Sister Hope to resolve that her private lamp should be always
trimmed, if not burning.

"Each member is to perform the work for which experience, strength, and taste best fit him," continued Dictator Lion. "Thus drudgery and disorder will be avoided and harmony prevail. We shall rise at dawn, begin the day by bathing, followed by music, and then a chaste repast of fruit and bread. Each one finds congenial occupation till the meridian meal; when some deep-searching conversation gives rest to the body and development to the mind. Healthful labor again engages us till the last meal, when we assemble in social communion, prolonged till sunset, when we retire to sweet repose, ready for the next day's activity."

"What part of the work do you incline to yourself?" asked Sister Hope, with a humorous glimmer in her keen eyes.

"I shall wait till it is made clear to me. Being in preference to doing is the great aim, and this comes to us rather by a resigned willingness than a wilful activity, which is a check to all divine growth," responded Brother Timon.

"I thought so." And Mrs. Lamb sighed audibly, for during the year he had spent in her family Brother Timon had so faithfully carried out his idea of "being, not doing," that she had found his "divine growth" both an expensive and unsatisfactory process.

Here her husband struck into the conversation, his face shining with the light and joy of the splendid dreams and high ideals hovering before him.

"In these steps of reform, we do not rely so much on scientific reasoning or physiological skill as, on the spirit's dictates. The greater part of man's duty consists in leaving alone much that he now does. Shall I stimulate with tea, coffee, or wine? No. Shall I consume flesh? Not if I value health. Shall I subjugate cattle? Shall I claim property in any created thing? Shall I trade? Shall I adopt a form of religion? Shall I interest myself in politics? To how many of these questions — could we ask them deeply enough and could they be heard as having relation to our eternal welfare — would the response be 'Abstain'?"

A mild snore seemed to echo the last word of Abel's rhapsody, for Brother Moses had succumbed to mundane slumber and sat nodding like a massive ghost. Forest Absalom, the silent man, and John Pease, the English member, now departed to the barn; and Mrs. Lamb led her flock to a temporary fold, leaving the founders of the "Consociate Family" to build castles in the air till the fire went out and the symposium ended in smoke.

The furniture arrived next day, and was soon bestowed; for the principal property of the community consisted in books. To this rare

library was devoted the best room in the house, and the few busts
and pictures that still survived many flittings were added to beautify
the sanctuary, for here the family was to meet for amusement, instruction, and worship.

Any housewife can imagine the emotions of Sister Hope, when she
took possession of a large, dilapidated kitchen, containing an old
stove and the peculiar stores out of which food was to be evolved for
her little family of eleven. Cakes of maple sugar, dried peas and
beans, barley and hominy, meal of all sorts, potatoes, and dried fruit.
No milk, butter, cheese, tea, or meat appeared. Even salt was considered a useless luxury and spice entirely forbidden by these lovers of
Spartan simplicity. A ten years' experience of vegetarian vagaries had
been good training for this new freak, and her sense of the ludicrous
supported her through many trying scenes.

Unleavened bread, porridge, and water for breakfast; bread, vegetables, and water for dinner; bread, fruit, and water for supper was
the bill of fare ordained by the elders. No teapot profaned that sacred
stove, no gory steak cried aloud for vengeance from her chaste gridiron; and only a brave woman's taste, time, and temper were sacrificed on that domestic altar.

The vexed question of light was settled by buying a quantity of
bayberry wax for candles; and, on discovering that no one knew how
to make them, pine knots were introduced, to be used when absolutely necessary. Being summer, the evenings were not long, and
the weary fraternity found it no great hardship to retire with the
birds. The inner light was sufficient for most of them. But Mrs. Lamb
rebelled. Evening was the only time she had to herself, and while the
tired feet rested the skilful hands mended torn frocks and little stockings, or anxious heart forgot its burden in a book.

So "mother's lamp" burned steadily, while the philosophers built a
new heaven and earth by moonlight; and through all the metaphysi-
cal mists and philanthropic pyrotechnics of that period Sister Hope
played her own little game of "throwing light," and none but the
moths were the worse for it.

Such farming probably was never seen before since Adam delved.
The band of brothers began by spading garden and field; but a few
days of it lessened their ardor amazingly. Blistered hands and aching
backs suggested the expediency of permitting the use of cattle till the
workers were better fitted for noble toil by a summer of the new life.

Brother Moses brought a yoke of oxen from his farm, — at least,
the philosophers thought so till it was discovered that one of the ani-

mals was a cow; and Moses confessed that he "must be let down easy, for he couldn't live on garden sarse entirely."

Great was Dictator Lion's indignation at this lapse from virtue. But time pressed, the work must be done; so the meek cow was permitted to wear the yoke and the recreant brother continued to enjoy forbidden draughts in the barn, which dark proceeding caused the children to regard him as one set apart for destruction.

The sowing was equally peculiar, for, owing to some mistake, the three brethren, who devoted themselves to this graceful task, found when about half through the job that each had been sowing a different sort of grain in the same field; a mistake which caused much perplexity, as it could not be remedied; but, after a long consultation and a good deal of laughter, it was decided to say nothing and see what would come of it.

The garden was planted with a generous supply of useful roots and herbs; but, as manure was not allowed to profane the virgin soil, few of these vegetable treasures ever came up. Purslane[5] reigned supreme, and the disappointed planters ate it philosophically, deciding that Nature knew what was best for them, and would generously supply their needs, if they could only learn to digest her "sallets" and wild roots.

The orchard was laid out, a little grafting done, new trees and vines set, regardless of the unfit season and entire ignorance of the husbandmen, who honestly believed that in the autumn they would reap a bounteous harvest.

Slowly things got into order, and rapidly rumors of the new experiment went abroad, causing many strange spirits to flock thither, for in those days communities were the fashion and transcendentalism raged wildly. Some came to look on and laugh, some to be supported in poetic idleness, a few to believe sincerely and work heartily. Each member was allowed to mount his favorite hobby and ride it to his heart's content. Very queer were some of the riders, and very rampant some of the hobbies.

One youth, believing that language was of little consequence if the spirit was only right, startled new-comers by blandly greeting them with "Good-morning, damn you," and other remarks of an equally mixed order. A second irrepressible being held that all the emotions of the soul should be freely expressed, and illustrated his theory by

---

[5]*Purslane:* An annual weed; sometimes used in salads.

antics that would have sent him to a lunatic asylum, if, as an unregenerate wag said, he had not already been in one. When his spirit soared, he climbed trees and shouted; when doubt assailed him, he lay upon the floor and groaned lamentably. At joyful periods, he raced, leaped, and sang; when sad, he wept aloud; and when a great thought burst upon him in the watches of the night, he crowed like a jocund cockerel, to the great delight of the children and the great annoyance of the elders. One musical brother fiddled whenever so moved, sang sentimentally to the four little girls, and put a music-box on the wall when he hoed corn.

Brother Pease ground away at his uncooked food, or browsed over the farm on sorrel, mint, green fruit, and new vegetables. Occasionally he took his walks abroad, airily attired in an unbleached cotton *poncho*, which was the nearest approach to the primeval costume he was allowed to indulge in. At midsummer he retired to the wilderness, to try his plan where the woodchucks were without prejudices and huckleberry-bushes were hospitably full. A sunstroke unfortunately spoilt his plan, and he returned to semi-civilization a sadder and wiser man.

Forest Absalom preserved his Pythagorean silence,[6] cultivated his fine dark locks, and worked like a beaver, setting an excellent example of brotherly love, justice, and fidelity by his upright life. He it was who helped overworked Sister Hope with her heavy washes, kneaded the endless succession of batches of bread, watched over the children, and did the many tasks left undone by the brethren, who were so busy discussing and defining great duties that they forgot to perform the small ones.

Moses White placidly plodded about, "chorin' raound," as he called it, looking like an old-time patriarch, with his silver hair and flowing beard, and saving the community from many a mishap by his thrift and Yankee shrewdness.

Brother Lion domineered over the whole concern; for, having put the most money into the speculation, he was resolved to make it pay, — as if anything founded on an ideal basis could be expected to do so by any but enthusiasts.

Abel Lamb simply revelled in the Newness, firmly believing that his dream was to be beautifully realized and in time not only little

---

[6]*Pythagorean silence:* Pythagoras was a sixth-century B.C. Greek philosopher and mathematician and founder of a secret religious order or society that stressed purification, moral asceticism, and the doctrine of the transmigration of souls.

Fruitlands, but the whole earth, be turned into a Happy Valley.[7] He worked with every muscle of his body, for *he* was in deadly earnest. He taught with his whole head and heart; planned and sacrificed, preached and prophesied, with a soul full of the purest aspirations, most unselfish purposes, and desires for a life devoted to God and man, too high and tender to bear the rough usage of this world.

It was a little remarkable that only one woman ever joined this community. Mrs. Lamb merely followed wheresoever her husband led, — "as ballast for his balloon," as she said, in her bright way.

Miss Jane Gage was a stout lady of mature years, sentimental, amiable, and lazy. She wrote verses copiously, and had vague yearnings and graspings after the unknown, which led her to believe herself fitted for a higher sphere than any she had yet adorned.

Having been a teacher, she was set to instructing the children in the common branches. Each adult member took a turn at the infants; and, as each taught in his own way, the result was a chronic state of chaos in the minds of these much-afflicted innocents.

Sleep, food, and poetic musings were the desires of dear Jane's life, and she shirked all duties as clogs upon her spirit's wings. Any thought of lending a hand with the domestic drudgery never occurred to her; and when to the question, "Are there any beasts of burden on the place?" Mrs. Lamb answered, with a face that told its own tale, "Only one woman!" the buxom Jane took no shame to herself, but laughed at the joke, and let the stout-hearted sister tug on alone.

Unfortunately, the poor lady hankered after the flesh-pots, and endeavored to stay herself with private sips of milk, crackers, and cheese, and on one dire occasion she partook of fish at a neighbor's table.

One of the children reported this sad lapse from virtue, and poor Jane was publicly reprimanded by Timon.

"I only took a little bit of the tail," sobbed the penitent poetess.

"Yes, but the whole fish had to be tortured and slain that you might tempt your carnal appetite with that one taste of the tail. Know ye not, consumers of flesh meat, that ye are nourishing the wolf and tiger in your bosoms?"

At this awful question and the peal of laughter which arose from some of the younger brethren, tickled by the ludicrous contrast be-

---

[7]*Happy Valley:* In *Rasselas* (1759), a philosophical romance by Samuel Johnson (1709–1784), the protagonist dwells in the "happy valley." Note the playful allusion to Hawthorne's "blithe/dale."

tween the stout sinner, the stern judge, and the naughty satisfaction of the young detective, poor Jane fled from the room to pack her trunk and return to the world where fishes' tails were not forbidden fruit.

Transcendental wild oats were sown broadcast that year, and the fame thereof has not yet ceased in the land; for, futile as this crop seemed to outsiders, it bore an invisible harvest, worth much to those who planted in earnest. As none of the members of this particular community have ever recounted their experiences before, a few of them may not be amiss, since the interest in these attempts has never died out and Fruitlands was the most ideal of all these castles in Spain.[8]

A new dress was invented, since cotton, silk, and wool were forbidden as the product of slave-labor, worm-slaughter, and sheep-robbery. Tunics and trousers of brown linen were the only wear. The women's skirts were longer, and their straw hat-brims wider than the men's, and this was the only difference. Some persecution lent a charm to the costume, and the long-haired, linen-clad reformers quite enjoyed the mild martyrdom they endured when they left home.

Money was abjured, as the root of all evil. The produce of the land was to supply most of their wants, or be exchanged for the few things they could not grow. This idea had its inconveniences; but self-denial was the fashion, and it was surprising how many things one can do without. When they desired to travel, they walked, if possible, begged the loan of a vehicle, or boldly entered car or coach, and, stating their principles to the officials, took the consequences. Usually their dress, their earnest frankness, and gentle resolution won them a passage; but now and then they met with hard usage, and had the satisfaction of suffering for their principles.

On one of these penniless pilgrimages they took passage on a boat, and, when fare was demanded, artlessly offered to talk, instead of pay. As the boat was well under way and they actually had not a cent, there was no help for it. So Brothers Lion and Lamb held forth to the assembled passengers in their most eloquent style. There must have been something effective in this conversation, for the listeners were moved to take up a contribution for these inspired lunatics, who preached peace on earth and good-will to man so earnestly, with empty pockets. A goodly sum was collected; but when the captain

---

[8]*castles in Spain:* Castles in the air; castles in fairy tales like the one built for Aladdin by the Genie of the Lamp that appear and then vanish.

presented it the reformers proved that they were consistent even in their madness, for not a penny would they accept, saying, with a look at the group about them, whose indifference or contempt had changed to interest and respect, "You see how well we get on without money"; and so went serenely on their way, with their linen blouses flapping airily in the cold October wind.

They preached vegetarianism everywhere and resisted all temptations of the flesh, contentedly eating apples and bread at well-spread tables, and much afflicting hospitable hostesses by denouncing their food and taking away their appetites, discussing the "horrors of shambles," the "incorporation of the brute in man," and "on elegant abstinence the sign of a pure soul." But, when the perplexed or offended ladies asked what they should eat, they got in reply a bill of fare consisting of "bowls of sunrise for breakfast," "solar seeds of the sphere," "dishes from Plutarch's chaste table,"[9] and other viands equally hard to find in any modern market.

Reform conventions of all sorts were haunted by these brethren, who said many wise things and did many foolish ones. Unfortunately, these wanderings interfered with their harvest at home; but the rule was to do what the spirit moved, so they left their crops to Providence and went a-reaping in wider and, let us hope, more fruitful fields than their own.

Luckily, the earthly providence who watched over Abel Lamb was at hand to glean the scanty crop yielded by the "uncorrupted land," which, "consecrated to human freedom," had received "the sober culture of devout men."

About the time the grain was ready to house, some call of the Oversoul[10] wafted all the men away. An easterly storm was coming up and the yellow stacks were sure to be ruined. Then Sister Hope gathered her forces. Three little girls, one boy (Timon's son), and herself, harnessed to clothes-baskets and Russia-linen sheets, were the only teams she could command; but with these poor appliances the indomitable woman got in the grain and saved food for her young, with the instinct and energy of a mother-bird with a brood of hungry nestlings to feed.

This attempt at regeneration had its tragic as well as comic side, though the world only saw the former.

[9]*Plutarch's chaste table:* Plutarch was a Roman historian, biographer, and philosopher (ca. 46–ca. 120).

[10]*Oversoul:* Refers to an essay (1841) by Ralph Waldo Emerson (1803–1882) that deals with his theory of cosmic unity — "it is the soul of the whole; the wise silence."

With the first frosts, the butterflies, who had sunned themselves in the new light through the summer, took flight, leaving the few bees to see what honey they had stored for winter use. Precious little appeared beyond the satisfaction of a few months of holy living.

At first it seemed as if a chance to try holy dying also was to be offered them. Timon, much disgusted with the failure of the scheme, decided to retire to the Shakers,[11] who seemed to be the only successful community going.

"What is to become of us?" asked Mrs. Hope, for Abel was heart-broken at the bursting of his lovely bubble.

"You can stay here, if you like, till a tenant is found. No more wood must be cut, however, and no more corn ground. All I have must be sold to pay the debts of the concern, as the responsibility rests with me," was the cheering reply.

"Who is to pay us for what we have lost? I gave all I had, — furniture, time, strength, six months of my children's lives, — and all are wasted. Abel gave himself body and soul, and is almost wrecked by hard work and disappointment. Are we to have no return for this, but leave to starve and freeze in an old house, with winter at hand, no money, and hardly a friend left; for this wild scheme has alienated nearly all we had. You talk much about justice. Let us have a little, since there is nothing else left."

But the woman's appeal met with no reply but the old one: "It was an experiment. We all risked something, and must bear our losses as we can."

With this cold comfort, Timon departed with his son, and was absorbed into the Shaker brotherhood, where he soon found the order of things reversed, and it was all work and no play.

Then the tragedy began for the forsaken little family. Desolation and despair fell upon Abel. As his wife said, his new beliefs had alienated many friends. Some thought him mad, some unprincipled. Even the most kindly thought him a visionary, whom it was useless to help till he took more practical views of life. All stood aloof, saying: "Let him work out his own ideas, and see what they are worth."

He had tried, but it was a failure. The world was not ready for Utopia yet, and those who attempted to found it only got laughed at for their pains. In other days, men could sell all and give to the poor,

[11]*Shakers:* A religious society founded in England by the visionary Ann Lee (1736–1784) and then relocated in the United States in the mid-1770s. They were pacifist, communitarian, and given their name because of the ecstatic dance they performed.

lead lives devoted to holiness and high thought, and, after the persecution was over, find themselves honored as saints or martyrs. But in modern times these things are out of fashion. To live for one's principles, at all costs, is a dangerous speculation; and the failure of an ideal, no matter how humane and noble, is harder for the world to forgive and forget than bank robbery or the grand swindles of corrupt politicians.

Deep waters now for Abel, and for a time there seemed no passage through. Strength and spirits were exhausted by hard work and too much thought. Courage failed when, looking about for help, he saw no sympathizing face, no hand outstretched to help him, no voice to say cheerily, —

"We all make mistakes, and it takes many experiences to shape a life. Try again, and let us help you."

Every door was closed, every eye averted, every heart cold, and no way open whereby he might earn bread for his children. His principles would not permit him to do many things that others did; and in the few fields where conscience would allow him to work, who would employ a man who had flown in the face of society, as he had done?

Then this dreamer, whose dream was the life of his life, resolved to carry out his idea to the bitter end. There seemed no place for him here, — no work, no friend. To go begging conditions was as ignoble as to go begging money. Better perish of want than sell one's soul for the sustenance of his body. Silently he lay down upon his bed, turned his face to the wall, and waited with pathetic patience for death to cut the knot which he could not untie. Days and nights went by, and neither food nor water passed his lips. Soul and body were dumbly struggling together, and no word of complaint betrayed what either suffered.

His wife, when tears and prayers were unavailing, sat down to wait the end with a mysterious awe and submission; for in this entire resignation of all things there was an eloquent significance to her who knew him as no other human being did.

"Leave all to God," was his belief; and in this crisis the loving soul clung to this faith, sure that the Allwise Father would not desert this child who tried to live so near to Him. Gathering her children about her, she waited the issue of the tragedy that was being enacted in that solitary room, while the first snow fell outside, untrodden by the footprints of a single friend.

But the strong angels who sustain and teach perplexed and troubled souls came and went, leaving no trace without, but working

miracles within. For, when all other sentiments had faded into dimness, all other hopes died utterly; when the bitterness of death was
nearly over, when body was past any pang of hunger or thirst, and
soul stood ready to depart, the love that outlives all else refused to
die. Head had bowed to defeat, hand had grown weary with too
heavy tasks, but heart could not grow cold to those who lived in its
tender depths, even when death touched it.

"My faithful wife, my little girls, — they have not forsaken me,
they are mine by ties that none can break. What right have I to leave
them alone? What right to escape from the burden and the sorrow I
have helped to bring? This duty remains to me, and I must do it manfully. For their sakes, the world will forgive me in time; for their
sakes, God will sustain me now."

Too feeble to rise, Abel groped for the food that always lay within
his reach, and in the darkness and solitude of that memorable night
ate and drank what was to him the bread and wine of a new communion, a new dedication of heart and life to the duties that were left
him when the dreams fled.

In the early dawn, when that sad wife crept fearfully to see what
change had come to the patient face on the pillow, she found it smiling at her, saw a wasted hand outstretched to her, and heard a feeble
voice cry bravely, "Hope!"

What passed in that little room is not to be recorded except in the
hearts of those who suffered and endured much for love's sake. Enough
for us to know that soon the wan shadow of a man came forth, leaning on the arm that never failed him, to be welcomed and cherished
by the children, who never forgot the experiences of that time.

"Hope" was the watchword now; and, while the last logs blazed
on the hearth, the last bread and apples covered the table, the new
commander, with recovered courage, said to her husband, —

"Leave all to God — and me. He has done his part, now I will do
mine."

"But we have no money, dear."

"Yes, we have. I sold all we could spare, and have enough to take
us away from this snowbank."

"Where can we go?"

"I have engaged four rooms at our good neighbor, Lovejoy's.
There we can live cheaply till spring. Then for new plans and a home
of our own, please God."

"But, Hope, your little store won't last long, and we have no
friends."

"I can sew and you can chop wood. Lovejoy offers you the same pay as he gives his other men; my old friend, Mrs. Truman, will send me all the work I want; and my blessed brother stands by us to the end. Cheer up, dear heart, for while there is work and love in the world we shall not suffer."

"And while I have my good angel Hope, I shall not despair, even if I wait another thirty years before I step beyond the circle of the sacred little world in which I still have a place to fill."

So one bleak December day, with their few possessions piled on a ox-sled, the rosy children perched atop, and the parents trudging arm in arm behind, the exiles left their Eden and faced the world again.

"Ah, me! my happy dream. How much I leave behind that never can be mine again," said Abel, looking back at the lost Paradise, lying white and chill in its shroud of snow.

"Yes, dear; but how much we bring away," answered brave-hearted Hope, glancing from husband to children.

"Poor Fruitlands! The name was as great a failure as the rest!" continued Abel, with a sigh, as a frostbitten apple fell from a leafless bough at his feet.

But the sigh changed to a smile as his wife added, in a half-tender, half-satirical tone, —

"Don't you think Apple Slump would be a better name for it, dear?"

MARY GOVE

On the Columbian Phalanx

Mary Gove (1810–1884) was a writer, reformer, and colorful cultural radical who espoused daring Fourierist ideas on sexual relations, marriage, free love, and divorce. Little is known about the Columbian Phalanx on the Muskingum River in Ohio that Gove visited, but her account of its internal disputes indicates the strains and tensions that afflicted many utopian communities.

Gove's report appeared in the form of a letter to John Allen — he was a member of Brook Farm and a lecturer on Fourierism — and it was published in the New York *Weekly Herald*, March 15, 1845. The text used here is a reprint in *A Documentary History of American Industrial Society*, ed. John R. Commons, vol. 7 (Cleveland: Arthur H. Clark, 1910), 277–80.

Dear John Allen:

Again I will try to give you some idea of my whereabouts, and what I have seen. . . . I have visited the Columbian Association, seven miles above Zanesville,[1] on the Muskingum. The site of the Ohio Phalanx was beautiful, but it cannot be compared with the Columbian. Though it is winter, and the trees bare, and a slight covering of snow on the ground, yet it is the fairest spot I ever looked upon or dreamed of. There are 2700 acres, including a beautiful island formed by the branching of the Muskingum. The timber, of which there is a large quantity, is very much finer than is usual in this region. They say they could pay for the place by carrying on cooper-ing[2] for a few years. They have suitable timber also for boat building. There are large quantities of bituminous coal, limestone, and iron ore on the domain. They have also a beautiful stone that will polish like dark colored marble. They have a quarry of grindstones too — indeed it is very difficult for Northern persons to imagine the riches of this region. They have steam-boat navigation from the Ohio to the Erie Canal at Dresden. They have paid about $10,000 on the land, the cost of which was $55,000. The natural riches of the place, coal, timber, lime, iron, &c., with the crops, would enable them to pay for their place, with the greatest ease, if they had a united band upon the ground. They have one field of wheat now, containing 137 acres. They have about 150 members, though they are not all on the ground, on account of accommodations. They have thirty log buildings about twenty feet square. They have the frame of a building erected one hundred feet in length and forty in breadth — two stories high. Their land lies both sides of the Muskingum. They are, as a whole, hardly in the alphabet of social science. A few of them look to a unitary edifice — I think about fifteen of them have some idea of Fourierism. Some friends of Association went with me from Zanesville, and gave me a favorable introduction. I walked over a large part of the Domain. One good man said to me, "I wish you would tell the New England people to come out here and join us — we should certainly succeed if they would." . . . The people gradually gathered together, and I preached Association and Grahamism[3] to them in earnest. I believe I saw only one man who did not consume

---

[1]*Zanesville:* A town in central Ohio on the Muskingum River, fifty miles east of Columbus.

[2]*coopering:* Barrel-making.

[3]*Grahamism:* Refers to Sylvester Graham (1794–1851), a reformer who spoke and wrote about health and personal hygiene.

quantities of tobacco, and just now enormous quantities on account of a quarrel they were engaged in, which made them "very nervous." This quarrel involves the very foundations of Association, and so I shall give you a little history of it as I understood it. The founder of this Phalanx, Mr. A. B. Campbell, had become obnoxious to those members who were not imbued with any principle of association on account of his heretical notions. I can give you but little account of him, from personal observation, as I only saw him about two hours. I however laid my hand upon his head, asked him a good many questions, and heard the statements of both sides respecting him. He seems to have great intellectual power, with limited education. He was formerly a Methodist minister. He has studied what writings he could come at on Association in English, evidently with great attention. He first lectured through this region, and gathered some friends and contracted for this place. Pious people who had an idea that they could make money by uniting, advanced what of the purchasing money has been paid. Other people of similar character wished to join, but Mr. Campbell had made himself very obnoxious by his lectures, in which he had criticized the religion of the day in rather the style of come-outism.[4] He had also spoken of civilized marriages very disrespectfully, and moreover he worked on Sunday. One of the principal members of the side opposed to him said to me, "Campbell is the wickedest man in the world — he has spoken against the Bible, he has spoken against marriage, he has worked on Sunday, he has taken in members without property, he has said he would as lief have a black man join as a white man." In view of all these offences, (or rather in view of their consequence, which was that several persons who wished to join and put in money, would not do it whilst the head of the Association spoke against marriage, and worked on Sunday,) the majority of the members of the Columbian Phalanx voted to expel Mr. Campbell. The day of my arrival on the Domain, he had left. They had no rule in their Constitution by which they could expel him, and no definite charge against him, except that he had attended a dance in the village, in a house which some persons thought was not respectable. He was expelled — driven away in mid-winter without a penny, or a peck of corn, with a wife and five children. I think he had been working for them with head or hand, about two years. About a dozen or fifteen, who have some idea of the principles of

---

[4]*come-outism:* A protest against and withdrawal from an established religious body or institution.

Association, adhered to Mr. Campbell, or as they said, to the right. The present leader who takes Mr. Campbell's place, is a sceptic, but quite an energetic man. His impiety has not yet been objected to by the members — probably will not be till it is found unprofitable. Day before I left, the Fourier portion of the phalanx came to Zanesville, and held a conversation with me respecting their difficulties and the hopes of Association generally. There were a dozen earnest young men who came, and Mr. Campbell was with them. I asked Mr. C. many questions. He is a Fourierist as far as he has gone, though his feelings are negative with regard to the sacred scriptures, I think, owing entirely to his present excoriation by the professed believers in the Bible. His friends, by his advice, will do all in their power to save their place. If they cannot, they will be valuable help to some association farther removed from chaos than this. I found that his ideas with regard to marriage had been entirely misunderstood by those, to whom all things are right that are according to law. The question of the relation of the sexes in Association is a momentous one; and though our friends may wish to evade or avoid it, fearing they shall be misunderstood, or that odium will attach to them if they speak out their thoughts — it must be met. . . .

Truly yours,

MARY S. GOVE.

ADIN BALLOU

On the Hopedale Community

Adin Ballou (1803–1890) was a clergyman, reformer, and leader of the Hopedale Community, a religious utopia in Milford, Massachusetts, which began in 1841. It floundered in the late 1850s but survived until 1868, when it merged with the Unitarian Hopedale parish. Ballou was the editor of the *Practical Christian*, the community's semimonthly publication, and the author of several books, including *Practical Christian Socialism* (1854) and the posthumous *History of the Hopedale Community* (1897). In the following excerpt from a tract published in 1851, Ballou reviews the Christian basis, tenets, and practical advantages of the community he led. The text is from John Humphrey Noyes, *History of American Socialisms* (Philadelphia: Lippincott, 1870), 120–27.

The Hopedale Community, originally called Fraternal Community, No. 1, was formed at Mendon, Massachusetts, January 28, 1841, by about thirty individuals from different parts of the State. In the course of that year they purchased what was called the "Jones Farm," *alias* "The Dale," in Milford. This estate they named Hopedale — joining the word "Hope" to its ancient designation, as significant of the great things they hoped for from a very humble and unpropitious beginning. About the first of April 1842, a part of the members took possession of their farm and commenced operations under as many disadvantages as can well be imagined. Their present domain (December 1, 1851), including all the lands purchased at different times, contains about 500 acres. Their village consists of about thirty new dwelling-houses, three mechanic shops, with water-power, carpentering and other machinery, a small chapel, used also for the purposes of education, and the old domicile, with the barns and outbuildings much improved. There are now at Hopedale some thirty-six families, besides single persons, youth and children, making in all a population of about 175 souls.

It is often asked, What are the peculiarities, and what the advantages of the Hopedale Community? Its leading peculiarities are the following:

1. It is a church of Christ (so far as any human organization of professed Christians, within a particular locality, have the right to claim that title), based on a simple declaration of faith in the religion of Jesus Christ, as he taught and exemplified it, according to the scriptures of the New Testament, and of acknowledged subjection to all the moral obligations of that religion. No person can be a member, who does not cordially assent to this comprehensive declaration. Having given sufficient evidence of truthfulness in making such a profession, each individual is left to judge for him or herself, with entire freedom, what abstract doctrines are taught, and also what external religious rites are enjoined in the religion of Christ. No precise theological dogmas, ordinances or ceremonies are prescribed or prohibited. In such matters all the members are free, with mutual love and toleration, to follow their own highest convictions of truth and religious duty, answerable only to the great Head of the true Church Universal. But in practical Christianity this church is precise and strict. There its essentials are specific. It insists on supreme love to God and man — that love which "worketh no ill" to friend or foe. It enjoins total abstinence from all God-contemning words and deeds;

all unchastity; all intoxicating beverages; all oath-taking; all slave-holding and pro-slavery compromises; all war and preparations for war; all capital and other vindictive punishments; all insurrectionary, seditious, mobocratic and personal violence against any government, society, family or individual; all voluntary participation in any anti-Christian government, under promise of unqualified support — whether by doing military service, commencing actions at law, holding office, voting, petitioning for penal laws, aiding a legal posse by injurious force, or asking public interference for protection which can be given only by such force; all resistance of evil with evil; in fine, from all things known to be sinful against God or human nature. This is its acknowledged obligatory righteousness. It does not expect immediate and exact perfection of its members, but holds up this practical Christian standard, that all may do their utmost to reach it, and at least be made sensible of their shortcomings. Such are the peculiarities of the Hopedale Community as a church.

2. It is a Civil State, a miniature Christian Republic, existing within, peaceably subject to, and tolerated by the governments of Massachusetts and the United States, but otherwise a commonwealth complete within itself. Those governments tax and control its property, according to their own laws, returning less to it than they exact from it. It makes them no criminals to punish, no disorders to repress, no paupers to support, no burdens to bear. It asks of them no corporate powers, no military or penal protection. It has its own Constitution, laws, regulations and municipal police; its own Legislative, Judiciary and Executive authorities; its own educational system of operations; its own methods of aid and relief; its own moral and religious safeguards; its own fire insurance and savings institutions; its own internal arrangements for the holding of property, the management of industry, and the raising of revenue; in fact, all the elements and organic constituents of a Christian Republic, on a miniature scale. There is no Red Republicanism[1] in it, because it eschews blood; yet it is the seedling of the true Democratic and Social Republic, wherein neither caste, color, sex nor age stands proscribed, but every human being shares justly in "Liberty, Equality and Fraternity." Such is The Hopedale Community as a Civil State.

3. It is a universal religious, moral, philanthropic, and social reform Association. It is a Missionary Society, for the promulgation of

---

[1]*Red Republicanism:* An extreme Republican of the French Revolution; an extreme radical in political reform.

New Testament Christianity, the reformation of the nominal church, and the conversion of the world. It is a moral suasion Temperance Society on the teetotal basis. It is a moral power Anti-Slavery Society, radical and without compromise. It is a Peace Society on the only impregnable foundation of Christian non-resistance. It is a sound theoretical and practical Woman's Rights Association. It is a Charitable Society for the relief of suffering humanity, to the extent of its humble ability. It is an Educational Society, preparing to act an important part in the training of the young. It is a socialistic Community, successfully actualizing, as well as promulgating, practical Christian Socialism — the only kind of Socialism likely to establish a true social state on earth. The members of this Community are not under the necessity of importing from abroad any of these valuable reforms, or of keeping up a distinct organization for each of them, or of transporting themselves to other places in search of sympathizers. Their own Newcastle[2] can furnish coal for home-consumption, and some to supply the wants of its neighbors. Such is the Hopedale Community as a Universal Reform Association on Christian principles.

What Are Its Advantages?

1. It affords a theoretical and practical illustration of the way whereby all human beings, willing to adopt it, may become individually and socially happy. It clearly sets forth the principles to be received, the righteousness to be exemplified, and the social arrangements to be entered into, in order to this happiness. It is in itself a capital school for self-correction and improvement. No where else on earth is there a more explicit, understandable, practicable system of ways and means for those who really desire to enter into usefulness, peace and rational enjoyment. This will one day be seen and acknowledged by multitudes who now know nothing of it, or knowing, despise it, or conceding its excellence, are unwilling to bow to its wholesome requisitions. "Yet the willing and the obedient shall eat the good of the land."

2. It guarantees to all its members and dependents employment, at least adequate to a comfortable subsistence; relief in want, sickness or distress; decent opportunities for religious, moral and intellectual cul-

---

[2]*Newcastle:* A city in England noteworthy for its coal production. "To carry coals to Newcastle" means to bring to a place what is already plentiful there.

ture; an orderly, well regulated neighborhood; fraternal counsel, fellowship and protection under all circumstances; and a suitable sphere of individual enterprise and responsibility, in which each one may, by due self-exertion, elevate himself to the highest point of his capabilities.

3. It solves the problem which has so long puzzled Socialists, the harmonization of just individual freedom with social co-operation. Here exists a system of arrangements, simple and effective, under which all capital, industry, trade, talent, skill and peculiar gifts may freely operate and co-operate, with no restrictions other than those which Christian morality every where rightfully imposes, constantly to the advantage of each and all. All may thrive together as individuals and as a Community, without degrading or impoverishing any. This excellent system of arrangements in its present completeness is the result of various and wisely improved experiences.

4. It affords a peaceful and congenial home for all conscientious persons, of whatsoever religious sect, class or description heretofore, who now embrace practical Christianity, substantially as this Community holds it, and can no longer fellowship the popular religionists and politicians. Such need sympathy, co-operation and fraternal association, without undue interference in relation to non-essential peculiarities. Here they may find what they need. Here they may give and receive strength by rational, liberal Christian union.

5. It affords a most desirable opportunity for those who mean to be practical Christians in the use of property, talent, skill or productive industry, to invest them. Here those goods and gifts may all be so employed as to benefit their possessors to the full extent of justice, while at the same time they afford aid to the less favored, help build up a social state free from the evils of irreligion, ignorance, poverty and vice, promote the regeneration of the race, and thus resolve themselves into treasure laid up where neither moth, nor rust, nor thieves can reach them. Here property is preeminently safe, useful and beneficent. It is Christianized. So, in a good degree, are talent, skill, and productive industry.

6. It affords small scope, place or encouragement for the unprincipled, corrupt, supremely selfish, proud, ambitious, miserly, sordid, quarrelsome, brutal, violent, lawless, fickle, high-flying, loaferish, idle, vicious, envious and mischief-making. It is no paradise for such; unless they voluntarily make it first a moral penitentiary. Such will hasten to more congenial localities; thus making room for the upright, useful and peaceable.

7. It affords a beginning, a specimen and a presage of a new and glorious social Christendom — a grand confederation of similar Communities — a world ultimately regenerated and Edenized. All this shall be in the forthcoming future.

The Hopedale Community was born in obscurity, cradled in poverty, trained in adversity, and has grown to a promising childhood, under the Divine guardianship, in spite of numberless detriments. The bold predictions of many who despised its puny infancy have proved false. The fears of timid and compassionate friends that it would certainly fail have been put to rest. Even the repeated desertion of professed friends, disheartened by its imperfections, or alienated by too heavy trials of their patience, has scarcely retarded its progress. God willed otherwise. It has still many defects to outgrow, much impurity to put away, and a great deal of improvement to make — moral, intellectual and physical. But it will prevail and triumph. The Most High will be glorified in making it the parent of a numerous progeny of practical Christian Communities. Write, saith the Spirit, and let this prediction be registered against the time to come, for it shall be fulfilled.

JOSEPH SMITH

The Wentworth Letter

Joseph Smith (1805–1844) was the American Mormon leader and founder of the Church of Jesus Christ of Latter-Day Saints. In the 1820s, he claimed to receive visions and revelations, which culminated in his discovery of golden tablets inscribed with sacred writings. Smith's reports of the tablets were transcribed and published in 1829 as the *Book of Mormon*. A seer and prophet (Hawthorne alludes to Smith, the "Mormon prophet," in ch. 23 of *The Blithedale Romance*), he and his followers established a series of churches and communities in New York, Ohio, and Missouri before settling in Nauvoo, Illinois. Smith faced bitter opposition both from the public and from within his own movement, and he and his brother were killed by a mob in Carthage, Illinois, in June 1844. After his death, leadership of the Mormons passed to Brigham Young (1801–1877), who led the great migration to the West (1846–47) and directed the settlement at Salt Lake City, Utah.

The document included here, the so-called Wentworth Letter, is a concise history of the church and its beliefs. It appeared in the *Times and Seasons*, the church's newspaper in the Nauvoo settlement, on March 1, 1842. The text is from *The Personal Writings of Joseph Smith*, ed. Dean C. Jessee (Salt Lake City: Deseret, 1984), 213–20, which preserves Smith's loose punctuation and sometimes awkward usages.

I was born in the town of Sharon Windsor co., Vermont on the 23rd of December, A.D. 1805. When ten years old my parents removed to Palmyra New York, where we resided about four years, and from thence we removed to the town of Manchester.

My father was a farmer and taught me the art of husbandry. When about fourteen years of age I began to reflect upon the importance of being prepared for a future state, and upon enquiring the plan of salvation I found that there was a great clash in religious sentiment; if I went to one society they referred me to one plan, and another to another; each one pointing to his own particular creeds as the summon bonum of perfection: considering that all could not be right, and that God could not be the author of so much confusion I determined to investigate the subject more fully, believing that if God had a church it would not be split up into factions, and that if he taught one society to worship one way, and administer in one set of ordinances, he would not teach another principles which were diametrically opposed. Believing the word of God I had confidence in the declaration of James; "If any man lack wisdom let him ask of God who giveth to all men liberally and upbraideth not and it shall be given him,"[1] I retired to a secret place in a grove and began to call upon the Lord, while fervently engaged in supplication my mind was taken away from the objects with which I was surrounded, and I was enwrapped in a heavenly vision and saw two glorious personages who exactly resembled each other in features, and likeness, surrounded with a brilliant light which eclipsed the sun at noon-day. They told me that all religious denominations were believing in incorrect doctrines, and that none of them was acknowledged of God as his church and kingdom. And I was expressly commanded to "go not after them," at the same time receiving a promise that the fulness of the gospel should at some future time be made known unto me.

[1]James 1:5.

On the evening of the 21st of September, A.D. 1823, while I was praying unto God, and endeavoring to exercise faith in the precious promises of scripture on a sudden a light like that of day, only of a far purer and more glorious appearance, and brightness burst into the room, indeed the first sight was as though the house was filled with consuming fire; the appearance produced a shock that affected the whole body; in a moment a personage stood before me surrounded with a glory yet greater than that with which I was already surrounded. This messenger proclaimed himself to be an angel of God sent to bring the joyful tidings, that the covenant which God made with ancient Israel was at hand to be fulfilled, that the preparatory work for the second coming of the Messiah was speedily to commence; that the time was at hand for the gospel, in all its fulness to be preached in power, unto all nations that a people might be prepared for the millennial reign.

I was informed that I was chosen to be an instrument in the hands of God to bring about some of his purposes in this glorious dispensation.

I was also informed concerning the aboriginal inhabitants of this country, and shown who they were, and from whence they came; a brief sketch of their origin, progress, civilization, laws, governments, of their righteousness and iniquity, and the blessings of God being finally withdrawn from them as a people was made known unto me: I was also told where there was deposited some plates on which were engraven an abridgement of the records of the ancient prophets that had existed on this continent. The angel appeared to me three times the same night and unfolded the same things. After having received many visits from the angels of God unfolding the majesty, and glory of the events that should transpire in the last days, on the morning of the 22d of September A.D. 1827, the angel of the Lord delivered the records into my hands.

These records were engraven on plates which had the appearance of gold, each plate was six inches wide and eight inches long and not quite so thick as common tin. They were filled with engravings, in Egyptian characters and bound together in a volume, as the leaves of a book with three rings running through the whole. The volume was something near six inches in thickness, a part of which was sealed. The characters on the unsealed part were small, and beautifully engraved. The whole book exhibited many marks of antiquity in its construction and much skill in the art of engraving. With the records was bound a curious instrument which the ancients called "Urim and

Thummin," which consisted of two transparent stones set in the rim of a bow fastened to a breastplate.

Through the medium of the Urim and Thummin I translated the record by the gift, and power of God.

In this important and interesting book the history of ancient America is unfolded, from its first settlement by a colony that came from the tower of Babel,[2] at the confusion of languages to the beginning of the fifth century of the Christian era. We are informed by these records that America in ancient times has been inhabited by two distinct races of people. The first were called Jaredites and came directly from the tower of Babel. The second race came directly from the city of Jerusalem, about six hundred years before Christ. They were principally Israelites, of the descendants of Joseph. The Jaredites were destroyed about the time that the Israelites came from Jerusalem, who succeeded them in the inheritance of the country. The principal nation of the second race fell in battle towards the close of the fourth century. The remnant are the Indians that now inhabit this country. This book also tells us that our Saviour made his appearance upon this continent after his resurrection, that he planted the gospel here in all its fulness, and richness, and power, and blessing; that they had apostles, prophets, pastors, teachers and evangelists; the same order, the same priesthood, the same ordinances, gifts, powers, and blessing, as was enjoyed on the eastern continent, that the people were cut off in consequence of their transgressions, that the last of their prophets who existed among them was commanded to write an abridgement of their prophesies, history &c., and to hide it up in the earth, and that it should come forth and be united with the bible for the accomplishment of the purposes of God in the last days. For a more particular account I would refer to the Book of Mormon, which can be purchased at Nauvoo, or from any of our travelling elders.

As soon as the news of this discovery was made known, false reports, misrepresentation and slander flew as on wings of the wind in every direction, the house was frequently beset by mobs, and evil designing persons, several times I was shot at, and very narrowly escaped, and every device was made use of to get the plates away from me, but the power and blessing of God attended me, and several began to believe my testimony.

On the 6th of April, 1830, the "Church of Jesus Christ of Latter-day Saints," was first organized in the town of Manchester, Ontario

[2]*tower of Babel:* See Genesis 11:1–9.

co., state of New York. Some few were called and ordained by the spirit of revelation, and prophesy, and began to preach as the spirit gave them utterance, and though weak, yet were they strengthened by the power of God, and many were brought to repentance, were immersed in the water, and were filled with the Holy Ghost by the laying on of hands. They saw visions and prophesied, devils were cast out and the sick healed by the laying on of hands. From that time the work rolled forth with astonishing rapidity, and churches were soon formed in the states of New York, Pennsylvania, Ohio, Indiana, Illinois and Missouri: in the last named state a considerable settlement was formed in Jackson co.; numbers joined the church and we were increasing rapidly; we made large purchases of land, our farms teemed with plenty, and peace and happiness was enjoyed in our domestic circle and throughout our neighborhood; but as we could not associate with our neighbors who were many of them of the basest of men and had fled from the face of civilized society, to the frontier country to escape the hand of justice, in their midnight revels, their sabbath breaking, horse racing, and gambling, they commenced at first ridicule, then to persecute, and finally an organized mob assembled and burned our houses, tarred, and feathered, and whipped many of our brethren and finally drove them from their habitations; who houseless, and homeless, contrary to law, justice and humanity, had to wander on the bleak prairies till the children left the tracks of their blood on the prairie, this took place in the month of November, and they had no other covering but the canopy of heaven, in this inclement season of the year; this proceeding was winked at by the government and although we had warrantee deeds for our land, and had violated no law we could obtain no redress.

There were many sick, who were thus inhumanly driven from their houses, and had to endure all this abuse and to seek homes where they could be found. The result was, that a great many of them being deprived of the comforts of life, and the necessary attendances, died; many children were left orphans; wives, widows; and husbands widowers. — Our farms were taken possession of by the mob, many thousands of cattle, sheep, horses, and hogs, were taken and our household goods, store goods, and printing press, and type were broken, taken, or otherwise destroyed.

Many of our brethren removed to Clay[3] where they continued until 1836, three years; there was no violence offered but there were

[3]*Clay:* Clay County, Missouri.

threatenings of violence. But in the summer of 1836, these threatenings began to assume a more serious form; from threats, public meetings were called, resolutions were passed, vengeance and destruction
were threatened, and affairs again assumed a fearful attitude, Jackson
county was a sufficient precedent, and as the authorities in that
county did not interfere, they boasted that they would not in this,
which on application to the authorities we found to be too true, and
after much violence, privation and loss of property we were again
driven from our homes.

We next settled in Caldwell, and Davies counties, where we made
large and extensive settlements, thinking to free ourselves from the
power of oppression, by settling in new counties, with very few inhabitants in them; but here we were not allowed to live in peace, but
in 1838 we were again attacked by mobs, an exterminating order was
issued by Gov. Boggs,[4] and under the sanction of law was organized
banditti ranged through the country, robbed us of our cattle, sheep,
horses, hogs &c., many of our people were murdered in cold blood,
the chastity of our women was violated, and we were forced to sign
away our property at the point of the sword, and after enduring every
indignity that could be heaped upon us by an inhuman, ungodly band
of marauders, from twelve to fifteen thousand souls men, women,
and children were driven from their own fire sides, and from lands
that they had warrantee deeds of, houseless, friendless, and homeless
(in the depth of winter,) to wander as exiles on the earth or to seek an
asylum in a more genial clime, and among a less barbarous people.

Many sickened and died, in consequence of the cold, and hardships they had to endure; many wives were left widows, and children
orphans, and destitute. It would take more time than is allotted me
here to describe the injustice, the wrongs, the murders, the bloodshed, the theft, misery and woe that has been caused by the barbarous, inhuman, and lawless, proceedings of the state of Missouri.

In the situation before alluded to we arrived in the state of Illinois
in 1839, where we found a hospitable people and a friendly home; a
people who were willing to be governed by the principles of law and
humanity. We have commenced to build a city called "Nauvoo" in
Hancock co., we number from six to eight thousand here besides vast
numbers in the county around and in almost every county of the
state. We have a city charter granted us and a charter for a legion the

---

[4]*Gov. Boggs:* Lillburn W. Boggs (1792–1860) was the Democratic governor of
Missouri (1836–40).

troops of which now number 1,500. We have also a charter for a university, for an agricultural and manufacturing society, have our own laws and administrators, and possess all the privileges that other free and enlightened citizens enjoy.

Persecution has not stopped the progress of truth, but has only added fuel to the flame, it has spread with increasing rapidity, proud of the cause which they have espoused and conscious of their innocence and of the truth of their system amidst calumny and reproach have the elders of this church gone forth, and planted the gospel in almost every state in the Union; it has penetrated our cities, it has spread over our villages, and has caused thousands of our intelligent, noble, and patriotic citizens to obey its divine mandates, and be governed by its sacred truths. It has also spread into England, Ireland, Scotland and Wales: in the year of 1839 where a few of our missionaries were sent over five thousand joined the standard of truth, there are numbers now joining in every land.

Our missionaries are going forth to different nations, and in Germany, Palestine, New Holland,[5] the East Indies, and other places, the standard of truth has been erected: no unhallowed hand can stop the work from progressing, persecutions may rage, mobs may combine, armies may assemble, calumny may defame, but the truth of God will go forth boldly, nobly, and independent till it has penetrated every continent, visited every clime, swept every country, and sounded in every ear, till the purposes of God shall be accomplished and the great Jehovah shall say the work is done.

We believe in God the Eternal Father, and in his son Jesus Christ, and in the Holy Ghost.

We believe that men will be punished for their own sins and not for Adam's transgression.

We believe that through the atonement of Christ all mankind may be saved by obedience to the laws and ordinances of the Gospel.

We believe that these ordinances are 1st, Faith in the Lord Jesus Christ; 2d, Repentance; 3d, Baptism by immersion for the remission of sins; 4th, Laying on of hands for the gift of the Holy Ghost.

We believe that a man must be called of God by "prophesy, and by laying on of hands" by those who are in authority to preach the gospel and administer in the ordinances thereof.

---

[5]*New Holland:* Refers to the Netherlands East Indies but often was used broadly to suggest India, Southeast Asia, and the Malay archipelago.

We believe in the same organization that existed in the primitive church, viz: apostles, prophets, pastors, teachers, evangelists &c.

We believe in the gift of tongues, prophesy, revelation, visions, healing, interpretation of tongues &c.

We believe the bible to be the word of God as far as it is translated correctly; we also believe the Book of Mormon to be the word of God.

We believe all that God has revealed, all that he does now reveal, and we believe that he will yet reveal many great and important things pertaining to the kingdom of God.

We believe in the literal gathering of Israel and in the restoration of the Ten Tribes. That Zion will be built upon this continent. That Christ will reign personally upon the earth, and that the earth will be renewed and receive its paradasaic glory.

We claim the privilege of worshipping Almighty God according to the dictates of our conscience, and allow all men the same privilege let them worship how, where, or what they may.

We believe in being subject to kings, presidents, rulers, and magistrates, in obeying, honoring and sustaining the law.

We believe in being honest, true, chaste, benevolent, virtuous, and in doing good to *all men;* indeed we may say that we follow the admonition of Paul "we believe all things we hope all things," we have endured many things and hope to be able to endure all things. If there is any thing virtuous, lovely, or of good report or praise worthy we seek after these things.[6]

Respectfully &c.

JOSEPH SMITH

HARRIET BEECHER STOWE

"The Quaker Settlement" (*From* Uncle Tom's Cabin)

Uncle Tom's Cabin, Harriet Beecher Stowe's anti-slavery novel, appeared first in serialized form from June 1851 to April 1852 in the Washington, D.C.–based *National Era* (1847–60), the official weekly journal of the American and Foreign Anti-Slavery Society, and was then pub-

[6]See 1 Corinthians 13:7, Philippians 4:8.

lished in book form. The five thousand copies of the first edition sold out in forty-eight hours, and for the next two years the presses never caught up with the demand, with three hundred thousand copies sold in 1852 alone. Total sales in the United States reached a million in the next seven years and were about the same in England.

A devout Christian, Stowe (1811–1896) claimed that God had inspired the novel. Through it, she sought to define and honor the Christian and family virtues that slavery violated. In "The Quaker Settlement" (ch. 13), Stowe describes a matriarchal Christian utopia, presided over by the benevolent figure of Rachel Halliday. The text is from *Uncle Tom's Cabin; or, Life among the Lowly, with an Introduction Setting Forth the History of the Novel and a Key to Uncle Tom's Cabin*, 2 vols. (Boston: Houghton Mifflin, 1896), 1:214–25.

A quiet scene now rises before us. A large, roomy, neatly-painted kitchen, its yellow floor glossy and smooth, and without a particle of dust; a neat, well-blacked cooking-stove; rows of shining tin, suggestive of unmentionable good things to the appetite; glossy green wood chairs, old and firm; a small flag-bottomed rocking-chair, with a patch-work cushion in it, neatly contrived out of small pieces of different colored woollen goods, and a larger sized one, motherly and old, whose wide arms breathed hospitable invitation, seconded by the solicitation of its feather cushions, — a real comfortable, persuasive old chair, and worth, in the way of honest, homely enjoyment, a dozen of your plush or brochetelle[1] drawing-room gentry; and in the chair, gently swaying back and forward, her eyes bent on some fine sewing, sat our fine old friend Eliza.[2] Yes, there she is, paler and thinner than in her Kentucky home, with a world of quiet sorrow lying under the shadow of her long eyelashes, and marking the outline of her gentle mouth! It was plain to see how old and firm the girlish heart was grown under the discipline of heavy sorrow; and when, anon, her large dark eye was raised to follow the gambols of her little Harry, who was sporting, like some tropical butterfly,

---

[1]*brochetelle:* Embroidered, brocaded.
[2]*Eliza:* Eliza Harris and her son Harry, having escaped from slavery, are reunited with George Harris, Eliza's husband, and given shelter in Ohio by this family of Quakers.

hither and thither over the floor, she showed a depth of firmness and steady resolve that was never there in her earlier and happier days.

By her side sat a woman with a bright tin pan in her lap, into which she was carefully sorting some dried peaches. She might be fifty-five or sixty; but hers was one of those faces that time seems to touch only to brighten and adorn. The snowy lisse crape cap, made after the strait Quaker pattern, — the plain white muslin handkerchief, lying in placid folds across her bosom, — the drab shawl and dress, — showed at once the community to which she belonged. Her face was round and rosy, with a healthful downy softness, suggestive of a ripe peach. Her hair, partially silvered by age, was parted smoothly back from a high placid forehead, on which time had written no inscription, except peace on earth, good will to men, and beneath shone a large pair of clear, honest, loving brown eyes; you only needed to look straight into them, to feel that you saw to the bottom of a heart as good and true as ever throbbed in woman's bosom. So much has been said and sung of beautiful young girls, why don't somebody wake up to the beauty of old women? If any want to get up an inspiration under this head, we refer them to our good friend Rachel Halliday, just as she sits there in her little rocking-chair. It had a turn for quacking and squeaking, — that chair had, — either from having taken cold in early life, or from some asthmatic affection, or perhaps from nervous derangement; but, as she gently swung backward and forward, the chair kept up a kind of subdued "creechy crawchy," that would have been intolerable in any other chair. But old Simeon Halliday often declared it was as good as any music to him, and the children all avowed that they wouldn't miss of hearing mother's chair for anything in the world. For why? for twenty years or more, nothing but loving words, and gentle moralities, and motherly loving kindness, had come from that chair; — headaches and heart-aches innumerable had been cured there, — difficulties spiritual and temporal solved there, — all by one good, loving woman, God bless her! . . .

The next morning was a cheerful one at the Quaker house. "Mother" was up betimes, and surrounded by busy girls and boys, whom we had scarce time to introduce to our readers yesterday, and who all moved obediently to Rachel's gentle "Thee had better," or more gentle "Hadn't thee better?" in the work of getting breakfast; for a breakfast in the luxurious valleys of Indiana is a thing complicated and multiform, and, like picking up the rose-leaves and trimming the bushes in Paradise, asking other hands than those of the original mother. While, therefore, John ran to the spring for fresh water, and Simeon the second sifted meal for corn-cakes, and Mary ground coffee, Rachel moved gently, and quietly about, making biscuits, cutting up chicken, and diffusing a sort of sunny radiance over the whole proceeding generally. If there was any danger of friction or collision from the ill-regulated zeal of so many young operators, her gentle "Come! come!" or "I wouldn't, now," was quite sufficient to allay the difficulty. Bards have written of the cestus of Venus,[3] that turned the heads of all the world in successive generations. We had rather, for our part, have the cestus of Rachel Halliday, that kept heads from being turned, and made everything go on harmoniously. We think it is more suited to our modern days, decidedly.

While all other preparations were going on, Simeon the elder stood in his shirt-sleeves before a little looking-glass in the corner, engaged in the anti-patriarchal operation of shaving. Everything went on so sociably, so quietly, so harmoniously, in the great kitchen, — it seemed so pleasant to every one to do just what they were doing, there was such an atmosphere of mutual confidence and good fellowship everywhere, — even the knives and forks had a social clatter as they went on to the table; and the chicken and ham had a cheerful and joyous fizzle in the pan, as if they rather enjoyed being cooked than otherwise; — and when George and Eliza and little Harry came out, they met such a hearty, rejoicing welcome, no wonder it seemed to them like a dream.

At last, they were all seated at breakfast, while Mary stood at the stove, baking griddle-cakes, which, as they gained the true exact golden-brown tint of perfection, were transferred quite handily to the table.

Rachel never looked so truly and benignly happy as at the head of her table. There was so much motherliness and fullheartedness even in the way she passed a plate of cakes or poured a cup of coffee, that it seemed to put a spirit into the food and drink she offered.

It was the first time that ever George had sat down on equal terms at any white man's table; and he sat down, at first, with some

[3]*cestus of Venus:* Belt worn by Venus, the Roman goddess of love.

constraint and awkwardness; but they all exhaled and went off
like fog, in the genial morning rays of this simple, overflowing kindness.

This, indeed, was a home, — *home*, — a word that George had
never yet known a meaning for; and a belief in God, and trust in his
providence, began to encircle his heart, as, with a golden cloud of
protection and confidence, dark, misanthropic, pining atheistic
doubts, and fierce despair, melted away before the light of a living
Gospel, breathed in living faces, preached by a thousand unconscious
acts of love and good will, which, like the cup of cold water given in
the name of a disciple, shall never lose their reward.

"Father, what if thee should get found out again?" said Simeon
second, as he buttered his cake.

"I should pay my fine," said Simeon, quietly.

"But what if they put thee in prison?"

"Couldn't thee and mother manage the farm?" said Simeon, smiling.

"Mother can do almost everything," said the boy. "But isn't it a
shame to make such laws?"

"Thee mustn't speak evil of thy rulers, Simeon," said his father,
gravely. "The Lord only gives us our worldly goods that we may do
justice and mercy; if our rulers require a price of us for it, we must
deliver it up."

"Well, I hate those old slaveholders!" said the boy, who felt as
unchristian as became any modern reformer.

"I am surprised at thee, son," said Simeon; "thy mother never
taught thee so. I would do even the same for the slaveholder as for
the slave, if the Lord brought him to my door in affliction."

Simeon second blushed scarlet; but his mother only smiled, and
said, "Simeon is my good boy; he will grow older, by and by, and
then he will be like his father."

"I hope, my good sir, that you are not exposed to any difficulty on
our account," said George, anxiously.

"Fear nothing, George, for therefore are we sent into the world. If
we would not meet trouble for a good cause, we were not worthy of
our name."

"But, for *me*," said George, "I could not bear it."

"Fear not, then, friend George; it is not for thee, but for God and
man, we do it," said Simeon. "And now thou must lie by quietly this
day, and to-night, at ten o'clock, Phineas Fletcher will carry thee on-

ward to the next stand, — thee and the rest of thy company. The pursuers are hard after thee; we must not delay."

"If that is the case, why wait till evening?" said George.

"Thou art safe here by daylight, for every one in the settlement is a Friend, and all are watching. It has been found safer to travel by night."

Brook Farm, painting by Josiah Wolcott, ca. 1844. Reproduced by permission of the Massachusetts Historical Society, © 1995.

3

Life at Brook Farm

It has been considered puzzling, even perverse, that Hawthorne chose to enroll in a utopian venture. Lindsay Swift, the historian of Brook Farm, has stated that "the whole experience stands as a thing apart and unrelated to the rest of his life," and the biographer E. H. Miller has portrayed Hawthorne as "the most unlikely" of utopians.

But for Hawthorne, Brook Farm seemed promising. The West Roxbury countryside, with its woods, meadows, and nearby river, was nearly ideal in its pastoral quality; as he said in a letter of May 3, 1841, to his sister Louisa: "This is one of the most beautiful places I ever saw in my life, and as secluded as if it were a hundred miles from any city or village." Hawthorne believed that he and his wife-to-be, Sophia, would prosper in such a setting and that his literary endeavors would thrive there.

Hawthorne found the farm work onerous, however; he missed his beloved Sophia's presence; his mother and sisters in Salem were upset that he was away from them; and he chafed at his loss of privacy and inability to get serious writing done. The letters included here illustrate both his initial delight in Brook Farm and the onset of his disappointment. By September, Hawthorne had concluded that "the real Me was never an associate of the community." He was different from the others, he suggested, *among* yet *apart* from them, and this same ambiguity of perspective and position is evident in his first-person narrator, Coverdale.

The other selections in this chapter provide interesting opportunities for contrast and comparison with Hawthorne's fictional and nonfictional representations of Brook Farm. George Ripley had the idea for the utopian project at Brook Farm; he was its leader and one of the editors of its journal, *The Harbinger,* and in the "Letter" he wrote to his congregation on October 1, 1840, one can see the liberal, generous, transcendentalist convictions that Ripley sought to instill in the community he founded — above all, his egalitarian belief that "there is a light" that "enligheneth every man that cometh into the world."

John Sullivan Dwight and Rebecca Codman Butterfield were Brook Farmers, and they bear witness to the value of what Ripley achieved — a point worth remembering when appraising Hawthorne's troubled, skeptical view. Butterfield's account is especially valuable for its insights into the role of women at Brook Farm and the freedom they enjoyed there. Ralph Waldo Emerson and Elizabeth Palmer Peabody were not members, but they knew much about Brook Farm's operation and personnel, and their writings make all the more vivid the religious and transcendentalist contexts for the Brook Farm enterprise.

The selections in this chapter should be used to enrich the reading and study of *The Blithedale Romance* rather than to tie Brook Farm too tightly to the novel. In a letter of July 24, 1851, to his friend William B. Pike, Hawthorne stated, "When I write another romance, I shall take the Community for a subject, and shall give some of my experiences and observations at Brook Farm." But in a letter of July 14, 1852, written after the novel was published, Hawthorne advised George William Curtis (a former Brook Farmer), "Do not read [*The Blithedale Romance*] as if it had anything to do with Brook Farm (which essentially it has not) but merely for its own story and characters." Blithedale both is and is not connected to Brook Farm — which is how Hawthorne wanted it.

GEORGE RIPLEY

From the "*Letter to the Church in Purchase Street*"

George Ripley (1802–1880) was an important Unitarian minister, reformer, literary critic, and editor. After graduating from Harvard in 1823 and completing his studies at Harvard Divinity School in 1826, he served as minister of the Purchase Street Church in Boston until 1841. Along with F. H. Hedge, Ralph Waldo Emerson, Amos Bronson Alcott, Margaret Fuller, and Theodore Parker, Ripley was a member of the Transcendental Club, and he contributed to its intellectual life through books such as *Discourses on the Philosophy of Religion* (1836) and essays. He organized — and edited, in part, himself — the fourteen volumes of *Specimens of Foreign Standard Literature* (1838–42), translations of such major European writers, theologians, and philosophers as Victor Cousin and Friedrich Schleiermacher. Ripley also helped to start the transcendentalists' journal, *The Dial* (1840–44).

Ripley is best known, however, as the founder of the cooperative community of Brook Farm, in West Roxbury, Massachusetts, the plan for which he developed and discussed with Emerson, Fuller, and others in 1840 and which he launched in the spring of 1841. He was a teacher at Brook Farm's school and the editor of and frequent contributor to its journal, *The Harbinger* (1845–49).

Ripley's October 1, 1840, letter to his congregation is a crucial document in the history of transcendentalism and nineteenth-century reform. In it he states his discontent with his role as minister, voices his commitment to free speech, and makes clear his belief that the principles of the New Testament must become ingrained in the social order — a social order that Ripley sees as being riven by poverty and deprivation. The text of this letter is from Octavius Brooks Frothingham, *George Ripley* (Boston: Houghton Mifflin, 1883), 63–91.

I have long been persuaded that we should offer a more spiritual worship, enjoy a more sincere communion with each other, and find our Sabbath services far more attractive and fruitful, were all such restrictions removed, even if we came together as the disciples did, in a large upper room, in a fisher's boat, or by the shore of the sea. The minister should take his stand where he can freely speak out all that is in his soul. He would be joined by those who find that he addresses a powerful and living word to their hearts, who are helped by him in their endeavors after a just and truthful life, and are drawn by a spiritual affinity with the message he declares, and who are too desirous that the truth of God should prevail to think of its external, temporary effects. Such an assembly would constitute the true church of the first-born. It would consist of those who are united by no other tie than faith in divine things; by the desire to cultivate the holiest principles of our nature, — reverence, justice, and love; to ascertain and follow the laws of Providence in the constitution of the inner spirit and of the outward world; and to convert the jarring elements of earth into materials for a pure, serene, and joyful life.

The basis of worship in such a church would be feeling, not speculation; the platform would be broad enough to welcome every seeking spirit, in whatever stage of its progress it might be; all should be encouraged, none should be excluded; and especially they who are yet feeling after God, if haply they may find him, should be taken by the hand, not driven from the fold. This would leave the investigation of truth entirely free. The sincerest convictions could be uttered without dread or misgiving. We should meet, not as having attained, but as learners; of course, every ray of light would be sought, not shunned; we should let the dead past bury its dead; we should look on life and truth with young eyes; and thus seeking to be as little children, we should enter the Kingdom of God, and we should know where we were by the divine peace and joy with which our hearts would overflow. In such a church there could be no cold or formal preaching. The instruction would be the overflowing of an individual soul; there would be no aim at effect. The topics of discourse would be taken from the experience of life; they would embrace the widest range of thought, and the more exciting and Soul-stirring the better. The infinite Bible of the Universe would be the text-book, and whatever the soul feels or forbodes, the commentary.

But so long as the questions which relate to the highest truth and duty, though discussed everywhere else, are virtually excluded from the pulpit; so long as the minister is expected to adapt himself to the state of the times, to popular opinion and prevailing prejudices; so long as he is valued more for his plausible and obliging spirit than for his fearless rebuke of sin and detection of error, we may be lulled into treacherous slumber by the services of the church, but they can never accomplish their purpose in arousing the guilty from their sleep of death, pouring light over the darkened mind, and advancing the reign of truth, justice, and love over the kingdoms of men.

This idea of social worship can be carried into effect only in a congregation where there is a prevailing harmony of sentiment between the people and the minister; where the questions which most interest his mind are those which they are also most desirous to hear discussed; where the arrangements of the society allow the most perfect freedom of departure to all who have ceased to be interested in the views that are advanced. Whenever the attention of the minister is strongly drawn to subjects which are not regarded as important by the hearer, the free, sympathetic chain which binds heart with heart is disturbed, no electric spark is drawn forth, the speaker loses his power, and the people are not moved.

Now this is precisely the position which one portion of our community holds towards another, and, in many cases, ministers and people share in its embarrassments. If a minister is stationary and his people are for progress, there is an interruption of sympathy. There is a similar interruption if a people is stationary, while the minister is for progress. And the same is true with regard to any other points on which the community is divided.

The attention of some good men is directed chiefly to individual evils; they wish to improve private character without attacking social principles which obstruct all improvement; while the attention of other good men is directed to the evils of society; they think that private character suffers from public sins, and that, as we are placed in society by Providence, the advancement of society is our principal duty. With regard to these questions there is a great difference of opinion. They compose the principal subjects of thought at the present day. They form what is called the exciting questions by which society is now agitated. I should not do justice, my friends, to you or myself, if I were to close this communication without noticing the ground I have occupied in regard to those questions. It has been made, as you are aware, the cause of some reproach. A popular cry has been started by many individuals against the advocates of new views on philosophy and the condition of society, and, in common with many others, you have heard accusations brought against principles by those who have failed even to explain the meaning of the terms by which they were denounced.

There is a class of persons who desire a reform in the prevailing philosophy of the day. These are called Transcendentalists, because they believe in an order of truths which transcends the sphere of the external senses. Their leading idea is the supremacy of mind over matter. Hence they maintain that the truth of religion does not

depend on tradition, nor historical facts, but has an unerring witness
in the soul. There is a light, they believe, which enlighteneth every
man that cometh into the world; there is a faculty in all — the most
degraded, the most ignorant, the most obscure — to perceive spiritual
truth when distinctly presented; and the ultimate appeal on all moral
questions is not to a jury of scholars, a hierarchy of divines, or the
prescriptions of a creed, but to the common sense of the human race.
These views I have always adopted; they have been at the foundation
of my preaching from the first time that I entered the pulpit until
now. The experience and reflection of nearly twenty years have done
much to confirm, nothing to shake, them; and if my discourses in this
house, or my lectures in yonder vestry, have in any instance displayed
the vitality of truth, impressed on a single heart a genuine sense of religion, disclosed to you a new prospect of the resources of your own
nature, made you feel more deeply your responsibility to God,
cheered you in the sublime hope of immortality, and convinced your
reason of the reality and worth of the Christian revelation, it was because my mind has been trained in the principles of Transcendental
Philosophy, — a philosophy which is now taught in every Protestant
university on the Continent of Europe, which is the common creed of
the most enlightened nations, and the singular misunderstanding of
which among ourselves illustrates more forcibly, I am ashamed to
say, the heedless enterprise than the literary culture of our countrymen. If you ask, why I have not preached the philosophy in the pulpit, I answer that I could not have preached without it, but my main
business as a minister, I conceive, has been, not to preach philosophy
or politics or medicine or mathematics, but the Gospel of Christ. If
you ask whether I embrace every unintelligible production of the
mind that is quoted from mouth to mouth as Transcendentalism, I
answer, that if any man writes so as not to be understood, be he
Transcendentalist or Materialist, it is his own fault, not another's; for
my own part, I agree with Paul, "that I had rather speak five words
with my understanding, that by my voice I might teach others also,
than ten thousand words in an unknown tongue."[1] There is another
class of persons who are devoted to the removal of the abuses that
prevail in modern society. They witness the oppressions that are done
under the sun, and they cannot keep silence. They have faith that
God governs man; they believe in a better future than the past. Their
daily prayer is for the coming of the kingdom of righteousness, truth,

[1]See 1 Corinthians 14:4.

and love; they look forward to a more pure, more lovely, more divine state of society than was ever realized on earth. With these views, I rejoice to say, I strongly and entirely sympathize. While I do not feel it my duty to unite with any public association for the promotion of these ideas, it is not because I would disavow their principles, but because in many cases the cause of truth is carried forward better by individual testimony than by combined action. I would not be responsible for the measures of a society; I would have no society responsible for me; but in public and private, by word and by deed, by persuasion and example, I would endeavor to help the progress of the great principles which I have at heart. The purpose of Christianity, as I firmly believe, is to redeem society as well as the individual from all sin. As a Christian, then, I feel bound to do what I can for the promotion of universal temperance, to persuade men to abandon every habit which is at war with their physical welfare and their moral improvement, and to produce, by appeals to the reason and conscience, that love of inward order which is beyond the reach of legal authority. As a Christian, I would aid in the overthrow of every form of slavery; I would free the mind from bondage and the body from chains; I could not feel that my duty was accomplished while there was one human being, within the sphere of my influence, held to unrequited labor at the will of another, destitute of the means of education, or doomed to penury, degradation, and vice by the misfortune of his birth. I conceive it to be a large share of the minister's duty to preach the gospel to the poor, to announce glad tidings of deliverance to all that are oppressed. His warmest sympathies should be with those who have none to care for them; he should never be so much in earnest as when pleading the cause of the injured. His most frequent visits will not be to the abodes of fashion and luxury, but to the dwellings where not many of the wise and mighty of this world are apt to enter; and if he can enjoy the poor man's blessing, whom he has treated like an equal and a brother in all the relations of life, whose humble abode he has cheered by the expression of honest sympathy, and whose hard lot draws tears from those unused to sorrow, he will count it a richer reward than the applause of society or the admiration of listening crowds. There is another cause in which I feel the strongest interest, and which I would labor to promote, — that of inward peace between man and man. I have no faith whatever in the efficacy or the lawfulness of public or private wars. If they have ever been necessary in the progress of society, as I know they have been unavoidable, it was owing to the prevalence of the rude, untamed animal passions of man over the higher sentiments of his nature. It should be the effort of every true man to abolish them altogether; to banish the principles from which they proceed; to introduce the empire of justice and love; and to abstain on all occasions from the indulgence of bitterness or wrath in his own conduct, and to offer no needless provocation for its indulgence in others. I believe in the omnipotence of kindness, of moral intrepidity, of divine charity. If society performed its whole duty, the dominion of force would yield to the prevalence of love, our prisons would be converted into moral hospitals, the schoolmaster would supersede the executioner, violence would no more be heard in our land, nor destruction in our borders. Our walls would be salvation, and our gates praise.

RALPH WALDO EMERSON

From "Man the Reformer"

In *Nature* (1836), in his two volumes of *Essays* (1841, 1844), and in such lectures as "The American Scholar" (1837) and the address before the Harvard Divinity School (1838), Ralph Waldo Emerson (1803–1882) announced and articulated nearly all of the themes of transcendentalism — though at the same time he stressed that there was no Transcendentalist party and no "pure" transcendentalism. Emerson encouraged his readers and audiences to feel the exaltation of their highest potential, to trust instinct and intuition (the signs of God's presence in persons), and to perceive Nature as a source for truths deeper and more profound than any that the current social order made available. Emerson's criticism of educational, social, and religious institutions, and his insistence that men and women remake them, were compelling to Ripley and other reformers.

Ripley discussed his plans for Brook Farm with Emerson in the summer and fall of 1840, not long after Emerson delivered a series of lectures in April and May on literature, politics, private life, reform, religion, ethics, education, and social tendencies. He tried to persuade Emerson to join the community, but Emerson refused, judging that he was well-situated for his life and work in Concord, and that a cooperative community of the kind that Ripley charted would threaten his freedom and independence.

"Man the Reformer" was first given as a lecture in January 1841 and was later published in *The Dial* 1 (April 1841), 523–38, from which this selection is taken. It is noteworthy for Emerson's comments on the value of "manual labor" and the barriers that forestall the progress of intellect and virtue.

The young man on entering life finds the ways to lucrative employments blocked with abuses. The ways of trade are grown selfish to the borders of theft, and supple to the borders (if not beyond the borders) of fraud. The employments of commerce are not intrinsically unfit for a man, or less genial to his faculties, but these are now in their general course so vitiated by derelictions and abuses at which all connive, that it requires more vigor and resources than can be expected of every young man, to right himself in them; he is lost in them; he cannot move hand or foot in them. Has he genius and virtue? the less does he find them fit for him to grow in, and if he would thrive in them, he must sacrifice all the brilliant dreams of boyhood and youth as dreams; he must forget the prayers of his childhood; and must take on him the harness of routine and obsequiousness. If not so minded, nothing is left him but to begin the world anew, as he does who puts the spade into the ground for food. We are all implicated, of course, in this charge; it is only necessary to ask a few questions as to the progress of the articles of commerce from the fields where they grew, to our houses, to become aware that we eat and drink and wear perjury and fraud in a hundred commodities. How many articles of daily consumption are furnished us from the West Indies; yet it is said, that, in the Spanish islands, the venality of the officers of the government has passed into usage, and that no article passes into our ships which has not been fraudulently cheapened. In the Spanish islands, every agent or factor of the Americans, unless he be a consul, has taken oath that he is a Catholic, or has caused a priest to make that declaration for him. The abolitionist has shown us our dreadful debt to the southern negro. In the island of Cuba, in addition to the ordinary abominations of slavery, it appears, only men are bought for the plantations, and one dies in ten every year, of these miserable bachelors, to yield us sugar. I leave for those who have the knowledge the part of sifting the oaths of our custom-houses; I will not inquire into the oppression of the sailors; I will not pry into the usages of our retail trade. I content myself with the fact, that the general system of our trade, (apart from the blacker traits,

which, I hope, are exceptions denounced and unshared by all reputable men,) is a system of selfishness; is not dictated by the high sentiments of human nature; is not measured by the exact law of reci-
procity; much less by the sentiments of love and heroism, but is a
system of distrust, of concealment, of superior keenness, not of giving
but of taking advantage. It is not that which a man delights to unlock
to a noble friend; which he meditates on with joy and self-approval in
his hour of love and aspiration; but rather that which he then puts
out of sight, only showing the brilliant result, and atoning for the
manner of acquiring by the manner of expending it. I do not charge
the merchant or the manufacturer. The sins of our trade belong to no
class, to no individual. One plucks, one distributes, one eats. Every
body partakes, every body confesses, — with cap and knee volunteers
his confession, yet none feels himself accountable. He did not create
the abuse; he cannot alter it; what is he? an obscure private person
who must get his bread. That is the vice, — that no one feels himself
called to act for man, but only as a fraction of man. It happens therefore that all such ingenuous souls as feel within themselves the irrepressible strivings of a noble aim, who by the law of their nature
must act for man, find these ways of trade unfit for them, and they
come forth from it. Such cases are becoming more numerous every
year.

But by coming out of trade you have not cleared yourself. The trail
of the serpent reaches into all the lucrative professions and practices
of man. Each has its own wrongs. Each finds a tender and very intelligent conscience a disqualification for success. Each requires of the
practitioner a certain shutting of the eyes, a certain dapperness and
compliance, an acceptance of customs, a sequestration from the sentiments of generosity and love, a compromise of private opinion and
lofty integrity. Nay, the evil custom reaches into the whole institution
of property, until our laws which establish and protect it seem not to
be the issue of love and reason, but of selfishness. Suppose a man is
so unhappy as to be born a saint, with keen perceptions, but with the
conscience and love of an angel, and he is to get his living in the
world; he finds himself excluded from all lucrative works; he has no
farm, and he cannot get one; for, to earn money enough to buy one,
requires a sort of concentration toward money, which is the selling
himself for a number of years, and to him the present hour is as sacred and inviolable as any future hour. Of course, whilst another
man has no land, my title to mine, your title to yours, is at once vitiated. Inextricable seem to be the twinings and tendrils of this evil,

and we all involve ourselves in it the deeper by forming connexions, by wives and children, by benefits and debts.

It is considerations of this kind which have turned the attention of many philanthropic and intelligent persons to the claims of manual labor as a part of the education of every young man. If the accumulated wealth of the past generations is thus tainted, — no matter how much of it is offered to us, — we must begin to consider if it were not the nobler part to renounce it, and to put ourselves into primary relations with the soil and nature, and abstaining from whatever is dishonest and unclean, to take each of us bravely his part, with his own hands, in the manual labor of the world.

But it is said, "What! will you give up the immense advantages reaped from the division of labor, and set every man to make his own shoes, bureau, knife, wagon, sails, and needle? This would be to put men back into barbarism by their own act." I see no instant prospect of a virtuous revolution; yet I confess, I should not be pained at a change which threatened a loss of some of the luxuries or conveniencies of society, if it proceeded from a preference of the agricultural life out of the belief, that our primary duties as men could be better discharged in that calling. Who could regret to see a high conscience and a purer taste exercising a sensible effect on young men in their choice of occupation, and thinning the ranks of competition in the labors of commerce, of law, and of state? It is easy to see that the inconvenience would last but a short time. This would be great action, which always opens the eyes of men. When many persons shall have done this, when the majority shall admit the necessity of reform in all these institutions, their abuses will be redressed, and the way will be open again to the advantages which arise from the division of labor, and a man may select the fittest employment for his peculiar talent again, without compromise.

But quite apart from the emphasis which the times give to the doctrine, that the manual labor of society ought to be shared among all the members, there are reasons proper to every individual, why he should not be deprived of it. The use of manual labor is one which never grows obsolete, and which is inapplicable to no person. A man should have a farm or a mechanical craft for his culture. We must have a basis for our higher accomplishments, our delicate entertainments of poetry and philosophy, in the work of our hands. We must have an antagonism in the tough world for all the variety of our spiritual faculties, or they will not be born. Manual labor is the study of the external world. The advantage of riches remains with him who procured them, not with the heir. When I go into my garden with a spade, and dig a bed, I feel such an exhilaration and health, that I discover that I have been defrauding myself all this time in letting others do for me what I should have done with my own hands. But not only health but education is in the work. Is it possible that I who get indefinite quantities of sugar, hominy, cotton, buckets, crockery ware, and letter paper, by simply signing my name once in three months to a cheque in favor of John Smith and Co. traders, get the fair share of exercise to my faculties by that act, which nature intended for me in making all these far-fetched matters important to my comfort? It is Smith himself, and his carriers, and dealers, and manufacturers, it is the sailor, and the hide-drogher,[1] the butcher, the negro, the hunter, and the planter, who have intercepted the sugar of the sugar, and the cotton of the cotton. They have got the education, I only the commodity. This were all very well if I were necessarily absent, being detained by work of my own, like theirs, — work of the same faculties; then should I be sure of my hands and feet, but now I feel some shame before my wood-chopper, my ploughman, and my cook, for they have some sort of self-sufficiency, they can contrive without my aid to bring the day and year round, but I depend on them, and have not earned by use a right to my arms and feet. . . .

I do not wish to overstate this doctrine of labor, or insist that every man should be a farmer, any more than that every man should be a lexicographer. In general, one may say, that the husbandman's is the oldest, and most universal profession, and that where a man does not yet discover in himself any fitness for one work more than another, this may be preferred. But the doctrine of the Farm is merely this, that every man ought to stand in primary relations with the work of the world, ought to do it himself, and not to suffer the accident of his having a purse in his pocket, or his having been bred to some dishonorable and injurious craft, to sever him from those duties; and for this reason, that labor is God's education: that he only is a sincere learner, he only can become a master, who learns the secrets of labor, and who by real cunning extorts from nature its sceptre.

---

[1]*hide-drogher:* A worker who attends to the drying of hides.

NATHANIEL HAWTHORNE

Letters to Sophia Peabody

In his journal in August 1843, Emerson recorded the following: "Hawthorne boasts that he lived at Brook Farm during its heroic age: then all were intimate and each knew the other's work: priest and cook conversed at night of the day's work. Now they complain that they are separated and such intimacy cannot be; there are a hundred souls." While there is more evidence of solidarity and community at Brook Farm than Emerson suggests, Hawthorne in *The Blithedale Romance* does point throughout to distance and separation between persons in the midst of their lives together. Hawthorne was most intensely connected not to anyone at Brook Farm, but, rather, to Sophia Peabody, whom he married in July 1842. (See the portraits on pp. 434–35.)

This group of letters to Sophia (there are others not included here) reveal the shifting nature of Hawthorne's attitude toward Brook Farm. He began enthusiastically, but by August 12, he was referring to himself as in "bondage" to Brook Farm and stating that "labor is the curse of this world."

Certain phrases and sentences in the letters, as when Hawthorne describes working at the manure pile, are close to passages that appear in *The Blithedale Romance*, and in this respect they are an important textual source. Sometimes one can detect multiple links between a single letter and the novel's language and action. The letter of April 13, for example, refers to Hawthorne's arrival in a snowstorm (see chs. 2 and 3), alludes to the Pilgrim settlers (chs. 2 and 14), mentions a cow kicking over a milk pail (ch. 8), comments on the kindly Mrs. Barker (Mrs. Silas Foster in ch. 2), and records the demands of manual labor (chs. 8, 10, and 24).

On other occasions, similar sentiments appear in a letter and in the novel, but with differences in language. Compare, for example, the September 3 letter ("the real Me was never an associate of the community") with the beginning of chapter / 17, in which Coverdale reflects that Brook Farm had been for him "part of another age." See also the October 18 letter on the dangers to Sophia of mesmerism ("the sacredness of an individual is violated by it") — which for comparison can be placed alongside the selections on mesmerism by Harriet Martineau and Margaret Fuller (see p. 476) — and Coverdale's observations in chapter 23 on the "epoch of rapping spirits" in the mesmerism scene at the village hall.

It is intriguing that Hawthorne chose not to give to Coverdale anything like the relationship he enjoyed with Sophia. Coverdale remains a bachelor given to regrets and reveries, somewhat like Ik. Marvel's (the pen name of Donald G. Mitchell [1822–1908]) protagonist in his best-selling blend of fiction and essay, *Reveries of a Bachelor; or, A Book of the Heart* (1851) — though by the end, Marvel's bachelor takes a wife and raises a family. (See the illustrations on pp. 436–37.)

The text is from *The Letters, 1813–1843*, ed. Thomas Woodson, L. Neal Smith, and Norman Holmes Pearson, in *The Centenary Edition of the Works of Nathaniel Hawthorne*, vol. 15 (Columbus: Ohio State UP, 1984), 526–29, 545–46, 565–67, 575–77, 588–90. For further comments by Hawthorne on Brook Farm, see *The American Notebooks*, ed. Claude M. Simpson, in *The Centenary Edition of the Works of Nathaniel Hawthorne*, vol. 8 (Columbus: Ohio State UP, 1972).

Oak Hill,[1] April 13th. 1841

Ownest love,

Here is thy poor husband in a polar Paradise! I know not how to interpret this aspect of Nature — whether it be of good or evil omen to our enterprise. But I reflect that the Plymouth pilgrims arrived in the midst of storm and stept ashore upon mountain snow-drifts; and nevertheless they prospered, and became a great people — and doubtless it will be the same with us. I laud my stars, however, that thou wilt not have thy first impressions of our future home from such a day as this. Thou wouldst shiver all thy life afterwards, and never realize that there could be bright skies, and green hills and meadows, and trees heavy with foliage, where now the whole scene is a great snow-bank, and the sky full of snow likewise. Through faith, I persist in believing that spring and summer will come in their due season; but the unregenerated man shivers within me, and suggests a doubt whether I may not have wandered within the precincts of the Artic circle, and chosen my heritage among everlasting snows. Dearest, provide thyself with a good stock of furs; and if thou canst obtain the skin of a polar bear, thou wilt find it a very suitable summer dress for this region. Thou must not hope ever to walk abroad, except upon snow-shoes, nor to find any warmth, save in thy husband's heart.

Belovedest, I have not yet taken my first lesson in agriculture, as

[1]*Oak Hill:* Located in West Roxbury, Massachusetts, near Brook Farm.

thou mayst well suppose — except that I went to see our cows fod-
dered, yesterday afternoon. We have eight of our own; and the number is now increased by a transcendental heifer, belonging to Miss
Margaret Fuller. She is very fractious, I believe, and apt to kick over
the milk pail. Thou knowest best, whether, in these traits of character, she resembles her mistress. Thy husband intends to convert himself into a milk-maid, this evening; but I pray heaven that Mr. Ripley
may be moved to assign him the kindliest cow in the herd — otherwise he will perform his duty with fear and trembling.

Ownest wife,[2] I like my brethren in affliction very well; and
couldst thou see us sitting round our table, at meal-times, before the
great kitchen-fire, thou wouldst call it a cheerful sight. Mrs. Barker[3] is
a most comfortable woman to behold; she looks as if her ample person were stuffed full of tenderness — indeed, as if she were all one
great, kind heart. Wert thou but here, I should ask for nothing
more — not even for sunshine and summer weather; for thou wouldst
be both, to thy husband. And how is that cough of thine, my
belovedest? Hast thou thought of me, in my perils and wanderings?
Thou must not think how I longed for thee, when I crept into my cold
bed last night, — my bosom remembered thee, — and refused to be
comforted without thy caresses. I trust that thou dost muse upon me
with hope and joy, not with repining. Think that I am gone before, to
prepare a home for my Dove, and will return for her, all in good time.

Thy husband has the best chamber in the house, I believe; and
though not quite so good as the apartment I have left, it will do very
well. I have hung up thy two pictures; and they give me a glimpse of
summer and of thee. The vase I intended to have brought in my arms,
but could not very conveniently do it yesterday; so that it still remains
at Mrs. Hillards,[4] together with my carpet. I shall bring them the next
opportunity.

Now farewell, for the present, most beloved. I have been writing
this in my chamber; but the fire is getting low, and the house is old
and cold; so that the warmth of my whole person has retreated to my
heart, which burns with love for thee. I must run down to the kitchen
or parlor hearth, where thy image shall sit beside me — yea be
pressed to my breast. At bed-time, thou shalt have a few lines more.

---

[2]*Ownest wife:* Hawthorne refers to Sophia as his wife, though they were not yet
married when these letters were written. She was living in Boston at the time.

[3]*Mrs. Barker:* Elise Barker, one of Brook Farm's neighbors.

[4]*Mrs. Hillards:* Susan Howe Hillard, the wife of George Stillman Hillard
(1808–1879), lawyer, editor, and critic, with whom Hawthorne had lived.

Now I think of it, dearest, wilt thou give Mrs. Ripley[5] a copy of Grandfather's Chair and Liberty Tree; she wants them for some boys here. I have several vols of Famous Old People.

April 14th. 10 A.M. Sweetest, I did not milk the cows last night, because Mr. Ripley was afraid to trust them to my hands, or me to their horns — I know not which. But this morning, I have done wonders. Before breakfast, I went out to the barn, and began to chop hay for the cattle; and with such "righteous vehemence" (as Mr. Ripley says) did I labor, that, in the space of ten minutes, I broke the machine. Then I brought wood and replenished the fires; and finally sat down to breakfast and ate up a huge mound of buckwheat cakes. After breakfast, Mr. Ripley put a four-pronged instrument into my hands, which he gave me to understand was called a pitch-fork; and he and Mr. Farley[6] being armed with similar weapons, we all three commenced a gallant attack upon a heap of manure. This affair being concluded, and thy husband having purified himself, he sits down to finish this letter to his most beloved wife. Dearest, I will never consent that thou come within half a mile of me, after such an encounter as that of this morning. Pray Heaven that this letter retain none of the fragrance with which the writer was imbued. As for thy husband himself, he is peculiarly partial to the odor; but that whimsical little nose of thine might chance to quarrel with it.

Belovedest, Miss Fuller's cow hooks the other cows, and has made herself ruler of the herd, and behaves in a very tyrannical manner. Sweetest, I know not when I shall see thee; but I trust it will not be longer than till the end of next week. I love thee! I love thee! I would thou wert with me; for then would my labor be joyful — and even now, it is not sorrowful. Dearest, I shall make an excellent husbandman. I feel the original Adam reviving within me.

                        Brook Farm, June 1st. 1841 — nearly 6 A.M.
Very dearest,
    I have been too busy to write thee a long letter by this opportunity; for I think this present life of mine gives me an antipathy to pen and ink, even more than my Custom House experience did. I could not

---

[5]*Mrs. Ripley:* Sophia Ripley (1803–1861), wife of George Ripley (1802–1880), founder of Brook Farm. Hawthorne refers in this passage to titles of several of his books.
    [6]*Mr. Farley:* Francis D. Farley, Brook Farm resident.

live without the idea of thee, nor without spiritual communion with thee; but, in the midst of toil, or after a hard day's work in the gold mine, my soul obstinately refuses to be poured out on paper. That abominable gold mine![7] Thank God, we anticipate getting rid of its treasurers, in the course of two or three days. Of all hateful places, that is the worst; and I shall never comfort myself for having spent so many days of blessed sunshine there. It is my opinion, dearest, that a man's soul may be buried and perish under a dung-heap or in a furrow of the field, just as well as under a pile of money. Well; that giant, Mr. George Bradford,[8] will probably be here to-day; so that there will be no danger of thy husband being under the necessity of laboring more than he likes, hereafter. Meantime, my health is perfect, and my spirits buoyant, even in the gold mine.

And how art thou belovedest? Two or three centuries have passed since I saw thee; and then thou wast pale and languid. Thou didst comfort me in that little note of thine, but still I cannot help longing to be informed of thy present welfare. Thou art not a prudent little Dove, and wast naughty to come on such a day as thou didst; and it seems to me that Mrs. Ripley does not know how to take care of thee at all. Art thou quite well now.

Dearest wife, I intend to come and see thee either on Thursday or Friday — perhaps my visit may be deferred till Saturday, if the gold mine should hold out so long. I yearn for thee unspeakably. Good bye now; for the breakfast horn has sounded, sometime since. God bless thee, ownest.

                                        Thy lovingest husband.

                                Salem Sept 3^d 1841 — 4 °clock P.M.
Most beloved. — Thou dost not expect a letter from thy husband; and yet, perhaps, thou wilt not be absolutely displeased should one come to thee tomorrow. At all events, I feel moved to write; though the haze and sleepiness, which always settles upon me here, will certainly be perceptible in every line. But what a letter didst thou write to me! Thou lovest like a celestial being, (as truly thou art) and dost express thy love in heavenly language; — it is like one angel writing

---

[7] *gold mine:* This was the ironic phrase that George Ripley used for the manure pile.
[8] *Mr. George Bradford:* George P. Bradford (1807–1890), Harvard graduate, resident of Brook Farm, and teacher of literature and language there.

to another angel; but alas! the letter has miscarried, and has been delivered to a most unworthy mortal. Now wilt thou exclaim against thy husband's naughtiness! And truly he is very naughty. Well then; the letter was meant for him, and could not possibly belong to any other being, mortal or immortal. I will trust that thy idea of me is truer than my own consciousness of myself.

Dearest, I have been out only once, in the day time, since my arrival. How immediately and irrecoverably (if thou didst not keep me out of the abyss) should I relapse into the way of life in which I spent my youth! If it were not for my Dove, this present world would see no more of me forever. The sunshine would never fall on me, no more than on a ghost. Once in a while, people might discern my figure gliding stealthily through the dim evening — that would be all. I should be only a shadow of the night; it is thou that givest me reality, and makest all things real for me. If, in the interval since I quitted this lonely old chamber, I had found no woman (and thou wast the only possible one) to impart reality and significance to life, I should have come back hither ere now, with the feeling that all was a dream and a mockery. Dost thou rejoice that thou hast saved me from such a fate? Yes; it is a miracle worthy even of thee, to have converted a life of shadows into the deepest truth, by thy magic touch.

Belovedest, I have not yet made acquaintance with Miss Polly Metis. Mr. Foote was not in his office when I called there; so that my introduction to the erudite Polly[9] was unavoidably deferred. I went to the Athenaeum[10] this forenoon, and turned over a good many dusty books. When we dwell together, I intend that my Dove shall do all the reading that may be necessary, in the concoction of my various histories; and she shall repeat the substance of her researches to me, when our heads are on the pillow. Thus will knowledge fall upon me like heavenly dew.

Sweetest, it seems very long already since I saw thee; but thou hast been all the time in my thoughts; so that my being has been continuous. Therefore, in one sense, it does not seem as if we had parted at all. But really I should judge it to be twenty years since I left Brook Farm; and I take this to be one proof that my life there was an unnat-

---

[9]*the erudite Polly:* Apparently refers to a woman in Salem; Hawthorne is punning on *polymetis* — crafty, shrewd, "of many devices" — a word that Homer applies to Odysseus.

[10]*Athenaeum:* The Boston Athenaeum, founded in 1805, was a library and reading room and well-respected cultural institution.

ural and unsuitable, and therefore an unreal one. It already looks like a dream behind me. The real Me was never an associate of the community; there has been a spectral Appearance there, sounding the horn at day-break, and milking the cows, and hoeing potatoes, and raking hay, toiling and sweating in the sun, and doing me the honor to assume my name. But be not thou deceived, Dove of my heart. This Spectre was not thy husband. Nevertheless, it is somewhat remarkable that thy husband's hands have, during this past summer, grown very brown and rough; insomuch that many people persist in believing that he, after all, was the aforesaid spectral horn-sounder, cow-milker, potatoe-hoer, and hay-raker. But such a people do not know a reality from a shadow.

Enough of nonsense. Belovedest, I know not exactly how soon I shall return to the Farm. Perhaps not sooner than a fortnight from to-morrow; but, in that case, I shall pay thee an intermediate visit of one day. Wilt thou expect me on Friday or Saturday next, from ten to twelve °clock on each day, — not earlier nor later.

Brook Farm, Septr 22^d 1841 — P.M.

Dearest love, here is thy husband again, slowly adapting himself to the life of this queer community, whence he seems to have been absent half a life time — so utterly has he grown apart from the spirit and manners of the place. Thou knowest not how much I wanted thee, to give me a home-feeling in the spot — to keep a feeling of coldness and strangeness from creeping into my heart and making me shiver. Nevertheless, I was most kindly received; and the fields and woods looked very pleasant, in the bright sunshine of the day before yesterday. I had a friendlier disposition towards the farm, now that I am no longer obliged to toil in its stubborn furrows. Yesterday and to-day, however, the weather has been intolerable — cold, chill, sullen, so that it is impossible to be on kindly terms with mother Nature. Would I were with thee, mine own warmest and truest-hearted wife! I never shiver, while encircled in thine arms.

Belovedest, I doubt whether I shall succeed in writing another volume of Grandfather's Library,[11] while I remain at the farm. I have not the sense of perfect seclusion, which has always been essential to

---

[11]*Grandfather's Library:* The title of Hawthorne's book of stories for children, published in April 1842.

my power of producing anything. It is true, nobody intrudes into my room; but still I cannot be quiet. Nothing here is settled — everything is but beginning to arrange itself — and though thy husband would seem to have little to do with aught beside his own thoughts, still he cannot but partake of the ferment around him. My mind will not be abstracted. I must observe, and think, and feel, and content myself with catching glimpses of things which may be wrought out here-after. Perhaps it will be quite as well that I find myself unable to set seriously about literary occupation for the present. It will be good to have a longer interval between my labor of the body and that of the mind. I shall work to the better purpose, after the beginning of No-vember. Meantime, I shall see these people and their enterprise under a new point of view, and perhaps be able to determine whether thou and I have any call to cast in our lot among them.

Sweetest, our letters have not yet been brought from the Post Of-fice; so that I have known nothing of thee since our parting kiss. Surely we were very happy — and never had I so much peace and joy as in brooding over thine image, as thou wast revealed to me in our last interview. I love thee with all the heart I have — and more. Now farewell, most dear. Mrs. Ripley is to be the bearer of this letter; and I reserve the last page for tomorrow morning. Perhaps I shall have a blessed word from thee, ere then.

Septr 23^d — Before breakfast — Sweetest wife, thou hast not writ-ten to me. Nevertheless, I do not conclude thee to be sick, but will be-lieve that thou hast been busy in creating Laura Bridgman.[12] What a faithful and attentive husband thou hast! For once he has anticipated thee in writing.

Belovedest, I do wish the weather would put off this sulky mood. Had it not been for the warmth and brightness of Monday, when I arrived here, I should have supposed that all sunshine had left Brook Farm forever. I have no disposition to take long walks, in such a state of the sky; nor have I any buoyancy of spirit. Thy husband is a very dull person, just at this time. I suspect he wants thee. It is his purpose, I believe, either to walk or ride to Boston, about the end of next week, and give thee a kiss — after which he will return quietly and contentedly to the farm. Oh what joy, when he will again see thee every day!

[12]*Laura Bridgman:* Bridgman (1829–1889) was a blind, deaf, and mute woman whom the reformer Samuel Gridley Howe (1801–1876) taught at the Perkins Institute for the Blind in Boston. Sophia sculpted an eighteen-inch-high bust of her.

We had some tableaux[13] last night. They were very stupid, (as, indeed, was the case with all I have ever seen) but do not thou tell Mrs. Ripley so. She is a good woman, and I like her better than I did — her husband keeps his old place in my judgment. Farewell, thou gentlest Dove — thou perfectest woman — thou desirablest wife.

Thine ownest Husband.

Brook Farm, October 18th [16]. Saturday. [1841]

Most dear wife, I received thy letters and note, last night, and was much gladdened by them; for never has my soul so yearned for thee as now. But, belovedest, my spirit is moved to talk with thee to-day about these magnetic miracles,[14] and to beseech thee to take no part in them. I am unwilling that a power should be exercised on thee, of which we know neither the origin nor consequence, and the phenomena of which seem rather calculated to bewilder us, than to teach us any truths about the present or future state of being. If I possessed such a power over thee, I should not dare to exercise it; nor can I consent to its being exercised by another. Supposing that this power arises from the transfusion of one spirit into another, it seems to me that the sacredness of an individual is violated by it; there would be an intrusion into thy holy of holies — and the intruder would not be thy husband! Canst thou think, without a shrinking of thy soul, of any human being coming into closer communion with thee than I may? — than either nature or my own sense of right would permit me? *I* cannot. And, dearest, thou must remember, too, that thou art now a part of me, and that by surrendering thyself to the influence of this magnetic lady, thou surrenderest more than thine own moral and spiritual being — allowing that the influence *is* a moral and spiritual one. And, sweetest, I really do not like the idea of being brought, through thy medium, into such an intimate relation with Mrs. Park![15]

Now, ownest wife, I have no faith whatever that people are raised to the seventh heaven, or to any heaven at all, or that they gain any insight into the mysteries of life beyond death, by means of this strange science. Without distrusting that the phenomena which thou

---

[13]*tableaux:* Scenes or pictures represented on stage with the characters dressed in costume.

[14]*magnetic miracles:* Mesmeric experiments and displays.

[15]*Mrs. Park:* Name of a mesmerist and clairvoyant (1807–?), well known to Brook Farmers.

tellest me of, and others as remarkable, have really occurred, I think that they are to be accounted for as the result of a physical and material, not of a spiritual, influence. *Opium* has produced many a brighter vision of heaven (and just as susceptible of proof) than those which thou recountest. They are dreams, my love — and such dreams as thy sweetest fancy, either waking or sleeping, could vastly improve upon. And what delusion can be more lamentable and mischievous, than to mistake the physical and material for the spiritual? What so miserable as to lose the soul's true, though hidden, knowledge and consciousness of heaven, in the mist of an earth-born vision? Thou shalt not do this. If thou wouldst know what heaven is, before thou comest thither hand in hand with thy husband, then retire into the depths of thine own spirit, and thou wilt find it there among holy thoughts and feelings; but do not degrade high Heaven and its inhabitants into any such symbols and forms as those which Miss Larned[16] describes — do not let an earthy effluence from Mrs. Park's corporeal system bewilder thee, and perhaps contaminate something spiritual and sacred. I should as soon think of seeking revelations of the future state in the rottenness of the grave — where so many do seek it.

Belovedest wife, I am sensible that these arguments of mine may appear to have little real weight; indeed, what I write does no sort of justice to what I think. But I care the less for this, because I know that my deep and earnest feeling upon the subject will weigh more with thee than all the arguments in the world. And thou wilt know that the view which I take of this matter is caused by no want of faith in mysteries, but from a deep reverence of the soul, and of the mysteries which it knows within itself, but never transmits to the earthly eye or ear. Keep thy imagination sane — that is one of the truest conditions of communion with Heaven.

Dearest, after these grave considerations, it seems hardly worth while to submit a merely external one; but as it occurs to me, I will write it. I cannot think, without invincible repugnance, of thy holy name being bruited abroad in connection with these magnetic phenomena. Some (horrible thought!) would pronounce my Dove an impostor; the great majority would deem thee crazed; and even the few believers would feel a sort of interest in thee, which it would be anything but pleasant to excite. And what adequate motive can there be

---

[16]*Miss Larned:* This woman seems to have been a friend or acquaintance of Sophia's and had taken part in spiritualist practices.

for exposing thyself to all this misconception? Thou wilt say, perhaps, that thy visions and experiences would never be known. But Miss Larned's are known to all who choose to listen. Thy sister Elizabeth would like nothing so much as to proclaim thy spiritual experiences, by sound of trumpet.

October 19th [18]. Monday. — Most beloved, what a preachment have I made to thee! I love thee, I love thee, I love thee, most infinitely. Love is the true magnetism. What carest thou for any other? Belovedest, it is probable that thou wilt see thy husband tomorrow. Art thou magnificent. God bless thee. What a bright day is here, but the woods are fading now. It is time I were in the city, for the winter.

Thine ownest.

ELIZABETH PALMER PEABODY

From *"Plan of the West Roxbury Community"*

Elizabeth Palmer Peabody (1804–1894), the sister of Hawthorne's wife, Sophia, was an educator, writer, and reformer. She was an assistant to Amos Bronson Alcott at his Temple School in Boston and described his educational theory in *Record of a School* (1835). She knew the major and minor New England writers, reformers, and intellectuals, and the bookshop she opened in Boston in 1840 was a literary gathering place where Margaret Fuller held her "conversations" on literature, philosophy, and classical mythology. This selection is taken from an essay on Brook Farm that appeared in *The Dial* 2 (January 1842), 361–72. In it Peabody gives an overview of the community's principles and practices during its first nine months of operation.

In the last number of the Dial were some remarks, under the perhaps ambitious title, of "A Glimpse of Christ's Idea of Society"; in a note to which, it was intimated, that in this number, would be given an account of an attempt to realize in some degree this great Ideal, by a little company in the midst of us, as yet without name or visible existence. The attempt is made on a very small scale. A few individuals, who, unknown to each other, under different disciplines of life, reacting from different social evils, but aiming at the same object, — of being wholly true to their natures as men and women; have been made acquainted with one another, and have determined to become the Faculty of the Embryo University.

In order to live a religious and moral life worthy the name, they feel it is necessary to come out in some degree from the world, and to form themselves into a community of property, so far as to exclude competition and the ordinary rules of trade; — while they reserve sufficient private property, or the means of obtaining it, for all purposes of independence, and isolation at will. They have bought a farm, in order to make agriculture the basis of their life, it being the most direct and simple in relation to nature.

A true life, although it aims beyond the highest star, is redolent of the healthy earth. The perfume of clover lingers about it. The lowing of cattle is the natural bass to the melody of human voices.

On the other hand, what absurdity can be imagined greater than the institution of cities? They originated not in love, but in war. It was war that drove men together in multitudes, and compelled them to stand so close, and build walls around them. This crowded condition produces wants of an unnatural character, which resulted in occupations that regenerated the evil, by creating artificial wants. Even when that thought of grief,

> "I know, where'er I go
> That there hath passed away a glory from the Earth,"[1]

came to our first parents, as they saw the angel, with the flaming sword of self-consciousness, standing between them and the recovery of spontaneous Life and Joy, we cannot believe they could have anticipated a time would come, when the sensuous apprehension of Creation — the great symbol of God — would be taken away from their unfortunate children, — crowded together in such a manner as to shut out the free breath and the Universal Dome of Heaven, some opening their eyes in the dark cellars of the narrow, crowded streets of walled cities. How could they have believed in such a conspiracy against the soul, as to deprive it of the sun and sky, and glorious apparelled Earth! — The growth of cities, which were the embryo of nations hostile to each other, is a subject worthy the thoughts and pen of the philosophic historian. Perhaps nothing would stimulate courage to seek, and hope to attain social good, so much, as a pro-

---

[1]William Wordsworth, "Ode: Intimations of Immortality from Recollections of Early Childhood" (1807), st. 2.

found history of the origin, in the mixed nature of man, and the exasperation by society, of the various organized Evils under which humanity groans. Is there anything, which exists in social or political life, contrary to the soul's Ideal? That thing is not eternal, but finite, saith the Pure Reason. It had a beginning, and so a history. What man has done, man may *undo*. "By man came death; by man also cometh the resurrection from the dead."[2]

The plan of the Community, as an Economy, is in brief this; for all who have property to take stock, and receive a fixed interest thereon; then to keep house or board in commons, as they shall severally desire, at the cost of provisions purchased at wholesale, or raised on the farm; and for all to labor in community, and be paid at a certain rate an hour, choosing their own number of hours, and their own kind of work. With the results of this labor, and their interest, they are to pay their board, and also purchase whatever else they require at cost, at the warehouses of the Community, which are to be filled by the Community as such. To perfect this economy, in the course of time they must have all trades, and all modes of business carried on among themselves, from the lowest mechanical trade, which contributes to the health and comfort of life, to the finest art which adorns it with food or drapery for the mind.

All labor, whether bodily or intellectual, is to be paid at the same rate of wages; on the principle, that as the labor becomes merely bodily, it is a greater sacrifice to the individual laborer, to give his time to it; because time is desirable for the cultivation of the intellect, in exact proportion to ignorance. Besides, intellectual labor involves in itself higher pleasures, and is more its own reward, than bodily labor.

Another reason, for setting the same pecuniary value on every kind of labor, is, to give outward expression to the great truth, that all labor is sacred, when done for a common interest. Saints and philosophers already know this, but the childish world does not; and very decided measures must be taken to equalize labors, in the eyes of the young of the community, who are not beyond the moral influences of the world without them. The community will have nothing done within its precincts, but what is done by its own members, who stand all in social equality; — that the children may not "learn to expect one kind of service from Love and Goodwill, and another from the obligation of others to render it," — a grievance of the common society stated, by one of the associated mothers, as destructive of the

[2]1 Corinthians 15:21.

soul's simplicity. Consequently, as the Universal Education will involve all kinds of operation, necessary to the comforts and elegances of life, every associate, even if he be the digger of a ditch as his highest accomplishment, will be an instructer in that to the young members. Nor will this elevation of bodily labor be liable to lower the tone of manners and refinement in the community. The "children of light" are not altogether unwise in their generation. They have an invisible but all-powerful guard of principles. Minds incapable of refinement, will not be attracted into this association. It is an Ideal community, and only to the ideally inclined will it be attractive; but these are to be found in every rank of life, under every shadow of circumstance. Even among the diggers in the ditch are to be found some, who through religious cultivation, can look down, in meek superiority, upon the outwardly refined, and the book-learned.

Besides, after becoming members of this community, none will be engaged merely in bodily labor. The hours of labor for the Association will be limited by a general law, and can be curtailed at the will of the individual still more; and means will be given to all for intellectual improvement and for social intercourse, calculated to refine and expand. The hours redeemed from labor by community, will not be reapplied to the acquisition of wealth, but to the production of intellectual goods. This community aims to be rich, not in the metallic representative of wealth, but in the wealth itself, which money should represent; namely, LEISURE TO LIVE IN ALL THE FACULTIES OF THE SOUL. As a community, it will traffic with the world at large, in the products of Agricultural labor; and it will sell education to as many young persons as can be domesticated in the families, and enter into the common life with their own children. In the end, it hopes to be enabled to provide — not only all the necessaries, but all the elegances desirable for bodily and for spiritual health; books, apparatus, collections for science, works of art, means of beautiful amusement. These things are to be common to all; and thus that object, which alone gilds and refines the passion for individual accumulation, will no longer exist for desire, and whenever the Sordid passion appears, it will be seen in its naked selfishness. In its ultimate success, the community will realize all the ends which selfishness seeks, but involved in spiritual blessings, which only greatness of soul can aspire after.

And the requisitions on the individuals, it is believed, will make this the order forever. The spiritual good will always be the condition of the temporal. Every one must labor for the community in a reasonable degree, or not taste its benefits. The principles of the organization therefore, and not its probable results in future time, will determine its members. These principles are coöperation in social matters, instead of competition or balance of interests; and individual self-unfolding, in the faith that the whole soul of humanity is in each man and woman. The former is the application of the love of man; the latter of the love of God, to life. Whoever is satisfied with society, as it is; whose sense of justice is not wounded by its common action, institutions, spirit of commerce, has no business with this community; neither has any one who is willing to have other men (needing more time for intellectual cultivation than himself) give their best hours and strength to bodily labor, to secure himself immunity therefrom. And whoever does not measure what society owes to its members of cherishing and instruction, by the needs of the individuals that compose it, has no lot in this new society. Whoever is willing to receive from his fellow men that, for which he gives no equivalent, will stay away from its precincts forever.

But whoever shall surrender himself to its principles, shall find that its yoke is easy and its burden light. Everything can be said of it, in a degree, which Christ said of his kingdom, and therefore it is believed that in some measure it does embody his Idea. For its Gate of entrance is straight and narrow. It is literally a pearl *hidden in a field*. Those only who are willing to lose their life for its sake shall find it. Its voice is that which sent the young man sorrowing away. "Go sell all thy goods and give to the poor, and then come and follow me." "Seek first the kingdom of Heaven, and its righteousness, and all other things shall be added to you."[3]

This principle, with regard to labor, lies at the root of moral and religious life; for it is not more true that "money is the root of all evil," than that *labor is the germ of all good*.

All the work is to be offered for the free choice of the members of the community, at stated seasons, and such as is not chosen, will be hired. But it is not anticipated that any work will be set aside to be hired, for which there is actual ability in the community. It is so desirable that the hired labor should be avoided, that it is believed the work will all be done freely, even though at voluntary sacrifice. If there is some exception at first, it is because the material means are inadequate to the reception of all who desire to go. They cannot go, unless they have shelter; and in this climate, they cannot have shelter

[3]This paragraph contains a number of references and allusions to the New Testament. The two direct quotations at the end are from Matthew 19:21, 6:33.

unless they can build houses; and they cannot build houses unless they have money. It is not here as in Robinson Crusoe's Island,[4] or in the prairies and rocky mountains of the far west, where the land and the wood are not appropriated. A single farm, in the midst of Massachusetts, does not afford range enough for men to create out of the Earth a living, with no other means; as the wild Indians, or the United States Army in Florida[5] may do.

This plan, of letting all persons choose their own departments of action, will immediately place the Genius of Instruction on its throne. Communication is the life of spiritual life. Knowledge pours itself out upon ignorance by a native impulse. All the arts crave response. "WISDOM CRIES." If every man and woman taught only what they loved, and so many hours as they could naturally communicate, instruction would cease to be a drudgery, and we may add, learning would be no longer a task. The known accomplishments of many of the members of this association have already secured it an interest in the public mind, as a school of literary advantages quite superior. Most of the associates have had long practical experience in the details of teaching, and have groaned under the necessity of taking their method and law from custom or caprice, when they would rather have found it in the nature of the thing taught, and the condition of the pupil to be instructed. Each instructer appoints his hours of study or recitation, and the scholars, or the parents of the children, or the educational committee, choose the studies, for the time, and the pupils submit, as long as they pursue their studies with any teacher, to his regulations.

As agriculture is the basis of their external life, scientific agriculture, connected with practice, will be a prominent part of the instruction from the first. This obviously involves the natural sciences, mathematics, and accounts. But to classical learning justice is also to be done. Boys may be fitted for our colleges there, and even be carried through the college course. The particular studies of the individual pupils, whether old or young, male or female, are to be strictly regulated, according to their inward needs. As the children of the community can remain in the community after they become of age, as

---

[4]*Robinson Crusoe's Island:* Daniel Defoe's *Robinson Crusoe* (1719) tells the story of a man shipwrecked on a desert island who saves himself through his faith and resourcefulness.

[5]*the United States Army in Florida:* The U.S. Army fought in Florida against the Seminole Indians, led by the warrior Osceola, from 1835 to 1842. The Seminoles were resisting forced removal from their homeland.

associates, if they will; there will not be an entire subserviency to the end of preparing the means of earning a material subsistence, as is frequently the case now. Nevertheless, as they will have had opportunity, in the course of their minority, to earn three or four hundred dollars, they can leave the community at twenty years of age, if they will, with that sufficient capital, which, together with their extensive education, will gain *a subsistence* anywhere, in the best society of the world. It is this feature of the plan, which may preclude from parents any question as to their right to go into this community, and forego forever all hope of great individual accumulation *for their children;* a customary plea for spending life in making money. Their children will be supported at free board, until they are ten years of age; educated gratuitously; taken care of in case of their parents' sickness and death; and they themselves will be supported, after seventy years of age, by the community, unless their accumulated capital supports them.

There are some persons who have entered the community without money. It is believed that these will be able to support themselves and dependents, by less work, more completely, and with more ease than elsewhere; while their labor will be of advantage to the community. It is in no sense an eleemosynary[6] establishment, but it is hoped that in the end it will be able to receive all who have the spiritual qualifications.

It seems impossible that the little organization can be looked on with any unkindness by the world without it. Those, who have not the faith that the principles of Christ's kingdom are applicable to real life in the world, will smile at it, as a visionary attempt. But even they must acknowledge it can do no harm, in any event. If it realizes the hope of its founders, it will immediately become a manifold blessing. Its moral *aura* must be salutary. As long as it lasts, it will be an example of the beauty of brotherly love. If it succeeds in uniting successful labor with improvement in mind and manners, it will teach a noble lesson to the agricultural population, and do something to check that rush from the country to the city, which is now stimulated by ambition, and by something better, even a desire for learning. Many a young man leaves the farmer's life, because only by so doing can he have intellectual companionship and opportunity; and yet, did he but know it, professional life is ordinarily more unfavorable to the perfection of the mind, than the farmer's life; if the latter is lived with

[6]*eleemosynary:* Charitable, philanthropic.

wisdom and moderation, and the labor mingled as it might be with study. This community will be a school for young agriculturalists, who may learn within its precincts, not only the skilful practice, but the scientific reasons of their work, and be enabled afterwards to improve their art continuously. It will also prove the best of normal schools, and as such, may claim the interest of those, who mourn over the inefficiency of our common school system, with its present ill-instructed teachers.

It should be understood also, that after all the working and teaching, which individuals of the community may do, they will still have leisure, and in that leisure can employ themselves in connexion with the world around them. Some will not teach at all; and those especially can write books, pursue the Fine Arts, for private emolument if they will, and exercise various functions of men. — From this community might go forth preachers of the gospel of Christ, who would not have upon them the odium, or the burthen, that now diminishes the power of the clergy. And even if *pastors* were to go from this community, to reside among congregations as now, for a salary given, the fact, that they would have something to retreat upon, at any moment, would save them from that virtual dependence on their congregations, which now corrupts the relation. There are doubtless beautiful instances of the old true relation of pastor and people, even of teacher and taught, in the decaying churches around us, but it is in vain to attempt to conceal the ghastly fact, that many a taper is burning dimly in the candlestick, no longer silver or golden, because compassion forbids to put it quite out. But let the spirit again blow "where it listeth," and not circumscribe itself by salary and other commodity, — and the Preached word might reassume the awful Dignity which is its appropriate garment; and though it sit down with publicans and sinners, again speak "with authority and not as the scribes."[7]

---

[7]*"with authority and not as the scribes"*: Mark 1:22 refers to the special authority with which Christ preached.

THE BROOK FARM PHALANX

Prospectus for The Harbinger

The Harbinger, published at Brook Farm from June 1845 to February 1849, was the successor to the transcendentalist journal *The Dial* and *The Phalanx,* the Fourierist monthly that Albert Brisbane had edited in New York City. George Ripley served as editor in chief, Charles A. Dana (1819–1897) was the associate editor, and John Sullivan Dwight (see the next selection) was the music and literary editor. *The Harbinger* focused on Fourier's ideas and on the general project of social reform, but it also included many articles on literature and the arts. This "prospectus" shows the triumph of Fourierism at Brook Farm, and it was published in *The Phalanx* 1, no. 23 (May 28, 1845), 354–55. The text used is from Octavius Frothingham, *George Ripley* (Boston: Houghton Mifflin, 1883), 177–80.

In *The Father: A Life of Henry James, Sr.* (1994), the scholar Alfred Habegger notes that *harbinger* is a bilingual pun, as the French word for *harbinger,* or *precursor,* is *fourrier.*

"All things, at the present day, stand provided and prepared, and await the light."[1]

Under this title it is proposed to publish a weekly newspaper for the examination and discussion of the great questions in social science, politics, literature, and the arts, which command the attention of all believers in the progress and elevation of humanity.

In politics "The Harbinger" will be democratic in its principles and tendencies; cherishing the deepest interest in the advancement and happiness of the masses; warring against all exclusive privilege in legislation, political arrangements, and social customs; and striving, with the zeal of earnest conviction, to promote the triumph of the high democratic faith which it is the chief mission of the nineteenth century to realize in society. Our devotion to the democratic principle will lead us to take the ground of fearless and absolute independence

[1] *"All things, at the present day, . . . ":* This phrase, taken from the Swedish mystic, theologian, and philosopher Emmanuel Swedenborg (1688–1772), appeared under the masthead of *The Harbinger.*

(Text continues on p. 439.)

Nathaniel Hawthorne, portrait by Cephas Giovanni Thompson, 1850. Reproduced by permission of the Grolier Club of New York.

Sophia Amelia (Peabody) Hawthorne, from an etching by S. A. Schoff, 1847.
Courtesy of the Peabody Essex Museum, Salem, MA.

From *Reveries of a Bachelor; or, A Book of the Heart,* by Ik. Marvel.
Ik. Marvel was the pseudonym of Donald Grant Mitchell
(1822–1908), whose *Reveries of a Bachelor* appeared in 1850. It was
a phenomenal best-seller, with more than one million authorized
sales and many more in pirated editions. It is possible that Mitchell's
sentimental, humorous sketches of a bachelor fretting about marriage
and family may have influenced Hawthorne's conception of
Coverdale. The difference, however, is that at the end of *Reveries,* the
bachelor decides to marry.

Rustic Dance after a Sleigh Ride, oil painting by William Sidney Mount, 1830. Mount (1807–1868) spent most of his life in Stony Brook, Long Island. He was a notable genre and portrait painter of the period, especially admired for his depictions of country life. Bequest of Martha C. Karolik for the M. and M. Karolik Collection of American Paintings, 1815–1865. Courtesy, Museum of Fine Arts, Boston.

in regard to all political parties, whether professing attachment to that principle or hostility to it. We know that fidelity to an idea can never be measured by adherence to a name; and hence we shall criticise all parties with equal severity, though we trust that the sternness of truth will always be blended with the temperance of impartial candor. With tolerance for all opinions, we have no patience with hypocrisy and pretense; least of all with that specious fraud which would make a glorious principle the apology for personal ends. It will therefore be a leading object of "The Harbinger" to strip the disguise from the prevailing parties, to show them in their true light, to give them due honor, to tender them our grateful reverence whenever we see them true to a noble principle; but at all times, and on every occasion, to expose false professions, to hold up hollow-heartedness and duplicity to just indignation, to warn the people against the demagogue who would cajole them by honeyed flatteries, no less than against the devotee of Mammon[2] who would make them his slaves.

"The Harbinger" will be devoted to the cause of a radical, organic, social reform, essential to the highest development of man's nature, to the production of these elevated and beautiful forms of character of which he is capable, and to the diffusion of happiness, excellence, and universal harmony upon the earth. The principles of universal unity as taught by Charles Fourier, in their application to society, we believe are at the foundation of all genuine social progress; and it will ever be our aim to discuss and defend these principles without any sectarian bigotry, and in the catholic and comprehensive spirit of their great discoverer. While we bow to no man as an authoritative, infallible master, we revere the genius of Fourier too highly not to accept with joyful welcome the light which he has shed on the most intricate problems of human destiny.

The social reform, of whose advent the signs are everywhere visible, comprehends all others; and in laboring for its speedy accomplishment, we are conscious of devotion to the enslaved, to the promotion of genuine temperance, and to the elevation of the toiling and down-trodden masses to the inborn rights of humanity.

In literature "The Harbinger" will exercise a firm and impartial criticism without respect of persons or parties. It will be made a vehicle for the freest thought, though not of random speculations; and with a generous appreciation of the various forms of truth and

---

[2]*devotee of Mammon:* Someone consumed by the desire for wealth and material possessions.

beauty, it will not fail to expose such instances of false sentiment, perverted taste and erroneous opinion, as may tend to vitiate the public mind or degrade the individual character. Nor will the literary department of "The Harbinger" be limited to criticism alone. It will receive contributions from various pens in different spheres of thought; and, free from dogmatic exclusiveness, will accept all that in any way indicates the unity of man with Man, with Nature, and with God. Consequently, all true science, all poetry and art, all sincere literature, all religion that is from the soul, all wise analyses of mind and character, will come within its province.

We appeal for aid in our enterprise to the earnest and hopeful spirits in all classes of society. We appeal to all who, suffering from a restless discontent in the present order of things, with faith in man and trust in God, are striving for the establishment of universal justice, harmony, and love. We appeal to the thoughtful, the aspiring, the generous everywhere, who wish to see the reign of heavenly truth triumphant by supplanting the infernal discords and falsehoods on which modern society is built, for their sympathy, friendship, and practical coöperation in the undertaking which we announce to-day.

JOHN SULLIVAN DWIGHT

On Life at Brook Farm

John Sullivan Dwight (1813–1893) graduated from Harvard in 1832 and from Harvard Divinity School in 1836 but spent only a brief period in the ministry. He joined Brook Farm in 1841, taught music and Latin there, and contributed to *The Dial* and *The Harbinger. Dwight's Journal of Music,* begun in 1852, was for three decades an important contribution to the development of music criticism and appreciation in America. In this transcription of an address given later in his career, Dwight tells of his arrival at and involvement in Brook Farm, and along the way he makes a skeptical point about *The Blithedale Romance.* He stresses that Hawthorne in fact knew little about the persons who dwelled at Brook Farm, and that only the setting and landscape figure as elements in the novel. The text of Dwight's account is taken from George Willis Cooke, *John Sullivan Dwight: Brook-Farmer, Editor, and Critic of Music* (Boston: Small, Maynard, 1898), 56–61.

It was my privilege . . . to know Mr. Ripley very intimately for a number of years before he conceived that experiment. When I came out of the Divinity School at Cambridge, he was my first warm, helpful, encouraging friend. I was at his house almost daily during that famous controversy with Andrews Norton.[1] I knew the whole of it as it went on. I talked with Mr. Ripley, and heard him read his manuscript.

After I lived in Northampton, I was very much attracted to his idea which resulted in Brook Farm. His aspiration was to bring about a truer state of society, one in which human beings should stand in frank relations of true equality and fraternity, mutually helpful, respecting each other's occupation, and making one the helper of the other. The prime idea was an organization of industry in such a way that the most refined and educated should show themselves practically on a level with those whose whole education had been hard labor. Therefore, the scholars and the cultivated would take their part also in the manual labor, working on the farm or cultivating nurseries of young trees, or they would even engage in the housework.

I remember the night of my first arrival at Brook Farm. It had been going on all the summer. I arrived in November. At that time it was a sort of pastoral life, rather romantic, although so much hard labor was involved in it. They were all at tea in the old building, which was called the Hive. In a long room at a long table they were taking tea, and I sat down with them. When tea was over, they were all very merry, full of life; and all turned to and washed the dishes, cups, and saucers. All joined in, — the Curtis brothers, Dana,[2] and all. It was very enchanting; quite a lark, as we say. Much of the industry went on in that way, because it combined the freest sociability with the useful arts.

The idea of most of us was that, beginning with what we felt to be a true system, with true relations to one another, it would probably grow into something larger, and that by bringing in others we should finally succeed in reforming and elevating society and put it on a

---

[1] *Andrews Norton:* Norton (1786–1853) was a Unitarian minister, theologian, biblical scholar, and critic of Ripley's and Emerson's liberal religious views. In 1839, in *A Discourse on the Latest Form of Infidelity,* Norton attacked Emerson's transcendentalist ideas; Ripley came to Emerson's defense in a pamphlet, *The Latest Form of Infidelity Examined,* also published in 1839.

[2] *the Curtis brothers, Dana:* James Burrill Curtis (1822–1895), George William Curtis (1824–1892), and Charles A. Dana (1819–1897) were Brook Farm members.

basis of universal co-operation. Communism it was not, because property was respected. Some were allowed to hold and earn more than others. Only justice was sought for in the matter of labor and in the distribution of any surplus, if there were any, which seldom occurred. Capital, labor, and skill each had their fair proportion in the division; and the same person might share under each of these heads. It gave labor the largest share, five-twelfths; capital, four-twelfths; and skill, three-twelfths. By skill is meant the organizing head to industry. That was the whole of our equality.

The great point aimed at was to realize practical equality and mutual culture, and a common-sense education for the children in a larger sense than prevails in ordinary society. The educational phase consisted partly in our education of one another and partly in the school, which was also one of the means of support of the community. Pupils were taken from outside, who lived there, and were taught by Mr. and Mrs. Ripley and others. There were some young people who came and lived there simply as boarders, from a certain romantic interest in the ideas, but not committing themselves to them by membership.

The social education was extremely pleasant. For instance, in the matter of music, we had extremely limited means or talent; and very little could be done except in a very rudimentary, tentative, and experimental way. We had a singing class, and we had some who could sing a song gracefully and accompany themselves at the piano. We had some piano music; and, so far as it was possible, care was taken that it should be good, — sonatas of Beethoven and Mozart, and music of that order. We sang masses of Haydn and others, and no doubt music of a better quality than prevailed in most society at that date; but that would be counted nothing now. Occasionally we had artists come to visit us. We had delightful readings; and once in a while, when William Henry Channing[3] was in the neighborhood, he would preach us a sermon.

Hawthorne was there then, but he left at about that time. He knew very little about it as an organized industrial experiment. But he was pleased to live on a farm, and he liked to drive oxen; and he would drive until he got himself tired through the day, and shut himself up in his room in the evening. So it was wholly a mistake that *The Blithedale Romance* describes Brook Farm. There is nothing of Brook Farm in it except the scenery. None of the characters represent people

[3] *William Henry Channing:* Channing (1810–1884) was a Unitarian minister and reformer.

at Brook Farm. It has been supposed that the heroine was Margaret Fuller, but she was never a member. She was only an occasional visitor, a friend of Mr. and Mrs. Ripley. She made us delightful visits.

We were never more than a hundred, often not that; and we had very little means and a poor farm, nearly two hundred acres, mostly grass and woods, and found it hard to get people enough of the right kind to do what work was required. Everybody went into the work heartily, and everybody tried to help every other. There was a great sweetness and charm in the sincerity of the life.

I do not think Brook Farm was wholly a dream. This aspect has been too strongly presented. I think it was very practical, for we had very practical and common-sense men and women among us. It was a great good to me. Every one who was there will say it was to him, though it is extremely hard to tell of it. The truth is, every resident there had his own view of it. Every one saw the life through his own eyes and in his own way. Naturally, they formed groups; and one group was not like another. Certain ones were just as individual as in any common society. I felt and still think that it was a wholesome life, that it was a good practical education. I have no doubt I should not have been living at this day if it had not been for the life there, for what I did on the farm and among the trees, in handling the hay and even in swinging the scythe. Those who have survived, and been active in their experiences, have certainly shown themselves persons of power and faculty, with as much common sense, on the average, as ordinary men.

REBECCA CODMAN BUTTERFIELD

From *"Reminiscences of Brook Farm"*

Rebecca Codman joined Brook Farm in March 1843 at the age of eighteen, accompanying her parents and two brothers. She and her family remained until the community dissolved in 1847. Her reminiscences were probably written sometime in the 1890s and have only recently been published in "Rebecca Codman Butterfield's Reminiscences of Brook Farm," ed. Joel Myerson, *New England Quarterly* 65 (December 1992): 603–30. Note in particular her discussion of the relationship and division of labor between the sexes, and the difference between her account of associative community and the one that Hawthorne offers in *The Blithedale Romance*.

Just before entering the driveway to the Farm, the road crossed a bridge thrown over a little brook, which here entered the Farm, and from which it derived its name. At each corner of this bridge stood a fine willow, under the pleasant shade of which the traveler would often linger to note the beauty of the scene, or to listen to the merry ripple of the little stream. On the upper side of this bridge the road sloped gently to the brook, making a convenient and well-used watering place for the animals of the farm, as well as for those of travelers over the road.

Crossing the brook and taking a sudden turn to the left, through a roadway with a few trees on either side one came immediately to the main building of the place, the original farmhouse, called by the Association "The Hive."

It was a large, two and one-half storied, wooden building with front door and hall in the middle, and rooms on either side. A long ell had been attached to the farmhouse, and together these contained the reception rooms, the large dining room, the kitchen, washrooms, and shed on the lower floor, one or two offices and numerous sleeping rooms on the second, and still more sleeping rooms in the attic. As an evidence of the luxuriousness of these attic apartments, I might mention one of my brothers awakening one winter morning, and seeing that the snow had blown in through a crack in the roof and formed a wedged-shaped pile some six inches high, over the body of the unconscious sleeper in a neighboring bed.

In front of this main house the banks sloped down to two pretty terraces, and these gradually again down to the pleasant meadow through which ran the little brook. On one side of the drive-way, over-arching it, as well as part of "The Hive," stood a grand specimen of our New England elms; the shade of which covered the entire yard near the Hive and was always a welcome and beautiful feature of the place. Back of "The Hive," separated from it only by the roadway leading to the other buildings, was a large barn. About a hundred and fifty feet from "The Hive" stood the workshop. Here was the wood-working, shoe making and other rooms. "The Harbinger," a paper devoted to the spread of Socialistic views and to musical and literary criticisms, was printed here. Power was supplied for the machinery of the workshop by a small steam engine in the basement. In the shop attic, there were also some sleeping arrangements.

An eighth of a mile further on stood "The Eyrie," a two storied, flat roofed building, perched upon the highest point of land on the place, and built on a bed of rocks — hence its name. It was used for library, music, study, and recitation rooms on the lower floor, with sleeping rooms for the students above. Near this stood a small brown house, "The Cottage," with the great attraction of a large and safely built swing. A short distance from "The Cottage" was another large wooden house, the lower story used for ironing and workrooms. It contained two very large parlors, with folding doors, which rooms thrown together were used often as a place for meetings. This was called the "Pilgrim House," after Mr. Morton of Plymouth, father of Mrs. Abby Morton Diaz.[1]

Communication was had between these houses by a roadway, winding around by the Pilgrim House to the Cottage and the Eyrie, and by shorter foot-paths over the hills. The longest distance between the houses was about a quarter of a mile.

The Farm was beautifully located in every respect, and was situated in what has been termed "the wild flower region" of Massachusetts. Within a circle of three or four miles, the greatest variety of wild flowers could be found. Prominent among those were the white and blue violet, columbine, field and water lily, anemone, swamp pink, lady's slipper, mountain laurel, blue gentian, orchis, poligulla, Solomon's seal, fleur de lis, and the brilliant cardinal flower. A half hour's visit to the woods or meadows would reward the lover of these beautiful Children of Nature with a bountiful bouquet, often rivalling in loveliness and brilliancy the productions of the greenhouse. These wild flowers, so numerous and lovely, added to our greenhouse plants and flowers, had an important influence in cultivating the love of the beautiful in that class who, heretofore, had known so little of anything but severe manual labor.

Just before my residence at the Farm commenced, various mechanical industries had been introduced, and some changes in the internal organization effected. Endeavoring in some measure to follow the plan suggested by Fourier, the various labors of the farm, household, and workshops were committed to general departments, called Series, and these again subdivided into smaller departments called Groups. For instance, all matters that related to agriculture were in charge of the Farming or Agricultural Series, and each department of that work, as the nursery, teaming, vegetable garden, barn work, etc., had its appropriate body of workers, or Group. Each Group had its head

---

[1]*Mr. Morton of Plymouth, father of Mrs. Abby Morton Diaz:* Ichabod Morton, from Plymouth, Massachusetts, stayed at Brook Farm for only two weeks; Abby Morton Diaz was Brook Farm's kindergarten teacher.

or chief, elected by the members of the Group (on the first of each month or at stated intervals), who had charge of the work allotted to the Group, and directed how and when it should be done. Each Group had, too, its Clerk, who kept a record of the amount of labor done by each member, and at the end of the month the books of the various groups were returned to the Directors, and the amount of work performed by each person passed to his or her credit, on account. Meetings of the various groups were as frequent as the nature or urgency of the work required, and in case more laborers were needed in any Group they were supplied upon application to the Officers of the Series, or by the directors.

A person wishing to leave his work temporarily, either furnished a substitute (which was easily done) or left the matter with the chief of the Group. This system of voluntary Groups worked very satisfactorily. All were interested in the welfare of the Institution, and the work to be done found willing hands to undertake it. Opportunity to work in a special Group, which contained some of the liveliest and most genial of our people, or had very light and attractive work, would perhaps be sought for by some; but every disagreeable duty found individuals enough to attend to it. Brook Farm, though at first called a Community, was never a "Community of Property" or Association wherein all property was held in common, as was the case in some of the socialistic experiments of that period. It was a joint stock corporation, like any bank or factory, and was incorporated under Massachusetts laws. Each person, upon joining, contributed to the common concern such property in money, household goods, machinery, tools, and so forth, as he was able or willing to invest, and for these he received certificates of stock, showing the amount contributed, on which interest at four percent per annum was payable.

Work, at Brook Farm, in the opinion of all who lived there, had a charm which it had nowhere else. This is accounted for partly upon the ground that in a great number of the occupations women were associated with men in performing the labor. Again, there was quite a variety of these occupations, and a person often worked in several of these groups in the course of a day. And, within a certain limit, there was an opportunity for each person to choose the occupation for which he or she had a natural qualification or was attracted to. The mingling of persons of different ages and degrees of culture served also to add attraction to labor. These circumstances gave a zest to the ordinary employments of the place, that prevented them from becoming monotonous or tiresome.

Fourier's idea was that all labor, even the most disagreeable, might be made attractive by the circumstances thrown around it, and we at Brook Farm realized most fully the correctness of this view. Many scholars from families whose children had not been accustomed to labor of any sort, found work with us not what they had deemed it, and became as efficient workers as any of our members. Our people labored as constantly and earnestly as the average in our cities, say from 8 to 10 hours per day. So far as practicable, a Group, either large or small, was assigned to each kind of work. This gave a social nature to all occupations. In passing over the farm, one would notice the animation and happiness attending all work. No one being directly responsible for his own support, it might be supposed there would have been a disposition to shirk, and to let those who would, do what was to be done, but such was not the case. Our success depended entirely on our own exertions, there being no means or capital of any account upon which to rely, and each, therefore, felt that he or she must labor constantly, in order to have the experiment prove a success.

We had a great many visitors and applicants for membership. At the time of which I write, there was a widespread interest in the question of Social Reform or "Association," as we called it. Societies were formed in a great many of the large cities of the Eastern, Middle, and Western States, and lecturers upon the subject traversed the county, awakening people to an interest in the movement. The record shows that in one year we had over four thousand visitors. Many of these came from curiosity, but large numbers hoping they might find an immediate home with us. Persons desirous of joining us, if encouraged by the Directors to apply for membership, were expected to make a statement of what they could bring to the Association, of their occupation or ability in any branch of industry, and any other matters supposed to bear upon the question of admission. If they were thought to be desirable persons for membership, they came, lived and worked with us for at least one month as applicants; after which they were voted upon, and if received as candidates, remained another month, when the vote was taken upon their final admission. This probationship saved us from being flooded with incompetent or useless members.

As an evidence of the devotion shown by our members, I would instance the following — At the end of a certain period it became necessary to reduce our expenses, or to increase our income, and not being evident how the latter could be accomplished it was voted to institute some system of retrenchment in the food. The living was already very simple; indeed it was regarded by many as very cheap and poor; very few delicacies were afforded; gingerbread was the only cake; meat was only occasionally furnished, never but once a day, and the food, though healthful and well cooked, was not equal to that ordinarily found upon a mechanic's table. In carrying out this system of retrenchment, butter was seldom furnished, meat less frequently than ever, and other changes of this sort were made; and yet all, without murmur, submitted to these privations. Had it been necessary to reduce the bill of fare to bread and butter, and our meals to two a day, I sincerely believe that nearly all of our members would have cheerfully acquiesced in the arrangement.

As a rule, the labors were divided between the sexes, as is usual in ordinary society; the women attending to the household duties, and the men to the work on the farm or in the workshops.

Wherever there was a portion of the household work more appropriate to the stronger muscle or tougher frame of the man, that portion was given to men to perform. In the kitchen as baker, in the washroom as assistant, in the dormitory to bring and carry water. I shall never forget the impression made upon my youthful mind on the occasion of my first visit to the Farm, as we drove into the yard (coming from the city as we did) at seeing one of the members (as we afterwards learned, a gentleman of great culture, education, poetic talent and refinement, from the town of Concord) engaged in hanging out the morning's washing! And yet, was not this appropriate work in rough weather for a man? Seldom did our women participate in outdoor work, though I remember on one or more occasions, when help in that direction was imperatively needed, a half dozen of our young women did very active work in the hay field. In several of the groups, notably the waiters' groups, the young men and women were about equally divided in numbers, and the same in some of the labors connected with the kitchen.

Dress

While each person at Brook Farm dressed according to his or her own taste or ability, the utmost simplicity prevailed. There was little occasion for the display of dress, and there was no encouragement for it; indeed the average condition of the individual finances did not admit of much expenditure. Other pleasures or enjoyments were more valued, and there was no superiority whatever conferred by it.

The most refined and cultivated of our teachers and scholars would be seen at times, at work in barn or field, dressed as any farmer engaged at such work. There was no false standard of merit based upon the style or quality of the clothing. Our companions were all judged by a higher test than that. In accordance with the practical spirit of our enterprise, and the spirit of economy that prevailed, the short dress was generally adopted by the girls, and by some of the women, as a working dress, and it was admirable for this purpose, and also for a walking dress — an exercise of which our women were remarkably fond; partly, no doubt, because of the ease with which it was accomplished in the short dress and skirts. Not only its lightness and convenience was appreciated by most of our women, but its healthfulness. The oldest and youngest, matron and maiden, teacher and scholar, enjoyed and appreciated it, and it was the only style of dress worn by some of our women, either on the Farm or away from it, when there were no sufficient reasons for not wearing it. Indeed, some of our women, years after leaving the Farm, wore it as a working and occasional dress. In summer it was made of light goods, generally pretty prints or ginghams; in winter of heavy woolen or mixed goods. The favorite dress of the men was the Tunic, very similar in cut to the Norfolk jacket of the present day. The summer Tunic was of brown linen; the winter one of Rob Roy or blue and black plaid flannel, with an occasional difference in color and style of making up. It served in place of vest and coat, and was worn with a black leather belt. As to style, little was attempted. What was most comfortable, and at the same time economical, was most satisfactory and sure to be adopted. In the neat, simple and cheap costume of Brook Farm, persons of means and culture felt as "well dressed" as when arrayed in the garments which were fashionable in the "outside world," as we used to term it. One of its most valuable results was, that it gave us opportunity for intellectual, moral, and social improvement, then — if not now — rarely found in ordinary society except by people of leisure. The relief to women, especially, by this freedom, was very great. . . .

Let me endeavor to give you a clearer idea of Brook Farm life by a brief description of a working day. At five o'clock (except in the hardest of winter weather), the waking horn sounded, a sort of bugle being used instead of a bell. Those belonging to the groups engaged in teaming, care of animals, barn or stable work, together with those who were to make ready the breakfast, were obliged to be up early attending to their duties; others having SPECIAL work to do, or desirous of gaining time, so as to be at liberty during some other portion of the day, would be found at their work before breakfast, but generally most of the labor was performed between breakfast and supper. At half past six o'clock, the horn again announced that in a half hour breakfast would be ready, giving those at the other houses time to reach "The Hive," where the kitchen and dining room were located. Then might be seen from fifty to a hundred persons wending their way, generally in groups of two or more, towards "The Hive." At seven o'clock, in one dining room (with six tables placed lengthwise, in two rows, each capable of seating from fifteen to twenty persons) would quickly gather most of our people. The tables were plain boards joined together and placed upon stands covered with white table cloths, the seats plain wooden benches. Though simple, everything in the arrangements connected with the tables, was extremely neat and cleanly. At morning and evening meals, six waiters, young women, one at each table, kept the tables supplied with the food and drink prepared for that meal. It was a pleasant social time; all joined in making the time spent at our meals the pleasantest part of the day's intercourse. Though the food was plain, it was abundant and very nicely prepared, and the good cheer attending the meals made them very enjoyable.

Breakfast over, each one started for the day's work, the scholar for his studies and recitations; the printer, shoemaker, and wood worker for the work-shop; the farmer for the barn and field; the editor to his editorial work; the teamster for his duties, and so on. At the same time, the women commenced the various labors in their departments; some joined the washing group or ironing, others to the kitchen, one group to dormitory or chamber work, another to the consistory or lamp work, another to the day nursery, another to the sewing. Here might be seen Mr. Ripley, dressed like any farmer, with half a dozen others, on the way to the potato field to engage in regular farm work; Mr. John S. Dwight or Mrs. Ripley surrounded by a group of students on their way to The Eyrie for recitation or study. Here, Mr. Charles A. Dana and a group of young men and boys with hoes, starting for the nursery to look after the needs of the young trees, and a jolly time they would have of it, at the same time being active and attentive to their work. In the dormitory group, one or two young men were always ready to do the heavy work, carrying water, etc. In the kitchen would be found a male assistant, in addition to the baker. In the washroom and ironing work, there was a man to assist in the labor requiring strength. Some of these labors, like mangling,[2] would employ the person the entire forenoon; others only a part of it, after which he would be free to join some other group near at hand.

At noon again, the horn gave notice of dinner a half hour later, allowing time for those in the fields and at a distance to prepare for the meal. Young men were the waiters at dinner, and prominent among them were Messrs. Charles A. Dana, John S. Dwight, Frederic Cabot, and John Orvis.

Though there was usually no loud laughter, there was always a great deal of fun and joviality consequent upon the number assembled together and the great freedom that existed at the Farm. The coming and going of so many visitors, many of them persons of note, added a good deal of life to the middle of the day.

After dinner the members again repaired to their various occupations until called to supper at 6 P.M. Here again, though simple the fare, the sociality of the occasion added a zest to the meal.

Supper being over, our young people enjoyed themselves in any way they were disposed. In summer with games, or in walks with their favorite companions along the beautiful road leading to West Roxbury. A happy group was always found around the large swing. For the older ones, there were Group or Series meetings; there business and pleasure were often intermingled; singing and other classes for adults as well as for the young; an extempore concert, a lecture from some visitor, books to be read from the library, various games in the members' rooms, and occasionally a dance. There was no prescribed hour for retiring, but generally all was quiet by 10 o'clock.

The assembling of our people as the hours for meals approached, gathered as they were from all classes, afforded great entertainment. In summer, collected as they were under the great elm in the front yard, or in winter in the reception rooms or entry of "The Hive" before and after meals, the social element had large scope, forming quite a feature in the ordinary enjoyment of the day.

In drawing this sketch to a close, let me mention a few of the principal points of difference between our life at Brook Farm and that of ordinary society. Perhaps I may, in this way, more clearly show you the attractions of the life and indicate in a measure my grounds for believing that some such form of social organization must supersede our present isolated imperfect one.

---

[2]*mangling:* Using a machine that ironed laundry between two heated rollers.

The Social Nature of the Life

The life at the Farm, as I have tried to show you, was of the most social character imaginable, and this, too, without the infringement of the individual privacy and rights of any member. From one hundred to two hundred persons associated as one family naturally gave great chance for the play of the social elements of character. You have all noticed how much animation and enthusiasm there is at a picnic, and how the work necessary to be done is, by the combined help, made to seem more like play than work. So it was at Brook Farm. Our trials seemed comparatively light, borne as they were by so many, and amid so much sympathy and love. In all of this, I see simply a leading demand of the soul supplied. In present society the social demands of our nature, if not actually starved, are poorly fed. Brook Farm showed how they can be better supplied if not wholly satisfied.

The Economies Resulting from a Combined Life, as Compared to Isolated Homes

Our productive industries were few, and we lacked the organizing talent to find new ones, and had it not been for the savings and economy resulting from the associated mode of life, we very much sooner would have been obliged to disband. (In the kitchen one cook and one baker, with some assistance, prepared the meals, which for the same number in our ordinary houses would have required twenty-five. In the washroom, four or five women, with one man and some machinery, did the work of twenty-five more, and the same in the ironing and dining rooms, and so on.) In the purchase of food and its cooking, heating, and so forth, the combination of individuals insures great economy.

Superior Educational Advantages for All

In the rearing and education of children, the associated life has immense advantages over ordinary society — while under a watchfulness and attention that few persons, even the wealthy, can give their little ones. The children of the community are far happier than those in isolated homes.

Young children of the members had the same opportunities for instruction as had our boarding scholars. Older children from twelve to sixteen years of age, worked at various employments in the forenoon, and attended school in the afternoon.

Adults wishing education in the English branches, languages, music, or dancing, had only to express their wish and they could have the benefit of the best teachers of the place, without expense.

The Mingling of the Sexes

Perhaps no more important advantage than this was realized by us. Much of the misunderstandings and unhappiness of married life springs from a faulty knowledge of each other, gained in the limited acquaintanceship allowed by our present imperfect social system. Young men and women rarely meet in relations to each other which admit opportunities to learn either the strength or the weakness of character, of the opposite sex. So, when close relations are established, they are surprised at finding in the character of the other what they did not expect, or at not finding what they confidently did expect.

At Brook Farm, opportunities for knowing each other thoroughly were constantly afforded, and the result was satisfactory in the highest degree. Not only did the sexes comprehend each other better; they had more respect for each other, more confidence in each other; a better appreciation of the wants and needs of each other.

The Combination of City and Country Life

We had this at Brook Farm. While living in the beautiful country, with all its attractions to eye and ear, its pure air, its healthfulness; we had the activity, social life, amusements, and other attractions which numbers gave. This was of great advantage, especially to the young; and it supplied what I believe to be one of the most serious and vital deficiencies of present society, and one which, more than any other, is the cause of intemperence and others of the grosser evils of our times.

The Doing Away with the False Relation of Employer and Employed, and the Disadvantages of What Is Called "Help"

Some of these ladies can appreciate the relief occasioned by this latter change. With us, it was brother and sister working together at labors which were all equally honorable.

The Satisfaction Resulting from the Belief
That We Were Helping to Solve One
of the Great Questions of the Future

You all know, I am sure, the luxury of working for objects which are deemed for the benefit of others. We were deeply impressed at Brook Farm, young as well as old, with the idea that only through the application of the principle of cooperation or association, could the spirit of Christianity be realized in actual life; and the belief that we were introducing co-operation in place of COMPETITION and AN-TAGONISM added very largely to our enthusiasm, contentment, and happiness.

The Full Recognition of the Equality
of the Sexes

To us Brook Farmers, the discussions of the questions concerning a woman's right to vote, to hold property, or office, and to equal privileges with her brother, seem like going back a generation or more and reviving questions then settled. For at Brook Farm no one questioned the right or propriety of a woman's doing any act, following any vocation, taking part in any enterprise in which men were engaged, that she felt fitted for or was disposed to undertake. Hence, no distinction was made between the sexes in the ordinary conduct of affairs. There might be a Group with one exception, of women, and that exception the chief, a man, or again, a Group mostly of men, with the leader a woman. So, upon all committees and councils, women were placed equally with men. To illustrate: A Council of "Arbiters" so called, was appointed, to whom individuals and departments were to bring all complaints, charges, or grievances not provided for in other ways, and who were to take cognizance of all matters relating to morals and manners. This Council was to consist of seven persons, a majority of them to be women.

The Social or Enlarged Home Was Found
to More than Fill the Place of the Private
or Isolated One

It is well known that there are but few persons, women especially, but what will say: "I could not have given up my private house and home for a combined one." But the women of Brook farm, coming from what is termed the highest ranks in society, as well as from the humbler ones, were unanimous in their expressions of contentment with the home there furnished, and acknowledged its superiority in a great variety of ways to all isolated ones.

Yᵉ MAY SESSION OF Yᵉ WOMAN'S RIGHTS CONVENTION—Yᵉ ORATOR OF Yᵉ DAY DENOUNCING Yᵉ LORDS OF CREATION.

"Women's Rights Convention" cartoon from *Harpers Weekly,* June 11, 1859. The Seneca Falls Convention, advocating women's rights, was held in July 1848, yet as this cartoon shows, such meetings, conventions, and conferences were still being satirized more than a decade later.

4

Women's Roles and Rights

Like other nineteenth-century reform movements, the struggle for women's rights was complex and diverse. Angelina E. Grimké and Catharine Beecher, for example, disagreed with each other on whether women should participate in public life and be involved in anti-slavery efforts, yet each in her own way believed she was working to expand women's roles, prospects, and powers. The women's movement included intellectuals like Lydia Maria Child and Margaret Fuller and middle-class activists like Elizabeth Cady Stanton and Susan B. Anthony, who met Stanton in 1851 and teamed with her in advancing feminist causes. It also included African American women and white working women like those who labored in the textile mills in Lowell, Massachusetts. By the 1830s and in increasing numbers in the 1840s and 1850s, women of many different backgrounds were calling for and beginning to enact changes in education, law, marriage, the workplace, and the family.

Feminism seems to have taken early root in temperance activism. As I noted in the Introduction, in the 1820s and 1830s, women formed roughly half of the membership of American Temperance Society auxiliaries and state societies. They ran societies of their own as well as joining those with a mixed-gender membership.

The "woman question" emerged most dramatically, however, as a by-product of anti-slavery. When the abolitionists Angelina Grimké and her sister Sarah were mobbed in the 1830s for speaking in public before audiences that included men, they were obliged to proclaim and defend their rights as women. Angelina Grimké, Child, Fuller, and Stanton pointed out that the struggle for freedom for African Americans clarified for white, middle-class women the nature of their own oppression and lack of full equality (e.g., no control of their property once they married, exclusion from most occupations and from advanced schooling). "The investigation of the rights of the slave," Grimké concluded, "has led me to a better understanding of my own."

The documents by Harriet Farley, who evokes the daydreams of a weaver at her loom in a textile mill, and by Hawthorne, who tells of the death by drowning of a Concord schoolteacher named Martha Hunt, give some indication of the cost and difficulty of the new roles women were occupying. Frequently, gender issues intersected with class issues, as is evident in the presentation of the wealthy Zenobia and the poor seamstress Priscilla in *The Blithedale Romance*. Social class and economic situation could either contribute to self-culture and a higher self for women or forestall them.

It is intriguing that Hawthorne took much of the description of Zenobia's death from his notebook entry on Hunt's suicide. Hunt, age nineteen, was closer perhaps to someone like Priscilla than to the radiant, privileged Zenobia. Hawthorne describes the search for her body, which, when found, was clenched and rigid, as is Zenobia's. Hunt knew both Fuller and Emerson, and they encouraged her intellectual pursuits and loaned books to her. But it was part of her pain that she was not, and could never become, someone like Fuller. Hunt's death jolted Fuller and her friends, because it proved that not everyone, and certainly not all women, could exchange a limited, monotonous reality for the ideals of transcendentalism and reform.

Similar ambiguities about gender — about women's *and* men's roles — circulate throughout *The Blithedale Romance*, and the points of view offered in the selections below enable us more keenly to reflect upon them. Zenobia displays self-dramatizing but charismatic passion for newness and experiment and intellectual discovery, and she is the most compelling figure in the novel. One might indeed be tempted initially to see her as an embodiment of the spirit of independence and self-assertion that Stanton and the other women who gathered at Seneca Falls, New York, in 1848, expressed in their "Declaration of Sentiments." Yet Zenobia is conflicted in her desires and self-tormentingly in love with a man she cannot have, and hence is portrayed as a women whose feminist principles are not in accord with her true needs.

At the end of the novel, Coverdale announces that he loves Zenobia's rival, her half-sister Priscilla. These words have puzzled (and sometimes exasperated) readers, nearly all of whom have found Zenobia to be far more complex and captivating than Priscilla. Some have even proposed that it is Hollingsworth whom Coverdale really loves, the man who tenderly nurses Coverdale back to health and whose seductive offer — that they forge a union in reform — Coverdale spurns. *The Blithedale Romance* studies divisions and tensions within individual gender roles and disturbances within male and female friendships.

ANGELINA E. GRIMKÉ

"Human Rights Not Founded on Sex"

Angelina Emily Grimké (1805–1879) and Sarah Moore Grimké (1792–1873) were sisters from Charleston, South Carolina, who became abolitionists and advocates of rights for women. Having been raised in a wealthy slaveholding family, they had a special authority in speaking on behalf of black slaves. But the idea of women as public speakers before mixed audiences was a highly contested one, and many Northerners, including clergymen and abolitionists (though not Garrison and Douglass), were adamantly opposed to it.

Angelina's first two pamphlets were her *Appeal to the Christian Women of the Southern States* (1836) and *Appeal to the Women of the Nominally Free States* (1837). Perhaps her best book is *Letters to Catharine Beecher* (1837), which consists of letters that had originally appeared in the anti-slavery papers *The Liberator* and *The Emancipator*. In these letters, Grimké replies to Beecher's *Essays on Slavery and Abolitionism with Reference to the Duty of American Females* (1837), which criticized abolition and women's public activity in anti-slavery campaigns. The following selection is taken from the revised edition of *Letters to Catharine Beecher,* published in 1838.

East Boylston, Mass. October 2, 1837.

Dear Friend:

In my last, I made a sort of running commentary upon thy views of the appropriate sphere of woman, with something like a promise, that in my next, I would give thee my own.

The investigation of the rights of the slave has led me to a better understanding of my own. I have found the Anti-Slavery cause to be the high school of morals in our land — the school in which *human rights* are more fully investigated, and better understood and taught, than in any other. Here a great fundamental principle is uplifted and illuminated, and from this central light, rays innumerable stream all around. Human beings have *rights*, because they are *moral* beings; the rights of *all* men grow out of their moral nature; and as all men have the same moral nature, they have essentially the same rights. These rights may be wrested from the slave, but they cannot be alienated: his title to himself is as perfect *now*, as is that of Lyman Beecher:[1] it is stamped on his moral being, and is, like it, imperishable. Now if rights are founded in the nature of our moral being, then the *mere circumstance of sex* does not give to man higher rights and responsibilities, than to woman. To suppose that it does, would be to deny the self-evident truth, that the "physical constitution is the mere instrument of the moral nature." To suppose that it does, would be to break up utterly the relations, of the two natures, and to reverse their functions, exalting the animal nature into a monarch, and humbling the moral [nature] into a slave; making the former a proprietor, and the latter its property. When human beings are regarded as *moral* beings, *sex*, instead of being enthroned upon the summit, administering upon rights and responsibilities, sinks into insignificance and nothingness. My doctrine then is, that whatever it is morally right for man to do, it is morally right for woman to do. Our duties originate, not from difference of sex, but from the diversity of our relations in life, the various gifts and talents committed to our care, and the different eras in which we live.

The regulation of duty by the mere circumstance of sex, rather than by the fundamental principle of moral being, has led to all that multifarious train of evils flowing out of the anti-christian doctrine of masculine and feminine virtues. By this doctrine, man has been converted into the warrior, and clothed with sternness, and those other kindred qualities, which in common estimation belong to his character as a *man*; whilst woman has been taught to lean upon an arm of flesh, to sit as a doll arrayed in "gold, and pearls, and costly array," to be admired for her personal charms, and caressed and humored like a spoiled child, or converted into a mere drudge to suit the con-

[1]*Lyman Beecher:* Beecher (1775–1863) was an eminent Presbyterian clergyman; his children included Catharine Beecher and Harriet Beecher Stowe.

venience of her lord and master. Thus have all the diversified relations of life been filled with "confusion and every evil work." This
principle has given to man a charter for the exercise of tyranny and
selfishness, pride and arrogance, lust and brutal violence. It has
robbed woman of essential rights, the right to think and speak and
act on all great moral questions, just as men think and speak and act;
the right to share their responsibilities, perils and toils; the right to
fulfill the great end of her being, as a moral, intellectual and immortal
creature, and of glorifying God in her body and her spirit which are
His. Hitherto, instead of being a help meet to man, in the highest,
noblest sense of the term as a companion, a co-worker, an equal; she
has been a mere appendage of his being, an instrument of his convenience and pleasure, the pretty toy with which he wiled away his
leisure moments, or the pet animal whom he humored into playfulness and submission. Woman, instead of being regarded as the equal
of man, has uniformly been looked down upon as his inferior, a mere
gift to fill up the measure of his happiness. In "the poetry of romantic
gallantry," it is true, she has been called "the last *best* gift of God to
man"; but I believe I speak forth the words of truth and soberness
when I affirm, that woman never was given to man. She was created,
like him, in the image of God, and crowned with glory and honor;
created only a little lower than the angels, — not, as is almost universally assumed, a little lower than man; on her brow, as well as on his,
was placed the "diadem of beauty," and in her hand the sceptre of
universal dominion. Gen: i. 27, 28. "The last *best gift* of God to
man"! Where is the scripture warrant for this "rhetorical flourish,
this splendid absurdity"? Let us examine the account of her creation.
"And the rib which the Lord God had taken from man, made he a
woman, and brought her unto the man." Not as a gift — for Adam
immediately recognized her *as part of himself* — ("this is now bone
of my bone, and flesh of my flesh") — a companion and equal, not
one hair's breadth beneath him in the majesty and glory of her moral
being; not placed under his authority as a *subject*, but by his side, on
the same platform of human rights, under the government of God
only. This idea of woman's being "the last gift of God to man," however pretty it may sound to the ears of those who love to discourse
upon "the poetry of romantic gallantry, and the generous promptings
of chivalry," has nevertheless been the means of sinking her from an
end into a mere *means* — of turning her into an *appendage* to man,
instead of recognizing her as *a part of man* — of destroying her individuality, and rights, and responsibilities, and merging her moral

being in that of man. Instead of *Jehovah* being *her* king, *her* lawgiver, and *her* judge, she has been taken out of the exalted scale of existence in which He placed her, and subjected to the despotic control of man.

I have often been amused at the vain efforts made to define the rights and responsibilities of immortal beings as *men* and *women*. No one has yet found out just *where* the line of separation between them should be drawn, and for this simple reason, that no one knows just how far below man woman is, whether she be a head shorter in her moral responsibilities, or head and shoulders, or the full length of his noble stature, below him, i.e. under his feet. Confusion, uncertainty, and great inconsistencies, must exist on this point, so long as woman is regarded in the least degree inferior to man; but place her where her Maker placed her, on the same high level of human rights with man, side by side with him, and difficulties vanish, the mountains of perplexity flow down at the presence of this grand equalizing principle. Measure her rights and duties by the unerring standard of *moral being,* not by the false weights and measures of a mere circumstance of her human existence, and then the truth will be self-evident, that whatever it is *morally* right for a man to do, it is *morally* right for a woman to do. I recognize no rights but *human* rights — I know nothing of men's rights and women's rights; for in Christ Jesus, there is neither male nor female. It is my solemn conviction, that, until this principle of equality is recognised and embodied in practice, the church can do nothing effectual for the permanent reformation of the world. Woman was the first transgressor, and the first victim of power. In all heathen nations, she has been the slave of man, and Christian nations have never acknowledged her rights. Nay more, no Christian denomination or Society has ever acknowledged them on the broad basis of humanity. I know that in some denominations, she is permitted to preach the gospel; not from a conviction of her rights, nor upon the ground of her equality as a *human being*, but of her equality in spiritual gifts — for we find that women, even in these Societies, is allowed no voice in framing the Discipline by which she is to be governed. Now, I believe it is woman's right to have a voice in all the laws and regulations by which she is to be *governed,* whether in Church or State; and that the present arrangements of society, on these points, are *a violation of human rights, a rank usurpation of power*, a violent seizure and confiscation of what is sacredly and inalienably hers — thus inflicting upon woman outrageous wrongs, working mischief incalculable in the social circle, and in its influence on the world producing only evil, and that continually. *If* Ecclesiastical and Civil governments are ordained of God, *then* I contend that woman has just as much right to sit in solemn counsel in Conventions, Conferences, Associations and General Assemblies, as man — just as much right to sit upon the throne of England, or in the Presidential chair of the United States.

Dost thou ask me, if I would wish to see woman engaged in the contention and strife of sectarian controversy, or in the intrigues of political partizans? I say no! never — never. I rejoice that she does not stand on the same platform which man now occupies in these respects: but I mourn, also, that he should thus prostitute his higher nature, and vilely cast away his birthright. I prize the purity of *his* character as highly as I do that of hers. As a moral being, *whatever it is morally wrong for her to do, it is morally wrong for him to do.* The fallacious doctrine of male and female virtues has well nigh ruined all that is morally great and lovely in his character: he has been quite as deep a sufferer by it as woman, though mostly in different respects and by other processes. As my time is engrossed by the pressing responsibilities of daily public duty, I have no leisure for that minute detail which would be required for the illustration and defence of these principles. Thou wilt find a wide field opened before thee, in the investigation of which, I doubt not, thou wilt be instructed. Enter this field, and explore it; thou wilt find in it a hid treasure, more precious than rubies — a fund, a mine of principles, as new as they are great and glorious.

Thou sayest, "an ignorant, a narrow-minded, or a stupid woman, cannot feel nor understand the rationality, the propriety, or the beauty of this relation" — i.e., subordination to man. Now, verily, it does appear to me, that nothing but a narrow-minded view of the subject of human rights and responsibilities can induce any one to believe in *this subordination to a fallible* being. Sure I am, that the signs of the times clearly indicate a vast and rapid change in public sentiment on this subject. Sure I am that she is not to be, as she has been, "*a mere second-hand agent*" in the regeneration of a fallen world, but the acknowledged equal and co-worker with man in this glorious work. Not that "she will carry her measures by tormenting when she cannot please, or by petulant complaints or obtrusive interference, in matters which are out of her sphere, and which she cannot comprehend." But just in proportion as her moral and intellectual capacities become enlarged, she will rise higher and higher in the scale of creation, until she reaches that elevation prepared for her by her Maker, and upon whose summit she was originally stationed, only "a little lower than the angels." Then will it be seen that nothing which concerns the well-being of mankind is either beyond her sphere, or above her comprehension: *Then* will it be seen "that America will be distinguished above all other nations for well educated women, and for the influence they will exert on the general interests of society."

But I must close with recommending to thy perusal, my sister's Letters on the Province of Woman, published in the New England Spectator, and republished by Isaac Knapp of Boston. As she has taken up this subject so fully, I have only glanced at it. That thou and all my country-women may better understand the true dignity of woman, is the sincere desire of

Thy Friend,

A. E. GRIMKÉ

CATHARINE BEECHER

From A Treatise on Domestic Economy

Catharine Beecher (1800–1878) was an influential writer on religion, health, housekeeping, and women's education. She taught in and founded schools for girls in Connecticut in the 1820s and later organized "female institutes" in several states in the Midwest. She promoted the right of women to an education, yet she also favored the traditional role of woman as homemaker, opposed suffrage for women, and argued against women's involvement in abolitionism, the cause that her sister Harriet later advocated in *Uncle Tom's Cabin* (1852). Beecher was the author of many books, but her best-known work is *A Treatise on Domestic Economy*, first published in 1841 and frequently reprinted. It is an excellent example of the widely popular tradition of the conduct manual or guide for women. In the following selection, Beecher surveys the duties and demands of the "domestic arrangements" for which women are responsible. Her observations stand in contrast to the position that Grimké presents on behalf of women's public role.

The discussion of the question of the equality of the sexes, in intellectual capacity, seems both frivolous and useless, not only because it can never be decided, but because there would be no possible advantage in the decision. But one topic, which is often drawn into this discussion, is of far more consequence; and that is, the relative importance and difficulty of the duties a woman is called to perform.

It is generally assumed, and almost as generally conceded, that women's business and cares are contracted and trivial; and that the proper discharge of her duties demands far less expansion of mind and vigor of intellect, than the pursuits of the other sex. This idea has prevailed, because women, as a mass, have never been educated with reference to their most important duties; while that portion of their employments which are of least value, have been regarded as the chief, if not the sole concern of a woman. The covering of the body, the conveniences of residences, and the gratification of the appetite, have been too much regarded as the sole objects on which her intellectual powers are to be exercised.

But as society gradually shakes off the remnants of barbarism, and the intellectual and moral interests of man rise in estimation above the merely sensual, a truer estimate is formed of woman's duties, and of the measure of intellect requisite for the proper discharge of them. Let any man of sense and discernment become the member of a large household, in which a well-educated and pious woman is endeavoring systematically to discharge her multiform duties; let him fully comprehend all her cares, difficulties, and perplexities; and it is probable he would coincide in the opinion, that no statesman, at the head of a nation's affairs, had more frequent calls for wisdom, firmness, tact, discrimination, prudence, and versatility of talent, than such a woman.

She has a husband, whose peculiar tastes and habits she must accommodate; she has children, whose health she must guard, whose physical constitution she must study and develope, whose temper and habits she must regulate, whose principles she must form, whose pursuits she must direct. She has constantly changing domestics, with all varieties of temper and habits, whom she must govern, instruct, and direct; she is required to regulate the finances of the domestic state, and constantly to adapt expenditures to the means and to the relative claims of each department. She has the direction of the kitchen, where ignorance, forgetfulness, and awkwardness are to be so regulated, that the various operations shall each start at the right time, and all be in completeness at the same given hour. She has the claims of society to meet, calls to receive and return, and the duties of hospitality to sustain. She has the poor to relieve; benevolent societies to aid; the schools of her children to inquire and decide about; the care of the sick; the nursing of infancy; and the endless miscellany of odd items constantly recurring in a large family.

Surely it is a pernicious and mistaken idea, that the duties which tax a woman's mind are petty, trivial, or unworthy of the highest grade of intellect and moral worth. Instead of allowing this feeling, every woman should imbibe, from early youth, the impression, that she is training for the discharge of the most important, the most difficult, and the most sacred and interesting duties that can possibly employ the highest intellect. She ought to feel that her station and responsibilities, in the great drama of life, are second to none, either as viewed by her Maker, or in the estimation of all minds whose judgement is most worthy of respect.

She, who is the mother and housekeeper in a large family, is the sovereign of an empire demanding as varied cares, and involving more difficult duties, than are really exacted of her, who, while she wears the crown, and professedly regulates the interests of the greatest nation on earth, finds abundant leisure for theatres, balls, horse-races, and every gay pursuit.

There is no one thing, more necessary to a housekeeper, in performing her varied duties, than *a habit of system and order;* and yet the peculiarly desultory nature of women's pursuits, and the embarrassments resulting from the state of domestic service in this Country, render it very difficult to form such a habit. But it is sometimes the case, that women, who could and would carry forward a systematic plan of domestic economy, do not attempt it, simply from a want of knowledge of the various modes of introducing it. It is with reference to such, that various modes of securing system and order, which the Writer has seen adopted, will be pointed out.

A wise economy is nowhere more conspicuous, than in the right *apportionment of time* to different pursuits. There are duties of a religious, intellectual, social, and domestic, nature, each having different relative claims on attention. Unless a person has some general plan of apportioning these claims, some will intrench on others, and some, it is probable, will be entirely excluded. Thus, some find religious, social, and domestic, duties, so numerous, that no time is given to intellectual improvement. Others, find either social, or benevolent, or religious, interests, excluded by the extent and variety of other engagements.

It is wise, therefore, for all persons to devise a general plan, which they will at least keep in view, and aim to accomplish, and by which, a proper proportion of time shall be secured for all the duties of life.

In forming such a plan, every woman must accommodate herself to the peculiarities of her situation. If she has a large family, and a small income, she must devote far more time to the simple duty of providing food and raiment, than would be right were she in affluence and with a small family. It is impossible, therefore, to draw out any general plan, which all can adopt. But there are some *general principles*, which ought to be the guiding rules, when a woman arranges her domestic employments. These general principles are to be based on Christianity, which teaches us to "seek first the kingdom of God,"[1] and to place food, raiment, and the conveniences of life, as of secondary account. Every woman, then, ought to start with the assumption, that religion is of more consequence than any worldly concern, and that whatever else may be sacrificed, this shall be the leading object in all her arrangements, in respect to time, money, and attention. It is also one of the plainest requisitions of Christianity, that we devote some of our time and efforts to the comfort and improvement of others. There is no duty so constantly enforced, both in the Old and New Testament, as the duty of charity, in dispensing to those who are destitute of the blessings we enjoy. In selecting objects of charity, the same rule applies to others, as well as to ourselves; that their moral and religious interests are of the first concern, and that for them, as well as ourselves, we are to "seek first the kingdom of God."

Another general principle, is, that our intellectual and social interests are to be preferred to the mere gratification of taste or appetite. A portion of time, therefore, must be devoted to the cultivation of the intellect and the social affections.

Another general principle, is, that the mere gratification of appetite is to be placed *last* in our estimate, so that, when a question arises as to which shall be sacrificed, some intellectual, moral, or social, advantage, or some gratification of sense, we should invariably sacrifice the last.

Another general principle, is, that, as health is indispensable to the discharge of every duty, nothing that sacrifices that blessing is to be allowed, in order to gain any other advantage or enjoyment. There are emergencies, when it is right to risk health and life, to save ourselves and others from greater evils; but these are exceptions, which do not vacate the general rule. Many persons imagine, that, if they violate the laws of health in performing religious or domestic duties,

[1]Matthew 6:33.

they are guiltless before God. But such greatly mistake. We as directly violate the law "thou shalt not kill," when we do what tends to risk or shorten our own life, as if we should intentionally run a dagger into a neighbor. True, we may escape any fatal or permanently injurious effects, and so may a dagger or bullet miss the mark, or do only transient injury. But this, in either case, makes the sin none the less. The life and happiness of all His creatures are dear to our Creator; and He is as much displeased, when we injure our own interests, as when we injure others. So that the idea that we are excusable if we harm no one but ourselves, is most false and pernicious. These, then, are the general principles, to guide a woman in systematizing her duties and pursuits.

The Creator of all things is a Being of perfect system and order; and to aid us in our duty, in this respect, he has divided our time, by a regularly returning day of rest from worldly business. In following this example, the intervening six days may be subdivided to secure similar benefits. In doing this, a certain portion of time must be given to procure the means of livelihood, and for preparing food, raiment, and dwellings. To these objects, some must devote more, and others less, attention. The remainder of time not necessarily thus employed, might be divided somewhat in this manner: The leisure of two afternoons and evenings could be devoted to religious and benevolent objects, such as religious meetings, charitable associations, Sunday school visiting, and attention to the sick and poor. The leisure of two other days might be devoted to intellectual improvement, and the pursuits of taste. The leisure of another day might be devoted to social enjoyments, in making or receiving visits; and that of another to miscellaneous domestic pursuits, not included in the other particulars.

It is probable that few persons could carry out such an arrangement, very strictly; but every one can make out a systematic arrangement of time, and at least *aim* at accomplishing it; and they can also compare the time which they actually devote to these different objects, with such a general outline, for the purpose of modifying any mistaken proportions.

Instead of attempting some such systematic employment of time, and carrying it out so far as they can control circumstances, most women are rather driven along by the daily occurrences of life, so that, instead of being the intelligent regulators of their own time, they are the mere sport of circumstances. There is nothing which so distinctly marks the difference between weak and strong minds, as the fact, whether they control circumstances, or circumstances control them.

It is very much to be feared, that the apportionment of time, actually made by a great portion of women, exactly inverts the order required by reason and Christianity. Thus the furnishing a needless variety of food, the conveniences of dwellings, and the adornments of dress, often take a larger portion of time, than is given to any other object. Next after this, comes intellectual improvement; and last of all, benevolence and religion.

It may be urged, that it is indispensable for most persons to give more time to earn a livelihood, and to prepare food, raiment, and dwellings, than to any other object. But it may be asked, how much time devoted to these objects is employed in preparing varieties of food, not necessary, but rather injurious, and how much is spent for those parts of dress and furniture not indispensable, and merely ornamental? Let a woman subtract from her domestic employments, all the time given to pursuits which are of no use, except as they gratify a taste for ornament, or minister increased varieties to tempt appetite, and she will find, that much, which she calls "domestic duties," and which prevent her attention to intellectual, benevolent, and religious, objects, should be called by a very different name. No woman has a right to give up attention to the higher interests of herself and others, for the ornaments of taste or the gratification of the palate. To a certain extent, these lower objects are lawful and desirable; but, when they intrude on nobler interests, they become selfish and degrading.

Some persons endeavor to systematize their pursuits, by apportioning them to particular hours of each day. For example, a certain period before breakfast, is given to devotional duties; after breakfast, certain hours are devoted to exercise and domestic employments; other hours to sewing, or reading, or visiting; and others to benevolent duties. But, in most cases, it is more difficult to systematize the hours of each day, than it is to sustain some regular division of the week.

In regard to the minutiæ of domestic arrangements, the Writer has known the following methods adopted. *Monday*, with some of the best housekeepers, is devoted to preparing for the labors of the week. Any extra cooking, the purchasing of articles to be used during the week, and the assorting of clothes for the wash, and mending such as would be injured without; — these and similar items belong to this day. *Tuesday* is devoted to washing, and *Wednesday* to ironing. On *Thursday*, the ironing is finished off, the clothes folded and put away, and all articles which need mending put in the mending basket, and attended to. *Friday* is devoted to sweeping and housecleaning. On

Saturday, and especially the last Saturday of every month, every department is put in order; the castors and table furniture are regulated, the pantry and cellar inspected, the trunks, drawers, and closets arranged, and every thing about the house put in order for *Sunday*. All the cooking needed for Sunday is also prepared. By this regular recurrence of a particular time for inspecting every thing, nothing is forgotten till ruined by neglect.

Another mode of systematizing, relates to providing proper supplies of conveniences, and proper places in which to keep them. Thus, some ladies keep a large closet, in which are placed the tubs, pails, dippers, soap-dishes, starch, bluing, clothes-line, clothes-pins, and every other article used in washing; and in the same or another place are kept every convenience for ironing. In the sewing department, a trunk, with suitable partitions, is provided, in which are placed, each in its proper place, white thread of all sizes, colored thread, yarns for mending, colored and black sewing-silks and twist, tapes and bobbins of all sizes, white and colored welting-cords, silk braids and cords, needles of all sizes, papers of pins, remnants of linen and colored cambric, a supply of all kinds of buttons used in the family, black and white hooks and eyes, a yard measure, and all the patterns used in cutting and fitting. These are done up in separate parcels and labelled. In another trunk, are kept all pieces used in mending, arranged in order, so that any article can be found without loss of time. A trunk like the first mentioned, will save many steps, and often much time and perplexity; while purchasing thus by the quantity makes them come much cheaper than if bought in little portions as they are wanted. Such a trunk should be kept locked, and a smaller supply, for current use, be kept in a workbasket.

The full supply of all conveniences in the kitchen and cellar, and a place appointed for each article, very much facilitates domestic labor. For want of this, much vexation and loss of time is occasioned, while seeking vessels in use, or in cleansing those used by different persons for various purposes. It would be far better for a lady to give up some expensive article in the parlor, and apply the money, thus saved, for kitchen conveniences, than to have a stinted supply where the most labor is to be performed. If our Countrywomen would devote more to comfort and convenience, and less to show, it would be a great improvement. Mirrors and pier-tables[2] in the parlor, and an unpainted,

---

[2]*pier-tables:* A pier-table is a table placed against a wall between two windows and usually under a pier glass (a large high mirror).

gloomy, ill-furnished kitchen, not unfrequently are found under the same roof.

Another important item, in systematic economy, is the apportioning of *regular* employment to the various members of a family. If a housekeeper can secure the cooperation of *all* her family, she will find that "many hands make light work." There is no greater mistake, than in bringing up children to feel that they must be taken care of, and waited on, by others, without any corresponding obligations on their part. The extent to which young children can be made useful in a family, would seem surprising to those who have never seen a *systematic* and *regular* plan for securing their services. The Writer has been in a family, where a little girl of eight or nine washed and dressed herself and little brother, and made their little beds before breakfast, set and cleared all the tables at meals, with a little help from a grown person in moving tables and spreading cloths, while all the dusting of parlors and chambers was also neatly performed by her. A little brother of ten, brought in and piled all the wood used in the kitchen and parlor, brushed the boots and shoes neatly, went on errands, and took all the care of the poultry. They were children whose parents could afford to hire this service, but who chose to have their children grow up healthy and industrious, while proper instructions, system, and encouragement, made these services rather a pleasure than otherwise to the children.

Some parents pay their children for such services; but this is hazardous, as tending to make them feel that they are not bound to be helpful without pay, and also as tending to produce a hoarding, money-making spirit. But where children have no hoarding propensities, and need to acquire a sense of the value of property, it may be well to let them earn money for some extra services, rather as a favor. When this is done, they should be taught to spend it for others, as well as for themselves; and in this way, a generous and liberal spirit will be cultivated.

There are some mothers, who take pains to teach their boys most of the domestic arts which their sisters learn. The Writer has seen boys mending their own garments, and aiding their mother or sisters in the kitchen, with great skill and adroitness; and at an early age they usually very much relish joining in such occupations. The sons of such mothers, in their college life, or in roaming about the world, or in nursing a sick wife or infant, find occasion to bless the forethought and kindness which prepared them for such emergencies. Few things are in worse taste, than for a man needlessly to busy himself in women's work; and yet a man never appears in a more interesting attitude, than when, by skill in such matters, he can save a mother or wife from care and suffering. The more a boy is taught to use his hands in every variety of domestic employment, the more his faculties, both of mind and body, are developed; for mechanical pursuits exercise the intellect, as well as the hands. The early training of New England boys, in which they turn their hand to almost every thing, is one great reason of the quick perceptions, versatility of mind, and mechanical skill, for which that portion of our Countrymen are distinguished.

The Writer has known one mode of systematizing the aid of the older children in a family, which, in some cases of very large families, it may be well to imitate. In the case referred to, when the oldest daughter was eight or nine years old, an infant sister was given to her as her special charge. She tended it, made and mended its clothes, taught it to read, and was its nurse and guardian through all its childhood. Another infant was given to the next daughter, and thus the children were all paired in this interesting relation. In addition to the relief thus afforded to the mother, the elder children were thus qualified for their future domestic relations, and both older and younger bound to each other by peculiar ties of tenderness and gratitude.

In offering these examples of various modes of systematizing, one suggestion may be worthy of attention. It is not unfrequently the case, that ladies, who find themselves cumbered with oppressive cares, after reading remarks on the benefits of system, immediately commence the task of arranging their pursuits, with great vigor and hope. They divide the day into regular periods, and give each hour its duty; they systematize their work, and endeavor to bring every thing into a regular routine. But in a short time, they find themselves baffled, discouraged, and disheartened, and finally relapse into their former desultory ways, with a sort of resigned despair. The difficulty, in such cases, is, that they attempt too much at a time. There is nothing which so much depends upon *habit*, as a systematic mode of performing duty; and where no such habit has been formed, it is impossible for a novice to start at once into a universal mode of systematizing, which none but an adept could carry through. The only way for such persons, is, to begin with a little at a time. Let them select some three or four things, and resolutely attempt to conquer at these points. In time, a habit will be formed of doing a few things at regular periods, and in a systematic way. Then it will be easy to add a few more; and thus, by a gradual process, the object can be secured, which it would be vain to attempt by a more summary course. Early rising is almost a *sine qua non* to success, in such an effort; but where a woman lacks either the health or the energy to secure a period for devotional duties before breakfast, let her select that hour of the day in which she will be least liable to interruption, and let her then seek strength and wisdom from the only true Source. At this time, let her take a pen and make a list of all the things which she considers as duties. Then let a calculation be made, whether there is time enough in the day or the week for all these duties. If there is not, let the least important be stricken from the list, as what are not duties and must be omitted. In doing this, let a woman remember, that, though "what we shall eat, and what we shall drink, and wherewithal we shall be clothed," are matters requiring due attention, they are very apt to take a wrong relative importance, while social, intellectual, and moral, interests, receive too little regard.

In this Country, eating, dressing, and household furniture and ornaments, take far too large a place in the estimate of relative importance; and it is probable that most women could modify their views and practice, so as to come nearer to the Saviour's requirements. No woman has a right to put a stitch of ornament on any article of dress or furniture, or to provide one superfluity in food, until she is sure she can secure time for all her social, intellectual, benevolent, and religious, duties. If a woman will take the trouble to make such a calculation as this, she will usually find that she has time enough to perform all her duties easily and well.

It is impossible for a conscientious woman to secure that peaceful mind, and cheerful enjoyment of life, which all should seek, who is constantly finding her duties jarring with each other, and much remaining undone, which she feels that she ought to do. In consequence of this, there will be a secret uneasiness, which will throw a shade over the whole current of life, never to be removed, till she so efficiently defines and regulates her duties, that she can fulfil them all.

And here the Writer would urge upon young ladies the importance of forming habits of system, while unembarrassed with multiplied cares which will make the task so much more difficult and hopeless. Every young lady can systematize her pursuits, to a certain extent. She can have a particular day for mending her wardrobe, and for arranging her trunks, closets, and drawers. She can keep her workbasket, her desk at school, and all her conveniences in proper places, and in regular order. She can have regular periods for reading, walking, visiting, study, and domestic pursuits. And by following this method, in youth, she will form a taste for regularity, and a habit of system, which will prove a blessing to her through life.

A NATURAL CONSEQUENCE.

MISS LUCY (*blushing extensively*).—Miss President and Ladies, It is my painful duty to resign my office as Corresponding Secretary of the Woman's Rights Association—for I am to be married to-morrow

"A Natural Consequence" and "Proper Prudence," cartoons from *Harper's New Monthly Magazine,* November 1852.

PROPER PRUDENCE.

Miss Prudence (*emphatically*).—Miss President, I repeat it – No conscientious Woman will ever marry until she is in a condition to support her Husband and Children in a suitable manner.

Margaret Fuller, engraving from a portrait by Alonzo Chappel. Reproduced by permission of the Concord Free Public Library.

TIME TABLE OF THE LOWELL MILLS,

Arranged to make the working time throughout the year average 11 hours per day.

TO TAKE EFFECT SEPTEMBER 21st., 1853.

The Standard time being that of the meridian of Lowell, as shown by the Regulator Clock of AMOS SANBORN, Post Office Corner, Central Street.

From March 20th to September 19th, inclusive.

COMMENCE WORK, at 6.30 A. M. LEAVE OFF WORK, at 6.30 P. M., except on Saturday Evenings.
BREAKFAST at 6 A. M. DINNER, at 12 M. Commence Work, after dinner, 12.45 P. M.

From September 20th to March 19th, inclusive.

COMMENCE WORK at 7.00 A. M. LEAVE OFF WORK, at 7.00 P. M., except on Saturday Evenings.
BREAKFAST at 6.30 A. M. DINNER, at 12.30 P.M. Commence Work, after dinner, 1.15 P. M.

BELLS.

From March 20th to September 19th, inclusive.

Morning Bells.	Dinner Bells.	Evening Bells.
First bell,...........4.30 A. M.	Ring out,..............12.00 M.	Ring out,...........6.30 P. M.
Second, 5.30 A. M.; Third, 6.20.	Ring in,...........12 35 P. M.	Except on Saturday Evenings.

From September 20th to March 19th, inclusive.

Morning Bells.	Dinner Bells.	Evening Bells.
First bell,...........5.00 A. M.	Ring out,...........12.30 P. M.	Ring out at...........7.00 P. M.
Second, 6.00 A. M.; Third, 6.50.	Ring in,.............1.05 P. M.	Except on Saturday Evenings.

SATURDAY EVENING BELLS.

During APRIL, MAY, JUNE, JULY, and AUGUST, Ring Out, at 6.00 P. M.
The remaining Saturday Evenings in the year, ring out as follows :

SEPTEMBER.	NOVEMBER.	JANUARY.
First Saturday, ring out 6.00 P. M.	Third Saturday ring out 4.00 P. M.	Third Saturday, ring out 4.25 P. M.
Second " " 5.45 "	Fourth " " 3.55 "	Fourth " " 4.35 "
Third " " 5.30 "		
Fourth " " 5.20 "	**DECEMBER.**	**FEBRUARY.**
OCTOBER.	First Saturday, ring out 3.50 P. M.	First Saturday, ring out 4.45 P. M.
First Saturday, ring out 5.05 P. M.	Second " " 3.55 "	Second " " 4.55 "
Second " " 4.55 "	Third " " 3.55 "	Third " " 5.00 "
Third " " 4.45 "	Fourth " " 4.00 "	Fourth " " 5.10 "
Fourth " " 4.35 "	Fifth " " 4.00 "	**MARCH.**
Fifth " " 4.25 "		First Saturday, ring out 5.25 P. M.
NOVEMBER.	**JANUARY.**	Second " " 5.30 "
First Saturday, ring out 4.15 P. M.	First Saturday, ring out 4.10 P. M.	Third " " 5.35 "
Second " · " 4.05 "	Second " " 4.15 "	Fourth " " 5.45 "

YARD GATES will be opened at the first stroke of the bells for entering or leaving the Mills.

⁂   *SPEED GATES commence hoisting three minutes before commencing work.*

Penhallow, Printer, Wyman's Exchange, 28 Merrimack St.

Timetable of the Lowell Mills, 1853. Reproduced by permission of the Museum of American Textile History.

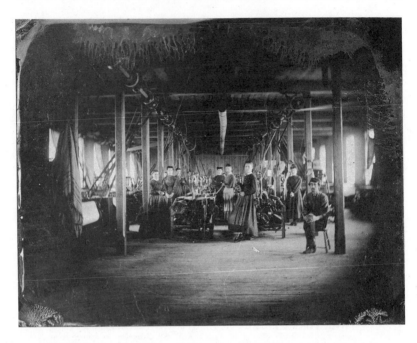

New England Textile Mill, ca. 1850. Reproduced by permission of George Eastman House.

LYDIA MARIA CHILD

On Women's Rights

Lydia Maria Child (1802–1880) was one of the most impressive writers and intellectuals of the nineteenth century. She worked and studied
with many reformers and writers in Boston and New York, such as Margaret Fuller, Elizabeth Peabody, and William Lloyd Garrison, and she
wrote dozens of books and countless articles, in addition to editing the
abolitionist weekly *The National Anti-Slavery Standard*. Her best work
includes *An Appeal in Favor of that Class of Americans Called Africans*
(1833) and her two volumes of *Letters from New York* (1843, 1845),
which collect many of her newspaper pieces. In the following selection
from the first volume of *Letters from New York*, Child notes the difference
between granting women *rights* and merely endowing them with *privileges*, and she offers a rejoinder to a lecture by Emerson. The text is from
Letters from New York, 3rd ed. (1843; New York: C. S. Francis, 1845).

Jan. 1843.

You ask what are my opinions about 'Women's Rights.' I confess,
a strong distaste to the subject, as it has been generally treated. On no
other theme probably has there been uttered so much of false, mawk-
ish sentiment, shallow philosophy, and sputtering, farthing-candle
wit. If the style of its advocates has often been offensive to taste, and
unacceptable to reason, assuredly that of its opponents have been still
more so. College boys have amused themselves with writing dreams,
in which they saw women in hotels, with their feet hoisted, and chairs
tilted back, or growling and bickering at each other in legislative
halls, or fighting at the polls, with eyes blackened by fisticuffs. But it
never seems to have occurred to these facetious writers, that the proceedings which appear so ludicrous and improper in *women*, are also
ridiculous and disgraceful in *men*. It were well that *men* should learn
not to hoist their feet above their heads, and tilt their chairs backward, nor to growl and snap in the halls of legislation, nor give each
other black eyes at the polls.

Maria Edgeworth[1] says, 'We are disgusted when we see a woman's

---

[1]*Maria Edgeworth:* Edgeworth (1768–1849) was an English novelist whose works
include *Castle Rackrent* (1800).

mind overwhelmed with a torrent of learning: that the tide of literature has passed over it should be betrayed only by its fertility.' This is
beautiful and true; but is it not likewise applicable to man? The truly
great never seek to display themselves. If they carry their heads high
above the crowd, it is only made manifest to others by accidental revelations of their extended vision. 'Human duties and properties do
not lie so very far apart,' said Harriet Martineau; 'if they did, there
would be two gospels and two teachers, one for man and another for
woman.'

It would seem indeed, as if men were willing to give women the
exclusive benefit of gospel-teaching. '*Women* should be gentle,' say
the advocates of subordination; but when Christ said, 'Blessed are
the meek,'[2] did he preach to women only? '*Girls* should be modest,'
is the language of common teaching, continually uttered in words
and customs. Would it not be an improvement for men also to be
scrupulously pure in manners, conversation and life? Books addressed to young married people abound with advice to the *wife*, to
control her temper, and never to utter wearisome complaints, or vex-
atious words when the husband comes home fretful and unreasonable from his out-of-door conflicts with the world. Would not the
advice be as excellent and appropriate, if the husband were advised
to conquer *his* fretfulness, and forbear *his* complaints, in consideration of his wife's ill-health, fatiguing cares, and the thousand dis-
heartening influences of domestic routine? In short, whatsoever can
be named as loveliest, best, and most graceful in woman, would likewise be good and graceful in man. You will perhaps remind me of
courage. If you use the word in its highest signification, I answer, that
woman, above others, has abundant need of it in her pilgrimage: and
the true woman wears it with a quiet grace. If you mean mere animal
courage, *that* is not mentioned in the Sermon on the Mount, among
those qualities which enable us to inherit the earth, or become the
children of God. That the feminine ideal approaches much nearer to
the gospel standard, than the prevalent idea of manhood, is shown by
the universal tendency to represent the Saviour and his most beloved
disciple with mild, meek expression, and feminine beauty. None
speak of the bravery, the might, or the intellect of Jesus; but the devil
is always imagined as a being of acute intellect, political cunning, and
the fiercest courage. These universal and instinctive tendencies of the
human mind reveal much.

[2]From Christ's Sermon on the Mount, Matthew 5–7, and Luke 6:20–49.

That the present position of women in society is the result of physical force, is obvious enough; whosoever doubts it, let her reflect why she is afraid to go out in the evening without the protection of a man. What constitutes the danger of aggression? Superior physical strength, uncontrolled by the moral sentiments. If physical strength were in complete subjection to moral influence, there would be no need of outward protection. That animal instinct and brute force now govern the world, is painfully apparent in the condition of women everywhere; from the Morduan Tartars,[3] whose ceremony of marriage consists in placing the bride on a mat, and consigning her to the bridegroom, with the words, 'Here, wolf, take thy lamb,' — to the German remark, that 'stiff ale, stinging tobacco, and a girl in her smart dress, are the best things.' The same thing, softened by the refinements of civilization, peeps out in Stephens's remark, that 'woman never looks so interesting, as when leaning on the arm of a soldier;' and in Hazlitt's[4] complaint that 'it is not easy to keep up a conversation with women in company. It is thought a piece of rudeness to differ from them; it is not quite fair to ask them a *reason* for what they say.'

This sort of politeness to women is what men call gallantry; an odious word to every sensible woman, because she sees that it is merely the flimsy veil which foppery throws over sensuality, to conceal its grossness. So far is it from indicating sincere esteem and affection for women, that the profligacy of a nation may, in general, be fairly measured by its gallantry. This taking away *rights*, and *condescending* to grant *privileges*, is an old trick of the physical-force principle; and with the immense majority, who only look on the surface of things, this mask effectually disguises an ugliness, which would otherwise be abhorred. The most inveterate slave-holders are probably those who take most pride in dressing their household servants handsomely, and who would be most ashamed to have the name of being *unnecessarily* cruel. And profligates, who form the lowest and most sensual estimate of women, are the very ones to treat them with an excess of outward deference.

There are few books which I can read through, without feeling insulted as a woman; but this insult is almost universally conveyed through that which was intended for praise. Just imagine, for a moment, what impression it would make on men, if women authors

---

[3]*Morduan Tartars:* Nomadic, Turkish-speaking, Muslim people living in Russia.
[4]*Hazlitt's:* William Hazlitt (1778–1830) was an English essayist and critic.

should write about *their* 'rosy lips,' and 'melting eyes,' and 'voluptuous forms,' as they write about *us!* That women in general do not feel this kind of flattery to be an insult, I readily admit; for, in the first place, they do not perceive the gross chattel-principle, of which it is the utterance; moreover, they have, from long habit, become accustomed to consider themselves as household conveniences, or gilded toys. Hence, they consider it feminine and pretty to abjure all such use of their faculties, as would make them co-workers with man in the advancement of those great principles, on which the progress of society depends. 'There is perhaps no *animal*,' says Hannah More,[5] 'so much indebted to subordination, for its good behaviour, as woman.' Alas, for the animal age, in which such utterance could be tolerated by public sentiment!

Martha More, sister of Hannah, describing a very impressive scene at the funeral of one of her Charity School teachers, says: 'The spirit within seemed struggling to speak, and I was in a sort of agony; but I recollected that I had heard, somewhere, a woman must not speak in the *church*. Oh, had she been buried in the church-*yard*, a messenger from Mr. Pitt[6] himself should not have restrained me; for I seemed to have received a message from a higher Master within.'

This application of theological teaching carries its own commentary.

I have said enough to show that I consider prevalent opinions and customs highly unfavourable to the moral and intellectual development of women: and I need not say, that, in proportion to their true culture, women will be more useful and happy, and domestic life more perfected. True culture, in them, as in men, consists in the full and free development of individual character, regulated by their *own* perceptions of what is true, and their *own* love of what is good.

This individual responsibility is rarely acknowledged, even by the most refined, as necessary to the spiritual progress of women. I once heard a very beautiful lecture from R. W. Emerson, on Being and Seeming. In the course of many remarks, as true as they were graceful, he urged women to *be*, rather than *seem*. He told them that all their laboured education of forms, strict observance of genteel etiquette, tasteful arrangement of the toilette, &c., all this *seeming* would not *gain hearts* like *being* truly what God made them; that

---

[5]*Hannah More:* More (1745–1831) was an English author of books on morality and religion.

[6]*Mr. Pitt:* William Pitt (1708–1778) and his second son, William "the Younger" (1759–1806), were eminent English orators and statesmen.

earnest simplicity, the sincerity of nature, would kindle the eye, light up the countenance, and give an inexpressible charm to the plainest features.

The advice was excellent, but the motive, by which it was urged, brought a flush of indignation over my face. *Men* were exhorted to *be*, rather than to *seem*, that they might fulfil the sacred mission for which their souls were embodied; that they might, in God's freedom, grow up into the full stature of spiritual manhood; but *women* were urged to simplicity and truthfulness, that they might become more *pleasing*.

Are we not all immortal beings? Is not each one responsible for himself and herself? There is no measuring the mischief done by the prevailing tendency to teach women to be virtuous as a duty to *man* rather than to *God* — for the sake of pleasing the creature, rather than the Creator. 'God is thy law, *thou* mine,' said Eve to Adam. May Milton[7] be forgiven for sending that thought 'out into everlasting time' in such a jewelled setting. What weakness, vanity, frivolity, infirmity of moral purpose, sinful flexibility of principle — in a word, what soul-stifling, has been the result of thus putting man in the place of God!

But while I see plainly that society is on a false foundation, and that prevailing views concerning women indicate the want of wisdom and purity, which they serve to perpetuate — still, I must acknowledge that much of the talk about Women's Rights offends both my reason and my taste. I am not of those who maintain there is no sex in souls; nor do I like the results deducible from that doctrine. Kinmont, in his admirable book, called the Natural History of Man, speaking of the warlike courage of the ancient German women, and of their being respectfully consulted on important public affairs, says: 'You ask me if I consider all this right, and deserving of approbation? or that women were here engaged in their appropriate tasks? I answer, yes; it is just *as* right that they should take this interest in the honour of their country, as the other sex. Of course, I do not think that women were *made* for war and battle; neither do I believe that *men* were. But since the fashion of the times had made it so, and settled it that war was a necessary element of greatness, and that no safety was to be procured without it, I argue that it shows a healthful state of feeling in other respects, that the feelings of both sexes were

---

[7]*Milton:* John Milton (1608–1674) wrote the epic poem *Paradise Lost* (1667), from which Child quotes here.

equally enlisted in the cause: that there was no *division* in the house, or the state; and that the serious pursuits and objects of the one were also the serious pursuits and objects of the other.'

The nearer society approaches to divine order, the less separation will there be in the characters, duties, and pursuits of men and women. Women will not become less gentle and graceful, but men will become more so. Women will not neglect the care and education of their children, but men will find themselves ennobled and refined by sharing those duties with them; and will receive, in return, co-operation and sympathy in the discharge of various other duties, now deemed inappropriate to women. The more women become rational companions, partners in business and in thought, as well as in affection and amusement, the more highly will men appreciate *home* — that blessed word, which opens to the human heart the most perfect glimpse of Heaven, and helps to carry it thither, as on an angel's wings.

> 'Domestic bliss,
> That can, the world eluding, be itself
> A world enjoyed; that wants no witnesses
> But its own sharers and approving heaven;
> That, like a flower deep hid in rocky cleft,
> Smiles, though 'tis looking only at the sky.'

Alas, for these days of Astor houses and Tremonts, and Albions! where families exchange comfort for costliness, fireside retirement for flirtation and flaunting, and the simple, healthful, cozy meal, for gravies and gout, dainties and dyspepsia. There is no characteristic of my countrymen, which I regret so deeply as their slight degree of adhesiveness to home. Closely intertwined with this instinct, is the religion of a nation. The Home and the Church bear a near relation to each other. The French have no such word as home in their language, and I believe they are the least reverential and religious of all the Christian nations. A Frenchman had been in the habit of visiting a lady constantly for several years, and being alarmed at a report that she was sought in marriage, he was asked why he did not marry her himself. '*Marry* her!' exclaimed he, — 'Good heavens! *where should I spend my evenings?*' The idea of domestic happiness was altogether a foreign idea to his soul, like a word that conveyed no meaning. Religious sentiment in France leads the same roving life as the domestic affections; breakfasting at one restaurateur's and supping at another's. When some wag in Boston reported that Louis Philippe had sent over for Dr. Channing[8] to manufacture a religion for the French people, the witty significance of the joke was generally appreciated.

There is a deep spiritual reason why all that relates to the domestic affections should ever be found in close proximity with religious faith. The age of chivalry was likewise one of unquestioning veneration, which led to the crusade for the holy sepulchre. The French revolution, which tore down churches, and voted that there was no God, likewise annulled marriage; and the doctrine, that there is no sex in souls, has usually been urged by those of infidel tendencies. Carlyle says, 'But what feeling it was in the ancient, devout, deep soul, which of marriage made a *sacrament*, this, of all things in the world, is what Diderot[9] will think of for æons without discovering; unless perhaps it were to increase the *vestry fees*.'

The conviction that woman's present position in society is a false one, and therefore re-acts disastrously on the happiness and improvement of man, is pressing by slow degrees on the common consciousness, through all the obstacles of bigotry, sensuality, and selfishness. As man approaches to the truest life, he will perceive more and more that there is no separation or discord in their mutual duties. They will be one; but it will be as affection and thought are one; the treble and bass of the same harmonious tune.

MARGARET FULLER

From Woman in the Nineteenth Century

Margaret Fuller's important book, *Woman in the Nineteenth Century* (1845), was a revised and expanded version of a long essay she published in the July 1843 issue of *The Dial*: "The Great Lawsuit: Man *versus* Men: Woman *versus* Women." The book is learned, difficult, and allusive (it shows the influence of Emerson, the Swedish mystic Emmanuel Swedenborg, Fourier, and Goethe). But while it is abstruse and faltering as a sustained argument, it is passionate and provocative in its claims for

---

[8] *Louis Philippe had sent over for Dr. Channing:* Louis Philippe (1773–1850) was the French king whose regime was marred by corruption and suppression of dissent; William Ellery Channing (1780–1842) was a Unitarian clergyman and author.

[9] *Carlyle . . . Diderot:* Thomas Carlyle (1795–1881) was a Scottish essayist, literary critic, and historian; Denis Diderot (1713–1784) was a French man of letters.

both the autonomy of women and the interdependence of women and men — claims that Fuller sought to show were not contradictory. In this excerpt, Fuller pays special heed to the kind of "influence" men typically say women should exercise, and she queries the conventional assumption that women cannot speak and act for themselves.

Readers have speculated that Hawthorne may have based his character Zenobia on Fuller, but they have differed about how much this is the case. Some, such as John Sullivan Dwight (see Ch. 3, p. 440), have maintained that Fuller is not the real-life model for Zenobia at all. The important point is perhaps that Zenobia embodies conflicted attitudes toward women's roles that are akin to those Fuller explores and seeks to resolve in her writings.

We will not speak of the innumerable instances in which profligate and idle men live upon the earnings of industrious wives; or if the wives leave them, and take with them the children, to perform the double duty of mother and father, follow from place to place, and threaten to rob them of the children, if deprived of the rights of a husband, as they call them, planting themselves in their poor lodgings, frightening them into paying tribute by taking from them the children, running into debt at the expense of these otherwise so overtasked helots. Such instances count up by scores within my own memory. I have seen the husband who had stained himself by a long course of low vice, till his wife was wearied from her heroic forgiveness, by finding that his treachery made it useless, and that if she would provide bread for herself and her children, she must be separate from his ill fame. I have known this man come to instal himself in the chamber of a woman who loathed him and say she should never take food without his company. I have known these men steal their children whom they knew they had no means to maintain, take them into dissolute company, expose them to bodily danger, to frighten the poor woman, to whom, it seems, the fact that she alone had borne the pangs of their birth, and nourished their infancy, does not give an equal right to them. I do believe that this mode of kidnapping, and it is frequent enough in all classes of society, will be by the next age viewed as it is by Heaven now, and that the man who avails himself of the shelter of men's laws to steal from a mother her own children, or arrogate any superior right in them, save that of superior virtue, will bear the stigma he deserves, in common with him who steals grown men from their mother land, their hopes, and their homes.

I said, we will not speak of this now, yet I have spoken, for the subject makes me feel too much. I could give instances that would startle the most vulgar and callous, but I will not, for the public opinion of their own sex is already against such men, and where cases of extreme tyranny are made known, there is private action in the wife's favor. But she ought not to need this, nor, I think, can she long. Men must soon see that, on their own ground, that woman is the weaker party, she ought to have legal protection, which would make such oppression impossible. But I would not deal with "atrocious instances" except in the way of illustration, neither demand from men a partial redress in some one matter, but go to the root of the whole. If principles could be established, particulars would adjust themselves aright. Ascertain the true destiny of woman, give her legitimate hopes, and a standard within herself; marriage and all other relations would by degrees be harmonized with these.

But to return to the historical progress of this matter. Knowing that there exists in the minds of men a tone of feeling towards women as towards slaves, such as is expressed in the common phrase, "Tell that to women and children," that the infinite soul can only work through them in already ascertained limits; that the gift of reason, man's highest prerogative, is allotted to them in much lower degree; that they must be kept from mischief and melancholy by being constantly engaged in active labor, which is to be furnished and directed by those better able to think, &c. &c.; we need not multiply instances, for who can review the experience of last week without recalling words which imply, whether in jest or earnest, these views or views like these; knowing this, can we wonder that many reformers think that measures are not likely to be taken in behalf of women, unless their wishes could be publicly represented by women?

That can never be necessary, cry the other side. All men are privately influenced by women; each has his wife, sister, or female friends, and is too much biased by these relations to fail of representing their interests, and, if this is not enough, let them propose and enforce their wishes with the pen. The beauty of home would be destroyed, the delicacy of the sex be violated, the dignity of halls of legislation degraded by an attempt to introduce them there. Such duties are inconsistent with those of a mother; and then we have ludicrous pictures of ladies in hysterics at the polls, and senate chambers filled with cradles.

But if, in reply, we admit as truth that woman seems destined by nature rather for the inner circle, we must add that the arrangements of civilized life have not been, as yet, such as to secure it to her. Her circle, if the duller, is not the quieter. If kept from "excitement," she is not from drudgery. Not only the Indian squaw carries the burdens of the camp, but the favorites of Louis the Fourteenth accompany him in his journeys, and the washerwoman stands at her tub and carries home her work at all seasons, and in all states of health. Those who think the physical circumstances of woman would make a part in the affairs of national government unsuitable, are by no means those who think it impossible for the negresses to endure field work, even during pregnancy, or the sempstresses to go through their killing labors.

As to the use of the pen, there was quite as much opposition to woman's possessing herself of that help to free agency, as there is now to her seizing on the rostrum or the desk; and she is likely to draw, from a permission to plead her cause that way, opposite inferences to what might be wished by those who now grant it.

As to the possibility of her filling with grace and dignity, any such position, we should think those who had seen the great actresses, and heard the Quaker preachers of modern times, would not doubt, that woman can express publicly the fulness of thought and creation, without losing any of the peculiar beauty of her sex. What can pollute and tarnish is to act thus from any motive except that something needs to be said or done. Women could take part in the processions, the songs, the dances of old religion; no one fancied their delicacy was impaired by appearing in public for such a cause.

As to her home, she is not likely to leave it more than she now does for balls, theatres, meetings for promoting missions, revival meetings, and others to which she flies, in hope of an animation for her existence, commensurate with what she sees enjoyed by men. Governors of ladies' fairs are no less engrossed by such a change, than the Governor of the state by his; presidents of Washingtonian societies[1] no less away from home than presidents of conventions. If men look straitly to it, they will find that, unless their lives are domestic, those of the women will not be. A house is no home unless it contain food and fire for the mind as well as for the body. The female Greek, of our day, is as much in the street as the male to cry, What news? We doubt not it was the same in Athens of old. The women, shut out

---

[1] *Washingtonian societies:* Temperance societies, which took their name from the nation's first president.

from the market place, made up for it at the religious festivals. For human beings are not so constituted that they can live without expansion. If they do not get it one way, they must another, or perish.

As to men's representing women fairly at present, while we hear from men who owe to their wives not only all that is comfortable or graceful, but all that is wise in the arrangement of their lives, the frequent remark, "You cannot reason with a woman," when from those of delicacy, nobleness, and poetic culture, the contemptuous phrase "women and children," and that in no light sally of the hour, but in works intended to give a permanent statement of the best experiences, when not one man, in the million, shall I say? no, not in the hundred million, can rise above the belief that woman was made, *for man*, when such traits as these are daily forced upon the attention, can we feel that man will always do justice to the interests of woman? Can we think that he takes a sufficiently discerning and religious view of her office and destiny, *ever* to do her justice, except when prompted by sentiment, accidentally or transiently, that is, for the sentiment will vary according to the relations in which he is placed. The lover, the poet, the artist, are likely to view her nobly. The father and the philosopher have some chance of liberality; the man of the world, the legislator for expediency, none.

Under these circumstances, without attaching importance, in themselves, to the changes demanded by the champions of woman, we hail them as signs of the times. We would have every arbitrary barrier thrown down. We would have every path laid open to woman as freely as to man. Were this done and a slight temporary fermentation allowed to subside, we should see crystallizations more pure and of more various beauty. We believe the divine energy would pervade nature to a degree unknown in the history of former ages, and that no discordant collision, but a ravishing harmony of the spheres would ensue.

Yet, then and only then, will mankind be ripe for this, when inward and outward freedom for woman as much as for man shall be acknowledged as a right, not yielded as a concession. As the friend of the negro assumes that one man cannot by right, hold another in bondage, so should the friend of woman assume that man cannot, by right, lay even well-meant restrictions on woman. If the negro be a soul, if the woman be a soul, appareled in flesh, to one Master only are they accountable. There is but one law for souls, and if there is to be an interpreter of it, he must come not as man, or son of man, but as son of God.

Were thought and feeling once so far elevated that man should esteem himself the brother and friend, but nowise the lord and tutor of woman, were he really bound with her in equal worship, arrangements as to function and employment would be of no consequence. What woman needs is not as a woman to act or rule, but as a nature to grow, as an intellect to discern, as a soul to live freely and unimpeded, to unfold such powers as were given her when we left our common home. If fewer talents were given her, yet if allowed the free and full employment of these, so that she may render back to the giver his own with usury, she will not complain; may I dare to say she will bless and rejoice in her earthly birth-place, her earthly lot. Let us consider what obstructions impede this good era, and what signs give reason to hope that it draws near.

NATHANIEL HAWTHORNE

On Margaret Fuller

In *Nathaniel Hawthorne and His Wife*, published in 1884, Julian Hawthorne made the controversial decision to print a passage from his father's notebooks describing Margaret Fuller as "a great humbug" — a passage that Hawthorne's wife, Sophia, had earlier excluded from her *Passages from the French and Italian Notebooks* (1872). Hawthorne's words are offensive and cruel, yet in their jaded way they also bring out Fuller's intensity, intellectual resolve, and desire for experience. In this respect, what Hawthorne says about Fuller as an individual may be less significant than the connections between his view of her life and career and his descriptions of intellectual women, presented through Coverdale, in *The Blithedale Romance*.

The text is from *The French and Italian Notebooks*, ed. Thomas Woodson, in *The Centenary Edition of the Works of Nathaniel Hawthorne*, vol. 14 (Columbus: Ohio State UP, 1980), 155–157.

From Greenough, Mr. Mozier passed to Margaret Fuller, whom he knew well, she having been an inmate of his during a part of her residence in Italy.[1] His developments about poor Margaret were very

---

[1]*Greenough . . . Mr. Mozier:* Horatio Greenough (1805–1852) was an American sculptor, born in Boston, who worked in Rome; Joseph Mozier (1812–1870) retired from his New York business in 1845 to study sculpture in Rome.

curious. He says that Ossoli's family,[2] though technically noble, is really of no rank whatever; the elder brother, with the title of Marquis, being at this very time a working bricklayer, and the sisters walking the streets without bonnets — that is, being in the station of peasant-girls, or the female populace of Rome. Ossoli himself, to the best of his belief, was Margaret's servant, or had something to do with the care of her apartments. He was the handsomest man whom Mr. Mozier ever saw, but entirely ignorant even of his own language, scarcely able to read at all, destitute of manners; in short, half an idiot, and without any pretensions to be a gentleman. At Margaret's request, Mr. Mozier had taken him into his studio, with a view to ascertain whether he was capable of instruction in sculpture; but, after four months' labor, Ossoli produced a thing intended to be a copy of a human foot; but the "big toe" was on the wrong side. He could not possibly have had the least appreciation of Margaret; and the wonder is, what attraction she found in this boor, this hymen without the intellectual spark — she that had always shown such a cruel and bitter scorn of intellectual deficiency. As from her towards him, I do not understand what feeling there could have been, except it were purely sensual; as from him towards her, there could hardly have been even this, for she had not the charm of womanhood. But she was a woman anxious to try all things, and fill up her experience in all directions; she had a strong and coarse nature, too, which she had done her utmost to refine, with infinite pains, but which of course could only be superficially changed. The solution of the riddle lies in this direction; nor does one's conscience revolt at the idea of thus solving it; for — at least, this is my own experience — Margaret has not left, in the hearts and minds of those who knew her, any deep witness for her integrity and purity. She was a great humbug; of course with much talent, and much moral reality, or else she could not have been so great a humbug. But she had stuck herself full of borrowed qualities, which she chose to provide herself with, but which had no root in her.

Mr. Mozier added, that Margaret had quite lost all power of literary production, before she left Rome, though occasionally the charm and power of her conversation would re-appear. To his certain knowledge, she had no important manuscripts with her when she

[2]*Ossoli's family:* During the time she lived in Italy, Fuller fell in love with Giovanni Angelo Ossoli, an Italian nobleman and supporter of the republican army and revolutionary cause, and she bore his son. It is unclear whether Fuller and Ossoli ever married. All three died tragically in a shipwreck off the coast of Fire Island, New York, in July 1850.

sailed, (she having shown him all she had, with a view to his procuring their publication in America;) and the History of the Roman Revolution, about which there was so much lamentation, in the belief
that it had been lost with her, never had existence. Thus there appears to have been a total collapse in poor Margaret, morally and intellectually; and tragic as her catastrophe was, Providence was, after
all, kind in putting her, and her clownish husband, and their child, on
board that fated ship. There never was such a tragedy as her whole
story; the sadder and sterner, because so much of the ridiculous was
mixed up with it, and because she could bear anything better than to
be ridiculous. It was such an awful joke, that she should have resolved — in all sincerity, no doubt — to make herself the greatest,
wisest, best woman of the age; and, to that end, she set to work on
her strong, heavy, unpliable, and, in many respects, defective and evil
nature, and adorned it with a mosaic of admirable qualities, such as
she chose to possess; putting in here a splendid talent, and there a
moral excellence, and polishing each separate piece, and the whole
together, till it seemed to shine afar and dazzle all who saw it. She
took credit to herself for having been her own Redeemer, if not her
own Creator; and, indeed, she was far more a work of art than any of
Mr. Mozier's statues. But she was not working on an inanimate substance, like marble or clay; there was something within her that she
could not possibly come at, to re-create and refine it; and, by and by,
this rude old potency bestirred itself, and undid all her labor in the
twinkling of an eye. On the whole, I do not know but I like her the
better for it; — the better, because she proved herself a very woman,
after all, and fell as the weakest of her sisters might.

NATHANIEL HAWTHORNE

On the Death of Martha Hunt

According to Annie Sawyer Downs, the daughter of a physician who
practiced in Concord in the 1840s, the Hunts were a farming family fi-
nancially pressed and outside the central currents of social life in the
town. Martha, a local schoolteacher, age nineteen, came to know Fuller
and Emerson, and they encouraged and loaned books to her. Pained by
her restricted life, however, she drowned herself one summer day in the
Concord River. The report of Hunt's death, which was published in the

July 11, 1845, issue of the Concord *Freeman*, concluded: "Miss Hunt was a very accomplished young lady — and it is supposed she committed the act in a momentary fit of insanity, brought on by intense study." A grim footnote to Hunt's death is that, years later, her sister killed herself in the same place and at the same hour of the day.

Hawthorne's account of Martha Hunt's death has been linked to his description of Zenobia's suicide in *The Blithedale Romance* and, furthermore, to Margaret Fuller's death by drowning in July 1850 in a shipwreck off the coast of Fire Island. But such connections, while intriguing, are hard to establish as intentional on Hawthorne's part, and it is difficult to know what conclusions to draw from them.

The text is from *The American Notebooks*, ed. Claude M. Simpson, in *The Centenary Edition of the Works of Nathaniel Hawthorne*, vol. 8 (Columbus: Ohio State UP, 1972), 261–67.

On the night of July 9th, a search for the dead body of a drowned girl. She was a Miss Hunt, about nineteen years old; a girl of education and refinement, but depressed and miserable for want of sympathy — her family being an affectionate one, but uncultivated, and incapable of responding to her demands. She was of a melancholic temperament, accustomed to solitary walks in the woods. At this time, she had the superintendence of one of the district-schools, comprising sixty scholars, particularly difficult of management. Well; Ellery Channing[1] knocked at the door, between 9 and 10 in the evening, in order to get my boat, to go in search of this girl's drowned body. He took the oars, and I the paddle, and we went rapidly down the river, until, a good distance below the bridge, we saw lights on the bank, and the dim figures of a number of people waiting for us. Her bonnet and shoes had already been found on this spot, and her handkerchief, I believe, on the edge of the water; so that the body was probably at no great distance, unless the current (which is gentle, and almost imperceptible) had swept her down.

We took in General Buttrick,[2] and a young man in a blue frock, and commenced the search; the general and the other man having long poles, with hooks at the end, and Ellery a hay-rake, while I steered the boat. It was a very eligible place to drown one's self. On

[1] *Ellery Channing:* William Ellery Channing (1817–1901) was a poet, essayist, and editor.
[2] *General Buttrick:* General Joshua Buttrick was the owner of a farm in Concord.

the verge of the river, there were water-weeds; but after a few steps, the bank goes off very abruptly, and the water speedily becomes fifteen or twenty feet deep. It must be one of the deepest spots in the whole river; and, holding a lantern over it, it was black as midnight, smooth, impenetrable, and keeping its secrets from the eye as perfectly as mid-ocean could. We caused the boat to float once or twice past the spot where the bonnet &c had been found; carefully searching the bottom at different distances from the shore — but, for a considerable time without success. Once or twice the poles or the rake caught in bunches of water-weed, which, in the star-light, looked like garments; and once Ellery and the General struck some substance at the bottom, which they at first mistook for the body; but it was probably a sod that had rolled in from the bank. All this time, the persons on the bank were anxiously waiting, and sometimes giving us their advice to search higher or lower, or at such and such a point. I now paddled the boat again past the point where she was supposed to have entered the river, and then turned it, so as to let it float broadside downwards, about midway from bank to bank. The young fellow in the blue frock sat on the next seat to me, plying his long pole.

We had drifted a little distance below the group of men on the bank, when this fellow gave a sudden start — "What's this?" cried he. I felt in a moment what it was; and I suppose the same electric shock went through everybody in the boat. "Yes; I've got her!" said he; and heaving up his pole with difficulty, there was an appearance of light garments on the surface of the water; he made a strong effort, and brought so much of the body above the surface, that there could be no doubt about it. He drew her towards the boat, grasped her arm or hand; and I steered the boat to the bank, all the while looking at this dead girl, whose limbs were swaying in the water, close at the boat's side. The fellow evidently had the same sort of feeling in his success as if he had caught a particularly fine fish; though mingled, no doubt, with horror. For my own part, I felt my voice tremble a little, when I spoke, at the first shock of the discovery; and at seeing the body come to the surface, dimly in the starlight. When close to the bank, some of the men stepped into the water and drew out the body; and then, by their lanterns, I could see how rigid it was. There was nothing flexible about it; she did not droop over the arms of those who supported her, with her hair hanging down, as a painter would have represented her; but was all as stiff as marble. And it was evident that her wet garments covered limbs perfectly inflexible. They took her out of the water, and deposited her under an oak-tree; and by the time we had got ashore, they were examining her by the light of two or three lanterns.

I never saw nor imagined a spectacle of such perfect horror. The rigidity, above spoken of, was dreadful to behold. Her arms had stiffened in the act of struggling; and were bent before her, with the hands clenched. She was the very image of a death-agony; and when the men tried to compose her figure, her arms would still return to that same position; indeed it was almost impossible to force them out of it for an instant. One of the men put his foot upon her arm, for the purpose of reducing it by her side; but, in a moment, it rose again. The lower part of the body had stiffened into a more quiet attitude; the legs were slightly bent, and the feet close together. But that rigidity! — it is impossible to express the effect of it; it seemed as if she would keep the same posture in the grave, and that her skeleton would keep it too, and that when she rose at the day of Judgment, it would be in the same attitude.

As soon as she was taken out of the water, the blood began to stream from her nose. Something seemed to have injured her eye, too; perhaps it was the pole, when it first struck the body. The complexion was a dark red, almost purple; the hands were white, with the same rigidity in their clench as in all the rest of the body. Two of the men got water, and began to wash away the blood from her face; but it flowed and flowed, and continued to flow; and an old carpenter, who seemed to be skilful in such matters, said that this was always the case, and that she would continue to "purge," as he called it, in this manner, until her burial, I believe. He said, too, that the body would swell, by morning, so that nobody would know her. Let it take what change it might, it could scarcely look more horrible than it did now, in its rigidity; certainly, she did not look as if she had gotten grace in the world whither she had precipitated herself; but rather, her stiffened death-agony was an emblem of inflexible judgment pronounced upon her. If she could have foreseen, while she stood, at 5 o'clock that morning, on the bank of the river, how her maiden corpse would have looked, eighteen hours afterwards, and how coarse men would strive with hand and foot to reduce it to a decent aspect, and all in vain — it would surely have saved her from this deed. So horribly did she look, that a middle-aged man, David Buttrick,[3] absolutely fainted away, and was found lying on the grass, at a

---

[3]*David Buttrick*: Buttrick lived on a farm north of Concord; his exact relationship to General Buttrick is not known.

little distance, perfectly insensible. It required much rubbing of hands and limbs to restore him.

Meantime, General Buttrick had gone to give notice to the family that the body was found; and others had gone in search of rails, to make a bier. Another boat now arrived, and added two or three more horror-struck spectators. There was a dog with them, who looked at the body, as it seemed to me, with pretty much the same feelings as the rest of us — horror and curiosity. A young brother of the deceased, apparently about twelve or fourteen years old, had been on the spot from the beginning. He seemed not much moved, externally, but answered questions about his sister, and the number of the brothers and sisters, (ten in all,) with composure. No doubt, however, he was stunned and bewildered with the scene — to see his sister lying there, in such terrific guise, at midnight, under an oak, on the verge of the black river, with strangers clustering about her, holding their lanterns over her face; and that old carpenter washing the blood away, which still flowed forth, though from a frozen fountain. Never was there a wilder scene. All the while, we were talking about the circumstances, and about an inquest, and whether or no it was necessary, and of how many it should consist; and the old carpenter was talking of dead people, and how he would as lief handle them as living ones.

By this time, two rails had been procured, across which were laid some boards or broken oars from the bottom of a boat; and the body, being wrapt in an old quilt, was laid upon this rude bier. All of us took part in bearing the corpse, or in steadying it. From the bank of the river to her father's house, there was nearly half a mile of pasture-ground, on the ascent of the hill; and our burthen grew very heavy, before we reached the door. What a midnight procession it was! How strange and fearful it would have seemed, if it could have been foretold, a day beforehand, that I should help carry a dead body along that track! At last, we reached the door, where appeared an old gray-haired man, holding a light; he said nothing, seemed calm, and after the body was laid upon a large table, in what seemed to be the kitchen, the old man disappeared. This was the grandfather. Good Mrs. Pratt[4] was in the room, having been sent for to assist in laying out the body; but she seemed wholly at a loss how to proceed; and no wonder — for it was an absurd idea to think of composing that

---

[4]*Mrs. Pratt:* Maria T. Pratt and her husband, Minot Pratt, were members of Brook Farm.

rigidly distorted figure into the decent quiet of the coffin. A Mrs. Lee had likewise been summoned, and shortly appeared, a withered, skin-and-bone looking woman; but she, too, though a woman of skill, was in despair at the job, and confessed her ignorance how to set about it. Whether the poor girl did finally get laid out, I know not, but can scarcely think it possible. I have since been told that, on stripping the body, they found a strong cord wound round the waist, and drawn tight — for what purpose is impossible to guess.

"Ah, poor child!" — that was the exclamation of an elderly man, as he helped draw her out of the water. I suppose one friend would have saved her; but she died for want of sympathy — a severe penalty for having cultivated and refined herself out of the sphere of her natural connections.

She is said to have gone down to the river at 5 in the morning, and to have been seen walking to and fro on the bank, so late as 7 — there being all that space of final struggle with her misery. She left a diary, which is said to exhibit (as her whole life did) many high and remarkable traits. The idea of suicide was not a new one with her; she had before attempted, walking up to her chin into the water, but coming out again, in compassion to the agony of a sister, who stood on the bank. She appears to have been religious, and of a high morality.

The reason, probably, that the body remained so near the spot where she drowned herself, was, that it had sunk to the bottom of perhaps the deepest spot in the river, and so was out of the action of the current.

HARRIET FARLEY

"A Weaver's Reverie"

The city of Lowell in northeastern Massachusetts was one of the major textile centers in the United States, and American reformers and visitors from abroad such as Charles Dickens were impressed by the conditions for women workers, the boardinghouses, reading rooms, and evening schools. Lowell's best citizens claimed it was the "Industrial Utopia."

For women, the Lowell mills were better than other choices, such as the life of a "city seamstress" — Zenobia's epithet for Priscilla in *The Blithedale Romance*. As the historian Catherine Clinton has pointed out in *The Other Civil War: American Women in the Nineteenth Century* (1984), the seamstress was among the most exploited members of the American working class; the piecework that she did at home earned her almost nothing despite long hours of labor. Such work was so poorly paid, Clinton observes, that reformers noted that often seamstresses were driven to prostitution.

Not all workers in Lowell concurred with the city fathers about its virtues, and women were prominent in labor activism. Five women in 1844 organized the Lowell Female Labor Reform Association, and membership reached six hundred in a year's time. These women joined with men in fighting for the ten-hour workday.

Harriet Farley (1813–1907), born and raised in a poor family in New Hampshire, left in 1837 to work in a Lowell mill, as did many girls from the countryside. In 1842, Farley became editor of *The Lowell Offering*, a periodical written by and for the mill girls, to which Farley had contributed as early as December 1840.

It has been said that the writings in *The Lowell Offering* were sentimental and escapist, too eager to speak affirmatively about the lives that the women workers led and unwilling to engage such controversial issues as the efforts to improve working conditions and achieve a ten-hour day. But while there is validity to this charge, it is also true, as the story below indicates, that Farley included pieces that revealed the hardships and longings of the young women whose lives were so highly regulated and confined.

The text is from *The Lowell Offering* 1 (1841): 188–90. For an 1853 timetable of the Lowell mills and a photograph of women workers in a New England textile mill, see pages 477 and 478.

It was a sunny day, and I left for a few moments, the circumscribed spot which is my appointed place of labor, that I might look from an adjoining window upon the bright loveliness of nature. Yes, it was a sunny day; but for many days before, the sky had been veiled in gloomy clouds; and joyous indeed was it to look up into that blue vault, and see it unobscured by its sombre screen; and my heart fluttered, like a prisoned bird, with its painful longings for an unchecked flight amidst the beautiful creation around me.

Why is it, said a friend to me one day, that the factory girls write so much about the beauties of nature?

Oh! why is it, (thought I, when the query afterwards recurred to me,) why is it that visions of thrilling loveliness so often bless the sightless orbs of those whose eyes have once been blessed with the power of vision?

Why is it that the delirious dreams of the famine-stricken, are of tables loaded with the richest viands, or groves, whose pendant boughs droop with their delicious burdens of luscious fruit?

Why is it that haunting tones of sweetest melody come to us in the deep stillness of midnight, when the thousand tongues of man and nature are for a season mute?

Why is it that the desert-traveler looks forward upon the burning, boundless waste, and sees pictured before his aching eyes, some verdant oasis, with its murmuring streams, its gushing founts, and shadowy groves — but as he presses on with faltering step, the bright *mirage* recedes, until he lies down to die of weariness upon the scorching sands, with that isle of loveliness before him?

Oh tell me why is this, and I will tell why the factory girl sits in the hour of meditation, and thinks — not of the crowded, clattering mill, nor of the noisy tenement which is her home, nor of the thronged and busy street which she may sometimes tread,—but of the still and lovely scenes which, in by-gone hours, have sent their pure and elevating influence with a thrilling sweep across the strings of the spirit-harp, and then awakened its sweetest, loftiest notes; and ever as she sits in silence and seclusion, endeavoring to draw from that many-toned instrument a strain which may be meet for another's ear, that music comes to the eager listener like the sound with which the sea-shell echoes the roar of what was once its watery home. All her best and holiest thoughts are linked with those bright pictures which called them forth, and when she would embody them for the instruction of others, she does it by a delineation of those scenes which have quickened and purified her own mind.

It was this love of nature's beauties, and a yearning for the pure, hallowed feelings which those beauties had been wont to call up from their hidden springs in the depths of the soul, to bear away upon their swelling tide the corruption which had gathered, and I feared might settle there, — it was this love, and longing, and fear, which made my heart throb quickly, as I sent forth a momentary glance from the factory window.

I think I said there was a cloudless sky; but it was not so. It was clear, and soft, and its beauteous hue was of "the hyacinth's deep blue" — but there was one bright, solitary cloud, far up in the cerulean vault; and I wished that it might for once be in my power to lie down upon that white, fleecy couch, and there, away and alone, to dream of all things holy, calm, and beautiful. Methought that better feelings, and clearer thoughts than are often wont to visit me, would there take undisturbed possession of my soul.

And might I not be there, and send my unobstructed glance into the depths of ether above me, and forget for a little while that I had ever been a foolish, wayward, guilty child of earth? Could I not then cast aside the burden of error and sin which must ever depress me here, and with the maturity of womanhood, feel also the innocence of infancy? And with that sense of purity and perfection, there would necessarily be mingled a feeling of sweet, uncloying bliss — such as imagination may conceive, but which seldom pervades and sanctifies the earthly heart. Might I not look down from my ærial position, and view this little world, and its hills, valleys, plains, and streamlets, and its thousands of busy inhabitants, and see how puerile and unsatisfactory it would look to one so totally disconnected from it? Yes, there, upon that soft, snowy cloud could I sit, and gaze upon my native earth, and feel how empty and "vain are all things here below."

But not motionless would I stay upon that ærial couch. I would call upon the breezes to waft me away, over the broad, blue ocean, and with nought but the clear, bright ether above me, have nought but a boundless, sparkling, watery expanse below me. Then I would look down upon the vessels pursuing their different courses across the bright waters; and as I watched their toilsome progress, I should feel how blessed a thing it is to be where no impediment of wind or wave might obstruct my onward way.

But when the beams of a mid-day sun had ceased to flash from the foaming sea, I should wish my cloud to bear away to the western sky, and divesting itself of its snowy whiteness, stand there, arrayed in the brilliant hues of the setting sun. Yes, well should I love to be stationed there, and see it catch those parting rays, and, transforming them to dyes of purple and crimson, shine forth in its evening vestment, with a border of brightest gold. Then could I watch the king of day as he sinks into his watery bed, leaving behind a line of crimson light to mark the path which led him to his place of rest.

Yet once, O only once, should I love to have that cloud pass on— on — on — among the myriads of stars; and leaving them all behind, go far away into the empty void of space beyond. I should love, for once, to be *alone*. Alone! where *could* I be alone? But I would fain be where there is no other, save the *Invisible*, and there, where not even one distant star should send its feeble rays to tell of a universe beyond, there would I rest upon that soft, light cloud, and with a fathomless depth below me, and a measureless waste above and around me, there would I ——

"Your looms are going without filling," said a loud voice at my elbow; so I ran as fast as possible, and changed my shuttles.

ELIZABETH CADY STANTON ET AL.

"Declaration of Sentiments" and "Resolutions," Seneca Falls Convention

In her autobiography, *Eighty Years and More* (1898), Elizabeth Cady Stanton (1815–1902) linked the inception of the Seneca Falls Convention on the rights of women to the difficulties that she and other women faced in caring for a family and managing a household. After moving from Boston to Seneca Falls, New York, Stanton found herself immersed in domestic duties, which were "too numerous and varied, and none sufficiently exhilarating or intellectual to bring into play my higher faculties." She added that "woman's best development" could not be achieved in "the isolated household," and that she had gained a new appreciation for the cooperative arrangements that Fourier had described. During the two days (July 19–20) of the convention, the three hundred delegates (including forty men), listened to speeches, engaged in debates, and adopted both a "Declaration of Sentiments" and a series of "Resolutions" that stated their principles and goals.

The text is from *The History of Woman Suffrage*, 6 vols. (New York: Fowler & Wells, 1881–1922), 1:67–74.

Declaration of Sentiments[1]

When, in the course of human events, it becomes necessary for one portion of the family of man to assume among the people of the earth a position different from that which they have hitherto occupied, but one to which the laws of nature and of nature's God entitle them, a

---

[1]The phrasing and structure of this document is patterned on the American Declaration of Independence of 1776.

decent respect to the opinions of mankind requires that they should declare the causes that impel them to such a course.

We hold these truths to be self-evident: that all men and women are created equal; that they are endowed by their Creator with certain inalienable rights; that among these are life, liberty, and the pursuit of happiness; that to secure these rights governments are instituted, deriving their just powers from the consent of the governed. Whenever any form of government becomes destructive of these ends, it is the right of those who suffer from it to refuse allegiance to it, and to insist upon the institution of a new government, laying its foundation on such principles, and organizing its powers in such form, as to them shall seem most likely to effect their safety and happiness. Prudence, indeed, will dictate that governments long established should not be changed for light and transient causes; and accordingly all experience hath shown that mankind are more disposed to suffer, while evils are sufferable, than to right themselves by abolishing the forms to which they were accustomed. But when a long train of abuses and usurpations, pursuing invariably the same object evinces a design to reduce them under absolute despotism, it is their duty to throw off such government, and to provide new guards for their future security. Such has been the patient sufferance of the women under this government, and such is now the necessity which constrains them to demand the equal station to which they are entitled.

The history of mankind is a history of repeated injuries and usurpations on the part of man toward woman, having in direct object the establishment of an absolute tyranny over her. To prove this, let facts be submitted to a candid world.

He has never permitted her to exercise her inalienable right to the elective franchise.

He has compelled her to submit to laws, in the formation of which she had no voice.

He has withheld from her rights which are given to the most ignorant and degraded men — both natives and foreigners.

Having deprived her of this first right of a citizen, the elective franchise, thereby leaving her without representation in the halls of legislation, he has oppressed her on all sides.

He has made her, if married, in the eye of the law, civilly dead.[2]

---

[2]*civilly dead:* Marriage in the United States followed the tradition of English law, in which women who married lost their separate legal status. Wives could neither enter into contracts nor own any property.

He has taken from her all right in property, even to the wages she earns.

He has made her, morally, an irresponsible being, as she can commit many crimes with impunity, provided they be done in the presence of her husband. In the covenant of marriage, she is compelled to promise obedience to her husband, he becoming, to all intents and purposes, her master — the law giving him power to deprive her of her liberty, and to administer chastisement.

He has so framed the laws of divorce, as to what shall be the proper causes, and in case of separation, to whom the guardianship of the children shall be given, as to be wholly regardless of the happiness of women — the law, in all cases, going upon a false supposition of the supremacy of man, and giving all power into his hands.

After depriving her of all rights as a married woman, if single, and the owner of property, he has taxed her to support a government which recognizes her only when her property can be made profitable to it.

He has monopolized nearly all the profitable employments, and from those she is permitted to follow, she receives but a scanty remuneration. He closes against her all the avenues to wealth and distinction which he considers most honorable to himself. As a teacher of theology, medicine, or law, she is not known.

He has denied her the facilities for obtaining a thorough education, all colleges being closed against her.

He allows her in Church, as well as State, but a subordinate position, claiming Apostolic authority for her exclusion from the ministry, and, with some exceptions, from any public participation in the affairs of the Church.

He has created a false public sentiment by giving to the world a different code of morals for men and women, by which moral delinquencies which exclude women from society, are not only tolerated, but deemed of little account in man.

He has usurped the prerogative of Jehovah himself, claiming it as his right to assign for her a sphere of action, when that belongs to her conscience and to her God.

He has endeavored, in every way that he could, to destroy her confidence in her own powers, to lessen her self-respect, and to make her willing to lead a dependent and abject life.

Now, in view of this entire disfranchisement of one-half the people of this country, their social and religious degradation — in view of the unjust laws above mentioned, and because women do feel themselves aggrieved, oppressed, and fraudulently deprived of their most sacred rights, we insist that they have immediate admission to all the rights and privileges which belong to them as citizens of the United States.

In entering upon the great work before us, we anticipate no small amount of misconception, misrepresentation, and ridicule; but we shall use every instrumentality within our power to effect our object. We shall employ agents, circulate tracts, petition the state and National legislatures, and endeavor to enlist the pulpit and the press in our behalf. We hope this Convention will be followed by a series of Conventions embracing every part of the country.

[Resolutions]

The following resolutions were discussed by Lucretia Mott,[3] Thomas and Mary Ann McClintock, Amy Post, Catharine A. F. Stebbins, and others, and were adopted:

WHEREAS, The great precept of nature is conceded to be, that "man shall pursue his own true and substantial happiness." Blackstone[4] in his Commentaries remarks, that this law of Nature being coeval with mankind, and dictated by God himself, is of course superior in obligation to any other. It is binding over all the globe, in all countries and at all times; no human laws are of any validity if contrary to this, and such of them as are valid, derive all their force, and all their validity, and all their authority, mediately and immediately, from this original; therefore,

Resolved, That such laws as conflict, in any way, with the true and substantial happiness of woman, are contrary to the great precept of nature and of no validity, for this is "superior in obligation to any other."

Resolved, That all laws which prevent woman from occupying such a station in society as her conscience shall dictate, or which place her in a position inferior to that of man, are contrary to the great precept of nature, and therefore of no force or authority.

Resolved, That woman is man's equal — was intended to be so by the Creator, and the highest good of the race demands that she should be recognized as such.

---

[3]*Lucretia Mott:* Mott (1793–1880) was a Quaker reformer, women's rights activist, and abolitionist.

[4]*Blackstone:* Sir William Blackstone (1723–1780), English jurist, author of an important multivolume history of English law, *Commentaries on the Laws of England* (1765–69).

Resolved, That the women of this country ought to be enlightened in regard to the laws under which they live, that they may no longer publish their degradation by declaring themselves satisfied with their present position, nor their ignorance, by asserting that they have all the rights they want.

Resolved, That inasmuch as man, while claiming for himself intellectual superiority, does accord to woman moral superiority, it is pre-eminently his duty to encourage her to speak and teach, as she has an opportunity, in all religious assemblies.

Resolved, That the same amount of virtue, delicacy, and refinement of behavior that is required of woman in the social state, should also be required of man, and the same transgressions should be visited with equal severity on both man and woman.

Resolved, That the objection of indelicacy and impropriety, which is so often brought against woman when she addresses a public audience, comes with a very ill-grace from those who encourage, by their attendance, her appearance on the stage, in the concert, or in feats of the circus.

Resolved, That woman has too long rested satisfied in the circumscribed limits which corrupt customs and a perverted application of the Scriptures have marked out for her, and that it is time she should move in the enlarged sphere which her great Creator has assigned her.

Resolved, That it is the duty of the women of this country to secure to themselves their sacred right to the elective franchise.

Resolved, That the equality of human rights results necessarily from the fact of the identity of the race in capabilities and responsibilities.

Resolved, therefore, That, being invested by the Creator with the same capabilities, and the same consciousness of responsibility for their exercise, it is demonstrably the right and duty of woman, equally with man, to promote every righteous cause by every righteous means; and especially in regard to the great subjects of morals and religion, it is self-evidently her right to participate with her brother in teaching them, both in private and in public, by writing and by speaking, by any instrumentalities proper to be used, and in any assemblies proper to be held; and this being a self-evident truth growing out of the divinely implanted principles of human nature, any custom or authority adverse to it, whether modern or wearing the hoary sanction of antiquity, is to be regarded as a self-evident falsehood, and at war with mankind.

At the last session Lucretia Mott offered and spoke to the following resolution:

Resolved, That the speedy success of our cause depends upon the zealous and untiring efforts of both men and women, for the overthrow of the monopoly of the pulpit, and for the securing to woman an equal participation with men in the various trades, professions, and commerce.

The only resolution that was not unanimously adopted was the ninth, urging the women of the country to secure to themselves the elective franchise. Those who took part in the debate feared a demand for the right to vote would defeat others they deemed more rational, and make the whole movement ridiculous.

But Mrs. Stanton and Frederick Douglass seeing that the power to choose rulers and make laws, was the right by which all others could be secured, persistently advocated the resolution, and at last carried it by a small majority.

Selected Bibliography

Bibliographies and Reference Works
on Hawthorne, Transcendentalism, and Brook Farm

Beebe, Maurice, and Jack Hardie. "Hawthorne Checklist." *Studies in the Novel* 2 (1970): 519–88.

Blair, Walter. "Nathaniel Hawthorne." In *Eight American Authors: A Review of Research and Criticism.* Ed. Floyd Stovall. 1956. New York: Norton, 1963. 100–52.

Boswell, Jeanetta. *Nathaniel Hawthorne and the Critics: A Checklist of Criticism, 1900–1978.* Metuchen, NJ: Scarecrow, 1982.

Clark, C. E. Frazer. *Nathaniel Hawthorne: A Descriptive Bibliography.* Pittsburgh: U of Pittsburgh P, 1978.

Cohen, Bernard, ed. *The Recognition of Nathaniel Hawthorne.* Ann Arbor: U of Michigan P, 1969.

Crowley, J. Donald, ed. *Hawthorne: The Critical Heritage.* New York: Barnes and Noble, 1970.

Gale, Robert L. *A Nathaniel Hawthorne Encyclopedia.* New York: Greenwood, 1991.

Guarneri, Carl J. "A Bibliography of American Fourierism." In Guarneri, *The Utopian Alternative: Fourierism in Nineteenth-Century America.* Ithaca: Cornell UP, 1991. 505–16.

Gura, Philip F., and Joel Myerson, eds. *Critical Essays on American Transcendentalism.* Boston: G. K. Hall, 1982.

Idol, John L., Jr., and Buford Jones, eds. *Nathaniel Hawthorne: The Contemporary Reviews.* New York: Cambridge UP, 1994.

Myerson, Joel, ed. *The American Renaissance in New England. Dictionary of Literary Biography,* vol. 1. Detroit: Gale Research, 1978.
———. *The Transcendentalists: A Review of Research and Criticism.* New York: MLA, 1984.
Ricks, Beatrice, et al. *Nathaniel Hawthorne: A Reference Bibliography, 1900–1971.* Boston: G. K. Hall, 1972.
Wilson, James C., ed. *The Hawthorne and Melville Friendship: An Annotated Bibliography, Biographical and Critical Essays, and Correspondence Between the Two.* Jefferson, NC: McFarland, 1991.

Biographies

Herbert, T. Walter. *Dearest Beloved: The Hawthornes and the Making of the Middle-Class Family.* Berkeley: U of California P, 1993.
Mellow, James R. *Nathaniel Hawthorne in His Times.* Boston: Houghton Mifflin, 1980.
Miller, Edwin Haviland. *Salem Is My Dwelling Place: A Life of Nathaniel Hawthorne.* Iowa City: U of Iowa P, 1991.
Mitchell, Thomas R. "Julian Hawthorne and the 'Scandal' of Margaret Fuller." *American Literary History* 7 (Summer 1995): 210–33.
Stewart, Randall. *Nathaniel Hawthorne: A Biography.* New Haven: Yale UP, 1948.
Turner, Arlin. *Nathaniel Hawthorne: A Biography.* New York: Oxford UP, 1980.

See also:

Gollin, Rita K. "The Matthew Brady Photographs of Nathaniel Hawthorne." In *Studies in the American Renaissance, 1981.* Boston: Twayne, 1981. 379–91.
———. *Portraits of Nathaniel Hawthorne: An Iconography.* DeKalb: Northern Illinois UP, 1983.

Critical Studies

Arvin, Newton. *Hawthorne.* Boston: Little, Brown, 1929.
Bauer, Dale M. *Feminist Dialogics: A Theory of Failed Community.* Albany: State U of New York P, 1988.
Baym, Nina. *The Shape of Hawthorne's Career.* Ithaca: Cornell UP, 1976.
Bell, Michael Davitt. *Hawthorne and the Historical Romance of New England.* Princeton: Princeton UP, 1971.

Berlant, Lauren. *The Anatomy of National Fantasy: Hawthorne, Utopia, and Everyday Life.* Chicago: U of Chicago P, 1991.

————. "Fantasies of Utopia in *The Blithedale Romance.*" *American Literary History* 1 (1989): 30–62.

Brodhead, Richard H. *Hawthorne, Melville, and the Novel.* Chicago: U of Chicago P, 1976.

————. *The School of Hawthorne.* New York: Oxford UP, 1986.

————. "Veiled Ladies: Toward a History of Antebellum Entertainment." *American Literary History* 1 (Summer 1989): 273–94.

Brown, Gillian. *Domestic Individualism: Imagining the Self in Nineteenth-Century America.* Berkeley: U of California P, 1990.

Cary, Louise D. "Margaret Fuller as Hawthorne's Zenobia: The Problem of Moral Accountability in Fictional Biography." *American Transcendental Quarterly* n.s. 4:1 (March 1990): 31–48.

Colacurcio, Michael J. *The Province of Piety: Moral History in Hawthorne's Early Tales.* Cambridge: Harvard UP, 1984.

Crews, Frederick. *The Sins of the Fathers: Hawthorne's Psychological Themes.* 1966. New York: Oxford UP, 1970.

Dryden, Edgar. *Nathaniel Hawthorne: The Poetics of Enchantment.* Ithaca: Cornell UP, 1977.

Gable, Jr., Harvey L. "Inappeasable Longings: Hawthorne, Romance, and the Disintegration of Coverdale's Self in *The Blithedale Romance.*" *New England Quarterly* 67 (June 1994): 257–78.

Howe, Irving, *Politics and the Novel.* Cleveland: World, 1957.

Hutner, Gordon. *Secrets and Sympathy: Forms of Disclosure in Hawthorne's Novels.* Athens: U of Georgia P, 1988.

James, Henry. *Hawthorne.* 1879. Ithaca: Cornell UP, 1966.

Levine, Robert S. *Conspiracy and Romance: Studies in Brockden Brown, Cooper, Hawthorne, and Melville.* New York: Cambridge UP, 1989.

Mackenzie, Manfred. "Colonization and Decolonization in *The Blithedale Romance.*" *University of Toronto Quarterly* 62 (Summer 1993): 504–21.

Matthiessen, F. O. *American Renaissance: Art and Expression in the Age of Emerson and Whitman.* 1941. New York: Oxford UP, 1972.

McIntosh, James. "The Instability of Belief in *The Blithedale Romance.*" *Prospects* 9. New York: Cambridge UP, 1984. 71–114.

Melville, Herman. "Hawthorne and His Mosses.:" 1850. Rpt. in *The Shock of Recognition.* Ed. Edmund Wilson. New York: Modern Library, 1955. 187–204.

Millington, Richard H. "American Anxiousness: Selfhood and Culture in Hawthorne's *The Blithedale Romance.*" *New England Quarterly* 63 (December 1990): 558–83.

Pearce, Roy Harvey, ed. *Hawthorne Centenary Essays*. Columbus: Ohio State UP, 1964.

Ponder, Melinda M. *"The Blithedale Romance."* In *Essex Institute Historical Collections*. Special issue on "The Presentation of Hawthorne's Romances." 127, no. 1 (January 1991): 50–68.

Schriber, Mary Suzanne. "Justice to Zenobia." *New England Quarterly 55* (March 1982): 61–78.

Tanner, Laura E. "Speaking with 'Hands at Our Throats': The Struggle for Artistic Voice in *The Blithedale Romance*." *Studies in American Fiction* 21 (Spring 1993): 1–19.

Tompkins, Jane. *Sensational Designs: The Cultural Work of American Fiction, 1790-1860*. New York: Oxford UP, 1985.

Van Doren, Mark. *Nathaniel Hawthorne: A Critical Biography*. 1949. New York: Viking, 1966.

Waggoner, Hyatt H. *Hawthorne: A Critical Study*. Cambridge: Harvard UP, 1955.

Yellin, Jean Fagan. "Hawthorne and the American National Sin." In *The Green American Tradition: Essays and Poems for Sherman Paul*. Ed. H. Daniel Peck. Baton Rouge: Louisiana State UP, 1989. 75–97.

On Brook Farm

Myerson, Joel. *Brook Farm: An Annotated Bibliography and Resources Guide*. New York: Garland, 1978.

Myerson, Joel, ed. *The Brook Farm Book: A Collection of First-Hand Accounts of the Community*. New York: Garland, 1987.

Sams, Henry W., ed. *Autobiography of Brook Farm*. 1958. Gloucester, Mass.: Peter Smith, 1974.

Swift, Lindsay. *Brook Farm: Its Members, Scholars, and Visitors*. New York: Macmillan, 1900.

On Utopian Communities

Clark, Christopher. *The Communitarian Moment: The Radical Challenge of the Northampton Association*. Ithaca: Cornell UP, 1995.

Fellman, Michael. *The Unbounded Frame: Freedom and Community in Nineteenth Century American Utopianism*. Westport, CT: Greenwood, 1973.

Fogarty, Robert S. *Dictionary of American Communal and Utopian History*. Westport, CT: Greenwood, 1980.

Guarneri, Carl J. *The Utopian Alternative: Fourierism in Nineteenth-Century America*. Ithaca: Cornell UP, 1991.

Hayden, Dolores. *Seven American Utopias: The Architecture of Communitarian Socialism, 1790–1975*. Cambridge: MIT P, 1976.

Kesten, Seymour R. *Utopian Episodes: Daily Life in Experimental Colonies Dedicated to Changing the World*. Syracuse: Syracuse UP, 1993.

Excerpts from Rebecca Codman Butterfield's diaries reprinted with the permission of the Massachusetts Historical Society.

Excerpt from *The Condition of the Working Class in England in 1844* by Friedrich Engels. Translated and edited by W. O. Henderson and W. H. Chaloner, with the permission of the publishers, Stanford University Press, and of Blackwell Publishers, Ltd. © 1958 Basil Blackwell.

"Earth's Holocaust" from *Mosses from an Old Manse,* volume X of the Centenary Edition of the Works of Nathaniel Hawthorne, is reprinted by permission. Copyright 1974 by the Ohio State University Press. All rights reserved.

Letters to Sophia Peabody, from *The Letters, 1813–1843,* volume XV of the Centenary Edition of the Works of Nathaniel Hawthorne, are reprinted by permission. Copyright 1984 by the Ohio State University Press. All rights reserved.

Notes on the death of Martha Hunt, from *The American Notebooks,* volume VIII of the Centenary Edition of the Works of Nathaniel Hawthorne, are reprinted by permission. Copyright 1972 by the Ohio State University Press. All rights reserved.

Notes on Margaret Fuller, from *The French and Italian Notebooks,* volume XIV of the Centenary Edition of the Works of Nathaniel Hawthorne, are reprinted by permission. Copyright 1980 by the Ohio State University Press. All rights reserved.

Karl Marx, excerpt from *Karl Marx: Selected Writings* by Karl Marx. © David McLellan 1977. Reprinted from *Karl Marx: Selected Writings,* edited by David McLellan (1977) by permission of Oxford University Press.

Joseph Smith, excerpt from *The Personal Writings of Joseph Smith,* ed. Dean C. Jessee, © 1984, reprinted with the permission of Deseret Book Company.